The Queen
of
Bedlam

The Queen

of
Bedlam

ROBERT
McCAMMON

POCKET BOOKS
New York London Toronto Sydney

Pocket Books
A Division of Simon & Schuster, Inc.
1230 Avenue of the Americas
New York, NY 10020

First Pocket Books trade paperback edition October 2007

POCKET and colophon are registered trademarks of Simon & Schuster, Inc.

For information about special discounts for bulk purchases, please contact Simon & Schuster Special Sales at 1-800-456-6798 or business@simonandschuster.com.

Manufactured in the United States of America

10 9 8 7 6 5 4 3 2 1

ISBN-13: 978-1-4165-5111-9
ISBN-10:   1-4165-5111-5

FOR MY DAUGHTER, SKYE.

One

The Masker

one

'TWAS SAID better to light a candle than to curse the dark, but in the town of New York in the summer of 1702 one might do both, for the candles were small and the dark was large. True, there were the town-appointed constables and watchmen. Yet often between Dock Street and the Broad Way these heroes of the nocturne lost their courage to a flask of John Barleycorn and the other temptations that beckoned so flagrantly on the midsummer breeze, be it the sound of merriment from the harbor taverns or the intoxicating scent of perfume from the rose-colored house of Polly Blossom.

The nightlife was, in a word, lively. Though the town awakened before sunrise to the industrious bells of mercantile and farming labors, there were still many who preferred to apply their sleeping hours to the avocations of drinking, gambling, and what mischief might follow those troublesome twins. The sun would certainly rise on the morrow, but tonight was always a temptation. Why else would this brash and eager, Dutch-groomed and now English-dressed town boast more than a dozen taverns, if not for the joy of intemperate companionship?

But the young man who sat alone at a table in the back room of the Old Admiral was not there to seek companions, be they of humankind or brewer's yeast. He did have before him a tankard of strong dark ale, which he sipped at every so often, but this was a prop to blend into the scene. One watching him would see how he winced and frowned at the drinking, for it took a true hardgut to down the Old Admiral's keel-cleaner. This was not his usual haunt. In fact he was well-known at the Trot Then Gallop, up on Crown Street, but here he was within a coin's throw of the Great Dock on the East River, where the masted ships whispered and groaned on the night currents and the flambeaux from fishermen's skiffs burned red against the eddies. Here in the Old Admiral the blue smoke of clay pipes whirled through the lamplight as men bellowed for more ale or wine and the crack of dice hitting tables sounded like the pistols of little wars. That noise never failed to remind Matthew Corbett of the pistol shot that had blown out the brains of . . . well, it had been three years ago, it was best not to linger on such a foregone picture.

He was only twenty-three years old, but something about him was elder than his span. Perhaps it was his grave seriousness, his austere demeanor, or the fact that he could always forecast rain from the aching in his bones like those of a toothless senior muttering in his pudding. Or, to be more correct, the ache of ribs below his heart and left arm at the shoulder, bones broken courtesy of a bear known as Jack One Eye. The bear had also left Matthew with a crescent scar that began just above his right eyebrow and curved into the hairline. A doctor in the Carolina colony had once said to him that ladies liked a young man with a dashing scar, but this one seemed to warn the ladies that he'd come close to a cropper with Death, and perhaps the chill of the mausoleum lingered in his soul. His left arm had been almost without life for over a year after that incident. He'd expected to live on the starboard for the rest of his days but a good and rather unorthodox doctor here in New York had given him arm exercises—self-inflicted torture involving an iron bar to which horseshoes were chained on either end—to do daily, along with hot compresses and stretching. At last came the miracle morning when he could rotate his shoulder all the way around, and with further treatment nearly all his strength had returned. Thus passed away one of the last acts of Jack One Eye upon the earth, gone now but surely never forgotten.

Matthew's cool gray eyes, flecked with dark blue like smoke at twilight, were aimed toward a certain table on the other side of the room. He was careful, though, not to stare too pointedly, but only to graze and jab and look into his ale, shift his shoulders, and graze and jab again. No matter, really; the object of his interest would have to be blind and dumb not to know he was there, and true evil was neither. No, true evil just continued to talk and grin and sip with puckered lips at a greasy glass of wine, puff a smoke ring from a black clay pipe, and then talk and grin some more, all while the gaming went on with its hollerings and dice-shots and shadowy men yelling as if to scare the dawn from ever happening.

But Matthew knew it was more than the humor and drinking and gaming of a tavern in a young town with the sea at its chest and wilderness to its back that brought out this festivity. It was the Thing That No One Spoke Of. The Incident. The Unfortunate Happenstance.

It was the Masker, is what it was.

So drink up wine from those fresh casks and blow your smoke to the moon, Matthew thought. Howl like wolves and grin like thieves. We've all got to walk a dark street home tonight.

And the Masker could be any one of them, he mused. Or the Masker could be gone the way he'd come, never to pass this way again. Who could know? Certainly not the idiots who these days called themselves constables and were empowered by the town council to patrol the streets. He reasoned they were probably all indoors somewhere as well, though the weather be warm and the moon half on the hang; they were stupid, yes, but not foolish.

Matthew took another drink of his ale and flicked his gaze again toward that far table. The pipesmoke hung in blue layers, shifting with the wind of motion or exhalation. At the table sat three men. One elder, fat and bloated, two younger with the look of ruffians. But to be sure, this was a rumpot of ruffians, so that in itself was not surprising. Matthew hadn't seen either of the men with the fat bloatarian before. They were dressed in rustic style, both with well-used leather waistcoats over white shirts and one with leather patches on the knees of his breeches. Who were they? he wondered. And what business did they have with Eben Ausley?

Only very seldom and just for a quick flash did Matthew catch the glint of Ausley's small black eyes aimed at him, but just as swiftly the man angled his white-wigged head away and continued the conversation with his two juniors. Anyone looking on would not realize that the young Corbett—with his lean long-jawed face, his unruly thatch of fine black hair, and his pale candlelit countenance—was a crusader whose quest had slowly, night upon night, turned to obsession. In his brown boots, gray breeches, and simple white shirt, frayed at the collar and cuffs but scrupulously laundered, he appeared to be no more than his occupation of magistrate's clerk demanded. Certainly Magistrate Powers wouldn't approve of these nightly travels, but travel Matthew must, for the deepest desire of his heart was to see Eben Ausley hanged from the town gallows.

Now Ausley put down his pipe and drew the table's lamp nearer. The companion on his left—a dark-haired, sunken-eyed man perhaps nine or ten years elder than Matthew—was speaking quietly and seriously. Ausley, a heavy-jowled pig in his mid-fifties, listened intently. At length Matthew saw him nod and reach into the coat of his vulgar wine-purple suit, the frills on his shirt quivering with the belly-strain. The white wig on Ausley's head was adorned with elaborate curls, which perhaps in London was the fashion of the moment but here in New York was only a fop's topping. Ausley brought from within his coat a string-wrapped lead pencil and a palm-sized black notebook that Matthew had seen him produce a score of times. There was some kind of gold-leaf ornamentation on the cover. Matthew had already mused upon the thought that Ausley was as addicted to his note-taking as to his games of Ombre and Ticktack, both of which seemed to have a hold on the man's mind and wallet. He could imagine with a faint smile the notes scribbled down on those pages: *Dropped a loaf this morning . . . a fig or two into the bucket . . . dear me, only a nugget today* . . . Ausley touched the pencil to his tongue and began to write. Three or four lines were set down, or so it appeared to Matthew. Then the notebook was closed and put away and finally the pencil as well. Ausley spoke again to the dark-haired young man, while the other one—sandy-haired and thick-set, with a slow oxen-like blinking of his heavy eyelids—appraised the noisy game of Bone-Ace going on over in the corner. Ausley grinned; the yellow lamplight fairly leaped off his teeth. A group of drinkers stumbled past between Matthew and his objects of interest. Just that fast Ausley and the other two men were standing up, reaching for their hats on the wallhooks. Ausley's tricorn displayed a dyed crimson feather, while the dark-haired man with the leather-patched breeches wore a wide-brimmed leather hat and the third gent a common short-billed cap. The group strolled to the tavern-keeper at the bar to settle their bills.

Matthew waited. When the coins were down in the money-box and the three men going out onto Dock Street, Matthew put on his own brown linen cap and stood up. He was a little light-headed. The strong ale, currents of smoke, and raucous noise had unhinged his senses. He quickly paid his due and walked into the night.

Ah, what a relief out here! A warm breeze in the face was cool compared to the heated confines of a crowded tavern. The Old Admiral always had such an effect on him. He'd tracked Ausley here on many earlier occasions so he ought to be immune to such, but his idea of an excellent evening was a drink of polite wine and a quiet game of chess with the regulars at the Gallop. He smelled on the breeze the pungence of harbor tarbuckets and dead fish. But there on the very same breeze, wafting past, was quite another scent Matthew had expected: Eben Ausley wore a heavy cologne that smelled of cloves. He nearly bathed in the stuff. The man might as well have carried a torch with him, to illuminate his comings and goings; it certainly helped to follow Ausley by on these nights. But tonight, it seemed, Ausley and his companions were in no hurry, for there they were strolling up ahead. They walked past the glow of a lantern that hung from a wooden post to mark the intersection of Dock Street and Broad Street, and Matthew saw their intent was to go west onto Bridge Street. Well, he thought, this was a new path. Usually Ausley headed directly back the six blocks north to the orphanage on King Street. Better keep back a bit more, Matthew decided. Better just walk quietly and keep watch.

Matthew followed, crossing the cobblestoned street. He was tall and thin but not frail, and he walked with a long stride that he had to restrain lest he get up the back of his bull's-eye. The smells of the Great Dock faded, to be replaced by the heady aromas of hay and livestock. In this section of town were several stables and fenced enclosures for pigs and cows. Warehouses held maritime and animal supplies in stacks of crates and barrels. Occasionally Matthew caught a glimpse of candlelight through a shutter, as someone moved about inside a countinghouse or stable. Never let it be said that all the residents of New York gamboled or slept at night, as some might rather labor clock-round if physical strength would allow.

A horse clopped past, its rider wearing polished boots. Matthew saw Ausley and the two others turn right at the next corner, onto the Broad Way near the Governor's House. He made the turn at a cautious pace. His quarry walked a block ahead, still just ambling. Matthew took note of candlelight in several upper windows of the white-bricked governor's abode beyond the walls of Fort William Henry. The new man, Lord Cornbury, had arrived from England only a few days ago. Matthew hadn't yet seen him, nor had anyone else of his acquaintance, but the notices plastered up announced a meeting in the town hall tomorrow afternoon so he expected to soon have a look at the gent who'd been awarded the reins of New York by Queen Anne. It would be good to have someone in charge of things, since the constables were in such disarray and the town's mayor, Thomas Hood, had died in June.

Matthew saw that the red-feathered cockatoo and his companions were approaching another tavern, the Thorn Bush. That nasty little place was even gamier than the Admiral, in all senses of the word. Matthew had been witness in there last November when Ausley had lost what must have been a small fortune on the game of Bankafalet. Matthew decided he wasn't up to any more tavern-sitting tonight. Let them go in and drink themselves blue, if they liked. It was time to go home and abed.

But Ausley and the two men kept walking past the Thorn Bush, not even pausing to look in the door. As Matthew neared the place, a drunk young man—Andrew Kippering, Matthew saw in the bloom of lamplight—and a dark-haired girl with a heavily painted face staggered out into the street, laughing at some shared amusement. They brushed past Matthew and went on in the direction of the harbor. Kippering was an attorney of some renown and could be a serious sort, but was not unknown to tip the bottle and frequent Madam Blossom's household.

Ausley and the others turned right onto Beaver Street and crossed Broad Street once again, heading east toward the river-front. Here and there lanterns burned on cornerposts, and every seventh dwelling was required by law to show a light. A dog barked fiercely behind a white picket fence and another echoed off in the distance. A man wearing a gold-trimmed tricorn and carry-ing a walking-stick suddenly turned a corner in front of Matthew and almost scared him witless, but with a quick nod the man was striding away, the stick tap-tapping on the brick sidewalk.

Matthew picked up his pace to keep Ausley in sight, but mak-ing certain to step carefully lest he mar his boots with any of the animal dung that often littered both bricks and cobbles. A horse-cart trundled past with a single figure hunched over the reins. Matthew walked on a narrow street between two walls of white stone. Ahead, by the illumination of a dying post-lamp, Ausley and the others turned right onto Sloat Lane. A fire had broken out here at the first of the summer and consumed several houses. The odor of ashes and flame-wrack still lingered in the air, commingled with rotten cloves and the smell of a pig that needed to be roasted. Matthew stopped and carefully peered around the corner. His quarry had slipped out of sight, between darkened wooden houses and squat little red brick buildings. Some of the houses farther on were blackened ruins. The lantern on the cornerpost ahead flick-ered, about to give up its ghost. A little prickling of the skin on the back of Matthew's neck made him look around the way he'd come. Standing a distance behind him was a figure in dark clothes and hat, washed by the candlelight on the cornerpost he'd just passed. This was not his area of habitation, and it struck him suddenly that he was very far from home.

The figure just stood there, seemingly staring at him though Matthew was unable to make out a face beneath that tricorn. Matthew's heart had begun to hammer in his chest. If this was the Masker, he thought, then damned if he'd give up his life without a fight. Good thinking there, boy, he told himself with a twinge of morbid humor. Fists against a throat-slashing blade always won the day.

Matthew was about to call to the figure—and say what? he asked himself. *Fine night for a walk, isn't it, sir? And by the by would you please spare my life?*—but abruptly the mystery man turned away, strode purposefully out of the lantern's realm and was gone. The breath hissed out of Matthew. He felt the chill of sweat at his temples. That wasn't the Masker! he told himself with a little stupid fury. Of course not! It might have been a constable, or someone just out walking, the same as himself! Only he was not out just walking, he thought. He was a sheep, tracking a wolf.

Ausley and his tavern companions had gone. There was no sight of them whatsoever. Now the question was, did Matthew continue along this ash-reeking lane or retrace his way back to where the Masker was waiting? Stop it, idiot! he commanded. That wasn't the Masker because the Masker has left New York! Why should anyone think the Masker was still lurking in these streets? Because they hadn't caught him, Matthew thought grimly. That's why.

He decided to go ahead, but with a watchful eye at his back in case a piece of darkness separated itself from the night and rushed upon him. And he had gone perhaps ten paces farther when a piece of darkness shifted not at his back, but directly in front of him.

He stopped and stood stone-still. He was a dried husk, all the blood and breath gone from him on a summer night suddenly turned winter's eve.

A spark leaped, setting fire to cotton in a little tinderbox, and from it a match was lighted.

"Corbett," said the man as he touched flame to pipe bowl, "if you're so intent on following me I ought to give you an audience. Don't you think?" Matthew didn't reply. Actually his tongue was still petrified.

Eben Ausley took a moment lighting his pipe to satisfaction. Behind him was a fire-blacked brick wall. His corpulent face seethed red. "What a wonder you are, boy," he said in his crackly high-pitched voice. "Laboring at papers and pots all day long and following me about the town at night. When do you sleep?"

"I manage," Matthew answered.

"I think you ought to get more sleep than you do. I think you are in need of a long rest. Don't you agree with that, Mr. Carver?"

Too late, Matthew heard the movement behind him. Too late, he realized the other two men had been hiding in the burned rubble on either side of—

A lumberboard whacked him square in the back of the head, stopping all further speculations. It sounded so loud to him that surely the militia would think a cannon had fired, but then the force of the blow knocked him off his feet and the pain roared up and everything was shooting stars and flaming pinwheels. He was on his knees and made an effort of sheer willpower not to go down flat on the street. His teeth were gritted, his senses blowsy. It came to him through the haze that Ausley had led him a merry traipse to this sheep-trap. "Oh, that's enough, I think," Ausley was saying. "We don't want to *kill* him now, do we? How does that feel, Corbett? Clear your noggin out for you?"

Matthew heard the voice as if an echo from a great distance, which he wished were the truth. Something pressed down hard upon the center of his back. A boot, he realized. About to slam him to the ground.

"He's all right where he is," Ausley said, in a flat tone of nonchalance. The boot left Matthew's back. "I don't think he's going anywhere. Are you, Corbett?" He didn't wait for a reply, which wouldn't have arrived anyway. "Do you know who this young man is, my friends? Do you know he's been trailing me hither and yon, 'round and about for . . . how long has it been, Corbett? Two *years?*"

Two years haphazardly, Matthew thought. Only the last six months with any sense of purpose.

"This young man was one of my dearest students," Ausley went on, smirking now. "One of my boys, yes. Raised up right there at the orphanage. Now I didn't take him off the street myself, my predecessor Staunton did that, you see. That poor old fool saw him as a worthwhile project. Wretched urchin into educated gentleman, if you please. Gave him *books* to read, and taught him . . . what was it he taught you, Corbett? How to be a damned fool, like he was?" He continued merrily along his crooked road. "Now this young man has gone a far travel from his beginnings. Oh yes, he has. Went into the employ of Magistrate Isaac Woodward, who chose him as a clerk-in-training and took him out into the world. Gave him a chance to continue his education, to learn to live a gentleman's life and to *be* someone of value." There was a pause as Ausley relit his pipe. "And *then*, my friends," Ausley said between puffs, "and *then*, he betrayed his benefactor by falling in with a woman accused of witchcraft in a little hole of a town down in the Carolina colony. A murderess, I understood her to be. A common tramp and a conniver, who pulled the wool over this young man's eyes and caused the death of that noble Magistrate Woodward, God rest his soul."

"Lie," Matthew was able to say. Or rather, to whisper. He tried again: "That's . . . a lie."

"Did he speak? Did he say something?" Ausley asked.

"He mumbled," said the man standing behind Matthew.

"Well might he mumble," Ausley said. "He mumbled and grumbled quite a lot at the orphanage. Didn't you, Corbett? If I had killed my benefactor by first exposing him to a wet tempest that half robbed his life and then breaking his heart by treachery, I'd be reduced to a mumbling wretch too. Tell me, how does Magistrate Powers trust you enough to turn his back on you? Or have you learned a bewitching spell from your ladyfriend?"

"If he knows witchcraft," another voice said, "it hasn't done him any good tonight."

"No," Ausley answered, "he doesn't know witchcraft. If he did, he'd at least make himself into an invisible pest instead of a pest I have to look at every time I venture out into the street. Corbett!!"

It had been a demand for Matthew's full attention, which he was able to give only by lifting his throbbing brain-pan on its weakened stalk. He blinked, trying to focus on Ausley's repugnant visage.

The headmaster of King Street's orphanage for boys, he of the jaunty cockatoo and the swollen belly, said with quiet contempt, "I know what you're about. I've always known. When you came back here, I knew it would start. And I warned you, did I not? Your last night at the orphanage? Have you forgotten? *Answer me!*"

"I haven't forgotten," Matthew said.

"Never plot a war you cannot win. Isn't that right?"

Matthew didn't respond. He tensed, expecting the boot to come down on his back again, but he was spared.

"This young man . . . boy . . . *fool*," Ausley corrected himself, speaking now to his two companions, "decided he didn't approve of my correctional methods. All those boys, all those grievous *attitudes*. Some of them like animals wild from the woods, even a barn was too good for them. They'd bite your arm off and piss on your leg. The churches and the public hospital daily bringing them to my door. Family perished on the voyage over, no one to take responsibility, so what was I to do with them? Indians massacred this one's family, or that one was stubborn and would not work, or this one was a young drunkard living in the street. What was I to *do* with them, except give them some discipline? And yes, I did take many of them in hand. Many of them I had to discipline in the most strict of manners, because they would abide no—"

"Not discipline," Matthew interrupted, gathering strength into his voice. His face had reddened, his eyes glistening with anger in their swollen sockets. "Your methods . . . might make the church elders and the hospital council think twice . . . about the charity they give you. And the money the town pays you. Do they know you're confusing discipline with sodomy?"

Ausley was quiet. In this silence, the world and time seemed to hang suspended.

"I've heard them scream, late at night," Matthew went on. "Many nights. I've seen them, afterward. Some of them . . . didn't want to live. All of them were changed. And you only went after the *youngest* ones. The ones who couldn't fight back." He felt the burn of tears, and even after eight years the impact of this emotion stunned him. He pulled in a breath and the next words tumbled out of him: "I'm fighting back for them, you jackal sonofabitch."

Ausley's laugh cracked the dark. "Oh ho! Oh ho, my friends! View the avenging angel! Down on the ground and fighting the air!" He came forward a few steps. In the next pull of the pipe and the red wash of cinder-light, Matthew saw a face upon the man that would have scared even the winged Michael. "You make me *sick*, Corbett! With your stupidity and your fucking *honor*. With your following me, trying to get under my feet and trip me up. Because that's what you're doing, isn't it? Trying to *find out* things? To *spy* on me? Which tells me one very important thing: you have nothing. If you had something—*anything*—beyond your ridiculous suppositions and made-up memories, you would have first fetched your dear dead magistrate Woodward upon me, or now your new dog Powers. Am I not correct in this?" His voice suddenly changed; when he spoke again he sounded like a nettled old woman: "Look what you've made me step in!"

Then, after a meditative pause: "Mr. Bromfield, drag Corbett over here, won't you?"

A hand grabbed Matthew's collar and another took hold of his shirt low on his back. He was dragged fast and sure by a man who knew how to move a body. Matthew tensed and tried to convulse himself, but a knuckled fist—Carver's, he presumed—jammed into his ribs just enough to tell him that pride led to breakage.

"You have a filthy mind," Ausley said, standing closer with his odors of cloves and smoke. "I think we should scrub it a bit, beginning with your face. Mr. Bromfield, clean him up for me, please."

"My pleasure," said the man who'd seized Matthew, and with diabolical relish he took hold of the back of Matthew's head and thrust his face down into the fly-blown mass of horse manure that Ausley's boot had found.

Matthew had seen what was coming. There was no way to avoid it. He was able to seal his mouth shut and close his eyes, and then his face went into the pile. It was, by reason of the analytical part of Matthew's brain that took the cool measure of all things, distressingly fresh. Almost velvety, really. Like putting one's face into a velvet bag. Warm, still. The stuff was up his nostrils, but the breath was stuck hard in his lungs. He didn't fight, even when he felt the sole of a boot press upon the back of his head and his face was jammed through the wretched excess near down to the cobblestones. They wanted him to fight, so they could break him. So he would not fight, even as the air stuttered in his lungs and his face remained pressed down into the filth under a whoreson's boot. He would not fight, so he might fight the better on his feet some other day.

Ausley said, "Pull him up."

Bromfield obeyed.

"Get some air in his lungs, Carver," Ausley commanded.

The flat of a hand slapped Matthew in the center of his chest. The air whooshed out of his mouth and nostrils, spraying manure.

"Shit!" Carver hollered. "He's got it on my shirt!"

"Step back then, step back. Give him room to smell himself."

Matthew did. The stuff was still jammed up his nose. It caked his face like swamp mud and had the vomitous odor of sour grass, decayed feed, and . . . well, and stinking *manure* straight from the rump. He retched and tried to clear his eyes but Bromfield had hold of his arms as strong as a picaroon's rope.

Ausley gave a short, high, and giddy laugh. "Oh, look at him now! The avenger has turned scarecrow! You might even scare the carrion birds away with that face, Corbett!"

Matthew spat and shook his head violently back and forth; unfortunately some of this unpalatable meal had gotten past his lips.

"You can let him go now," Ausley said. Bromfield released Matthew and at the same time gave him a solid shove that put him on the ground again. Then, as Matthew struggled up to his knees and rubbed the mess out of his eyes, Ausley stood over him and said quietly, the menace in his voice commingled with boredom, "You are not to follow me again. Understand? Mind me well, or the next time we meet shall not go so kindly for you." To the others: "Shall we leave the young man to his contemplations?"

There was the sound of phlegm being hawked up. Matthew felt the gob of spit hit his shirt at the left shoulder. Carver or Bromfield, showing their good breeding. After that, the noise of boots striding away. Ausley said something and one of the others laughed. Then they were gone.

Matthew sat in the street, cleaning his face with his sleeves. Sickness bubbled and lurched in his stomach. The heat of anger and the burn of shame made him feel as if he were sitting aboil under the noonday sun. His head was still killing him, his eyes streaming. Then his stomach turned over and out of him flooded the Old Admiral's ale and most of the salmagundi he'd put down for his supper. It came to him that he was going to be laboring over a washpot tonight.

Finally, after what seemed a terrible hour, he was able to get up off the ground and think about how to get home. His roost on the Broad Way, up over Hiram Stokely's pottery shop, was going to be a good twenty-minute walk. Probably a long, malodorous twenty minutes, at that. But there was nothing to be done but to get to doing it; and so he started off, seething and weaving and stinking and being altogether miserable in his wretched skin. He searched for a horse trough. He would get himself a bath in it, and so cleanse his face and clear his mind.

And tomorrow? To be so impetuous as to once more haunt the dark outside the King Street orphanage, waiting for Ausley to appear on his jaunt to the gambling dens and so spy on him in hopes of . . . what, exactly? Or to stay home in his small room and embrace cold fact, that Ausley was right: he had absolutely nothing, and was unlikely to get anything at this pace. But to give up . . . to give up . . . was abandoning them all. Abandoning the reason for his solemn rage, abandoning the quest that he felt set him apart from every other citizen of this town. It gave him a purpose. Without it, who would he be?

He would be a magistrate's clerk and a pottery sweeper, he thought as he went along the silent Broad Way. Only a young man who held sway over a quill and a broom, and whose mind was tormented by the vision of injustice to the innocent. It was what had made him stand up against Magistrate Woodward—his mentor and almost father, truth be told—to proclaim Rachel Howarth innocent of witchcraft in the town of Fount Royal three years ago. Had that decision helped to carry the ailing magistrate to his death? Possibly so. It was another torment, like the hot strike of a bullwhip ever endlessly repeating, that lay upon Matthew's soul in every hour lit by sun or candle.

He came upon a horse trough at Trinity Church, where Wall Street met the Broad Way. Here the sturdy Dutch cobblestones ended and the streets were plain hard-packed English earth. As Matthew leaned down into the trough and began to wash his face with dirty water, he almost felt like weeping. Yet to weep took too much energy, and he had none of that to spare.

But tomorrow was tomorrow, was it not? A new beginning, as they said? What a day might change, who could ever know? Yet some things would never change in himself, and of this he was certain: he must bring Eben Ausley to justice somehow, for those crimes of wanton evil and brutality against the innocent. Somehow, he must; or he feared that if he did not, he would be consumed by this quest, by its futility, and he would wither into slack-jawed acceptance of what could never in his mind be acceptable.

At last he was suitable to proceed home, yet still a ragamuffin's nightmare. He still had his cap, that was a good thing. He still had his life, that was another. And so he straightened his shoulders and counted his blessings and went on his way through the midnight town, one young man alone.

two

ON THIS BRIGHT MORNING, neither of Matthew's breakfast hosts knew of his tribulations of the night before; therefore they merrily jaylarked about the day with no regard to his headache and sour stomach. He kept these injuries to himself, as Hiram Stokely and his wife, Patience, went about the sunny kitchen in their small white house behind the pottery shop.

Matthew's plate was filled with corncakes and a slice of salted ham that on any other day he would have considered a delight but today was a little too discomfited to properly appreciate. They were good and kind people, and he'd been fortunate to find a room over the shop. His responsibility to them was to clean the place and help with the throwing and kiln, as much as his limited talents allowed. They had two sons, one a merchant sea captain and the other an accountant in London, and it seemed to Matthew that they liked having the company at mealtimes.

The third member present of the Stokely family, however, definitely found something peculiar with Matthew this morn. At first Matthew had thought it was the salted ham that made Cecily, the pet pig, nose about him to the point of aggravation. Considering he was putting knife and fork to one of her relations, he could well fathom her displeasure, yet she was surely by now used to these cannibals who'd taken her in. Surely she knew that after two years of this coddled life she wasn't destined for the plate, for she was a smart piece of pork. But the way she snorted and pushed and carried on this day made Matthew wonder if he'd gotten all the horse manure out of his hair. He'd almost scrubbed his skin off with sandalwood soap in the washbasin last night, but perhaps Cecily's talented snout could find some lingering stink.

"Cecily!" said Hiram, after a particularly hard push from the rotund lass to Matthew's right kneecap. "What's the matter with you today?"

"I'm afraid *I* don't know," was Matthew's response, though he presumed Cecily was reminded of rolling in the sty by some aroma he was emitting, even though he wore freshly cleaned trousers, shirt, and stockings.

"She's nervous, is what." Patience, a large stocky woman with gray hair pinned up under a blue cotton mob cap, looked up from her hearth, where she was using a bellows to fan the biscuit-pan fire. "Something's got her gristle."

Hiram, who was just as physically sturdy as his wife, with white hair and beard and pale brown eyes the color of the clay he worked so diligently, took a drink from his mug of tea. He watched Cecily make a circle in the kitchen before she went back under the table to give out a snort and push Matthew's knee again. "She was like this a morning or two before the fire, you remember? She can tell when there's trouble about to happen, is what I believe."

"I didn't realize she was such the fortune-teller." Matthew scooted his chair back from the table to make room for Cecily. Unfortunately, the lady continued to shove her snout at him.

"Well, she likes you." Hiram gave him a quick, joshing smile. "Maybe she's trying to tell you something, eh?"

A day late, Matthew thought.

"I recall," Patience said quietly, as she went back to her work, "when Dr. Godwin came to visit us last. To get his plates. Do you remember, Hiram?"

"Dr. Godwin?" Hiram's eyes narrowed a fraction. "Hm," he said.

"What about Dr. Godwin?" Matthew asked, sensing something that perhaps he ought to know.

"It's not important." Hiram drank from his mug again and began to eat the last piece of corncake on his platter.

"I imagine it *is*," Matthew insisted. "If you brought it up at all, it must be."

Hiram shrugged. "Well, it's just . . . Cecily, that's all."

"Yes? And Cecily had what to do with Dr. Godwin?"

"She acted like this that day, when he came to get his plates."

"That day?" Matthew knew exactly what the man meant, but he had to ask it: "You mean the day he was murdered?"

"It's nothing, really," Hiram said, though he squirmed in his chair. He figured he ought to be used to Matthew's ravenous questions and particularly the penetrating expression the young man gave when he knew he'd been thrown a hook. "I don't know if it was that day, exactly, or some other day. And thank you, Patience, for bringing this subject to light."

"I was thinking out loud," she said, rather apologetically. "I meant no harm in the saying."

"Will you *stop that*?" Matthew, his nerves on edge, stood up to get away from Cecily. The knees of his trousers were sopping with sow spit. "I'd better go; I've got an errand before work."

"The biscuits are almost done," Patience said. "Sit down, the magistrate will—"

"I'm sorry, no. Thank you for the breakfast. I presume I'll see both of you at Lord Cornbury's address?"

"We'll be there." Hiram stood up as well. "Matthew, it doesn't mean anything. It's just a pig, playing with you."

"I know it doesn't mean anything. I didn't say it did. And I reject the idea that there's any connection between Dr. Godwin and myself. I mean . . . in terms of being murdered." Dear Lord, he thought. Do I have fever? "I shall see you this afternoon," he said, and dodged Cecily making another snorting circle around him as he got out through the door and walked along the fieldstone path that led to the street.

Ridiculous! he told himself as he strode southward. To let a pig's so-called premonitions cloud his mind, as if he really believed in such a thing. Well, some did, of course. Some said animals could foretell changing weather and such before the human breed, but to foretell murder . . . that smacked of dabbling in witchcraft, didn't it? As if he held any stock in *that*, either!

On this fine morning it seemed the entire population of New York was out and about on the public ways. They meandered, squatted, scurried, and barked all around him, and those were just the cats, goats, chickens, and dogs. The town was becoming a veritable menagerie, as on some of those vessels arriving from England. The three-month journey had killed half the people and left their livestock to enjoy the greener pastures of North America.

The Stokelys' pottery shop was one of the last structures of the town proper. Just north beyond their door lay the High Road, which led across rolling fields and hills crowned with thick green woodland to the distant town of Boston. The sun shimmered in gold flakes on the waters of the East and Hudson rivers, and as Matthew followed the Broad Way over a hilltop he took in the panoramic view of New York he saw every morning on his way to work.

Haze from cooking hearths and blacksmith fires hung above the yellow-tiled roofs of scores of houses, shops, and sundry buildings spread before him. On the streets moved the industrious citizens, either on foot or by horse and ox-cart. The higglers were out, selling baskets and rope and all kinds of middling merchandise from their street-corner wagons. So too on the move was the rag-and-bone man, scooping up the night's animal manure into his bucket-like cart for sale at the farmers' market. Matthew knew where the man might find a right treasure of a pile over near Sloat Lane.

Three white-sailed skiffs advanced before the breeze along the East River. A larger sailing ship, piloted out of the harbor by two long rowers, was leaving the Great Dock to a small gathering of well-wishers and a ringing of bells at the wharfside. The area of the piers was of course a center of business and was like a beehive even before dawn, with its assemblage of canvasers, anchorsmiths, cod-men, pulleymakers, riggers, tarboys, shipwrights, treenail makers, and all such cast of seaplay characters. Then, looking to the shops and buildings to the right of the docks, one peered into the domain of the warehousers and merchandisers who held sway over goods either leaving the town or coming in, which gave occupations to packers, tollers, tally-clerks, stevedores, tide waiters, scriveners, out-criers, and perchemears. At the center of town stood the stone structures of the Custom House, the mayor's home, and the newly built City Hall, which had been constructed to bring together in one place the offices of those townsmen who oversaw the day-to-day politics and essentials of New York, such as the ward officers, the department of records, the legal staff, the high constable, and the chief prosecutor. Basically, as Matthew thought, they were there to keep rival businessmen from killing one another, for this might be the new world but the old savage sensibilities of London had also made the Atlantic crossing.

Matthew walked downhill into the town, his pace brisk and his destination deliberate. By the dint of repetition and the sundial that stood before Madam Kenneday's bakery, he knew he had half-an-hour until Magistrate Powers arrived at the office. Before Matthew put a quill to paper this morning he was determined to light a fire under a pair of blacksmith boots.

For all of its cattle corrals, stables, skinning shops, warehouses, and rough taverns, New York was a pretty town. The Dutch pioneers had left their mark in the distinctive narrow facades, high stepped-gable roofs, and their penchant for weather-vanes, decorative chimneys, and simple but geometrically precise gardens. All the structures south of Wall Street bore the Dutch signature, while the houses and buildings north of that demarcation were of the typically four-square English variety. Matthew had gotten into a conversation about that subject a few nights ago at the Gallop; it would be seen in the future, he contended, that the Dutch were of a pastoral mind and so strived to beautify their surroundings with gardens and parks, but the English were eager to jam their boxes onto every available space in the name of commerce. One just had to cross Wall Street to see the difference between London and Amsterdam. Of course he'd not been to either of those cities, but he had his collection of books and he was always interested in the stories of travellers. Plus he was always armed with an opinion, which made him either the hero or goat of these conversant evenings at the Gallop.

It was true, he mused as he ventured along the Broad Way toward the steeple of Trinity Church, that New York was becoming . . . well, how would one put it? *Cosmopolitan*, perhaps? That its presence and future was beginning to be noticed around the world? Or so it seemed. On any day one might see walking the cobblestones brightly robed visitors from India, or Belgian financiers the picture of serious intent in dark suits and black tricorns, or even Dutch merchants in gilt waistcoats and elaborate wigs puffing powder at each stride, indicating that enemies could meet quite profitably at the counting table. Found planning the trade of coin over wine and codfish at the alehouses day or night might be Cuban sugar merchants from Barbados, Jewish gemstone traders from Brazil, or German tobacco buyers from Stockholm. Indigo dye suppliers from Charles Town or ambassadors from numerous businesses in Philadelphia and Boston regularly visited. A sight not uncommon was that of Sint Sink, Iroquois, and Mohican Indians bringing into the town cartloads of deer, beaver, and bear skins and causing a right hullabaloo among people and dogs alike. Of course slave ships arrived at dock from Africa or the West Indies, and those slaves who weren't purchased for duty here were sent off for auction to other localities like Long Island. Perhaps one New York household in every five held a slave; though the slaves were forbidden by town decree to gather beyond two in number, there were alarming reports from dockside merchants of night-roaming gangs of slaves who, perhaps continuing to fight old tribal feuds, attacked one another over perceived territories.

Matthew wondered, as he walked, if becoming cosmopolitan meant an eventual emulation of the sprawl, debasement, and utter calamity of London. The tales he'd heard of that pandemetro chilled his blood—everything from the twelve-year-old prostitutes to the freak-show circuses and the joy of the mob at the hangman's theater. Possibly, with that latter revulsion, he was remembering how near Rachel Howarth had come to being burned alive in Fount Royal, and how the merry crowd would have howled as the ashes flew up. He wondered what would be the future of New York, in a hundred years. He wondered if fate and human nature decreed that every Bethlehem become in time a Bedlam.

As he crossed Wall Street before Trinity Church and the black iron fence around the church cemetery, he gave a glance at the trough in which he'd cleaned himself of his night's misfortune. The Dutch fortress wall that had stood here, made of logs twelve feet tall, had been constructed to guard that avenue of attack from the British before the settlement changed hands some thirty-eight years ago. It occurred to Matthew that New York no longer faced an adversary from without, as barring severe epidemic or some unforeseen catastrophe the place was securely fixed. He thought that the next threat to the survival of this town might well come from within, and bear from the consequences of forgetting the perils of human greed.

On his left, also on Wall Street, was the yellow stone City Hall and the town gaol, before which a notorious pickpocket named Ebenezer Grooder was on public view, confined to the pillory. A basket of rotten apples lay within reach of any citizen who wished to apply further justice. Matthew continued south, entering the smoke-hazed realm of stables, warehouses, and blacksmitheries.

It was one of those establishments, whose affixed sign read simply *Ross, Smith*, that was the aim of his arrow. He went into the open barn door of the place, into the dim light where hammers rang on iron and orange flames seethed in the black-bricked forge. A thick-set young man with curly blond hair was at work on the bellows cord, making the fire flare and spit. Beyond him, the elder master Marco Ross and the second apprentice were hammering out the vital commodity of horseshoes on their respective anvils. The noise was a kind of rough music, as one hammerblow was pitched higher than the other. All the smiths wore leather aprons to protect their clothes from flying shards of red-hot metal, and the heat and strenuous activity already at this early hour made the men sweat through the backs of their shirts. Cart-wheels, plows, and other bits of farm implements were arranged in wait for inspection, showing that Master Ross was at no sorrow for work.

Matthew crossed over the bricked floor to stand near the young man at his bellows labor. He waited until finally John Five sensed him there and turned to look over his shoulder. Matthew nodded; John returned the nod, his cherubic face ruddy in the heat and his eyes pale blue beneath thick blond brows, and then he returned to what he was doing without a word, since speaking was useless so long as the hammers did the talking.

At last John knew Matthew would not be denied; Matthew saw it, in the slump of the younger man's shoulders. That alone gave him an indication of how their meeting must go, but he had to pursue it. John Five ceased the bellows work, waved his arm in the air to get Master Ross to see, and then held up five fingers to ask for that much time. Master Ross gave a curt nod, with a stern glance at Matthew that said *Some of us have work to do* and laid in again on the hammer-and-tongs.

Outside, in the smoky sunlight, John Five wiped his sparkling forehead with a cloth and said, "How are you, Matthew?"

"Well, thank you. And you?"

"Well also." John was not as tall as Matthew, but had the wide shoulders and thick forearms of a man born to command iron. He was four years Matthew's junior, yet far from being a youth. In the King Street almshouse—then known as the Sainted John Home for Boys, before it was expanded to include two more buildings for orphaned girls and adult paupers—he had been the fifth John of thirty-six boys, thus his identity. John Five had one ear; the left had been hacked off. Across his chin was a deep scar that pulled the right corner of his mouth down into a perpetual sadness. John Five remembered a father and mother and a cabin in a wilderness clearing, perhaps an idealized memory. He recalled two infant siblings, both brothers he believed. He recalled the logs of a fort, and a man in a tricorn with goldleaf trimming talking to his father and showing him the shaft of a broken arrow. His memory could pull up the shrill sound of a woman screaming and blurred figures bursting through the window shutters and the door. He saw the glint of firelight on an upraised hatchet. Then the candle of his mind went out.

One thing he remembered quite clearly—and this he told Matthew and some of the others, one night at the orphanage—was a thin rail of a man with black teeth, tipping a bottle to his mouth and telling him to *Dance, dance, you little shit! Dance for our supper! And smile or I'll carve one in that fuckin' face!*

John Five recalled dancing in a tavern, and seeing his small shadow thrown on the wall. The thin man took coins from the customers and put them in a brown pot. He remembered the man drunk and swearing on a nasty bed in a little room somewhere. He remembered crawling under the bed to sleep, and two other men breaking into the room and beating the drunk man to death with cudgels. And he remembered thinking, as the man's brains flew upon the walls and the blood flowed over the floor, that he had never really liked to dance.

Soon after that, a travelling parson had brought the nine-year-old John to the orphanage and left him in the care of the demanding but fair-minded Headmaster Staunton, but when Staunton had left two years later to answer the call of a dream bidding him to take God's salvation to the Indian tribes, the position had been filled by Eben Ausley, newly arrived with commission in hand from jolly old England.

Standing with John Five alongside Master Ross' blacksmith shop, as the town began to speed itself into the rhythms of another day of trade and citizens passed by in their own currents of life like so many fish in the rivers, Matthew looked down at his shoes and measured his words carefully. "When we spoke last, you said you'd consider my request." He looked up into the younger man's eyes, which he could read like any book in his collection. Yet he had to go on. "Have you?"

"I have," John answered.

"And?"

John gave a pained expression. He stared at the knuckles of his hands, which he closed into fists and began to work together as if fighting a private battle. And Matthew knew this was entirely true. Still, Matthew had to persist: "You and I both know what needs to be done." There was no response, so Matthew plowed deeper. "He thinks he's gotten away with everything. He thinks no one cares. Oh yes, I saw him last night. He crowed like a madman, about how I hadn't gone to the magistrate because I have nothing. And you know the high constable is one of his gaming friends. So I have to have proof, John. I have to have *someone* who'll speak up."

"Someone," John said, with just a trace of bitterness.

"Myles Newell and his wife moved to Boston," Matthew reminded him. "He was willing, and close to it, but now that he's gone it's up to you."

John remained silent, still pressing his fists together, his eyes shadowed.

"Nathan Spencer hanged himself last month," Matthew said. "Twenty years old, and he still couldn't put it to rest."

"I know very well about Nathan. I was at the funeral too. And I've thought about him, many days. He used to come here and talk, just like you do. But tell me this, Matthew," and here John Five peered into his friend's face with eyes that were at once racked with anguish and as hot as the forge, "was it Nathan who couldn't put it to rest . . . or was it you?"

"It was both of us," Matthew said, truthfully.

John gave a quiet grunt and looked away again. "I'm sorry about Nathan. He was tryin' very hard to move on. But you wouldn't let him, would you?"

"I had no idea he was planning to kill himself."

"Maybe he wasn't, until you kept pesterin' him. Did you ever think about that?"

In truth, Matthew had. It was something, though, that he'd forced away from himself; he couldn't bear to admit to the shaving mirror that his pleadings with Nathan to make witness against Eben Ausley in front of Magistrate Powers and Chief Prosecutor James Bynes would result in a rope thrown over the rafters of the young man's garret.

"Nathan wasn't well," John Five went on. "In the head. He was weak. You should have known that, you bein' such the scholar."

"I can't bring him back, and neither can you," Matthew said, with more spice than he'd meant; it sounded too much like the curt dismissal of responsibility. "We have to go on, from where we—"

"*We?*" John scowled, an expression of menace not to be taken lightly. "What is this *we*? I haven't said I wanted anythin' to do with this. I've just listened to you talk, that's all. For the sake that you're such a high-collar now, and I have to say you're a fine smooth talker, Matthew. But talkin' can only go so far."

Matthew, as was his wont, took the initiative. "I agree. It *is* time for action."

"You mean time to put my neck in a noose too, don't you?"

"No, I do not."

"Well, that's what would happen. I don't mean hangin' myself. No, I'd never do that. But I mean ruinin' my life. And for what?" John Five drew a long breath and shook his head. When he spoke again, his voice was quieter and almost disconsolate. "Ausley's right. No one cares. No one will believe anythin' that's said again' him. He has too many friends. From what you've told me, he's lost too much money at them gamin' tables to go behind bars, or be banished from the town. His debtors wouldn't stand for it. So even if I spoke out—even if *anyone* spoke out—I'd be called a madman, or devil-possessed, or . . . who knows what would happen to me."

"If you're afraid for your life, I can tell you that Magistrate Powers will—"

"You talk and talk," John Five said, and stepped forward upon Matthew with a grimness that made the elder man think their friendship—an orphans' comraderie, as it were—was about to end with a broken jaw. "But you don't *listen*," John went on, though he checked his progress. He gazed toward the street, at the gents and ladies passing, at a horse-cart trundling by, at some children chasing each other and laughing as if all the world was a merriment.

"I've asked Constance to be my wife. We're to be joined in September."

Constance Wade, Matthew knew, had been John's love for nearly a year. He never thought John would get up the nerve to ask her, since she was the daughter of that stern-faced, black-garbed preacher William Wade, the man of whom it was said birds hushed singing when he cast the unblinking eye of God at them. Of course Matthew was happy for John Five, for Constance was certainly a fair maid and had a quick and lively mind, but he knew also what this meant.

John didn't speak for a moment, and Matthew likewise held his tongue in check. Then John said, "Phillip Covey. Have you asked *him*?"

"I have. He steadfastly refuses."

"Nicholas Robertson? John Galt?"

"Both I've asked, several times. Both have refused."

"Then why *me*, Matthew? Why keep comin' to *me*?"

"Because of what you've gone through. Not only from Ausley, but before. The Indian raid. The man who took you around and made you dance in the taverns. All that being knocked down, all that darkness and trouble. I thought you'd want to stand up and make sure that Ausley's put away where he ought to be." There was no response from John Five to this; the younger man's face was emotionless. Matthew said firmly, "I thought you'd want to see justice done."

Now, to Matthew's surprise, a hint of emotion did return to John's face, but it was the faintest trace of a knowing smile—or a slyness of knowledge, to be exact. "Justice done? Is that really it? Or do you just want to make me dance again?"

Matthew started to answer, to protest John's point, but before he could the younger man said quietly, "Please hear me, Matthew, and make true of it. Ausley never touched you, did he? You were of an age he thought . . . older than he cared to bother, isn't that right? So you heard things at night—cryin' maybe, a scream or two—and that was all. Maybe you rolled over on your cot and you had a bad dream. Maybe you wished you could do somethin', but you couldn't. Maybe you just felt small and weak. But if anyone was to want to do somethin' about Ausley *now*, Matthew, it would be me, and Covey, and Robertson, and Galt. We don't. We just want to go on with our lives." John paused to let that sink in. "Now you talk about justice bein' done, and that's a fine sentiment. But justice can't always see clear, isn't that the sayin'?"

"Nearly."

"Near enough, I guess. If I—or any of the others—got up on the stand and swore again' Ausley, there's no for certain he'd get more than ol' Grooder's gettin' right now. No, he wouldn't even get that. He'd talk his way out of it. Or buy his way out, with that high constable in his pocket. And look what would become of *me*, Matthew, to admit to such a thing. I'm to be married in September. Do you think the Reverend Wade would say I was good enough for his daughter, if he was to know?"

"I think he and Constance might both appreciate your courage."

"Ha!" John had almost laughed in Matthew's face. His eyes looked scorched. "I don't have that much courage."

"So you're just dismissing it." Matthew felt sweat on his forehead and on the back of his neck. John Five had been his last hope. "Just dismissing it, for all time."

"Yes," came the reply without hesitation. "Because I've got a life to live, Matthew. I'm sorry for all them others, but I can't help 'em. All I can do is help myself. Is that such a sin?"

Matthew was struck dumb. He'd feared that John Five would say no in this way—and indeed the tenor of their meetings had never indicated compliance, but hearing it outright was a major blow. Thoughts were spinning through his mind like whirlagigs. If there was no way to entreat any of Ausley's earlier victims to speak out—and no way to get into the almshouse to gain the testimonies of new victims—then the Headmaster from Hell had indeed won the battle and the war. Which meant Matthew, for all his belief in the power and fairness of justice, was simply a piece of sounding brass without structure or composition. One reason he'd come to

New York after leaving Fount Royal was to plan this attack and see it to the finish, and now—

"Life's not easy for anyone," John Five said. "You and me, we ought to know that better than most. But I think sometimes you've got to let bad things go, so you can move on. Just thinkin' about it, over and over again, and keepin' it in your head . . . it's no good."

"Yes," Matthew agreed, though he didn't know why. He'd heard himself speak as if from a vast distance.

"You ought to find somethin' better than this to hold on to," John said, not unkindly. "Somethin' with a future to it."

"A future," Matthew echoed. "Yes. Possibly you're right." Inwardly, he was thinking he had failed himself and failed the others at the orphanage and failed even the memory of Magistrate Woodward. He could hear the magistrate, speaking from his deathbed: *I have always been proud of you. Always. I knew from the first. When I saw you at the almshouse. The way you carried yourself. Something different and indefinable. But special. You will make your mark. Somewhere. You will make a profound difference to someone . . . just by being alive.*

"Matthew?"

I have always been proud of you.

"Matthew?"

He realized John Five had said something he'd not caught. He came back to the moment like a swimmer gliding up through dark and dirty water. "What?"

"I *asked* if you would be goin' to the social on Friday night."

"Social?" He thought he'd seen an announcement about it, plastered up on a wall here and there. "What social?"

"At the church. Friday night. You know, Elizabeth Martin has got quite the eye for you."

Matthew nodded vacantly. "The shoemaker's daughter. Didn't she just turn fourteen?"

"Well, what of it? She's a fine-lookin' girl, Matthew. I wouldn't turn up my nose at such a prize, if I were you."

"I'm not turning up my nose. I just . . . don't feel in the spirit of companionship these days."

"Who's talkin' about *companionship*, man? I'm talkin' marriage!"

"If that's so, your kettle's got a crack in it."

"Suit yourself, then. I'd best get back to work." John made a motion toward the doorway and then hesitated. He stood in a shard of sunlight. "You can beat your head 'gainst a wall 'til it kills you," he said. "It won't ever knock the wall down, and then where'll *you* be?"

"I don't know," came the answer, in a weary and soul-sick breath.

"I hope you'll figure it out. Good day, Matthew."

"Good day, John."

John Five returned to the blacksmith shop, and Matthew—still hazy in the head, whether from his disappointment or the knock he'd taken last night—walked away to New Street and thence northward to Wall Street and the City Hall office of Magistrate Powers. Before he reached that destination, he passed again by the pillory where Ebenezer Grooder was so justly confined, since he himself had heard the facts of this particular case as the magistrate's clerk.

Grooder, he noted, had company. Standing next to the basket of ammunition was a slim dandy in a beige-colored suit and a tricorn of the same color. He had pale blond hair, almost white, that was tied back in a queue and fixed with a beige ribbon. Grooder's visitor wore tan boots of expensive make and rested a riding-crop against his left shoulder. The tilt of his head said he was examining the pickpocket's predicament with interest. As Matthew watched, the man plucked an apple from the basket and without hesitation fired it into Grooder's face at a distance of more than twenty feet. The apple smacked into Grooder's forehead and exploded upon contact.

"Ah, you miserable bastard!" Grooder shouted, his fists clenched through the pillory's catch-holes. "You damned wretch!"

The man silently and methodically chose another fouled apple and threw it smack into Grooder's mouth.

He'd chosen an apple with some firmness to it, for this time Grooder didn't holler insults as he was too busy spitting blood from his split upper lip.

The man—who ought to be a grenadier with aim that true, Matthew thought—now took a third apple, cocked his arm to throw as Grooder found his ragged profane voice again, and suddenly froze in mid-motion. His head swivelled around and found Matthew watching him, and Matthew looked into a face that was both handsome for its regal gentility and fearsome for its utter lack of expression. Though there was no overt animosity from the other, Matthew had the feeling of looking at a coiled reptile that had been mildly disturbed by a cricket lighting on a nearby stone.

The man's piercing green eyes continued to hold him for several seconds, and then suddenly—as if some decision had been made about Matthew's threat or more precisely the *lack* of threat from a passing cricket—he turned away and delivered the third apple again with cold ferocity into the pickpocket's bloody mouth.

Grooder gave an anguished noise, perhaps a cry for help muted by broken teeth.

It was not for Matthew to intercede. It was, after all, Magistrate Powers' sentence on Grooder, that he stand at the pillory by daylight hours and that the pleasure of the citizens be to punish the man in such a fashion. Matthew strode past, quickly now because he had much work to do. Still . . . it *was* terribly cruel, wasn't it?

He glanced back and saw that the man in the beige suit was swiftly crossing the street, heading in the opposite direction. Grooder was quiet, his head bowed and blood dripping down into a little gory puddle below him. His hands kept clenching and unclenching, as if grappling the air. The flies would be all over his mouth in a few minutes.

Matthew kept walking. He'd never seen that man before. Possibly, like many others, he'd recently come to New York by ship or coach. So what of him?

Yet . . . it had occurred to Matthew that the man had taken great pleasure in his target practice. And never be it said that

Grooder didn't merit such attention, but . . . it was unpalatable, to his taste.

He continued on, to the yellow stone edifice of the triple-storied City Hall, in through the high wooden doors meant to signify the power of government and up the broad staircase to the second floor. The place still smelled of raw timbers and sawdust. He went to the third door on the right. It was locked, as the magistrate had not yet arrived, so Matthew used his key. Now he had to harness his power of will, and force all thoughts of injustice, disappointments, and bitterness from his mind, for his working day had begun and the business of the law was indeed a demanding mistress.

three

B Y THE PENDULUM CLOCK it was sixteen minutes after eight when Magistrate Nathaniel Powers entered the office, which was a large single room with a lead-paned glass window viewing upon the northward expanse of the Broad Way and the forested hills beyond.

"Morning, Matthew," he said, as he instantly and by constant habit shed his rather dimpled dove's-gray tricorn and the gray-striped coat of a suit that had known more needle-and-thread than a petticoat army. These he placed carefully, as always, upon two pegs next to the door.

"Good morning, sir," answered Matthew, as always. Truth be told, he'd been day-dreaming out the window, turned around at his desk upon which lay two ledger books, his bottle of good black India ink, and two goose-feather quills. He'd been quick enough, with the noise of boots on the corridor's boards and the *click* of the doorhandle, to dip his quill and return to his transcription of the most recent case of Duffey Boggs, found guilty of hog thievery and sentenced to twenty-five lashes at the whipping-post and the branding of a "T" on the right hand.

"Ah, the letters are ready?" Powers walked to his own desk, which befitting his status was central in the room and perhaps twice as large as Matthew's. He picked up the packet of more than a dozen envelopes, which were stamped with red wax seals of the magistrate's office and were bound for such destinations as varied as a city official down the stairs and a law colleague across the Atlantic. "Good work, very neatly done."

"Thank you," Matthew replied, as he always did when this compliment was offered him, and then he returned his attention to the thief of hogs.

Magistrate Powers sat down at his desk, which faced Matthew. "And what is on the docket for today, then?"

"Nothing at court. At one o'clock you have an appointment with Magistrate Dawes. Of course you're expected to attend Lord Cornbury's address at three o'clock."

"Yes, that." He nodded, his face amiable though deeply lined and care-worn. He was fifty-four years old, was married, and had three children: a married girl with her own family and two sons who wished nothing to do with books or judgments of law and so occupied themselves as workmen on the docks, though one had risen to the rank of foreman. The thing was, the two boys were likely paid quite a sum more than their father, the salaries of civil servants being as low as a mudcat's whiskers. Powers had dark brown hair gone gray with fatigue at the temples, his nose as straight as his principles and his brown, once hawk-like eyes in need of spectacles from time to time. He had been a tennis champion in his youth, at the University of Cambridge, and he spoke often of greatly missing the cheers and tumult of the galleries. Sometimes Matthew thought he could see the magistrate as a young, supple, and handsome athlete drinking in the approval of the crowd, and times as well he wondered if the man's silent reveries replayed those days before his knees creaked and his back was bent under the weight of a pressing judgment.

"Edward Hyde is his given name," Powers said, interpreting Matthew's silence as an interest in the new governor. "Third Earl of Clarendon. Attended Oxford, was a member of the Royal Regiment of Dragoons and a Tory in Parliament. My ear-to-the-ground also says he'll have some interesting observations about our fair town."

"You've met him, then?"

"Me? No, I've not been so favored. But it seems those who *have*—including High Constable Lillehorne—wish to keep the particulars to themselves and the rest of us in suspense." He began to go through the tidy stack of papers that had been arranged on the desk for his appraisal courtesy of his clerk, who had also prepared his quills and gathered some legal books from the shelves in anticipation of impending cases. "So tomorrow morning is our interview with the widow Muckleroy?"

"Yes sir."

"Casting a claim for stolen bedsheets on Barnaby Shears?"

"She contends he sold the bedsheets and bought his mule."

"Well, his entire house isn't worth an ass," Powers said. "One wonders how these folk get together."

"Not without some effort, I'm sure." The widow Muckleroy weighed near three-hundred pounds and Shears was a rascal so thin he could almost slide between the iron bars of his gaol cell, where he was now being held until this matter was cleared up.

"Friday, then?" the magistrate inquired, looking through his notes.

"Friday morning, nine o'clock, is the final hearing before sentence on George Knox."

Powers found some writing he'd done on the subject and spent a moment studying the pages. It was a matter of violence between rival owners of two flour mills. George Knox, when raging drunk, had hit Clement Sandford over the head with a bottle of ale in the Red Bull Tavern, causing much bloodshed and subsequent disorder as the supporters of both men in their dispute over prices and territories began a melee that had spilled out into Duke Street.

"It amazes me," the magistrate said quietly, in his appraisal of the facts, "that in this town prostitutes may give sewing lessons to ladies of the church, pirates may be consulted for their opinions on seaworth by shipbuilders, Christians and Jews may stroll together on a Sunday, and Indians may play dice games with leatherstockings, but let one silver piece fall in a crack between two members of the same profession and it's a bloody war." He put aside his papers and scowled. "Don't you get sick of it, Matthew?"

"Sir?" Matthew looked up from his writing; the question had honestly surprised him.

"Sick of it," Powers repeated. "*Sick*. As in *ill*. Of the pettiness and the never-ending pettifoggery."

"Well . . ." Matthew had no idea how to respond. "I don't—"

"Ah!" Powers waved a hand at him. "You're still a young fish, not a cranky old crab like I am. But you'll get here, if you stay in this profession long enough."

"I hope to not only stay in this profession, but to advance in it."

"What? Quilling transcripts, hour after hour? Arranging my papers for me? Writing my letters? And to become a magistrate some day? The honest fact is that you'd have to go to law school in England, and do you know the expense of that?"

"Yes sir, I do. I've been saving my money, and—"

"It will take *years*," the magistrate interrupted, staring steadily at Matthew. "Even then, you must have connections. Usually through social ties, family, or church. Didn't Isaac go over all this with you?"

"He . . . told me I'd need to be further educated in practical matters, and that . . . of course I'd have to formally attend a university, at some point."

"And I have no doubt you'd be an excellent university student and an excellent magistrate, if that's the professional path you choose to follow, but when were you planning on applying for placement?"

Matthew here had a jolt of what he might later term a "brain check," in light of his interest and aptitude for playing chess; he realized, like a drowsy sleeper hearing a distant alarm bell, that since the death of Isaac Woodward the passage of days, weeks, and months had begun to merge together into a strange coagulation of time itself, and that what at first had seemed slow and almost deceptively languid was indeed a fast bleeding of a vital period of his life. He realized also, not without a sharp piercing of bitterness like a knife to the gut, that his fixation on bringing Eben Ausley to justice had blinded him to his own future.

He sat motionless, the quill poised over paper, his precise lettering spread out before him, and suddenly the quiet *thrump* of the pendulum clock in the corner seemed brutally loud.

Neither did Powers speak. He continued to stare at Matthew, seeing the flash of dismay—*fright*, even—that surfaced on the younger man's face and then sank away again as false composure took its place. At length Powers folded his hands together and had the decency to avert his eyes. "I think," he said, "that when Isaac sent you to me he considered you'd stay here only a short while. A year, at the most. Possibly he believed your wage would be better. I think he meant for you to go to England and attend school. And you still can, Matthew, you still can; but I have to tell you, the climate at those universities is not kind to a young man without pedigree, and the fact that you were born here and raised in an orphanage . . . I'm not sure your application wouldn't be passed over a dozen times, even with my letter as to your character and abilities." He frowned. "Even with the letters of every magistrate in the colony. There are too many formidable families with money who wish their sons to become lawyers. *Not* magistrates for America, you understand, but lawyers for England. The private practice always pays so much better than the public welfare."

Matthew found his voice, albeit choked. "What am I going to *do*, then?"

Powers didn't reply, but he was obviously deep in thought; his eyes were distant, his mind turning something over and over to examine it from all angles.

Matthew waited, feeling like he ought to excuse himself to go home and spend the last of his remaining pocket-money on a few tankards full of the Old Admiral's ale, but of what use was a drunken escape from reality?

"You could still go to England," the magistrate finally said. "You might pay a captain a small amount and work on the ship. I might help you in that regard. You might find employ with a law office in London, and after a period of time someone there with more political currency than I possess might offer to champion you to a university of merit. If you really wanted to, that is."

"Of course I'd want to! Why wouldn't I?"

"Because . . . there might be something better for you," Powers answered.

"Better?" Matthew asked incredulously. "What could be better than *that?*" He remembered his place: "I mean . . . sir."

"A future. Beyond the hog thieves and the ruffians fighting in the streets. Look at the cases we've heard together, Matthew. Did any of them stand out, particularly?"

Matthew hesitated, thinking. In truth, the majority of cases had involved small thefts or various petty acts of criminality such as vandalism and slander. The only two real cases that had intrigued him and gotten his mind working had been the murder of the blue beggar, the first year he'd come to work in New York, and the matter of the deadly scarecrow on the Crispin farm last October. Everything else, it seemed to him now, had been an exercise in sleepwalking.

"As I thought," Powers went on. "Nothing much to report except the usual humdrum details of human malfeasance, carelessness, or stupidity, yes?"

"But . . . it's those things that are usual in any pursuit of justice."

"Rightly so, and that is the nature of public work. I'm just asking you, Matthew, if you really wish to give your life to those— how shall I put it—*mundanities?*"

"It's suited you well enough, hasn't it, sir?"

The magistrate smiled faintly and held up his frayed sleeve cuff. "Let's not speak of *suits*, shall we? But yes, I've been happy in my chosen profession. Well . . . *pleased* is the proper word, I suppose. But *satisfied* or *challenged?* Of those I'm not so sure. You see, I didn't volunteer for this position, Matthew. In the course of my work in London I made some judgments which unfortunately secured me some influential enemies. The next thing I knew, I was pushed out of a position and the only avenue open to my family and myself was a sea route to either Barbados or New York. So I've done the best I could, considering the situation, but now . . ." He trailed off.

Matthew had had the feeling that there was more to this line of thought than met the ear. He prodded, "Yes, sir?"

The magistrate scratched his chin and paused, constructing his next comment. Then he stood up and walked to the window, where he leaned against the casement to look down upon the street. Matthew swivelled around to follow his progress.

"I'm leaving my position at the end of September," Powers said. "And leaving New York, as well. That's what I'm speaking to Magistrate Dawes about today . . . though he doesn't know it yet. You're the first I've told."

"*Leaving?*" Matthew had received no inkling of this, and his first thought was that the man's health demanded a change. "Are you *ill*, sir?"

"No, not ill. In fact, since I made up my mind I've been feeling very perky lately. And I only did decide in the last few days, Matthew. It's not something I've been keeping from you." He turned from the window to give the younger man his full attention, the sunlight spilling across his shoulders and head. "You've heard me mention my elder brother Durham?"

"Yes sir."

"He's a botanist, I believe I've told you? And that he manages a tobacco plantation for Lord Kent in the Carolina colony?"

Matthew nodded.

"Durham has asked me to help him, as he wishes to concentrate only on the botanical aspects. Lord Kent keeps buying more land, and the place has gotten so large everything else is overwhelming him. It would be legal work—contracts with suppliers and such—and also managerial in nature. Not to mention three times the money I'm currently making."

"Oh," Matthew said.

"Judith is certainly well for it," the magistrate continued. "The social harridans here have never exactly welcomed her with open arms. But there's a town beginning to thrive near the plantation, and Durham has great expectations for it. I haven't mentioned this to the boys yet. I expect Roger may travel with us, but Warren will likely stay, his job being so important. Abigail of course has her own family and I shall miss the grandchildren, but my mind is settled."

"I see," was Matthew's response. His shoulders slumped. He wondered if this was the personal calamity Cecily had smelled on him this morning. All in all, he ought to go do some drinking and then back to bed.

"That's not all I have to tell you," Powers said, and the bright tone of his voice instantly made Matthew sit up straight, whether expecting more bad news or not he wasn't sure. "Don't think I'm going to leave here and not find something of interest for you. Do you wish to clerk for another magistrate?"

What are my choices? Matthew asked himself, but didn't speak it.

"If you do, that's simple enough. Either Dawes or Mackfinay would take you on today, if they could. But I want you to know where I've been this morning."

"Sir?" Now Matthew was totally lost.

"Where I've *been*," the magistrate repeated, as if conversing with an imbecile. "Or, more importantly, who I've met. I received a messenger at home yesterday evening, asking if I would meet with a Mrs. Katherine Herrald at the Dock House Inn. It seems we share some enemies, to the extent that she wished to speak with me. I went this morning, and . . . though I regretted that I could not be of assistance to her, I told her I knew someone who might be, and that I'd have you meet her at one o'clock tomorrow afternoon."

"*Me?*" Matthew truly thought the magistrate had lost a few coins from his treasury. "Why?"

"Because . . ." Powers stopped and seemed to think better of it. "Just because, and that's all I'm going to say. We have our interview with the widow Muckleroy at ten o'clock, yes? So you'll have time for a good lunch and then off to the Dock House with you."

"Sir . . . I'd really like to know what this is about. I mean, I appreciate any help you might give me, but . . . *who* is Mrs. Katherine Herrald?"

"A businesswoman," came the reply, "with a very intriguing plan. Now hush with the questions and contain yourself. Finish that transcript by noon and I'll take you to Sally Almond's, but only if you'll order the lamb's broth and biscuits." So saying, he returned to his desk and began to prepare his notes for the widow's questioning, while Matthew stared at his back and wondered what kind of insanity had infected the town today.

"Sir?" he tried again, but Powers waved an impatient hand at him and thus signalled the absolute end of any further discussion of the mysterious Mrs. Herrald.

At length Matthew had to put his curiosity aside, for nothing more would be forthcoming. He dipped his quill into the inkpot and put it to paper once again, as indeed he did need to finish the transcript and the Tuesday special at Sally Almond's tavern was not to be missed.

four

As the time approached for the arrival of Lord Cornbury, the meeting room in City Hall became first crowded, then packed, and then overflowing with citizens. Matthew, who had secured a seat on the third row pew with Magistrate Powers to his left and the sugar merchant Solomon Tully to his right, watched this infusion of human beings with great interest. Along the aisle of butter-yellow pinewood strode both the illustrious and infamous personages of New York, all bathed in the golden afternoon light that streamed through the tall multi-paned windows as if the place were rival to Trinity in its beatific acceptance of the good, the bad, and the unfortunately featured.

Here came strutting the prime businessmen of the town, their boots clattering on the boards as they pushed through the rabble; here came sauntering the shop-owners and warehouse masters, eager to find places behind the business leaders; here came shoving the lawyers and doctors demonstrating that they too sought the sunlight of recognition; here were the mill owners and tavernkeepers, the sea captains and craftsmen, the sweepers and menders and bakers, the shoemakers and tailors and barbers, those who pushed and those who were pushed, in a tide of humanity that surged from the street and were pressed shoulder-to-shoulder in the pews and in the aisle, and behind them a massed knot of people jammed up in the doors and out upon the cobblestones where no one could move so much as Ebenezer Grooder in his pillory. And all these personages, it appeared to Matthew, had gone home after lunch to pull from closets and chests their finest bits of peacock feathers to stand out from their fellow peacocks in a riot of color, fancy breeches, lace-collared and cuffed shirts, waistcoats of every hue from sea-green to drunkard's purple, rolled-brim tricorns of not only stolid black but also red, blue, and a particularly eye-inflaming yellow, embroidered coats and stockings, thick-soled chopine shoes that made men of medium height tall and tall men nearly topple, elaborate walking-sticks of ash, ebony, and chestnut capped with gold and silver grips, and all the rest of the fevered fashion that supposedly illuminated the signature of a gentleman.

It was a true carnival. With all the hollering of greetings, hail-fellows, and laughter meant to be heard in Philadelphia, the meeting room was quickly devolving into a Saturday eve tavern scene, made only more common by the number of pipes being smoked and not just a few of those fist-thick black Cuban cigars that had recently arrived from the Indies. In a short while smoke was billowing through the streams of sunlight and the slaves stationed around with large cloth fans to cool the air were having a hard time of it.

"How do they look?" Solomon Tully asked, and when both Matthew and Powers gave him their attention he grinned widely to show his bright white set of choppers.

"Very nice," the magistrate said. "And I presume they cost a small fortune?"

"Of course! Would they be worth a damn if they hadn't?" Tully was a stout and gregarious citizen in his early fifties, his face hard-lined but chubby-cheeked and ruddy with health. He, too, was a clothes-horse today, dressed in a pale blue suit and tricorn and a waistcoat striped dark blue and green, the chain of his London-bought watch gleaming from a prominent pocket.

"I suppose not," Powers replied, for the sake of conversation though he and Matthew knew full well that Mr. Tully—as friendly as he was and as charitable to the public welfare—would soon move from conversation to braggadocio.

"Only the best, is what I say!" Tully went on, as expected. "I said, give me the finest, cost be damned, and that's what I got. The ivory's direct from Africa, and the springs and gears were made in Zurich."

"I see," said the magistrate. His eyes were beginning to water, with all the smoke.

"They surely look expensive," Matthew offered. "Rich, I should say." He had to admit that they helped strengthen Mr. Tully's face, which had begun to recede in the mouth area due to an unfortunate set of decayed God-given dentals. Tully had only returned from England two days ago with his new equipment, and was justly proud of the compliments that had lately set him beaming.

"Rich is right!" Tully grinned more broadly still. Matthew thought he heard a spring twang. "And you can be sure they're of first-rate quality, young man. Why do anything if not first-rate, eh? Well, they're fixed in there all right, too. Want to look?" He started to tilt his head and stretch his mouth wider for Matthew's inspection, but fortunately at that moment one of the few women to arrive for the occasion came along the aisle in a parting of men like the miracle of the Red Sea and Tully turned around to see what the sudden lack of uproar was about.

Madam Polly Blossom was, like the Red Sea, a force of nature. She was a tall and handsome blond woman aged thirty-something, with a square no-nonsense jaw and clear blue eyes that saw all the way through a man to his wallet. She carried at her side a rolled-up parasol and she wore a bright yellow bonnet fastened below her chin with blue ribbons. Her silvery-blue mantua gown was covered, as was her custom, with embroidered flowers in hues of bold and subdued greens, lemon-yellow, and pink. She was ever the elegant-looking lady, Matthew thought, save for the black boots with metal filagree at the toes. He'd heard she could give a drunken customer a kick to the buttocks that would land him on Richmond island without need of a ferryboat.

As the pipes puffed and the gallery keenly watched this new entertainment, Polly Blossom strode along to the second row on the right side and stopped there to stare down upon the gentlemen who occupied that pew. All faces there were averted and no one spoke. Still the lady Blossom waited, and though Matthew couldn't see her face from this angle, he was certain her beauty had somewhat hardened. At last the young Robert Deverick, all of eighteen and perhaps wishing to show that courtesy was still in fashion to ladies of all situations, stood up from his seat. Abruptly the elder Pennford Deverick grasped his son's arm and shot him a scowl that were it a pistol had blown his son's brains out. This caused a current of whispers to go flying about the room and culminate in a few wicked chuckles. The young man, fresh-faced and scrubbed and wearing a pin-striped black suit and waistcoat in echo of his wealthy father's attire, looked torn for a moment between individual chivalry and family solidarity, but when Deverick hissed *"Sit down,"* the decision was made. The youth turned his eyes away from Madam Blossom and, his cheeks inflamed with red coals, sank back down into his seat and his father's control.

But instantly a new hero arose upon the stage of this play. The master of the Trot Then Gallop, the stout and gray-bearded Felix Sudbury in his old brown suit, stood up from the fourth row and graciously motioned that the lady in need could find refuge where he'd been sitting between the silversmith Israel Brandier and the tailor's son Effrem Owles, who was one of Matthew's friends and who played a wicked game of chess on Thursday nights at the Gallop. Some gallant gadfly began to applaud as Sudbury gave up his place and the lady slid in, and then several others clapped and guffawed until Pennford Deverick swept his gray-eyed gaze around like a battle frigate positioning a cannon broadside and everyone shut up.

"There's a sight, eh?" Solomon Tully dug an elbow into Matthew's ribs as the noise of conversation swelled once more and the linen fans flapped against the roiling smoke. "Madam Blossom coming in here like she owned the damned place and seating herself right in front of the Reverend Wade! Did you ever see such?"

Matthew saw that, indeed, the madam of Manhattan—who probably *could* own the building, with all the money he'd heard she and her doves were making—was sitting directly in front of the slim, austere, black-suited, and tricorned William Wade, who stared solemnly ahead as if through the lady's skull. Another note of interest, he saw, was that John Five—dressed in a plain gray suit for the occasion—was seated to the right of his father-in-law-to-be. Whatever might be said about Reverend Wade's rather grim personality, let it never be said that he wasn't fair-minded, Matthew thought. It was quite a feat for the minister to give his daughter over to marriage with a man whose past was largely a blank, and what wasn't blanked were memories of brutal violence. Matthew considered that the reverend was giving John Five a chance, and perhaps that was the most Christian gift.

Someone else caught his eye. Matthew's stomach clenched. Three rows behind John Five and Reverend Wade sat Eben Ausley, dressed up like a watermelon in a green suit and a vivid red velvet waistcoat. For this important day he was wearing a white wig with rolled curls that spilled down over his shoulders in emulation of formal judicial style. He had chosen to seat himself amid a contingent of young attorneys, among them the law associates Joplin Pollard, Andrew Kippering, and Bryan Fitzgerald, as if sending a message to Matthew and all those concerned that he was well-protected by the stupidity of the law. He did not deign to glance at Matthew, but smiled falsely and kept up a conversation with the aged but greatly respected Dutch physician Dr. Artemis Vanderbrocken, who sat on the pew in front of him.

"Pardon me, pardon me," said someone who stepped into Matthew's line-of-sight and leaned over the pew toward Magistrate Powers. "Sir, may I have a moment?"

"Oh. Yes, Marmaduke, what is it?"

"I was wondering, sir," said Marmaduke Grigsby, who wore spectacles on his moon-round face and had a single tuft of white hair sticking up like a little plume atop his otherwise-barren scalp. His eyes were large and blue and above them his heavy white eyebrows jumped and twitched, a clear sign to Matthew that the printmaster of New York was nervous in the magistrate's presence. "If you'd come to any further conclusions about the Masker?"

"Keep your voice down about that, please," the magistrate warned, though it was hardly necessary amid the returned hullabaloo.

"Yes sir, of course. But . . . do you have any further conclusions?"

"One conclusion. That Julius Godwin was murdered by a maniac."

"Yes sir." The way that Grigsby smiled, all lips and no teeth, told Matthew the questions were not to be turned aside so quickly. "But do you believe this presumed maniac has left our fair town?"

"Well, I can't say if—" Powers abruptly stopped, as if he'd bitten his tongue. "Now listen, Marmy. Is this more grist for that rag of yours?"

"Broadsheet, sir," Grigsby corrected. "An humble broadsheet dedicated to the welfare of the people."

"Oh, I saw that yesterday!" Now Solomon Tully showed an interest. "The *Bedbug*, is it?"

"For the last issue, Mr. Tully. I'm toying with calling it the *Earwig* next time. You know, something that bores in deeply and refuses to let loose."

"You mean there's going to be *another* one?" the magistrate asked sharply.

"Yes sir, absolutely. If my ink supply holds out, I mean. I'm hoping Matthew will help me set the type, just as he did the last time."

"He *what*?" Powers glared at Matthew. "How many occupations do you have?"

"It was an afternoon's work, that's all," Matthew said, rather meekly.

"Yes, and how many slips of the quill happened the next day because of it?"

"Oh, Matthew could work us both into our graves," Grigsby said, with another smile. It faltered under the magistrate's cool inspection. "Uh . . . I mean, sir, that he is a very industrious young—"

"Never mind that. Grigsby, do you know the kind of fear you've put into people? I ought to put you out there in the stocks for inciting a public terror."

"This lot doesn't look very terrified, sir," said the printmaster, holding his ground. He was sixty-two years old, short and rotund and stuffed into a cheap and ill-fitting suit the color of brown street mud—or to be more charitable, the good earth after a noble rain. Nothing about Grigsby seemed to fit together. His hands were too large for his arms, which were too small for his shoulders, which were too bulky for his chest, which caved in above the swell of his belly, and on down to his too-big-buckled shoes at the end of beanpole legs. His face was constructed with the same unfortunate proportions, and appeared at various times and in various lights to be all slab of a creased forehead, then overpowered by a massive nose shot through with red veins (for he did so love his nightly rum) and at its southern boundary made heavy by a low-hanging chin pierced by a cleft the size of a grapeshot. His formidable forehead was of special note, for he'd displayed to Matthew his ability to crack walnuts upon it with the heel of his hand. When he walked he seemed to be staggering left and right as if in battle with the very gravity of the world. Snowy hairs sprouted from the curls of his ears and the holes of his nose. His teeth had such spaces between them one might get a bath if he was full-bore on his esses. He had nervous tics that could be alarming to the uninitiated: the aforementioned twitching of the eyebrows, a sudden rolling of the eyes as if demons were playing bouncy-ball in his skull, and a truly wicked jest from God that caused him to uncontrollably break wind with a noise like the deepest note of a bass Chinese gong.

Yet, when Marmaduke Grigsby the printmaster decided to stand his ground this almost-misshapen creature became a man of self-assured grace. Matthew saw this transformation happen now, as Grigsby coolly looked down through his spectacles at Magistrate Powers. It was as if the printmaster was not complete until faced with a challenge, and then the strange physical combination of left-over parts from a giant and a dwarf were molded under pressure into the essence of a statesman.

"It is my task to inform, sir," said Grigsby, in a voice neither soft nor harsh but, as Hiram Stokely would say about a fine piece of pottery, well baked. "Just as it is the right of the citizens to *be* informed."

The magistrate had not gotten to be a magistrate by sitting on his opinions. "Do you really think you're informing the citizens? By making up this . . . this damned *Masker* business?"

"I saw Dr. Godwin's body, sir. And I was not the only one who remarked upon that bit of cutting. Ashton McCaggers also speculated the same. In fact, it was he who mentioned it first."

"McCaggers is nearly a fool, the way he carries on!"

"That may be so," Grigsby said, "but as coroner he does have the authority to examine the dead for the benefit of High Constable Lillehorne. I trust you believe he's fit for that task?"

"Is all this bound for your next broadsheet? If so, I think you'd best direct your questions to the high constable." Powers frowned at his own remarks, for he was not a man suited to show a foul temper. "Marmy," he said, in a more conciliatory tone, "it's not the broadsheet that bothers me. Of course we'll have a proper newspaper here sooner or later, and perhaps you're the man to publish it, but I don't approve of this appeal to the low senses. Most of us thought we were leaving that behind in London with the *Gazette.* I can't tell you the harm an ill-reported or speculative story might do to the industry of this town."

It never hurt London, Matthew almost said, but he did think silence was the wisest course. He read the *Gazette* religiously when copies arrived by ship.

"I reported only the facts of Dr. Godwin's murder, sir," Grigsby parried. "As far as we know, I mean."

"No, you made up this 'Masker' thing. And perhaps it did come from McCaggers, but the young man didn't set it in type, you did. That kind of presumption and fear-mongering belongs in the realm of fantasy. And I might add that if you wish in the future to improve your list of subjects as to whom you will check facts, you should at the present time constrain your imagination."

Grigsby started to reply, but he hesitated whether by force of the magistrate's argument or his own desire not to disrupt a friendship. "I see your point, sir," he said, and that was all.

"Well, it's a damnable thing," Solomon Tully said. "Julius was a fine man and an excellent physician, when he wasn't in his cups. You know, he's the one who recommended my dental work. When I heard he'd been murdered, I couldn't believe my ears."

"Everyone had kind words to say about Dr. Godwin," the printmaster offered. "If he had any enemies, they weren't apparent."

"It was the work of a maniac," said Powers. "Some wretch who crawled off a boat and passed through town. It's been almost two weeks now, and he's well gone. That's both my opinion and that of the high constable."

"But it *is* odd, don't you think?" Grigsby lifted his eyebrows, which seemed a Herculean task.

"What?"

"Odd," said the printmaster, "in many ways, not least the fact that Dr. Godwin had so much money in his wallet. And the fact that his wallet was right there inside his coat. Untouched. Do you see what I mean?"

"Emphasizing the fact that a maniac killed him," Powers said. "Or possibly someone frightened the man off before he got the wallet, if indeed robbery was a motive."

"A maniacal robber, then?" Grigsby asked, and Matthew could see his mental quill poised to scribe.

"I'm speculating, that's all. And I'm telling you before witnesses I don't wish to see my name in the *Bedbug* . . . or *Earwig* or whatever you're calling it next. Now find a place to prop yourself, here come the aldermen."

The official door at the opposite end of the room had opened and the five aldermen—representing the five wards of the town— filed in to take their seats at the long, dark oak table that usually served to give them a surface to pound their fists on as they argued. They were joined by twice their number of scribes and clerks, who also took their chairs. Like the waiting crowd, the aldermen and lesser lights were dressed in their finest costumes, some of which had probably not seen sunshine from out a trunk since the Wall had come down. Matthew noted that the old Mr. Conradt, who oversaw the North Ward, looked gray and ill; but then again, he always appeared thus. So too, the Dock Ward alderman Mr. Whitakker was hollow-eyed and pale, as if all the blood had left his face, and one of the scribes spilled his papers onto the floor with a nervous twitch of his arm. As Marmaduke Grigsby retired from the aisle, Matthew began to wonder what was up.

At last the crier came to the speaker's podium that stood before the council table, drew in a mighty draught of air, and bellowed, "Hear ye, hear ye, all——" Then his voice cracked, he cleared his throat like a bassoon being blown, and he tried it again: "Hear ye, hear ye, all stand for the honorable Edward Hyde, Lord Cornbury, Governor of the Queen's colony of New York!"

The crier stepped back from the podium and the assemblage stood up, and from the door came with a rustle of lace and a swoop of feathers not Lord Cornbury but—shockingly, scandalously— one of Polly Blossom's bawds seeking to make a laughingstock of the sober occasion.

Matthew was struck senseless, as was everyone else. The woman, who made her madam look like a pauper's princess in her yellow-ribboned gown and her high lemon-hued sunhat topped with an outrageous sprouting of peacock feathers, marched right past the aldermen as if she—as Solomon Tully might have said— owned the damned place. She wore white kidskin gloves with gaudy sparkling rings displayed on the outside of the glove-fingers. From underneath her skirt of flouncing ribbons came, in the silence, the sharp *clack-clack* of high French heels on the English wood. The sunhat and feathers tilted at a precarious angle above a snow-white, elaborately curled wig decorated with glitter-stones and piled high to the moon, and the result of this was that she appeared to be a giantess of a woman, well over six feet tall.

Matthew expected someone to holler or storm the podium, or

one of the aldermen to leap to his feet in outrage, or Lord Cornbury himself to burst through the door red-faced and raging at having a prostitute upstage his entrance in such a way. But none of these things happened.

Instead, the wanton spectacle—who Matthew suddenly noted did not *glide*, as might be expected by a woman of leisure, but had a decidedly ungraceful gait—went right past the crier, who seemed to shrink into himself until he was just eyes and a nose at the collar of a shirt. Still no one rose or protested to stop her progress. She reached the podium, grasped it with gloved hands, regarded the citizens with her long, rather horsey pale-powdered face, and from her pink-rouged lips came the voice of a man: "Good afternoon. You may be seated."

five

N O ONE SAT DOWN. No one moved.
From far back of the room Matthew thought he heard
the sound of a bass Chinese gong, muffled. He caught a movement beside him and looked over at Solomon Tully, whose mouth
was stretched wide open and whose new choppers, wet with spit,
were sliding out of the gaping aperture. Without a thought,
Matthew reached out and pushed them back in until something
clicked. Tully continued to stare open-mouthed at the colony's
new governor.

"I said, you may be seated," Lord Cornbury urged, but the
way his peacock feathers swayed had some already mesmerized.

"God above," whispered Magistrate Powers, whose eyes were
about to pop, "the lord's a lady!"

"Gentlemen, *gentlemen*!" a voice boomed from the back.
There came the tap of a cane's tip, followed by the noise of boots
clumping on the pineboards. High Constable Gardner Lillehorne, a study in purple from his stockings to the top of his tricorn, strode up to the front and stood at ease, one hand resting
on the silver lion's head that adorned his black-lacquered cane.
"Ladies also," he amended, with a glance toward Polly Blossom.
"Lord Cornbury has asked you to be seated." He heard, as did the
whole assemblage, the noise of giggling and scurrilous chatter-

ings back where the crowd became a mob. Lillehorne's nostrils flared. He lifted his black-goateed chin like an axeblade about to fall. "*I*," he said, in a louder voice, "would also ask you not to show discourtesy, and to remember the manners for which you are so justly famous."

"Since when?" the magistrate whispered to Matthew.

"If we are not seated," Lillehorne went on against what was mostly still shock instead of resistance, "we will not witness Lord Cornbury's address this day . . . I mean, his *remarks* this day." He stopped to pat his glistening lips with a handkerchief that bore the new fashion, an embroidered monogram. "Sit, sit," he said with some annoyance, as if to wayward children.

"I'll be damned if my eyes haven't gone," Tully told Matthew as they sat down and the others got themselves settled again, as much as was possible. Tully rubbed his mouth, vaguely noting that the corners of his lips felt near split. "Do you see a man up there, or a woman?"

"I see . . . the new governor," Matthew answered.

"Pray continue, sir!" Lillehorne had turned around to face Lord Cornbury, and perhaps only Matthew saw that he squeezed his lion's head so hard his knuckles were bleached. "The audience is yours." With a gesture of his arm that would have made competent actors challenge Lillehorne to a duel for the honor of the theater, the high constable retreated to his place at the back of the room where, Matthew considered, he could watch the reactions of the crowd to see how the popular wind ruffled Cornbury's feathers.

"Thank you, Mr. Lillehorne," said the governor. He gazed out upon his people with his purpled eyes. "I wish to thank all of you as well for being here, and for showing me such hospitality as I and my wife have enjoyed these last few days. After a long sea voyage, one needs time to rest and recuperate before appearing properly in public."

"Maybe you need more time, sir!" some wag shouted back in the gallery, taking advantage of all the swirling smoke to hide his face. A little laughter swelled up but it froze on Lillehorne's wintry appraisal.

"I'm sure I do," agreed Lord Cornbury good-naturedly, and then he gave a ghastly smile. "But rest will do for some other day. On this afternoon I wish to state some facts about your town—*our* town now, of course—and offer some suggestions as to a future avenue toward greater success."

"Oh, mercy," quietly groaned Magistrate Powers.

"I have been in consultation with your aldermen, your high constable, and many business leaders," Cornbury went on. "I have listened and, I hope, learned. Suffice it to say I have not accepted this position lightly from my cousin, the Queen."

Lillehorne thumped his cane tip against the floor, daring anyone to chortle for fear of a night in the gaol.

"My cousin, the Queen," Cornbury repeated, as if chewing on a sweet. Matthew thought he had very heavy eyebrows for such a lady. "Now," the governor said, "let me outline where we are."

For the next half-hour, the audience was held not in rapture but rather by the droning on of Cornbury's less-than-majestic vocal skills. The man might be able to carry a dress, Matthew mused, but he couldn't manage a decent speech. Cornbury meandered through the success of the milling and shipbuilding businesses, the fact that there were nearly five thousand residents and that now in England people saw New York as not a struggling frontier town but a steady venture able to return sterling investment on the pound. He gave his lengthy opinion on how someday New York might surpass both Boston and Philadelphia as the central hub of the new British Empire, but added that first a shipment of iron nails that had accidentally gone to the Quaker town from the old British Empire must be retrieved so as to rebuild the structures unfortunately burned in the recent fire, as he did not trust treepegs. He waxed upon the potential of New York as a center for farming, for apple orchards and pumpkin fields. And then, going on forty minutes in his dry dissertation, he hit upon a subject that made the citizens sit up.

"All this potential for industry and profit must not be wasted," Cornbury said, "by late-night carousings and the resulting problem of slugabeds. I understand the taverns are not

closed here until the last . . . um . . . gentleman staggers out."
He paused a moment, surveying the audience, before he clumsily plowed ahead. "Forthwith, I shall decree that all taverns close at half past ten." A murmur began and quickly grew. "Also, I shall decree that no slave is to set foot in a tavern, and no red Indian shall be served—"

"Just a moment, sir! Just a moment!"

Matthew and the others up front looked around. Pennford Deverick had stood up and was casting an eagle-eye at the governor, his brow deeply furrowed as a sign of his own discontent. "What's this about the taverns closing early, sir?"

"Not early, Mr. Deverick, isn't it?"

"That's right. Mr. Deverick it is."

"Well. Not early, sir." Again the hideous smile emerged. "I wouldn't call ten-thirty at night early, by any stretch. Would you?"

"New York is not a town constrained by a bedtime, sir."

"Well, then, it ought to be. I've done a study on this. Long before I set out from England, many wise men afforded me their opinions on the wastage of available manpower due to—"

"The blazes with their opinions!" Deverick said sharply, and when he spoke sharply it was like a very loud knife to the ears, if a knife might be loud. Matthew saw the people around him flinch, and beside him Robert Deverick looked as if he wished to crawl under the nearest stone. "Do you know how many people here *depend* on the taverns?"

"Depend, sir? On the ability to consume strong drink and in the morning be unable to go about their duties to themselves, their families, and our town?"

Deverick was already waving him off with the governor's ninth word. "The taverns, Lord Cornblow . . ."

". . . *bury*," said the governor, whose quiet voice could also be cutting. "Lord Corn*bury*, if you please."

"The taverns are meeting places for businessmen," Deverick continued, sworls of red beginning to come up on his cheeks not unlike the governor's rouge. "Ask any tavern owner here." He pointed toward various personages. "Joel Kuyther over there. Or Burton Lake, or Thaddeus O'Brien, or—"

"Yes, I'm sure the assembly is well-stocked," Cornbury interrupted. "I presume you are also a tavern owner?"

"Lord Governor, if I may?" Again the smooth and rather oily High Constable Lillehorne slid forward, the lion's head on his cane nodding for attention. "If you haven't been properly introduced to Mr. Deverick other than by name, you should know that he represents, in a way, *all* the taverns and their owners. Mr. Deverick is a goods broker, and it is by his untiring enterprises that the establishments are properly stocked with ale, wine, foodstuffs, and the like."

"Not only that," Deverick added, still staring squarely at the governor. "I supply most of the glasses and platters, and a majority of the candles."

"And to also mention a majority of the candles used by the town," said Lillehorne, who Matthew thought was up to getting free wine for a year at his own favorite haunt.

"And, not least," Deverick pressed on, "the majority of lanterns that hold those candles, supplied to the town's constables for a reasonable allowance."

"Well," Lord Cornbury said after a short rumination, "it seems you run the town then, sir, is that not so? For all your good works procure both the peace and—you would have me believe—prosperity of New York." He lifted his gloved hands to show the palms, in an attitude of surrender. "Shall I sign over my governing charter to you, sir?"

Don't ask that of Lillehorne, Matthew thought. The high constable would use his own blood for want of ink.

Deverick stood very straight and stiff and tall, his face with its craggy boxer's nose and high creased forehead taking on an expression of composed nobility that perhaps Lord Cornbury could do well to emulate. Of course Deverick was a rich man. Possibly one of the wealthiest in the colony. Matthew didn't know much about him—who did? for he was certainly a lone wolf—but he'd heard from Grigsby that Deverick had fought his way out of the London rubbish piles to stand here, grandly clothed and as cold as midwinter's pond ice, staring down an official popinjay.

"I have my own fields of governance," replied Deverick, with a slight lift of his chin. "I should stay within their boundaries lest I trip over another man's fence. But before I release this subject, let me please ask you to meet with myself and a committee of the tavern owners to discuss the matter at your convenience ere you decide upon a fixed course of action."

"Oh, he's *good*," Powers whispered. "I didn't know there was so much lawyer in old Pennford."

Lord Cornbury again hesitated, and Matthew thought the man was not so schooled in diplomacy as he ought to be. Surely his feminine nature would seize upon a truce, if not so much to appease a very influential man but to get through his first public display without a riot.

"Very well," the governor said flatly, with no trace of interest in hearing any other opinion. "I shall delay my decree for one week, sir, and thank you for your remarks." With that gesture, Pennford Deverick returned to his seat.

Some of the discordant hubbub that had been brewing back in the mob pot began to simmer down now, but there were occasional hoots and hollers out on the street that proclaimed the verdict of the common man. Matthew wondered if a live governor such as the one standing before them could be worse than a dead mayor; well, time would tell.

Cornbury now launched upon another speech in which he praised every gentleman—and gentle lady, of course—for their support and recognition of the need for strong leadership in this growing and all-important town. Then, his smug horse half whipped to death, he said, "Before I ask that this meeting be adjourned, are there any comments from you? Any suggestions? I want you to know I am an open-minded man, and I shall do my best to solve whatever problems may arise, small or large, to aid this town in its orderly and profitable progress. Anyone?"

Matthew had in mind something to ask, but he warned himself against it because it was sure to anger Lillehorne and in his position that wasn't wise. He'd already in the past month left two letters with the high constable's clerk outlining his thoughts and had heard nothing back, so what was the point of further expressing an opinion?

Suddenly old wild-haired Hooper Gillespie stood up and said in his raspy wind-weathered voice, "See here, sir! I've got a problem needs fixin'!" He sailed on, as was his way, without waiting for a response. "I run the ferry between here and Breuckelen and I'm sick and tired of seein' them bullywhelp boys a-roamin' the river. You know they set fires out on Oyster Island to run them boats on the rocks, enough to make ye weep to see a good ship wrecked thataway. They got a cove they's hidin' in, I can point it out to ye quick enough. Holed up there in a shipwreck hulk, they got 'emselves a right nice hidin' place there all covered with weeds and sticks and such, 'nuff to make a beaver throw a jealousy. Well, it's gonna come to killin' if them boys ain't brought to justice, and I see 'em all the time a'-workin' their mischiefs and bad intents. And you know they come up alongside me a night back first a' June and robbed me, robbed all my passengers right there pretty as you please. Next time I'm feared if we don't have no coin or drink to scold 'em off with they're gonna run somebody clean through, 'cause their leader, that young fella thinks he's the like of Kidd hisself, well he carries a rapier sword and I tell you I don't like havin' a blade so near my throat on a night the Devil wouldn't be out there on that damn river. What do ye say?"

Lord Cornbury said nothing, for the longest spell. His eyes had gotten very large, which did nothing for his beauty. Finally, he asked of the audience, "Can anyone here translate that into proper English?"

"Oh, Mr. Gillespie's prattling on, sir," said Cornbury's new favorite middleman, the high constable. "He's mentioning a problem with some river trash that I am planning to clean up very soon indeed. It's nothing you need think about."

"What'd he say?" Gillespie asked the man sitting next to him.

"Sit down, Hooper!" commanded Lillehorne, with an imperial wave of that cane. "The governor doesn't have time for your little situations."

Afterward, Matthew wondered why he did it. He thought it was because of those two words. *Little situations*. To Gardner Lillehorne, everything that did not pertain to himself was a *little situation*. The robbers that used the river as their highway was a *little situation*, though they'd been at it for almost a year. The murder of Julius Godwin was a *little situation*, according to how much effort Lillehorne had put into it. So, too—and it seemed that all wickedness, sloth, and corruption came back to this point—the crimes of Eben Ausley surely would have been a *little situation* to the constable, whom Matthew had seen gaming with the headmaster on many occasions.

Well, it was time to make a big display of a little situation, Matthew thought.

He stood up, steeled himself in an instant, and when Lord Cornbury looked at him with those painted eyes he said, "I'd like to ask that some measure of attention be given to the problem of the constables, sir. The problem being that, as the town has increased in population and unfortunately so has the incidence of criminal behavior, the number and efficiency of the constables has not kept pace."

"Please identify yourself," Cornbury requested.

"His name's Corbett, sir. He's a clerk for one of the town's—"

"Matthew Corbett," came the steadfast and rather loud reply, as Matthew was determined not to be shot down by the high constable's crooked musket. "I am clerk for Magistrate—"

"—magistrates, Nathaniel Powers," Lillehorne kept talking, speaking directly to the governor, his own voice getting louder, "and I am well aware of this—"

"—Nathaniel Powers, sir," continued Matthew, battling the war of tangled voices, and then suddenly he was swept by a storm of images from his *little situation* with Magistrate Woodward at Fount Royal in the Carolina colony, where he had fought as a champion for the life of the accused witch Rachel Howarth. He remembered skeletons in a muddy pit, and the vile killer who'd tried to murder them in the middle of the night; he remembered the evil smell of the gaol and the beautiful naked woman dropping her cloak and saying defiantly *Here is the witch*; he recalled the fires that burned across Fount Royal, set by a diabolical hand; he saw in that storm the mob surging toward the gaolhouse doors, the shouting for the death at the stake of a woman whom Matthew had come to believe was innocently embroiled in a plot demonic far beyond even the ravings of that mad Reverend Exodus Jerusalem; he saw the lifeforce of Isaac Woodward waning, even as Matthew risked everything for—as the magistrate had put it—his "nightbird"; he saw all these scenes and more awhirl in his mind, and as he turned his face upon High Constable Lillehorne he knew one thing certain about himself: he had earned the right to speak as a man.

"—problem, fear not. We have on hand a score of good men, loyal citizens who nightly heed their civic du—"

"*Sir!*" Matthew said; it hadn't been a shout, but it was as startling as a pistol report in the chamber, for no one dared raise a voice against Lillehorne. Instantly the place could have been a tomb, and Matthew thought he'd indeed put the first shovel to his grave.

Lillehorne stopped speaking.

"I hold the floor," Matthew said, the heat rising in his face. He saw Eben Ausley give a mean little smile and then hide it behind the hand that cupped his chin. *Later for him,* Matthew thought. *Today for me.*

"What did you *say?*" Lillehorne came forward, a slow step at a time. This was a man who could glide. His narrow black eyes in the long pallid face were fixed upon his enemy with almost delicious anticipation.

"I hold the floor. I have the right to speak freely." He looked at Cornbury. "Do I not?"

"Um . . . yes. Yes, of course you do, son."

Ugh, Matthew thought. *Son?* He stood sideways to the high constable, not prepared to fully turn his back on the man. Beside him, Magistrate Powers said *sotto voce*, "Give your best."

"Please," Lord Cornbury urged, evidently feeling quite the benignant ruler now. "Do speak freely."

"Thank you, sir." One more uneasy glance at Lillehorne, who'd stayed his forward progress, and then Matthew gave all his attention to the man in the dress. "I wished to point out that we— our town—suffered a murder two weeks ago, and that—"

"Just *one* murder?" Cornbury interrupted, with a lopsided grin. "Mind you, I just made a sea voyage from a city where a dozen murders a night is commonplace, so bless your stars."

Some laughter ensued from this, notably Lillehorne's chortle and a repugnant noseblow guffaw from none other than Ausley. Matthew kept his face expressionless and continued. "I do bless my stars, sir, but I'd rather look to the constables for protection."

Now Solomon Tully and the magistrate laughed, and across the aisle Effrem Owles gave a little gleeful yelp.

"Well." The governor's smile was not so hideous, or perhaps Matthew was getting accustomed to the face. "Do go on."

"I'm aware of London's mortality rate." The *Gazette* made sure of that, with all its grisly descriptions of throat-cuttings, decapitations, strangulations, and poisonings of men, women, and children. "Also of the fact that London has an advanced force of civic organization."

"Not too well organized, unfortunately," Cornbury said, with a shrug.

"But think of how many murders there might be a night, without that organization. And add to that all the other criminal acts that occur between dusk and dawn. I'm proposing, sir, that we as a community take London's model into example and do something now to stem criminal violence before it becomes . . . shall we say . . . rooted."

"We don't have any criminal violence here!" shouted someone from the back. "That's just hog's breath, is all!"

Matthew didn't look around; he knew it was one of those so-called score of good men defending his woe-begotten honor. Other shouts and hollers burbled around, and he waited until they quieted. "My point," he said calmly, "is that we need organization before we have a problem. When we're chasing the cart it might be too late."

"You have suggestions, I assume?"

"Lord Governor!" Lillehorne, from the sound of the anguish in his voice, had been holding his breath while this discourse—this affront to his authority—was taking place. "The clerk is free to write his suggestions and give them to my clerk, just as any man or woman in this room or this town or this *colony* can do. I don't see the need for this public laundering!"

Was there any point in reminding Lillehorne of the letters already written and obviously rejected or discarded outright? Matthew didn't think so. "I do have a few suggestions," he said, still speaking directly to Cornbury. "May I state them, for the public record?" He nodded toward the scribes with quills poised over parchment paper at the aldermen's table.

"You may."

Matthew thought he heard a hissing sound from behind him. Lillehorne was not having a good day, and it was likely to get worse. "The constables," Matthew began, "need to meet at a common place before their rounds begin. They should sign their names in a ledger, indicating what time they arrive for duty. They should also sign out, and so receive permission from a higher authority before they go back to their homes. They should sign an oath not to drink on duty. And, to be honest, the drunkards among them should be culled and sent packing."

"Really?" Cornbury adjusted his hat, as the peacock feathers had begun to droop over into his eyes.

"Yes sir, really. The higher authority at this . . . this *station*, call it . . . should be responsible for making sure they're fit for service, and passing out to them lanterns and some sort of noise-making devices. Say a ratchet crank. Those are used in London, are they not?" The *Gazette* said so, therefore no need to wait for Cornbury's verification. "Something the Dutch used to do, and we for whatever reason ceased doing, was giving green-glassed lanterns to the constables. Therefore when you saw a green lantern's glow, you knew at whom you were looking. I think there also ought to be a program of training for the constables. They should all be able—"

"Hold, hold!" Lillehorne nearly shouted. "The constables are picked from the common stock! What kind of training are you talking about?"

"They should all be able to read and write," Matthew said. "Also it wouldn't hurt if they were men whose eyesight was proven not to be faulty."

"Listen to this!" The high constable was now back on stage, playing to the crowd. "The clerk makes it seem as if we're a town full of dunce-caps!"

"One dunce-cap is too many," Matthew answered; and with that he knew his future would be a battleground. Lillehorne was ominously silent. "I would also suggest, Lord Cornbury, that for the purpose of finding the best individuals for this nightly task, they should be paid from the common fund."

"*Paid?*" Cornbury managed to look both bemused and shocked at the same time. "In *money?*"

"Just as for any job. And let this central station be a serious workplace, not a warehouse or stable used as an afterthought. I think there are other details worth looking into, as well. Larger candles that burn longer, for instance. And more of them afforded to the constables and also placed in lanterns on *every* street corner. I'm sure Mr. Deverick might help with that."

"Yes of course," Deverick spoke up quickly, but everyone including Matthew knew he was already counting the extra lucre. "I also like the idea of the green lanterns. I can get those as a special order."

"This has not passed my approval *yet*, sir!" Cornbury obviously had no liking for Pennford Deverick, and wasn't about to let the moneywagon run away from him. "Please withhold your pleasure!" Then he directed a piercing stare at Matthew, who felt the power of royalty like a fist balled up to knock him down. "How is it you've given such thought to this, and the high constable has heard nothing of it?"

Matthew pondered this. Everyone waited, with some expectation. Then Matthew said, "The high constable is a busy man, sir. I'm sure these ideas would have come clear to him, eventually."

"Or perhaps not." Cornbury frowned. "Dear me, I've seen men duel to the death over lesser affronts to offices as this. Mr. Lillehorne, I assume you have the good of the town in mind, and that would preclude any offense you might take at this young man's bravura. Yes?"

Gardner Lillehorne said with the hint of a hiss, "My lord, I am only here to *sssserve*."

"Very good. Then I shall read over these remarks from the public record and I shall ask you at some point to meet with myself and, of course, the aldermen for further discussion. Until then, Mr. Deverick, I don't wish to see any green lanterns floating about in the dark. And you may sit down, Mr. Corbett, with thanks for your thoughtful suggestions. Anyone else?"

Matthew sat down, having been thoroughly dismissed. But Tully jabbed an encouraging elbow into his ribs and Powers said, "Good show."

"Sir? I have a question, if you please?"

The voice was familiar. Matthew looked around to see his chess-playing comrade stand up. Effrem Owles was twenty years old, but already the gray streaks were pronounced on the sides of his bird's-nest thatch of brown hair. His father, the tailor, had gone completely silver-haired by age thirty-five. Effrem was tall and thin and wore round spectacles that made his intelligent dark brown eyes seem to float out of his face. "Effrem Owles, sir," he said. "I do have a question, if it's not so . . . improper."

"I'll be the judge of impropriety, young man. Ask away."

"Yes sir, thank you. Well then . . . why is it you're dressed as a woman?"

A gasp went up that might have been heard 'round the world. Matthew knew Effrem had asked the question in all sincerity; it was not the younger man's nature to show cruelty or ill-will, but his vice—if such could be called—was a plain-spoken curiosity that sometimes rivalled even Matthew's.

"Ah." Lord Cornbury lifted a gloved and ringed finger. "Ah, that. Thank you for asking, Mr. Owles. I do understand how some—many, even—might not fathom my attire today. I am not always dressed so, but I decided that I should today at our first meeting show my respect and solidarity of spirit with the royal lady who has given me this wonderful opportunity to represent her interests so far from the mother shore."

"You mean—" Effrem began.

"Yes," Lord Cornbury said, "my cousin—"

"The Queen," supplied some harsh-voiced rascal from back amid the mob.

"There you have it." The governor smiled at his citizens as if he were the very sun. "Now I must retire from you and go about my business. Your business, of course. I promise to obey your call and your needs, as much as is humanly possible. Never let it be said that Edward Hyde is not responsive to the people. Good day, all of you, and I trust that at our next meeting we shall all have progress to report. Good day, gentlemen," he said to the aldermen, and with a sharp turn he made his way back toward the door and out of the chamber, leaving voices both calling and cat-calling, and Matthew wondering how many hours it had taken the man to practice flouncing in that gown. The crier, still visibly shaken, managed to croak that the meeting was ended and God save Queen Anne and the town of New York.

"That's that," said Magistrate Powers, which suitably summed everything up.

On his way out through the converging crowd, which seemed torn between near-hysterical laughter and sheer speechless shock, Matthew caught Effrem's eye and gave a lift of the chin that said *Good question*. Then with the next step he was aware of the sweet scent of flowers and Polly Blossom was passing him, leaving her provocative perfume up his nostrils. No sooner was she past than Matthew's forward progress was stopped by a silver lion's head pressed firmly against his collarbone.

Up close, Gardner Lillehorne was not a large man. In fact, he was three inches shorter than Matthew and wore too-large suits that did not hide his spindly frame but served to hang from it like baggy washing on a clothesline. His face was long and thin, accentuated by the precisely trimmed black goatee and mustache. He did not wear wigs, yet the blue sheen of his black hair pulled back with a dark purple ribbon suggested artificiality, at least for the season's latest dye from India. His nose was small and pointed, his lips like those of a painted doll's, his fingers small and his hands almost childlike. Nothing about him at close range was large or imposing, which Matthew thought had to do with why he was never likely to be granted a mayorship or governor's charter; the big, sprawling English empire liked big, sprawling men as their leaders.

At least Lord Cornbury appeared to be a large man, under the dress. That was an area Matthew wished not to think about too much. Yet at this moment, for all his near-diminutive stature, High Constable Lillehorne appeared to have filled his guts and lungs and fleshy cavities with angry bile, for he seemed swollen to twice his size. Matthew had once, as an urchin living on the waterfront before he'd gone to the orphanage, captured a small gray frog that in his hand expanded itself until it was twicefold all slippery slick skin, pulsating warts, and glaring enraged black eyes as big as duit coppers. Looking upon Lillehorne reminded Matthew of this maddened toad, which had promptly squirted his hand with piss and jumped into the East River.

"How very kind of you," said the goateed and livid puffer, in a quiet voice strained through clenched teeth. "How very, very decent of you . . . Magistrate Powers."

Matthew realized that, though Lillehorne was staring daggers at him, the high constable was addressing Powers at his right side.

"To ambush me in such a fashion, before the new governor. I knew you wished me out of a job, Nathaniel, but to use a *clerk* as your weapon of removal . . . it doesn't suit a gentleman like yourself."

"I heard Matthew's suggestions the same as you," Powers said. "They were his own."

"Oh, of course they were. For certain. You know what

Princess said to me, just this morning? She said, 'Gardner, I hope the new governor will shine a little light on you, and possibly report back to the Queen herself what a good job you're doing in a thankless situation.' Can't you see her face as she said that, Nathaniel?"

"I suppose," came the answer. Matthew knew that, though the true name of Lillehorne's rather socially voracious wife was Maude, she preferred to be called "Princess," since her father was known in London as the "Duke of Clams" after his shellfish eating-house on East Cheap Street.

"You and I have had our differences over one case or another, but I hardly expected this. And to hide behind a *boy*!"

"Sir?" Matthew had decided to stand firm, though the lion's head was trying to shove him off-balance. "The magistrate had nothing to do with this. I spoke for myself, pure and simply."

Lillehorne produced a mocking half-smile. "Pure? I doubt it. Simple-*minded*, yes. The time wasn't right to bring this issue to the forefront. *I* have the governor's ear, *I* could make these changes in our system *gradually*."

"We might not be able to wait for such gradual change," Matthew said. "Time and the criminal element may overtake us, and whatever system you believe we have."

"You are an impudent *fool*." Lillehorne gave Matthew's chest a painful thrust with the cane and then, thinking better of any further public display, brought the instrument down to his side. "And don't think I won't be watching you in case you want to overstep your bounds again, clerk."

"You're missing the point, Gardner," said Powers in an easy, nonthreatening voice. "We're all on the same side, aren't we?"

"And what side might that be?"

"The law."

It wasn't common that Lillehorne couldn't come up with a stinging response, but this time he fell silent. Suddenly an even worse visage came up alongside the high constable's shoulder. A hand touched the shoulder.

"Tonight at the Blind Eye?" Ausley inquired, pretending that neither Matthew nor the magistrate stood before him. "Montgomery's vowing to go double-or-nothing at Ombre."

"I shall bring my wallet, in order to hold the winnings from Montgomery's and your own."

"Good afternoon, then." Ausley touched the brim of his tricorn and glanced at Powers. "And good afternoon to you, sir." Then he waddled along with the stream of citizens past Matthew, leaving in his wake the overpowering odor of cloves.

"Just remember your *place*," the high constable warned Matthew, not without some heat, and Matthew thought he might be pissed on yet. But Lillehorne suddenly put an odious smile on his face, called to one of the sugar mill owners, and sidled away from Matthew and Powers to put the grab on another man of greater financial influence.

They got out of the chamber, out of the building, and onto the street where the sunlight was still bright and groups of people stood about discussing what they'd witnessed.

The magistrate, who looked tired and worn in the more glaring illumination, said he was going home to have a spot of tea in his rum, put his backside in a chair, and ponder on the differences not only between men and women but between talkers and doers. Then Matthew himself started up the incline hill of the Broad Way toward home, figuring there were always pots to be done and that the wheel and the work had a wonderful way of smoothing even the wicked edges of the world into a more comfortable shape.

six

UPON AWAKENING from his dream of murdering Eben Ausley, Matthew lay on his bed in the dark and pondered how easy it would be to murder Eben Ausley.

Think of it. To wait for him to emerge from a tavern—the Blind Eye, say—after a long night of gambling and drinking, and then fall in behind him and keep away from the lamps. Better still, to go on ahead and lie in wait at a place of one's choice. Here come the footsteps, heavy on the stones. Best to be sure it's him, though, before you strike. Sniff the air. Rotten cloves? That's our man.

Closer he comes, and closer yet. Let him come on, as we decide how to do the deed. We must have an implement, of course. A knife. Terribly messy. Turn on a bone and he escapes, screaming for his life. Blood all over the place. A hideous misfortune. Well then, a strangulation cord. Yes, and best of luck getting a rope around that fat neck; he'd shake you off like a flea before you got his eyes popped.

A club, then. Yes, a nice heavy bastard of a club with skull-cleaving knots all over it. The kind of club the blackguards sell to each other in the murder dens of Magpie Alley, according to the *Gazette*. Here you may offer your coins to the shadow-faced villains and take your pick of brainers. Ah, there's the one we want! The one with a hard ridge running the length of the bopper, the better to bust with. Right there, under the monkey's-claw blade and the little fist-sized bag of nails.

Matthew sat up, lit a match from his tinderbox on the bedside table, and touched the candle in its brown clay holder. As the welcomed light spread, so fled the ridiculous—and rather sickening, really—images of murder. In his dream, everything had been flailing blurred motion, but he'd known he was following Ausley for the dark purpose and when he came up behind him he killed the man. He wasn't sure how, or with what, but he did remember seeing Ausley's face staring up from the stones, the eyes glazed and the mocking little lip-twisted smile gone crooked as if he'd seen what the Devil had waiting for him down in the fire-hole.

Matthew sighed and rubbed his forehead. He might wish to with all his heart and soul, but he could no more kill Ausley than be alone in a room with him.

You ought to find somethin' better than this to hold on to, John Five had said. *Somethin' with a future to it.*

"Damn it," Matthew heard himself mutter, without realizing he was going to say it.

John Five was nothing, if not to the point.

The point being, it was over. Matthew had long ago realized his hopes of seeing Ausley brought to justice balanced on a slender thread. If only he'd been able to get one of the others—Galt, Covey, or Robertson—to bear witness. Just one, and then Ausley's pot would've been cracked. But think now what had befallen Nathan Spencer, who'd seen better to hang himself than let everyone in New York know how he'd been brutalized. What sense was there in that? Nathan had been a quiet, timid boy; too quiet and too timid, it seemed, for even as Matthew had offered him a hand out of the morass Nathan had been contemplating suicide.

"Damn it," he repeated, in spite of all reason. He didn't want to think, as John Five had maintained, that his intrusions into Nathan Spencer's life had aided the death-wish along. No, no; it was better not to think along that line, or one might become too cosy with the idea of death-wishes.

You ought to find somethin' better than this to hold on to. Matthew sat on the edge of his bed. How long had he been asleep? An hour or two? He didn't feel very sleepy anymore, even after murdering Eben Ausley. Through his windows there was no hint of dawn. He could go down and check the clock in the pottery shop, but he had the feeling just from repetition of sleep and time that it was not yet midnight. He stood up, his nightshirt flagging about him, lit a second candle for the company of light, and looked out the window that faced the Broad Way. Everything quiet out there, and mostly dark but for the few squares of other candlelit windows. No, no; hear that? Fiddle music, very faint. Laughter carried on the night breeze, then gone. As Lord Cornbury had put it, the last gentleman had not yet staggered out.

At supper this evening the Stokelys, who'd attended the governor's address but had been back in the crowd closer to the street, had praised Matthew's suggestions for the constables. It was past time the town got up to snuff in that regard, Hiram had said; the thing about the station where they were to meet made sense, too. Why hadn't Lillehorne thought of that?

As for Lord Cornbury's appearance, Hiram and Patience were less positive. The man might be meaning to represent the Queen, Hiram said, but couldn't he have worn a man's clothes just as well? It was a peculiar day, Patience said, when the governor of New York town was dressed in more ribbons and puffs than Polly Blossom.

Meanwhile, under the table, Cecily kept knocking her snout against Matthew's knees, reminding him that whatever premonition she foresaw had not yet come to pass.

Matthew turned from the window and surveyed his room. It was not large nor particularly small, just a garret tucked behind a trapdoor at the top of a ladder above the shop. There was a narrow bed, a chair, a clothes chest, the bedside table, and another table on which rested his washbasin. In a hot summer one could cook up here and in a cold winter the thickness of a blanket spared him from frostbite, but one didn't complain about such things. Everything was clean and neat, well-swept and well-ordered. He could cross from wall to wall with six steps, yet this was a favorite part of his world because of the bookcase.

The bookcase. There it stood, beside the clothes chest. Three shelves, made of lustrous dark brown wood with diamond-shaped mother-of-pearl insets. Underneath the bottom shelf was burned a name and date: Rodrigo de Pallares, Octubre 1690. It had arrived in New York last May, on a privateer's vessel, and was offered at waterfront auction along with many other items taken from Spanish ships. Matthew had bid on it, as a birthday gift to himself, but was outbid by half again as much by the shipbuilder Cornelius Rambouts. Suffice it to say, it was an amazement when Magistrate Powers, who'd been present at the auction, announced to Matthew that Corny had decided to sell that "old worm-eaten piece he'd picked up at the dock" for Matthew's original bid just to be rid of a Spanish captain's tobacco-pipe smell.

The books that were jammed into these three shelves had also come off ships. Some were water-damaged, others missing front or back covers or large sections of pages, some yet almost perfect for their tribulations of sea travel, and all to Matthew were wonderful miracles of the human intellect. It helped that he was fluent in Latin and French, and his Spanish was coming along. He had his favorites, among them John Cotton's *A Discourse About Civil Government*, Thomas Vincent's *God's Terrible Voice in the City of London*, Cyrano de Bergerac's *A Comic History of the Society of the Moon*, and the short stories of *The Heptameron* compiled by Margaret, Queen of Navarre. In truth, though, all these volumes spoke to him. Some in voices soothing, some angry, some that had confused madness with religion, some that sought to build barriers and others that sought to break them; all the books spoke, in their own way. It was left to him to listen, or not.

He contemplated taking the chair and rereading something heavy, like Increase Mather's *Kometographia, Or a Discourse Concerning Comets*, to get these demons of murder out of his mind, yet it was not the dream that weighed on him so much. He found himself dwelling more on the memory of Nathan Spencer's funeral. It had been a bright and sunny June morning when Nathan had gone into the ground; a day when the birds sang, and that night the fiddles had played in the taverns and the laughter had gone on just as every night, but Matthew had sat in this room, in his chair, in the dark. He had wondered then, as he wondered now—as he wondered many nights, long before John Five had said it—if he'd killed Nathan. If his adamance and thirst for justice—no, call it what it was: his unflagging ambition to bring Eben Ausley to the noose—had led Nathan to uncoil the rope. He'd thought Nathan would crack, under his unrelenting pressure. And surely Nathan would do the right thing, the courageous thing. Surely Nathan would bear witness before Magistrate Powers and Chief Prosecutor Bynes to those terrible things done to him, and later be willing to repeat those same atrocities before a court of the town of New York.

Who wouldn't do such, if they were truly in need of justice?

Matthew looked into the flame of the nearest candle.

Nathan had needed only one thing: to be left alone.

I did kill him, he thought.

I finished what Ausley began.

He drew a long breath and let it out. The flame flickered, and strange shadows crawled upon the walls.

The funny thing, he thought. No . . . the tragic thing, was that the same all-consuming fire for justice in himself that had saved the life of Rachel Howarth in Fount Royal had . . . probably . . . most likely . . . almost certainly? . . . caused Nathan Spencer to take his own life.

He felt constricted within these walls; his shoulders felt pinched. He had the most uncommon need for a strong drink to calm his mind. He needed to hear the fiddle play across the room, and to be welcomed in a place where everyone knew his name.

The Gallop would still be open. Even if Mr. Sudbury was just cleaning the tables down, there'd be time enough for one good blast of brown stout. He had to get dressed and hurry, though, if he wished to end this night in the presence of friends.

Five minutes later he was going down the ladder wearing a fresh white shirt, tan-colored breeches, and the boots he'd polished before retiring to bed. The pottery shop was as neatly kept as Matthew's room, seeing as how it was also Matthew's responsibility. Arranged on shelves were various bowls, cups, plates, candle-holders, and such, either waiting for a buyer or awaiting further ornamentation before firing. It was a firmly built place, with upright wooden posts supporting the garret floor. A large window that displayed select pieces of the potter's art faced the street to entice customers. Matthew paused to fire a match and light the pierced-tin lantern that hung on a hook next to the door, deciding that tonight—though he was determined to steer clear of the Blind Eye and any sighting of Ausley—he could use more illumination to beware any attack from the headmaster's stomperboys.

As he walked down the Broad Way he saw moonlight glitter silver on the black harbor water. The Gallop was on Crown Street, about a six-minute's brisk pace, and thankfully a good distance north of the rougher taverns such as the Thorn Bush, the Blind Eye, and the Cock'a'tail. He had no need for danger or intrigue tonight, as his head was still not quite comfortable on his neck. One drink of stout, a little conversation—probably about Lord Cornbury, if he knew anything about the public taste for gossip— and then to bed until morning.

He turned left onto Crown Street, where at the corner stood the Owleses' tailor shop. The sound of fiddling came again, coupled with laughter. The music and hilarity was issuing from the lamp-lit doorway of the Red Barrel Inn, across the street. Two men staggered forth, singing some off-key ditty whose words Matthew could only make out were not of the Sunday language. Following behind them a thin woman with black hair and dark-painted eyes came to the door and heaved a bucketful of who-knew-what at their backs, then screeched a curse as her dowsed targets laughed as only those who are truly stoggered may. One of the men fell to his knees in the dirt and the other began to dance a merry jig around him as the woman hollered for a constable.

Matthew put his head down and kept going, knowing that one might see anything at any time on the streets of this town, which particularly after nightfall had aspirations to rival the coarser deeds of London.

But how could it not be so? Matthew knew that, after all, London was in the blood of these people. There was talk of *New York-ers*, those who were born here, but the majority of citizens still had London grime on their bootsoles and London soot in their lungs. It was still the mother city, from whence came ships bearing more Londoners determined to give birth to New Yorkers. Matthew surmised that in time New York would forge its own complete identity, if it survived to become a city, but for now it was a British investment shaped by the will of Londoners for the pocketbooks of London. How could it not take that city as its model of growth, industry, and—unfortunately—vice? Which was exactly why Matthew was concerned about the lack of organization concerning the constables. He knew from his newspaper reading that the mother city was nearly overcome by the criminal element, with the "Old Charlies" unable to cope with the daily flood of murders, robberies, and other demonstrations of the darker heart.

As more business grew to profit in New York, the ships would be bringing over experienced wolves intent on chewing the bones of a whole new flock of sheep. He fervently hoped that High Constable Lillehorne—or whoever was in charge by then—would be ready when it happened.

The Gallop was just a block ahead, across Smith Street. A black cat with white feet shot out along the street and tore after what appeared to be a large rat, the effect causing Matthew's heart to give a leap up somewhere behind his uvula.

And then, from his right down Smith Street, came a thin gurgled cry.

"Murder!"

And again, now louder and more urgent: *"Help! Murder!"*

Matthew stopped and lifted his lantern, his heart still lodged in his throat. A figure was running toward him; more stumbling and shambling than running, but making an effort at keeping a straight line. The sight of this figure coming at him almost made him concurrently pee in his breeches and hurl the lantern in self-defense.

"Murder! Murder!" the young man shouted, and then he seemed to see Matthew for the first time and he held up his arms

for mercy as he all but fell forward, his face bleached and his red-dish-brown hair wild. *"Who's 'at?"*

"Who are—" He recognized the face then, by the lantern's glow and the added light of the lamp nailed up to the Smith Street cornerpost. It was Phillip Covey, one of Matthew's friends from the orphanage. "It's Matthew Corbett, Phillip! What's happened?"

"Matthew, Matthew! Heesh all cut up!" Covey grabbed hold of Matthew and almost tumbled them both to the dirt. The smell of liquor off Covey's breath nearly knocked Matthew down any-way. Covey's eyes were shot with red and dark-circled, and what-ever he'd seen had caused his nose to blow because gleaming threads of snot were dangling down over his lips and chin. "Heesh had it, Matthew! God help 'im, heesh all cut!"

Covey, a small-boned young man about three years younger than Matthew, was so drunk Matthew had to put an arm around him to hold him from falling. Still Covey trembled and flailed and began to sob, his knees buckling. "God Lord!" he cried. "God Lord, I near stepped on 'im!"

"Who? Who is it?"

Covey looked at him blankly, tears streaking his cheeks and his mouth twisted. "I dunno," he managed, "but heesh all cut up over there."

"Over there? Over *where?*"

"There." Covey pointed back along Smith Street, and then Matthew saw the wet blood on not only the hand with the point-ing finger but Covey's other hand and red smears and grisly clumps of black mess all over Matthew's white shirt.

"My God!" Matthew cried out, and when he jerked back Covey's knees gave way and the younger man pitched down to the street where he blurbled and gagged and began to puke up his guts.

"What is it? What's the noise?"

Two lanterns were coming from the direction of the Trot Then Gallop, and in another few seconds Matthew made out four men following the light.

"Here!" Matthew shouted; a stupid, confused thing to say in a moment of chaos, he realized. They were coming this way anyhow. To make things more clear, Matthew shouted, "I'm here!" which was perhaps the most ridiculous thing because at that moment the double lantern light fell upon him and there was a gasp and stumble as four men saw his bloody shirt and collided with each other like pole-struck oxen.

"*Matthew*? You're all torn up!" Felix Sudbury aimed his light at Covey. "Did this bastard do it?"

"No sir, he——"

"*Constable! Constable!*" the second man behind Sudbury began to shout, in a voice that might batter in doors and break shutters.

Matthew turned away from this ear-shattering yawp and walked quickly past Phillip Covey, his lantern uplifted to reveal whoever lay grievously injured further along Smith Street. He saw no one lying within the reach of his light. Along the street, candles were showing in windows and people were beginning to emerge from their houses. Dogs were barking up a riot. From somewhere on his left Matthew heard a donkey heehawing, probably in response to that leather-lunged gentleman behind him who now cupped his hands to his mouth and shouted "*Connnnstable!*" into the night loud enough to surely alarm the fire-winged citizens of Mars.

Matthew kept walking south. Felix Sudbury called behind him, "Matthew! Matthew!" but he didn't reply. Within the next few paces he made out someone in black kneeling on the ground under the red-striped awning that marked the doorway to the Smith Street Apothecary, closed for the night. A solemn face turned toward him. "Bring the light here."

Matthew obeyed, but not without reticence. Then he saw the entire picture: two men were kneeling over a body stretched out on its back. A black pool of blood shimmered in the English dirt. The man who'd spoken—none other than Reverend William Wade—reached up as Matthew approached and took the lantern to give more light to his compatriot.

Old Dr. Artemis Vanderbrocken also held a lamp, which

Matthew had not seen because the reverend's figure blocked the light. The doctor's instrument bag was beside him, and Vanderbrocken was leaning over peering at the body's throat.

"Quite a cutting," Matthew heard the aged physician say. "A little more and we'd be burying a body and a head."

"Who is it?" Matthew asked, leaning over to look but not really wanting to get that close. The coppery smell of blood was heavy and sickening.

"Not certain," answered Reverend Wade. "Can you tell, Artemis?"

"No, the face is too swollen. Here, let's try the coat."

Sudbury and the others joined the scene, as did several people from the southerly direction. Another drunk pushed forward to see, his pock-marked face ruddy with ale and the liquor smell hanging 'round him like a dank mist. "It's me brother!" he suddenly shouted. "Dear Christ, it's me brother, Davy Munthunk!"

"It's Davy Munthunk!" hollered the yell-king, who was standing right behind Matthew and almost took his ears off. "Davy Munthunk's been murdered!"

"Davy Munthunk's been murdered!" somebody else shouted down the street.

A second ruddy face pushed through the crowd at knee-level. "Who the fuck murdered me, then?"

"Watch that mouth!" Wade said. "Stand back, all of you. Matthew, are you honest?"

"Yes sir."

"Hold these." He gave Matthew a dark blue velvet wallet, bound with a leather cord, that was heavy with coins. Then he handed over a gold pocketwatch. "It's got blood on it, be careful." He seemed to see Matthew's gore-smeared shirt for the first time. "What happened to *you*?"

"I was—"

"Here! William, look at these!" Vanderbrocken lifted the lantern and showed the reverend something Matthew was unable to see. "Ornamentation," the doctor remarked. "Someone has a wicked wit to go along with that blade."

"We have to leave him," Matthew heard the reverend say. "You're sure he's dead?"

"Sorry to say, he's already travelled far beyond *this* world."

"But who *is* it?" Matthew asked. He was being pushed and shoved as others formed a crowd around the body. In just a brief span, if Matthew knew the mob mentality as he thought he did, the muffin man would pull his wagon up to the spectacle, the higglers would start hollering for attention, the harlots would flirt for late-night customers, and the pickpockets would start sharking for loot.

Reverend Wade and the doctor stood up. It was then that Matthew caught a glimpse of what might have been a light blue nightshirt under Dr. Vanderbrocken's gray cloak.

"Here." Wade returned the lantern to Matthew's hand. "You look and tell."

The reverend stepped aside. Matthew moved forward and shone the light down upon the dead.

The face was a red and swollen shockmask. Blood had streamed copiously from mouth and nostrils, but the hideous cutting was across the throat. Yellow cords and glistening dark matter were laid bare in that cavity, which looked like a grotesque and gaping smile under the sag of the chin. What had once been a white linen cravat was now black with matted gore. Big green flies were at work on the wound, as well as crawling about the lips and nostrils, oblivious to the shouts and furors of the human kind. As much as Matthew was distressed by the ugly violence, he also found himself focused on details: the rigid right hand resting on the belly, the fingers and thumb splayed as if signifying surprise and, in a way, acceptance; the tousselled, thick iron-gray hair; the obviously expensive and well-tailored pin-striped black suit and waistcoat and the glossy black shoes with silver buckles; the black tricorn lying just a few feet away, which as Matthew looked at it was crushed under the clumsy boots of the onlookers who pushed forward in an excitement nearing frenzy.

The dead man's face was unrecognizable for its swelling and death-convulsions, which seemed to have unseated the jaw and thrust it forward to expose the glint of the lower teeth. The eyes were thin slits in the mottled flesh, and as Matthew leaned closer still—as close as he dared, with all that blood and the whirling flies—he made out what appeared to be distinct cuts just above the eyebrows and below the sockets.

"God, what a mess!" Felix Sudbury said, standing alongside Matthew. "Can you tell who it is? *Was*, I mean?"

"Make way! Make way for a constable!" came a hoarse shout, before Matthew could respond. Someone was trying to fight through the crowd, which didn't give a damn to part shoulders.

"Murder! Oh Lord, murder!" a woman was screaming. "My boy Davy's been murdered!" Then, before the constable could get through the madhouse, the two-hundred-forty pounds of Mother Munthunk shoved into view, pushing people aside like ten-pins. The woman, wife of a sea captain and keeper of the Blue Bee Tavern off Hanover Square, was a fearsome sight in her kindliest disposition, but tonight behind her wild mane of gray-streaked hair, her hatchet-nosed face, and eyes black as London's secrets she was frightening enough to make even the drunk Munthunk brothers bleat.

"Ma! Ma! Davy's alive, Ma!" Darwin shouted, though with all this racket it would've been hard to hear a cannon go off over your right shoulder.

"I'm alive, Ma!" hollered Davy, still on his knees.

"By God, I'll skin ye raw!" The hulking female reached down and with one huge scabby hand plucked Davy to his feet. "I'll whip ye 'til your mouth farts and your ass cries 'Mercy'!" She got her fingers locked in his hair and he howled with pain as she pulled him from one storm into another.

"Make way for a *constable*, damn it!" Then the constable pushed through, and Matthew recognized him as the little barrel-chested bully Dippen Nack, who carried a lantern in one hand and brandished a black billyclub in the other. He took one look at the corpse, his beady eyes in the rum-ruddy face grew twice their size, and he squirted away in a blur like any rabbit would run.

Matthew saw that with no control over this crowd the scene of the crime was being stomped to ruins. Now some people—perhaps those who'd been roused from their last round at the taverns—were daring to come in and look closer at the face, and in so doing they were stepping on the body as those behind them pushed forward to get a gander. Suddenly beside Matthew appeared Effrem Owles, wearing a coat over a long white nightshirt and his eyes huge behind his glasses. "You'd best move back!" he warned. "Come on!"

Just as Matthew was about to retreat he saw the boot of a staggering lout step right down upon the corpse's head, and then the lout himself stumbled and fell across the body. "Get up from there!" Matthew shouted, anger flaming his cheeks. "Get back, everyone! It's not a damned circus!"

A bell began to be rung steadily and deliberately, its high metallic sound piercing the uproar. Matthew saw someone pushing through the human shoals. The ringing of the bell caused people to come to their senses and make way. Then High Constable Lillehorne appeared, holding a small brass bell in one hand and a lantern in the other. He kept up the bell-ringing until the noise quietened to a dull murmur. "Step back!" he commanded. "Everyone step back *now* or you'll spend the night behind bars!"

"We just wanted to see who it was got murdered, that's all!" protested a woman in the crowd, and others shouted agreement.

"If you want to see so much, I'll volunteer you to carry the body to the cold room! Anyone wish to make that trip?"

That shut everyone's trap up good and proper. The cold room, in the basement of City Hall, was Ashton McCaggers' territory and not a place citizens wished to go unless they required his services, at which point they would be beyond caring.

"Go on about your business!" Lillehorne said. "You're making fools of yourselves!" He looked down at the corpse and then directly at Matthew. His eyes widened as he saw the bloody shirt. "What have you done, Corbett?"

"Nothing! Phillip Covey found the body. He ran into me and . . . got this all over me."

"Did he also loot the corpse, or is that your own doing?"

Matthew realized he was still holding both the watch and the wallet together in one hand. "No, sir. Reverend Wade took this from the coat."

"Reverend Wade? Where is the reverend, then?"

"He's—" Matthew searched the faces around him for Wade and Dr. Vanderbrocken, but neither of them were anywhere in sight. "He was just here. Both he and—"

"Stop your yammering. Who is this?" Lillehorne aimed the light down. To his credit, his expression remained composed and emotionless.

"I don't know, sir, but—" Matthew opened the watch's case with his thumb. There was no scrollwork monogram inside, as he'd hoped. The time had stopped at seventeen minutes after ten, which might be an indication of when the spring had wound out or when the trauma of a falling body had broken the mechanism. Still, the watch was an indicator of lavish wealth. Matthew turned to Effrem. "Is your father here?"

"He's right over there. Father!" Effrem called, and the elder Owles—who also wore round spectacles and had the silver hair that Effrem was soon to possess—came through the crowd.

"Are you giving the orders here, Corbett?" Lillehorne asked. "I might have a spot for you in the gaol tonight, too."

Matthew chose to ignore him. "Sir?" he said to Benjamin Owles. "Would you examine the suit and tell us who made it?"

"The suit?" Owles distastefully regarded the bloody corpse for a moment, but then he hoisted his courage and nodded. "All right. If I can."

A suit would bear the maker's mark in its weave and structure, Matthew surmised. In New York there were two other professional tailors and a number of amateurs who did clothes work, but unless this suit had made the voyage from England, Owles ought to be able to identify the workmanship.

Owles had just bent down and examined the coat's lining when he said, "I recognize this. It's a new lightweight suit, made at the first of the summer. I know, because *I* made it. In fact, I made two of the same material."

"Made them for whom?"

"Pennford and Robert Deverick. This has a pocket for a watch." He stood up. "It's Mr. Deverick's suit."

"It's Penn Deverick!" someone called into the dark.

And on along the street went the news, more swift than any article of brutal murder in the *Gazette* might be passed: "Penn Deverick's dead!"

"It's Pennford Deverick been murdered!"

"Old Deverick's a-layin' there, God rest him!"

"God rest him, but the Devil's got him!" some heartless scoundrel said, but not many might disagree.

Matthew kept quiet and decided to let the high constable find for himself what Matthew had already seen: the cuttings around Deverick's eyes.

They were the same wounds Marmaduke Grigsby had remarked upon in his article on the murder of Dr. Julius Godwin in the *Bedbug*.

Dr. Godwin unfortunately also suffered cuttings around the eyes that Master Ashton McCaggers has mentioned in his professional opinion appeared to form the shape of a mask.

Matthew watched while Lillehorne bent over the body, taking care not to get his boots in the blood. Lillehorne waved away the flies with his bell-hand. It would just be a few seconds before . . . and yes, there it was.

Matthew saw the high constable's head give a slight jerk, as if he'd been struck by a fist somewhere in the area of the upper chest.

He knew, as Matthew clearly did, that the Masker had claimed a second kill.

seven

TUESDAY NIGHT BECAME Wednesday morning. Thirteen steps down, Matthew stood in the grim domain of Ashton McCaggers.

The cold room, reached by a door behind the City Hall's central staircase, was lined with gray stone and had a floor of hard-packed brown clay. Originally an area to store foodstuffs in case of emergency, the chamber was deemed by McCaggers cool enough, even in the heat of midsummer, to delay the deterioration of a human body. However, no reckoning had yet been taken of how long a corpse might lie here on the wooden slab of a table before it broke down into the primordial ooze.

The table itself, at the center of the twenty-two-foot-wide chamber, had been prepared to host the body of Pennford Deverick by being covered with a sheet of burlap and then a layer of crushed chestnut hulls and flax and millet seeds so as to soak up the fluids. Matthew and the others commanded to be present by Gardner Lillehorne—including Effrem and Benjamin Owles, a still-woozy Phillip Covey, Felix Sudbury, and the onerous first-constable-on-the-scene Dippen Nack—had stood under a wrought-iron chandelier that held eight candles and watched as the corpse had slid down a metal chute from a square opening at the rear of the building. Then McCaggers' slave, the formidable bald-headed and silent man known only as Zed, had come down the thirteen stone steps after his task of wheeling the body-cart along Smith Street and had proceeded to lift the dead man onto another wheeled table. After this, Zed then prepared the examination table, pushed the body over, and lifted Deverick—still fully clothed so that the master of investigation might see the corpse as it was discovered—onto the bed of hulls and seeds. Zed worked diligently and without even glancing at his audience. His physical strength was awesome and his silence absolute, for he had no tongue.

To say the least, it was disturbing to all to see Pennford Deverick in such condition. His body was stiffening, and beneath the yellow candlelight he looked to be no longer truly human but rather a wax effigy whose facial features had melted and been re-formed with a mallet.

"I'm going to heave again, Matthew," Covey croaked. "I swear I am."

"No, you're not." Matthew caught his arm. "Just look at the floor."

There was nothing wrong with Zed's ears, but he paid the visitors no heed. All his attention was directed to the dead. He went about lighting four candles with tin reflectors behind them, and these he placed on the table one on either side of the corpse and one above the head and below the feet. He next opened the lid of a barrel, scooped two buckets into it, and placed the buckets—full of ordinary water, Matthew saw—on top of the wheeled table. A third bucket, empty, was placed along with them. From a cupboard he brought several pieces of folded white linen and placed these also beside the three buckets.

Next, he brought an artist's easel from its place in a corner and set this up alongside the corpse, as well as a pad of white document sheets and a clay jar that held black and red wax crayons. After this was done, he seemed to go to sleep standing up, his thick arms at his sides and his eyes half-closed. Under the candlelight, the strange upraised tribal scars that covered his face were deep purple against the ebony flesh, and somewhere in those markings were the stylized *Z, E,* and *D* shapes for which McCaggers had named him.

The death-jurists didn't have much longer to wait. Lillehorne came down the stairs, followed by a pale young man of medium height, whose light brown hair was receding from a high forehead and who wore an unremarkable suit of nearly the same hue. McCaggers, who was only three years Matthew's senior, carried a brown leather case with tortoise-shell clasps. He wore spectacles, had deep-set dark eyes, and was in need of a shave. As he descended the stairs he was the picture of cool and poised professionalism, but Matthew knew—as they all knew—what would happen when he reached the floor.

"He's a mess," Lillehorne said, referring to the corpse and not to McCaggers, though he well could be. "The blade almost took his head off."

McCaggers didn't reply, but as he came off the bottom step and his eyes found the body the sweat beads leaped from the pores of his face and in a matter of seconds he was as wet as if he'd been dowsed. His entire form had begun to shiver and quake, and when he put his toolcase up onto the table beside the buckets he had so much trouble with the clasps that Zed quickly and with practised grace opened it for him.

From the leather case gleamed and glinted calipers, forceps, little saws, knives of various shapes and sizes, tweezers, probes, and things that resembled many-pronged forks. The first item McCaggers chose, with a trembling hand, was a silver bottle. He uncapped it, drank down a good chug, and waved it under his nose.

He gave a quick glance at the corpse and then away. "We are absolutely certain the deceased"—his frail voice cracked on that word, which he repeated—"deceased individual is Mr. Pennford Deverick? Does anyone wish to verify?"

"I'll verify," said the high constable.

"Witnesses?" asked McCaggers.

"I'll verify," Matthew said.

"Then . . . I pronounce Mr. Deverick dead." He cleared his throat. "Dead. Verify?"

"Yes, I verify," said Lillehorne.

"Witnesses?"

"Dead as a fish in a frypan," said Felix Sudbury. "But listen, shouldn't we wait for his wife and boy? I mean . . . before anything else is done?"

"A messenger's been sent," Lillehorne said. "In any case, I wouldn't want Mrs. Deverick to see him as he is, would you?"

"She may *wish* to see him."

"Robert can make that decision, after he"—Lillehorne was momentarily interrupted by the noise of McCaggers vomiting into the empty bucket, but then he forged ahead—"views the body."

"I'm feelin' awful faint," Covey said, his knees starting to sag.

"Just hold up." Matthew was still supporting him. He watched as Zed dipped one of the linen cloths into a water bucket and moistened his master's pallid, agonized face. McCaggers took another snort and sniff of his stimulant.

It was the town's fortune—for good or otherwise—to have a man who was so skilled in anatomy, art, and memory as Ashton McCaggers, for it was said McCaggers could speak to you on Monday and on Saturday recite to you the exact time of day you'd spoken and virtually every line of your speech. He had been a promising art student, that much was clear, as well as a promising medical student—up until the moment of dealing with anything having to do with blood or dead flesh, and then he was a carriage wreck.

Still, his skills outweighed his deficiencies in the position the town had given him, and though he was no physician—and never would be, until blood became rum and flesh cinnamon cake—he would do his best, no matter how many buckets he filled.

This, Matthew thought, looked like a four-bucket job.

Zed was staring solemnly at his master, waiting for a signal. McCaggers nodded, and Zed went to work cleaning the clotted blood away from the dead man's face with another cloth dipped into the second water bucket. Matthew saw the point of the bucket trio now: one for the water to clean the body, one for water to revive McCaggers, and one for . . . the other.

"We are all in accord, then, as to the cause of death?" McCaggers asked Lillehorne, the sweat bright on his face once again.

"A blade to the throat. Say you?" The high constable regarded his jurists.

"Blade to the th'oat," croaked Dippen Nack, and the others gave either a nod or a vocal agreement.

"Duly noted," McCaggers said. He watched the cloth Zed used becoming dark with gore, and then he gave a lurch and turned once more to the bucket of other.

"This one picked Mr. Deverick's pockets, sir!" Nack put his billyclub up against Matthew's chin. "Caught him redhanded with the booty!"

"I told you, Reverend Wade gave this to me to hold. He and Dr. Vanderbrocken were examining the body."

"Therefore, what became of the good reverend and doctor?" Lillehorne lifted his thin black eyebrows. "Did anyone else see them?" he asked the group.

"I saw someone," Sudbury offered. "Two men, over the body."

"The reverend and the doctor?"

"I couldn't really tell who they were. Then of a sudden, with all that crowd around, I didn't see them anymore."

"Corbett?" Lillehorne peered into Matthew's eyes. "Why did they not stay on the scene? Don't you think it odd that both of those illustrious men should . . . shall we say . . . slip away into the crowd as they've supposedly done?"

"You'll have to ask them. Perhaps they had somewhere else to go."

"Somewhere more important than where Pennford Deverick lay dead on the ground? I should like to hear that story." Lillehorne took the wallet and gold watch from Matthew's hand.

"May I point out that this wasn't a robbery?" Matthew asked.

"You may point out that it might have been an *interrupted* robbery, yes. Covey!"

Phillip Covey almost shot out of his shoes. "Yes sir?"

"You say you were drunk and you almost tripped over the body, is that correct?"

"Yes sir. Correct, sir."

"You were coming from which tavern?"

"The . . . uh . . . the . . . I'm sorry, sir, I'm a bit nerved about all this. I was coming from . . . the . . . uh . . . the Gold Compass, sir. No, wait . . . it was the Laughing Cat, sir. Yessir, the Laughing Cat."

"The Laughing Cat is on Bridge Street. You live on Mill Street, don't you? How was it that you'd gone completely past Mill Street and were walking up Smith Street in the opposite direction of your house?"

"I don't know, sir. I suppose I was on my way to another tavern."

"There are *many* taverns between Bridge Street and where you supposedly almost tripped over the body. Why did you not go into one of those?"

"I . . . I guess I was—"

"How did you find the body resting?" McCaggers suddenly asked.

"Resting, sir? Well . . . on its back, sir. I mean, *his* back. I nearly stepped on him."

"And you got the blood on your hands how?"

"I tried to wake him up, sir." What came out next was in frantic haste. "I thought it was . . . you know . . . another drunk, lying there asleep. So I got down with him, trying to wake him up. Just for somebody to pal with, I guess. I took hold of his shirt . . . and then I saw what I'd gotten into."

McCaggers paused to dip a hand into the water bucket and cool his forehead. "Did you search this young man for a knife, Gardner?"

"I did. Nothing was found, but he could easily have tossed it."

"Did you find anything else on him?"

"Some coins, that's all." Lillehorne frowned. "*Should* I have found anything else?"

McCaggers must have felt something rising, for he hurriedly leaned over the bucket. He made a retching noise, but it was clear he was coming to the end of the second tasting of his supper.

"Gloves to guide a slippery knife handle," McCaggers said, when he could manage it. "A blade-sheath. Anything of value belonging to the victim. A *motive*. The young man didn't kill Mr. Deverick. Nor did he kill Dr. Godwin."

"Dr. Godwin? What are——"

"No need to play at denial. The same person who did this murdered Dr. Godwin."

There was a long silence during which Lillehorne watched Zed as the cleaning progressed, cloth to blood, to bucket, wrung out, back to blood once more. Now Deverick's face was almost scrubbed.

Lillehorne's voice was hollow when he finally spoke. "Go home, all of you."

Dippen Nack was first up the stairs, followed by Covey. As Matthew started to go up after Mr. Sudbury, Effrem, and Mr. Owles, Lillehorne said, "All except *you*, clerk."

Matthew stopped. He'd known he wasn't going to get out of here that easily.

"Hello? Hello? May I come down?"

The voice was unmistakable. Lillehorne winced. Marmaduke Grigsby appeared at the top of the stairs, his shirtsleeves rolled up to say he was ready for work.

"You're not needed here, Grigsby. Go home."

"Pardon, sir, but there's a frightful rabble of people out front milling about. I did my best to escort Mrs. Deverick and Robert through the crowd. Shall I bring them down?"

"Just the boy. I mean . . . send him down, and keep Mrs. Deverick——"

"The high constable wishes to see your son first, if you please, madam," they heard Grigsby say to the family beyond the door. Then young Robert—looking shocked and wan, his eyes puffed from sleep and his curly dark brown hair in disarray—came into view and slowly, dreadfully descended the stairs. Grigsby followed like a bulldog. "Shut that door!" Lillehorne commanded. "From the *other* side!"

"Oh yes sir, how disrespectful of me." Grigsby closed the door with a solid *thunk* but he remained on the cold room side. He came down, his face resolute.

Matthew saw that now Zed was cleaning the throat wound. McCaggers, who was still beset by fits of trembling, had regained some composure and with a black crayon was drawing on a sheet of paper a precise outline of the body as it lay on the table.

Robert Deverick, wearing a dark blue cloak studded with gold buttons over a blue-striped nightshirt, stopped at the foot of the stairs. His eyes moved from Lillehorne to the table and back again, and his lips moved but made no sound.

"Your father was murdered on Smith Street," Lillehorne said quietly but with force. "It happened"—he opened the watch, having the same idea as Matthew—"between ten o'clock and ten-thirty, it appears. Can you tell me where he'd been tonight?"

"Father . . ." Robert's voice faltered. His eyes glittered, but if there were tears it was hard to tell. "Father . . . who could've murdered my father?"

"Please. Where had he been?"

The young man continued to stare at the corpse, transfixed perhaps by the violence that had been inflicted upon human flesh. Matthew thought how much difference twelve hours could make; yesterday afternoon at the meeting Penn Deverick had been vibrant, boastful, and arrogant—his usual self, or so Matthew had heard—and now he was as cold and insensate as the clay underfoot. Matthew watched Robert trying to gain control of himself. Veins in the throat twitched, a muscle in the jaw jumped, the eyes narrowed and swam. Matthew understood that remaining in London were an elder brother and two sisters. Deverick had been a goods broker there, as well, and Robert's brother now ran that business.

"Taverns," Robert managed at last. Grigsby slid past him, ignoring Lillehorne's look of absolute scorn, and sidled up next to the corpse. "He went out. Before eight o'clock. To make the rounds of the taverns."

"For what reason?"

"He was . . . infuriated . . . about Lord Cornbury's opinion . . .

that the taverns should be closed early. He intended to fight the governor. With a petition. Signed by all the tavern owners and . . ." Robert drifted off, for the deep and hideous wound that had been his father's throat was being fully revealed to the light. McCaggers, his face slick with sweat and his hands trembling, leaned over and measured the cut with his calipers. Matthew saw that in McCaggers' eyes was the mad gleam of a terror no one should have to endure, yet he carried on.

"Go on, please," Lillehorne urged.

"Yes. I'm sorry . . . I'm . . ." Robert put his hand to his forehead to steady himself. He closed his eyes. "The taverns," he said. "He wished to get support . . . to fight Lord Cornbury's edict, should it be made official. That's where he was tonight."

"It would be beneficial," Matthew offered before he thought better of it, "to find out the last tavern he visited, what time, and who he might have—"

"Already in mind," the high constable interrupted. "Now Robert, let me ask you this: do you have an idea—any inkling—of who might have wished your father harm?"

Again with grim fascination the young man watched McCaggers at work. McCaggers was using a probe to examine the exposed tissues, after which he gagged and leaned over his bucket once more yet nothing came up. When McCaggers went back to his examination his face was as gray as a whore's sheet and his eyes behind the spectacles were two small black bits of coal.

"My father," said Robert, "used to have a credo. He said . . . business is war. And he fervently believed it. So . . . yes, he had enemies, I'm sure. But in London, not here."

"And how can you be so sure?"

"Here he had no competition."

"But then, perhaps he did. Perhaps someone wanted him out of his position, so—"

"That's a stretch," McCaggers said, as Zed wiped his forehead with the moist clean cloth. "Did someone also wish Dr. Godwin out of his position? I'm telling you, the same person has committed these crimes."

"Really?" Grigsby might not have had a notebook at hand, but he was eager to record. "You're positive of that?"

"Don't speak to him, McCaggers!" Lillehorne warned. Then, to Grigsby, "I've told you to get out! If you linger one more minute, you'll stay in the gaol for a week!"

"You don't have that authority," Grigsby said, in an easy voice. "I'm breaking no law. Am I, Matthew?"

The furious sound of McCaggers drawing something on the easel-paper caught their attention. When he stepped back, they saw he'd used the red crayon to indicate the throat wound on the black-outlined figure. "Here is my answer," he said, and then he drew a red triangle framing each eye. When he marked the cut connecting them across the bridge of the nose, it was with such force that his crayon snapped.

"The Masker," Grigsby said.

"Call him what you please." McCaggers' face was nearly dripping in the yellow light; he looked almost dead himself. "It was the same hand." He changed to the black crayon and began writing notations alongside the body-figure that Matthew was unable to decipher.

"You're saying . . . the same person who murdered Dr. Godwin murdered my father?" Robert asked, stricken anew.

"We're not certain of that." Lillehorne fired a glance at McCaggers that said *hold your tongue.* "There's still work to be done."

"I'll keep the body through tonight," McCaggers said, speaking to all and to no one in particular. "Then to Mr. Paradine tomorrow morning."

Jonathan Paradine was the town's funeral master, whose business stood on Wall Street near Trinity Church. When the corpse left here, wrapped in sailcloth, it would be delivered to Paradine for proper shrouding and fitting to a suitable casket of the Deverick family's choice.

Matthew had noted that, even as strong as he was, Zed was not required to carry the body up those steps. Instead, above the chute there was a system of pulleys and ropes constructed by the town's engineer for the purpose of hauling the deceased up the way he or she had arrived. By no means did all the dead of New York come to the cold room; most by far went directly from deathbed to Paradine. This was a place solely for the investigation—such as it was—of foul play, of which there'd been four instances since Matthew had been working with Magistrate Powers: the fatal beating of a woman by her peddler husband, the knifing of a sea captain by a prostitute, the murder of Dr. Godwin, and now Mr. Deverick.

"I'll have my report for you this afternoon," McCaggers said to the high constable. He took off his spectacles and rubbed his eyes. His hands were still shaking. Matthew reasoned that he would never overcome his dread of blood and death, even were he to examine forty corpses a year.

"May I see that report as well?" Grigsby asked.

"You may not, sir." Lillehorne turned his attention once more to the young Deverick. He handed over the wallet and gold pocketwatch. "These are yours now, I think. I'll go up and speak to your mother with you, if you like."

"Yes, I'd appreciate that. I wouldn't know what to say by myself."

"Gentlemen?" Lillehorne motioned Matthew and Grigsby up toward the door.

Without turning from the notes he was writing, McCaggers said, "I'll speak to Mr. Corbett."

Lillehorne's backbone went rigid, his lips so tight he could hardly squeeze a word between them. "I don't think it wise to—"

"I'll speak to Mr. Corbett," came the reply, both an order and a curt dismissal. It was obvious to Matthew that in this lower realm McCaggers was king and the high constable at best a jester.

Still, Lillehorne had his ton of pride. "I shall have a word with Chief Prosecutor Bynes over this misplacement of loyalty to the office."

"Whatever that means, you may do so. Goodnight to you. Rather . . . good morning."

With no further protest other than a little angry exhalation of air, Lillehorne escorted Grigsby and the young Deverick up the stairs. At the top, Grigsby reached back and firmly closed the door.

Matthew stood watching McCaggers write his notes, look at the body, write again, check with the calipers, write, and have his sweating face mopped with a wet cloth by the silent and impassive Zed.

"I attended the meeting today," said McCaggers, when Matthew thought the man's concentration had forced out all memory of his being there. McCaggers continued to work as if indeed he, Zed, and the corpse were a trio. "What do you make of Lord Cornbury?"

Matthew shrugged, though McCaggers didn't see it. "An interesting choice of hats, I'd say."

"I know some of his history. He has a reputation as a meddler and a buffoon. I doubt he'll be with us very long." McCaggers paused to take another drink from his bottle of courage, and he allowed Zed to once more blot the sweatbeads from his forehead. "Your suggestions were well-put. And well-needed, too, I might say. I hope they'll be implemented."

"As do I. Especially now."

"Yes, especially now." McCaggers leaned over to peer closer at the corpse's face, and then he gave an involuntary shudder and returned to his writing. "Tell me, Mr. Corbett. Is it true, what's said of you?"

"What's said of me?"

"The witchcraft business, in the Carolina colony. That you resisted the will of a magistrate and sought to have a woman freed from a death sentence?"

"It is."

"Well?"

Matthew paused. "Well *what*, sir?"

McCaggers turned to look at him, the candlelight sparking on his spectacles and his damp cheeks. "Was she a witch?"

"No, she was not."

"And you just a clerk? How is it you had such conviction?"

"I've never cared for unanswered questions," Matthew replied. "I suppose I was born that way."

"A freak of birth, then. Most accept the easiest answer to the most difficult question. It's more comforting, don't you agree?"

"No sir, not for me."

McCaggers grunted. Then: "I presume Mr. Grigsby wishes to write another article in his sheet? On 'The Masker,' as he so colorfully states?"

"He does."

"Well, he missed half of what I told him last time." McCaggers put down his crayon and turned, with an agitated look, toward Matthew. "How can a man publish a sheet if he has tin ears and his eyes can't see what's in front of him?"

"I don't know, sir," said Matthew, becoming a little disturbed at McCaggers' sudden vivacity. Or perhaps more disturbing was the fact that Zed was staring at him with those black and fathomless eyes. Matthew understood that Zed had arrived tongueless at the marketplace; if one knew the slave's history, it might be a tale for a night's horror.

"I told him it wasn't an ordinary knife. It was a knife with a hooked blade. A backhanded strike, drawn from left to right." McCaggers placed a finger on the red crayon of the throat cut to demonstrate the motion. "This is a knife designed to slice through the throat of an animal. Drawn with no hesitation and with full strength. I would look for someone who has experience in a slaughterhouse."

"Oh. I see," said Matthew.

"Pardon me." McCaggers, who had gone pale with his own recitation of violence, stopped to press the wet cloth up against his mouth.

"The cuttings around the eyes," Matthew ventured. "Do you have any idea what—"

McCaggers shook his head and held up a hand palm-outward to beseech Matthew's silence.

Matthew waited uneasily as McCaggers composed himself and Zed stared at him like the living visage of some massive and ominous African carving.

"A statement, of course," McCaggers said quietly when he lowered the cloth and took a breath. "Exactly the same as delivered to Julius Godwin. In the Italian tradition, carnival masks are sometimes decorated with colored diamond or triangle shapes around the eyes. Particularly the harlequin masks of Venice." He saw that Matthew was waiting for more. "That's all I have, concerning the marks. But come closer and look here."

Matthew walked nearer the corpse and the immobile Zed. McCaggers stayed where he was beside the easel. "Look at the left temple. Here is the place." He chose another red crayon from the jar and drew a circle on the outlined-figure's head. Matthew looked at the body at that spot and saw on the swollen flesh a black bruise about three inches long.

"That blow to the head began the play," McCaggers explained. "Mr. Deverick was dazed and unable to cry out, but not dead. I believe the killer lowered him to the ground on his back, put away the cudgel—a small one, easily concealed—took hold of Mr. Deverick's hair to steady the target, and did his work. Then the marks around the eyes saved for last, is my best guess. Mr. Deverick was left laid out; your friend got the blood on his hands and then onto that wretched shirt of yours. Am I correct?"

"The part about the shirt, for certain."

"The whole thing probably took only a matter of seconds. As I say, he is an experienced cutter. Also, by way of Dr. Godwin, an experienced murderer."

Matthew was staring closely at the imprint of the cudgel, the dead face before him now simply an item of clinical interest and a question unanswered. "You say his throat was cut from the front? A backhanded motion?"

"I can tell that from the depth of the wound. Deep to shallow, the severed cords and clots of tissue pushed to the killer's right. Hold a moment." McCaggers swayed and trembled and stared down at the floor until his fit of dread had passed. Zed offered the wet cloth, but McCaggers shook his head.

"How do you know his throat wasn't cut from behind?" Matthew asked.

"The killer would have had to be left-handed. I think he was—is—right-handed. If he'd come up behind Mr. Deverick, he likely would've used his cudgel to squarely strike the back of the skull. And look at Mr. Deverick's right hand."

Matthew did. The rigid hand that lay across the belly, the fingers and thumb spread. *Acceptance*, he'd thought at the scene of the crime. It came clear to him in an instant. "He was about to shake his killer's hand."

"The shock of the blow splayed his fingers. Should we be looking for a gentleman? Someone Mr. Deverick knew and respected?"

The impact of this brought something else clearly to Matthew's mind. It was chilling, in its implication of evil. "Whoever did this wished Mr. Deverick to see his face. To know, perhaps, that he was about to die. Yes?"

"Possibly, but you might have it the wrong way about," McCaggers said. "The killer might have wished to make sure he saw *Mr. Deverick's* face, probably because he wasn't carrying a lantern. I think this is not the random act of a madman, and neither was the murder of Dr. Godwin. Because Dr. Godwin was also struck on the left temple, leaving that same bruise in almost exactly the same place."

Matthew couldn't reply, for he was left thinking about the preparations the killer must have made in order to be quiet, quick, and successful. Wear dark clothes, no lantern, cudgel at the ready, perhaps a belt under a nightblack cloak to hold the instrument, then the blade in a sheath close at hand. From the ground, the blood wouldn't have spurted so far up that the killer—who was also ready for that fountain of gore—couldn't have avoided most of it. Gloves, of course, in case the knife handle did become slick. The cuttings around the eyes, and gone back into the dark.

"What was the connection between Dr. Godwin and Mr. Deverick?" Matthew asked, only if to hear himself voice the question.

"You find it," said McCaggers. Then with an air of finality he turned his back on Matthew to concentrate solely on his notations.

Matthew waited for a few moments longer, but it was clear his welcome had passed. When McCaggers made a motion to Zed and the slave began cutting away the dead man's clothes with an expertly applied razor, Matthew knew it was time to pick up his lantern from the floor, its candle burned to a stub, and return to the world of the living.

His ascent toward the door, however, was briefly interrupted. "Sometimes," McCaggers said, and Matthew knew from the echo of the voice that his back was still turned, "it's not wise to reveal all to a watchful eye. I leave to your judgment what to tell Grigsby and what to keep concealed."

"Yes sir," Matthew answered, and with that he left the cold room.

eight

"WELL? LET'S HAVE IT!"

Matthew had barely gotten through the door of City Hall before Marmaduke Grigsby collared him. The printmaster got alongside, step-for-step, but had to struggle to keep up with Matthew's long strides. "What did McCaggers think? Did he say more about the murder weapon?"

"I think we should not turn this into a public forum," Matthew cautioned, for even at this hour long past midnight there were still a few men—refugees from the taverns, no doubt—gathered on the street puffing their pipes and discoursing on the callous quickness of the pale rider. Matthew kept walking and turned the corner onto the Broad Way with Grigsby at his elbow. Even as he did, he thought that he had quite a distance to travel on such a dark night, with the Masker now blooded by two killings. The street-corner lanterns had almost burned themselves out, and clouds had slipped in on a damp seabreeze to blank the moon. He slowed his pace. Though he carried his own meager light and occasionally could be seen a lantern here and there as another nocturnal citizen moved about, he decided it was best to have company after all.

"We should not let this linger," Grigsby said. "We should compare notes and come up with an article for the *Earwig* at once.

I have other announcements and sundry items to fill up the sheet, but this by far merits the ink."

"I have a full day tomorrow. Today, I mean. Possibly I can help you on Thursday."

"I'll go ahead and write what I know to be true. You can go over the article and add your facts and impressions afterward. Then we'll get to work setting the type. You *will* help me with that, won't you?"

It was a tedious task that nearly blinded a person, since the type had to be set up backward. It could take—regardless of what he'd told Magistrate Powers was "an afternoon's work"—the whole of a day and well into the night. But the operation did require at least two men, one to "beat" the type with ink and the other to "pull" the lever that pressed the page.

"Yes, I'll help," Matthew agreed. He did like Mr. Grigsby and certainly admired his spirit. He also enjoyed having a hand in putting the sheet together, and being the first eyes to see some of the items Grigsby had written concerning drunken tavern brawls, fights between husbands and wives, chases of bulls and horses loose in the streets, who was seen dining at what eating-house in the company of whom, and the more mundane stories of what cargo had arrived and what was shipping out, what vessels were due in port from which destination, and the like.

"I knew I could count on you. We'll need to speak with Phillip Covey, of course, since I understand he was first on the scene. And you *second* there, how fortunate for me! For the sheet, I mean. Then perhaps we can get an official statement from Lillehorne. Improbable, but not impossible. You know, I think we might even gather a statement from Lord Cornbury, this being such a . . ."

Matthew had just about stopped listening at the phrase *first on the scene*. As Grigsby rambled on with his grandiose plans, Matthew was thinking about who had really been *second* and *third* on the scene. He recalled Reverend Wade saying to Dr. Vanderbrocken *We have to leave him*.

And go where?

He decided this was an instance of what perhaps should not be shared with Grigsby, at least until he'd had a chance to hear what Lillehorne would learn about those two gentlemen, and where they'd been going that was more important than waiting for a constable at a murder scene. Had perhaps they heard or seen something that bore telling? If so, they were poor witnesses to be such town pillars, for they'd surely disappeared this night.

"How did Mrs. Deverick take the news?" Matthew asked as they neared Trinity Church.

"Stoically," remarked Grigsby. "But then, Esther Deverick has never been known to display emotion in public. She lifted her handkerchief and hid her eyes, but whether she shed a tear or not is up for question."

"I should like to interview Robert again. Surely he knows *something* about who might have wished his father harm. Or maybe he knows, but doesn't realize it."

"You're making the assumption, then, that the Masker"— Grigsby was aware of how his voice carried down the Broad Way's silent length, and he lessened the volume considerably—"that the Masker has a plan and a purpose? How do you come to the conclusion that we don't simply have a lunatic in our midst?"

"I didn't say the killer wasn't a lunatic, or at least half-mad. It's the other half that concerns me and ought to equally concern Lillehorne. If two people have been murdered by the same hand, why shouldn't we expect a third, or a fourth, or . . . however many. But I'm not sure this is so random."

"Why? Because of some information McCaggers gave you?"

Matthew could feel Grigsby tensed like a lightning rod. Once the printer's ink got in a man's veins, it ran there through all of life's ambitions. "I can get the final report through Magistrate Powers," he said, not wishing to comment on the possibility that Deverick might have been struck down in the process of recognizing a fellow gentleman or—God forbid—business leader. It had come to Matthew that the Masker might indeed wear his own mask of community service and industry fellowship, and that this "half-madness" had been festering into action for months if not years. "I think it best to wait for McCaggers' opinions before we——"

Both he and Grigsby were startled as a well-dressed man in a beige suit and tricorn hat came around the corner of King Street, quickly walked past them without a word, and disappeared into the further dark. Matthew had just had a few seconds to register that the man was even there, but he'd thought he recognized him as the individual who'd thrown apples so viciously into the face of Ebenezer Grooder.

What was more interesting, however, was that in the breeze of the man's passage Matthew imagined he caught the faint aroma of clove-scented cologne.

But then again, Ausley's realm was only a block to the east, where the iron fence and gate stood around the building of leprous-colored walls on the corner of King and Smith. Whenever Matthew walked so near to that place, his skin crawled and his nostrils flared, so perhaps Ausley's reek emanated from the yellow bricks here, or from the very air as it moved past the shuttered windows and darkened doors.

"Um . . . Matthew," Grigsby said, as he looked at the little flickering flame from the tallowcandle lamp on the cornerpost. "Please don't think me cowardly in my elder age, but . . . would you mind walking with me a little further on?" He correctly read Matthew's hesitation to leave his own straight route home. "I do have something important to ask of you."

Matthew wasn't certain what was important enough to get killed for, on an early morning when New York seemed not quite the familiar town it had been yesterday, but he did think that whoever the Masker was, the murder of Mr. Deverick might have been to him as much an aid to sated sleep as a hot toddy. "All right," he agreed.

Soon they were walking past the almshouse. Grigsby didn't speak, perhaps in deference to Matthew's history there, though of course he knew nothing of Ausley's nocturnal punishments to his charges. Matthew looked neither right nor left, but kept his gaze fixed upon the middle distance. What had been one orphanage building in Matthew's time had now expanded to become three buildings, though still known collectively as the "almshouse." The eldest and largest still housed the boys of the streets, the castoffs of broken families, the victims of violence both by Indian and colonist hands, those who were sometimes nameless and bore no recollection of a past nor hope for a happy future. The second building kept orphaned girls and was watched over by a Madam Patterson and her staff, who'd come from England sponsored by Trinity Church for the purpose. The third building, the most recently constructed but still ugly for its gray brick and black slate roof, was under the jurisdiction of the chief prosecutor and contained those debtors and impoverished miscreants whose actions were not exactly criminal but who would be expected to work the blemishes off their records by physical labor on behalf of the town. This building, with its low squat structure and barred windows, had lately become better known as the "poorhouse" and was guaranteed to give a shiver down the spine of every working man and woman whose coins could not equal their credit when the bills came due.

Matthew allowed himself to look at the boys' orphanage building before they passed. It was completely dark and oppressive in its stillness, its wretched weight of bricks and mortar, its hidden secrets. And yet . . . and yet . . . did the faint shine of candlelight move past a bolted shutter? Was Ausley on the move in there, crossing from room to room, listening to the breathing of the young and defenseless? Did he pause by a particular cot in a chamber and cast the dirty light down upon a sleeping face? And did his older "lieutenants," recruited to keep violent order among those who had known only brutality and suffering, turn their eyes away from that light and settle again into their own night's refuge?

That kind of thinking led nowhere. Without witnesses, there was nothing. Yet still in the future someone might emerge from that place willing to reveal their torments to the law, and on that day Matthew might still see Ausley hauled away in the back of a wagon.

They continued past more houses and business establishments, but in this area of town with the almshouse at their back and the harbor ahead of them by two long blocks there was a gray cast to the air even on the sunniest day, and night seemed darker still. Not far distant, to their right, was a slave cemetery; on their left was a paupers' field, the occupants identified—as much as possible—with painted names written on small wooden crosses. A Dutch farmer named Dircksen still worked two acres of corn just east of the paupers' graveyard, and his sturdy white brick farmhouse looked as if it might last the ages.

"My granddaughter is arriving soon," said Grigsby.

"Sir?" Matthew wasn't sure he'd heard correctly.

"Beryl. My granddaughter. She's arriving . . . well, she should have been here three weeks ago. I've asked Reverend Wade to put up a prayer for me, on her behalf. More than one, actually. But of course everyone knows how errant those ship schedules can be."

"Yes, of course."

"They might have lost the wind for a time. They might have had problems with a sail, or a rudder. Everyone knows how difficult those voyages can be."

"Yes, very difficult," Matthew said.

"I expect her any day now. Which is what I wished to ask you."

"Sir?"

"Well, it *connects* to what I wished to ask you. Beryl is very headstrong. Very much like her father. Full of life and energy and . . . really, too much for an elder statesman like myself to handle."

"I didn't know you had a granddaughter."

"Oh, yes. I have a second son, also, and two grandsons. They saw me off at the wharf, when I left to make my name in the colony. They're all fine and settled. But Beryl . . . she needs guidance, Matthew. She needs . . . how shall I say this? . . . watching."

"Watching? You mean, supervision?"

"Yes, but . . . she also has a great appetite for . . . *adventure*, I suppose is the word."

Matthew was silent. They were getting close to Grigsby's

house amid the grouping of houses and nautical wares establishments ahead.

"She's just turned nineteen. A difficult age, wouldn't you say?" Grigsby continued when Matthew advanced no comment. "She did have a position, though. For eight weeks she was a school teacher in Marylebone, before the school burned down."

"Pardon?"

"No one was injured, thankfully. But Beryl has now found herself adrift. I don't mean that literally, of course. She assured me the ship she booked passage on has made the crossing six times, so I should think the captain knows the way. Wouldn't you?"

"I would," Matthew said.

"But it's her *temperament* I really worry about, Matthew. She wants to find a position here, and at my urging—and due to that very flattering article on Mrs. Brown's bakery in the last sheet—headmaster Brown has offered to give her a chance at the school. First she'll have to prove her ability and her seriousness to the task. So: are you up to it?"

Matthew was taken aback by the question and certainly didn't know what Grigsby was talking about. He smelled apples on the breeze. There was an orchard on a hill nearby, and a house whose elderly Dutch family refined the most wonderful cider in town. "Up to *what*?" he asked.

"Up to squiring Beryl about. You know. Ensuring she doesn't get into any trouble before the headmaster has a chance to make up his mind."

"Me? No, I don't think I'm suited for it."

Grigsby stopped walking and looked at him with such amazement that Matthew had to stop as well. "Don't think you're *suited* for it? Lord, boy! You're the only one I can think of who *is* suited for it! You're serious, no-nonsense, and down-to-earth. You're reliable and trustworthy. You don't get drunk and you don't go chasing every skirt you see."

Matthew gave a slight frown. "I didn't know I was so boring."

"No, I mean what I say. Your influence would be very good for

Beryl. A steadying hand, from someone nearer her own age. Someone to set an example for her. You see?"

"An example? Of absolute crushing boredom? Come on, I have to get home." He started walking in the direction of Grigsby's house again, and the printmaster quickly caught up with him. Or, to be more accurate, quickly caught up with the circle of lantern light.

"Think about it, won't you? Just to squire her around a bit, introduce her to some trustworthy people, make her feel comfortable here?"

"I would think that was the grandfather's job."

"It is! Yes of course it is! But sometimes, for all his good efforts, a grandfather is only an old fool."

"Your house," said Matthew, as they approached it. Grigsby's abode, flanked on one side by an anchorsmith's workshop and on the other by a roper's establishment, was just beyond the apple orchard and faced the East River. The house was made of simple white brick but had been personalized by Grigsby with a bright green door and shutters, and above the door was a carved sign that read *M. Grigsby, Printer*. Alongside the house was a small brick outbuilding, a cool house with a step-down floor that had once been a Dutch dairy, where Grigsby kept supplies of paper, ink, and sundry press parts.

"Will you at least think about it?" Grigsby asked on the front step. "I do need your help in this situation."

"I'll give it some thought, but no promises."

"Splendid! That's all I can expect. Well, thank you for your company and the light." He fished his key from his pocket and hesitated with one hand on the latch. "Listen to me, now. You be careful going home. Very careful. Understand?"

"I do, and thank you."

"All right. See me on Thursday, if at all possible, and let's get to work on the next sheet."

Matthew said goodnight and started for home, heading north on Queen Street along the river. There were many things in his mind this early morning, but he found himself pondering the situation of Grigsby's granddaughter. For one thing, he hoped the ship hadn't gone down in a storm. Three weeks late? Of course wind and currents could be fickle, but still . . .

He knew the real reason he didn't care to become involved with squiring Beryl Grigsby around, and it shamed him because it was purely selfish yet perfectly understandable. He thought Marmaduke hung the moon, but the printmaster's misshapen figure and strange characteristics—from spraying spittle between those gaping teeth to gong-farting—were not the most desirable to find in a young girl. In fact, Matthew shuddered to think what manner of gnome Beryl might be. There was a reason she was on a ship crossing the stormy Atlantic toward a rude colonial town, and it likely had little to do with a fire at a Marylebone school.

Besides, he was too busy for such galavanting. Too busy by far.

Right now he only wanted to get this damned bloody shirt off, wash his face, and get to bed. There was the widow Muckleroy's testimony to take at ten o'clock—oh, what a task that was going to be!—and then at one o'clock the real mystery Matthew looked forward to solving: the identity and purpose of Mrs. Katherine Herrald.

Though his lantern candle expired well before he got to safety and his vivid imagination told him he was being stalked by a figure who remained perhaps twenty yards behind, content to wait for another night, he reached the pottery shop without incident and climbed up the ladder and through the trapdoor to the security of his own humble kingdom.

nine

A S THE DEVIL was beating his wife, Matthew entered the red-carpeted lobby of the Dock House Inn through a pair of doors with insets of frosted glass. It was a handsome structure of red and black brick, three floors tall, built in 1688 where an earlier inn, the Van Pouwelson, had stood before being gutted by a fire. The walls within were dark oak, the sturdy furniture crafted for those who appreciated the difference between necessity and comfort. In a vaulted alcove stood a spinet adorned with paintings drawn from scenes of *A Midsummer Night's Dream,* and used in well-attended concerts played by several local musicians. Everything about the Dock House Inn, from its rich Oriental carpets to its oil portraits of famed New York business leaders, spoke of affluence and influence. It was difficult to realize that less than a hundred yards from the entrance the hulls of masted ships ground against the pilings and rats skittered under the boots of the sweating cargo crews.

Matthew had worn his best dark blue suit, white cravat, white shirt, and silver-buttoned waistcoat for his interview today with Mrs. Herrald. The rain that had showered from a sunny sky—the tears of the Devil's wife as she was being beaten, said the Dutch folk—had managed to catch him on Broad Street, just around the corner. His hair was drenched and his coat soaked across the shoulders, for thus had been the weather this day as clouds had passed before the sun, spat rain upon the town, and moved on. The sun had steamed the streets, the clouds had gathered, and the Devil's wife had cried again, and on and on since midmorning.

He had no time now to concern himself with his sodden appearance. It was enough that he *make* an appearance, since a broken-down timber wagon had snarled cart and pedestrian traffic on his route and disrupted his schedule enough to throw him at least three minutes late. Four times between the Gold Compass, where he and Magistrate Powers had eaten lunch, and the Dock House Inn he'd been stopped by acquaintances who wished to know more about his experiences of the night before. Of course it seemed everyone in town knew about the murder of Mr. Deverick, to the extent that Matthew was left wondering of what use was a proper broadsheet when word-of-mouth travelled at such speed. Even the widow Muckleroy, at ten o'clock this morning, had been more constant in her inquiries about the murder than she'd been in her testimony concerning the stolen bedsheets. In truth, the magistrate had been so disturbed by Matthew's story—and the evidence that the so-called "Masker" had done another deed—that he barely seemed able to focus on the woman's responses.

Powers had wished Matthew luck but had offered no further information concerning his appointment. Now Matthew pushed back his rain-wet hair, ran a finger across his teeth to clear away any remnant of the codfish pie he'd eaten, and approached the elaborately bewigged Mr. Vincent at the ledger desk, behind which a pendulum clock with a dial displaying the astrological signs showed Matthew as indeed being three minutes late.

"Matthew Corbett to see Mrs. Katherine Herrald," Matthew said.

"Mrs. Herrald is waiting in the parlor," came the stiff answer, from the rather stiff-necked proprietor. "That way." He flicked a finger.

"Thank you."

"Uh . . . one moment, young man. Have I heard correctly that you were fresh on the scene of that tragedy last night?"

"I was, sir, but please pardon me, I have to go." As he spoke,

Matthew was already on his way toward the other side of the lobby, where two steps led up to a closed set of double doors and the parlor beyond.

"Mind that you stop back by when you're done!" What might have been a request became a command when spoken by the imperial Gilliam Vincent. "Mr. Deverick was a very good friend to the Dock House!"

Matthew walked up the steps, started to open the doors but then decided to knock first.

"Enter," came a woman's voice.

For better or for worse, Matthew thought. He took a deep breath and went in.

If the lobby was refined, the parlor was opulent with its maroon-colored fabric wall coverings, its stone fireplace with a small mantel-clock, and its cowhide-upholstered chairs. A gaming table, complete with marble chessboard, stood in the light of a paned glass window from which one could view the shipmasts and harbor activity just beyond. This was the room where businessmen representing London, Amsterdam, Barbados, Cuba, South America, and greater Europe met to weigh the bags of money and sign agreements. On a desk under an artist's landscape of New York was a row of quill pens in leather sheaths, and it was the dark red-upholstered chair of this desk where the woman sat, turned to view the doorway.

She stood up as Matthew entered, which took him by surprise because usually a gentlewoman remained seated and allowed the man to advance, offering her hand—or the quick flip of a painted fan—as a gesture of recognition. But then she was on her feet and Matthew saw she was almost as tall as himself. He halted his approach to offer a courteous bow.

"You are late," the woman said, in a quiet voice that was not as accusatory as simply making the honest statement.

"Yes, madam," Matthew answered. He thought perhaps two seconds about offering an excuse, but he decided the fact spoke for itself. "I apologize."

"Then again, you *did* have an interesting night, did you not?

I'm sure those circumstances might have had some effect upon your progress."

"You *know* about last night?"

"Mr. Vincent informed me. It seems Mr. Deverick was a well-respected individual."

"Yes, he was."

"Unfortunately, however," said Mrs. Herrald with a slight pause, "not so well-liked." She motioned with a lavender-gloved hand toward a chair situated to her left. "Would you sit here, please?"

As Matthew sat down, Mrs. Herrald seated herself and so Matthew had a few seconds to complete an examination of her that had begun as soon as he'd entered the room.

She wore a lavender-colored gown with small white ruffles at the throat and over it a deep purple jacket accented with gold buttons. On her head was a cocked riding-hat, the same hue as her gown, with no feather or ornamentation. She was a trim woman, about fifty years old, her features sharp and her blue eyes clear and unwavering as she also took in her examination of him. There were lines of age around her eyes and across her forehead yet there was nothing aged about her, for she was straight-backed and elegant and seemed perfectly comfortable in her own skin. Her dark gray hair, with streaks of pure white at the temples and at a pronounced widow's-peak, was fashionably combed and arranged yet not piled high and glittering with golden geegaws as Matthew had seen done by many older women of means. And there was no doubt she was a woman of means; to book an accommodation at the Dock House one had to have money, and there was just something about Mrs. Herrald—the lift of the square chin, the cool appraisal of the intelligent eyes, the confidence the woman seemed to have in herself—that indicated she was used to the greater privileges of the world. Tucked at her side was a small black leather case, the kind in which Matthew had seen wealthy men carrying their important contracts and introduction letters.

"What do you think of me?" she asked.

The question took him aback, but he kept his composure. "I suppose I should ask what *you* think of *me*."

"Fair enough." She steepled her fingers together. The expression in her eyes was not altogether lacking mischief. "I think you are a smart young man, raised rather crudely in the orphanage here, and you wish to advance in the world but at present you don't know your next step. I think you are well-read, thoughtful, trustworthy though a bit lacking in your organization of time— even though I always consider *late* to be better than *never*—and I think you are older than your years would proclaim. In fact, I think you've never really been a *youth*, have you?"

Matthew didn't reply. Of course he knew she'd gotten all this from Magistrate Powers, but he was interested in the road she was travelling.

Mrs. Herrald paused, waiting for his response. Then she nodded and went on. "I think you have always felt *responsible*. For whom or what, I don't know. But responsible to others, in some way. That's why you've never been a youth, Mr. Corbett, for responsibility makes the young aged. It unfortunately also separates one from his peers. Sets him apart, causes him to perhaps retreat inward even more than the hardships of life already have. Therefore, without true friends or a sense of his place in the world, he turns to still further serious and steadying influences. Voracious reading, say. The mental workings of chess, or imagined problems that must somehow be solved. Without a sense of purpose, those imagined problems might become overwhelming, and command the mind day and night . . . to no resolution. From that point one begins to wander a path that leads to a very bleak and unrewarding future. Do you agree?"

Matthew not only had no answer, but he was also aware that he wasn't just damp from the rain. He was sweating under his arms. He shifted in his chair, feeling like a cod on a hook. Had the woman made the rounds of New York inquiring about him? He didn't know whether to feel flattered by her attention or flattened by such crushing insights. She had to have gone around town discovering his habits! Damn it, he ought to put on a face of effrontery, rise from his chair, and stalk out of here.

But instead he kept his expression mild, his eyes calm, and he stayed where he was.

"So do you now have an opinion of *me*?" she asked, in a buttery voice.

"I think . . . you enjoy the process of discovery," he replied, and that was all.

"How true," came her answer. Then they sat staring at each other as darkness grew in the room, a sudden shower pelted the window, the shadows moved, and sunlight streamed down again through the paned glass.

"I am a businesswoman," Mrs. Herrald said. "I'm sure Nathaniel . . . I mean to say . . . Magistrate Powers told you?"

"He told me you were in business, yes. But not what *kind* of business, or why you might be interested in me."

"It's *because* of your responsibility. That's why I'm interested. Your youth, even your *lack* of youth. Your mind. Your pursuits. Even your history with Magistrate Woodward."

Matthew couldn't suppress a start. Now this maddening woman was really treading too near a grave. "Magistrate Powers told you about that, as well? To what extent?" He remembered his manners. "If I may ask?"

"Of course. He told me the whole story. Why would he not, if I asked? It was a difficult time for you, yes? But you certainly kept to your convictions, even though it caused grief to both yourself and to your . . . shall I call him your *mentor*? I'm sure you had a strong allegiance to him, since he secured you from the orphanage. Did you consider what you were doing a betrayal?"

"I considered what I was doing," Matthew said evenly, though he wished to grit his teeth, "as a search for justice."

"And you assumed that in this case you knew more than the experienced and highly competent Magistrate Woodward?"

Matthew looked at his hands and worked his knuckles. He could feel Mrs. Herrald carefully watching him, perhaps looking for a sign of weakness or a flaw in what had been until now a well-maintained veneer. He concentrated on breathing steadily and quietly, and in showing not a whit of emotion. Then he was ready. He looked up and squarely met her cool gaze.

"I believed that I was right," he said, "based on not only the existing evidence but the *lack* of evidence. In my experience—a rather limited experience, as you so correctly point out—sometimes the questions easily answered are not the right questions. Sometimes the questions easily answered are meant to lead one into darkness. Therefore, to get my light—as it were—I look to the questions that no one else might ask. The unpopular questions. The uncivil, impolite questions. I harp on them and I pound on them, and often my strategy is to drive into the ground those who refuse to answer what I wish to know. I grant that I don't have many friends and I grant that I have perhaps retreated too much into myself, but—" He stopped, because he realized he'd walked right into the little devious snare of self-revelation that Mrs. Herrald had set out for him. *She made me angry*, he thought. *She broke my control, and now I am spilled*.

"Go on," she urged, still in a quiet voice. "You were speaking of impolite questions."

"Yes, impolite." Matthew had to take a few seconds to gather his wits. "In Fount Royal, with Magistrate Woodward . . . everything was moving so quickly. Moving toward a burning at the stake. I didn't . . . I didn't feel some . . . many . . . of the more difficult questions had been answered. And yes, he was my mentor. My friend, as well. But . . . I couldn't let those unanswered questions lie there. I couldn't. Not with those townspeople so eager to take her life."

"*Her* life?"

"Rachel Howarth was her name. The accused woman."

Mrs. Herrald nodded and looked out the window toward the forest of masts for a time. Then she asked, "What was the first thing you did this morning?"

"Well . . . I ate breakfast with the Stokelys. I live above their pottery—"

"After that," she interrupted.

He frowned, puzzled. "I . . . walked to work."

"Is that completely true? Or did you go somewhere before that?"

He realized what she was getting at. "I walked down Smith Street to where Mr. Deverick's body was found."

"Why?"

"I wished to see it in daylight. To see if there might be anything in the dirt that . . . may have been left. A button, for instance, from the killer's coat. Anything, I suppose."

"And you found what?"

"Nothing. Sand had already been spread to blot up the blood, and the dirt raked. I suppose that was on the high constable's order, getting things back to normal."

"Hardly normal," she said. "Two murders within the space of as many weeks? Who do you think the high constable should be looking for?"

Before Matthew could think about it, he spoke what had been on his mind since awakening this morning: "A gentleman executioner."

"Hm," she said, but offered no more. Then she cleared her throat, angled her head, and looked at him as if clearly for the first time. "I presume you've never heard of the Herrald Agency?"

"No, madam, I haven't."

"Founded by my husband. My late husband. In London, in 1685. He was a lawyer of some renown in his younger years, and later gave his aid to many individuals who required it. Legal aid and advice, yes, but the Herrald Agency specializes in . . ." She gave him the hint of a smile. "As you put it so astutely, the process of discovery."

"Oh," Matthew said, though he had no clue what she was talking about.

"We now have two offices in London, one in Edinburgh, one soon to open in Amsterdam, and we plan—I plan—to consider opening an office in New York. We have a dozen agents all with varying specialties in problem solving. Most of them have backgrounds in law enforcement, though several have been recruited from the opposite camp. As cities grow, it seems, so grows our business. Needless to say, I believe New York—as well as Boston and Philadelphia—will soon make the transition from town to city. Therefore I wish to find a central location for—"

"Pardon me, please," said Matthew, and he leaned forward in his chair with a perplexed expression. "Forgive the interruption, but what exactly do you mean by 'problem solving'?"

"I shall answer with an example. In April the young son of a very influential banking family misplaced one of his mother's diamond bracelets by giving it to his fiancee, a rather disreputable Dutch actress. The mother wanted it back, but it seemed that the fiancee had suddenly and completely vanished after the opening night. Furthermore, she was the female companion of a criminal figure whose very name turned the London law hawks into frightened pigeons. So it was brought to us to find and return the bracelet, and also to make certain that our criminal acquaintance—who had known nothing about his companion's dalliances—did not do to her with an axe what he had done to two previous ladies, because the young son still wished to marry her. The problem was solved, but unfortunately bride and groom had a falling-out over dinner plates for the home and besides, theater season was about to open in the Netherlands."

"By problems," Matthew said, "you mean . . . personal difficulties?"

"Missing documents, forged letters, theft of money or property, questions of sincerity and loyalty as applied to either business or marriage, missing persons, reconstruction of accidents, courier for valuable items or bodyguard for important persons, discovery of any question that might be asked as to the truth or falsity of any given situation. All those, and more." Mrs. Herrald paused to give him time to take all this in. "In addition," she continued, "we are often asked by law enforcement officials to explore the more dangerous territory of the professional criminal and the criminal organizations, of which there is no lack and which are likely—

given human corruption and the greed for both power and money—to grow beyond all current recognition. I might also point out that the investigation of murder is one of our specialties, and we have a sterling record of success. Do you have any questions?"

Matthew was speechless. He'd had no idea anything such as this existed. It made the thoughts of law school fly out of his head like old, slow geese. "I . . . well . . . what do you want with *me*?"

"Now don't be thick!" she scolded, but with good nature. "And also don't be modest. You are highly regarded by Nathaniel Powers, or you wouldn't be sitting here."

"But . . . is this an interview for *employment*?"

"It's an interview to determine whether you're interested or not. Are you?"

"Yes," Matthew said, almost at once. "Certainly I am. But what exactly would I be doing?"

"Discovery," said Mrs. Herrald. "Problem solving. Thinking quickly, in dangerous situations. Taking your life in your hands sometimes, to be truthful. Or trusting your life to the hands of someone else. Picking up a question like a . . . like a chess piece, and determining how it fits in the game. If you're interested in doing that, in being the first member of the Herrald Agency in America and being paid very well for it, then you will do what I next require of you."

Matthew listened, but said nothing.

Mrs. Herrald opened the black leather case at her side and brought out a white envelope. "Do you know the DeKonty estate?"

"I do." It was about eight miles from town along Manhattan Island. Matthew and Magistrate Powers had been there a little over a year ago to attend a party for the town's legal staff hosted by August DeKonty, who had owned both a stone quarry and one of the largest lumbermills in the colony.

"You're aware that Mr. DeKonty passed away in March? And that his widow and daughter have moved to Boston?"

"I am."

"Also are you aware that the new owner of the estate is a Mr. Hudson Greathouse, a business consultant who has just recently taken occupancy?"

"That I didn't know."

"He's a very private individual. You will meet him today, and give him this letter." She handed it to Matthew. The first thing he did was turn it over and look at the red wax seal embossed with the letter *H*. "You are *not* to open it. If the seal is broken, I personally take a sizeable loss of both money and reputation and you may return to your position with Nathaniel Powers."

"May I ask what's in it?"

"Amendments to the deed that need a signature. There was some difficulty over the DeKonty landholdings, and this is a clarification procedure. Therefore you will take this letter to Mr. Greathouse, stand by in his presence as he signs it, and bring it back to me by seven o'clock this evening. Oh . . . here." She reached into the case and brought out another object, which she gave him without hesitation. "Wind it now. The mantel clock reads twelve minutes before two."

In Matthew's hand was a gleaming silver watch. He opened the lid and gazed down upon the beautiful white dial, the black numerals and hands. If the mantel clock was correct—and he was sure the finicky Mr. Vincent wound it by the hour—then the watch was also correct. Still, Matthew took hold of the winding stem and very carefully and slowly turned it several times until the spring gave resistance.

"Can you secure a horse?" Mrs. Herrald asked.

Matthew nodded, still giving all his attention to the silver watch. Had there ever been silver that shone so brightly, or a dial so white, or Roman numerals shaped as if by the etching-pen of an emperor?

"I am here," she said. "Look at me."

He did.

"A horse. You can ride?"

"I can, yes madam." If he couldn't handle a horse by now, with all the travelling through the colony he and Magistrate Powers had done, then he would have to settle for the most broken-down donkey at Tobias Winekoop's stable.

"Direct your expenses to my bill here. Now listen to me with care, Matthew: I am offering you this opportunity to show me how reliable you are. There is a financial value to the content of that envelope, though you personally could not benefit from it. Some, however, with the right resources in unfit places might. Any such item carries a risk. Do you understand?" She waited until he'd given a nod. "Bear in mind the serious nature of being a courier. Do not dawdle, do not leave the main road, do not stop to help any damsel or dandy in distress because that is the oldest trick in the book for highway robbers."

"*Robbers?*" Matthew felt his heartbeat quicken and his stomach give a lurch. He'd not considered the fact that a deed with a monetary value might attract highwaymen—or highwayladies, as the case might be.

"Do you carry a pistol? A sword?"

"No," Matthew answered, feeling a little stunned. "I don't know how to use either one."

"We'll have to rectify that, *if* you succeed this afternoon. Well, it's probably for the best though. If you're not an expert with a pistol or sword, you have no business killing yourself by trying to use one. Just be aware of your surroundings and, as I say, don't stop."

Matthew realized he must have had a look of terrible distress on his face, because Mrs. Herrald's voice softened. "I'm a worrier by nature. I see a plot in every plan. Do know that if you're robbed, it's only a copy yet it bears an extremely valuable signature and seal from the royal office of land transfers. The original can be recopied, of course, though it would take months to get the signature and seal redone. But don't throw your life away on my account. Are you ready to go?"

He didn't reply, for his tongue was not in working order.

Mrs. Herrald said, "If you have misgivings, you may return the envelope. I'll give you money for dinner and a glass of wine at the tavern of your choice, and we shall write this meeting off as an exercise in verbiage. What do you wish?"

"Do I have to give back the watch?" Matthew managed to ask.

"Yes, and polish it, too."

He stood up, watch in one hand and dangerous envelope in the other. "I'll go."

Mrs. Herrald remained seated. "Seven o'clock," she said firmly.

Matthew wondered what would happen if his body wasn't found until eight. But he pulled himself tall, got his legs moving, and left the parlor.

"Wait! Corbett! Wait, I said!" shouted Mr. Vincent as he came out from behind his desk, but Matthew carried a watch now and time waited for no man.

ten

MATTHEW SET OFF on a middle-sized, brown-and-white paint mare named Suvie that he'd secured on previous business trips from Mr. Winekoop's stable. She was a plodder, but she was easily managed and had never been known—at least according to the amiable, pipe-smoking Winekoop—to throw a rider. So, with Suvie under him, his hands in the reins, boots in the stirrups, and wax-sealed envelope tucked in an inner coat pocket and fastened down with a button, he rode along the Broad Way to the north, mindful of pedestrians, wagons, wandering mendicants, merchants hawking their wares from little pull-carts, dogs chasing cats chasing chickens, slop and the essence of chamberpot thrown into the street, and other sundry obstacles to be avoided.

He wished he'd thought to bring a hat, because here came another brief shower that wet him and then passed on in favor of the sun. He decided to keep going past the pottery shop, though, for he wanted to keep to a strict time-schedule.

It had been almost two-thirty when he'd left the stable. There'd been an important task he'd needed to accomplish at City Hall, and also to ask Magistrate Powers for permission to make this journey though the afternoon was free and he'd known the magistrate would give his blessing. The magistrate, however, had not been in the office and so Matthew had left a note, completed his task, and then hurried back down the stairs where he'd run into High Constable Lillehorne and Chief Prosecutor Bynes on their way up.

"Ho there, Matthew!" said Bynes, a large-bellied and jovial man with a florid face and trimmed gray beard. "Where to in such a hurry?"

"Hello, sir. I'm sorry, I do have an appointment."

"A moment, then." Bynes reached out and put a ham-sized grip on Matthew's shoulder. Lillehorne tried to squeeze past them but was unable to advance. "Two things. I meant to speak to you earlier about your suggestions at the meeting. They were very interesting and could be useful, and I'm sure the high constable intends to properly study them. Isn't that right, Gardner?"

"Yes sir," Lillehorne said, his voice suddenly bright. "I intend to study them at great length."

"Grand!" That was the chief prosecutor's highest and all-purpose praise. Then his face darkened and a voice that could call down thunder and cataclysm in the courtroom became almost fatherly. "And last night. You happened upon that tragic scene. Gardner painted the whole picture for me, and I've looked in upon the body. Those marks around the eyes . . . very disturbing, are they not?"

"Yes sir, they are."

"I understand that our rather eccentric printmaster mentioned that term again when he was unlawfully present in the cold room. Yes?"

"Term, sir?" Matthew knew exactly what he meant, but he wouldn't speak it. Besides, he wasn't sure it had been "unlawful" for Grigsby to be present. Unless they were rewriting the town code at night when everyone slept.

"You do know." Bynes applied just a little more pressure to Matthew's shoulder. "We—all of us—are in this together, Matthew. We are all professionals. Craftsmen, in our own way. Make no mistake, we shall bring this murderer to justice. Unfortunately, no good is done when Marmaduke Grigsby starts declaring . . . you know . . . that term for all to see in his sheet. It causes an unease, which breeds fear, which breeds panic, which breeds citizens uncertain of the protective power of their legal officials. Not good. Yes?"

"Yes. I mean . . . no. I suppose."

"Now I think it's fine for Grigsby to run his little paper. Talk about the ships coming in, the cargoes, the energy of New York, the social scene and . . . yes, of course, even the minor squabblings in the streets which any town of merit must endure." Bynes paused, his cool blue eyes ready to strike lightning to go along with a storm-dealing throat. "But Grigsby cannot be—and will not be—allowed to make this murderer into more than simply a lunatic who most probably has now fled town."

"Pardon, sir," Matthew said, "but I think that's what was advanced after Dr. Godwin's murder. Obviously it wasn't true."

"We don't know that it isn't true *now*. I'm not saying Grigsby shouldn't run a small bit about the incident. I'd have to be a fool not to know that the whole town's talking about it, but we must *control* public opinion, Matthew. For the good of the people. If Grigsby makes a big splash about it, how will that help anything? Yes?"

Matthew had no idea whether he ought to agree or disagree. But he said, "I do know of one thing that would greatly aid the good of the people, sir. To actively investigate the murder and find this person before he—"

"Shhhhh." A thick finger went to Bynes' lips. "We *are* investigating, you can be sure of that, and we shall find this lunatic if he is insane enough to remain in New York."

Something about that music sounded off-key, but Matthew let it go. He turned his attention to the high constable. "A question for *you*, sir. Have you been able to question Reverend Wade and Dr. Vanderbrocken?"

"I have, if you really need to know."

"May I ask what was their explanation of such a quick disappearance?"

Lillehorne cast a glance at Bynes that said *Oh the fools I have to suffer*. Then, to Matthew with a hint of disdain, "The good reverend was on his way to attend to church business. The good doctor was on his way to see a sick patient. They obviously were on the south side of the street and heard Phillip Covey's shout, just as you heard it from the north side. Each apologized for not remaining there to wait for a constable, but they had their separate destinations."

"Their separate destinations," Matthew repeated.

"That's what I said. Are you in need of an ear-horn?"

"Pardon, but did you ask exactly *what* church business and *who* was the patient?"

"No, because I'm respectful to those two gentlemen and their explanations have satisfied me. Any further probing would be *disrespectful* and possibly *sinful* in the case of Reverend Wade. Really, Corbett!" He tried again to get past Bynes. "Shall we go, sir?"

Bynes released Matthew's shoulder. He flicked an imaginary something off Matthew's left lapel. "Speak to your friend, won't you? Both as a friend to him and a friend to me? Yes?" He smiled broadly. "Grand!"

As Matthew guided Suvie up the Broad Way hill past the pottery shop toward the lush green forest beyond, he was thinking about the phrase *separate destinations*. That was odd, because he distinctly remembered Reverend Wade saying to Dr. Vanderbrocken *We have to leave him*.

Was he mistaken, or didn't that sentence imply the reverend and doctor were travelling together toward a *common* destination?

The doctor's bag had been on the ground. It appeared he'd been wearing a nightshirt under his cloak, which also had an implication of emergency. If the two men had been travelling together, why had they not just said so to Lillehorne?

Of course, there were many slips between Lillehorne's cup and his lips, so it was certainly possible he'd misunderstood they weren't together or his questions had come out bungled. But still, it was very odd.

How serious was it, for a man of God to tell a lie?

Matthew had to shake these questions out of his brain. What did it matter, anyway? He didn't believe for an instant that either the reverend or doctor had had anything to do with the murders.

As Lillehorne had said, they were coincidentally on the south side of the street when they heard Covey shouting.

We have to leave him.

Something didn't fit, Matthew thought. He hated when that happened, because it meant he was going to have to go speak to Reverend Wade and Dr. Vanderbrocken himself, just for the sake of clarity, when he returned to town.

The last few houses on the edge of New York slipped past. On either side were farmfields and orchards, stone boundary walls, and cattle in their pastures. He rode past the large old windmill atop Common Hill, and then he was truly on the Boston Post Road as it curved along the huge green deep of Collect Pond on the left and thick woodland on the right sloping all the way down to the river.

The rain showers had thankfully settled the dust on the Post Road. The road itself was not nearly as rugged as that miserable path from Charles Town to Fount Royal, but certainly could still bring a civil engineer to his knees. Matthew considered that one of the most gruelling jobs in the colony had to be driving a coach between New York and Boston, and feeling those bumps and gullies nearly knock the wheels off under you. But then again, it was a road well-travelled by local farmers and occupants of the larger estates further north and of course as a route not only to Boston but also to East Chester and New Rochelle.

It was a hilly route, with large stretches of wilderness between cultivated farmland. Here too, as in the Carolina colony, the massive trees in places overhung the road with gnarled branches that had been old in the days of Henry Hudson. Deer occasionally jumped in the undergrowth at the sight of Matthew and Suvie. Dark flights of insects whirled over swamp ponds and clear streams gurgled over smooth-worn stones. There was also, as in Carolina, the feeling that one was always being watched by Indian eyes, yet for a white man to see an Indian who didn't wish to be sighted was a near impossibility. The clouds bellied, a shower fell, the clouds broke apart, and the bright sun shone down through ten-thousand green leaves above Matthew's head.

He kept Suvie at a walk, intending to pick her up into a trot a little further along. He judged it would take about a half-hour from this point to reach the more narrow road, marked by a pile of white stones, that turned to the left off the Post Road and wound to a number of estates either once or currently held by Dutch residents. Then he could work Suvie into speed and possibly cover the remaining four miles in about forty minutes. It interested Matthew why someone would choose to live out here in the wilderness so far from town, but as he understood it these particular people owned businesses—like Mr. DeKonty's stone quarry and lumbermill—that demanded both space and resources. He understood there was a vineyard out here somewhere and a winery starting up, but he hadn't yet seen it. These were hardy, fearless people who seemed to have no problem with Indians showing up for tea, but never let it be said that New York would ever grow without fearless people.

Rays of sunlight streamed through the forest, but now lower to the ground. Ahead the road curved to the right beyond the thicket of trees. The noise of birdsong was loud and reassuring though from the western distance came a faint low rumble of thunder. Occasionally he caught a glimpse of green cliffs rising up below a blue haze. He hated to be caught out in a real rainstorm, not just these passing summer drizzle-fits, but even if he became soaked at least the envelope was well-protected.

Now the road curved to the left and climbed a hillock. At the top it descended and went right again, a capricious trickster. He guided Suvie around the bend and saw the oak branches interlocking over the road ahead like the arbored ceiling of a green cathedral.

The road stretched out straight and flat. This would be a good place to urge Suvie into a trot, he decided, but no sooner had this thought come to mind than three quail burst from the thicket to his right, flying past him like arrows, and following with a crash of breaking underbrush came a big chestnut horse with a white-starred face.

The muscular animal was being ridden by a man wearing a

black tricorn with a raven's-feather tucked in the scarlet band, a white ruffled shirt, dark blue coat, and white breeches. Unfortunately, Matthew saw, he was no ordinary equestrian out for an afternoon's jaunt, for he wore a dark blue kerchief across the lower half of his face and bore a pistol whose barrel looked equally as long as Matthew's forearm. The business-hole in that barrel was trained on Matthew, whose first rather frantic idea of digging his heels into Suvie's sides and riding like a scalded-ass demon flew away as quickly as a scared quail.

"Hold your horse," the highwayman directed, as Suvie gave a shudder of alarm and started to sidestep. Matthew did as he was told and pressed his knees in, at the same time giving as smooth a pull on the reins as he could manage. Suvie whinnied and snorted but complied with her rider. The highwayman approached, the pistol resting across his lap. Matthew's heart was pounding so hard he knew his ears must be twitching.

"Keep the reins and step down," came the next command. When Matthew didn't immediately obey—being somewhat frozen solid at this sudden attack—the highwayman placed the pistol's barrel against Matthew's right knee. "I won't kill you, young man," he said, his voice low and husky though not altogether ungentlemanly, "but I shall blow your knee off if you fail to do as I say. This being a well-travelled road, I'm sure a wagon will come along in three or four hours."

Matthew climbed down off Suvie, still holding the reins.

The highwayman now dismounted, and Matthew was aware that he was a broad-shouldered monster of a man perhaps three inches above six feet. Gray sides showed below the tricorn, as well as half a craggy face, the bridge of a formidable nose, and deep-set eyes dark as tarpits. The left charcoal-gray eyebrow was sliced by a jagged and nasty-looking scar.

"What do you have?" the man asked, laying the barrel against Matthew's left ear.

"Nothing." It was all he could do to speak, but he knew that he had to steady up.

"Why is it *everyone* says that? Well, not everyone. Some beg to give me their money, after I shoot them through the ear. Wish to answer that question again?"

"I have a little money."

"Oh, ho! From *nothing* to *a little*! Progress of sorts, I'd say. Soon we'll have you richer than Midas. Where is this pittance?"

"Saddlebag," Matthew said, but only with great reluctance because he knew what else was in there. He thought he could hear the ocean roaring in the pistol's barrel.

"Open it." The man took Suvie's reins and stepped back.

Matthew tried to take his time at undoing the leather straps, but the highwayman said, "I'm going to take what you have, so cease the nonsense." When Matthew had opened the bag, the man commanded, "Step off the road," and Matthew backed up into the high grass. Then the raven of the roads strode forward, reached into the bag, brought out Matthew's brown leather drawstring wallet, and . . . the indignity of it . . . the silver watch just presented to him two hours before.

"Shiny," the highwayman commented. "I like this very much, thank you." The watch disappeared into his coat with practised grace. Next was the undoing of the wallet, and this time the half-face gave a menacing scowl. "What's your job? Professional beggar? How is it you carry a silver watch of wealth and a wallet of poverty?"

"My station in life," Matthew answered. "The watch belongs to someone else."

The highwayman stared at him impassively for a moment, looked into the empty saddlebag once more, and then gave Suvie a flathand whack on the rump that caused her to squall like an infant and shoot forward, her eyes wide with terror and her ears back against her head. She galloped wildly away along the road, heading in the direction of the DeKonty estate, and Matthew thought he heard the chestnut horse give a whicker that for all the world sounded like an evil little laugh.

Matthew slowly let go of the breath that had lodged in his lungs. He knew full well he was up to his ears in what his face had been pushed into two nights ago.

"Open your coat," came the next directive.

Instinctively, Matthew's fingers went to his coat just over the envelope. He winced and dropped his hand down as if seared by unearthly fire.

"Open it." The highwayman came forward until he was an arm's length from Matthew. The tarpit eyes glittered and the pistol rose up to rest against his own shoulder.

"I have no more—"

In the next instant Matthew's coat was wrenched open, a button flew from within, and a hand pulled the envelope out before the button could fall into the grass. The robber checked the other side of Matthew's coat for another pocket but, finding nothing, turned his attention to the waistcoat. Its small pocket was empty and so too was the pocket of his breeches; therefore the highwayman took two steps back and looked down at the envelope, starting to turn it over to the sealed side.

Matthew stepped forward, damp sweat prickling his face. At once he had the highwayman's full concentration and the pistol barrel at one nostril.

"Listen," Matthew said in a voice that was near breaking, "that doesn't concern you. It's an official document. Amendments to a deed, but worthless to you. Please give it back to me and let me go on my—"

Still staring callously at him, the highwayman broke the seal. Bits of red wax fell down into the grass. He backed away six paces, the pistol yet aimed at Matthew, and then he drew the document out, unfolded it, and spent a moment examining it. There was nothing written on the back of the parchment, but something on the front must have appealed to the brigand because Matthew could tell he was grinning wolfishly even under the kerchief.

"Well," he said, "this bears some very nice signatures. I expect my friends in Boston who have a talent for handwriting might wish to see this, do you think?"

Matthew put a hand to his eyes. Slowly, his hand moved down to cover his mouth and his eyes went cold.

The highwayman crumpled the envelope and threw it down

upon the road. He refolded the document and slid it into his own coat. "I thank you, young man. You've made the day of a lowly wanderer that much brighter." He shoved his pistol into a belt holster and then, taking the reins, swung himself up into the chestnut's saddle with smooth and powerful economy of motion. Thunder spoke from the west again, and the robber cocked an ear toward it. "I shouldn't waste too much time around here," he advised. "It might not be safe."

He turned his horse along the Post Road and galloped off in the direction of Boston, and the last view Matthew saw of him was a horse's ass carrying a horse's ass.

Matthew listened to the birds singing. The air was warm, the trees beautiful, the summer at its full height of glorious bounty.

It was a damned hell of a day.

After a time he wiped the sweat off his face with his cravat, and then he stood staring down at the crumpled envelope in the road. He looked southwest, toward New York, then back at the envelope.

Interesting, he thought.

He made no attempt to pick the envelope up. It was a dead thing.

Then he turned to the northeast and began walking, first at a moderate pace and then faster still. He had a way to go, of course, and he didn't wish to wear himself out before he got there but some speed was essential. Possibly he might find Suvie up ahead, eating grass in a meadow. He hoped.

As he walked, he remained aware of not only what was ahead but also what might be coming up behind, and he was ready at any moment to jump into the underbrush.

Again Matthew walked alone, but the strength of his purpose was company enough.

eleven

L ATE AFTERNOON'S SHADOWS had fallen across Manhattan, painting the wooded hills deep green and gold.

Weary but still determined, Matthew covered what he felt must be the last quarter-mile along the winding wilderness road, and then he recognized the waist-high rock wall of the DeKonty estate through the trees ahead. A pair of closed iron gates guarded the trail leading up to the house, which couldn't be seen for all the foliage. He guided Suvie off the road and into the forest, thankful that he'd found her chewing apples in an orchard about a half-mile from the point where she'd been rump-slapped, and thankful also that she had graciously accepted him back on after being so rudely treated.

Now there was a score to be settled.

He said quietly, "Whoa, girl," and reined her in. Then he climbed off and walked her deeper into the woods, where she couldn't be seen from the road. He tied her securely to a branch, gave her one of the apples he'd put into his saddlebag, and then he was ready to go.

Best not to enter through the gates, he decided. Possibly they were locked anyway, and he wished to find his own route in. He walked along the wall, remembering that the DeKonty house was set well back from the road and was surrounded by tulip gardens that had been Mrs. DeKonty's pride.

After a few minutes he climbed over the wall, terribly mauling his best suit, but then he was over and into some manicured shrubs and he crouched down thinking that if Mr. Hudson Greathouse kept a mastiff or wolfhound to guard the place his suit would be the least thing mauled today. But there was no bark and roar of one of those beasts rushing to break his bones and so he rose up—carefully, cautiously—and walked through a little grassy paradise where butterflies swam amid the seas of flowers and a path of raked gravel led off beside a fieldstone well. It was a meticulously kept estate, Matthew thought, and then he came upon a hillock where four sheep were grazing and he saw how the grass was so evenly trimmed.

Up past the sheep, the trail that led from the road curved up toward the main house, which stood surrounded by huge oaks and as he recalled overlooked the river on the far side. It was a structure obviously built by a wealthy merchant in the quarry business, for it was two levels made of dark brown and tan stones with a gray slate roof. At the apex stood a brown-painted cupola topped by a brass weathervane in the shape of a rooster. The front door was a big slab of tea-colored wood with a knocker the size of the highwayman's fist.

He remembered a barn and a carriage-house back behind the main dwelling, and also on the riverfront side there was another garden where the party had been held. Over there as well were glass-paned doors that led into a study where Mr. DeKonty had gone on at length about the various grades of lumber. A place of education then had become of interest now, and as Matthew headed around toward the back of the house to make a circuitous path to his destination he heard the distant *clang* of metal and knew that someone had just unlocked the gates.

He had to hurry now. He walked quickly past a hitching-post in the shade of a green-mossed oak and made a mental note to buy new boots if he was going to do any more hiking such as this, for his heels were rubbed raw.

On the river side, the water shimmering down at the bottom of a rather high slope and the forest unbroken beyond, Matthew found the double doors he knew to be there. Closed, yes. But locked, no. The brass handles gave as he carefully turned them. A set of dark red drapes was drawn across the entrance. He couldn't see beyond into the room, but he would have to risk the chance that it was not empty. He opened the doors, parted the drapes, stepped into an empty study, and closed the doors behind him.

Within the walls of dark wood were bookshelves, a writing desk with quills and inkpot, a chair at the desk, and two other chairs. Across the back of one chair he saw hung in a leather scabbard a rapier with a bone-white grip and an undecorated metal handguard and pommel. A workman's sword, he thought. Made for use instead of threat. A man's coat hung on a wallhook across the room, next to a closed door.

Then he heard voices approaching from the other side, and he thought it wise to retreat behind the drapes and stay as still and quiet as mind over nerves would allow.

". . . unfortunate, really," said a man's muffled voice. "He gave it away so . . ." and here the door opened and the voice became clear ". . . easily. He practically showed me where it was."

"And how was that?" A woman's voice, behind the man.

Matthew had to grin just a bit. It seemed that Mrs. Herrald would not be at the Dock House Inn at seven o'clock.

"He *touched* his coat pocket," said the highwayman, whose voice had become much less that of the raven of the road and much more the English gentleman. "The outside of it, *here*." He was displaying the motion for Mrs. Herrald. "Furthermore, as I took the envelope he *told* me what it contained. He altogether lost his nerve."

Matthew decided to say *Better than losing my knee*, but he wished to make a grand entrance. He pushed aside the drapes, stepped forward . . . and two things happened in a blur.

Mrs. Herrald, who had removed her riding-hat since arriving at the house, gave a startled cry. In the next instant the supposed highwayman, still a huge man no matter his masquerade, moved faster than Matthew had ever seen a human being react in his life. There was a hissing sound of leather spitting steel, a bright spark of sunlight leaped in an arc across the walls, and very suddenly Matthew had the sharp tip at the end of thirty inches of rapier up under his throat where all the life flowed.

Matthew froze. The swordsman also became a statue, as did Mrs. Herrald, but the weapon did not waver a nose-hair.

"I surrender," Matthew said, and slowly lifted his hands palm-out.

"By *God*!" the man thundered, shaking the glass in the door panes. "Are you *insane*? I almost ran your neck through!"

"I thank you for your hesitation in that regard." Matthew tried to swallow and found his Adam's-apple in jeopardy. "I have a delivery for a Mr. Hudson Greathouse."

"A *delivery*? What are you——"

"Mr. Greathouse," said Mrs. Herrald quietly, "please lower your sword from our courier's throat." Her face was still blanched but some humor had returned to her eyes, and Matthew thought that even by what the man Greathouse had told her, she knew his trick.

The sword dropped, but Greathouse kept it at his side unsheathed. Matthew felt it was a compliment, in a way. The man's rugged, hawk-nosed face bore the rather dazed and confused expression Matthew had seen on six-month-long sea voyage passengers as they staggered onto the dock encountering long-forgotten stability.

"May I deliver the envelope?" Matthew asked.

"I already *took* it," growled Greathouse.

"Yes sir, but . . . no, sir. You did take an envelope, yes. But the right one, no." Matthew shrugged off his coat, reached back underneath his waistcoat, and retrieved the envelope where it was lodged between shirt and breeches-band. "I apologize," he said as he handed it over. "It's a little sweat-damp."

Greathouse turned the envelope to look at the red wax seal with its embossed *H*. "This can't be! I broke the seal on the envelope I took from his pocket!"

"That envelope *did* have a wax seal, yes sir. The color of red used on the real envelope is probably a shade or two lighter than that used in Magistrate Powers' office, where I did the work before I left. But I didn't believe it would be a problem. I think, Mrs. Herrald, that you've bought your envelopes from the same source as does City Hall, namely Mr. Ellery's Stationer's Shop on Queen Street. If not, the envelopes are nearly the same in size." He looked back and forth between Mrs. Herrald and Hudson Greathouse. "I couldn't duplicate the correct seal, of course," he said, enjoying their silence, "so I had to divert the highwayman's . . . um . . . Mr. Greathouse's attention from examining it too closely before it was broken. Then again, if he'd seen it was not embossed with an *H* and he'd shown any reaction, he would've given himself away even before he pretended to read official signatures on a blank piece of paper."

"*Really?*" Mrs. Herrald's eyes sparkled, as she was obviously relishing the display.

"Yes, madam. His six paces stepped backward might have been far enough to keep me from seeing there was nothing written on the paper, but I already knew there wasn't." That part had been comical to Matthew, and he'd had to put his hand over his mouth to hide a wicked smile as the "highwayman" had read the "signatures" and boasted of his forger "friends in Boston." They had to be quite some forgers, to forge names out of nothing.

"And how did you know I wasn't a real highwayman?" Greathouse asked. "How did you know that when I saw a blank piece of paper I wouldn't just cave your head in?"

Matthew shrugged. "I didn't. But you had my wallet and the watch. Why should you get so upset over nothing?"

Mrs. Herrald nodded. "Prior preparation, using the envelope and wax. Very clever. Misdirection, with your hand over your pocket. Again, clever, but Mr. Greathouse should have been aware of that old trick. Anything else?"

"Yes madam, the fact that you were arriving was very clear. Mr. Greathouse threw the torn envelope down onto the road as a signal to let you know the game had been played out, in case I walked so far to find my horse that you missed me on my supposed trip back to town."

"True. All true. But for one small hitch-knot, young man. Mr. Greathouse, would you open your delivery?"

Greathouse broke the seal and opened the envelope. A smile flickered at the edges of his mouth. "Oh," he said. "I see the amendments to the deed came." He held up an official parchment written in an expansive, flowing hand and bearing half-a-dozen fat-fingered signatures.

"It arrived by ship's post, two hours before my meeting with Mr. Corbett," Mrs. Herrald said, still speaking to Greathouse. "I was unfortunately unable to tell you in time that our courier would be protecting a *real*, and very valuable, document."

Matthew looked down at the floor's oak boards and tasted a little sour remnant of his Gold Compass codfish.

"I should sign it now, while it's in front of me." Mrs. Herrald took the parchment, sat down at the desk, dabbed quill into ink, and wrote her name in stately script below the other names.

"This is *your* house?" Matthew asked.

"Yes. Oh, there's a matter of some landholdings, but this settles it once it's back in London." She smiled up at him. "I'll take it to the post myself."

"You smacked me, boy!" hollered Greathouse, who slapped Matthew on the back so hard Matthew thought he might wind up head-over-heels in the garden. The man grinned with square white teeth that looked cut from DeKonty's quarry. "Well done!"

When Matthew had gotten all the wind back in his lungs and could speak again, he said, "Pardon, Mrs. Herrald, but . . . if your plan was for me to be waylaid on the road and the envelope taken, then what was the point of all this?"

She spent a moment refolding the parchment. Then she looked up at him and in her eyes Matthew thought he saw a new appreciation. Or respect, as the case might be. She said, "I know your history from Nathaniel Powers. I know your motivations concerning that situation in Fount Royal, and I know your desire for success. What I didn't know was how you would deal with failure."

She stood up, now regarding him face-to-face. "As a member

of the Herrald Agency, you will do your best to succeed, but in spite of that, many times you will fail. That is the nature of the world, and the truth of life. But when you find your horse again, will you go back, or will you go forward? That was what I had to know.

"Welcome," she said, and she offered her hand.

Matthew realized he stood at an important crossroads, and one that should not be lightly negotiated. If dealing with a false highwayman was the worst of it, fine; yet Matthew thought today's incident was likely a frivolity, considering the danger of this line of work. Yet, for the chance to use his mind and his instincts, to further the career that Magistrate Woodward had begun by removing him from the orphanage, to make something of himself in this rowdy and riotous world, wasn't it worth at least a try?

It was, he decided, though he knew he'd decided this when he'd left town by the Post Road.

It was.

He took Mrs. Herrald's hand, and rightaway received another slap on the back from Hudson Greathouse that made him think he couldn't survive many more congratulations.

"You'll stay for dinner," Mrs. Herrald announced. "Mr. Greathouse will make his famous Irish beef and ale stew. I presume your horse is somewhere nearby, so I'd suggest you go ride it properly up here, get it watered and settled in the barn. The key to the gate is hanging on a peg next to the front door." She motioned him off. "Go!"

As twilight gathered, the stormclouds grew and thickened and at last the devilishly playful showers of the day became a driving rain. In the dining-room of Mrs. Herrald's house, candles burned as rain beat against the windows and Matthew sat at the polished walnut table realizing that Mr. Greathouse's stew was not so famous for its beef as for its ale, which had been poured in by the brewer's jug. Matthew ate lightly and Mrs. Herrald more lightly still, yet Greathouse drank a mug of ale to go along with his ale and showed no effect other than a proclivity to fill up the room with his voice.

Matthew had not been told directly, but he surmised as they talked about various things—the state of the town, the new governor, the high constable and such chit-chat—that they were employer and employee, yes, but also something more. Not so personally involved as sharing a professional . . . what would be the word? Matthew thought. *Elan*, possibly? A bond of purpose? That they greatly respected each other was obvious and paramount, in their patterns of speech and their responses to the other's comments, but again there was something more than respect present here. Matthew had the impression that Greathouse was Mrs. Herrald's "right-hand man," so to speak, and might even be second-in-command of the agency. In any case, she listened intently when he spoke and he did the same for her, and Matthew thought this was not simply a professional courtesy but rather a deep alliance of kindred minds.

As Greathouse quaffed his ale and talked about how he and Mrs. Herrald were trying to decide between two suitable office locations on either Stone Street or New Street, Matthew studied him and wondered what his history might be. Sitting there with the sleeves of his white shirt rolled up to the elbows and his full head of gray hair pulled back into a queue and tied with a black ribbon, Greathouse might have been a schoolmaster discoursing on geometrics. Yet his voice had a military quality about it; that is, Matthew thought, his voice had a patina of confidence and an edge of urgency that might be suited to battlefield command. Certainly his physical size and quickness spoke of an active life, as did the jagged scar through his left eyebrow and his familiarity with the rapier. Greathouse also bore one telltale sign of a man who had wielded a sword in earnest: the forearm of his right hand, his sword arm, swelled larger than the left.

He appeared to be a man who pretended to be more rough-hewn than he was, Matthew decided. Sometimes Greathouse started to reach for the napkin to dab his mouth and seemed to remind himself not to; or sometimes he did it anyway, while speaking. A man with an education in manners who played his role with a more common touch. Matthew wondered if he might be an aristocrat, raised amid wealth, who for one reason or another felt more comfortable in the light of a lesser candle. Matthew guessed his age in the mid-to-late forties, probably just a bit younger than Mrs. Herrald.

And he could surely go on, once he got started. "Did you know," he said, "that we're near the place this island got its name? Some of the first settlers brought kegs of brandy in for the Indians and everyone wound up soused at a ceremonial feast. When the settlers later asked the name of the island, the Indians made it up on the spot: *Manahacktantenk*. In their lingo it meant 'the place where everybody got drunk.' "

He lifted his ale mug high. "To Manahacktantenk," he said, and drank it down.

Toward the end of their dinner, with darkness fully fallen and rain still tapping on the windows, Mrs. Herrald said, "Matthew, I wish to ask your opinion on something. Excuse me." She rose from her chair, as did the two gentlemen, and she left them for a moment at the table. When she returned, she had with her to Matthew's great surprise an item with which he was most familiar.

She seated herself again and put down upon the table a copy—smudged, one of the imperfect dogs that had gotten loose, but still legible—of the *Bedbug*. "I was most interested in this broadsheet. I was wondering if you knew the printer."

"I do. His name is Marmaduke Grigsby. In fact, I helped him lay down the type and work the press."

"A man of many occupations, it seems," said Greathouse, eating another portion of his famous stew.

"Just helping a friend, that's all. But what of it?"

"I was wondering how many he prints, and when he's printing the next sheet. Do you know?"

"I believe we printed three-hundred copies of that one." And every six-hundred back-and-fronts recalled by the muscles of his shoulder in levering that damned press down upon the typeface form and holding each one at pressure for fifteen seconds. "I understand Mr. Grigsby wants to print the next sheet within a few days, if possible."

"Even though we're still negotiating for an office, I think we should consider asking your friend to run a notice for us. Something quiet, of course. Just that the Herrald Agency is opening soon, and that we specialize in finding . . ." She paused. "What is lost," she decided. "And finding answers to delicate questions."

"I'd like to see the response to *that*," Greathouse said, as he pressed the napkin to each corner of his mouth with a huge hand. "Farmer Jones wishes to know the answer to why his daughter Lovey comes to dinner with hay in her hair."

"To start, one must begin," Mrs. Herrald answered, with a slight shrug. "Isn't that true?" She'd directed the question to Matthew.

"It is," he agreed, "but I do wonder why you've chosen this place, at this time. I understand much valuable cargo passes through New York, and many wealthy people with items of value. But, after all, New York isn't London. I can verify that the criminal element here is not exactly overpowering the judicial system." He realized he was echoing the statement of High Constable Lillehorne. "Why, exactly, have you chosen New York?"

Mrs. Herrald stared into his eyes, and by the steady candlelight Matthew thought there was a serenity and certainty of purpose about her that was almost unsettling, being from a woman. He wondered if those who sat in the presence of Queen Anne felt such an emanation of cool willpower as he felt now from Katherine Herrald. He had to sit back in his chair a bit, for the force of it was almost like a fist against his chest.

"Now you've asked for it." Greathouse stood up. "Want a glass of wine?"

"No, thank you."

"I'll help myself, then. Don't mind me." He clomped off toward the rear of the house.

Mrs. Herrald said, her eyes still fixed on his, "Matthew, New York is *the* town."

"Yes, madam, I know it's the town."

"Not just any town," she corrected. "*The* town. I've kept up with the colonies. With the other towns in Massachusetts, Pennsylvania, and down through Virginia and Carolina. I've educated myself on the reports that find their way from this new world to the old one. The census figures. The harbor logbooks. The credits and payments that bear international stamps and are fussed over by all the Queen's men. I do have friends in places both high and low, Matthew, and they tell me what I already know: this is *the* town."

"Pardon," Matthew said, feeling he must be thick-headed, "but I'm not following you."

"The future," she replied patiently, "is here. In New York. Now please don't misunderstand. Boston will become a great city, as will Philadelphia. Even New Rochelle, most likely, and Orangeburg too. But I look at New York, and I see an uncommon city that will not be matched by any town on the coast. Boston is growing by leaps and bounds, yes, but the weather there is more inclement and the Puritans still run the place. Philadelphia has its potential as a world port, but the Free Society of Traders went bankrupt there twenty years ago, so the jury is still out. The Dutch set up a very organized system of international trade in New York, and we English took that over when we took the colony. I think the Dutch were relieved, really. Now they can make money as business partners and not have to spend it on maintaining a colony."

"I see," Matthew said, though he was waiting for her point.

She gave it to him. "New York is the future business center of perhaps the entire English endeavor. It's not much to look at now, no, though it has its certain . . . charms. But I believe that in ten years, twenty years, or thirty . . . however long it takes . . . this town will be a city that may even dare to rival London."

"Rival *London?*" Matthew almost laughed at that one, but he kept a straight face. "I agree that the town has potential, but New York has a long way to go before it rivals London. Half the streets are still dirt!"

"I didn't say it would happen soon. London was born at the dawn of time, if you listen to the balladeers on Golding Lane. But New York will find its time, and I believe there will be fortunes to be made and lost here, even with half the streets dirt."

Matthew nodded pensively. "I'm glad you have such belief in the town's future. So that's why you wish to open the office?"

"Not only that. If *I* have done my research and come to this belief, others also have."

"Others?"

Mrs. Herrald didn't answer for a moment. She picked up her fork and used it to slowly stir the remaining liquid in the bowl before her, as if she were probing for the bottom of a swamp.

She said, "You can be sure, Matthew, that the criminal element of not only England but also greater Europe is looking in this direction, and has already seen the potential. Whatever it might be: kidnapping, forgery, public and private theft, murder for hire. Domination of the mind and spirit, thereby to gain illicit profit. I could give you a list of the names of individual criminals who will most likely be lured here at some time or another, but it's not those petty thugs who concern me. It's the society that thrives underground, that pulls the marionette strings. The very powerful and very deadly group of men—and women—who even now are sitting at dinner just as we are, but they hold carving knives over a map of the new world and their appetites are ravenous."

She ceased her stirring and again locked her gaze with his. "You say that currently the criminal element is not overpowering the judicial system. That's today. There are going to be many tomorrows in the life of this colony and this city, Matthew. If we don't prepare for the future, it will be taken from us by those who do." She lifted her arched eyebrows. "Please don't be blind to the fact that there's already an element of . . . shall we say . . . *evil* at work here? The 'Masker,' as Mr. Grigsby calls him. There have been several murders in Boston and Philadelphia that are still unsolved and unlikely to be as more time goes past. Oh, it's already here, Matthew. And it will thrive unless the enforcement of law is strong and organized. Which it currently is not."

Greathouse came back in with a wineglass full to the brim. "Have I missed the sermon?"

"I was just getting to the 'amen,' " Mrs. Herrald answered. "I hope I haven't frightened our junior associate too very much."

"There were some, I recall, who up and bolted." Greathouse settled himself in his chair. "What say, Matthew? Still in the game?"

It was time for Matthew to ask an indelicate question, but one that must be posed. "How much money am I to be paid?"

"Ah!" Greathouse grinned. He lifted his glass in a toast. "That's the spirit!"

"To be negotiated," said Mrs. Herrald. "You can be sure it's more money than you've ever seen, and will continue to be improved as your experience and training improves."

"Training? What training?"

"Had to be a catch," Greathouse said.

"Your training from *junior* to full associate, which may take some time," came the reply. "You won't be given anything you can't handle, that I promise." Matthew didn't like the sound of that *training* part, yet he assumed it probably had to do with learning a new language or improving his processes of logic and deduction by further reading. Still, his hesitation made Greathouse say, "You know what the dockmen say in London, Matthew? 'Don't sweat over the small crates, and everything's a small crate.' "

"I would say some crates are not as small as others, but I echo the sentiment . . . I suppose," said Mrs. Herrald with a slight smile. "We need you, Matthew. You'll be well-paid and well-challenged. Probably well-travelled too, before long. Certainly well-educated in the complexities of life, and of the criminal mind. Have I frightened you off?"

"No, madam," Matthew answered quickly and firmly. "Not in the least."

"That's what I wished to hear." She looked out the window and saw a flash of lightning in the distance, toward town. "I don't think you should try the road this time of night, and in this weather. If you'd care to stay, you can sleep in the downstairs bedroom. Get an early start at sunup, if you like."

Matthew thought that would be the wisest course, and thanked Mrs. Herrald for her hospitality. As the night moved on, Greathouse brought a chessboard and pieces from another room, set it up on the table, and had a game with Matthew as he downed a second brimful glass of wine. Matthew assumed Greathouse would be an easy victim with all that liquor in his brain, but the man caused grievous difficulty with his knights before Matthew shredded him with a queen-and-bishop combination.

After a second game in which Matthew showed no mercy from the beginning and coldly cut Greathouse to pieces left and right until the swordsman's king was trapped in a corner like a miserable rat, Greathouse yawned and stretched his huge self until his backbone cracked. Then he said goodnight and retired to the carriage-house, where he resided.

Mrs. Herrald had already gone to bed during the second chess game, so Matthew went into the small but comfortable bedroom downstairs, took off his clothes, and put on a nightshirt she'd laid out for him. He washed his face in a waterbowl, cleaned his teeth with a brush and peppermint dental powder left for his convenience, blew out his candle, and went to bed as the distant lightning flashed and flared over Manhattan.

There was much to think about. To deeply ponder and consider. Matthew spent about three minutes thinking about Mrs. Herrald's "sermon" at the table before the weariness crashed over him and he was out as quickly and absolutely as his candle.

Thus it was with some confusion and grogginess that he came back to his senses with someone pulling at him and a lantern in his face. The rain was still falling from the dark, hitting the bedroom's window. He sat up, squinting in what seemed like noonday's sun thrown in his eyes.

"Up and dressed," said Hudson Greathouse, standing over him. His voice was all business and as sober as Sunday. "Your training starts *now*."

twelve

MATTHEW WAS URGED by Hudson Greathouse through the drizzling rain toward the brown stone carriage-house, where illumination showed at the windows. He doubted he'd been allowed to slumber for more than two hours, and he was dog-tired and heavy-limbed. He walked before the light of Greathouse's lantern through the open doorway, finding himself standing on a dirt floor with eight more lanterns set about in a large circle.

Greathouse closed the door and, to Matthew's unease, dropped the bolt across it. There was no carriage in the place, but a set of steps led up to a second level and what must have been Greathouse's living area. Greathouse set the lamp he was carrying on a wallhook, and it was then that Matthew saw the glint of yellow light on the grips and handguards of four swords in scabbards also resting horizontally on hooks. That wasn't all of the man's arsenal. On display along with the swords were two pistols, three daggers, and—of all things—an oversized slingshot.

"Mrs. Herrald tells me you know nothing about swords or pistols. Correct?"

"Yes sir. I mean . . . correct." Matthew had been about to yawn before he'd seen the weapons, but now he was as fully awake as a healthy jolt of fear could make a person.

"You've never held a sword, then?"

"No. Well . . ." He *had* briefly picked up a sword in a gaol cell in Fount Royal, but it was more to get rid of it than use it and so he didn't think that incident counted for much. "When I was a boy . . . I mean, a very *young* boy . . . I was running with a gang at the harbor. Not a real gang, I mean. But just . . . you know . . . boys. Orphans, like I was."

"There's a point to this?"

"Yes sir. We used to fight each other with sticks and pretend they were swords. You know. Mock wars."

"Ever kill anyone with a pretend sword?" Greathouse approached him, looming over Matthew like a giant and getting larger still, if just in Matthew's sensibility, as his shadow was thrown across the wall.

"No sir."

"Ever kill anyone with *anything*?"

"No sir."

"Can you fight? Use your fists?"

"I'm . . . sure I remember fighting with the gang. But it was a long time ago, and I really was a different person. I've changed since then."

"You should have kept that part of yourself." Greathouse stopped before him and sized him up from toe to head as if for the first time. Washed with lanternlight, the man's face was haughty and dismissive. It occurred to Matthew that either Greathouse had tremendous recuperative abilities over the effects of alcohol or he could simply drink a keg down and keep going.

"You're spindly," Greathouse said, and began to walk in a circle around him. "You look weak as water and pale as a moonbeam. Don't you ever get outside in the daylight and *work*?"

"My work is . . . predominantly mental, sir."

"That's the trouble with young people these days. They sit on their mental and call it work. Well, you think you're so smart, don't you? So clever at chess. I think you've let yourself go to rot. You're more a ghost than a man. How'd you get that scar on your head? Fall down and hit it on a damned *chessboard*?"

"No sir," Matthew said. "I . . . got it in a fight with a bear."

Greathouse stopped his circling.

"If I may ask," Matthew ventured, "how did you get *your* scar?"

Greathouse paused. Then at last he said, "Broken teacup. Thrown by my third wife."

"Oh."

"You don't ask the questions," the man snarled. "*I* ask the questions, do you understand?"

"Yes sir."

Greathouse continued his circling, around and around. Then he stopped directly in front of Matthew. "If you want to see a scar, take a gander at this." He unbuttoned his ruffled shirt and displayed a truly ugly brown scar that began just beneath the left collarbone and crossed to the center of the chest. "Dagger strike, fifth of March, 1677. He was going for my heart, but I caught his wrist in time. An assassin, dressed in monk's robes. And here." He pulled the shirt off his right shoulder to show a dark purple crater. "Musket ball, twenty-second of June, 1684. Knocked my arm out of the socket. I was lucky there, no bones broken. The ball went through the woman who was standing in front of me at the time. Look here, then." He angled his body so Matthew could see a third gruesome scar across the ribs on the right side. "Ninth of October, 1686. That's what a rapier can do to you, even when it doesn't bear a cutting edge. The bastard swung instead of lunged. I did suffer two ribs broken on that one. Spent a month laid up, almost lost my mind but for the dear Contessa." He touched the injury gently, as if in reverence. "I can foretell rain by three days." He shrugged his shirt back into place and buttoned it once more, his expression now more pleased than petulant.

Matthew had to ask, "Is that what I have to look forward to?"

Instantly Greathouse pressed a finger against Matthew's chest so hard Matthew thought he was about to receive his first battle-mark. "Not," Greathouse said, "if you're smart. Not if you're lucky. And not if you let me teach you how to defend yourself."

Matthew said nothing, but Greathouse seemingly read his mind. "I will tell you," said the swordsman, "that I was fighting four men when one got his rapier swing past my guard, so yes I *can* be a competent instructor. Anyway, he had no rhythm and he was all herky-jerky panic. It was good luck for him and bad luck for me. Until I got my breath back and spilled his puddings all over the alley floor. I gave another one a cut to the face that went through one cheek and out the other and then they all ran for their lives."

"Did you spare them?"

Greathouse examined his gnarled knuckles, which Matthew noted also were marked with numerous small scars. "I followed the blood and tracked the wounded one down. A thrust to the throat and he was finished. It was a dark night, though. Only that saved the other two, though I suppose my own blood and broken ribs also might have slowed me a step." Abruptly he walked to the armory and chose two swords. He unsheathed both, turned one, and offered Matthew the grip. "Take it. Thrust at me."

"*Sir?*"

"Take the rapier and thrust at me."

Matthew accepted the sword. It was a damned heavy thing. Unbalanced, it felt to him. An unnatural way to get yourself killed, trying to move this sluggish piece of steel through the air. He wagged the sword back and forth, watching the light glint and jump from its surface. It seemed to him that the business point was too slow by far to get where he intended it.

"You're holding it like a baby with a rattle," Greathouse said. "Take a man's grip and lock that thumb down. All right now, just thrust at me."

"How do I stand?"

"Don't worry about the stance yet. Come on, do as I say."

"I don't feel comfortable with this. Do you have one that's not so heavy?" Already Matthew could feel the muscles of his forearm protesting. A swordsman he was not meant to be.

"That's the lightest of the bunch, moonbeam. Just hold the sword out, then. Bend your elbow a little. All right. Tight grip. Tighter. Drop your shoulder. Not your arm, your shoulder. Right there, stay still." Greathouse brought his sword around and hit

Matthew's flat-to-flat with a ringing sound and, though not with much power, the vibration coursed up Matthew's arm right to the skull. "Just get a feel for it," Greathouse said, as he brought his sword around on the other side and struck again. He continued from one side to the other. The carriage-house sounded like a belfry. "The rapier has two parts, the blade and the hilt. Of the hilt there is the pommel—that little ball at the end of the hilt—the grip, and the guard. The parts of the blade are the strong—the *forte* near the grip—and the weak, which would be the *feeble* near the point." The two swords continued to sound out their steel music. "Always block—or parry—a strike or thrust at the *forte*, you see as I'm allowing here. If you try to parry a blow at the *feeble*, you likely will either lose your weapon or have it broken. Or you'll be run through. The rapier is not fashioned for cutting strikes, though of course you've seen it *can* cut with enough force behind it. It's meant for lunging strikes, using the sharp tip to drive through your target. You're weakening your grip, hold it steady. Now we shall get you accustomed to the feel of the weapon, and then we'll move to the fundamentals of *quarte*, *terce*, approach, lunge stretch, distance measure, break measure, the feint, the riposte, beating, binding, time and—"

"I think I have this under control," Matthew interrupted, though his forearm ached like a bad tooth.

"I'm glad you think so," said Greathouse, who instantly brought his rapier around with a little more power and at a different angle and suddenly Matthew's fingers shot open as if his hand had been hornet-stung and the sword flew away like one of Increase Mather's comets.

"I'm sorry, I lost my grip," Matthew said, as he tried to shake the sting out of his hand.

"You never *had* a grip. I told you to keep that thumb locked down. Go get the sword and come back right where you stand."

Matthew obeyed. Greathouse said, "Make your body thin. As if it isn't thin enough, but at least that's to your advantage. Show only your right side. Keep your feet in line with me. Not so far apart. Now they're too close. You want to have optimum power when you thrust, but keep your feet not too close or your balance will be unsteady. All right, that's much better." He walked in a slow circle just beyond the lanterns. "Keep your sword pointed outward, don't let it slope down unless your opponent is three inches tall. Very well, sink down as if you're about to sit. A little more. Left arm behind you, like a rudder." He stopped in front of Matthew again. "Sword tip pointed. Slightly higher than the hilt. All right, that's good. Now you're going to stretch forth your right arm and step forward with your right foot as far as you can, keeping left arm, body, and sword in line. Thrust at me. Do it!"

Matthew pushed himself forward. Long before his sword broke the circle, it was knocked aside by Greathouse's blade.

"Again," Greathouse said. "Keep your body in line. Don't lift your left foot or let it drag. And when I say thrust, I don't mean *jerk* like a sun-addled mule. I'm looking for economy of motion; speed will come later."

Once more Matthew thrust, once more his sword was nearly knocked from his hand.

"I held it!" he said proudly. "Did you see?"

"Yes, my mistake." Greathouse took a single step forward, his blade came in with a quick twist, and again Matthew's hand spasmed open and the sword stabbed dirt ten feet away.

"The next time you lift that thumb up," Greathouse glowered, "you shall need only nine-fingered gloves. Go get it and return to your position."

Matthew again obeyed. His forearm was killing him, but he gritted his teeth and was determined to make at least a show of fortitude.

"Take the *quarte*. That's the position I just showed you. Now I want you to just move the sword. Cut to the right, return to position, thrust in the center, return to position, cut to the left, thrust in the center. Keep your back firm. Bend your knees a little more. More still, you won't fall. Keep moving the sword until I say to stop."

Bastard, Matthew thought. He didn't know how much more of this his arm could take, but damned if he'd give up.

"You're losing your form," said Greathouse as he walked the circle again. "You have no power in your arm, do you? Keep going. Don't lift that left foot. Are you deaf? I said to keep your body in line!"

Sweat glistened on Matthew's face as he continued to cut and thrust. The rapier now felt as if it weighed near an anvil and his forearm was just nerveless meat. His shoulder, however, was screaming bloody murder.

After what seemed at least fifteen minutes, Greathouse said, "Stop."

Matthew lowered the weapon and tried to rub the life back into his arm. He was breathing hard. It amazed him how much strength and energy was demanded just to handle the damned sword, much less use it in a combat situation. "How long will it take me to become proficient?" he asked, in between breaths.

Greathouse had sheathed his rapier and hung it by a leather strap across his shoulder. Now he produced a short-stemmed clay pipe from his breeches pocket, lit it with a match from a small tinderbox, and blew out a plume of gray smoke that floated past Matthew's head. "Ten years," he answered. "Give or take." He tucked the tinderbox away.

"Ten *years*?"

"You're starting a little late. I began lessons when I was eight years old."

"Well, maybe I should begin with a sword fit for a child, then."

"I don't think I could teach while convulsed with laughter. Anyway, I don't believe in using wooden blunts for adults. You have to strengthen your hand and forearm and keep your body in line. Blunts only give you a false sense of progress."

"I'm not sure this is anything I can ever progress at, blunts or not."

Greathouse took Matthew's sword, indicating their night's training was at an end. "Maybe not, and certainly not all men are suited to using a rapier or any other kind of sword. I know there's a lot to remember."

"It's much more complicated than I thought," Matthew said.

"Unfortunately, the surface of that complication has barely been nicked." Greathouse returned the weapons to their places on the wall. He reached down to the floor and picked up a small brown bottle, which he uncorked and gave to Matthew. "Take a sip of this."

Matthew smelled the liquor long before it got near his nose, but he had a good long drink of it anyway. His eyes were watering when he returned the brandy. "Thank you."

Greathouse drank, corked the bottle again, and then returned the pipe to his mouth. "Chess is complicated, too, isn't it?"

"It is. I mean, at first. Before you can comprehend the pieces and their patterns of movement."

"So it is with the use of a sword, but instead of trying to checkmate a king and defend yourself from check, you're trying to kill a man and defend from being killed. Think about sword-play as being akin to chess in this way: both are concerned with taking and defending space. Equally important are approach and retirement, which would be the offense and defense in chess. You are always thinking ahead to the next move, the next parry, the next feint. You are building toward a completion, and you must take dominance of the action from your opponent." Greathouse let a little thread of smoke spill out over his lower lip. "Let me ask this: how long has it taken you to become so proficient at chess?"

"I suppose . . . many years. I still make too many mistakes for my liking, but I've learned how to recover."

"The same as in swordplay," said Greathouse with a lift of his chin. "I don't expect you to ever become an expert, but I do expect you to learn enough to recognize a mistake and recover from it. That may keep you alive long enough to pull out a pistol and shoot your opponent."

It took a few seconds for Matthew to realize Greathouse was jesting, though the man's expression remained dead serious.

"I want you here at nine o'clock on Saturday morning," Greathouse said. "You'll spend the day here. Literally, in this carriage-house. We'll continue the rapier lessons and also add loading and use of the pistol, and use of the fists at close quarters as well."

That sounded like a grand way to spend a Saturday, Matthew thought. "What's the slingshot for?"

"Squirrels," Greathouse said. "I roast them with potatoes and peppers." He took another pull from his pipe, puffed the smoke, and then knocked the dottle out with the heel of his hand. "Your training is not only to include physical exertion. I want to know how well you can read and follow maps, for instance. Or draw a map yourself, from a verbal description of a place. I want to know how well you can recall the description of a person, and I want to see you handle a horse with a bit more spirit than that old slogger in the barn." He did smile just a hint now, at Matthew's pained expression. "As Mrs. Herrald said, you'll never be given anything you can't handle. And you might take comfort in the fact that you're just the first recruit we've chosen. There'll be others, over time. We're looking at one in Boston and two more in New York right now."

"Really? Who?"

"If I told you it wouldn't be a secret, and for now Mrs. Herrald wishes to keep it so."

"All right," Matthew said, but his imagination was already at work wondering who the others might be. One thing more he felt he had to ask: "What about Mrs. Herrald?"

"What about her, exactly?"

"Her story. She told me her husband founded the agency. What happened to him?"

Greathouse started to reply, but he seemed to check himself. "That can wait," he decided. "Dawn breaks in four hours. I think you'd best get some sleep."

Matthew didn't have to ponder very long to agree. However much sleep he got for the remainder of the night, it was going to be a long day. He wasn't sure his right arm was going to be worth much, either, and he did have some work to do for Magistrate Powers. "Goodnight," he said to Greathouse, who replied with,

"Make sure you wipe your boots. Mrs. Herrald hates mud on her floor."

Matthew walked back to the house in what had become a drifting mist, obliged the madam of the house by wiping his boots clean on the iron bootscrape at the door, and within ten minutes had abandoned all thoughts of swordplay, chess, and roasted squirrels and fell into a deep and solid slumber.

A polite bell rung outside his door awakened Matthew to a gray dawn. He washed his face, dressed, forsook shaving as there was no razor offered, and also decided he could hold his bladder long enough until he got on the road as he did not wish to yellow the chamberpot. On leaving his room he found a hearty breakfast of eggs, ham, and biscuits along with a pot of strong dark tea awaiting him at the dining-table. Set next to his plate was his wallet and the silver watch.

Mrs. Herrald joined him but Greathouse didn't make an appearance, though Matthew assumed he had made the breakfast since he seemed to be the cook of the house.

"Take this to Mr. Grigsby, if you please." Mrs. Herrald handed him an envelope that was again secured with her red wax seal. "I assume he'll want payment in advance to publish the notice, so you'll find some additional coins in your wallet. By my calculations those should well satisfy both Mr. Grigsby and the livery stable. I understand you're due back to meet with Mr. Greathouse at nine o'clock Saturday morning." It was a statement, plainly stated. "Please take care to arrive on time."

"Yes, madam."

"Eat up, then. The rain's stopped, and I have letters to write."

Suvie had already been brought around from the barn and was standing at the hitching-post as Matthew walked out of the house. He put his wallet and the watch into his saddlebag and rode away as a few weak rays of sun pierced the clouds. In another moment he found Greathouse standing at the open gate.

"Good day to you," Greathouse said. "Oh. You might want to rub liniment on that forearm and shoulder when you get to town. By tonight you'll be in some pain."

"Thank *you*," Matthew answered, not without a jab of sarcasm. He rode through the gate, heard it swing shut behind him, and settled himself in the saddle for the journey home. Within half-an-hour the last of the clouds wisped away, the sky became bright blue and brighter still, the sun shone in full golden force, and Matthew slept with his chin resting on his chest as Suvie plodded the road to town.

Two

The Madness

thirteen

IT WAS FORTUNATE that Magistrate Powers had consented for Matthew's appointment with Mrs. Herrald, for on going to the magistrate's office on Thursday morning Matthew was unable to hold a quill steady enough to write a single line. The magistrate wanted to know everything that had happened and Matthew obliged him, accentuating the midnight rapier "training" that caused him now to be so useless to the cause of scribing.

"Off with you, then," Powers advised. "I'll poach another clerk. You go home and rest."

"I think I'll stop by the apothecary for some liniment," Matthew said, rubbing his shoulder. "I'll be ready for the Knox hearing tomorrow morning, though."

"I'm not so sure of that. I don't think Magistrate Mackfinay has anything on his docket. I'll ask if I might borrow his clerk." Powers waved him out the door. "You just rest your arm."

"Thank you, sir. I *will* try to do my job tomorrow."

"If not, not. Don't worry yourself about it." He looked at Matthew appreciatively. "I'm pleased I could help you start on a new course. Your being chosen by Mrs. Herrald for this position shines just as much a light on me as it does on you. And I'm certain she'll get her money's worth. They *are* going to pay you well, aren't they?"

"We haven't actually talked about the figures."

"Seems to me you may need a bit of legal representation yourself. If you want a proper contract drawn up, I'll be glad to advise."

"Thank you." Matthew was about to leave, but he hesitated at the door.

"Something else?" Powers looked up from his papers.

"Yes sir. I was wondering about Mrs. Herrald. Do you know anything more about her?"

"Such as?"

"You mentioned that you both shared enemies. May I ask what you meant by that?"

The magistrate spent a moment inspecting—or at least pretending to inspect—the first few lines of the letter atop his stack of correspondence. "Mrs. Herrald didn't inform you?" he asked. "Of her history?"

"She told me her husband began the agency. I understood that he is deceased. Is there something more I should know?" It came to him then. "Ah. You and Mrs. Herrald knew each other in London. That's why she sent the messenger. Was the messenger Mr. Greathouse?"

"It was Hudson, yes."

"You're on the basis of first names with him? That's an impressive feat. I assume you had some dealings with Mrs. Herrald, then?"

The magistrate summoned up a crooked smile. "Now I see what it's like to be on the witness stand. Shall I plead guilty and throw myself on the mercy of the court, Mr. Prosecutor?"

"I'm sorry, sir." Matthew had to smile as well, more to hide his embarrassment than to display humor. "I do get carried away."

"So I constantly note. To answer, I did know Katherine Herrald in London. I met her when Rich brought her to a Saturday supper at the fraternity."

"Rich?"

"Richard Herrald. He was a member of my law fraternity at Cambridge. Damned good tennis player, too. Almost as good as myself. And he became an excellent lawyer, specializing in criminal prosecution for the city. Yes, he brought that beautiful Katherine Taylor to the Saturday supper and afterward all the lot of us put down bets as to when they'd be married. I lost, but not by much."

"What happened to Mr. Herrald?"

Again, the magistrate focused false attention on his papers. Matthew knew there was definitely something he wished to say, but perhaps decorum forbade it. "I think," Powers said at last, "that Mrs. Herrald should answer your question."

"But the part about the 'shared enemies,' " Matthew persisted. "Shouldn't *you* answer that one?" He remembered to give due respect. "Sir."

"I should," Powers agreed. He said nothing more for a moment, staring into space. Then: "But my answer hinges upon Mrs. Herrald's, and so I leave it to her."

"Sir, I'm not asking for a legal decree. I'm asking only for—"

"If you're not out of this office in five seconds," Powers said, "I should think your mouth could dictate these letters to the quill of Mackfinay's clerk. So are you going, or are you staying?"

"Going."

"Then *be* gone."

The door closed at Matthew's back.

On the way out he nearly ran into Chief Prosecutor Bynes once again, so he had to hold his progress until the man had descended the stairs. Then he went down and walked into the bright midmorning sunlight. With an eye in the back of his head he entered the stream of citizens coming and going, ducked around a haywagon and started up Smith Street for the apothecary.

Matthew couldn't help but linger under the apothecary's red-striped awning and again examine the ground where Deverick had fallen. He'd found nothing yesterday, and today found the same. So it was into the apothecary, with its counter behind which were shelves of elixir bottles, heartburn chalk, various tree barks to treat fevers, calamine lotion, leech jars, dental powder, crushed flowers and herbs, medicinal vinegars and the like, and after a short time of speaking to Mr. Oosterhout he came back onto the street with a small paper-wrapped vial of yarrow oil which he was to apply twice a day. He turned right at the intersection of Smith and King, which took him unfortunately past Eben Ausley's domain—which to him looked no kinder by sun than by the dark of the moon—and to the printmaster's shop.

Soon he was in the company of Marmaduke Grigsby, who already had been scribing articles and from them arranging the small blocks of metal typeface in their sticks. The device of note, at the center of the most sun-illuminated room, was a bulky old monster that might have been used by the hand of Gutenberg himself. Looking at such a contraption, it was hard to believe it was the medium by which parchment sheets pressed with lamp-black and linseed varnish ink went out announcing events and proclaiming news to the citizens.

"Come to help with the type, I hope?" Grigsby asked. "Then if all goes well we can get to the pressing tomorrow."

"I have this." Matthew gave him the envelope, and waited as it was opened.

Grigsby read it carefully. "The Herrald Agency? Letters of inquiry to go to the Dock House Inn? What's this about?"

"For you, money." Matthew opened his wallet and offered one of the remaining silvers. "Will that do for a one-time announcement?"

"Of course!" Grigsby examined the coin so closely Matthew thought he was going to eat it. "What's this in the notice, though? 'Problem-solving'? What kind of problems?"

"Just run the notice as it is, if you please. I'm sure it will speak for itself to those who have an interest."

"All right, then. Now come sit down at the desk and let me get some fresh paper. I want to hear your story of how you came to find Deverick's body." Grigsby held up a hand before Matthew could protest. "I *know* you weren't first on the scene, but my interview with Phillip Covey was less than substantial. I want to know your impressions of the moment, and what McCaggers told you about the Masker. Come, come! Sit down!"

As Matthew took a seat in the cane-backed chair, he was fit-fully aware of McCaggers advising him to guard his information and of Bynes' more forceful advice at City Hall. He waited until the printmaster was ready with a dipped quill, and then he said, "I can give you my impressions of the moment true enough, but I have to refrain from repeating anything told me by the coroner."

Grigsby's thick white eyebrows began to convulse. "Oh no, Matthew! Not you, as well!"

"Me as well *what*?"

"You're not turning against me, are you? Hiding information that Lillehorne wants kept from public view? Or is it Magistrate Powers who's choked your chain?"

Matthew shook his head. "You know me better than that. McCaggers simply pointed out that it might not be in the best interest of the investigation to divulge any more about the Masker."

"Ah!" Grigsby leaned over the paper. "Then he *did* use the name again?"

"I believe he made it clear he thinks the killer of both men is one and the same."

"Then *Masker* it is!" said Grigsby, spraying spittle upon the paper as he began to scribe with a fury only a writer might know.

Matthew winced, hearing in his mind the awesome thunder that would break from Bynes' mouth when the chief prosecutor read this article. "McCaggers didn't use that term, exactly. I'm not sure it's wise to—"

"Nonsense!" came the quick, clipped retort. "The *Gazette* would use it, and if it's good enough for the *Gazette*, it's good enough for the *Earwig*!" He dipped his quill again. "Now, let's have your story from the beginning."

An hour later, Matthew left the printmaster's shop so worn down by Grigsby's constant grinding that, being as fuddled as he was from his poor night's sleep, he wasn't sure what he'd told the man or what he'd kept secret. Grigsby could take a one-sentence comment and craft a paragraph out of it. Matthew had had to beg off helping any further, due not so much to a pain in his shoulder as to a pain in the neck, and Grigsby had been disappointed but had vowed to get Effrem Owles to help with the pressing on Friday.

Matthew walked home, was impressed by Hiram Stokely to sweep the pottery, and, as he felt it his duty to work for his lodging, he did the sweeping vigorously and without complaint. His labor was at first more strenuous than it might have been, for he had to continually dodge Cecily's snorting round-rosies and snout-shoves to his knees until Stokely had mercy on him and put the pig outside. At last Matthew was done and declared his intention to retire to his loft and catch a nap, though his progress up the ladder to the trapdoor was momentarily delayed while he assured the potter he wasn't ill and did not need a doctor.

In his room, Matthew opened the window to allow the warm air exit, took off his coat and shirt, and applied yarrow oil to his right forearm and shoulder. Even thinking about what he was going to have to do on Saturday wore him out. He was a mental spirit, not a sportsman or swordsman. It was ridiculous, to have to go through such labors that would never suit him were he to practice with a rapier ten hours a day for a month. How did anyone ever learn to use a weapon like that, anyway? They had to start off with arms and constitutions like iron.

I think you've let yourself go to rot, Hudson Greathouse had said.

Little did he know, Matthew thought. Anyone could handle a sword if they were six-foot-three and constructed like a warship. And a pistol could be aimed by any idiot, so what was the point?

You're more a ghost than a man.

Strong words from a weak mind, Matthew thought. Well, damn him! Ordering people around like a sandpit general! Damn him to blazes!

Matthew lay on his bed and closed his eyes, but even so his fit of anger would not be stilled. Gone out there all that way, just to be tricked. Tried to make a fool out of me. But they didn't do a very good job of that, did they? No siree! It takes a smarter pair than those two to make a fool of Matthew Corbett! Now this "training" business, trying to test my mettle! Trying to make me do something I've never done before and likely can *never* do. Sword-fighting and fist-fighting and acting like a common lout! If I'd wanted to spend my life wallowing in violence I could've stayed an orphan with the harbor gangs!

He had a clear vision of Katherine Herrald, seated behind her desk. Fixing him with those keen blue eyes like lamps shining underwater.

Many times you will fail, she said. *That is the nature of the world, and the truth of life. But when you find your horse again, will you go back, or will you go forward?*

And then she lifted her hand from the desk, made a fist, and knocked down upon the wood. Once . . . twice . . . a third time . . .

"Matthew? Matthew?"

He sat up with a start, realizing how dramatically the light had faded.

Again came three knocks. "Matthew? Open up, please!"

It was Hiram Stokely's voice. He was up on the ladder, knocking at the underside of the trapdoor. "Matthew?"

"Yes sir! Just a minute!" Matthew got his feet on the floor and rubbed his eyes. He was feeling much better now, but what time was it? His watch was in his coat pocket. By the fading light he thought it must be near five o'clock. He pulled open the trapdoor and looked down into Stokely's face.

"Sorry to bother you," Stokely apologized, "but you have a visitor."

"A visitor?" Then Stokely moved aside for Matthew to see and there standing at the foot of the ladder was someone he'd never expected.

" 'lo, Matthew," said John Five. He must've just come from the blacksmith's shop, for though he wore an ordinary white shirt, brown breeches, and boots his face was still ruddy from the furnace fire. "Can I climb up?"

"Yes. Of course. Come on." Matthew held the trapdoor open

as Stokely descended and John Five climbed the ladder. When John was up in the room, Matthew eased the trapdoor shut and went about lighting a couple of candles.

"Nice place," John said, gazing around. "All those books. I should have known."

"Pardon me." Matthew spent a minute washing his face at the waterbasin. He retrieved his watch from his coat and saw that it was indeed almost ten minutes after five. He wound the watch and held it to his ear to hear the ticking.

"Oh, that's a fine thing! I didn't know you made *that* kind of money!"

"It was a gift. It *is* nice, isn't it?"

"Somethin' I'll likely never have. Can I hold it?"

Matthew gave it to him and prepared a dish of shaving soap while John Five listened to the watch at his remaining ear.

"Ticks pretty, huh?" John Five asked.

"It does."

John set the watch down on the bedside table and sniffed the air. "What's that smell?"

"Yarrow oil. I have a sore shoulder."

"Oh. I could've used that, many a time."

Matthew applied the soap to his stubble and began to shave with his straight-razor. He could see John Five standing behind him in the small round mirror over the basin. John kept looking around the room, his brow knit. Something was coming, but Matthew had no idea what it was.

John cleared his throat. "Take you to supper."

Matthew turned around. "I'm sorry?"

"Supper. I'll take you to supper. My coin."

Matthew continued his shaving, scraping his chin clean, but he watched John Five in the mirror. "What's this about, John?"

A shrug was the first reply. John walked over and peered out the window onto the Broad Way. "Doesn't fit you, holdin' a grudge," he said. "You know what I'm talkin' at."

"I know you're referring to our disagreement over a certain course of action. But I want you to know as well that I've thought

a lot about what you've said. About Nathan and all the rest of it."
Matthew paused with the razor at his upper lip. "Even though I
wish things might be different, I know they can't be. So I'm doing
my best to let that go, John. I really am."

"Does that mean you *don't* hold a grudge?"

Matthew finished the lip before he answered. "It does."

"Whew!" said John Five, with visible relief. "Thank God for
that!"

Now Matthew was really curious. He washed the blade off
and put it aside. "If your visit is just to discern if I hold a grudge
against you, I can promise I don't. But I'd say that's not exactly
why you're here. Is it?"

"No, it's not."

Matthew began to wipe his face with a clean cloth. When it
was obvious John Five was not going to advance without prod-
ding, Matthew said, "I'd like to hear it, if you'd like to tell me."

John nodded. He rubbed his hand over his mouth and stared
at the floor, all signs that Matthew took to be the steadying of
nerves. Matthew had never seen John Five so jittery, and this alone
doubled his curiosity.

"Take you to supper," John said. "I can tell you about it there.
Say the Thorn Bush, at seven?"

"The Thorn Bush? Not my favorite place."

"Food's good and cheap there. And they let me run a bill."

"Why not just tell me about it *now*?"

"Because," John said, "I eat supper every Thursday evenin' at
five-thirty with Constance and Reverend Wade. Tonight, especially, I wouldn't be wantin' to not show up."

"And why is tonight so special, then?"

John drew in a long breath and slowly let it out. "Because," he
said quietly, "it's the reverend I need to talk to you about. Constance thinks . . . she thinks . . ." He hesitated; it was something
he couldn't quite force himself to spit out.

"Thinks what?" Matthew urged, just as quietly.

John lifted his gaze to Matthew's. His eyes looked sunken and
haunted. "Constance thinks her father is losin' his mind."

The sentence hung between them. Outside, a woman—Mrs. Swaye, from two houses down—was calling for her little boy Giddy to come to supper. A dog barked and a wagon creaked as it was pulled past the window.

"More than that," John continued. "Things she can't understand. I've got to go, Matthew. I've got to go sit at that table and know what Constance is thinkin', and I've got to look in Reverend Wade's face and wonder what I'm seein'. Please meet me at the Thorn Bush at seven. You've got to eat *somewhere*, don't you?"

Matthew had planned to eat with the Stokelys, but this put a new coat of paint on the fence. The rough-edged Thorn Bush was certainly not the place Matthew would have chosen, though he realized John Five probably wished to go there for one reason other than his credit, which was more easily obtained at the Thorn Bush than at any other tavern in town: you could be faceless in there, if you pleased. The gambling tables and roaming prostitutes focused all attention upon themselves. And it was surely not an establishment into which Reverend Wade nor any of the minister's friends might wander.

"All right," he said. "If you wish, seven o'clock at the Thorn Bush."

"Thank you, Matthew." John started to clap Matthew on the right shoulder, but he saw the slick shine of the yarrow oil and stayed his hand. "I'll see you there," he said, and Matthew lifted the trapdoor to let him descend the ladder.

After John Five was gone, Matthew pondered the startling statement he'd just heard. *Losing his mind?* And how was this condition revealing itself? he wondered.

We have to leave him, Wade had said to Vanderbrocken, over the dead man in the street.

Had they been travelling separately, or together? And if together, to what destination?

One step at the time, Matthew thought. First, to listen to what John Five had to say, and then to determine what it might mean.

He carefully folded his razor and put it away, thinking that the most dangerous edges often lay close at hand.

fourteen

JOHN FIVE WAS WAITING for Matthew outside the Thorn Bush when he got there just before seven. It was the beginning of a fine night in New York. The stars were showing, the breeze was warm, candles burned in the street-corner lamps, and a man with a bloody nose sat in front of the tavern throwing curses at everyone who passed by.

"Damn you!" hollered the man at Matthew. "Think you've got me whipped, do you?" Obviously he was drunk as well as battered. He struggled to get to his feet, but John Five placed a boot at his shoulder and nonchalantly shoved him back down on his ass.

Beyond the door with its five triangular glass panes—three of them cracked—and a depiction of thorns and leaves carved into the wood, the place was lit by dirty lanterns hanging from the ceiling beams. The smoke from a thousand pipes had turned the beams as black as printer's ink. A current haze thickened the air. The front room, where the bar was prominent, held tables where sat a dozen or so men all in various degrees of intoxication while feathered and buckled women swooped and cawed around them. Matthew had seen this picture before, during his nights of tracking Eben Ausley. He understood that the more attractive of these ladies—the better dressed and better mannered, if manners counted for anything—came from Polly Blossom's rose-colored house on Petticoat Lane, while some of the others who seemed unkempt and desperate had come over on the ferry from New Jersey.

At once four women aged probably from seventeen to forty-seven converged upon John Five and Matthew with lip-licking expressions of seduction on their painted faces so ridiculous that Matthew might have laughed had he not been a gentleman. Anyway, business was business and the competition was fierce. Still these ladies knew who was buying and who was not; when John Five shook his head and Matthew said, "No, thank you," they turned away almost as one, shrugged their bared shoulders, and life went on.

Now the noise of men yelling came from a second room. Matthew knew the gambling fiends were in their element. A drowsy-looking barmaid carrying a pitcher of wine approached, and John Five said, "We're going all the way back. My friend wants some supper."

"Mutton pie with turnips and beef brains with boiled potatoes," she answered, reciting the evening's fare.

"May I have mutton pie with boiled potatoes?" Matthew asked, and she speared him a look that told him he might get what he wanted and then again he might not.

"Two glasses of wine," John added. "The port."

She went off to the kitchen and Matthew followed John into the gambling room, where the smoke of Virginia's finest was truly dense. The men in here at first appeared to be more shadows than flesh, either sitting at tables where cards were being slapped down or hovering over boards where dice clattered as they were thrown toward a series of painted numbers. Then another uproar went off like an explosion and someone slammed a fist against wood and yelled, "Fuck it all, Hallock! Everything on the black!"

Matthew wondered if some madhouses—bedlams, as they were called—weren't more sane than this. Certainly more peaceful. The yelling died down, the cards were turned or the bones were tossed and then again the throat of Hell seemed to open to allow out a quick hot breath of chaos. Matthew thought that for some of these men winning or losing was not really the attraction; it was that chaotic instant of joy or terror, both made so pure in their intensity that all else of life paled in their shadows.

"Look here!" someone said to Matthew's left as he was going through a group of men in the gambling room. "It's Corbett, isn't it?"

Matthew looked in the direction of the voice and found himself standing alongside a dice table in the presence of the two young lawyers Joplin Pollard and Andrew Kippering. Both had ale tankards in their hands and appeared a bit woozy. Of special notice was the dark-haired and not unattractive prostitute of about twenty years of age hanging on to Kippering's left arm, her ebony eyes deep-sunken and vacant as the burned-out houses on Sloat Lane.

"See, Andrew?" Pollard said, with a wide grin. "It *is* him. He. Whatever. The one and only, eh?"

"I am who I am, I suppose," Matthew replied.

"Good man!" Pollard hit his sore shoulder with the tankard. Worse than that, he slopped some ale on the light-blue shirt Matthew wore, which was the last clean shirt in his possession. "Always be who you are. Eh, Andrew?"

"Always," Kippering said, with a lift of his tankard and then a long drink. The prostitute pressed forward and Kippering obliged her by pouring some of the stuff down her throat as well.

"And who's this, then?" When Pollard motioned toward John Five, Matthew was able to step back and avoid another spillage. "Hold a minute!" Pollard turned toward the dice table and the men who were wagering there. "I'm in on this one too, damn it! Three shillings on anchor!"

Matthew saw they were playing the popular game of Ship, Captain, and Crew, in which the shooter had five throws with a pair of dice to come up with a six, five, and four in that order, which stood for the ship, captain, and crew. Others could bet on any variation of success or failure. Pollard had just wagered on "anchor," which was a three to show up in the first throw.

"My friend John Five," Matthew said when Pollard had

returned his attention. "John, Misters Joplin Pollard and Andrew Kippering, both of whom are attorneys."

"First throw! Crew without a ship and an ace!" came the call from the table, with its resulting moment of chaos. Four and one. Then the wagering began once more at the pitch of frenzy as silver coins were tossed into an iron pot.

Pollard just shrugged. "To hell with it. John *Five*, did you say?"

"Yes sir." John was a bit distracted, as the prostitute had begun chewing on Kippering's left ear. "I've seen you both around town."

"You're Constance Wade's beau," Kippering said, trying carefully to get his ear free.

"Yes sir, I am. May I ask how you know about that?"

"I don't think it's a *secret*. I was speaking to the reverend just lately and he mentioned your name, in passing."

"Are you a friend of the family?"

"Double anchors!" cried the caller. Once more the gamblers hollered or cursed and the entire room with its whirling smoke, brays of laughter, and shouts for liquid courage made Matthew feel he was on the pitching deck of a rudderless ship. He had noted that the prostitute's left hand was crawling down toward Kippering's crotch.

In the tumult of noise before Kippering's response to John's question, Matthew had the chance to sum up what he knew about the two attorneys. Joplin Pollard—boyish and clean-shaven, his reddish-blond hair close-cropped and his brown eyes large and sparkling with good humor—was in his early thirties and had come to the colony in 1698 to join the older and established lawyer Charles Land. Hardly a year later Land had inherited a large sum of money from a family estate in England and returned to the home country with his wife to become, as Matthew understood from Magistrate Powers, a rich art patron and dabbler in politics.

Thus Pollard—a "green gent," Powers had called him—had been forced to sink or swim in his own firm, and had hired Bryan Fitzgerald from a Boston partnership soon afterward. He was obviously doing well enough now, though, as attested by his taste in his fine light-gray linen suit, his ruffled royal-blue cravat and expensive black boots polished to a gloss.

Completing the trio of blazing youth was Kippering, who'd come from England two years ago with an excellent reputation as a business lawyer but who had, as the magistrate had heard from Pollard, dallied with one banker's wife too many and paid for his sins by expulsion from the gentlemen's club. It was assumed he was doing penance in the colony until he might attempt a comeback in the grander arena, but at the ripe age of twenty-eight Kippering—lean and wolfishly handsome, two days past a shave, a comma of thick black hair fallen over his forehead and his eyes so icy blue the expression from them was nearly fearsome—was obviously not ready for the embrace of a leather armchair when there were painted dollies prancing about and the wine flowed smooth and dark from tavern casks. Neither was he in a hurry to join the best-dressed list, for his plain black suit, simple white shirt, and scuffed black shoes had seen better years.

Kippering caught the young woman's hand before it reached his jewels and firmly but gently confined it with his own. "I've given advice to the reverend. *Not* anything concerning his daughter. But he felt compelled for whatever reason to inform me of the impending situation."

"You mean our marriage?"

Kippering shuddered. "Please restrain the profanity."

"This isn't a place the good reverend might approve of for his future son-in-law," said Pollard, as his mouth spread into a sly smile. "Do you think?"

"Probably not," Matthew spoke up, "but the food's good and cheap. I've eaten here many times. Besides, my friend and I are seeking privacy, which I believe can be found in the back room."

"Of course. I would inquire what might be so furtively private between a magistrate's clerk and a reverend's future son-in-law, visiting the back room of a den such as this, but then I'd be overstepping my bounds, wouldn't I?"

"Come off your horse, Joplin!" Kippering scowled. "The young man's not married *yet*! Since he's so determined to go down the road to disaster, he ought to be praised for his courage. Hell, *I* wouldn't have the guts to ask that crow for his daughter's hand. Would you?"

"Sir!" said John, with a heat in his voice that made Matthew think violence might be imminent. "I'd ask you not to refer to Reverend Wade in that disrespectful manner."

"Apologies, no harm meant." Kippering lifted his tankard. "It's the ale talking."

"Yes," said Pollard, "and that loquacious ale is going to get you skewered someday. But listen, Corbett. About Robert Deverick. He was my client, you know."

"Our client," Kippering amended.

"Yes, *our* client. And I might add our *best* client. You saw him stretched out there in the street. Terrible way for a man of his means to go."

"A terrible way for any man to go," Matthew said. He winced as another holler and harumpdedoo from the dice table blasted his eardrums. Across the way, someone was cursing a foul blue streak at one of the card games.

"Any ideas about it?" Pollard asked. "I mean, your being so fresh on the scene, according to Lillehorne. And since you seemed to have such an opinion on the enforcement of law before our dandy new governor."

"No ideas other than the obvious. I would ask if you knew of any enemies Mr. Deverick had." It was a shot in the dark since he doubted Deverick would have greeted an enemy with a hand-shake, but it *was* at least a starting-point.

"We've already covered that one with Lillehorne." Kippering was trying to hold the prostitute back from going through his coat pockets; it was like trying to get a firm grip on a weasel. "Deverick has had his business enemies, yes. In London, though. He's had supply problems from some unreliable merchants whom we've had to threaten with lawsuits, but nothing went beyond the point of sword-rattling. That's all."

"There must be something else."

Pollard said, "You must be wondering then if Dr. Godwin had

enemies, if indeed as I understand it the same maniac murdered both men. But then again, does a maniac need a reason for murder?" He answered his own question: "Absolutely not!"

"I'm wondering," Matthew said, "if the Masker may be not so much a maniac as a clever individual hiding a motive."

"What kind of motive?" Kippering asked, though his attention was divided. Being unsuccessful at looting her companion's pockets, the prostitute now began to kiss and lick his neck.

"I have no idea, but I'd like to know if there is some connection between Dr. Godwin and Mr. Deverick. Do you know of any?"

Another uproar came from the gamblers, some bitter loser slammed a hand down on a card table, a prostitute wearing a high crimson wig and white facepaint slid past Matthew like a jungle cat and pinched his behind on the way, and then Pollard turned back toward the dice game and shouted over the noise of wagering, "Don't roll those 'til I get my bet in! Who's got the throw? Wyndham?"

"I can't think of a connection," said Kippering, who had his hands full with his squirmy minx. "They weren't doctor and patient, if that's what you're assuming. Neither was Dr. Godwin a client of ours."

Matthew shrugged. "I didn't think it would be that simple, anyway. We'd best go. Good evening to you."

"Evening to you both," he managed to respond. "And good luck with . . . whatever your business might be." Then he got a lockhold on the girl and also turned to rejoin the hubbub.

The room at the back of the Thorn Bush was at the end of a short corridor where a sign was posted on the wall reading *No Gambling, No Women Allowed.* It was the tavern's stab at a "dining-room" for gentlemen where business might be discussed in relative quiet. True, the noise from the gamblers still carried in, but it was at least tolerable. The room was dimly lit by a few lanterns. Three other men sat together at one of the six tables, which were set far apart for the sake of privacy. The trio were all puffing long clay churchwarden pipes and were wreathed with smoke, their conversations serious and muted; none of them even glanced up as the new arrivals entered. Matthew and John Five sat at a table on the opposite side of the room, furthermost from the door.

Before they got completely settled, the barmaid came in with their glasses of port and left again. Matthew spent a moment rubbing what looked like a dried clump of food off the rim of his glass. He hoped it wasn't the beef brains.

John Five took a long drink of his wine and then said, "I couldn't figure who else to go to, Matthew. When Constance told me, I said she shouldn't be worryin'. I said things would work themselves out, but . . . I don't know, Matthew. It's not gettin' any better."

"You ought to start at the beginning," Matthew advised.

"She says it started back about a month ago. Late May, early June. Her father always liked to walk, around sundown. Said it helped him breathe. She never took a mind to it. But all of a sudden he was goin' out later and later. Now it's after ten o'clock most nights. And then when he gets back, he's . . ." John hesitated, obviously uncomfortable with this direction.

"Go on," Matthew urged. "He is what?"

"Different," John said. He swirled the port around in his glass and drank again. "Constance said he was . . . is . . . dark-spirited when he comes back. Does that make any sense to you?"

"Does she mean he's angry? Melancholy?"

"That, I guess. If it means sad. Or just . . . I don't know . . . like he didn't *want* to go where he went, but that he *had* to. Listen, Matthew." John looked across the table at his friend, the expression in his eyes at once steadfastly serious and almost pleading. "None of this can get out. I know many around here think William Wade's a stiff-backed Bible-thumper, but he's never been anythin' but kind to *me*. Constance loves him dearly, and accordin' to her there could be no better father. And he's a smart man, too. Not just about religious things, either. He goes fishin' every chance he gets, did you know that?"

"I didn't."

"Yep. Got his own favorite spot up at the end of Wind Mill

Lane. I've gone with him, of a Saturday mornin'. He can talk about anythin' you please. He can read the weather, and he's raised a garden back behind their house that would knock Granny Coquer flat down."

"Really?" That was impressive, since at eighty-three years Granny Coquer—who had been all of fifteen when she arrived in Dutch New Amsterdam—was growing tomatoes, corn, beans, and melons that brought a mob to her stall at the farmers' market.

"What I'm sayin' is, Reverend Wade is not one of those wild men who pass through town from time to time, yellin' 'fear God' at the top of their lungs and robbin' every Peter, Paul, and Mary they can get their touch on. Do you know the type I mean?"

Matthew nodded. He very well knew that type, by the name of Exodus Jerusalem.

"William Wade is a decent man," John said. "If he's in some kind of trouble, it's not of his own makin'."

"Trouble?" Matthew frowned. "Why do you put it that way?"

"Somethin's chewin' him up," came the grim response. "Constance says he can hardly sleep at night anymore. She says she hears him get up from his bed and walk in his room. Just pacin' the boards, back and forth. *Wait* . . . here's your food."

The barmaid had entered again, carrying a tray on which sat a brown bowl. She put it down in front of Matthew, gave him a wooden fork and spoon, and said, "Coin or credit?"

"On my bill, Rose," John Five said, and she shrugged as if such things mattered not a whit and exited the room, leaving Matthew with the distinct impression that this Thorn Bush's Rose was indeed a prickly specimen.

In the bowl was a muddy-looking stew that contained elements impossible to identify. Matthew stirred the stuff around with his spoon but was unable to determine if it was mutton pie, beef brains, boiled potatoes, turnips, some combination of everything, or a cook's surprise. He was hungry enough to try it, though, and found with a small sip that whatever it was it was smoky and peppery and really very good. So score minus for presentation, but double plus for taste. He started in on it with relish, indicating by a nod for John to continue.

"Pacin' his room, as I said," John went on. "One night Constance thought she heard him cry out in a bad dream. Then another night . . . she just plain heard him give a sob that near broke her heart."

"I assume she's asked him what the trouble might be?"

"She's not exactly used that word, but she *has* asked. The one time he'd talk about it at all, he said everythin' was goin' to be fine, soon enough."

" 'Soon enough'? That was his statement?"

John nodded. "Accordin' to Constance, I mean. She told me he sat her down, took both her hands, looked her in the eyes, and said he knew he'd been actin' peculiar, but she wasn't to worry. He said it was his problem, and he had to solve it his own way. He asked her to trust him."

Matthew took a drink of his port. "But obviously she feels this 'problem' hasn't gotten any better? That he's still worried to the point of distraction?"

"And he's still goin' out late at night, too. Take what happened on Tuesday night."

Matthew stopped eating. "Deverick's murder?"

"No, not that. On Tuesday night, near eleven o'clock, there came a knock at the reverend's door. He told Constance to stay in her room, and he went to see who was callin' at such an hour. She heard him talkin' to somebody, then he got his street clothes on and told her not to worry but that he had to go out. And she said his eyes were scared, Matthew. She said it was a terrible thing, to see such fear on her father's face." John drank down the rest of his port and looked as if he wished he had another full glass. "When he left the house . . . Constance went to a window and looked out, east along Maiden Lane. She saw the reverend walkin' with someone else carryin' a lantern. A man, she thought. It was a man's voice she'd heard at the door. An old man, she thought it might be. But up ahead, waitin' with a lamp at the corner of Maiden Lane and Smith Street, was a woman."

"A woman," Matthew repeated. "She was sure of that?"

"She could see the woman's gown and bonnet, but she couldn't make out the face."

"Hm," Matthew said, for it was all he could think to say. He was putting together in his mind what might have happened that night. Reverend Wade and his daughter lived in a small house on Maiden Lane between Nassau and Smith streets. Artemis Vanderbrocken had knocked on the door to summon the reverend, who'd hurriedly dressed and left the house. Wade had been walking south on Smith Street in the company of Vanderbrocken and the unknown woman when behind them came the shout from Phillip Covey. Or perhaps not *behind* them, but nearly *beside* them. Perhaps they were just passing when Covey began his cry of alarm, and that was why they'd been so quick on the spot.

Interesting, Matthew thought. What had happened to the woman?

"After Reverend Wade had gone," John continued, "it wasn't long before Constance heard commotion goin' on and a bell ringin'. That was at the murder scene, I suppose. She was afraid to go out. She got on her knees and prayed that her father was all right, but she couldn't get back to sleep. He came home maybe an hour or so later and went straight to his room."

"Did she ask where he'd been?"

"No. She wants him to tell her in his own time, and she *does* trust him, Matthew."

"I see. So Constance has no idea you're meeting with me?"

"No idea," John said.

"May I ask then, why are you here with me? Isn't this a betrayal of her trust for her father?"

John didn't answer. He cast his eyes down. "I love Constance, Matthew. With all my heart. I don't want her to be hurt. I don't want her to know the bad things of life. The ugly things. If I can shield her from those things—or delay her from bein' hurt, even by her own father—I'm goin' to do my best. If he's mixed up in somethin' he shouldn't be, I want to know first before Constance does. So maybe I can soften it for her. And maybe . . . I can help

Reverend Wade get free of whatever it is, if I only can find out." He nodded, his eyes still lowered and dark in their sockets. "If that's betrayin' a trust, to save a girl's heart from bein' broke and her soul from bein' scarred . . . I'll do it gladly, many times over."

Matthew now had the full picture. "You don't wish to follow Reverend Wade yourself, in case you might be seen, so you want *me* to follow him."

"I do." John looked up, hopefully. "I can pay a little money, if that would suit you."

Matthew finished his wine but did not respond. He was thinking that if he did follow the reverend he might well discover where he and Vanderbrocken were going and why they'd lied about heading toward different destinations the night of Deverick's murder.

"What say?" John prodded.

Matthew cleared his throat. "Do you know if the reverend went out last night?"

"Constance said he stayed home. That's the thing, see. He's not stayed home these last three weeks two nights in a row. Even when it's rained, he's gone out. That's why she thinks he'll be goin' out tonight, most likely between nine-thirty and ten."

"But she can't be positive of the night, or of the time?"

"No, I guess not."

Matthew didn't have to consider very long before he said, "All right. I'll try for tonight, between nine-thirty and ten. If I have to, I'll wait until ten-thirty, but after that I'm going home." He knew he'd stay until eleven or so, but he didn't wish to sound too eager.

"Thank you, Matthew. God bless you for helping with this thing. Do you want some money?"

"No. I'll do it to show I don't hold a grudge." And also, Matthew thought, to clear up his own questions about Wade and Vanderbrocken. But the woman was a new piece to the puzzle. First of all, who was she? Secondly, why had she waited at the corner of Maiden Lane and Smith Street instead of approaching the house with Dr. Vanderbrocken?

The barmaid returned with more wine, but Matthew had

what he needed and was ready to go. On the way to the front where John would sign his bill of credit they went again through the gambling room, which with the passage of half-an-hour had become even more smoke-filled, crowded, and boisterous. The prostitutes in gaudy gowns and dyed wigs, their faces all but obscured by white powder, red rouge, and dark eyeshadow, roamed amid the tables seeking stacks of coins, the men who owned them being only obstacles to a purpose. Matthew didn't see Pollard or Kippering in the room any longer, but they might have been there and just moved to a different table.

Matthew and John Five were about halfway through the room when their progress was impeded by two heavily made-up dollies who seemed to appear through the smoke alongside the dice table intent on physical ambush. One was an elder the size of Hiram Stokely and the other was a thin wraith who might have been thirteen years old. Their grins, showing black and crooked teeth, were frightening to behold. John Five held off the big-bellied one with a forearm. When the child reached for Matthew he sidestepped, got around two men who were standing in the way, and then he took a blow to the stomach when he saw Eben Ausley sitting at a card table to his left, within dice-throwing distance.

Ausley sat in the company of three other men, but Matthew didn't recognize any of them as the stomperboys who'd gotten the better of him on Monday night. The gamblers were focused on the play as cards were being dealt. Matthew noted that Ausley's pile of silver was the smallest of the lot, and sweat sparkled on the man's jowls and forehead. His white wig was crooked.

As Matthew watched, more transfixed by the enemy's presence rather than interested in the game, he saw the gamblers throw down their coins and cards, there was a great hurrah from one of the men, and Ausley scowled as if a snake had crawled out of the ale tankard on his right. Ausley blew out a big breath that might have been disgust or despair, reached for his omnipresent black notebook with its gold-ornamented cover, opened it, and began to scribble there with his string-wrapped pencil. Marking his losses, Matthew thought. May they ever increase.

Suddenly, like a feral beast sensing it was being observed, Ausley looked up from his notebook directly into Matthew's eyes. They stared at each other through the shifting smoke while at other tables cards were played and dice tossed, winners shouted and losers cursed, prostitutes whispered and even a brown dog scurried around trying to steal a scrap.

Then, just as abruptly, Ausley dismissed him, finished his note-writing, closed the book with a little *slap*, and pounded the table with his hammy fist for the next round to be dealt.

Matthew also turned away. He got out to the front room, where John Five had just signed his credit for the tavern-keeper.

"I thought I'd lost you in that crowd," John said. "Are you all right?"

"I am," Matthew answered, "but I could use some fresh air." He walked onto the Broad Way, his mind now turning from Eben Ausley to the task he needed to perform tonight, and John Five joined him, oblivious to the small and silent scene that had just played out.

fifteen

NEAR TEN O'CLOCK, Dippen Nack stopped at the well in the middle of Maiden Lane. He put aside his lantern and short-handled pitchfork, lowered the well's bucket, and took a drink of water, which he then followed with a tremendous gulp from a leather flask produced from under his coat. Then he retrieved his items and circled the well, swinging his lamplight back and forth over the house and storefronts with his pitchfork at the ready and calling that a decent inspection. He walked off along Maiden Lane to the west, heading in the direction of the Broad Way.

Matthew edged around the corner of Jacob Wingate's wig shop, where he'd been hiding, to watch the insufferable little man strut away like a bantam cock. Nack was one of the constables Matthew felt gave the position a bad name. Quick to accuse an innocent citizen and quick to flee from any perceived danger, Nack also had a mean disposition. He'd been warned by several of the magistrates—among them Magistrate Powers—to refrain from filching the gaol-keeper's keys and going into the gaol late at night to piss on the prisoners as they slept.

Keeping watch on Reverend Wade's house was more difficult than Matthew had expected, for Nack was the second constable he'd recognized on Maiden Lane within an hour. The other one, Sylvester Coppins, had been armed with an axe. It wouldn't do to allow himself to be seen skulking around, but fortunately there was a three-foot-wide space between Wingate's shop and the next structure, a house, which was sufficient to hide him within its depth. Very few structures fit up exactly alongside one another on these streets, and Matthew wondered if the Masker hid from public view just in the same way, moving from concealment to concealment as he fled the murder scenes. It seemed to Matthew, though, that perhaps the constables had been instructed to walk more quickly on their rounds than usual, which meant either that Lillehorne wanted more of a display of protection for the citizens or that the constables themselves were in a hurry to keep moving. Nack's drink of water before he downed his jolt told Matthew the man wished to stay more alert than was normal for a cowardly drunkard, even one armed with a pitchfork.

Matthew wished he at least had a lamp, but on this night he courted the dark. He might have done with a rapier or pistol, as well. Even a slingshot, for that matter. He was very aware of his lack of defenses, thus he took care to watch his back lest anything swoop on him out of the same space that gave shelter.

It was really madness to be out here, he'd thought more than once. A few citizens had gone past, several of them stumbling drunk, others striding with quick purpose to get indoors. He doubted that the bravery of the constables would last much after eleven, as the lantern candles melted down. It might be also that Reverend Wade didn't come out tonight, for though he was a man of God he was fully cognizant of what the Devil could do.

Perhaps it *was* best to go home at ten-thirty, Matthew decided as his watch ticked in his pocket. Then a movement from the right caught his attention, his heart jumped, and he swiftly retreated to his hiding-place. Two gentlemen carrying lanterns and walking-sticks crossed his field of vision and continued at a brisk pace until they were beyond sight. New York was a nervous town, and Grigsby's *Earwig* wasn't even out yet. Matthew had spent some time at the Gallop after leaving John Five and had learned from the usuals there that Effrem Owles was indeed helping Grigsby with the printing tonight, a task that would likely continue into the early hours.

Time passed. Matthew thought it must nearly be ten-thirty. There'd been no movement on Maiden Lane since the two men had walked by. He crouched down to rest his legs and then stood up again a while later when his knees began to protest. By habit he looked left and right, then over his shoulder, but he kept his attention fixed on the door of the Wade house across the street and up two houses.

Eleven o'clock, he decided it must be. There wasn't enough light here to see his watch. Just a little longer and he would call it quits.

Perhaps three minutes after he'd made that decision, he saw a candle pass by one of Reverend Wade's front windows. He waited, now hoping that either the minister or his daughter was just moving around in the house and there would be no nocturnal journey.

But suddenly the door opened and the stiff-backed and somber figure in a black suit and black tricorn emerged from the house in the yellow circle of the punched-tin lantern he was carrying. William Wade closed the door behind him, came down the four front steps to the street, and walked past Matthew, heading east at a pace neither rapid nor what might be called languid, as Matthew pressed himself against the wig shop's wall. Wade turned right onto Smith Street, and the pursuit had begun.

Matthew followed but gave the reverend plenty of room to get well ahead. They were alone on Smith Street as they passed, one before the other, the place where Deverick had been murdered. Matthew felt his spine crawl and imagined himself to be watched just as he watched Reverend Wade. He'd thought of taking a lantern from one of the cornerposts, but to remove town property was a crime that could result in the branding of the T on the right hand. Also he didn't wish to show a light to his quarry. Night had never before seemed so dark, but for better or worse he was at its mercy.

He soon discovered that, murderous Masker or not, some of the town's citizens refused to go home. Lively fiddle music came from the Cat's Paw, just along Wall Street to the left. Across Wall Street and down near the wharfside slave market, a group of men stood outside the Cock'a'Tail, their voices rising, tangling in argument or spirited discussion, and then fading away again. The place drew both rowdies and high-pockets, and more than one man had been killed down there in those spirited discussions over such mundanes as speculation on the prices of corn meal and whale oil.

Still Reverend Wade walked south along Smith Street and Matthew followed at a respectful distance. Several other men in groups of twos and threes passed, going in the opposite direction, but Wade kept his head lowered and his stride purposeful. Matthew as well looked into no one's face, for anyway just about everyone he passed seemed if not drunk then at least tipsy. But no one looked into his face, either, and Matthew considered that though these nighttime ramblers played a fine game they were—as was he—gripped by fear of the unknown.

They passed the flickering lantern on the cornerpost of Sloat Lane, where Matthew had trailed Ausley to that nasty encounter on Monday night. It came to him that he was likely following the "mystery man" in black clothes and tricorn who'd paused to watch him on that occasion. Matthew wondered if the reverend had recognized him or had simply recognized some kind of danger brewing in that dark and burnt passageway. In any event, Wade's destination that night had probably caused him to hold his tongue.

Reverend Wade turned right onto Princes Street, just past the gunsmith's shop, and Matthew took the turn as well but at a cautious pace. They were walking west toward Broad Street and passed the Blind Eye, another infamous den of gambling that Matthew understood was one of Gardner Lillehorne's favorite haunts. The place was still doing business, as muffled shouts from the patrons could be heard through the door above which hung a sign with a painted white-pupilled eye. As was said, whatever happened at the Blind Eye, no one saw it.

On crossing Broad Street, the reverend angled his course slightly to the south and entered narrow Petticoat Lane.

Matthew followed, noting that Wade's pace had slowed. They went past the shuttered shops and silent houses, yet on the night air came a woman's laughter like the sound of silver coins falling upon the cobblestones.

Standing at about the middle of Petticoat Lane, on the right-hand side of the street and separated from the surrounding structures by shoulder-high hedges, was a two-story brick house painted rose pink. It was a handsome place, originally built by a Dutch fur exporter, with tall windows under a gabled roof and two chimneys, one on each end of the house. As Matthew watched, the reverend stopped in the street directly in front of the house and stared up at it, his lantern down by his side. The wash of candles shone through the gauzy curtains that hung at the windows, and Matthew could see the movement of shadows within.

Reverend Wade remained where he was. Matthew realized the man had reached his destination, and was simply staring at the house with an expression that was impossible to read.

It was the house of Polly Blossom. Beyond those walls lived, as Matthew understood, anywhere from four to eight doxies, depending on who told the story. Madam Blossom was a hard taskmaster who groomed her ladies for their role, demanding a certain amount of work from them and a certain amount of income in return for their lodging. She herself was not above the labor in the case of special customers. Matthew knew nothing of her history, other than that she'd come from London to set up shop in 1694. Many young doves of unfortunate circumstance had lodged there, and of course a multitude of men had passed through. It was a fact of life, and hardly anyone in New York cast a bitter eye or word toward the house since Madam Blossom made a point of donating so much money to public works, such as upkeep of the wells.

But that was that and this was this: what was Reverend Wade doing *here*, of all places?

Matthew had the sudden horror that the reverend was going to go through the pink-painted iron gate between the hedges, climb the steps to the front door, and knock to make his entry; then Matthew would hold knowledge that would damn the man in this town. Enlightened as New York might be, it would not breach a man of God dallying with prostitutes. But abruptly the door opened, a man came out to the stoop and turned to speak to a woman behind him, and just that quickly Reverend Wade had vanished off the street. Matthew as well pressed against the doorway of the house at his back. In a moment footsteps approached, the recent customer of the Blossom enterprise walked past trailing smoke from his pipe, and Matthew thought this is where the Masker ought to stand if he wished to kill men who were half-dazed and the other half addled.

Slowly and carefully, Matthew looked out again along Petticoat Lane. The reverend was nowhere in sight. *Gone*, Matthew thought. *But no, no . . . he couldn't have just disappeared like that.* Matthew waited, as about fifteen seconds passed.

Then there came a little blush of lamplight and Wade emerged from between two houses like a snail from its shell. In fact, he only showed his head and shoulders. Again, he kept the lantern well down so as to spread the light across the cobbles. He just seemed to be staring at the Blossom house as if transfixed.

Now what was the matter here? Matthew wondered. He was still terrified that he was about to witness a minister's fall, yet if Wade was enthralled by one or more of the ladies here and he made these regular journeys then why did he not just go in?

Because there was something more than just the walk and the house, Matthew decided. There was Dr. Vanderbrocken and the woman who'd been waiting at the corner. There was urgency, and secrecy, and . . .

And there was the fact that Matthew saw Reverend Wade lean his head against the stones of the house beside him, saw the man cover his eyes, and heard him give a quiet yet soul-broken sob.

Matthew felt shame at witnessing this scene. He stared down at the sidewalk bricks. This whole thing had taken a bent that made him wish he'd never agreed to it. Now he was part of the secret too, and because he knew his own nature of counting the angels on the heads of pins he knew he would have to find out why Wade sobbed before a house where tears were never shed.

In another moment he heard the sound of footsteps, coming

closer. The reverend was on the move again. Matthew looked up and saw Wade following his light on the other side of the street, retracing his path back the way he'd come. Matthew realized he was in danger of being revealed by the wash of light if Wade happened to lift the lantern in his direction; he flattened himself against the doorway and held his breath.

The reverend continued on, his face downcast. Whatever worry—or trouble, as John Five had expressed it—was such a burden on the man that he looked neither right nor left but passed by Matthew, who had taken the attitude of a statue. He crossed Broad Street, and only then did Matthew dare to move. From the corner Matthew watched him enter Princes Street, probably retracing his path back home.

Matthew had no more heart for following anyone this night. He wished only to go home, perhaps read something that would set him to slumber, and wake up with the sunlight. He started north on Broad Street, which was deserted except for a moving lantern a few blocks up at Wall Street. That, too, disappeared in a westerly direction.

What to do about this information weighed heavily on Matthew's mind. When John Five wished to know where the reverend had been, what was he to say? He had no certainty that Wade went and stood before Polly Blossom's house *every* night. But in this case, once was enough. What possible motive could there be for a man of God to—

A walking-stick covered with black knobs suitable to knock someone's brains out was thrust at Matthew, who was struck hard on the left collarbone and sent reeling.

"I *knew* it was you! You little bastard! I *knew* it!"

The stick had come from the left, around the corner of Silas Jansen's credit-and-loans office at the meeting of Broad and Barrack streets. Now behind it and into the weak light of the fading cornerpost lamp staggered Eben Ausley, who had somewhere tonight lost his wig. His face was puffed and florid. Sweat gleamed on his forehead and wet the strands of gray hair stuck to his scalp. At his side he held a lantern, the candle of which was barely a flick-

ering nub behind the glass. His mouth twisted and he held the
stick up for a more brutal blow. "I *told* you not to follow me, didn't
I? Damn your soul, I'll teach you a lesson!"

Matthew easily sidestepped the strike. "Stop it," he said.

"You don't *command* me! How *dare* you!" Again the stick was
lifted and swung, but this time Ausley lost his balance and fell
back against Jansen's wall. Ausley stood there enraged, his chest
heaving, but his liquid amusements had put lead in his legs. "I'll
kill you," he managed to croak. "See you dead and buried before
I'm done!"

"I don't think so," Matthew answered. He thought that if he
liked he could wrest that stick away from Ausley and give him
some bruises to count tomorrow. He could beat the man over the
head so hard people would think his new wig was purple and
lumpy. He could knock Ausley's legs out from under him and
smash that ugly face with a good, soul-satisfying kick.

But the problem was, his soul didn't need that kind of satisfaction.

There were no stomperboys around. No constables either.
This was Matthew's chance to take revenge on behalf of all those
who'd suffered at the orphanage. Revenge for himself, too, for
being too weak to do anything when he'd walked out of the
Sainted John Home for Boys in the employ of Magistrate Woodward. Now he could have what he'd thought about and planned
for so long; he could take a pound of flesh for all of them, including Nathan Spencer.

"I saw you following me!" Ausley seethed, unsteady on his feet
and in his senses. "Back there when I left the Admiral! Well here I
am, then! What the hell do you *want*?"

It was a good question, but Matthew felt the need to address
the accusation first. "I haven't been following you. And I haven't
even been *near* the Old Admiral tonight."

"You dirty *liar*! I saw you step back around the corner!"

"I doubt you can see straight, but it wasn't me. In fact," said
Matthew, "I don't really care to waste any more time on you." He
realized it was true even as he spoke it; he had a direction now, and

a purpose with the Herrald Agency. Why should he spend a moment longer even speaking to this vile animal?

But Ausley pulled himself up to his full height, be that still considerably shorter than Matthew, and he attempted some dignity. He thrust his collection of chins out and forced his thin mouth into a replica of a smile. "Just so you know," he said, "and bear well the fact, that I have beaten you, boy. No one will witness against me. Not yesterday, not today, nor tomorrow. And why might that be? Possibly because they all know—all of them, they all do—that they *deserved* what they got? That they took themselves to be more mighty than they were, and I brought them back down to size. Well, someone had to do it! Had to teach those boys a lesson, and one they won't ever forget! That's what my job is, that's my profession!"

Matthew couldn't even begin to respond to this tipsy tirade, so he remained silent. The old anger of even two days before had faded, though. He had begun to realize that his life was ahead of him, with all its opportunities and adventures, and Eben Ausley was part of his past. Maybe the man had escaped proper justice and maybe that was neither fair nor right, but Matthew had done all he could. He was ready now, after all this time, to let it go.

"Beaten you," Ausley repeated, his mouth wet with saliva. "Beaten you." He nodded, his eyes glazed and heavy-lidded, and then he lurched away from Matthew and staggered west along Barrack Street, steering himself with his walking-stick and his lantern flickering at his side. For a moment Matthew thought he was truly a pathetic spectacle. And then he came to his senses, spat on the ground to clear the bad taste out of his mouth, and continued on his northward trek.

He was shaking a little from the encounter. A solid blow from that stick would've crowned him good and proper. He pulled his mind away from Ausley and looked ahead, thinking about what he was going to say to John Five. Maybe he should refuse to make a comment on the man's destination until he followed Reverend Wade a second night. He wondered what Mrs. Herrald would suggest. After all, she was the expert in such—

He took one more pace and stopped.

He listened carefully to the night, his head cocked. Was it his imagination, or had he just heard glass break?

Behind him a distance. He looked back.

The street was deserted.

If he'd indeed heard glass break, the sound had come from Barrack Street.

Ausley's lantern, Matthew thought. The drunken fool had dropped his lantern.

I saw you following me, he'd said.

I saw you step back around the corner.

A dog was barking a few streets over. From somewhere else, a man was singing in a ragged and incomprehensible voice, the noise fading in and out as if carried by the whims of the night breeze.

Matthew stared back toward the corner of Barrack Street.

I saw you following me.

"Ausley?" he called, but there was no reply. He walked to the corner and looked up the dark length of Barrack. And louder: "Ausley!"

Leave the bastard, Matthew thought. Lying drunk up there, that's all. Just leave him and go home.

It was amazing how alone one could feel in a town of five-thousand souls.

Matthew's throat clenched. He thought he saw something moving in there. A darkness against the darkness, hard at work.

He put his hand on the dirty lantern that hung from the cornerpost and lifted the lamp off its nail. He had an instant of thinking that he ought to be right now shouting for a constable but he wasn't sure what he was seeing. His heart slamming, he began walking cautiously along Barrack Street.

There the dim light found Eben Ausley lying on the sidewalk on his back, the broken lantern nearby. A little red flame still burned in a puddle of wax. Next to Ausley's right hand was the walking-stick, as if it had slipped from a nerveless grasp.

Matthew tried to say *Get up* but at first he couldn't speak. He tried again and still only managed a hoarse whisper.

The man did not move, and as Matthew stood over him and shone the blue eye of light down upon the body it was clear—terribly, bloodily, throat-cuttingly clear—that Eben Ausley had seen his final turn of cards.

As repulsed as Matthew was, as much as panic wanted to shoot along his nerves and send him running, the cool analytical center of himself took control. It sharpened his senses and steeled his will, and so he stood looking down at the body and taking impressions with the same clinical and almost distant judgment as did him well at his games of chess.

Ausley's throat had been brutally slashed, that much was perfectly clear. The blood was still jumping. So too were Ausley's hands, which involuntarily shivered as if finding that the bannisters on the stairs leading down to Hell were icy. His mouth was open in shock, as were his eyes, which had become bloodshot and gleamed like sea-damp oysters. A knife had been at work on Ausley's face as well as throat, for Matthew saw the glistening red shapes around his eyes as the blood oozed down. If not fully expired the man had only seconds to live, as his flesh was taking on that chalk-colored waxy look so popular among corpses. There was nothing to be done for him short of sewing his head back on his shoulders, and Matthew doubted even Benjamin Owles could save this suit.

As Matthew stared down at the dying man, himself in a kind of trancelike state, he was aware of a slow, almost liquid movement in the dark beyond.

Matthew saw it then: a shape, all black and black within black, sliding out of a doorway twenty feet up Barrack Street. Matthew lifted his lantern, caught the white blur of a face, and saw that the man—or was it a man?—wore a midnight-hued cloak with a high collar and a black stocking-cap covering the head. In that instant of realizing he was looking at the Masker, he saw the object of his attention begin running with a burst of speed toward the Broad Way, and it was only then that Matthew got his throat working and the cry came up into the night: *"Help! Help! Constable!"*

The Masker not only killed quickly, but he was quick on the run. By the time a constable got here, the Masker would be in Philadelphia. *"Help! Somebody!"* Matthew shouted, but he was already reaching down for Ausley's walking-stick. He let out one more *"Constable!"* so Dippen Nack might hear it in his bedchamber, and then he had to save his breath because he shot forward in pursuit.

sixteen

A T A FULL RUN the Masker wheeled to the left at the corner onto New Street and Matthew followed, narrowly missing banging his knee against a watering-trough.

It was true that Matthew was neither a sportsman nor a swordsman, but it was equally true that he could run. This skill had probably been refined during his days as a waterfront urchin before he was forcibly taken to the orphanage, as it took the fleet of foot to steal food and dodge billyclubs. Now it served him well, as he was catching up to his quarry; also paramount in his mind was the fact that it was safer to keep the Masker in front of him, yet he was ready at any second for the man to whirl around with an outstretched blade. Ausley didn't need the walking-stick any longer, but Matthew clung to it like life.

"Constable!" Matthew shouted again, and now the Masker took a severe turn to the left and, cloak flying, disappeared into the space between the silversmith's and the house next door. Matthew lifted the lantern with its paltry light; his pace faltered and he had only seconds to decide whether to go in or not before the Masker would be lost.

He held up the stick to ward off an attack, took a breath, and darted to the chase. The little passageway was so narrow it nearly scraped his shoulders. He came to another opening and found himself in someone's garden. A brick pathway led off to the right, with a white wall and a gate on the left. A dog began barking furiously to the right and in that direction the voice of some frightened citizen shouted, "Who's there? Who's there?"

Matthew could hear shouts also from over on Barrack Street. Ausley's body had been discovered. In for a penny, in for a pound, he thought. He began running again along the pathway and in a moment passed under a rose arbor. Then there was another wall ahead of him with the wooden gate open, and when Matthew went through this there was a holler, "I see you, damn you!" from the house on his right. With a flash and a bang a pistol discharged from an upper window and a lead ball shrieked past Matthew's ear. He didn't wait for further introductions; he took to his heels, went over a waist-high picket fence, and then the dog that had been barking lunged at him with snapping teeth and wild eyes but its night-chain yanked it back before flesh could be served.

Now Matthew didn't fear the Masker so much as whatever else lay in wait, but going through another gate he came around a privy where the lantern's light picked out a dark shape climbing over a stone wall about eight feet high. The Masker had dragged a barrel over to stand on, and as Matthew shouted again for a constable the dark figure secured the heights, paused to kick over the barrel, and then dropped onto the other side. Matthew heard footsteps running on stones, heading toward the docks.

He righted the barrel, climbed up, and also went over. He landed on the uneven stones of a narrow alley that ran behind the houses and shops of New Street. This was an excellent place to twist an ankle, a fact he could only hope the Masker had already discovered. He continued on along the alleyway but at a walk. His light was almost out, he was breathing hard, and unless the Masker had circled around behind him with intent to claim a second victim this night, the man was gone.

From the sounds of the yelling on Barrack Street, the barking of more dogs, and the calling of neighbors one to another, the entire town was coming awake. If I were the Masker, Matthew thought, I'd call a finish to this night and go to my secure place, wherever that might be. Still, there were many places the Masker could be hidden in ambush as Matthew approached. On the left was a barn. Beside it lay a jumble of debris, old broken buckets, coils of rope, wagon wheels, and the like. On the right was the rear of a store and a root cellar. Matthew tried the root cellar's door but it was bolted from within. He went on, shining his fading lamp to both sides. Most of the houses and shops had root cellars, and here and there were gates that led either into more Dutch gardens or out to the right onto New Street or to the left onto Broad Street.

As Matthew walked on, his lantern uplifted and the walking-stick thrust out like a rapier, he kept watch for any trace of movement beyond the edges of light. From the noise on Barrack Street, the demise of Eben Ausley had caused either a riot or a party.

The end of the alleyway, which was about as wide as a horse-cart, was not far distant. It opened onto Beaver Street, where Matthew could see the shine of a cornerpost lamp on a glass window. He kept moving his lantern from side to side, looking at the stones for anything the Masker might have dropped in his haste to escape. It would be a good idea, he decided, to retrace the path he'd come. But then again, that was best left to daylight for he was not about to be shot at twice in one night.

And then, quite suddenly, the light showed him something that stopped him in his tracks.

On the handle to a root cellar door on his left was a dark red smear.

He bent over it and examined it more carefully. His heart, which had not had an easy time of it during the last few minutes, began to pound anew. It was a small smear, yes. But it was wet and fresh, and it might have come from a bloody glove.

He hooked a finger under the door's handle and tried to lift it, but it was locked. He stepped back and looked at the structure. A two-story brick house or a shop of some kind? It was hard to tell from here. No lights shone in any of the windows. He found a pathway to the front and a wrought-iron gate that opened onto Broad Street. Just as he was about to go through, two men with lanterns came running past on their way to, presumably, the mur-

202 • Robert McCammon

der scene. He decided to give them time to make some distance, as he didn't wish to be either interrupted or assaulted by some terrified constable. When the men were gone, Matthew emerged through the gate onto Broad Street and looked up at the building before him.

Now he could see illumination, two or three candles' worth it appeared, up in a room on the second floor. He could also make out the sign on its hooks above the door.

Pollard, Fitzgerald, and Kippering, Attorneys.

Matthew went up the three front steps and used the brass knocker, which sounded equally as loud as the gunshot.

He waited, looking south along Broad Street in case anyone else came running past. There was no reply from within the lawyers' office, yet upon an appraisal of the upstairs window it did appear that at least one of the candles had moved. Matthew hated to knock again, as the noise sounded as if it could wake the dead, but he was determined to get in.

Perhaps ten seconds passed, with no response. He was about to use his fist when he heard a latch being undone. The door opened, and at that instant the last light of Matthew's lantern fizzled out.

Another candle was thrust almost into his face.

"*You?* What the hell do you want?"

Matthew squinted in the glare of a fresh wick. He knew the voice. "I hate to bother you, sir, but I assume you've heard a little noise just lately?"

"I have," said Kippering. "Fools shouting the town down, and what sounded like a gun going off. What's happened?"

"Haven't you been curious enough to venture out to see?"

"Should I have been?"

"Do you make a habit of answering a question with a question?"

"When the question is from a clerk at my office door near midnight, yes." Kippering lowered the candle, which was set in a pewter holder. Matthew noted that the man was wearing the same rather tatty black suit he'd worn at the Thorn Bush, and now Kippering's appearance matched his clothing. He looked haggard and tired with dark circles under his eyes, his mouth slack and his blue eyes more watery than icy. At that moment three men and a woman were going past on the sidewalk, heading north. Two of the men were armed, one with a musket and the other with an axe. "Here!" Kippering called to them. "What's happened?"

"Another murder," answered one of the men. "The Masker's cut somebody's head off!" They rushed on, almost gleefully.

"A little exaggeration," Matthew said, "but centrally true. The Masker has killed Eben Ausley. He's lying up there on Barrack Street."

"Who?" Kippering blinked heavily. "The Masker or Ausley?"

"Ausley. Are you ill?"

"A matter of conjecture, I'm sure." Kippering ran a hand through his thick and unruly hair, and the black comma fell back onto his forehead. "So Ausley's dead, is he?" He seemed to look at Matthew fully for the first time, and then his gaze found the walking-stick. He took it from Matthew's hand and examined it more closely in the light. "If I'm not mistaken—and I'm not—this belongs to Ausley. He had it at the Thorn Bush. Almost brained Tom Fletcher. May I ask what you're doing in possession of it?"

"You may, but first I have to ask if I might inspect your cellar."

"Inspect my *cellar*? What are you going on about?"

Matthew said, "I was first on the scene when Ausley was killed. I saw the Masker, just as he'd finished his work. I took the stick as a weapon and chased after him. He led me here."

"*Here?*" Kippering scowled. "You're the one who's ill, boy."

"He led me to the alley behind your office. On the door to your root cellar is a blood smear. From a glove, perhaps. I should like to have a look down there." Matthew reached out and grasped the stick. When he tried to pull it away, he met a little resistance; then Kippering released his grip and gave it up. "Will you show me, or shall I go for a constable?"

"The cellar door's bolted from within. It's always bolted."

"That may be so, but someone left blood on the doorhandle. I'd like to take a look."

"What are you saying? That *I'm* the Masker?" Kippering offered up a crooked grin. "Oh, certainly! After the night I've had, I surely gathered up the energy to go out prowling the streets and ended my festivities by murdering *another* of our clients. At this rate we'll be out of business in a week."

"Ausley was your client? I didn't know."

Kippering seemed to be listening to the noise over on Barrack Street. A few more people rushed past the office door. He gave a long, weary sigh. "I suppose I ought to go represent the estate. Keep the fools from trampling him flat." He refocused his gaze on Matthew. "You *saw* the Masker?"

"I did. Not his face, unfortunately."

"There's blood on the cellar door?"

Matthew nodded.

"Come in." Kippering opened the door wider, and Matthew entered. When Kippering started to close the door, Matthew said, "I'd appreciate it if you'd leave that open."

"I can assure you that the only thing I've killed tonight is half a bottle of brandy and a lot of time."

"Please leave the door open," Matthew insisted in a calm voice, and Kippering shrugged.

"This way." Kippering led him past a narrow staircase to another door. He paused to light a second candle in a pewter holder that was sitting atop a stack of books on a table and this he gave to Matthew, who laid aside the dead lantern. "I hope you're not afraid of spiders," he said. He unhooked a latch and opened the door into the cellar's darkness. "Watch your step, these stairs are older than my grandmother."

Before they descended, Matthew requested that Kippering also leave that door open and go down first. "You're *serious*, aren't you?" Kippering asked, but then he took appraisal of Matthew's expression and obeyed. As he followed down the rickety old stairs, Matthew thought that sometimes it did pay to carry a big stick.

The candles seemed to throw more shadows than illumination. It was a large cellar with a dirt floor and brick walls. The old yellowish-white bricks, Matthew noted, that had originally come over as ballast on some of the first Dutch ships. Filling the place almost up to the raftered ceiling were battered wooden shelves full of decaying law books, parcels of papers wrapped in twine, and stacks upon stacks of more yellowed documents. Matthew thought that, though there was a sea dampness to the air, if a fire ever got loose in here it would burn steadily for a month. Discarded buckets, two broken chairs, a desk that looked as if it had been chewed by a beaver, and other odds-and-ends of office decor littered the chamber. Matthew went directly to the cellar door and inspected the bolt.

"Anything there?" Kippering asked.

"No," came the answer. There was no blood on this side of the door. But that didn't stop Matthew from shining his candle around to check the steps and the floor. There were many footprints in the dirt, but why would there not be? He continued searching around boxes of papers. "What *is* all this?" he asked.

"The underbelly of the legal profession." Kippering sat down on a large wooden trunk. "This is where the old deceased records lie in rotting perpetuity. Most of it dates back to before Charles Land took the firm over from Rolf Gorendyke. He left it all here for us to clean up, except Bryan thinks there'll be value to it someday as history and he wants to keep it. If Joplin and I had our way, we'd toss it tomorrow."

"Toss it *where?*"

"Yes, well that's the problem, isn't it? We've thought of burning it, but . . ." He shrugged. "Maybe Bryan's right. Someday someone might give a damn about what went on here."

Matthew was still poking around and finding nothing but a rat's nest, both figuratively and literally. "You say Eben Ausley was your client?" he asked as he explored the room. "You don't seem so concerned that he's lying dead over on the next street."

"I had limited dealings with him. Joplin handled most everything. Records of contributions. Contracts for supplies and labor. Paperwork when the orphans found homes. Things such as that."

"I assume those more current documents are kept in better circumstances?"

"File cabinets upstairs."

Matthew kept looking, but this path was showing no promise. "Aren't you at all curious?" he asked.

"About what?"

"Two things. Who killed Ausley, and what the smear of blood on the door looks like?"

Kippering grunted and smiled thinly. "I *hear*," he said, "that Ausley had lost a lot of money on the tables. He'd borrowed heavily, and lost most of that as well. The man was what you might call a gambling fanatic. In case you don't know, there are individuals in this town who lend money and aren't pleased when it's not promptly repaid. Ausley unfortunately did not have the most charming personality, either. I think it was only a matter of time before someone either beat him to death or cut his throat, so this Masker person may have simply cheated the pawnbroker. As for the blood smear, I've seen them before. Still, I'll take your bait." He stood up with his candle, walked to the door, and threw back the bolt. Then he pushed the door open and stuck his head out to see.

Suddenly Matthew heard a frightened voice call from outside, "Hold there! Hold!"

"I'm just having a look around," Kippering explained to the unseen person.

"Just hold right there, I said! Do you have a weapon?"

"Settle down, Giles. It *is* Giles Wintergarten, isn't it? It's me, Andrew Kippering. Look." Matthew envisioned him holding the light nearer his face.

"Dear God, Mr. Kipperin', you scared the shit into my drawers pokin' your head out like that! Don't you know there's been another murder right up the way? I might have run you through!"

Matthew got the picture. A constable had been in the alley when the cellar door had opened. Carrying a sword, too, by the sound of it.

"The Masker's been at work, yessir!" said Wintergarten. "Cut the life out of Eben Ausley and left him like a bloody bag up there on Barrack! But he got his, too, he did! Ol' Emory Coody shot him good and proper!"

"Emory Coody?" Kippering asked. "The one-eyed weather-spy?"

"That's him! Lives right up the way!"

As the two spoke, Matthew found himself staring at the trunk upon which Kippering had been sitting. He walked to it, saw that there was no lock, and lifted the lid. His light fell upon what was inside, and after the jolt of surprise had subsided he thought, *Now I've found you*.

"Look here, Giles," Kippering was saying. "On the door-handle. Blood. See it?"

"Yessir. Yessir, that does 'pear to be blood, don't it?"

"I think the Masker came along here and left his mark. Possibly he tried to open the door, but it was locked from the inside. You might want to take a careful stroll up and down the alley and check all the other cellar doors, yes?"

"Yessir, that would be the thing to do. I ought to go get some help, though."

"All right, but be careful. Oh, and listen: will you inform High Constable Lillehorne of this, and tell him I'd be happy to help him in any way possible?"

"I will, sir. You ought to get in yourself now, Mr. Kippering. Work such as this ought to be left to the professionals."

"My thoughts exactly. Goodnight, Giles."

" 'Night, sir."

Kippering closed the door, rebolted it, and turned to face Matthew. "As I said, all blood smears look the same." He glanced at the open trunk. "What are you searching for *now*? Costumes for the dance?"

"There are *clothes* in here," Matthew said, his voice tight.

"Yes, there are."

"There are *gloves* in here." Matthew held up a pair. They were black and made of thin cloth.

"Your powers of observation are stunning. You might also observe that those are women's gowns and underclothing." He held up a large hand, took two strides forward, and demonstrated how small the glove was. It looked to fit a child. "Women's gloves.

I think there may be some men's shirts and a coat or two down there at the bottom, but I haven't gone all the way through. You'll note that everything is moldering and musty and is probably over twenty years old."

Matthew was flustered. He was so eager to believe he'd found the Masker's hidden cache of clothes that the first black gown on top had addled his brain. "Well . . . where did all this *come* from?"

"We're not sure, but we think one of Gorendyke's clients used the trunk as payment for legal services. Or it might have come from the estate of someone who died aboard ship on the way over. We're going to throw it out, sooner or later. Are you done?"

Matthew nodded, his brow furrowed.

Kippering closed the lid. "If you didn't hear, I showed Giles Wintergarten the blood smear and I told him to inform Lillehorne. I think the Masker either really did try to get in—though I didn't hear anything as I've been upstairs for at least an hour—or being such a clever murderer as you feel him to be, he deliberately left a mark for your benefit."

"For *my* benefit? Why?"

"Well, he stopped your following him, didn't he?"

"He couldn't have known I would see the mark," Matthew said.

"No, but he might have reasoned the odds were on his side that you would." Kippering gave a smile, which on his usually handsome but now dark-shadowed face seemed a little ghastly. "I think the Masker might also be a gambler. Don't you?"

Matthew cast his eyes down. He didn't know what to think. As he was pondering what to him was an appalling lack of mental acuity, he saw his candlelight gleam on an object that leaned against one of the shelves. It was a strange object to be down here, he thought. A pair of hammered-brass firetongs, yet there was certainly no fireplace in the cellar.

He walked to the firetongs and picked them up. The business end of the tongs had been thinned by some scraping instrument or grinding wheel, it appeared. "What's this for?"

Kippering took the tongs, turned away, and reached up to a

top shelf to grasp a packet of papers, which he brought down trailing dust. He waved the papers in front of Matthew's face before returning them to where they'd been likely situated for years.

Matthew sniffed, holding back a sneeze, and rubbed his nose.

"Want a drink?" Kippering asked. "I've got that half-bottle of brandy left. You can help me celebrate the fact that I only lost five shillings and eight pence at gambling tonight, and that I overpaid by twice for a cheap bottle of wine at Madam Blossom's."

"No," Matthew said, already feeling thoroughly debilitated. "Thank you."

"Then may I give you some free legal advice?" Kippering waited for Matthew to give him his full attention. "I would refrain from mentioning to anyone that you discovered Ausley's body. That is, if you wish to remain free to walk around town."

"Pardon?"

"You were nearly first on the scene with Mr. Deverick, weren't you? And now first to find Ausley? I'd hate to think what Lillehorne might do with that, since he seems to consider you such an outspoken boon to his authority."

"I didn't *murder* anyone. Why should I not tell Lillehorne?"

"Because," Kippering said, "the high constable will find your presence at both murders so interesting that he will wish to know what you were doing out tonight. And even though you and I may believe that Lillehorne is not entirely up to the job, he is relentless when it suits him to be. Thus he will wish to know in exacting detail your progress through this night, and he may well feel you are best questioned behind the security of iron bars. He will ask questions here and there and there and here, and sooner or later he'll find out that you and the future husband of our good reverend's daughter were meeting at a rather dismal little drinking and gambling establishment festooned with whores. For *privacy*, did you say? Do you see my direction?"

Matthew did, but he remained sullenly silent.

"Of course you do," Kippering went on. "Now I don't know what you and Mr. Five were talking about in that back room, but you can be sure Lillehorne will find out."

"That has nothing to do with the Masker. It's private business."

"Yes, you keep using that word, and that will only feed Lillehorne's desire to root out whatever secret you have." He paused to let Matthew feel the sting of that particular fish-hook. "Now in a few minutes I'm going to put on my official lawyer's face, straighten my suit and comb my hair, and walk out to stand alongside Ausley's corpse until the body-cart pulls up. I suggest you go home, go to bed, and in the morning you are as surprised to hear of Eben Ausley's death as anyone in New York. How does that settle with you?"

Matthew thought about it, though there wasn't a lot of thinking to be done. It wouldn't do for questions to be asked about Matthew's jaunts this night, not with Reverend Wade's problem still unknown. He said quietly, "It settles."

"Good. Incidentally, I'm sure Giles will carry that information about the blood smear straight to Lillehorne, in case you're thinking this is an attempt to keep you from telling anyone. I assure you I couldn't care less, just so long as he doesn't come up behind *me* on a dark night." Kippering motioned Matthew toward the stairs.

At the front, Matthew hesitated in the doorway before Kippering could shut him out. He gazed up at the candle-illuminated window. "Tell me, if you will," he said, "why you're at work so late."

Kippering kept the faint smile on his face. "I don't sleep very well. Never have. Goodnight. Oh . . . two last things: I should avoid the crowd up there on Barrack, and I should beware not the Masker but some frightened rabbit with a blunderbuss." So saying, he pushed the door shut and Matthew heard the latch fall.

Matthew looked toward City Hall and saw the wash of candlelight in two of the attic's small square windows. He'd never been up there before, as access to that area was by invitation only; that portion was the office and also the living quarters of Ashton McCaggers, whose abilities as coroner more than made up for his eccentricities. It appeared McCaggers was awake and preparing for another session in the cold room.

Zed would be hauling the body-cart past here soon. It was time to go.

Matthew crossed Broad Street to Princes Street, intending to go back up Smith and then to the Broad Way and home, thus bypassing that noisy rabble gathered around the corpse of Eben Ausley. As he made his way past the late-flickering lamps on their cornerposts, the warm breeze moving about him with its leathery smells of dockside tar and sewer ditch, he knew he would find sleep a troubling companion this night. There would be many echoes in his mind calling for recognition or resolve, and many that might never be resolved. In truth, he felt fortunate to have survived not only a gunshot and dog attack but the Masker himself, who might easily have turned on him and cut him to pieces with a hooked blade.

As for Ausley, he felt . . . nothing.

No anger, no sadness, no loss, no gain, no sense of justice, no exultation at the death of a wicked man.

He felt as if a slate within him upon which he'd marked balances for such a very long time had been wiped clean. Just that.

When he reached the safety of the pottery, he left the walking-stick on the ground alongside the building. He intended to rise with the sun, take the stick out to the East River, and consign it to dark water, where it might vanish in time from sight and memory like its late owner.

Matthew went up to bed, remembering to wash his hands.

seventeen

BECAUSE AT BREAKFAST the Stokelys had not yet heard about the murder of Eben Ausley, Matthew's first real test of monitoring his mouth came when he took his clothes to his laundress, the widow Sherwyn, as was his habit every Friday.

She was a big, robust, white-haired woman who'd outlived two husbands, owned a little stone house and attached laundry shop on Queen Street, and who collected gossips and town-tales as someone else might pin butterflies onto black velvet. Furthermore, she was an excellent laundress and very fair in her prices, so even at this early morning hour she'd already had half-a-dozen customers bringing in not only stained gowns and dirtied shirts but all the news of the night. It was for no little reason that Marmaduke Grigsby brought his clothes here and lingered over apple cider and gingerbread to trade topics, as when he left here he had enough bustarole to fill a month of *Earwig*s though if he printed most of it he'd have been either shot or hanged.

"Baaaaad night," said Widow Sherwyn as Matthew entered the shop with his bundle. It was said with grim foreboding, yet the color in her cheeks was as merry as a three-penny play. "But I suppose you've already heard?"

"Pardon?" was all he could say.

"Another *murder*," she explained. "Happened on Barrack Street, around midnight I hear. And guess who's the dead gent?"

"Um . . . I'm not good at guessing, madam. You'll have to tell me."

She waved a hand at him to say he was no fun. "Eben Ausley. The headmaster at the orphanage. Well, you ought to look more shocked than *that*! Didn't you say you grew up in that wretched place?"

"It wasn't so wretched . . ." He almost said *before Ausley got there*. ". . . when I was growing up," he finished. "I regret Ausley's death, of course. I have four shirts and three pair of breeches today." The shirt that had been bloodied by Phillip Covey was not among them, as it was now only suited for rags.

"What about that shirt you're wearing? Right wicked stain on the front."

Courtesy of Joplin Pollard's tipsy hand, Matthew thought. He'd put water on it when he'd gotten home, but too late. Actually he counted himself lucky the Thorn Bush ale hadn't burned a hole in it. "My last shirt," he said. "Have to do."

"Liquor stain?" she asked, narrowing her eyes. "You out and about last night?"

"Yes and yes."

"I can smell the pipe smoke. Gentlemen's habits, indeed! You fellows mess up, we women *clean* up. All right then, I'll have these ready for you on Monday. Tuesday if I fall behind. Hey." She beckoned him closer with a forefinger. "Have you seen my Marmaduke lately?"

"Mr. Grigsby? Yes." *My* Marmaduke? Evidently these two had more going on than the sharing of tidbits.

"Well, when you see him again, tell him I have it on good authority that *some* fine lady on Golden Hill ordered a silver service that arrived yesterday from Amsterdam and when the bill was presented her husband made a cannon sound meek. Well, she shot one back at him too. Then the battle began. You could hear them wrangling from there to Long Island. Almost put out on the street, is what happened."

"Who? The wife?"

"Naw! The *husband*! Shosh, everybody knows Princess rules that—oopsie, look what you've made me go out and spill! I never said that name, now, Matthew!"

"Princess Lillehorne?"

"Never never never did I say that name! Go on about your business, now! But don't believe that everything on Golden Hill is gold! You'll pass that along to 'Duke, won't you?"

"Very well." Matthew started for the door, but sometimes getting away from Widow Sherwyn was like walking through a puddle of tar.

"What tavern did you acquaint last night, Matthew?"

There was no need for a lie, as she could run one down like a hound after a hare. "I spent some time at the Thorn Bush."

"My lord!" Her sky-blue eyes widened. "Have you put aside those celestial books and decided to join the rest of us earthbound heathens?"

"I hope that one night and one stain doesn't mean a fall from grace."

"Well, you might have fallen *into* Grace! That's the name of Polly's new whore, you know. Grace Hester. She's been working the Thorn Bush."

"I'm sure I didn't know." Suddenly Matthew was struck by the fact that not a teacup could be filled, broken, or peed in without Widow Sherwyn hearing of it. Her outsized personality was a lamp—no, a lighthouse—that drew to her the tales of joy, sorrow, and intrigue that no magistrate nor constable would ever hear. He realized then what a treasure she was, particularly for someone in his new-found profession of problem solver. And, also, how useful she might be simply as a sounding-board.

"Why are you looking at me like that?" she asked, pausing in her folding of clothes from one basket to another.

"No reason," Matthew answered. "Just thinking how you know everyone, and how much you know *about* everyone. You've been in this location for how long?"

"Twenty-eight years in the town. Twelve years here. Proud of every day of it."

"Well you should be." He offered her his best smile. "I'm sure *I* couldn't get along without you."

"Sure you could. There are three other laundresses in New York, take your pick. Except don't go to Jane Neville, she's too expensive by half. Thievery, I call it. Outright larceny, and she doesn't even boil enough fat in her soap." Widow Sherwyn stopped herself, as the dawn of understanding bloomed on her face. "Oh, I see your drift. You're wanting to know what about whom?"

Matthew glanced toward the door to make sure no one else was coming in. "General impressions. Andrew Kippering."

"Why?"

"I saw him at the Thorn Bush last night. He and his partner, Pollard. In fact, this stain came from Pollard's tankard of ale. They were both gambling at one of the dice tables."

"You still haven't said *why*." The widow's expression was now solidly serious.

"I'm curious," Matthew explained, "as to why attorney Kippering keeps such late hours." He decided to leave it at that.

Widow Sherwyn cocked her head and stared at him intently. "If you're wanting to mingle with the ordinary folk," she said, "I expect you shouldn't start with Kippering, as from what I hear he might drag you into an early grave."

"He leads an active life, I presume?"

"Drinking, gambling, and whoring, probably not in that order. But that's common knowledge, isn't it?"

"Tell me something that's not," Matthew urged.

"Kippering is not one of my customers. Neither is Pollard. But Fitzgerald comes in regularly. I'll tell you something about *him*, if you wish to know."

"I do."

"Fitzgerald is a serious young man with a wife and two children. Lives on Crown Street, in a simple house. If one is to believe

Fitzgerald—and I do—he does most of the work. The 'cleaning-up,' as he once put it, for both his partners. Is paid very well also, but he and his wife are of Puritan stock and they have no want for luxuries . . . beyond *my* service, I mean. So my impression of all three of those gentlemen is that Pollard is the one with ambition, Fitzgerald the one with brains, and Kippering the one trying to kill himself."

"To kill himself?" Matthew asked.

"Surely. And this doesn't come from Fitzgerald, but I have it from a good source that Kippering is one of Polly's best customers. Stands to reason, of course, but there's a misery to it. He comes in drunk, sleeps with a whore—and sometimes just sleeps—and then off again. Sometimes stays there the whole night. Keeps a room in Mary Belovaire's house across from Sally Almond's tavern. Cot and a desk, is what I hear. In and out all hours. Mary's had to help him up the steps many nights, or many early mornings as might be. Pays his bills all right, but he gambles an awful lot. It'll catch up to him, sooner or later. Has no desire for a wife and fam-ily—though Lord knows Mary's got a line of ladies wanting to meet him, or used to before he got so sotted. Even the most foolish of the young pretties don't want to ride a rumpot stallion. So he drinks himself into stupors, throws his money away gambling, and almost has his name burned on a door at Polly Blossom's. Doesn't that sound to you like someone who pretends to enjoy life but really is in a great hurry to die?"

"It sounds to me," said Matthew, "like how three-quarters of the young men in New York would live, if they could."

Widow Sherwyn gave a mocking smile. "He's supposed to be smarter than most. And he's not *that* young."

"Interesting," Matthew said, but inwardly he gave a shudder. He had to wonder what Widow Sherwyn would say about *him*, if someone were to inquire.

"Now you owe me," she announced.

"Owe you?" He realized this woman reduced him to sounding like a dunce.

"Yes, indeedy. Did you think this caboodle was *free*? You pass along a good word for me to 'Duke, and when you come back to pick up your clothes you bring me a tidbit I don't know."

"The first is easy. I'm afraid the second may be impossible."

"I'll accept that as a compliment, but not as a bribe. Find me something of interest. Now scat, tomcat!"

Matthew got out of the place before he had to promise up his first-born child. It was another beautiful morning, the sky bright blue with only hints of wispy clouds. The scents of gardens and good earth wafted on the breeze. Even the smells of rotting timbers of old Dutch wharfs and a dead turtle the size of a cart-wheel had not dismayed Matthew this morning, as he'd consigned Ausley's stick to the East River at sunup. He turned right, intending to follow Queen Street to the Broad Way and then south into the bustling town. His plan was to go to City Hall and do his clerking for Magistrate Powers in the case of the rowdy George Knox. His arm was still a little sore but the yarrow oil had done wonders for it, and he did think his hand could manage a quill without wandering out of line.

About a half-block west, though, his eye caught a white brick house trimmed with dark green across the street. A white picket fence ran around the property, upon which were planted two large oak trees that spread a cool blue shade. On the fence next to the white entrance gate was the small sign *A. Vanderbrocken, Physician*.

Matthew slowed his pace. He stood looking at the house for a moment, debating his course of action. According to his newly wound watch, it was almost eight-thirty. The final hearing before sentencing of George Knox would start promptly at nine. He recalled Magistrate Powers saying a clerk could be poached from another office if Matthew wasn't up to the task, but Matthew hated not to be there when he was needed. But was he needed anymore, really? It seemed he was easily replaceable, and with the magistrate announcing his retirement the caseload—such as it was—would be further reduced. But be that as it may, the job of clerk was still his occupation until he was paid by the Herrald Agency, and when that might happen he had no clue. In fact, at a distance the whole Herrald Agency idea sounded to him like a barleybone, a sugar candy that easily melted in the heat of day.

Still, he had his own hungry curiosity to feed. Right across the street was Dr. Vanderbrocken's house, and Matthew had a few minutes to spare. He crossed to the doctor's gate.

Going through the gate and up the path to the front door, he was about to ring the brass ship's bell that hung there when he heard music coming from somewhere. It was a melody being drawn from a violin, and was quite pleasing though a touch melancholy. He realized the music was not coming from beyond the door, but rather from around the house. Leading to the back-yard was another pathway, which Matthew followed under the spread of one of the large oaks.

A second wooden gate, chest-high, blocked his progress into a garden burst into its midsummer majesty of red and purple flow-ers and ornamental shrubs. The violin player seemed to mangle a few notes here and there, but otherwise sounded quite proficient at the difficult instrument. Matthew listened as the music soared up and then quietened to a whisper, and in the ensuing sound of birdsong from the trees he rapped on the gate with his knuckles. "Hello? Can I have a moment, please?"

"Who is it?" came the doctor's voice, perturbed at being inter-rupted.

"Matthew Corbett, sir. May I speak to you?"

"Are you ill?"

"No, sir, I'm glad to say I'm not."

"Go away, then. I'm occupied." The violin music began again, this time a bit more lively as if to demonstrate the player's ability.

"A nice tune, sir," Matthew offered. "You ought to play some evening at the Dock House."

The music screeched to a stop. "Oh, for the sake of Heaven! Aren't you *gone* yet?"

"I had no idea you could play so well, sir."

There was a pause, and then came a creaking noise as weight left a chair. Matthew waited. Around the corner of the house appeared Artemis Vanderbrocken, wearing what appeared to be the exact same pale blue nightclothes Matthew had seen under his cloak the night of Deverick's murder. On the man's feet were leather slippers, and he carried a violin of such rich color it might have been carved from amber. Vanderbrocken's expression could have scared the music from a cat, as though he was so well-respected for his abilities he was also known for a surly demeanor that brooked no nonsense or—in this case—intrusion. He was of slim build and medium height, bald but for a halo of white hair, had a sharp nose and long chin garnished with a white goatee. His dark eyes behind round spectacles seemed lit with red, or perhaps that was just the sunlight off his violin. He was seventy-six if a day and had a plentitude of wrinkles in his face, yet commanded a straight-backed bearing and energy that belied his elder status. Right now, though, he just looked ready to break Matthew's teeth.

"I think you're mistaken, Mr. Corbett," he said testily. "You must have an illness of the ears, not to hear me plainly say I am *occupied*."

Matthew tried for a smile, but it didn't stick under the red heat of the doctor's glare. "But sir," he parried, "if my ears were so ill I couldn't have enjoyed the music that drew me here. I had no idea you were so—"

"Cease the bullshitting," said Vanderbrocken. "What is it you want?"

This was going to be a tough nut. Matthew wasted no time before the doctor could turn his back and stalk away. "I was on Smith Street the night Mr. Deverick was murdered."

"Were you? I'm sure many others were, as well."

"Yes sir, that's true, but I came up as you and Reverend Wade were over the body. I think you were pronouncing him dead."

"I didn't pronounce him dead. That was McCaggers' job."

"An unofficial pronouncement," Matthew went on. "You know that I work for Magistrate Powers."

"Yes, what of it?"

"Well sir . . . I also come into contact from time to time with High Constable Lillehorne, and he was telling me that—"

"Are you going to finish this *today*, young man?"

"Yes sir, please bear with me and I won't take but a minute more."

"I'm usually paid for my minutes."

Matthew could only nod and smile. "Yes sir. You mentioned to High Constable Lillehorne that you were going to see a patient that night. Might I ask who your patient was?"

"You might," came the indignant reply, "but I wouldn't answer."

"Understandable, sir, but you might be able to answer this, as it's a simple question and doesn't require you to betray an oath of confidence: were you and Reverend Wade travelling to the same destination?"

Vanderbrocken was silent. He lifted a hand to adjust his spectacles, which had slipped down to the sharp tip of his nose.

"I know you were in a hurry that night," Matthew continued, daring the fates and the doctor's temper. "I saw you were wearing a nightshirt under your cloak. Possibly the same one you have on now. So you must have been summoned from here, it being so late. And summoned for an urgent purpose, is my guess, but of course any question in that regard—"

"Is none of your business," Vanderbrocken interrupted. His nostrils flared. "Are you here on behalf of the high constable?"

"No sir."

"Then what the *hell* do you care whether William Wade and I were travelling to the same destination or not? Who are *you*, to be bothering me with ridiculous questions?"

Matthew stood his ground. He felt a stirring of anger, like hornets buzzing in his guts. He might even have raised his voice a bit to meet the doctor's infuriated tone. "With a murderer on the loose," he said while staring forcefully into the red-glared glasses, "I'd think there are *no* ridiculous questions, sir. Only questions that are either answered or evaded. You know Eben Ausley was killed by the Masker last night?"

Vanderbrocken's mouth opened a little wider, but that was all the reaction. "I didn't. Where did it happen?"

"Barrack Street."

"His throat cut the same? And the marks around the eyes?"

"It would seem so."

"My God," the doctor said quietly, and he looked at the ground. He drew a long breath and when he exhaled he seemed to shrink in his clothes. "What's happening to our town?" It was a question directed to the earth, or the air, or the birds that chirped in the trees. Then he took control of himself again and lifted a still-fiery gaze to Matthew. "I'm sorry about Ausley's death, as I would regret the passing of any citizen, but what does that have to do with Reverend Wade and myself?"

"I'm trying to clarify some information that the high constable was given. Am I correct in understanding that you met the reverend and were on your way to a common destination the night of Mr. Deverick's death?"

"Young man, I'm still not comprehending what business this is of yours. Have you become a constable yourself? Are you asking these things with the authority of Lillehorne or Magistrate Powers?"

"No sir," Matthew said.

"Ah, then you're simply a private citizen wishing to . . . what? Cause me distress?"

"I regret the distress," Matthew replied, "but I would like an answer."

Vanderbrocken took a step forward and now stood almost chest-to-chest with Matthew, the gate between them. "All right, you listen to me. My comings and goings are none of your concern, do you understand that? As for Reverend Wade's destination that night, I wouldn't presume to say. I *will* tell you that I have taken on some of the late Dr. Godwin's practice, and for that I am kept away from the fruits of retirement that I would otherwise be enjoying, including early nights and the freedom to pursue the violin in my own garden. So I'm not in the best of moods these days, Mr. Corbett, and if you fail to leave my sight within the interval I go into my house to get my loaded pistol and return I might show you what a man who seems to have no more privacy than a goldfish in a bowl is capable of."

With that, the good doctor abruptly turned and walked quickly around the house, and Matthew reckoned it was past time to get to City Hall.

eighteen

A S HE APPROACHED CITY HALL, it was clear to Matthew that—even taking into account last night's murder—this was to be far from an ordinary day.

In front of the building milled a group of forty or so men who by dint of facial expressions and loudness of mouth did not resemble happy citizens. He noted some of the men held broadsheets that could have only been Grigsby's latest edition. The newborn *Earwig* would have been on sale for the breakfasters at Sally Almond's tavern, at the Dock House Inn, and at several other locations around town. What the discord was about Matthew couldn't tell and didn't linger to learn, as he made his precarious way through the crowd and into the front door.

On the second floor he found that Magistrate Powers' office was locked. The magistrate was likely already at court. Matthew was fishing for his key when another clerk of his acquaintance, Aaron Lupton by name, stopped with a sheaf of papers on his path down the hallway between offices and told Matthew the morning's tale. The day's scheduled court proceedings had been cancelled and all magistrates and aldermen, as well as the high constable and other ranking officials, had been summoned by Lord Cornbury to a meeting in the main hall. The word, Lupton confided, was that they were thrashing out the language of a Clear

Streets Decree . . . and by the way had he heard about the third murder last night? Matthew assured Lupton he had, and Lupton went on to say that Cornbury was likely going to order the taverns closed early, and already the owners and their best customers had gotten wind of the meeting and were gathering in the street.

Also, Lupton said, Lord Cornbury today wore a blue gown that did nothing for his figure. Matthew thought there could be such a thing as too much information, but he thanked Lupton and unlocked the door intending to at least straighten up the office and check any correspondence that the magistrate might have put into his "to-reply" box. The first thing he saw was the fresh *Earwig* that either Grigsby or a hired boy had slipped under the door. The second thing that leaped to his attention, as he retrieved the sheet from the floor, was the dark line of type that read *Masker Has Struck Again* and below that, more horribly, *Interview of Coroner By Young Witness*.

"Shit," he heard himself say. He closed the door and almost broke the latch when he jammed it home. Then he sat down at his desk, the better to have a firm foundation beneath him.

Marmaduke and Effrem had had a hard time of it, judging from all the monks and friars on the page—the monks being letters too faint for want of ink and the friars being too dark for too plenty of ink—but the imperfections weren't enough to obscure Matthew's name in the central article.

> *Murder most foul was dealt upon town business leader Penn-*
> *ford Deverick near ten-thirty o'clock on Tuesday night, as the*
> *Masker has committed his second crime against reason and*
> *humanity. Ashton McCaggers, official coroner of New York*
> *town, was interviewed by Matthew Corbett, a friend of this sheet*
> *and a clerk in the employ of Magistrate Nathaniel Powers, in*
> *regard to this heinous act and the fiend who ended the honorable*
> *Mr. Deverick's life.*
>
> *According to Mr. McCaggers and our Mr. Corbett, the*
> *Masker has not vacated town as was first advanced by some of our*
> *town nobles, for Mr. Deverick lies dead with the exact same*

masklike cuttings about his eyes as was delivered to Dr. Julius Godwin two weeks past. It is Mr. McCaggers' opinion, says our interviewer, that the Masker struck Mr. Deverick down with a blunt instrument before the dirty work was done.

Matthew didn't recall telling Grigsby that, but he might have let it slip. Must have, as a matter of fact, for Marmaduke was quick to sew details together.

Our Mr. Corbett was a witness at the terrible scene. He tells us that Mr. Deverick was brutally attacked and yet made no attempt to escape, indicating that he may have known his killer. One blanches at the fact that, also according to Mr. McCaggers, a face familiar to many of us hides a murderer's rage.

Again, Matthew had only the slight memory of saying anything even remotely close to this. He thought it had been a statement along the line of, "Deverick didn't seem to put up a struggle. I think McCaggers believes it was someone he may have known."

Mr. Deverick was discovered on Smith Street by Mr. Phillip Covey and was pronounced dead near midnight by Mr. McCaggers. Questions asked of High Constable Gardner Lillehorne were referred to Chief Prosecutor James Bynes, who demurred to the opinions of Governor Lord Cornbury, who was unavailable for comment.
It is this publication's hope that the Masker is quickly brought to account for these deeds. Our condolences are offered to Mr. Deverick's widow, Esther, his son Robert and the extended family.

There followed a brief biography of Deverick, which Matthew assumed Grigsby had gotten from the widow, and then the news continued with the description of Cornbury's first meeting with his citizens. The story diplomatically called the new governor "a stylish addition to the town he so pleasantly intends to manage." Matthew turned the sheet over and saw there at the bottom—

below articles such as a lumber wagon accident on the Broad Way and items concerning ships in harbor and cargoes received—the announcement for the Herrald Agency. Well, at least that had turned out as planned.

He looked over the article about the Masker once again. There really wasn't anything in it that he thought McCaggers might object to and he believed he'd done a good job at keeping Grigsby at bay. Then again, there *was* that part about the "familiar face" and the "murderer's rage" that Matthew was sure would not go over lightly with Chief Prosecutor Bynes. Add to that the fact that it sounded as if Matthew was now reporting back to Grigsby on the doings—or misdoings—at City Hall. Not pretty.

He decided he would take this broadsheet with him, get out of here by the quickest, and enjoy a day off.

In the hallway he paused to lock the office door. As he was walking to the staircase he heard the noise of voices below him and boots tramping on the steps. Men were coming up. It seemed the meeting had ended. And not too amicably, it sounded, for there were shouts and language that turned the air blue. He thought he heard Bynes' thunder in that approaching storm, and here he stood like a lightning-bolt.

There was no time to get back into the magistrate's office. Matthew took the only avenue available to him, which was the more narrow staircase up to the third floor. Even here, though, he heard boots stomping up the steps after him. The chief prosecutor's office was to the right, at the end of the hall. To the left, past some records rooms, was a doorway. Matthew opened that door and stood on a short flight of stairs leading to another closed door. Perhaps ten feet above him was Ashton McCaggers' domain. As the voices grew louder and several men came up from the second level, Matthew shut the door to a crack and stood waiting for everything to quiet down. He couldn't help but find it ironic that he'd rather face the Masker at midnight than Bynes before lunch.

"The man's *impossible!*" he heard someone say in the corridor. "He's mad if he thinks there won't be a riot in the streets tonight!" It was Lillehorne's whine.

"The gaol will be full by eleven o'clock!" That voice Matthew couldn't place for certain; it might have been one of the other magistrates. "What to do with the night-fishermen? What to do with the harbor watch? If a ship sends up a signal after midnight, shall it be denied a pilot boat?"

"He wants those taverns closed, that's the crux of it!" Now that was for sure the voice of James Bynes, and it was far from being happy. "And putting *twenty* more constables on the street? Where are we to find the volunteers? Shall we force them before a musket? Well, I have my own headaches right here! I tell you, Grigsby should be arrested for this!"

Matthew heard the noise of paper being crumpled in a fist.

"He can't be arrested," the magistrate said. "Who'll print the decree notices?"

"Damn him!" Bynes raged. "Let him print the notices! Then we'll see if we can't stick him with intent to disrupt the public welfare!"

A door slammed and the voices were muffled. Following this, Matthew heard what was most decidedly the *crack* of a pistol shot, him being so recently acquainted with the noise, and his first thought was that Bynes was shooting a gun off to ease his anger.

When the next shot came just seconds after the first, Matthew realized the gunplay was not going on down the hall but instead up the stairs and beyond the attic door.

What McCaggers was doing up there was anyone's guess, but Matthew had a few questions for him and now seemed the appropriate time to pursue them, flintlock or no. He ascended to the ominous door and knocked firmly upon it, then waited not with a little trepidation of the unknown.

At length a small square aperture in the door was flipped up and an eyeglassed dark brown eye peered out. The eye looked angry at first, then softened at the recognition of its owner's visitor. "Mr. Corbett," said the coroner. "What may I do for you?"

"I'd like to come in, if I might."

"Well . . . I *am* busy at present. Perhaps later this afternoon?"

"I'm sorry, sir, but I probably won't be coming back to City

Hall today. Make that *definitely* not coming back. Won't you spare me a few minutes?"

"All right then, a few minutes." A bolt was unlocked, the doorgrip turned, and Matthew found himself granted entrance to what had been a cryptic area of the building.

He crossed the threshold and McCaggers, who wore a pair of brown breeches and a white shirt with the sleeves rolled up, closed the door at Matthew's back. The bolt was thrown again, which Matthew thought demonstrated McCaggers' desire for privacy. He realized in another moment, by the smoky golden light streaming through the attic windows, that McCaggers had created a world for himself up here, in the uppermost of the tallest building in town, and not all of this creation was easy to look upon.

The first items that caught Matthew's attention were the four human skeletons, three adult-sized and one a child, that hung suspended from the rafters. Also adorning the walls were perhaps thirty or more skulls of various sizes, some whole and some missing lower jawbones or other portions. Here and there, as macabre decorations, were the wired-together bones of legs, arms, hands, and ribcages. Atop a row of honey-colored wooden file cabinets were more complete skulls and skull fragments. On the wall behind the cabinets was a display of what appeared to be frog and bat skeletons. It was a veritable boneyard, yet everything was spotless and sterile. The pride of the collector, Matthew thought. McCaggers collected human and animal bones as he himself gathered books.

That wasn't all of the surprises in McCaggers' realm. Next to a long table topped with beakers of fluid in which things of uncertain origin floated, there stood a rack of swords, axes, knives of many sizes, two muskets, and three pistols as well as fierce-looking weapons such as wooden clubs studded with nails, brass knuckledusters, and crude spears. Amid the items were two spaces where pistols were missing, and Matthew smelled the sharp tang of burned gunpowder.

"I expect you heard my shots," McCaggers said. He picked up

two pistols that were lying amid a stack of books on a desk at his side. "I was shooting at Elsie."

"*Elsie?*"

"Yes, that's her." He motioned toward a dress-maker's form standing about twenty feet away. The thing was shot full of holes. "Elsie today. Sometimes Rosalind." He indicated a second form that was in even more pitiful shape. "She's not feeling well lately." He looked up, as did Matthew, at a hatch in the roof through which showed the blue sky. A rope ladder was hanging from it. Gunsmoke was still drifting out, and Zed's ebony face with its purplish upraised tattoos was peering down into the attic. "We have a visitor," McCaggers announced, revealing that Zed knew at least some English. "Mr. Corbett."

Zed withdrew, his expression impassive. Matthew wondered if he lived up there on the roof, and what the socialites of Golden Hill would say if they knew a slave commanded the highest point of New York.

"I have some new pistols I'm testing," McCaggers explained. He put the guns back in their proper places. "From the Netherlands. More power than the ones I've seen before. I'll dig the balls out of Elsie and measure the wounds. I mean, of course, the *impressions*. I do enjoy keeping notes, and one never knows when the information might be useful." He came back to the desk, where Matthew saw a notebook lying open and a quill pen next to an ink bottle. "Today the weapon of choice is the blade," McCaggers said as he made a few notations in his book. "Tomorrow it will be the pistol, once it's made small enough to conceal and able to fire multiple balls without reloading." He glanced up and caught Matthew's skeptical expression. "Both those conceits are being studied in Europe as we speak."

"I sincerely hope you don't literally mean *tomorrow*." Matthew couldn't imagine a pistol that would fire more than one ball. It would be the most dangerous weapon ever created.

"There are already pistols with multiple barrels in Prussia. As far as the reduction in size and weight to afford concealment, I'd venture fifty years, more or less. Barring the appearance of a new technology, of course, but the gunsmiths are nothing if not inventive." McCaggers saw the broadsheet in Matthew's hand. "Ah! The latest news?"

Matthew gave it over. "Just out this morning. I regret that Mr. Grigsby painted me as an interviewer. I tried my best to be selective in what I told him."

"I see you were." It only took a few seconds for McCaggers to get the gist of the story. "Oh, that part about the 'town nobles' will vex some people. Lillehorne, most particularly. It won't go over well with Bynes, either. *A face familiar to many of us hides a murderer's rage.* Grigsby doesn't shy from frightening the citizens, does he?" He turned the sheet to its second side and began to read as Matthew cast a wandering eye over the rest of the attic chamber.

A bookcase held a dozen thick ancient-looking tomes bound in scabby leather. Medical books? he wondered. Anatomy? He couldn't make out the titles. Near it stood a massive old black chest-of-drawers, next to which was a cubbyhole arrangement that held rolled-up scrolls of white paper. Over on the far side of the attic, past shelves on which were folded various items of clothing, was a simple cot and a writing table. Obviously there was no fireplace here, so McCaggers would have to take all his meals in the taverns unless—as was more likely, due to his penchant for privacy—he had an arrangement with a local household.

"*The Herrald Agency,*" McCaggers said, and Matthew saw he was reading the notice. "*Letters of inquiry to go to the Dock House Inn.* Well, that's interesting."

"It is?"

"Yes, I've heard of them before. Didn't know they were over here yet. Their motto used to be 'The Hands and Eyes of the Law.' " McCaggers looked up from the sheet. "Private investigators. More muddy water ahead for the high constable, if these people open an office."

"Really," Matthew said, trying to sound unconcerned one way or the other.

"Grigsby missed the night's news, didn't he?" McCaggers handed the *Earwig* back to Matthew. "I presume you've heard?"

"I have."

"Another nasty throat-cutting. The same blow to the head, the same shapes carved around the eyes. Oh." McCaggers' face had begun to blanch at the memory of what he'd seen in the cold room. He pressed one hand against his mouth as if to stem a rising tide. "Pardon," he said after a moment. "I do let my weakness get away from me."

This seemed the right time for Matthew to clear his throat and ask, "What weakness, sir?"

"Now you're being obtuse!" McCaggers lowered his hand. "You know exactly what I mean. Everyone knows, don't they?" He nodded. "They know, and they snigger about it behind my back. But what am I to *do*? I'm cursed, you see. Because I was born for this profession, yet I despise the . . ." He abruptly stopped. A faint glimmer of sweat had surfaced on his cheeks. He paused, waiting for his gullet to sink again. Then he forced a twisted smile upon his mouth and motioned up toward the skeletons. "You see my angels?"

"*Angels*, sir?"

"My *unknown* angels," McCaggers corrected. He gazed up at them as if they were the most splendorous objects of art. "Two— the young man and woman—came with me from Bristol. The other two—the older man and little girl—were found here. My angels, Matthew. Do you know why?"

"No," Matthew said. And he wasn't sure he *wished* to know, either.

"Because they represent everything that to me is fascinating about life and death," the coroner went on, still staring up at his possessions. "They are perfect. Oh, not to say they don't have bad teeth, or a cracked knuckle or an old knee injury, but just those minor things. The two from Bristol hung in my father's office. He was a coroner, too, as was my grandfather. I remember my father showing them to me in an afternoon's twilight, and saying, 'Ashton, look here and look deep, for all of life's joy, tragedy, and mystery are here on display.' Joy, he said, because they were children of purpose, as are we all. Tragedy, he said, because we all must come to this. And mystery . . . because where does the light go, from those houses, to leave only the foundations behind?"

Matthew saw a shine in McCaggers' eyes that some might have mistaken for madness, yet he had seen it in his own eyes in a mirror in Fount Royal when presented with a problem that seemingly had no solution.

"None of them," McCaggers said, "should have died. I mean, yes of course, eventually they would have passed, but I recall my father saying about those first two that they were simply found dead and no one could identify them. No one ever claimed them. The same with my two. The older man was found dead in the back of a tinker's wagon, but the tinker didn't know when or where he'd climbed aboard. The little girl died aboard a ship. And the astonishing thing, Matthew, is that there was no record of her ever being a passenger *on* the ship. No one knew her name. She slept on the deck and took food with the others, but no one ever asked about her or her parents. For all those many weeks, no one cared to know. Did she make herself invisible? Did she simply have a way about her that caused others to assume she was taken care of? Fourteen years old, she was. Where did she come from, Matthew? What was her story?"

"Of what did she die?" Matthew asked, gazing up at the smallest skeleton.

"Ah, now that's the question." McCaggers rubbed the point of his chin. "I studied her. The older man, too. I used my books and my notes. I used all the material my father had left to me, and that my grandfather had left to him, and I came up with . . . nothing. No injuries, no illnesses that I could identify. Nothing. And nothing left of them now but those foundations, for their lights have gone. But I'll tell you what I believe, Matthew. What I've put together as must be the only answer.

"I believe," he said quietly, as he regarded his angels, "that human beings need friends, and love, and the touch of humanity. I believe that if those things are denied long enough, an older man or a young girl might crawl into the back of a tinker's wagon or steal onto the gangplank of a ship and find their destination is still the same lonely path. I think these people died of something not found in my books, or my father's and grandfather's. I think somewhere their hearts were broken, and when all hope was extinguished they died, for they simply could not bear to live anymore."

"But look at the *bones*," McCaggers whispered. "How they fit together, how they protect what they hold within. The foundations of our houses are magnificent, Matthew, even if our hearts become darkened or our minds clouded. It was always the bones that drew me to this profession. The clean, precise geometry of them, the noble and unerring purpose. The bones are miracles of creation." He blinked, and seemed at that instant to return to the hard floor of reality. "It's the jelly I can't bear. The cracked clay, and what comes out." Again his hand pressed to his mouth, the lips drawn tight.

"I assume," Matthew said to change the subject, "that your father is still in Bristol?"

"Yes." It was spoken in a strange, faraway voice. "Still in Bristol. He will *always* be in Bristol."

This subject, too, seemed fraught with danger, for suddenly McCaggers gave a shudder and said, "Please. I'm not feeling well."

"I'm sorry."

"You wished to ask me something?"

"Yes. Uh . . ." Matthew hesitated, for he didn't wish to further sicken the coroner, yet he had to know. "It has to do with Ausley," he said. "Do you mind?"

"It's my *job*," came the answer, with a bitter edge.

"I've heard that a blood mark was found last night. On a root cellar door near Barrack Street."

"Yes, so Lillehorne's told me. Found on the root cellar door of the office belonging to the three lawyers Pollard, Fitzgerald, and Kippering. What of it?"

"I was just wondering if it was true." What Matthew had really wanted was to make sure the information had gotten to the high constable. "Do you know if there were any other blood marks found nearby?"

McCaggers turned toward Matthew and stared at him without blinking. "A curious line of questioning, I think. Why not ask Lillehorne yourself?"

"He . . . uh . . . was in a meeting this morning. With Lord Cornbury."

"I've only heard of the one mark," McCaggers said. "Evidently the Masker tried to get into their root cellar. If you're really intrigued, Lillehorne's already searched the cellar and found nothing."

"Why *their* root cellar?" Matthew had to ask. "I mean, Beaver Street is right there at the end of the alley, isn't it? Why would the Masker try to get into a root cellar when he could have easily turned either left or right onto Beaver Street?"

"It may have been that he was undone by the shouting, which I understand was profuse, and he feared the constables were converging on him." McCaggers picked up one of the swords from the rack and used a white cloth to wipe the blade. "You know, there *is* a question Lillehorne posed to me last night. I couldn't answer it. Why is it, do you think, that the person who started the alarm hasn't come forward?"

Before Matthew could think of a reply, McCaggers replaced the sword and picked up a second one to wipe down. "Lillehorne's very interested in finding this person. He's found any number of people who *heard* the shouting, but not the person who began it. What do you make of that?"

Matthew took a deep breath and said, "With three murders to investigate, I'd think the high constable would save his interest for the Masker, not an innocent witness who may have happened onto the scene."

McCaggers nodded and returned the sword to the rack. "Four murders," he said.

Matthew wasn't sure he'd heard correctly. "Sir?"

"Four," McCaggers repeated. "Murders. In the past three weeks. Ausley was the fourth, not the third."

"I don't think I'm following you."

McCaggers went to the series of cubbyholes and pulled out one of the paper scrolls. He opened it and studied the drawing of a body and the notes written there in black and red crayon. "As you're so adept at both questions and answers, I'll tell you that four days before Dr. Godwin was killed, a body washed up from the Hudson River on the property of a farmer named John Ormond. His farm is about ten miles out of town. The body was that of a young man, aged eighteen or nineteen, twenty at the oldest. Here, see for yourself." He gave Matthew the paper and then stepped back as if distancing himself from the scene.

Matthew wasn't quite sure what he was looking at, for some of the coroner's notations seemed to be in a scrivener's code unknown to him. He did note first and foremost the red crayon drawn in the eye sockets. "The man's eyes were injured?" Matthew asked.

"His eyes were *gone*. You see the stab wounds to the body?"

Matthew counted the red lines. "*Eight?*"

"Three to the chest. One to the base of the neck. Three to the back and one to the left shoulder. From what I could tell, the blades were all different shapes and widths. You'll also see in my notations that his wrists were bound behind him with cords."

"He was murdered by a mob?" Matthew asked.

"Actually, the frontal and nasal bones of his skull were shattered and three of the vertebrae in his neck broken. I think he fell from a considerable height along the river. Bear in mind, he was in the water at least five days before Ormond found him."

That would have been a pleasant picture, Matthew thought. The river, a warm summer day, and a decayed, eyeless corpse with eight stab wounds must have been McCaggers' idea of a picnic in Hell. "This was certainly a vile work," Matthew said. An understatement, he decided. Even the Masker didn't tie a man's hands behind the back before he struck. The victim would have had to know what was about to happen to him, once the cords were knotted.

"*Four* murders within three weeks," said McCaggers. "That is a new and very disturbing fact for the colony's book of records."

Matthew handed the document back. "I can understand why Lillehorne wanted to keep this one quiet. Who was he?"

"No idea." McCaggers rolled up the paper and returned it to

its cubbyhole. "The body was . . . not suitable for travel. Neither was anything—pardon me a moment—was anything left of the . . . uh . . . left of the—"

"The face?" Matthew finished for him.

"That, exactly. Fish and turtles. They . . . probably took the eyes first." McCaggers looked a little fish-eyed himself, but he carried on. "The clothes were inspected but the pockets were empty. After I finished my notes, Lillehorne ordered Zed to dig the grave. The case remains open, but so far no one has reported anyone missing."

"And he had no wallet? Nothing at all?"

"Nothing. Of course he might have been robbed, by either his murderers or the river." McCaggers lifted a finger, as if something had come to mind. "I have something to ask *you*. I'm to understand you grew up in the orphanage?"

"I did." Matthew surmised the coroner had gotten that information either from Magistrate Powers or Lillehorne.

"Did you know Ausley very well?"

"No, not well."

McCaggers crossed to the large black chest and pulled open a drawer. In it, Matthew saw, was a bundle wrapped in brown paper. Also in the drawer was a cheap brown cloth wallet, a pencil wrapped with string, a set of keys, a small pewter liquor flask, and what appeared to be a vial half-full of oily amber-colored liquid.

"I was wondering," McCaggers said, "if you'd ever heard Ausley speak of his next-of-kin."

Ah, Matthew thought. Here they were, then. The last possessions of Eben Ausley as he was carved out of the earth to reap his reward. His clothes wrapped in the paper. The vial had to be the sickening cloves cologne. The keys to the locks of the orphanage. The pencil to record Ausley's gambling losses, meals, comings-and-goings, and whatever else lay in his mind's brackish swamp.

"I haven't, no," Matthew answered. He felt a little itch at the back of his brain.

"I presume someone will come along, eventually. The second-in-charge at the almshouse, perhaps. Or I'll just put all this in a box and store it away." McCaggers closed the drawer. "Did he never talk about a family?"

Matthew shook his head. And then he realized what was making his brain itch. "Pardon me, but would you open that again?"

McCaggers did, and stepped aside as Matthew approached.

It only took a few seconds, actually. Hardly an inspection to see what was missing. "Ausley's notebook," Matthew said. "Where is it?"

"I'm sorry? Where is what?"

"Ausley always carried a small black notebook with gold ornamentation on the cover. I don't see it here." He looked into the coroner's face. "Might it be wrapped up with the clothes?"

"Positively not. Zed is meticulous in his removal of items from the clothing."

Far be it from Matthew to question Zed's meticulosity. In fact, he had the keen sensation of being watched and when he glanced up at the roof hatch he saw the slave standing there staring down at him with an expression one might afford a tadpole in a teacup.

Matthew looked at the objects in the drawer again, but he didn't really see them for his eyes were clouded. "The notebook isn't here," he said quietly, mostly to himself.

"If it isn't here," McCaggers offered, "it wasn't on the body." He pushed the drawer shut once more, and then walked to the weapons rack and chose another two pistols. He took them to a small round table where Matthew saw a box of lead balls, a powderhorn, and a number of flints arranged in readiness for the next assault on Elsie. "Would you care to take a shot?" he asked.

"No, thank you. I do appreciate your time, though." Matthew was already moving toward the door. He'd noted several holes in the wall beyond Elsie and two broken windowpanes. It amazed him that some gentleman or lady hadn't gotten a sting in the wig by now.

"Good day, then. Please feel free to come up from time to time, as I enjoy your company."

Coming from the eccentric—some would say half-mad—

coroner, that was high praise indeed, Matthew thought. But now it was time to bite the lead ball and see if he could get out of this building without unpleasantries in the form of a diminutive high constable or a blowhard chief prosecutor. He left the attic, closed the door behind him, and descended toward the cruel and common earth.

nineteen

BEFORE MATTHEW COULD PROCEED with his intent to have
lunch at the Gallop and settle into what would hopefully be a
quiet afternoon, even as some in the town were organizing protests
against the forthcoming Clear Streets Decree, he had a mission to
complete.

He'd been considering what he was to tell John Five about the
reverend's journey last night, and still—as one step after another
took him nearer to Master Ross' blacksmithery—he was unsure. It
wouldn't do to wait for John Five to come to him. As Matthew had
been asked in all good faith to perform this duty, he felt obligated
to report on his findings with proper speed, but yet . . . had he
really *made* any findings? Of course he'd seen Wade sob in front of
Madam Blossom's house, but what did it *mean*? Sometimes,
Matthew knew, there was a vast gulf between what was seen and
what there was to be understood, and therein lay his problem.

He entered the sullen heat of the smith's shop, found John
Five at his usual labor, and invited him outside to speak. The ritual
of asking a few minutes from Master Ross was repeated, and
shortly Matthew and John Five were standing together at about
the same spot they'd been on Tuesday morning.

"So," John Five began, when Matthew was hesitant in speaking. "You followed him?"

"I did."

"Busy night, that was. A terrible night, for Ausley."

"It was," Matthew agreed.

They were silent for a moment. Pedestrians passed on the sidewalk, a wagon carrying sacks of grain trundled by, and two children ran along rolling a stick-and-hoop.

"Are you gonna tell me, or not?" John asked.

Matthew decided to say, "Not."

John frowned. "And *why* not?"

"I did discover his destination. But I'm not sure it was his *usual* destination. I don't feel ready to tell you where it was, or what I witnessed there."

"Did you not understand how serious this thing is?"

"Oh, I did and do understand. That's exactly why I need more time."

"More time?" John Five thought about that. "You're sayin' you're gonna follow him again?"

"Yes," Matthew said. "I want to see if he goes to the same place. If he does . . . I may wish to speak to him first. Then, according to how things progress, he may tell either you or Constance himself."

John ran a hand through his hair, his expression perplexed. "It must be bad."

"Right now, it's neither good nor bad. My observations are unsupported, and thus I have to refrain from saying any more." Matthew realized John Five was waiting for something else—anything he might grasp upon as a spar of hope—and so Matthew said, "There's likely going to be a Clear Streets Decree tonight. The taverns will be closing early and there'll be more constables on the streets. I doubt if Reverend Wade will be making his late-night walks until the decree is lifted, and when that will be I have no idea."

"He might not walk," John said, "but his trouble won't go away so easy."

"I think you're absolutely right in that regard. For the time being, though, there's nothing either of us can do."

"All right," John Five said in a dispirited voice. "I don't like it, but I guess it'll have to be."

Matthew agreed that it would, wished his friend a good day, and promptly walked farther along the street to Tobias Winekoop's stable where he secured Suvie for the next morning at six-thirty. His Saturday training session with Hudson Greathouse was looming ever more darkly in his mind, but at least he knew what to expect.

Now there was one more errand he wished to conduct before lunch and this one had been prompted by Widow Sherwyn's gossip of Golden Hill. Among the fine houses there was the red brick mansion belonging to the Deverick family. Matthew doubted that Lillehorne had spent much time—if any—interviewing Deverick's widow Esther and son Robert about the elder man's business affairs. Even if they were near neighbors, the Lillehornes and Devericks were not cut from the same cloth. It seemed to Matthew that if a connection was to be found between Dr. Godwin, Deverick, and now—of all unlikely persons—Ausley, such a link might be discovered in the business realm. He realized he might indeed be far off the mark, as how in the world could an orphanage headmaster with a gambling fetish be involved with a wealthy goods broker who had clawed his way up from the bitter streets of London? And furthermore, then, how was an eminent and much-admired physician involved with both of them?

He intended to at least, as McCaggers might have said, take a shot at it. He started off northward toward the area known as Golden Hill, which was a row of palatial houses and gardens east of the Broad Way the length of Golden Hill Street between Crown and Fair.

As Matthew approached this avenue of opulence he sidestepped a farmer's wagon bringing hogs to market and looked up toward the heights where the rich folk lived. Golden Hill Street might be made of plain hard-packed dirt, but the residences were inhabited by the town's gilded families. And what residences they were! Two-storied with ornate constructions of red, white, or yellow brick, cream-colored stone and gray rock, with balconies, terraces, and cupolas and cut-glass windows that gazed in all directions upon harbor, townscape, and woodland as if marking what had passed and what was to pass in the history and future of New York. No doubt about it, these were the families who had created something of great value to this enterprise and were justly rewarded for their influence and financial bravery. All except Lillehorne, of course, who lived in the smallest house at the western end of the street and whose money came from his father-in-law, yet it was in the interest of those other stalwarts that a high constable be kept among the club if only as errand-boy.

Here the street was neatly raked and kept free of those irritating mounds of manure otherwise endured by the ordinary joseph and josephine. Huge shade trees invited lingering where no lingering was tolerated, and bursts of flowers in geometric gardens wafted into the warm air complex aromas that seemed perhaps a little too sophisticated for nostrils assailed by dockyard tar and fried sausages in the small chaos called life down below.

Matthew advanced eastward on the sidewalk, passing through pools of shade and again into bright sunlight. Everything seemed quieter up here, more restrained, *tighter* somehow. He could almost hear from marbled vestibules the *thrum* of pendulum clocks that were old before he was born, marking time for the servants as they moved from room to room. Even with his penchant for getting into places where he wasn't welcomed, Matthew was a bit awed by these displays of wealth. He'd walked on Golden Hill Street many times, of course, but he'd never been on such a mission as this where he'd actually intended to go knocking at a door dismantled from a Scottish castle. Warehouse captain, sugar mill general, credit and loan earl, lumberyard duke, slave trade baron, real estate prince, and shipyard emperor all lived here where the grass was green and the gravel of the carriage driveways smooth and white as infants' teeth.

He came along a five-foot-high wrought-iron fence topped with spear-tips and there was the simple iron nameplate *Deverick*. He faced a gate that challenged him from continuing up a fieldstone walkway to the front door yet it was unlocked and easily conquered. He noted how quiet were the hinges as they allowed him entry; he'd been almost expecting a scream of outrage. Then he went up the walkway and under the blue bloom of a canopy above the front steps. He climbed them, six in number, and as he reached for the polished brass door knocker he had a moment of self-doubt in that he was still, after all, a simple clerk. What business did he have bothering the Devericks when this ought to be the high constable's task? It was up to Lillehorne to pursue the Masker, as part of his official duty.

True, all true. Yet Matthew knew from past observation how the high constable's mind worked, in square circles and circular squares. If one waited on him to put paid to the Masker's bill, even the outlandish idea of a daily *Earwig* couldn't keep up with the murders. There was something to this link between the doctor, the broker, and the orphanage chief that Matthew thought only he might uncover, and now this new fact that nettled him like a mosquito in the mind: what had become of Ausley's notebook?

He pulled his willpower back up to his ears again, took firm hold of the knocker, and let it be known Matthew Corbett had come to call.

Promptly the door was opened. An austere whipcord of a woman wearing a gray dress with lace around the throat peered out at him. She was about forty years of age, had a severe cap of ash-blond hair and deep-set hazel eyes that looked him up and down—lingering on the shirt stain—and shot out a negative opinion on seemingly everything from his forehead scar to the scuffs on his shoes. She didn't speak.

"I'd like to see Mr. Deverick, please," Matthew said.

"Mr. *Davarick*," she replied with a heavy foreign accent that Matthew thought might be Austrian or Prussian but certainly from somewhere in old Europe, "iss *decissed*. He iss bean bearit thiss afternun at two o'cluck."

"I'd like to see the *younger* Mr. Deverick," Matthew corrected.

"Iss nut pozzible. Goot day." She started to close the door on him, but he reached out and put his hand against it.

"May I ask why it's not possible?"

"Mrs. *Davarick* iss *oot*. I am nut giffen parmizzion."

"Gretl? Who is that?" came a voice from beyond the servant woman.

"It's Matthew Corbett!" he took the opportunity to shout, a bit too loudly for this quiet neighborhood because Gretl looked as if she wished to kick him where it hurt with one of her polished square-toed black boots. "May I have a moment?"

"My mother's not home," Robert said, still standing out of sight.

"I haf *tolt* him ssso, sssir." That one was almost a spit in Matthew's face.

"It's you I'd like to speak with," Matthew persisted, braving the elements. "Concerning your father's . . ." He had a choice of words here, and he chose ". . . murder."

Gretl glared at him, waiting for Robert's reaction. When young Deverick gave none, she said "Goot day" again and began to push the door shut with a strength that Matthew thought might break his elbow were he to try and resist.

"Let him in." Robert now made an appearance, if only as a shadow in the cool dimness of the house.

"I am nut giffen par—"

"I'll give you permission. Let him in."

Gretl gave a little stiff-necked lowering of the head, though her eyes flashed with fire. She opened the door, Matthew walked past her almost expecting a boot up the arse, and Robert came forward on the dark parquet floor to meet him.

Matthew held his hand out and Robert shook it. "I regret bothering you today, as"—the door was rather roughly closed and Gretl glided past Matthew into a carpeted hallway—"obviously you have much on your mind," Matthew continued, "but thank you for the time."

"I can only give you a few minutes. My mother's out."

Matthew could only respond with a nod. Robert's curly brown hair had been neatly brushed and he wore an immaculate black suit and waistcoat, cravat and crisp white shirt, yet at close range his face was chalky and his gray eyes dark-shadowed and unfocused. Matthew thought he looked years older than he'd appeared at the meeting on Tuesday. The shock of a brutal murder had sapped his youth, and from what Matthew had heard of this family, Robert's eighteen-year-old spirit had long ago been damaged by his father's heavy hand.

"The parlor," Robert said. "This way."

Matthew followed the younger man into a room with a high vaulted ceiling and a fireplace made of black marble with two Greek goddesses holding what appeared to be ancient wine amphoras. The rug on the floor was blood-red trimmed with gold circles, the walls made of varnished dark timbers. The furniture— writing desk, chairs, an octagonal table with clawed feet—were all fashioned of glossy black wood save for a red fabric sofa set in front of the hearth. The room was as deep as the house, for one diamond-paned glass window gave a view onto Golden Hill Street while a second window of the same design looked out upon a flowering garden decorated with white statues and a small pond. The wealth this single room represented was enough to almost steal Matthew's breath away. He doubted if in his entire life he would ever hold enough money to even buy such a fireplace, which seemed large enough to burn treetrunks. But then again, he wondered why he would ever want to; it seemed to him that pineknots kept one just as warm, and everything beyond that was wasteful. Still, it was a magnificent chamber in a majestic house, and Robert must have seen this awestruck expression before because he said almost apologetically, "It's just a room." He motioned toward a chair. "Please sit down."

Matthew sat carefully, as if the chair might bite him for being ill-born.

Robert also sat down, in the chair at the writing desk. He rubbed his forehead with the heel of his hand, and Matthew thought he was trying to clear his mind before the conversation began.

Matthew was coming up with his first sentence when Robert said, his eyes still hazy, "You found my father."

"No, not exactly. I mean to say, I was *there*, but actually—"

"Is that the new broadsheet?"

"Yes, it is. Would you care to see it?" Matthew got up and placed the *Earwig* on the desktop blotter, then returned to his seat.

Robert spent a moment reading the article concerning his father's demise. His expression never changed; it remained almost blank, only faintly touched with sadness at the edges of the mouth. When he finished reading he turned the paper over. "Mr. Grigsby told me it was coming out today. I enjoyed his last edition." His gaze briefly flickered toward Matthew and then away again. "I understand there was another killing last night. I heard my mother talking about it, with Mr. Pollard."

"Mr. Pollard? He was here this morning?"

"He came for her. He's our lawyer, you know."

"And she went somewhere with Mr. Pollard?"

"To City Hall. There was going to be a meeting, Mr. Pollard said. About the taverns, and a Clear Streets Decree. He told my mother about Mr. Ausley. I expect that's why Lord Cornbury wants to close the taverns early, isn't that right?"

"Yes."

"Mr. Pollard told my mother she should be there with him at the meeting. He said she should wear her funeral gown, the better to remind Lord Cornbury that she also has been a victim, but that she wishes the taverns and the town to operate as usual just the same. It's a lot of money for us, you know."

"I would imagine so," Matthew said.

On the desktop were a number of envelopes and a blue glass ball paperweight. Robert picked up the ball and gazed into it as if searching for something there. "My father has said many times that we are enriched whenever a candle is lighted in the taverns, or a glass of wine drunk. Whenever a cup cracks, or a platter breaks." He looked over the ball at Matthew. "You see, that *is* a lot of money."

"I'm sure a fortune's been made on many Saturday nights alone."

"But it's a difficult task, as well," Robert went on, almost as if speaking to himself. "Getting the best price for the goods. Dealing with the suppliers, keeping everything moving as it should. Some items have to come across the sea, you know. Then there's the warehouse and the inventory. The wine barrels have to be inspected. The food animals chosen and prepared. There are so many details to keep up with. It's not as if we wish these things and make them happen."

"Certainly not," Matthew said, willing to wait for what destination Robert was travelling toward.

The younger Deverick was silent as he turned the paperweight between his hands. "My father," he finally said, "was a man of direct action. A self-made man. No one gave him anything, ever. And he never asked for favors. He created it all, himself. That is a thing to be proud of, don't you think?"

"Very proud."

"And a *smart* man," Robert continued, though now there was a harsher edge to his voice. "But he never had a formal education. Far from it. He said . . . many times . . . that his education was gotten from the streets and the public markets. He never knew his own father, you see. What he remembered of his mother . . . was a woman in a small room who drank herself to death. It wasn't easy for him. Not for Mr. Deverick, no. Yet he made all this." Robert nodded, his eyes as glassy as the paperweight. "Yes, my father *was* a smart man. I think he was right, when he said I wasn't fit for the business. Did I tell you he said that?"

"No," Matthew replied.

"A direct man, he was. Not unkind, though. Just . . . a man of action. Such men are dying breeds, my mother says. And now look here, my father's dead." A quick and terrible smile flashed across Robert's mouth, yet his eyes were wet with crushed misery.

The room seemed much smaller to Matthew than it had a few minutes before. He had the sensation of ghostly movement in the dark-timbered room, as if the vaulted ceiling was slowly lowering itself upon his head and the fireplace opening wider like an ebony mouth. The light from the windows seemed more dim, and more distant.

"Oh," Robert said, almost a gasp of surprise. He touched his right cheek like a slow-motion slap. "I'm prattling. I'm sorry, I didn't mean to go on."

Matthew kept silent, but Robert's moment of self-revelation was done. The younger man put aside the blue ball, straightened his spine against the chairback, and stared inquisitively at Matthew through red-rimmed eyes from the pallid face.

"Sssir?" Gretl was standing in the doorway. "My edvize iss to esk thiss vizitor to leaf now."

"It's all right, Gretl. Really it is. Besides, I've been just prattling on, haven't I, Mr. Corbett?"

"We're just talking," Matthew said.

Gretl gave him not even a disdainful glance. "Mrs. *Davarick* dit nut giff me parmizzion to—"

"My mother is not *here*," Robert interrupted, and the sound of his voice cracking on the last word made Matthew flinch. Red whorls had risen on the white cheeks. "Now that my father is gone, *I* am the head of this house when my mother is not here! Do you understand that?"

Gretl said nothing, but just stared impassively at him.

"Leave us alone," Robert said, his voice weaker now and his head beginning to slump, as if the act of asserting himself had drained him.

She gave another slight nod. "Vateffer you sey." And then she was gone into the guts of the house like a drifting wraith.

"I don't mean to be a problem," Matthew offered.

"You're *not* a problem! I can have a visitor if I like!" Robert caught himself and seemed to be struggling with this sudden rush of anger. "I'm sorry. Forgive me, it's been of course a terrible week."

"Of course."

"Don't mind Gretl. She's been the housekeeper here for years and she thinks she runs the place. Well, perhaps she does. But the last time I looked, my name was still Deverick and this was my house, too, so no, you're not a problem."

Matthew thought it was time he presented his questions to Robert, as he was beginning to fear the consequences if the widow

Deverick returned and found him here without "parmizzion." He said, "I won't take up too much more of your time. I know you have an unfortunate task this afternoon and a lot weighing on your mind, but I'd like to ask you to think about this: can you identify any connection whatsoever between Dr. Godwin, your father, and Eben Ausley?"

"No," Robert said almost at once. "None."

"Just consider it for a moment. Sometimes things aren't so obvious. For instance, did your father—and excuse me for being indelicate about this—like to go to the taverns himself and perhaps play the dice or cards?"

"Never." Again, it was spoken quickly and with resolve.

"He didn't gamble?"

"My father *despised* gambling. He thought it was a sure route for fools to throw their money away."

"All right." That seemed to close that particular avenue of advancement, but Matthew had to wonder what the deceased would have said about his dice-throwing young lawyers. "Do you know if your father ever visited Dr. Godwin? Either professionally or socially?"

"Our physician for years has been Dr. Edmonds. Besides, my mother couldn't stand Dr. Godwin."

"Really? May I ask why?"

"Well, everyone *knows*," Robert said.

"Everyone but me, then." Matthew gave a patient smile.

"The *ladies*," Robert said. "You know. At Polly Blossom's."

"I know there are prostitutes at Polly Blossom's house, yes. Is there something else?"

Robert waved a hand at him, as if in irritation at Matthew's thick skull. "My mother says everyone knows Dr. Godwin is physician to the ladies. *Was*, I mean. She says she wouldn't let him put a finger on her."

"Hm," Matthew replied, more of a thoughtful response than a word. He hadn't known that Dr. Godwin was physician-on-call to Polly Blossom's investments, but then again such an item would not necessarily have crossed his horizon as a topic of conversation. He marked the information, though, as something to pursue.

"If your next question is to be whether or not my father dallied at Polly Blossom's, I can tell you emphatically that he did not," said Robert, a little haughtiness husking his voice. "My father and mother—while not exactly the picture of passion—were devoted to one another. I mean . . . no one has a perfect life, do they?"

"I'm sure no one does," Matthew agreed, and he let that sit like a bone in a stewpot for a few seconds before he said, "I assume, then, that you *won't* be taking over the business?"

Robert's eyes were unfocused again. He seemed to be staring past Matthew. "A letter was sent to my brother Thomas in London yesterday morning. I expect he'll be here by October."

"But who'll be in charge between now and then?"

"We have capable managers. My mother says. She says everything will be taken care of. The business will go on, I'll return to school in August, and Thomas will take over. But you know, I was being groomed for it. Supposedly. Groomed with my business education. But my father said . . ." Here Robert hesitated, a muscle clenching in his jaw. "My father said . . . for all my education, something was left out of me. Isn't that humorous?" He smiled, but on that strained and bitter face it was more tragedy than comedy. "With all the grades I've been getting, all that studying in a cubbyhole night after night to make him . . . make them both . . . proud . . . that he should say something was left *out* of me? Oh yes, he had proper words for me. When I dealt with the man who shortchanged our beef order, last month. I had not made him *afraid* enough, my father said. I had not plunged the dagger in and twisted it, to make that man fear the Deverick name. That's what it's about, you know: power and fear. We step on the heads of those below us, they step on the lower heads, and down and down until the snails are crushed in their shells. That's what it will always be about."

"Your father didn't think you were hard enough with a swindler? Is that it?"

"My father always said business is war. A businessman should be a warrior, he said, and if someone dares to challenge you then . . . destruction has to be the only response." Robert blinked heavily. "I suppose school can't put that into a person's soul, if it's not there. All the grades in the world . . . all the honors . . . nothing can put that there, if you're not born with it."

"You're describing a man who must have made a lot of enemies over the course of his career."

"He had them. But mostly they were competitors in London. As I've told you before, here he had no competitors." There came the noise of horse hooves on the street. Matthew saw through the front window a black carriage pulling up to the curb. "My mother's returned," Robert said, listlessly.

With almost frightening speed the gruesome Gretl was out the front door and striding toward Mrs. Deverick's carriage to, Matthew presumed, fry his bacon. Matthew considered his options. He could either try to get out like a scalded dog or face the situation like a gentleman. In another moment, however, the scalded-dog option was out the window because just as Matthew had risen to his feet and was walking out of the parlor, Mrs. Deverick entered the vestibule with Joplin Pollard following behind and Gretl in the rear almost slobbering with evil anticipation of a fiery scene.

"I *tolt* him!" Gretl was hissing, even though there were no esses to be hissed. "Thet rud boy!"

"And here he stands," Pollard said, with a dry smile that did not involve the eyes. "Hello, Mr. Corbett. Just leaving, I presume?"

"Just leaving, Mr. Pollard."

But before Matthew could get out the door there was a formidable presence in a black funeral gown and hat with a black-lace veil over the face that had to be passed, and this was going to be no easy voyage. Mrs. Deverick set herself between him and the outside world, and one of her black-gloved hands rose up in front of his face with a lifted index finger that had the power, like the wand of a witch, to stop him in his tracks.

"One moment," Esther Deverick said quietly, her voice as frosty as a January eve. "What are you doing here, on our day of sorrow?"

Matthew dug deep but couldn't find anything to say. He saw Gretl grinning beyond Joplin Pollard.

"Mother?" Robert stepped forward. "Mr. Corbett was kind enough to bring us the new broadsheet." He lifted his right hand, and in it was the *Earwig*.

"I have one already." Mrs. Deverick lifted her black-gloved left hand, and in it was the *Earwig*. "Would someone care to tell me who this young man *is*?"

"Matthew Corbett is his name," Pollard spoke up. "A clerk for Magistrate Powers."

"A *clark*!" Gretl nearly cackled.

"He's the young man featured in the article," said Pollard. "You said you wished to meet him, not an hour ago. Here he is, at your command."

"Yes, isn't that so very convenient." The woman lifted her veil. Her narrow dark brown eyes under thin-pencilled brows and her white, high-cheekboned face made Matthew think of an insect, one of those preying things that ate their mates. Her hair, a fixed mass of elaborate curls, was so black it had to be either a wig or poured from a bottle of India ink. She was thin and small, actually, with a fashionably cinched waist for a woman her age, which Matthew guessed at between fifty and fifty-five, about three or four years her deceased husband's junior. It was as much the voluminous folds of the gown as her queenly bearing that made her seem to fill up the vestibule with no possible escape for Matthew until she deigned to free him. Which she did not. "I asked you what business you have here. Close that door, Mr. Pollard."

Thunk, it went.

"Speak," said Mrs. Deverick.

Matthew had to first clear his throat. He was painfully aware of all the eyes watching him. "Pardon my intrusion, madam. I . . . well, I was going to say I was passing by, but that would be an untruth. I came here for the purpose of interviewing your son concerning Mr. Deverick's murder."

"Now is probably not the time, Corbett," Pollard cautioned.

"Did I require you to *intercede* for me, sir?" The narrow dark eyes flicked at Pollard like a whipstrike and then returned to Matthew. "On whose authority do you conduct this so-called interview? The printmaster? The high constable? Talk, if you have a tongue!"

Matthew felt a bit weak-kneed under this barrage, but he steeled himself and said, "My own authority, madam. I want to know who killed Dr. Godwin, your husband, and Eben Ausley, and I intend to pursue the matter to the best of my ability."

"I forgot to tell you," Pollard offered, "that Mr. Corbett has the unfortunate reputation of being what might be called in impolite circles a 'sammy rooster.' His crowing and bluster seem to exceed his good taste."

"I consider myself a competent judge of taste, good or bad," came the rather stinging reply. "Mr. Corbett, how is it that you think yourself suited to pursue this subject when the town has a high constable employed to do so? Isn't that a presumption on your part?"

"I imagine it is. I'm presuming from prior experience and observation that Mr. Lillehorne couldn't pursue his path from his bed to his bedpan."

Pollard rolled his eyes, but the lady of the house showed no response.

"I think there was a common bond among the three victims," Matthew went on, before he lost his momentum. "I think the Masker is not an errant lunatic, but a cunning and very sane killer—if one may call murder an act of sanity—determined to make some kind of statement. If I can deduce that statement, I believe I can unmask the Masker, as it were. Others may yet die before that happens, I don't know. I assume the Clear Streets Decree is going through?"

Still Mrs. Deverick didn't speak. At last Pollard said, "Tonight the taverns will close at eight o'clock. The decree begins at half past eight. We're going to fight it with a petition, of course, and we fully expect to have this unfounded burden lifted after—"

"Save your red rag for the court." Mrs. Deverick continued to stare forcefully into Matthew's eyes. "Why have I never heard of you?"

"We turn in different circles," Matthew said, with a slight bow of respect.

"And what's in this for you? Money? Fame? *Oh*." Now a light seemed to appear in those eyes and a fleeting smile crossed the thin pursed lips. "You want to show Lillehorne *up*, don't you?"

"I have no need to show anyone up. I strive for the solution of the matter, that's all." But even as he said this, he realized he'd been stuck with a small sharp knife of truth. Maybe he *did* want to "show Lillehorne up," as she so acidly put it; or, more to the point, he wanted to demonstrate to the town that Lillehorne was ineffectual, buffle-headed, and probably corrupt as well.

"I don't believe you," Mrs. Deverick replied, and let it hang. Then she cocked her head to one side as if inspecting an interesting new growth that had sprouted in her garden. She was trying to decide if it was a flowering plant or a noxious weed. When Pollard made a noise to speak, Mrs. Deverick lifted that single commanding finger again and he instantly shut his mumbler.

To Matthew Mrs. Deverick said in a low, calm voice, "There are three things that greatly displease me. The first being an uninvited visitor. The second being the theory that my husband was in any way associated with the two deplorable men whose names you have spoken. The third being a certain imposter to civility on this street named Maude Lillehorne." She paused and, for the first time it seemed to Matthew, blinked. "I will choose to overlook the first according to your motive and I will grant you a certain small amount of leeway on the second according to your curiosity. As to the third," she said, "I will pay you ten shillings to discover the Masker's identity before there's another killing."

"*What?*" Pollard sounded as if he'd been struck in the bellypipes.

"Every night the decree continues, the Deverick family will lose money," the woman continued, still solely addressing Matthew. "I agree that the high constable is beyond his depth in this situation. I would like to see him—and by extenuation his wife—skewered on the wit of a magistrate's clerk. *If* you have wit enough, which will remain to be seen. Therefore I wish this problem to be solved before Lord Cornbury is given more reason to drag the decree out, court or no court. Ten shillings is my offer, and it is an offer of which I believe my husband—God rest him— would have approved."

Pollard said, "Madam, may I give advice that you not—"

"The time for advice is over. It is time for action, and I believe this young man may save the day for us." She turned her face toward Pollard. "My husband lies *dead*, sir. He will not rise like Lazarus. It is up to *me* now, to guide this endeavor until Thomas arrives." She didn't even pretend to acknowledge that Robert stood only a few feet away. Then, once more facing Matthew, "Ten shillings. Find this murderer before he strikes again. Yes or no?"

Ten shillings, Matthew thought. It was an outlandish amount. It was more money than he'd ever been paid in one sum in his life. He thought he must be dreaming, but of course he said, "Yes."

"If there's another killing, you get not a duit. If the high constable achieves the unlikely goal of solving this problem, you get not a duit. If the individual is uncovered by any other citizen, you—"

"Get not a duit," Matthew said. "I understand."

"Good. Then there's one further thing. I wish to know *first*. Not for the sake of revenge or any un-Christian motive, but . . . if there is indeed any connection between the three, I wish to be notified before Mr. Grigsby can print it for the town to devour."

"Forgive me," Matthew said, "but that sounds as if you might . . . how shall I say this? . . . have some reason to be concerned."

"My husband kept much to himself," she replied. "It was his nature. Now please leave, as I must rest before the funeral."

"May I return at a more convenient time and continue the interview? Both with yourself and your son?"

"You may write your questions down, give them to Mr. Pollard, and they will be contemplated."

Contemplated did not necessarily mean *answered*, Matthew thought, but he was in no position to contradict. "Very well."

"Good day, then. And I shall add *good hunting*." With that curt dismissal, she moved past him with a stormy rustle of stiffened fabric and lace, motioning for Robert to accompany her.

On Matthew's way out the door, which Gretl held wide for his exit, Pollard said, "Wait at the curb a moment and I'll give you a lift. I'm heading back to the office."

"No thank you," Matthew decided. "I think better when I walk." He went out and the door was shut at his back with a resounding finality. He didn't care. He strode in the sunlight past the waiting carriage and driver along Golden Hill Street west toward the Broad Way.

It occurred to him that, Herrald Agency or not, he'd just been hired to solve his first problem as a private investigator.

twenty

B Y TEN O'CLOCK on Saturday morning, Matthew reckoned that he had lunged forward and stabbed a bale of hay with his rapier about a hundred times. Now, approaching twelve, he was going through slow-motion fencing lessons with Hudson Greathouse in the carriage-house, as pigeons spectated from the rafters and the heat-sweat rolled down Matthew's face and back under his sodden shirt.

Greathouse seemed above such concerns as sweltering heat and physical discomfort. While Matthew struggled to keep his breath and his balance, Greathouse breathed with ease and moved nimbly to demonstrate the half-pace, whole-pace, slope-pace, encroachment, and circular-pace, and when Matthew happened to relax his grip he found his sword flicked from his hand by a sudden powerful movement that left his fingers thrumming and his face screwed up with anger.

"How many times do I have to tell you to keep that thumb locked down? And getting mad won't help you win a fight," Greathouse said, pausing to mop his forehead with a cotton cloth. "Just the opposite. If you try to play chess in anger, what happens? You stop thinking and start reacting, and then you're playing to your opponent's pace. The key to this is keeping your mind calm, your rhythm intact, and your options open. If your opponent steals your rhythm, you are *dead*." He pushed his sword down into the soft ground and rested his hand on the pommel. "Is any of this getting through?"

Matthew shrugged. His right arm and shoulder were just dull throbbing pieces of meat, but damned if he was going to do any complaining.

"If you want to say something," Greathouse growled, "then *say* it."

"All right." Matthew pushed his sword down into the ground as well. He felt as if his face was twice its size and the color of a ripe tomato. "I don't know why I'm having to do this. I'll never become a swordsman. You can teach me all day and all *year* about these foot-movements and circulations and what-not, but I don't see the reason."

Greathouse nodded, his expression calm and impassive. "You don't see the reason." It was a statement, not a question.

"No sir."

"Well then, I'll try to explain this in a fashion you might understand. First of all, Mrs. Herrald requires this training. She has some strange notion that there may be danger in your prospective line of work, and she expects you to live beyond your initial encounter with a frog-bellied ruffian who wields his sword like a hayseed's pitchfork. Secondly, *I* require this of you, both as an education in self-confidence and as a reawakening of the physical strength you have put to sleep amid your drowsy books. Thirdly . . ." Here he stopped, his brow knit. "You know," he said after a few seconds' pause, "you may be right, Matthew. All these time-honored and rational foundations of fencing technique may be just so much fundament to you. What care you for the thwart, or the imbrocatta, or the understanding of wards? After all, you are such a *smart* young man." He pulled his rapier up from the ground and brushed dirt off the gleaming steel. "I imagine you can only learn and appreciate the use of a rapier the same way you learned to play chess, is that correct?"

"And what way would that be?" Matthew asked.

"Trial and error," came the reply.

It was followed by a tongue of lightning that came at him so fast he barely had time to suck in a breath, much less jump back out of range. He realized in a split-second of decision that this time Greathouse's rapier was not going to feint in and withdraw; the shimmering blade-tip was aimed straight for the middle button on his shirt and just that fast his aching shoulder drew his arm up and the two swords rang together. The hum of the blades vibrated up Matthew's arm, down his spine, and through his ribs as the attacking rapier was turned aside. Then Greathouse was lunging forward again, crowding Matthew's space, angling his body slightly so the blade was going to strike Matthew's left hip. Matthew watched the sword coming in as if in slow-motion, his singular power of concentration taking hold to shut out everything in the world save the rapier intent on piercing his soul-cage. He stepped back, keeping his form for that was the most efficient use of speed, and struck aside the blow but almost too late, as the blade grazed his hip and snagged breeches-cloth in its passage.

"Damn it!" Matthew shouted, backing away toward the wall. "Are you mad?"

"I am!" Greathouse hollered in return. His eyes were wild and his lips tight. "Let's see what you've got, Chess Boy!" With a look of determination that scared Matthew out of all sense of pain or fatigue, Greathouse pressed in to the attack.

The first move was a feint to his left side that Matthew misjudged and tried to parry. Greathouse's blade came sweeping past Matthew's shoulder in a forehand cut that made the air sizzle like a sausage on a hot pan. Matthew staggered back, almost falling over the haybale he'd so thoroughly killed earlier in the day. Greathouse drove in at him again, the rapier's wicked point coming for his face, and it was all Matthew could do to knock the blade aside the best he could and back away another few steps to find breathing room.

Now Greathouse, grinning like a demon, cut at Matthew's legs but Matthew saw the strike coming, locked his thumb down, and parried the blade away with a blow that sounded more like the crack of a pistol than the meeting of steel. For an instant

Greathouse's torso was open and Matthew thought to bring his blade back in line, lunge forward, and give the brute a scare, but almost as soon as the thought took hold his rapier was knocked aside and he jerked his head back as a glint of steel flashed two inches away from the tip of his nose. It would not do to return to New York noseless, Matthew thought as he again retreated, the sweat beaded on his face and not all of it from simple exertion.

Still Greathouse came on, feinting left and right though Matthew had begun to read cues in the man's movements—extension of shoulder and set of the forward knee—to determine strike from disguise. Greathouse suddenly went low and then angled the rapier upward in a lunge that Matthew thought would have driven through a man's lower jaw and out the back of his neck, but fortunately Matthew was having none of it and had put more distance between them.

"Ha!" Greathouse suddenly shouted, combining the noise of insane joviality with a thrust at Matthew's ribs on the right side that Matthew was just able to clash aside. But it was a weak blow, for Greathouse's sword swung around like a deadly wheel and now came for Matthew's ribs on the side sinister. This time Matthew stood his ground. He gritted his teeth and parried the strike with his rapier as the man had taught him, *forte* against *feeble*.

Yet there was nothing remotely feeble about Hudson Greathouse. He backed up a step only and then came on the attack again with tremendous power, a lion in its element of mortal combat. When Matthew parried the blade—this time only by the thin whisker of a skinny man's beard—he felt the strength of Greathouse's blow nearly not only remove the sword from his hand but his shoulder from its socket. Another strike darted in at his face almost before Matthew could see it coming, more a silvery glint like a fish streaking through dark water. Matthew jerked his head aside but felt a bite as his left ear was nicked before he could get his own rapier up on guard.

My God! he thought with a surge of mortifying fear. *I'm bleeding!*

He backed away again, his knees gone wobbly.

Greathouse slowly advanced, his rapier held out at extension, his face damp with sweat, and his red-shot eyes turned toward some remembered battlefield where heads and limbs lay in bloody heaps.

It came to Matthew to shout for help. The man had lost his mind. Surely if Matthew yelled loudly enough, Mrs. Herrald would hear it. He presumed she was in the house, though he hadn't seen her today. God only hope she was in the house! He started to open his mouth to let loose a caterwaul and then the frightening mass of Hudson Greathouse sprang upon him swinging the rapier's brutal edge at Matthew's head.

Matthew could only respond instinctively, trying to put order to the collection of bewildering sword-facts that rattled in his brain. He locked his thumb down tight, tighter than tight, breaking-point tight, judged the distance and speed, and deflected the attacking rapier with his own blade. But suddenly Greathouse's sword was coming at him from a lower angle—a silver blur, a murderous comet—and yet once more Matthew turned aside the blow, the noise ringing through the carriage-house and the shock almost loosening his teeth. Greathouse himself seemed to be a distortion of the heated air, a monstrous creature half-human and half-weapon as the rapier flashed and feinted high, feinted low, flicked to left and right, and then struck like a serpent. Again Matthew parried it aside just short of his chest, but when he retreated two more steps his back met a wall.

He had no time to scurry away from this trap, for his enraged teacher was on him as the thunder follows the lightning. Matthew just had an instant to get his sword angled up across his body and then Greathouse's blade slammed into his rapier, locked *forte* to *forte* as the man pushed in on him with crushing strength. Matthew held on to his sword, trying to resist what he knew to be Greathouse's intention to tear it from his hand by brute power alone. The blades made a *skreek*ing sound as they fought each other, steel sliding against steel. Matthew feared his wrist was about to break. Greathouse's face and glaring eyes seemed as big as demonic planets, and it occurred to Matthew at this moment near bone-breakage that the man smelled like a goat.

Abruptly the pressure against his rapier was gone. Greathouse said, "You are *dead*."

Matthew blinked. He felt something sharp jabbing into his stomach and when he looked down he saw the black handle of a six-inch-long dagger gripped in the man's left hand.

"Some hide documents," Greathouse said, with a tight smile. "Others hide knives. I just sliced your stomach open. Your insides should begin to boil out in a few seconds, depending on how much you scream."

"Lovely," Matthew managed to reply.

Greathouse stepped back and lowered both rapier and dagger. "You *never* let your opponent get that close to you. Do you understand? You do whatever you have to do to keep a sword's distance. You see my thumb, how it's locked on that handle?" He lifted the dagger to show Matthew his grip. "Nothing but a broken wrist could stop me from driving that blade all the way through your bread-basket and, believe me, into the stomach is where a knife will go when you're caught at close quarters. The wound is painful and gruesome and puts an end to all arguments."

Matthew took a deep breath and felt the carriage-house spin around him. If he fell down right now he'd never hear the end of it, so by God he was *not* going to fall. One knee may have sagged and his back bent, but he kept on his feet.

"You all right?" Greathouse asked.

"Yes," Matthew answered, with as much grit as he could muster. He wiped sweat out of his eyebrows with the back of his hand. "Doesn't seem a very gentlemanly way to kill someone."

"There *is* no gentlemanly way to kill." Greathouse slid the dagger into the sheath at his lower back. "You see now what a real fight is like. If you can remember your technique and use it, fine. That would put you at an advantage. But a real fight, when it's either kill or be killed, is a nasty, brutish, and usually very quick encounter. Gentlemen may duel to draw blood, but I can promise—*warn* is the better word, I suppose—that you'll someday cross swords with a villain who'll long to get a short blade in your belly. You'll know him, when the time comes."

"Speaking of gentlemen and time," came a quiet voice from the doorway, and Matthew looked over to see Mrs. Herrald standing framed in the sunlight. He had no idea how long she'd been there. "I believe it's lunchtime for you two gentlemen. By the way, Matthew, your left ear is bleeding." She turned around and, regal as ever in a dark blue dress with white lace at the collar and cuffs, walked away toward the house.

Greathouse threw a clean cloth to Matthew. "Just a nick. You dodged the wrong way."

"But I *did* do well, didn't I?" Matthew took note of the man's sour expression. "All right then, *fairly* well?"

"You only struck one offensive blow. Or *attempted* to strike one, that is. It was weak and completely undisciplined. You did not keep your form, as your body was too wide a target. You have to remember to keep your body *thin*. Never once did you step forward to meet an attack, even as a feint. Your footwork was pure panic, and you were always retreating." He took the rapier from Matthew and wiped it down before placing it in its scabbard.

"So," Matthew said a little indignantly to hide his disappointment, "I did nothing right?"

"I didn't say that." Greathouse put Matthew's rapier on the armory's hooks. "You met two of my best blows with very well-done parries and you were reading some of my feints. The rest I let you get away with. In fighting even a middling swordsman, you would have been punctured at least six times. On the other hand, I left myself open several times and you did nothing to seize the advantage." He looked at Matthew as he wiped down his own rapier. "Don't tell me you didn't *see* your opportunities."

"I told you before, I'm not a swordsman." The more he fiddled with his ear, which was cut near the top, the more it stung so he left it alone. The cloth was marked with a blotch of blood, but the wound was not so large nor as grievous as it felt.

"That may be so." Greathouse sheathed his sword and put it

on the hooks. "But I intend to make you one, in spite of yourself. You have a natural speed and balance that I find very promising. Also, you have a good sense of measure. I like how you kept your sword up and didn't let it fall. And you're a lot stronger than you look, I'll say that for you. The most important thing is that you didn't let me run over you, and twice I really tried to knock that sword out of your hand." Greathouse motioned with a lift of his chin. "Come on, let's get our lunch and we'll return to this in an hour or so."

This waking nightmare was not yet over, Matthew realized with a sinking heart. He bit his tongue to keep from saying anything he might regret and followed Greathouse out of the humid interior.

It had been an interesting morning. When Matthew had gotten Suvie from the stable, Mr. Winekoop had given him the news of the night. Three tavern owners, including Mother Munthunk, had refused to close up at eight o'clock and had been taken to the gaol by a group of constables headed by Lillehorne himself. A fight had ensued between the lawmen and the Munthunk brothers, who valiantly tried to free their *mater* and thus joined her behind bars. The festivities had been just beginning, according to Winekoop's ear. Before ten, there were twelve men and two New Jersey prostitutes in the gaol as well as the others, which made that place the scene of a merry crowd. One of the constables, challenging a group of decree-breakers on Bridge Street, had been kicked in the stones and anointed with a piss-bucket. Someone had pelted City Hall with rotten tomatoes and after midnight a rock had broken one of the windows in Lord Cornbury's manse. All in all, a fine New York summer's eve.

But, so far as Winekoop had heard, there had been no murder last night. The Masker, it seemed, was after all a man cognizant of official decree and had stayed home from the party.

Lunch was a bowl of corn soup with a slice of ham and a thick piece of rye bread, served not in the house but on a table set up under an oak tree that overlooked the river. A pitcher of water was much appreciated by Matthew, who gulped down two glasses before Greathouse told him to drink slowly. Matthew had earlier given the man a copy of the *Earwig* brought from town, primarily to show the announcement on the second page, but it was the article on the Masker's activities that had caught Greathouse's interest.

"So," Greathouse said as they ate, "this Masker person. A third murder, you say?"

Matthew nodded, his mouth full of the ham and bread. He'd told Greathouse about the killing of Eben Ausley, but had omitted his own role in that evening's events.

"And no one has a clue as to who this individual might be?"

"No one," Matthew said after he'd had another drink. "Well, Mr. McCaggers believes from the skill and quickness of the cutting that the Masker may have had experience in a slaughterhouse."

"Ah yes, the coroner. I hear some strange stories about him. For instance, he can't abide dead bodies?"

"He does have some difficulties, yes. But he's very good at his job."

"How does he manage?"

"He has a slave, by the name of Zed, who helps him." Matthew took a spoonful of the corn soup and then another bite of the ham. "Lifting the bodies, cleaning up the . . . um . . . leavings and so forth. An interesting man, that one. Zed, I mean. He can't speak, as he has no tongue. He has scars or some kind of tattoos all over his face."

"Really?" There was an odd note of interest in Greathouse's voice.

"I've never seen a slave quite like him," Matthew continued. "Very distinctive and not a little unsettling."

"I would imagine so." Greathouse sipped from his water glass and gazed down upon the slowly moving river. He said after a moment, "I should like to meet that man."

"Mr. McCaggers?" Matthew asked.

"No. Zed. He might be of use to us."

"Of *use*? How?"

"I'll let you know after I've met him," Greathouse answered, and Matthew knew that was his final word on the subject for now.

"I should tell you," Matthew ventured after a little time had passed and his lunch was almost history, "that I'm to be paid ten shillings by Deverick's widow if I discover the Masker's identity before there's another murder. I had an encounter with her yesterday, and that offer resulted from it."

"Good for you." Greathouse sounded indifferent. "Of course it would be a pity if the Masker murdered *you* before you could be of value to the agency."

"I just wanted you and Mrs. Herrald to know. Actually I could put the money to good use."

"Who couldn't? Well, the only problem I could see is if some official contacted the agency to do the same job. Then we'd have a little conflict of interests, wouldn't we?"

"I seriously doubt if anyone representing the town will ask for help. High Constable Lillehorne wouldn't stand for it."

Greathouse shrugged and poured himself the last of the water. "Go on about your little investigation, then. I doubt you're up to that task yet, but at least you'll get some experience."

The way Greathouse had expressed that rankled Matthew to the marrow of his bones. *I doubt you're up to that task yet.* This man was becoming insufferable! *Your little investigation.* He prided himself on his investigative skills, on his ability to ferret out answers to the difficult questions, and this lout sitting here was nearly mocking him. His ear wound was still hurting, he was tired, and his last clean shirt was a sweat-rag. And here this man sat before him all but sneering at him.

Matthew pushed down his anger and said off-handedly, "I've also gleaned a new item of interest from Mr. McCaggers."

Greathouse leaned his head back so the sun could shine into his face through the oak branches. He closed his eyes and appeared to be about to catch a nap.

"The murder of Eben Ausley was not the third here lately. It was the fourth. A body was found in the Hudson River a few days before Dr. Godwin was killed. It washed up on a farm two or three miles north of here, as a matter of fact."

There was no response from Greathouse. Matthew expected to hear him start snoring at any minute.

"It was an unidentified young man," Matthew went on, "who seems to have been murdered by a mob. Mr. McCaggers counted eight stab wounds, all from blades of different shapes and widths. Also, the man had no eyes."

With the mention of that last word, Greathouse opened his own eyes and squinted up at the sun.

"The body was in poor condition, having been in the water for at least five days, so Lillehorne ordered Zed to bury it where it was found. One other interesting—and disturbing—fact is that the wrists were bound behind him with cords." Matthew waited for some further response, but there was none. "I'm the only other person to know about this. So you see, I *do* have a little value as a—"

Greathouse suddenly stood up. He stared out upon the river. "Whose farm?"

"Sir?"

"The farm where the body washed up. Whose farm?"

"John Ormond. It's about—"

"I know Ormond's farm," Greathouse interrupted. "We've bought some produce from him. How long in the water, did you say?" Now Greathouse shifted his gaze to Matthew and there was nothing left of naptime. "Five days?"

"Five days is what Mr. McCaggers presumed." This line of interest was making Matthew more than a bit nervous. He'd meant this just as an example of how he could both obtain and retain information, and now it was taking on a life of its own.

"Found how many days before the doctor's murder?"

"Four."

"And that was more than two weeks ago?" Greathouse made a face that looked as if he'd bitten a lemon. "It won't be a pretty sight, that's for sure."

"*Sir?*"

"Stand up," Greathouse commanded. "We can let the afternoon's lesson go. Right now we have an errand."

Matthew stood up, but slowly and with the greatest of trepidation. Greathouse was already striding toward the carriage-house. "What errand?" Matthew asked.

"We're going to dig up the body," Greathouse replied over his shoulder, and Matthew felt his guts go all twisty-quisty. "Come on, let's get the shovels."

twenty-one

UP UNTIL THE MOMENT Hudson Greathouse went into the barn and began to saddle a second horse for Matthew, this one a lean gray stallion far more spirited than the placid Suvie, the young clerk had thought this so-called errand was another of Greathouse's rather irritating jokes. But as Matthew soon came to realize, the joke was on him; with shovels bound up and tied to the saddle of Greathouse's own horse, they were on their way to exhume a corpse.

The sun was warm, the air still, the summer birds singing, and the insects awhirr in the gilded shafts of light spilling through the boughs. Matthew struggled to keep his horse in control. The beast was much stronger than Suvie, headstrong as well, and kept wanting to veer off the road. "What's this creature's name?" Matthew asked toward Greathouse's back.

"Buck," came the reply. "He's a fine animal. Just let him have his head, he'll do all right."

"He wants to leave the road!"

"No, he wants to pick up his *pace*. You're holding him back like an old woman." Greathouse suddenly urged his mount into a canter and said, "Come on, I want to get there before tomorrow!"

Matthew just had to press Buck's sides with his knees to cause the horse to nearly leap forward, an action for which Matthew was

totally unprepared and almost unseated into a tangle of green bri-
ars. He hung on, resisted the urge to pull the horse back to a more
comfortable speed—and somewhat doubted Buck would heed
him, anyway—and soon he was travelling neck-to-neck with
Greathouse's horse instead of nose to tail.

They followed the road through a wilderness of thick-trunked
trees that Matthew thought could never be felled by a hundred
axemen working a hundred days. Redbirds fluttered in the high
branches and a fox skittered across the road as the horses
approached. After a while, Greathouse settled his horse back into
an easy trot and Matthew did the same with Buck. A stone wall
soon appeared along the left side of the road, and knowing the
Ormond farm must be within a mile or so, Matthew said, "What's
this about? We're not really going to dig up a grave, are we?"

"We didn't bring shovels to knock apples out of the trees."

"But *why*? What's so urgent about this particular corpse?" He
got no answer, so he tried another tack. "I told you everything Mr.
McCaggers told *me*. There's nothing more to see. Anyway, I don't
think it's proper to disturb the dead."

"I won't tell if you won't. There's the turn ahead."

Greathouse took the next road to the left and Matthew kept
up with him, or rather had no choice as he had begun to suspect
Buck had been trained to follow Greathouse no matter who
thought they guided the reins. "Listen," Matthew persisted, "I'm
not used to this kind of thing. I mean . . . what's the point of it?"

Greathouse abruptly drew his horse up, causing Buck to stop
almost immediately as well. "All right," Greathouse rumbled, with
a nod. "I'll tell you why. The way you described the murder set me
to remembering something. I can't tell you what that is. Not yet.
And I'm going to insist that you not mention anything of this to
Mrs. Herrald, either. Just help me dig, that's all I'm asking."

Matthew caught a note in the man's voice that he'd not heard
before. It was not exactly fear, though there was indeed an element
of that, as it was more abhorrence. Of what? Matthew wondered.
The corpse? Surely not just that, for it was likely Greathouse had
seen—and created—his share of them. No, this was something

else entirely. Something that went deep, and was yet to be revealed.

Greathouse continued on, and so Buck followed with Matthew along for the ride. In another few minutes a more narrow track turned off again to the left and this was the route they took to the Ormond farm.

It was a well-worked plot consisting mostly of apple and pear trees, along with plantings of corn, turnips, beans, and a few rows of tobacco. As the two riders approached a farmhouse of brown stones that sat beside a barn and animal corral, chickens squawked and fluttered for shelter and a half-dozen hogs looked up inquisitively from their pen. From the barn appeared a burly man wearing a wide-brimmed straw hat, a brown shirt, and gray trousers with patches on the knees. Accompanied by a barking cinnamon-colored dog, he came out to meet his visitors as a wide-hipped woman opened the farmhouse's door and two small children peered around her skirts.

"Mr. Ormond!" Greathouse called as he reined his horse. "It's Hudson Greathouse."

"Yes sir, I recall ye." The farmer had a long dark beard and eyebrows as thick as wooly caterpillars. He eyed the shovels. "Plannin' to dig up your own turnips?"

"Not exactly. This is my associate Matthew Corbett. May we step down?"

"Come ahead."

That civility done, Greathouse waited until the dog had calmed down and was content to lope around sniffing at everyone's shoes before he continued. "It's been brought to my attention," he said, "that a body was discovered on your property."

Ormond regarded the ground and pressed a stone with the toe of his boot. He said in a slow, thick voice, "True enough."

"And it was buried beside the river?"

"Where it come up." He lifted his gaze and took stock of the shovels again. "Oh, Mr. Greathouse! I wouldn't want to be doin' what you've got a' mind."

"Mr. Corbett and I are not what you might call constables, in the strictest sense," Greathouse explained, "but we *are* representatives of the law. I feel it's my duty—our duty—to examine the corpse."

Speak for yourself, Matthew thought. The sun seemed terribly warm, and more brutal than bright.

"Not much left," said Ormond.

"We'd still like to look."

Ormond drew in a long breath and let it slowly leak out between his teeth. "I'd best put the dog in the house. Come on, Nero! Come on, boy!"

Greathouse unbound the shovels from his saddle and gave one to Matthew, who took it as if it were a venomous reptile. When the dog was put away and the wife and children also behind the closed door, Greathouse and Matthew walked with Ormond along a wagon track that led across the orchard.

"Nero found him," Ormond said. "Heard the dog barkin' up a fury, thought he'd treed a bobcat. Thank the Lord my children didn't go runnin' down there. I went to town that very afternoon, walked right into City Hall and asked for the biggest constable they've got."

Matthew might have made an inner comment about this statement, but he was too fixated on the river he'd begun to see beyond the trees.

"They said they couldn't handle him. Gettin' him from here to town, I mean," Ormond went on. "So I said just bury him. The coroner wrapped him up with a bedsheet and that big slave put him under. He's over this way here."

They came out from the orchard and there was the shimmering blue expanse of the river winding between the forested banks. Ormond led them about forty yards farther to a mound of dirt with a headstone of three ash-colored rocks. "Washed up there, he was." Ormond stood on a flat boulder and pointed down the hillside to a dead tree that had uprooted and fallen into the water. "Hung in those branches."

"Who has the next property upriver?" Greathouse was already at work moving aside the rocks.

"Farmer by the name of Gustenkirk. Good enough fella, keeps to himself. Wife and family, four children. Got a wooden leg."

"And the next property after that?"

"Another farm. Fella's name is Van Hullig. I spoke to him once, on the road to town. Older man, in his sixties. He can hardly speak anythin' but Dutch. After that, I guess there are some more farms 'til you get to the ferry crossin' and you're almost to the end of the island."

"The body might have been carried *across* the river," Matthew said as Greathouse got his shovel ready for the first blow against earth. He looked out upon what seemed a vast unbroken wilderness on the Jersey shore. "Mr. McCaggers said the young man died from a fall. Shattered his skull and broke his neck. That would suggest a more severe cliff than a sloping hillside."

"We'll see." Greathouse struck hard with the shovel and removed the first scoop of dirt. He worked so methodically, his head lowered to the task and his eyes fixed on the grave, that Matthew felt shamed at just standing there. Matthew realized the body was coming up whether he liked it or not, so he stepped forward, clenched his teeth, and started digging.

"Gents," said Ormond uneasily, after a moment or two, "I've had my say over this fella, whoever he was, and I wish him God rest. You toss a care if I go back to work?"

"Go ahead. We'll put him back down when we're done." Greathouse had spoken without a pause in his shovelling.

"Thank you kindly." Ormond hesitated. A whiff of decay had soured the air. "You want to wash afterward, I'll get you some soap and a bucket of water," he said, and then he turned and walked quickly back toward the orchard.

Within another few thrusts of the shovel, Matthew wished he'd brought a handkerchief and a bottle of vinegar. The smell of corruption was rising from the earth. Matthew had to walk away and breathe fresh air if there was any to be found. He felt sickened and in fear of showing his lunch, but damned if he'd do that in front of Greathouse. He realized he was made stronger by his determination not to appear weak before the man.

Matthew heard the noise of Greathouse's shovel sliding into something soft. He grimaced and tried mightily to steel his insides. If anything flooded up, he'd be ruined for corn soup and ham for a long time to come.

"You can stay there if you like," Greathouse said, not unkindly. "I can finish it alone."

And I'll never hear the end of it if I stand here, Matthew thought. He said, "No, *sir*," and he walked back to the hole and what lay within.

It appeared to be simply a dirty wrapping of bedsheets, without human form. About five feet, five inches in length, Matthew figured. Death and the river would have stolen the young man's height as well as weight. It came to him that the smell of rot was not unlike that of ancient mud at the river's bottom, a heavy dark layer of accumulated matter that had settled year after year, covering all secrets with slime. He cursed the day he'd walked up those stairs to McCaggers' realm.

"All right." Greathouse put his shovel aside. "Wasn't buried very deeply, but I suppose he didn't care. You ready?"

"I am." *Not*, Matthew thought.

Greathouse took the knife from its sheath at his back, bent down and began cutting the cloth away from where he thought the head must be. Matthew bent down as well, though his face felt burned by the reek of decay. Shadows passed over him and when he looked up he saw crows circling.

As Greathouse worked with his knife, Matthew noticed something odd about the winding-sheet. In it were perhaps a dozen or more small holes, ragged around the edges as if musket balls had gone through.

One layer was cut away, and then another. At this depth the sheet took on a yellowish-green stain. River stain, Matthew thought. That's what it was, of course.

Greathouse kept cutting, and then he took hold of the sheet and gave a slow but steady pull. A section of mottled cloth ripped and fell away, and there exposed to the sun was the dead man's face.

"Ah," Greathouse said quietly, more of a gasp, or a sickened statement on the cruelty of men.

Matthew's throat seemed to close up and his heart stuttered, but he forced himself to look and not turn away.

There was no possibility of ascertaining what this man's features had been in life. Gray flesh still clung to the bone of chin and cheeks, yes, but it was not enough to form a face. The forehead was smashed inward, the nose caved, the eyes pale sockets with some kind of dried yellow matter in their depths. On the scalp was a thatch of light brown hair. As a final mockery of the life that had been, a cowlick stuck up stiff and dry at the back of the head. The mouth was open, showing broken teeth and the interior flesh and tongue that was a bloodless and terrible waxy white, and it was this sight, this last gasp that had pulled in river and mud and the secretive slime, that made Matthew go cold beneath the burning sun and turn his face toward the wilderness.

"I'm going to cut some more of the sheet away," said Greathouse, his voice strained. He began to work with the knife again, his hand careful and reverent to the deceased.

When the sheet had been cut open and pulled aside, the shrivelled victim lay in all the horror of murder, his knees pulled up in a frozen attitude of prayer and his thin arms crossed upon the chest, a gesture of Christian burial that Matthew presumed Zed had done after the cords were cut. The body was dressed in a shirt that might have been white at one time, but was now a miasmic hue of gray, green, and splattered black. The shirt was unbuttoned, probably by McCaggers for inspection, and both Matthew and Greathouse could clearly see four of the stab wounds—three in the chest and one at the base of the neck—which were vivid purple against the spoiled-milk color of the flesh. The body wore breeches whose color and fabric had turned to something nearly like mud, and on the feet were brown boots.

Matthew had to put his hand up to his mouth and nose, for the smell of this was horrendous. He saw movement in a nearby tree; a few of the crows had landed and were waiting.

"There's part of the cord." Greathouse carefully pulled at it, finding too late that it was sealed by decomposition to the chest when a long piece of skin peeled off like soft cheese. It was a thin but tough little piece of rope, frayed on both ends. "You see the marks around the wrists where he was bound?"

"Yes," Matthew said, though he didn't bend over to look too closely. One thing he did note, however. "The left hand. The thumb's missing."

"First joint only. Looks like an old injury because the bone's grown smooth." Greathouse dared to touch it, and then his hand went toward one of the stab wounds. At first Matthew thought the man was going to probe one of those purple fissures with his fingers, which would have been the last straw on this hayload, but Greathouse's hand made a circle in the air. "I see four wounds, but I'm not going to turn him over to find out if your Mr. McCaggers was accurate in his count." He pulled his hand back and looked up at Matthew. His eyes were red-rimmed, as if hazed by thick and pungent smoke. "I want to tell you," he said, "that I've seen something like this before. I can't be for certain, and I ought not to speculate, but—"

Matthew gave a cry and stepped back, his eyes the size of one of Stokely's platters. He thought it must be the shimmer of heat, or the noxious vapors rising from the grave, but he imagined that the corpse had just given a quick tremble.

"What is it?" Instantly Greathouse was on his feet. "What's wrong with you?"

"He moved," Matthew whispered.

"He *moved*?" Greathouse looked back at the corpse to make sure, but a corpse was a corpse. "Are you *mad*? He's as dead as King James!"

They both stared at the body, and therefore they both saw the body give another fleeting tremble as if awakening from its Thanatostic slumber. The movement, Matthew realized in his dumbstruck terror, was more of a *vibration* than an action of muscle and sinew, which in the case of this unfortunate had turned to calf's-foot jelly.

Greathouse stepped nearer the grave. Matthew did not, but

he heard what Greathouse did: a thin, faint chittering noise that made the hairs on the back of his neck prickle.

Even as Greathouse realized what it must be and quickly reached for his shovel, the pale amber-colored roaches boiled from the cavity of the dead man's nose and out of the open mouth like an indignant army. They rushed back and forth in a frenzy over the eyeless face and more began to stream out of the knife wounds like yellow drops of blood. Matthew thought it must have been a jarring of the body or the unwelcome heat of the sun that had disturbed them from their dank banquet hall, and now he knew what had burrowed all those holes in the winding-sheet.

Greathouse began throwing the dirt back in like a man who has seen the devil's horns pushing up from the inferno. There was no time nor need for niceties, as the soul that had departed from this husk at the bottom of the hole had to be in a better place. Matthew came forward to help, and together he and Greathouse first covered over the face with its mask of swarming insects and then shovelled dirt upon the body until it was seen no more. When the grave was a mound again, Greathouse threw aside his shovel and without a word walked down the hillside to the river. He got on his knees where earth met water and splashed his face while Matthew sat on a boulder above and let the sun steam away the cold sweat that had burst up from his pores.

When Greathouse came back up the hill, he looked to Matthew to have aged five years in a matter of moments. His eyes were dark-shadowed, his jaw slack, even his gait tired and heavy. He stopped between Matthew and the grave, sliding a sideways glance at the dirt mound to make sure nothing was crawling out. At last he gave an almost imperceptible shudder and sat down on a rock a few feet to Matthew's left. "You did well," he said.

"As did you," Matthew answered.

"I'd have liked to have gone through the pockets."

"Really?"

"No," Greathouse said. "Not really. Anyway, I'd bet my horse he was picked clean before his wrists were tied."

"I'm sure either Zed or Lillehorne inspected the clothes," Matthew said. "As much as was possible, I mean."

"Most likely," Greathouse agreed. He looked up at the crows, which had left the tree and were again circling. They cawed sharply a few times, like robbers cursing at being robbed.

Matthew also watched them go 'round. The sky seemed more starkly white now than pure blue, and the river tinged with gray. The afternoon heat had become oppressive. Across the river the breeze blew through the forest and bent trees to its will, yet where the two men sat they neither heard the noise of the wind nor felt it, for on this bank the air was thick and motionless, still holding the smell of death.

Greathouse said, "I have seen two bodies like that before. Both in England. I can't be sure, of course, that what I'm about to tell you has come to pass. I could speculate that the man might have been killed by highwaymen for his money, or murdered by the enraged occupants of a tavern for cheating at cards, or some such reason that would not explain why he was bound." He rubbed his knuckles and stared off across the river. "I think . . . this may have been done by someone whom Mrs. Herrald and I know very well."

"You *know* who did this?"

"I believe I know who may have been the . . . what would be the right word? The *originator* of this method of operation. Meaning that he might not be physically present himself, but those who follow him may be close at hand."

"If you know," Matthew said, "you should go straight to the high constable."

"Well, there's the problem. I don't know for certain. And even if I went to Lillehorne, I doubt there's much he could do." Greathouse turned his gaze toward Matthew. "Have you ever heard of someone called Professor Fell?"

"No. Should I have?"

Greathouse shook his head. "You wouldn't have, except if Nathaniel—Magistrate Powers, that is—happened to mention this individual."

Matthew frowned, completely lost. "What does the magistrate have to do with this?"

"Nathaniel is in New York *because* of Professor Fell," came the reply. "He took his family out of England to guard their lives. He left a well-established and lucrative legal career in London, because the word had gotten to him that Professor Fell was angry at a prosecution case Nathaniel was making against one of his associates. No one makes Professor Fell angry and lives very long. Unless you put an ocean in between . . . and even then . . ." He trailed off.

"So you're saying this Professor Fell person is a *criminal*?"

"A *criminal*," Greathouse repeated quietly, with a bitter smile that quickly slipped away. "London is a collection of huts. The Thames is a stream. Queen Anne is a lady with a nice chair. Yes, Professor Fell is a criminal. No one knows his first name. No one knows really if 'he' is a man or woman, or if 'he' ever was a professor at any school or university. No one has ever given an age for him or a description, but I'll tell you this: you saw the workings of his mind, when you looked upon that body in the grave."

Greathouse was silent and Matthew was silent, waiting.

"There is an underworld you can't imagine. Not even the *Gazette* frames it accurately." Greathouse's eyes were dark; he stared at nothing, yet seemed to be seeing something that stirred fear and revulsion even in his heart of oak. "In England and in Europe. It's existed for . . . who can say how long. We know the names of the most vile elements. Gentleman Jackie Blue. The Thacker Brothers. Augustus Pons. Madam Chillany. They're in the business of counterfeiting, forgery, theft of both state and private papers, blackmail, kidnapping, arson, murder for hire, and whatever else offers them a profit. For many years they've fought over territory. Over countries, as if fighting for the seats at a dinner table nearest the roast beef platter. Their gang wars have been brutal and bloody and have gotten them nowhere. But in the last fifteen years, all that began to change. Professor Fell emerged—from where we don't know—and has through guile, intelligence, and not a small amount of head-chopping—united the gangs into a criminal parliament."

Still Matthew made no response. He was focused solely on taking in what Greathouse had to say.

"How exactly Fell gained the leadership role, we don't know. We have had our informants, but the information is unreliable. More than one songbird disappeared from a cage thought to be perfectly secure. The first ended up stuffed into a trunk on a ship bound for Aberdeen. The second—a woman—was found wrapped in burlap and weighed with stones in the Cherwell River. An unfortunate swimmer came upon her, a month or so after she'd vanished. You already know in what condition both corpses were found."

"Multiple stab wounds," Matthew reasoned. "Made by different blades."

"The man had been stabbed twenty-six times, the woman twenty-two. Then both their skulls were bashed in. The cords remained around their wrists, tied behind them. They were meant to be discovered, after a certain amount of time, as a show of power. We have a theory."

When Greathouse didn't immediately continue, Matthew prodded, "I'd like to hear it."

"Mrs. Herrald came up with it, actually. Judging from the fact that both victims were stabbed front and back, but no knife wounds were struck below the waist. She thinks Fell punishes the offenders or the disobedient by running them through a gauntlet, where everyone present gets a stab, so to speak. Maybe there's even a trial of some kind, before the spectacle begins. The guilty person—guilty for violating the code of silence or behavior—is made to run this gauntlet until they're nearly dead, and then their skulls are broken. I'd say that's a powerful method to secure loyalty, wouldn't you?"

Matthew said nothing.

"Or maybe there's no gauntlet," Greathouse said. "Maybe they just throw the victims into a room and the others set on them like wild dogs. But it's the cords, you see. Only the wrists are tied, not the ankles. The victims are meant to run, or stagger as the case may be. They are meant to know there is no escape, and that death will be a slow and painful process no matter how many times they run back and forth through the blades." Greathouse wore a sickened expression, as if he were imagining a torch-lit dungeon where firelight glinted off the knives and a shadow ran pleading for life amid other shadows pledged to murder. "We think there have been others, of course, but their bodies have either not been discovered yet or have been destroyed. Or it may be that by now Fell is on the cusp of creating what we think he desires: a criminal empire that spans the continents. All the smaller sharks—deadly enough in their own oceans—have gathered around the big shark, and so they have swum even here, up this river to wherever our young man in the grave was murdered for . . . what? An act of disobedience? A refusal to bow at the proper moment, or to polish the boots of someone his senior? Who can say? He may have been an example. A lesson of the day, for a minor infraction." Greathouse ran the back of his hand across his mouth and sat slumped over, his shoulders sagging. He didn't speak for a while, as the crows cawed ever more faintly in the sky. At last he said, "I need to get out of here," and stood up.

On their way back through the orchard, carrying their dirt-smeared shovels with them, Matthew asked, "But you can't be sure about this, can you? You can't be sure that Fell is here. As you said, the man may have been killed by highwaymen."

"Yes, I did say that. And you're right, I can't be sure. Not absolutely sure, anyway. I'm just telling you what I'm thinking: this is the professor's method of vengeance, and whether *he* is here or not, someone very near is applying his . . . shall we say . . . teachings."

Before they reached the farmhouse, Greathouse stopped at the orchard's edge and caught Matthew's sleeve. "Don't mention that name to anyone, not just yet. This is between us, do you understand?"

"Yes."

"We've been expecting him or his compatriots to come to the colonies, sooner or later. That's one of the reasons Mrs. Herrald decided to make a permanent office in New York. I suppose I should've been prepared for it, but I wasn't." Greathouse's expression had changed since leaving the graveside. A few minutes before, he'd appeared almost pole-axed by this development, but now Matthew saw the color was back in his face and his eyes had that fierce old-bastardy look to them again. He was, in spite of himself, pleased to see the return. "On Monday morning I'll come to town and have a look at the property maps at City Hall," Greathouse declared. "We'll find out who owns the land up north of Van Hullig. I agree that the body might have been carried from the other side of the river, but we've got to start somewhere."

They used the soap and bucket of water Ormond offered to wash as best as possible the odor of human decay from their hands and faces, but the main use of the soap was to get its sharp green scent of pine oil up the nostrils. Greathouse thanked the farmer for his help and gave him a few small coins in appreciation. Before they mounted their horses, Greathouse opened his saddlebag, brought out his brown bottle of brandy, uncorked it, and offered the first drink to Matthew, who took down a swallow that on any other day would have set fire to his insides but on this afternoon just managed to make him feel not quite so cold. Greathouse quaffed a healthy swig, also perhaps to burn away some demons, and then swung himself up into the saddle.

The ride back to Mrs. Herrald's was done in silence. Matthew found himself actually using the reins and his knees more confidently, and though Buck gave an occasional whicker of indignation the horse seemed to appreciate the fact that his rider had taken firmer command. Matthew had figured that nothing could be worse today than what he'd already been through, not even a buck from Buck, so the devil with this horse thinking he was the master.

Matthew did note one thing, and tucked it away. From time to time Greathouse glanced back along the road they travelled, his eyes dark and darting, as if making sure that through the glare of afternoon sunlight and swirl of dust a creature to be feared was not even now bearing down on them, like a hydra of many heads, arms, and knives.

There was more to this story of Professor Fell, Matthew decided as he watched Greathouse check the road at their backs. *I've only been told a part of it.* There was still some grim—and perhaps personal—secret that Greathouse kept bound up inside himself as surely as with murderer's ropes. What that might be would have to wait for a safer hour.

twenty-two

"FORGIVENESS CAN BE our greatest strength, yet also our greatest weakness. We all may understand, with the grace of Christ, what it means to forgive an enemy. To look in the eye someone who has deceived us, or wronged us, either in private or public, and offer a hand of compassionate forgiveness. Sometimes that takes a strength beyond the ken of man, does it not? Yet we do it, if we walk with God. We put aside the injustices others have set upon us, and we continue our forward progress on this earth. Now think well on what may be the most difficult act of forgiveness for many of us. To look in the eye of the mirror and forgive *ourselves* of deceits and wrongs we have accumulated over the many seasons of life. How may we truly forgive others if we cannot come to grips with the sins of our own souls? Those sins and torments brought upon ourselves *by* ourselves? How may we approach with a fresh soul anyone in need of deliverance, if our own souls remain injured by self-inflicted wounds?"

Reverend William Wade was speaking from his pulpit in Trinity Church on Sunday morning. It was as usual a full sanctuary, for Wade was a powerful speaker and had the rare quality of mercy over his listeners; he didn't often speak more than two hours, which made him a favorite of the elderly who had to hold their earhorns. Matthew sat in the fourth row of pews, alongside Hiram and Patience Stokely. Directly behind him sat Magistrate Powers, his wife, and daughter, and in front of him was Tobias Winekoop and his family. Shutters were closed at the windows to restrain the morning sun and also, according to the church elders, concentrate the attention of the congregation on Reverend Wade and not the weather or some other outside distraction, such as the cattle pen within spitting distance. The church was illuminated by candles and smelled of sawdust and weeping pine, for construction of some kind or another was always in progress. A few pigeons fluttered in the rafters, having made a nest up there after the roof was damaged by a storm the first week of May. Matthew had heard that Reverend Wade was seen at least twice putting out a platter of seeds and bread crumbs, though the elders were incensed about the pigeon droppings getting all over the pineboards and wanted to hire an Indian to bring them down with a bow-and-arrow. So far, though, no bowstring had been pulled in Trinity Church.

"Note here," said the reverend as he surveyed his flock, "I do not speak of self-forgiveness as a golden key to unlock further sins of mind, spirit, and flesh. I do not speak of self-forgiveness as a dreamer's potion that has the power to undo all that has gone before. Far from it. I speak of self-forgiveness as Paul writes in Second Corinthians, chapter the seventh, verses the ninth, the tenth, and the eleventh. I speak of self-forgiveness as letting go of the worldly sorrow that leads to death. Children of God, we hurt and we suffer, and that is the plight of Adam. We have been commanded from the Garden for our sins, yes, and we must come to dust as the world must turn through spring to winter, but why must we waste our moments in this life burdened with sins of the heart that we *can not forgive*?"

As the reverend spoke, Matthew listened with both ears but his eyes were watching John Five and Constance Wade, who sat together—at a decent distance apart, of course—on the front pew. John wore a brown suit and Constance was dressed in dark gray, both of them models of attentiveness to the message being preached. No one would know from looking at them that they feared for the sanity of the black-garbed man at the pulpit. Neither would anyone guess from regarding Matthew that this day was any different for him than any other Sabbath he'd attended church. He did not let his gaze linger on Reverend Wade with suspicion, but rather kept his expression as remote as Heaven sometimes seemed to be in the affairs of ordinary men, and wondered what wrenching sadness was hidden behind the somber face.

Last night had been another little carnival, Matthew had heard from both Magistrate Powers and Magistrate Dawes when he'd arrived at church. Fifteen more men and three women had been arrested for breaking the decree, necessitating throwing some of the previous night's haul out of gaol to make room. A dice game at the house of Samuel Baiter on Wall Street had led to a drunken brawl in which six men had beaten each other bloody and one's nose had nearly been bitten off. At a tick past eight-thirty, Dippen Nack had put his black billyclub up between the shoulderblades of a tall, heavy-set doxy at the corner of the Broad Way and Beaver, announced an arrest, and suddenly found himself looking into the blue-shaded eyes of Lord Cornbury, who was—according to Cornbury according to Nack according to what Dawes had heard—out for an "evening constitutional." All in all, another night for the record books.

But, again, the decree must be having some impact beyond chaos and clownish hilarity, for the Masker had not added another stone to the cemetery.

Matthew's dream last night had been unsettling. He'd gone to bed dreading what would spill from his mind after that exhumation on the Ormond farm, and so he was rewarded for his trepidation.

He'd been sitting at a table in a smoke-filled room—a tavern, perhaps—playing cards with a dark figure across from him. Five cards were dealt by a black-gloved hand. What the game was, Matthew didn't know. He only knew that the stakes were high, though there was no money in evidence. There were no voices, no humpdaroo, no fiddle music, nothing but the silence of the void. Suddenly the black glove laid down not a card but a knife with a bloody blade. Matthew knew he had to reply with a card, but when he set his down it was not a card but a lantern with broken glass and a small puddle of tallow burning within. The black glove moved again across the scarred table, and there lay Eben Ausley's missing notebook. Matthew had felt the stakes were getting higher, yet the game was still unknown. He had put down his highest card, a queen of diamonds, and found it changed to an envelope with a red wax seal. Then his opponent offered a challenge, and what lay before Matthew he couldn't quite recognize until he picked it up, held it close, and by the guttering tallow realized it was the first joint of a man's thumb.

He had gotten out of bed before dawn and sat at his window watching the sky lighten, trying to arrange the pieces of his dream that way and this, this way and that. But dreams being such gossamer and fleeting impressions, only Somnus knew their riddles.

In the pocket of Matthew's coat, as he sat listening to Reverend Wade, was indeed an envelope secured not with red sealing wax but with white dripped from a common taper. It was addressed *To Madam Deverick, From Your Servant Matthew Corbett*. Inside was a piece of paper that bore three questions written as cleanly as a sword-sore shoulder would allow:

> *Would you please recount for me any discussion your late husband might have had with you concerning any business matters out-of-the-ordinary in the length of your recollection?*
>
> *Did Mr. Deverick make any recent trips, either for business or pleasure? If I may add to this query, where did he go and whom did he see?*
>
> *At the risk of rejection or dismissal, may I ask why you indicated such displeasure when I mentioned the names of Dr. Julius Godwin and Mr. Eben Ausley in connection with that of your late husband?*
>
> *I thank you for your time and helpful efforts and trust you understand this information will remain strictly confidential unless required by a court of law.*
>
>
>
> *With All Respect,*
> MATTHEW CORBETT
>
>

Even now the widow Deverick and Robert were sitting over on the right side of the church, surrounded by a company of Golden Hill residents. It seemed to Matthew, judging from the thrust of the woman's jaw and sidelong glances at her neighbors, that she wore her mourning dress with some degree of pride, as if making the statement that she was both too strong and too civilized to either collapse at her husband's funeral yesterday or to show a tear today. Her hat with its twin black and blue feathers was elegant and likely expensive, yes, but a bit too jaunty for this sorrowful world. By contrast Robert, in his pale gray suit, his face still shock-white and eyes full of dazed pain, was nearly an invisible boy.

Matthew intended to give his letter of questions not to Joplin Pollard but to the widow herself after the service had ended. For one thing, he wished not to have to wait for Monday morning to begin this inquiry, and for another he bridled at the fact that she expected Pollard to read the questions first and, in essence, censor them. So hang the instructions he'd be given, he was doing this his own way. Still, he'd liked to have included a few more personal questions, about how she and Deverick had met and their earlier life in London, just to get some background on the man, but he'd decided she was definitely not going to answer those and it was a waste of ink. Anyway, it had taken the rest of the yarrow oil rubbed into his shoulder for him to scribe the letter as it was.

Actually he was sore not only at the shoulder but in the forearm, the legs, the chest, the rib cage, and the neck, not to mention the rapier cut on his left ear though tar soap had removed the dried blood. *Moonbeam*, he recalled Greathouse saying with derision that first training session. *You've let yourself go to rot.*

Matthew realized he could be as indignant as he pleased, but it was a show put on for the sake of pride. Greathouse was right. His position as a clerk and his interests in chess and books had left him in poor condition for physical activity. Not that he planned to forsake chess and reading, as he thought these kept his mind sharp and would mean the difference between success and failure at the Herrald Agency, but he knew also from the pain in his muscles and joints that he was a house in need of reconstruction. The lack of physical endurance might not only cost him success at the agency, it might cost him his life. He needed a rapier to practice with at home, and by jingo he intended to find one.

". . . how heavy our hearts are burdened," Reverend Wade was saying, his hands clasped tightly before him atop his podium. "How heavy our souls are laden, with this tonnage of guilt we bear. We live in the sorrow of the world, dear children, and this sorrow brings death to all the great possibilities that Christ would have us know. Look at what Paul says, in that verse the eleventh. He would urge us to clear ourselves, so that our minds and souls become fresh. To clear ourselves, and let go of . . ."

The reverend stopped speaking.

Matthew had thought Wade was simply pausing to take a breath, or to fashion a particular phrase, but three seconds went past and then five and then ten and still the reverend did not speak. The ladies of the congregation who were using their fans ceased almost as one. In front of Matthew, Magistrate Powers leaned forward as if to try to urge Wade to continue. The reverend stared blankly into space for a few seconds more before he blinked and recovered himself, but his face had taken on a damp sheen.

"Let go of our *responsibilities*," he said, and then his mouth twitched as if in an attempt to recover the word. "I'm sorry, that is not what I meant to say. Let go of our self-recriminations. Our failings. Our harsh verdicts of ourselves, that prevent us from finding . . ."

Again Reverend Wade hesitated, and this time his eyes darted from face to face and his mouth moved to make words but no words were born. Matthew saw the cords in Wade's neck standing out, and the man's hands clenched together so tightly it appeared the knuckles must crack. Wade looked up toward the ceiling, perhaps searching past the pigeons for the face of God, but it seemed that even an appeal to God would not suffice, for the reverend was struck mute.

John Five stood up, but already two of the church elders were on their feet and were rushing to the pulpit. Reverend Wade watched them coming, his eyes wide as if he didn't fully understand what was happening, and Matthew feared the man was going to collapse before they reached him.

"I'm all right." It was more of a gasp than speech. The reverend lifted a hand to assure his flock, but Matthew and everyone else saw how badly it trembled. "I'm sorry, I'm sorry, but I cannot continue today."

It was a shocking moment. The sight of the normally eloquent and resolute minister being reduced to a shaking apologist stunned even Matthew, who had already seen Wade at a weak moment. But events took a quick turn as Wade's apologies were overshadowed by the sudden tolling of a bell. It was being rung from outside in the distance, its high thin cry penetrating the shutters. At once Matthew and the others knew what it was. Heard rarely, and only in case of emergency, it was the harbormaster's bell at the Great Dock raising an alarm and a summons.

Several men put on their tricorn hats and were out the door at a run. Others followed, and even some of the women pushed out to see what trouble the bell was announcing. Perhaps with relief and looking near tears, Reverend Wade turned from the pulpit like a sleepwalker and started toward the door that led to his sanctum. He was supported by the two elders and by John Five, who had gone to the reverend's side with Constance right behind him. In another moment the congregation was in a state of utter confusion and seemed to be split between those going to the reverend's aid and those leaving the church for the dock. Still the bell rang on, as pigeons flew madly about the rafters in emulation of the human disorder below.

The Stokelys were in the aisle and going toward the street. Matthew saw Magistrate Powers striding up to give his help to Reverend Wade, but Wade was almost through the door and it appeared he was being held at both shoulders and arms by a dozen hands. Familiar faces went past, this way and that, all grimly serious. Matthew watched the door close behind Wade and his knot of churchmen, and then he thought perhaps selfishly to look for Esther Deverick but she had left her pew. Her two-feathered hat was somewhere among the well-dressed contingent of Golden Hill residents going out onto the Broad Way.

Matthew decided to also get to the street. By the time he was successful at doing this through the throng, however, the Broad Way was a clatter trap of wagons, horses, and citizens on their way to the dock. Sunday might be a day strictly of sermons, Godly contemplation, and rest in other towns, but in New York business rarely took a breather and so the streets, stockyards, counting-houses, and most other establishments were nearly as busy as usual, per the discretion and religious conviction of their owners. The Golden Hillers were being helped by servants into their carriages lined up in front of the church. Matthew saw the widow's hat before he saw her, and he made his way to the carriage before the driver could flick his whip.

"Pardon me! Pardon me!" Matthew called to the woman, who was seating herself in the plush cream-colored interior across from Robert. She looked at him incuriously, as if she'd never seen him before. Matthew took the letter from his coat and held it toward her. "The questions, madam. If you'd be so kind to—"

"Were my instructions not clear?" She tilted her head, her narrow eyes devoid of emotion but for perhaps the smallest little irritated ember. "Were they muddy, or foggy, or shrouded in mist? I told you to give your questions to my lawyer. Good day."

"Yes, madam, I know, but I thought you might—"

"Good *day*," she repeated, and then to the driver: "Home, Malcolm."

The whip came down, the two horses pulled the carriage away, and Matthew was left holding the letter and feeling as if the Trinity Church pigeons had just deposited on his head their own opinions of the situation.

twenty-three

THE BELL WAS STILL being rung. It was placed atop a watchman's tower at the dock, where in turn the watchman monitored through a spyglass the signal flags from another watchtower on Oyster Island. Whatever the bell was proclaiming, its primary purpose was to call men to either take up arms to defend the harbor against attack or to crew the rescue boats. Matthew returned the letter to his coat and started walking to the dock. In another moment he caught up with the Stokelys and then almost collided with the bulk of Chief Prosecutor Bynes moving through the gathering crowd, but at the last instant he checked his progress and Bynes went past hollering for the attention of some other official just ahead.

True to the spirit of New York, the fiddlers and squeezeboxers were already out on the dockside making a din of music with their tin cups offered, two young women dressed up like gypsies were dancing around also holding out money cups, three or four higglers were hawking from wagons such items as sausage pies, cheap parasols, and spyglasses, the enterprising baker Mrs. Brown was selling sugar cookies to children from a cart, and dogs chased after cats that chased after harbor rats scurrying wildly under all these feet.

Past the coiled ropes, tar barrels, and piled crates of cargo either coming or going, past the sturdy tall-masted merchant vessels tied to the dock that groaned against the breeze and current like sleepers dreaming of the open sea, out there just this side of Oyster Island could be seen a ship coming to port. Craning his neck to get a good look, Matthew could tell that the ship was in dire straits, as the old sea dogs might say. It was missing half of its mainmast and its mainsail, and was careening back and forth like a tipsy drunk to catch wind with its foresail and jibs. Two longboats—the rescue craft—were already in the water and being rowed out by eight men apiece to give aid, for even this close to safe harbor it appeared the damaged vessel might at any moment lose all rudder and turn upon the rocks that circled Oyster Island.

With the longboats going out, the alarm bell that had called the crews to action now fell silent, leaving the noise of fiddle and accordion, higglers hollering, and general calls of relief that either a pirate fleet was not intent on sacking the town or the Dutch navy had not decided to buy its colony back with a few well-placed cannonballs.

Matthew felt someone jostle him and suddenly Marmaduke Grigsby was standing at his side. The printmaster was as disheveled as Matthew had ever seen him. He must have hurried here from a job in progress for he wore an ink-stained apron over his clothes, a great black smear lay across his bulbous chin, and black ink specks dotted the lenses of his spectacles. His white eyebrows were jumping, each to their own mysterious rhythm. "Has anyone said what ship this might be?" he asked Matthew, with a note of urgency.

"No."

"I pray it's the *Sarah Embry*. God's will, it *has* to be!"

Matthew realized Grigsby's granddaughter must be a passenger on the *Embry*, but whether that long-delayed ship was the crippled vessel struggling to make port on three sails and a prayer had yet to be seen.

Grigsby took a dirty cloth from a pocket of his apron and studiously inspected it until he could find a less dirty portion with which to wipe his eyeglasses. Matthew glanced at him and saw sweat glistening on the gnomish man's forehead and cheeks, but then again it *had* become a hot day.

"I'll buy you a cup of cider," Matthew offered, motioning toward one of the higglers who was selling the drink from a small keg on a pullcart. "Come on."

"Oh . . . yes. All right. Thank you, Matthew. I *am* a pitiful old wretch, aren't I?"

With two cups of cider down their hatches, Matthew and Grigsby stood together watching the longboat crews throw ropes to the miserable ship. It would have to be towed the remaining distance. Now that the excitement of the alarm bell had dwindled and the noontime sun was bearing down, many of the gawkers began to drift away. The fiddlers left, the squeezeboxers silenced their accordions, the gypsy dancers flitted off—probably with a number of valuables, therefore Matthew had kept his hand firmly over the pocket that held his watch and wallet—and the higglers ceased their calls and also packed up their goods and left. Perhaps twenty or so people stayed on the dock watching the nautical drama unfold.

"If it's not the *Sarah Embry*," Grigsby said after a long silence, "I fear Beryl is lost."

"Ships are always late," Matthew reminded him gently. "You said as much yourself."

"I know I did. I also know how easily a storm can break a ship in half. I'm telling you, Matthew, Beryl is lost if this is not the *Embry*." He put a hand to his forehead and rubbed between the thick eyebrows, as if to calm their excitations. "I have to tell you something I've always found amusing about Beryl. Something I always dismissed . . . but now it may be tragic." He finished his eyebrow massaging and let his hand fall to his side. "She has thought for the longest time that she is an object of bad luck. That she *foists* unfortunate happenings upon others, with no ill wish toward anyone. The first young beau she ever had an eye for was injured in a riding accident, snapped his tailbone, and lay in a hospital for a solid two months. Now he goes by the monicker of Bowlegged Ben."

"It was probably just an ornery horse that threw him," Matthew said.

"He wasn't thrown from a horse. He was trying out a new saddle in the stable, the thing somehow came uncinched, and he fell on his kadoodle right there in front of Beryl. She said she heard the bone break. The fellow wouldn't return any of her letters. I think it must have been an embarrassment for him, because he'd talked himself up as such a grand equestrian."

"That's not too terrible a tragedy. Accidents happen all the time."

"Yes, that's what I wrote to Beryl. Then soon after that was the young man who broke out in red blotches and whose face swelled up like a strawberry when Beryl accompanied him to a party hosted by his accounting firm. After he frightened his host's children to tears his future at the firm did not appear as bright as the morning star."

"Not bad luck," said Matthew, watching the ship draw nearer. "Just happenstance."

"As I told her. The other things, as well, I told her were easily explained."

Matthew's throat felt a little dry. "Other things?"

"The Marylebone fire, for one. I said she probably shouldn't have taken the goat to school, but who would have known such a thing might happen? And the coach wreck next to her house, that wasn't her fault, either. Trees often fall across the road after heavy rains. It was just the *timing* of it, so soon after she'd pruned the branches."

"I see," Matthew said, though he did not.

The longboats were doing a masterful job of rowing the decrepit ship in, and what a disaster the vessel was. The entire bow under the figurehead looked to have been caved in and repaired with odd pieces of planking, jagged wood remained thrusting upward where the main mast had been torn away, ropes trailed in tangles over the sides, and the whole picture was one of both mishap and misfunction. As the longboats neared the dock and the towed craft loomed larger, one of the harbor crew cupped his hands to his mouth and yelled, "Ho! What ship?"

Came from a man on the nearest longboat the shouted reply: "The *Sarah Embry!*"

"Oh my God! Oh Christ be praised!" Grigsby grasped at Matthew's arm to steady himself from falling, but even so his knees buckled. His weight almost took them both to the ground. "Oh Lord, she's not drowned, she's not drowned!" Tears had sprung to Grigsby's eyes behind his glasses. Matthew in decorum focused his attention on the scene as the longboats, the rowers straining, pulled the *Embry* in and the harbor crew prepared to receive lines from the ship and lash them fast to the dock.

It was perhaps fifteen more minutes before the *Embry* was tied up and its anchor rattled into the murky drink, but desperate faces could be seen crowded at the portside railing. As a gangway was secured between ship and wharf, suddenly a long-bearded man wearing blue breeches and a filthy shirt that may have once been white scrambled down the planks and fell sobbing upon the dock. He was followed along the gangway by a procession of dazed, dirty people in all manner of clothing both regal and ragged but all covered with the same gray grime and green mildew, carrying bags and bundles and staggering about as if their legs had become twirly-tops. It was impossible to discern one face from another but for the fact that all men had dirty beards, all women were bedraggled wild-haired slatterns, and all children were small filthy moppets who resembled poisonous forest mushrooms.

"My God, what a voyage this must have been!" Grigsby might be a fearful old grandfather, but he was also an opportunistic scribbler with an *Earwig* to fill. Even without quill and pad at hand, he began working on a story. "Where's the captain?" he asked two befuddled travellers who seemed to have lost their ability to understand English and so stumbled past. "The captain!" Grigsby demanded of a gray-bearded, sunken-eyed gent whose mossy suit had fit him better twenty pounds ago. "Where is he?"

The man pointed a trembling finger at the sobbing figure laid out on the dock and then staggered on, leaving one of his buckled shoes at Matthew's feet. Matthew and Grigsby both saw the captain cease his crying long enough to kiss the planks so hard his lips were surely pierced with splinters.

"Grand*da*!" came a half-shout, half-shriek.

"Beryl! Beryl!" Grigsby shouted in return, and pushed forward toward a figure the color of clay and dressed in what appeared to be tattered rags. The girl, if that's indeed what it was for under all that grime it was hard to tell, dropped the two canvas bags she'd been carrying and tried to run to meet her grandfather yet running was a proposition her sea-legs would not permit. Two long strides, a stagger and down she went upon the dock as if whacked across the back with a longboat oar. At once Grigsby knelt down to help Beryl up. Matthew reached them just as several other passengers were aiding the captain to his feet and so was directly in the line of fire when the bearded nautican bellowed like a six-cannon fusillade: *"That girl!"*

Beryl, whose bleeding nose scraped in her tumble gave her the only color beside the dingy gray hue somewhere between dust and fungus that covered her clothing, arms, legs, face, and thick-matted hair, sat up and blinked toward the captain as if she'd been slapped.

"*She* cursed this voyage!" the man hollered. He made a lurch toward her but the others were holding him back, which caused them all to lurch as one and almost go down again. "Two weeks out of Portsmouth, and she knocks Reverend Patrickson right o'r the side! That's when all our troubles started up, that's when we hit the leviathan and all *Hell* broke loose!"

Beryl was standing up, though with the splayed-leg grace of a gin-house dolly.

"That piece a' meat stuck there at the bow, and them sea lawyers swimmin' round and round day and night!" The captain's voice was harsh and strangled and altogether deranged. "You know you done it! You know you put the wrath of God on us!"

"I know," said Beryl, her own voice hoarse but remarkably calm, "I only dropped the soap."

"Only dropped the soap, she says!" the captain shouted to the onlookers. "Only dropped the soap!" Then he seemed to go completely paddy-whacky, as he tore loose from those arms restraining him and began to spin in a circle and remove his clothes as he whirled. He had his shirt and shoes thrown off and his breeches down around his ankles and was hopping along the pier clad only in stockings and tattoos when several of the townsmen seized him for the sake of propriety and someone tried to wrap a horse blanket around him. This was a failed objective, as the captain broke free, kicked off his impediments to nudity, and began to run along the dock in the direction of Hanover Square yelling "Only dropped the soap! Only dropped the soap!" with eight or ten men and three dogs chasing him down.

"That's all I did, Grandda," said Beryl, as she leaned heavily against Grigsby. She sounded listless and near fainting. "I promise . . . that's all."

"We'll get you home," Grigsby promised, his face flushed. "Get some food in you, and let you rest. Dear Christ, I thought I'd never lay eyes on you again! Matthew, would you be a friend and carry her bags to the house?"

"I will." He picked them up off the planks and found them so heavy he doubted Hudson Greathouse could have shouldered such a load, but he was determined to manage it. Grigsby began guiding his granddaughter off the dock and Matthew followed until he noted Andrew Kippering standing amid the remaining knot of people watching this sorry spectacle. Kippering squinted in the sun. He looked as if he'd just awakened from a long sleep in his wrinkled clothes.

"Marmaduke!" Matthew called. "I'll be along in a few minutes!" Grigsby waved and went on with Beryl nearly dragging at his side, and then Matthew approached the whore-mongering lawyer.

"This is a fine commotion, isn't it?" Kippering asked, his eyes bleary from perhaps the depths of a drunken stupor. Matthew guessed the man had neither combed his hair, taken a bath, nor shaved since Thursday night. "Can't a fellow get any sleep on a Sunday afternoon?"

"I have a favor to ask." Matthew set down the bags, reached

into his coat, and brought out the letter. "Would you give this to Mr. Pollard?"

Kippering made no move to accept it. "What is it?"

"It's for Mr. Pollard to give to Mrs. Deverick. Would you please make sure that he gets it? Today, if you happen to see him."

"I doubt I will. Haven't seen him since Friday afternoon. He's off on an errand for another client."

"Well then, would you *keep* it for him? And make sure he gets it first thing in the morning?"

Kippering scratched his head and yawned. He watched the harbor crew at work taking mildewed boxes and crates off the *Sarah Embry*. "I'm not working today and I want no responsibilities. Get it to Pollard yourself."

Matthew lost his temper like the flash of a powder cartridge. It perhaps had been building since Mrs. Deverick had so rudely spurned the letter, treating him like a mongrel in need of a lesson in manners, and now he struck out at this insufferable man partly because he had not stood his ground with the woman and partly because he envied Kippering's status as a lawyer, yet Kippering was seemingly intent on throwing away a career that once had been Matthew's most cherished ambition. "Oh, excuse me. I thought you were just as much Mrs. Deverick's lawyer as is Mr. Pollard." Matthew felt his mouth curve into a sarcastic smile. "But I'm sure you'd rather spend your otherwise productive time with a bottle of rum and . . ." He caught hold of the name supplied to him by the widow Sherwyn. "Grace Hester."

Kippering stared fixedly at the ship being unloaded. More people were still coming off the *Embry*, whether passengers or crewmen of this broken vessel it was hard to say, for they all were equally reeling as they stepped upon dear solidity.

Suddenly Kippering's eyes turned upon Matthew and something had crept into them that had not been present a few seconds before. Matthew couldn't say exactly what it was, but their icy blue now had centers of cold fire.

"How do you know that name?" Kippering asked, and though he meant it to sound like a relaxed, easy question—a passing inquiry between two gentlemen on a Sunday afternoon—there was just the quietest note of tension in the voice.

Matthew had the sensation of watching Greathouse approach him with the rapier, ready to carve him into small pieces if he didn't quickly learn how to defend himself. He realized Kippering had just pushed forth a pawn, and now Matthew must reply, for this game had taken a turn he didn't understand yet had to play out. "Grace Hester," he repeated slowly, searching Kippering's eyes for a further reaction. To the lawyer's credit, there was none. Matthew decided to offer a pawn of his own, and if it was a mistake he would soon know. Assuming that the dark-haired young prostitute who'd been hanging off Kippering might be the belle in question, Matthew said, "She was with you at the Thorn Bush."

"Was she?" Kippering now wore a lopsided and completely false smile.

"I think you'd better go back to Madam Blossom's and finish your bottle," Matthew said. He decided to follow Greathouse's advice and attack, if just with a sharp little dagger. "I'm sure Miss Hester would appreciate the company."

Matthew had had enough of this gent. It was a sin for him to have risen through education and hard work to the position of attorney and then do his best to throw away all his sense and sensibilities. *Trying to kill himself*, the widow Sherwyn had said. Matthew leaned down to pick up the two canvas bags and felt Kippering's arm go across his shoulders and lock with a strength no sot should possess. Before Matthew could brace his legs, Kippering was pulling him along the pier into the shadows thrown by merchant masts and looming hulls, the Mighty Walls of Empire.

After they'd gone a distance from the onlookers, Kippering released his shoulders but kept a hand clenched to Matthew's left arm. The lawyer's head leaned forward, his eyes keen and face as composed as that in an oil-painting and equally daubed with tones of somber blues and grays. "Corbett," he said, in a voice meant to travel only to Matthew's ear and no further. "I don't fully understand you or what you're about. I'm *trying*, but you're a difficult nut. Now tell me this, and I ask you to be as truthful to me as you would be to your magistrate: what is it you know about Grace Hester?"

Matthew was at a loss. At the risk of being cracked, he decided to stall. "You're not my magistrate."

"No, I'm not. But I want to be your friend. I fear you're making that a little difficult right now."

The pressure on Matthew's arm had become a bit more intense, as if in emphasis of that last statement. Matthew saw people standing about twenty yards away, beyond the edge of the ships' shadows. Kippering wasn't going to become too violent, but what the hell was this all about? "I'd appreciate not being mauled or threatened today, sir," Matthew said calmly. And then he added, "What I know about Grace Hester doesn't merit a shout for a constable, does it?"

Instantly Kippering's grip relaxed. The man stepped away from Matthew a few paces, giving them both room to breathe. Then Kippering suddenly turned upon Matthew again, his mouth partway open and a glint of realization in his eyes. "John Five found out, didn't he? And that's what your so-called meeting was about that night?"

Matthew shrugged. He felt as if he were balancing on a razor.

"Don't try to be evasive," came the stern reply. "Has he told Constance?"

Here was a question he thought he should answer as honestly as possible. "No."

"So what is it you two are after? Money? If you're thinking of picking the reverend's pockets, I can tell you they're very shallow. I thought that damned one-eared blacksmith was so much in *love* with her."

"He is. Money is not the issue."

"What, then?" Kippering advanced on him once more, but Matthew did not retreat. "Who else knows? And how did John find out?"

Matthew held out a hand, palm thrust outward, to stop the man's approach. Kippering obeyed. This certainly must have something to do with Wade's nocturnal walks, with his show of emotion before Polly Blossom's house. Matthew took a few seconds to formulate a rational answer, and then he said, "I don't know who else has this knowledge, nor do I know how John discovered it." Was it a lie, if he had no idea what Kippering was going on about? Call it a necessary fiction. "I *will* be truthful, in telling you that John and I care only for Reverend Wade's welfare. His peace of mind lately has been sorely tested."

"Yes, and no *wonder*!" Kippering said. "Wouldn't *you* be torn up about it, if you were in his shoes?"

After a pause to gauge the weather, Matthew ventured, "I would be."

"Damn right." Kippering strode away another few paces from Matthew again and stood looking out past the ships toward Oyster Island and the open sea. "I pity him, really. He thought he was strong, until this happened. Some things even the strongest man can't bear." He glanced quickly over his shoulder. "This can't get out, do you understand? Tell John. And whoever told *him* ought to be horse-whipped. John hasn't been dipping his wick at Polly's, has he?"

"No."

"Have *you* been?"

"Again, no. The secret is safe for now. I don't think it'll be travelling any further."

"Secrets have wings in this town. I told William he ought to face it and do what needs doing, but he can't make himself. So he won't listen to my advice, which is to tell the church elders to go hang if it comes to that. But he says the situation will take care of itself, and of course it will . . . though I'm not sure William will ever forgive *him*self."

William, Matthew thought. He'd had no idea Kippering and Reverend Wade were obviously either close friends or close confederates to a cause. He recalled John Five telling him at the Thorn Bush what Constance had said about a talk with her father concerning the "problem": *The one time he'd talk about it at all, he said everythin' was goin' to be fine, soon enough.*

Soon enough. Matthew wondered at those two words. They carried a fatalism about them, and also a finality.

"Give me your damn letter."

Matthew focused his attention again on Kippering, who was holding out his hand.

"Come on. The letter. I'll go put it on Joplin's desk, if it's so important."

For all his suspicions and anger toward Kippering, Matthew did feel the man could be trusted. "My thanks," he said, as he gave the letter over.

Kippering inspected the writing on the front of the envelope. "Joplin told me you fancied yourself a . . . how shall I put this . . . ?"

"A sammy rooster?" Matthew supplied.

"A smart young man who can put two and two together." Kippering held the letter down at his side. "Joplin says you probably wish to become high constable yourself, someday. Is that your ambition?"

"Hardly. I did wish to be a lawyer at one time. Now I . . ." He decided to forgo any mention of the agency. "I have other plans."

"So I take it from my impressions of you that some career involving *justice* is your ambition?"

"Yes."

Kippering grunted. "Well, being a lawyer is not all that and a pot of porridge. Many times I've had to stand and watch justice— call it *fair play*, in the world of business schemes and contracts—be subverted due to a lying tongue or a bag of dirty money. No matter how highly you begin, such things have a way of chewing your lofty ideals down to the size of rum bottles and any warm female body you can afford, so please don't begrudge my choice of exquisite brainwash."

"I don't begrudge anything. I just think a professional man in your position should fly a straighter course."

"Oh, I see." A faint mocking smile moved across Kippering's face. "The professional man should keep his hands clean, is that it? For the sake of honor? Nice sentiment, if you can live in the realm of dreams." His smile went away. "I can't."

There seemed nothing more to say, for Kippering waved a

hand at him as if to dismiss all of Matthew's precepts of gentlemanly and professional behavior. Matthew decided it was best to retreat before he made a verbal slip that would suggest he knew nothing of the mysterious Grace Hester but the name. As Matthew turned to walk along the dock and retrieve Beryl's bags, Kippering said in a hollow voice, "I'm trusting you and John not to cause Reverend Wade any further distress or complications. Do I have your word?"

"You do," Matthew replied without hesitation. "And my word for John, as well. He wouldn't think of doing anything to cause Constance grief." He had an instant of wishing he'd used the more simple word *worry* here, but his streak of bluffing still held.

"The reverend will come out of this, sooner or later. You can mark that."

"I will. Good day, sir." Matthew walked away from Kippering toward the canvas bags still lying where he'd left them. He felt light-headed. Large drops of sweat were crawling like beetles from his armpits down his sides. When he dared to glance back at Kippering he couldn't tell the man from the shadows. Then he hefted the bags and, his mind about to burst with questions that could not yet be answered, he started off toward the printmaster's house.

twenty-four

MAGISTRATE POWERS had been assigned by the chief prosecutor a portion of the cases involving decree-breakers, and Matthew was writing down the names in a ledger book when Hudson Greathouse entered the office just after eight o'clock on Monday morning.

Matthew wondered who could be more surprised at this appearance, he or the magistrate. "Hudson!" Powers said as he laid aside his own quill and stood up. Obviously he hadn't been expecting the visitor. "Good morning!"

"Morning to you, Nathaniel." Greathouse came forward and as he shook Powers' hand he also clasped the magistrate's shoulder. He gave Matthew a quick nod but did not speak. Matthew thought he looked as if sleep had not been kind to him since their grave-digging excursion.

"Glad to see you as always," Powers said. "What may I do for you?"

"You can take a walk with me," came the reply.

"Of course." The magistrate had quickly guessed, as had Matthew, that whatever the occasion of this visit, the situation was serious. And also deserving of privacy. He went to the two pegs next to the door and shrugged into his gray-striped suit coat, then put on his dove's-gray tricorn. "Excuse us, Matthew. I'll be back as soon as possible."

"Yes sir."

Powers and Greathouse left the office. Matthew wrote down another name and then paused to take stock of what the "walk" might entail. Possibly Greathouse wanted to tell the magistrate about the body, and about his suspicions concerning Professor Fell. If this chairman of crime held a grudge against Powers, it was likely Greathouse was advising him that an even earlier retirement than the end of September might be judicious.

Matthew turned his chair around to gaze out the window. Enough rain had fallen before sunrise to wet the streets, but had stopped before Matthew had gone to get his laundry from the widow Sherwyn. Now the rain was holding off, though the sky was low and milky-white. He wished he hadn't told her about the dead man, but when she'd caught him full-bore with those piercing blue eyes, pressed her hand down upon his bundle of clean shirts and breeches, leaned toward him, and said, "Well? What bit do you have for me? Hm?" he'd felt spun up by a whirlwind.

At first he'd attempted to play dumb. "Madam, I'm sorry to say I don't have anything. I was very busy over the last two days and—"

"Bullcocks and hogwash," she snapped. "You have *something*." Unsmiling, she was more a fearsome ogress than a mischievous laundress. "In fact," she sniffed at the shirt he wore and instinctively he stepped back, "you have been *into* something. What died?"

Matthew had washed this shirt in a soapbucket twice on Saturday night and had detected no further odor of the grave. The woman possessed an educated nose, to say the least.

"Listen here," she told him. "I know just about everything that goes on in this town. Things that are easy to know, things that are hard to find out. I give you something, you give me something. That's my rule." She tapped his chest. "You might wish to know someone's secret some time, and who will you go to? Me. But if you don't want to have such an arrangement—and I don't offer it to everyone—you can walk right out of here and take your business to Jane Neville, for all I care."

"Well . . . why do you offer this particular service to *me*?"

"Because," she said slowly, as if enunciating for a simpleton, "you obviously have a *use* for it. I saw that right off. You didn't ask about Andrew Kippering for the sake of idle gossip, did you? Well, some would of course, but you're not that type. Your questions have a purpose, am I not right?"

"You are." There was no use trying to hide anything from this woman. She knew the secrets in every dirty collar.

"Have to do with your work, I suppose? At the magistrate's office?"

"My work, yes," Matthew said.

"Then you understand how I could be of value to you. An ear to the ground, so to speak. And all I ask is some little bit of information in return." She looked up toward the door, as she'd thought someone was coming in, but the shadow passed. "So. A bit for a bit. What do you have?"

Matthew did indeed realize the widow Sherwyn could be of value to him, if she could ferret out information useful to the Herrald Agency. But could she be trusted to be discreet? He said, "You do realize that this information passed between us must be . . . how shall I say . . ."

"Kept on the low," she suggested.

"Exactly. For instance, I wouldn't want anyone to know I'd been asking questions."

"Wouldn't want your water to be boiled," she said.

"Right. Very uncomfortable to be sitting in boiling water. So I'd ask you to keep any inquiry I might offer here as the utmost secrecy." It occurred to him that he might even pay her a few coins, if he was ever paid, but best not to mention that possibility yet.

"Absolute secrecy." Her eyes were bright and shining again. "So what do you have?"

"Well . . . Mr. Grigsby's granddaughter Beryl arrived yesterday. It seems that two weeks out of port, the women were—"

"Washing their hair on deck while the Reverend Patrickson stood up on a stool giving a sermon. The girl dropped the soap, another woman stepped on it, slip-slid into Captain Billops and then he fell right into the preacher and knocked the man over the side. Either the preacher busted his head on the railing or he filled up with water pretty quick, because he went right down. Then they hit the whale."

Matthew nodded. He'd heard all this from one of the mildewed passengers at the Trot yesterday afternoon, but it was fascinating to him how Widow Sherwyn gathered news so quickly and completely.

"The whale was already bloody. Bit by sharks, most like. Anyway, the *Embry* plows right into this whale before a hard wind and a piece of meat the size of a haywagon gets jammed right in the bow boards. Awful mess, must've been. Then the sharks came by the hundreds. Swimming 'round and 'round that ship, day and night. Whittling that whale meat down to nothing, and the *Embry* taking water at the bow and getting lower and lower every hour."

"You've heard this already," Matthew said.

"No sooner did they get the bow shored up, but the rain comes. Then the lightning, the thunder and the big waves." The widow, her own storm, kept on rolling. "That's when the mainmast cracked and fell. And after the tempest, the sun beat down and the wind went dead and there they sat on a sea of glass for day after day. That captain went crazy and wanted to throw the girl over the side, but the others stopped him because they knew it had just been an accident. Anyway, *he* was the one who knocked the preacher over. So yes, I've already heard this, and what else do you have?"

Matthew wondered if she might want to know that Cecily was still snout-slapping his knees under the breakfast table every morning. Then he glanced quickly at the door to make sure no one was coming in, opened his mouth, and before he could think better of it said, "Another murder victim was found a few days before Dr. Godwin's death. Washed up out of the Hudson onto a farm about ten miles out of town. The high constable has been sitting on the information."

She grasped the reason why. "Four murders instead of three. It was the Masker's doing?"

"That, I can't say. I *can* say the victim was a young man, still unidentified." He decided to give her one more bit. "Multiple stab wounds."

She gave a quiet whistle of appreciation. "And how did *you* come by this?"

"Again, I can't say, but I can tell you that I've seen the body."

"At close range, I presume. I think you'd best go home and change shirts before you draw buzzards, and I might add I consider our account even, for now."

Sitting at his desk in the magistrate's office, Matthew didn't know how wise it had been to give up that information, but the widow Sherwyn was bound to be a useful fount of knowledge so count it as a payment on future business.

Perhaps ten minutes passed before Powers and Greathouse came back into the office. Matthew noted that Greathouse must have told the magistrate about Professor Fell, because Powers' face was tight and his eyes hooded. He took off his coat and hat and put them in their places on the pegs. Then he said, "Matthew, you are relieved of your duties."

"Sir?"

"Relieved of your duties," the magistrate repeated.

"I'm almost done here, sir."

"You *are* done. For today and tomorrow and forevermore. I release you from all duties of this office. You are now in the full employ of the Herrald Agency and Mr. Greathouse has an announcement for you."

Greathouse held up an envelope. "We have a letter of inquiry, delivered to the Dock House Inn yesterday afternoon. You and I are going on a trip."

"A *trip*? To where?"

"You ask too many questions for a junior associate. Don't just sit there. Put away your pen and let's get going."

Matthew set his quill in its rest. He capped his ink bottle, not without a little anxiety at realizing this might be—would be—for the final time. "Sir?" he said to the magistrate as he stood up. "Won't you be *needing* me anymore?"

Powers' severe, almost grim expression slowly softened. He summoned up a wry smile. "No," he said, "I won't be. I think you're needed elsewhere now, far away from these cases of decree-breakers, hog thieves, and pickpockets. You recall what I told you? About finding a future profession suitable to your talents? Well, I believe—as does Hudson—that you can use your talents to far greater effect out there in the world as opposed to in this office, behind that desk. Anyway, there's never going to be a shortage of clerks. So onward with you, and good luck."

Matthew didn't know what to say. Of course he'd known this moment was coming, but now that it was here he didn't think himself ready.

His hesitation clearly showed, for Greathouse said, "We have almost a day's ride ahead of us. I'd appreciate a little more speed."

Magistrate Powers sat down at his desk, shuffled some papers, and cleared his throat. He began to inspect a letter that Matthew knew had already been read this morning.

Greathouse went to the door and opened it.

"Sir?" Matthew said, and Powers looked up. "I wanted to thank you for taking me in. Giving me the opportunity of working here. I *have* learned a lot."

"I think your education is just beginning," the magistrate replied. "Now before you go, promise me you'll come to my retirement celebration. All right?"

"Yes sir, I promise."

"Good. And if you need anything, I'll be right here. For a time, at least." He motioned toward Greathouse and the open door. "Go."

Matthew still hesitated. Suddenly that open door seemed terribly fearsome, and the open world beyond it a place of uncertainty and danger. Matthew reckoned that once he passed through it in the company of Hudson Greathouse, he would be today and tomorrow and forevermore removed from the life he had known as a simple clerk. He knew Greathouse's patience would not last very much longer. It was time to move from one world into another. He said to the magistrate, "Thank you again, sir," and he started toward where Greathouse stood waiting.

The door closed, with Matthew on the outside.

Greathouse was already striding toward the stairs. Matthew had no further qualms about which direction to go. He caught up with the man and followed him down and onto the street under the low milky sky. Greathouse's big chestnut horse with the white-starred face was secured to a hitching-post nearby. "Get yourself a horse," Greathouse told him. "A man's horse with some fire in it, not that lady's pony you've been riding. You can handle it, if you could handle Buck. Take the horse for overnight, as we won't be back until sometime tomorrow. Meet me back here as soon as you're able. Oh, and take this with you and read it." He gave Matthew the envelope he'd showed. "*Today*, if possible."

"Right." Matthew hurried toward Tobias Winekoop's stable, the envelope in hand. At the stable he announced to Mr. Winekoop that he would not be requiring Suvie today, and was told in return that the only two other horses available were named Volcano and Dante, the first known to throw inexpert riders in an explosive fit of pique and the second a moody, unpredictable animal that had once bitten Chief Prosecutor Bynes on the shoulder during a Sunday afternoon outing. Matthew decided on Dante, figuring Bynes' portly bulk might have had something to do with the showing of equine teeth, and besides, he and Dante had at least a little bit in common.

As Mr. Winekoop saddled the horse, Matthew opened the envelope that had *To the Attention of the Herrald Agency* written on it. A man's handwriting, Matthew thought; the letters were steady and well-formed, yet had a spiky quality that he attributed to male expression whereas a woman's hand was more rounded. Unfolding the paper, he read:

> *Dear Sir or Madam,*
>   *My greetings and solicitations. I am Dr. David Ramsendell,*
> *chief physician of the New Jersey Colony's Publick Hospital for*

the Mentally Infirm located near the township of Westerwicke some thirty miles to the southwest of New York along the Philadelphia Pike. My attention was drawn to your printed notice due to a situation involving a patient and more I cannot say in a letter. If you would be so kind as to respond to this missive at your convenience, I am in hopes your agency might provide a valuable service to both ourselves and our patient. Whatever your fee might be in this matter, I bow to your expertise and good graces.

With All Respect and Regards,
DAVID RAMSENDELL

Dante came snorting at the bit. He was an ebony horse with a red-tinged mane and cunning eyes that Matthew thought searched for a soft place to bite. The beast was equally as big as Greathouse's horse, if not larger, and looked damnably dangerous. Winekoop gave Matthew a pear to feed him, or rather appease him with, and one crunch did away with it. Matthew decided he would keep as far away as possible from those giant teeth. He eased up into the saddle. Dante trembled and stomped around a little as Matthew said quietly, "Easy, boy, easy," while he stroked a mane that felt stiff enough to double as broomstraw. Winekoop stepped back and waved him on, so Matthew began urging Dante out onto the street while lizards scurried in his stomach. The monstrous animal obeyed the command, much to Matthew's surprise and relief, and they went on at a walk while pedestrians got out of the way and even other horses pulling carts and wagons seemed to look down at the ground in the manner of men avoiding the glance of a ruffian. Matthew sat tighter than he should have, fearing a toss, but Dante at least for the present was a perfect gentleman.

Greathouse was waiting in front of City Hall. His horse gave a high nicker that Matthew imagined sounded somewhat nervous, and there was a low rumbling response from deep in Dante's throat. But, again at least for now, the two horses did not attack each other as Matthew had reckoned was a possibility. "Now *that's* a ride," Greathouse said with admiration. He turned his animal toward East King Street and the ferry to Weehawken, and Matthew followed with what felt like a mountain of muscle and bone moving beneath him.

At Van Dam's shipyard, which was the terminus of the flat-bottomed barge across the Hudson, they dismounted and had to wait for the ferry to make its return trip. Greathouse retrieved the letter from Matthew and asked him what he made of it.

"A patient in a hospital?" Matthew answered. "I don't see how we can be of any help there."

"Not just a hospital. A *mental* hospital. You know. What do they call those places?"

"Bedlam," Matthew said. The term for insane asylums had been used for many years, and originated in the clamor and rav-ings of the mad persons locked within.

"Well, we shall see. Oh, I've asked Nathaniel to get us a listing of the property owners north of the Ormond farm. We'll pursue that when we come back. I understand your Masker obeyed the decree again last night."

"*My* Masker?"

"He's your boy, isn't he? Worth ten shillings to you?"

"Only if I find out who he is before he murders anyone else."

"Then you'd best hope he stays at home again tonight, because we won't be back before tomorrow afternoon. There's our boat." Greathouse motioned toward the ferry, its white sail spread as it slowly approached across the gray water, and at bow and stern men using oars to steer a relatively straight path against the current. On the opposite bank, mist drifted over the rooftops and chimneys of the Weehawken settlement. The air was wet and heavy, the sunlight cut to a murky haze. Matthew had the feeling of gloom and doom, not just because of the Masker or Professor Fell, or Reverend Wade's agony or Andrew Kippering's mysterious Grace Hester, but also because of this letter that called Greathouse and him across the water to Bed-lam. He had the sensation of unknown shapes moving over there in the mist, of secrets waiting to be revealed, and puzzles of life and death that could be arranged into a picture if one could only find the missing pieces.

But it was just Weehawken, after all.

The ferry came, the crew threw ropes and lowered anchor, and Matthew and Greathouse led their horses over the gangplank along with a few other travellers. In another few minutes, with the animals secured and everyone aboard, the boat set off again for the far shore.

Three

The Message

twenty-five

THE PHILADELPHIA PIKE was sometimes a road and sometimes a wish. As Matthew and Greathouse followed its
progress across the hilly and wooded Jersey landscape, they passed
through a world in flux: here was a fledgling village of perhaps a
dozen houses and a central church hacked out of the forest, there
the remnants of a previous village being reclaimed by green vines
and underbrush. Many farms had thrived and were impressive
with their orderly fields of corn and beans, but some farms had also
withered. There stood a bare stone chimney, its structure burned
to black ruin around it. At the edge of another village—this one
with a score of houses, a stable, blacksmith's shop, and white-
painted tavern—a sign announced *Welcome to New Town* and a little
army of children came running out to tag along with the riders,
asking them questions about where they were from and where
they were going until the road curved again into the forest and the
children stopped following.

The air was still heavy and wet, tendrils of fog caught in the
heights of the tallest trees. Occasionally deer halted in the woods
to watch the riders go by or ran across the track before them.
Matthew noted that some of the stags had antlers so big it was
amazing the animals could stay upright. Greathouse and Matthew
urged their horses into a gallop when the road was good enough,

trying to make as much time as possible. About four hours into the journey, near a roadsign that had painted upon it *Inian's Ferry 8 miles*, they met a family travelling by wagon on their way to New York. Greathouse spoke to the father and learned that Westerwicke was twelve miles away, on the other side of the ferry that crossed the Raritan River.

They pressed on. As they approached the river, the forest gave way to more farms and industries such as a sawmill, lumberyard, cooper's shop, and, at the edge of a huge apple orchard, a brewery. Houses stood clustered together. Wooden frames were going up for other buildings. The influence of the river, and of river traffic moving inland, was steadily constructing a town. Matthew and Greathouse came to the ferry crossing at the Raritan and had to wait twenty minutes for the next boat, but they were intrigued to see four silent Indians in colorful beads and other tribal regalia come off the barge and begin to head northeast at a pace that would have left the palefaces gasping for breath within a hundred yards.

At last, as the hazy daylight began to further weaken, a sign announced the town of Westerwicke. The pike became Westerwicke's main street, with houses of wood and brick standing on both sides. Beyond the dwellings were well-groomed farmfields and orchards. Horses and cattle shared fenced pastures and sheep grazed on a distant hillside. Westerwicke had two churches, two taverns, and a small business district where residents paused their errands or conversations to watch the strangers pass. Greathouse pulled his horse up in front of one of the taverns, its sign depicting an offered hand and the legend *The Constant Friend*, and called to a young man who had just come out. Directions to the Publick Hospital indicated that their journey would end in another half-mile at a road branching off to the right.

It was with great relief to Matthew's tailbone when that final half-mile was history. The branch road took them through a grove of trees to three buildings. The first, constructed of wood and painted white, stood near a well and was about the size of a normal house. Before it was a horse trough and hitching-post, and a lighted lantern hung on a nail beside the front door. The second structure, connected to the first by a well-worn pathway, was much larger and made of rough stones with a steeply angled roof from which protruded two chimneys. Some of the windows were shuttered. Matthew thought that this was where the patients must be housed, yet the building looked as if it might have been meant for an original purpose of serving as a grain warehouse or even a meeting-hall. He wondered if a village had preceded Westerwicke, had perished due to fever or some other misfortune and this was all that remained of it except possibly some ruins in the forest.

The third building was fifteen or twenty yards beyond the stone structure. It was a little larger than the first and also painted white. He noted that two of its windows were also shuttered. A flowering garden complete with statuary and benches tucked amid the foliage stood nearby. Another road led back to what appeared to be a stable and several other small outbuildings. All in all, this was certainly not the place of misery and confusion that Matthew had imagined they would find. Birds were singing their late-afternoon songs in the trees, the light was fading to blue, and the atmosphere of the hospital and its grounds were far more restful than the squalid scenes of madness Matthew had read about London's asylums in the *Gazette*. Still, he did see bars on some of the unshuttered windows of the stone building, and now a few white faces peered through and hands came out to grasp the bars but the inspection of the visitors was made in silence.

Greathouse dismounted and tied his horse to the hitching-post. As Matthew did the same, the front door of the stone building opened and a man in gray clothes emerged. He paused to do something at the door—lock it behind him, Matthew guessed—and then he gave a start as he saw the new arrivals. He lifted his hand in greeting and came walking rapidly toward them.

"Hello!" Greathouse called. "Are you Dr. Ramsendell?"

The man continued right up to them. When he got within an arm's-length of Matthew he abruptly stopped and said with a crooked grin and a mangled voice, "I'm Jacob. Have you come to take me home?"

Matthew reckoned that the man was only five or six years elder than himself, though it was hard to tell for his face was deeply lined with hardship. His temple on the right side was crushed inward. An old jagged scar began at his right cheek and sliced up across a concave patch on his scalp where the hair no longer grew. His eyes were bright and glassy and there was something both hideous and pitiful about his fixed grin.

"I'm Jacob," he said again, in exactly the same way it had already been spoken. "Have you come to take me home?"

"No." Greathouse's voice was firm but careful. "We've come to see Dr. Ramsendell."

Jacob's grin never faltered. He reached up and touched the scar on Matthew's forehead before Matthew could think to step back. "Are you mad like me?" he asked.

"Jacob! Give them some room, please." The door to the first building had opened and another man came out, followed by a second, both of them wearing dark breeches and white shirts. Instantly Jacob retreated two paces but kept staring at Matthew. The man who'd spoken was tall and slim with a thatch of reddish-brown hair and a neatly trimmed beard. He also wore a tan-colored waistcoat. He said, "I heard my name called. What may I do for you gentlemen?"

"I think this one's mad." Jacob pointed at Matthew. "Somebody broke his head."

Greathouse continued on his verbal path with only a quick sidelong check to make sure Jacob, who was obviously a resident here, did not move any closer. "I'm Hudson Greathouse and this is Matthew Corbett. We represent the Herrald Agency. We've come from New York to—"

"*Excellent!*" said the bearded man with an expression of joy. He glanced at his companion, who was shorter and stockier, had gray hair, and wore spectacles perched on a hooked nose. "I *told* you they'd come! Oh ye of little faith!"

"I stand corrected and reproved," the second man answered, speaking to Greathouse and Matthew. "Also much impressed by your speed in this matter, gentlemen."

"I was in New York today," Jacob offered. "I flew on a bird."

"Pardon my bad manners." The bearded man held out his hand first to Greathouse and then to Matthew. "I am Dr. Ramsendell and this is Dr. Curtis Hulzen. Thank you for coming, gentlemen. I can't thank you *enough*. I know you've had a long trip. May I invite you into the office for a cup of tea?"

Greathouse showed him the envelope. "I'd like to know about *this*."

"Ah. Yes, the letter. I left it at the Dock House Inn yesterday. Come, let's talk in the office." Ramsendell motioned them toward the door. Matthew was acutely aware of Jacob walking almost on his heels.

"I was on a bird," Jacob said, to no one in particular. "It was fat and shiny and took people in its stomach."

"Jacob?" Ramsendell paused at the door. He spoke kindly to the afflicted man, rather as one would speak to a wayward child. "The gentlemen, Dr. Hulzen, and I have some important business to discuss. I'd like for you to complete your task."

"I have bad dreams," said Jacob.

"Yes, I know you do. Go along now. The sooner you finish, the sooner you can have your supper."

"You're going to talk about the Queen."

"That's correct, we are. Go on, now. The laundry won't fold itself."

Jacob seemed to ponder this for a few seconds, and then he gave a nod and a grunt and turned away, walking past the stone structure in the direction of the road that led to the outbuildings.

"Three years ago he was foreman at the sawmill by the river," Ramsendell explained quietly as Matthew and Greathouse watched Jacob leave. "Had a wife and two children. One careless accident—not his doing, by the way—and his injury reduced him to a second childhood. He *does* make improvement and he takes responsibility for small jobs, but he can never live out there again."

Out there. Matthew thought he'd spoken that as if the world beyond was the frightful place instead of this asylum.

"Please, come in." Ramsendell held the office door open for them.

The front room might have been any legal office in New York, as there were two desks, a larger conference table with six chairs, a file cabinet, shelves full of books, and on the plank floor a simple dark green woven rug. Another door at the back was open, and through it Matthew could see what appeared to be an examination table and a cupboard where he presumed drugs or medical instruments were stored. He caught movement back there and saw a gray-dressed woman with long black hair cleaning glass vials with a blue cloth. She seemed to sense she was being watched, for her head swivelled and for a few seconds she regarded Matthew with dull, sunken eyes. Then she focused again on her labor as if no one else existed in the world and no task was more vital.

"Sit down, won't you?" Ramsendell waited until Matthew, Greathouse, and Hulzen had taken chairs at the table. "May I offer you some tea?"

"If you don't mind," Greathouse said, "I could use something a bit stronger."

"Oh, I'm sorry. We have no drinking alcohol on the premises. We do have some apple cider left, though. Would that suit you?"

"Fine," Greathouse said, though Matthew knew the man was wishing for a tankard of stout black ale.

"Cider for me also," Matthew said.

"Mariah?" Ramsendell called, and the black-haired woman ceased her cleaning and peered out. Her mouth was slack and her left eye twitched. "Would you please go to the kitchen and pour two cups of apple cider for our guests? Use the pewter cups, if you will. Anything for you, Curtis?" Hulzen shook his head; he was busy loading tobacco from a deerskin pouch into a clay pipe with a diamond design on its sides. Ramsendell added, "A cup of tea for me, please."

"Yes sir," the woman replied, and went off toward the rear of the house.

"They need tasks," Ramsendell offered as he took a seat at the table. "To keep their dexterity up and give them a challenge. Some can't use their hands very well, though. And of course there are some who either cannot or will not move from their beds. Every case is different, you see."

Greathouse cleared his throat. Matthew thought that for all the man's toughness he looked ready to jump out of his skin. "I'm afraid I *don't* see. Where do these people come from? And how many are here?"

"Well, at present our patients number twenty-four men and eight women. They're kept in separate sections of the hospital, of course. And then there are holding areas for those who exhibit violence or who . . . how shall I put this? . . . choose to ignore their chamberpots. What we're trying to teach them here is that, even in their state of disarray, they still have the power to make choices. They *can* learn."

"Unfortunately, not all still retain that ability." Hulzen had fired a match and was lighting his pipe. Blue smoke spilled from his lips as he spoke. "There are some who are beyond help. Those we must constrain, so as not to hurt themselves or others, but at least here they do have food and shelter."

"The point is, we don't treat our patients as animals." Ramsendell looked from Greathouse to Matthew in order to emphasize his statement. "Curtis and I both have experience in the mental health system as practised in London, and we both abhor the idea of shackles and chains as a common method of control."

"The patients come from where?" Matthew asked, repeating Greathouse's query.

"Some from New Jersey, some from New York, some from Pennsylvania," said Ramsendell. "From small villages and larger towns alike. Some are wards of the court, others have been placed here by relatives. Some, like Jacob, are the victims of accidents that have affected the mental fluid. Others were born, it would seem, under unfortunate stars. In the last few years, with the financial reversals in Philadelphia, the asylum run there by the Quakers has come upon hard times; therefore we've taken in several of their patients. Then there are the people who are simply found wandering in woods or fields, and no one knows their names or histories. In some of those cases, a terrible shock of some kind—witnessing an accident, violence, or even a murder—has blanked the mind, so they may eventually be returned to normal lives if the care is successful."

Greathouse frowned. "Must be a tremendous expense to keep all these people up."

"This property was given to us by the colony and we have generous Christian benefactors who help with our costs," Hulzen said through his shifting blue cloud. "The town of Westerwicke has been very supportive, as well. Their physician, Dr. Voormann, sees to the medical problems of our patients for a nominal fee. Some of the women there prepare the meals, again for a small fee. So yes, there is some expense involved, but we know that if this hospital were to fail, it would mean putting our patients out upon the road."

"Well," Greathouse said, and perhaps only Matthew could detect his unease, "I'm sure no one would want that."

"We are modern in our approach," said Ramsendell as Mariah returned bearing a tray with two pewter cups of cider and a wooden cup of tea. She set it down upon the table, Ramsendell thanked her, and then he returned his attention to Greathouse as she went back to her work. "You'll note neither Curtis nor I wear checked shirts."

Greathouse had already plucked up his cider and taken a drink. "Pardon?" he asked.

"Checked shirts," Ramsendell repeated. "Medieval physicians wore checked shirts when they approached an insane person. They believed the demonic spirits of madness couldn't get through the checked cloth into the soul."

"Nice to know," Greathouse said, with a quick grimace that had meant to serve as a polite smile.

"Your work here is very beneficial, I'm sure," Matthew spoke up, "but I don't see what we can do for you."

"First things first." Ramsendell drank from his tea and turned the cup between his hands. "Again, we appreciate the speed of your response, but I think Curtis and I would like to hear something about your agency before we go any further."

Matthew nodded and remained silent while Greathouse held forth for the next five minutes on the history and purpose of the Herrald Agency, emphasizing their high standards and tradition of success in the field of "problem solving." He recounted cases involving recovered jewels, artwork, stolen legal documents, missing persons, forged diplomatic papers, and also gave mention of an assassination attempt in London undone by himself just the past December. "But I have to inform you gentlemen," he concluded, "that our professional services do not come cheaply. Our time, like yours, is valuable. We charge a flat fee for investigations and also require the payment of all expenses. Of course the fee will vary, according to the task."

"Do you charge to hear the particulars of the problem?" Hulzen asked, puffing on his second pipeful.

"No sir," Greathouse said. "We begin only when a contract of agreement is signed."

The two doctors were silent. Matthew finished off his cider while waiting for them to speak again. Hulzen stared at the ceiling as he smoked his pipe and Ramsendell twined his fingers together before him on the table.

"We're not sure you can help," Ramsendell said at last. "Not sure at all, really."

"You must have at least *thought* we could." Greathouse leaned back in his chair, making the legs creak. "We've come a long way. We'd at least like to hear the problem."

Ramsendell started to speak and then looked at Hulzen, who took one more draw from the pipe, expelled smoke in a thin stream, and said, "We have a young man—a resident of Westerwicke—who goes to New York to buy medical supplies for us at the Smith Street Apothecary. His last trip was on Thursday. He stayed overnight, at a boarding house in your town, and came back on Friday. He brought something with him that . . . well . . ." He glanced at Ramsendell as a prompt to continue.

"He had breakfast in a tavern there," Ramsendell said, "and brought back a copy of your broadsheet."

"The *Earwig?*" Matthew asked.

"The very same." Ramsendell offered a tight smile that faded. "We have a patient who likes to be read to. A *special* patient, I suppose you could say."

Greathouse tensed at that one. "Special? How?"

"Oh, certainly not violent. In fact, she's extremely docile. The others call her the Queen."

"The *Queen?*" Matthew recalled Jacob using that term outside.

"That's correct." Ramsendell watched Matthew's eyes for a reaction. "Did you ever think that *here* you might meet a queen? The Queen of Bedlam, as it were?"

"Our problem," said Hulzen, "is that we wish to find out who she is. Her proper name, and where she comes from. Her history, and . . . why she's in her current state."

"What state would that be?" Greathouse almost flinched as he waited for a response.

"Locked," Ramsendell replied.

There was a silence. Smoke still drifted at the ceiling, and beyond in the other room the black-haired woman continued to diligently polish the gleaming glass vials.

"I think we ought to meet her," Matthew said.

"Yes." Ramsendell pushed his chair back and stood up. "I'll make the introductions."

twenty-six

To the surprise of both Matthew and Greathouse, the two doctors did not lead them into the stone building after they left the office. Instead, they began walking on a pathway along the asylum toward the other house at the garden's edge.

The light was dwindling. Poles that held lanterns were set up at intervals, as on the streetcorners of New York, and a gray-clad man with a bald pate was touching a match to the candlewicks. "Good evening, sirs," said the man cheerfully as the group passed, and Dr. Ramsendell answered, "Evening, Charles."

"That was another patient?" Greathouse asked when they'd distanced themselves. When Ramsendell nodded, Greathouse said, "Call me slow, but I'm not fully understanding why you're letting lunatics out and about when they ought to be locked up."

"As I said, we have an enlightened attitude here. Unlike the London asylums, which to be honest are so overburdened the doctors there have little choice but to throw all the patients together into one mass. I will admit that we take some risks in giving a few of our charges special privileges and responsibilities, but not without proper evaluation."

"Don't any of them try to run away if they get the chance?"

"We are very careful in assigning freedoms," said Hulzen, who trailed smoke from his pipe. "It's true that we had two escapes seven years ago, the first year we began operation, but on the whole the patients who are afforded tasks are pleased to be trusted. And of course we make sure their minds are firm enough to understand the consequences of imprudent action."

"What might that be?" Greathouse prodded. "Whipping them until their backs are bloody?"

"Not at all!" There was a little heat in the response and smoke almost blew in Greathouse's face. "We detest the primitive approach. The most drastic punishment here would be solitary confinement."

"You might like to know," Ramsendell added as they continued walking the length of the asylum, "that Charles and two other patients serve as night watchmen. Of course we do have a pair of men from Westerwicke who are paid to act as guards during the day."

"Dr. Ramsendell!" someone called. It was a husky voice yet silkily pleasant. "Dr. Ramsendell, might I have a word?" The voice of a salesman, Matthew thought.

Instantly Ramsendell seemed to tense. His pace faltered, nearly causing Matthew to collide with him.

"Dr. Ramsendell, won't you show a little Christian pity to a sick and sorrowful man?"

Matthew saw a face peering through the bars of one of the asylum's unshuttered windows. The eyes caught his and held them with almost an unbreakable force, so much so that Matthew felt his own stride slowing to a stop.

"Oh!" said the man. He grinned. "Hello there, young dandy."

"Come along, Mr. Corbett," Ramsendell urged.

"Mr. *Corbett*, is it?" The grin widened, showing very large teeth. "Dr. Ramsendell is a very fine man and a wonderful physician, Mr. Corbett. If he says you need a stay here, you should well believe it is for your good and the good of all society. But beware his wrath, for one small lapse of judgment might mean you must eat your supper all alone."

The others had stopped just beyond Matthew, and now

Hulzen came back to his side and said quietly, "It's best not to speak."

"And Dr. Hulzen thinking not only am I mad, but also *deef*!" The man made a clucking sound and shook his head. "For *shame*!" He curled big-knuckled hands around the bars and pressed his face forward. He had a wide, square-jawed face with pale blue eyes that held such pure merriment no one would believe it was the moonshine of madness. His hair was straw-colored, parted straight up the middle and the sides turning to gray. His thick mustache was more gray than straw. He looked to be a large man, his head almost to the top of the window and his chest a massive bulk in the gray asylum uniform. His fleshy lips moved, wet with saliva. "I'll repeat my offer to shave you, Dr. Ramsendell. I'll polish that beard right off. Give your chin and throat a *fine* going-over. Eh?" He began to laugh, a frog's croak from deep in that barrel chest, and suddenly the glint in his eyes caught red and for a passing instant Matthew thought he might be looking into the face of Satan himself. Then the glint went out like a fire under a trapdoor and the man's voice, soft and salesmanlike again, reached out for him. "Step nearer, dandy. Let's have a look at *your* throat."

"Mr. Corbett?" Ramsendell stepped in front of Matthew and looked into his face, as if to shield him from a wicked spell. "We really should be going on."

"Yes," Matthew agreed. He felt sweat at his temples. "All right."

"I'll remember you!" the man behind the bars called as his audience walked away. "Oh, I'll remember *all* of you!"

"Who in blazes was *that*?" Greathouse asked, glancing back once and then not daring to glance again because the big hands were running up and down the bars as if seeking a weak place to crack.

"*That*," Ramsendell answered, and for the first time Matthew and Greathouse heard distaste—and perhaps a shudder of fear—in his voice, "was a problem we shall be ridding ourselves of soon. He was sent to us almost a year ago from the Quaker institution in Philadelphia. He's more cunning than insane, I can tell you. He fooled me into giving him work privileges, and the first chance he got he tried to murder poor Mariah back at the red barn." He motioned toward the road that led to the outbuildings. "Well, the Quakers have found out it seems he was a barber in London and he may have been involved with a dozen murders. We're expecting a letter in the autumn instructing us to take him to the New York gaol to wait for ship transfer to England. A constable will of course be coming over as well to make sure he arrives in irons."

"If it was up to me, I'd take him on the road and blow his brains out," Greathouse said. "A pistol could save a lot of wasted money."

"Unfortunately, we have signed a decree with the Quakers verifying that he will be delivered to New York in good health. On our Christian honor." Ramsendell took another two steps and then said thoughtfully, "You know, if this business goes well with the Queen, you gentlemen might consider our hiring you to escort Mr. Slaughter to New York."

"Mr. *Slaughter?*" Matthew asked.

"Yes. Tyranthus Slaughter. An unfortunate name though possibly well-deserved. But do consider that task if at all feasible, sirs. Just thirty-some miles. What could go wrong? Ah, here's our destination."

They had reached the house by the garden. Matthew smelled the scents of honeysuckle and mint. A few fireflies were sparking in the branches of the elm trees beyond. Ramsendell took a leather cord holding several keys from a pocket of his waistcoat, slid a key into the front door's lock, and opened it. "Watch your step, gentlemen," he said, though it was an unnecessary precaution for the open door had exposed a lamp-lit corridor with a long dark blue runner upon the floor. One lantern sat upon a small table and about midway along the corridor was a wrought-iron chandelier of four lamps, previously lit by—Matthew assumed—either Charles or one of the other trustees. As Matthew followed the two doctors in—and Greathouse lagged a few steps behind as if mistrustful of this unknown but perfectly normal-looking residence—he noted four closed doors, two on either side of the hall.

"This way, please." Ramsendell continued to the last door on the right. He rapped softly on it, waited a few seconds, and then said, "Madam? It's Dr. Ramsendell and Dr. Hulzen. We've brought two visitors to meet you." There was no response. He looked at Matthew. "She never answers but we think she appreciates the formality." He pushed another key into the lock and turned it. "Also we do respect her privacy." Then, louder, and aimed toward the lady within: "I'm opening the door now, madam."

That particular action also brought neither word nor rustle of motion. The doctors entered first, then Matthew and a decidedly timid Greathouse. Matthew caught another sweet scent; not of the garden this time, but rather of some flowery perfume or oil within the room. It was still dim here, blue twilight spilling between the open shutters of two windows. Matthew saw that the windows in this chamber were not barred, but were wide to the evening and the outside world. One faced the garden, while another was situated toward the forest where the fireflies pulsed.

Hulzen lit a match. He touched it to the triple candlewicks of a lantern that sat upon a table below the garden-facing window. The flames strengthened, illuminating in gold what appeared to be the parlor of any well-kept house in New York. But more than well-kept, Matthew decided as he gazed around. Richly maintained would be more accurate, for on the floor was a beautiful rug of small purple, gray, and blue squares, and upon the pale blue-painted walls were paintings within gleaming gilt frames. Hulzen went about lighting a second three-candle lantern that stood on a pedestal across the room, now revealing a white-canopied bed with ornate scrollwork, a pair of high-backed chairs with gray upholstery, and a round oak table that bore at its center a wooden bowl holding a few ripe apples and pears. Near the bed was a large wardrobe of some dark and luxurious wood so sinuously jointed that Matthew thought it must have been crafted by a true master's hand and cost a small fortune. Little red flowers and green leaves had been meticulously painted around the edges of the wardrobe's doors, which were opened by a latch that appeared to be if not pure gold then very near it.

Hulzen lit a third lamp. Its glow spread upon the opposite side of the room from which Matthew and Greathouse stood. Illuminated was a small fireplace, cold now in the midst of summer. What was remarkable there was the fireplace screen, an intricate golden metalwork of tree branches upon which perched painted birds—cardinal, robin, bluebird, and white dove—in richly daubed original colors. Above the mantel was a framed painting that Matthew stepped closer to see; it depicted a scene of the waterways of Venice at what seemed to be blue sunset much like the current horizon.

He swept his gaze across other objects, his mind taking in a treasure of details: small bottles with blown-glass flower caps sitting atop a dresser, a silver hairbrush and handmirror beside them; a set of six little horses that looked to be carved from ivory; thimbles arranged in perfect order beside a pair of spectacles; on another small table a Bible, a stack of slim pamphlets, and . . . yes, there was the latest *Earwig* too.

"May I introduce you?" asked Dr. Ramsendell.

Matthew looked up from his discoveries. Ramsendell was standing next to the window that afforded a view toward the forest. Beside him was the high back of a dark purple chair, and now both Matthew and Greathouse could see that someone with white hair was sitting there.

Ramsendell was speaking to the woman in the chair. "Madam," he said in a quiet voice, "I'd like you to meet Mr. Hudson Greathouse and Mr. Matthew Corbett. They've ridden from New York to see you. Would you come forward, gentlemen?"

"After you," Greathouse said under his breath.

Matthew approached Ramsendell, as Dr. Hulzen stepped back and watched.

"This is our Queen, sirs. We call her 'Madam,' for the sake of propriety."

Matthew stopped. He was looking down at a small-boned, frail woman who paid him not the least notice, but who continued staring out the window at the display of sparkling lights in the trees. He thought she must be well over sixty. Sixty-five, possibly. Closer to seventy? It was hard to tell. She was almost swallowed up by her silken homegown, which was the pink hue of the palest rose. On her feet were slippers of the same material and color but adorned with small bows. The woman had a cloud of thick, neatly brushed white hair, and her face, which Matthew saw in profile, was heavily lined yet innocent and almost childlike in its repose. She stared straight ahead, her soft brown eyes glittering with lamplight. She was focused entirely upon the dance of the fireflies. Below an uptilted, elegant nose her mouth moved occasionally as Matthew watched, as if she were posing questions to herself, or making some observation that was silent to her audience. Her hands, which clasped the armrests, bore no rings and neither did she wear any necklaces or other personal statements of fashion. Or statements of *identity*, Matthew thought.

"Does she have a wedding ring?" he asked, thinking aloud.

"She arrived with no jewelry," Ramsendell said, "but all the furnishings here came with her. We have taken the liberty of searching for letters or any other identifying papers. Nothing gives us any clue as to who she might be, though it's obvious she is— was—a woman of means."

"No name or initials in the Bible?"

"A new volume, it appears. Not even a fingermark on it."

"Maker's marks on the furniture?"

"Someone thought of that," Hulzen said. "The marks have either been rubbed away or, where they were burned into the wood, cut out with a small chisel."

Greathouse came forward and stood beside Matthew. "Can she *hear* us?" It had been spoken in what for him was nearly a whisper.

"She can hear perfectly well. But rarely does she respond to anything, and then it's either a quick 'yes' or 'no' or—at best— some cryptic statement neither Curtis nor I can fathom."

Matthew saw the woman cock her head slightly to the left, as if listening a little more intently, but her placid gaze did not change and she made no further motion. Since it appeared that Hudson Greathouse was paralyzed in the presence of the mentally infirm, Matthew decided it was up to him to steer the course. "I think we ought to be told the whole story."

Ramsendell nodded. He regarded the woman with a tender expression as he spoke. "She came to us in April of 1698—"

"*Came* to you?" Matthew interrupted; he was in his element now, and he could almost feel the blood flowing in his brain. "Exactly how?"

"Was *brought* to us," Ramsendell corrected. He answered the next question before Matthew could ask it. "By a lawyer in Philadelphia. Icabod Primm, of Market Street. He had written us previously, and visited us, to make certain his client would be satisfied."

"Hold on." Greathouse was totally bumfuddled. "His *client*? I thought you said you didn't know who she was. *Is*, I mean."

"We don't." By Hulzen's sour expression, he was beginning to think Greathouse was something of a lout. "We're trying to tell you."

"More directly then, please," said Matthew crisply. "How is it this woman arrived here nameless yet represented by a Philadelphia lawyer?"

"Mr. Primm," came the reply from Ramsendell, "never spoke to her by any other term but either 'Madam' or 'Lady.' *If* he spoke to her at all, which as I remember was not very often and anyway she was in the exact same state you see her in now. His letters mentioned a 'client' but no name whatsoever. We are paid a yearly fee—quite a large fee, by the way—to keep Madam in her present accommodations, apart from the other patients and living amid familiar objects from her . . . shall I say . . . previous life. She has never had a visitor, but every April sixteenth the money has come by messenger from Mr. Primm, who told us that very first April, four years ago, that any effort on our part to discover Madam's identity and history will result in his immediately removing her from this hospital. He has stated that his client has given him full power of representation, and so we signed the letter of admittance according to the terms."

"His client." Greathouse spoke it with some distaste. "Some young cur who married a wealthy older woman and then stashed her here when her mind went? So he takes the fortune and even strips her wedding ring off?"

"We considered that and rejected it." Hulzen had fired up his pipe again and was standing beside the window with the garden view. "What you must understand, Mr. Greathouse, is that we are involved in an experimental treatment here. We have the belief that persons with mental disorders might be *helped*, and someday possibly returned to society. That's why we built these four rooms in this house, so we might pursue that treatment with patients who would benefit from being in more familiar surroundings rather than the austerity of the asylum. At least we hoped that, when we began."

"A room in this part of our hospital is, as I said, very expensive," Ramsendell continued. "We doubt that someone would—as you put it—'stash' a relative here, or care to provide all these beautiful furnishings. No, we feel certain that Mr. Primm's client cares very deeply for Madam's welfare. Obviously Primm must have looked into the Quaker institution for similar living accommodations and was told about our hospital by them."

"Is this lady the only current occupant here?" Matthew asked.

"No, there's another elderly woman in the first room. Unfortunately she's bedridden. But we do know her name and her circumstances, and her son and two daughters make frequent visits. We are gratified to say that we've helped her regain some of her power of speech."

"This makes no sense," Greathouse said, a horn's pitch too loudly. "Why are you trying to find out anything about this woman at all, if—" He stopped, for the lady in the chair had given the softest whisper of a sigh. Her mouth moved again, making no noise. Matthew saw her eyes follow a bluejay that darted past the window. When Greathouse spoke again, it was the verbal equivalent of walking on eggs. "*If*," he said, "you've been forbidden to do so by Mr. Primm?"

"Simply put," answered Ramsendell, "we are not whores."

"Well," Greathouse said, with a nervous laugh, "I never suggested such."

"My point being, we are physicians. Professional healers. Madam has been here for four years with no change whatsoever. Curtis and I believe that if we knew her history, we might be able to"—he paused, assembling his sentence—"help her out of this shell she has constructed to keep the world at bay. We think she has suffered a severe shock, and this is her mind's method of survival." He waited to make sure Greathouse and Matthew had grasped his diagnosis. "Yes, we have gladly accepted the money from Mr. Primm and put it to good purpose in the hospital. And yes, we signed the letter of terms fully aware of its limitations. But that was four years ago. You are here today, gentlemen, because we wish you to discover Madam's identity and history without the involvement of Mr. Primm."

Matthew and Greathouse looked at each other. Their unspoken question was *Can it be done?*

"There's another thing you might find of interest." Ramsendell walked to the table where the *Earwig* lay. He picked the broadsheet up and held it for the visitors to see. "As I said, Madam likes to be read to. Occasionally she nods or makes a soft sound that I take to be approval as I'm reading the Bible or one of the other books. On Friday evening after supper I was reading to her from this sheet. For the first time, she repeated a word that she heard me say."

"A word? What was it?" Greathouse asked.

"To be exact, it was a *name*." Ramsendell put his finger upon the news item. "Deverick."

Matthew remained silent.

"I read the article again, but there was no response," said Ramsendell. "No *spoken* response, that is. I saw by the lamplight that Madam was weeping. Have you ever seen anyone weep without making a noise, sirs? Or changing their expression from what it is day in and day out, hour after hour? But there were the tears, crawling down her cheeks. She demonstrated an emotional reaction to that name, which is extremely remarkable because we've seen no emotion from her for the four years of her residence."

Matthew stared down at the woman's profile. She was perfectly immobile, not even her lips moving to betray the secret thoughts.

"I read the article to her several times with no further incident. I've spoken the name to her and gotten only a sigh or shift of position. But I saw your notice and I began to wonder if you might help, for this is certainly a problem to be solved. So Curtis and I discussed this, I went to New York on Saturday, left the inquiry, and came back yesterday."

"The mention of one name doesn't mean anything," Greathouse scoffed. "I'm surely no expert, but if she's not right in the head, then why should the name have meaning for her?"

"It's the fact that she made the *effort*." Hulzen's face was daubed orange as he put another match to his pipe. "Also the evidence of the tears. We feel very strongly that she does know that name, and in her own way was trying to tell us something."

Now Greathouse began to get his back up. "Beg pardon, but if that evidence was stuffing for a mattress you'd be sleeping on a board."

Matthew decided to do one simple thing before the wrangling could grow into argument. He knelt down beside the woman, looked at her profile, which was as still as a portrait, and said quietly, "Pennford Deverick."

Was there a brief flicker of the eye? Just the merest tightening of the mouth, as a line deepened almost imperceptibly at its corner?

"Pennford Deverick," he repeated.

The two doctors and Hudson Greathouse watched him without comment.

There was no response from Madam that Matthew could tell, yet . . . did her left hand clutch the armrest a fraction more firmly?

He leaned closer. He said, "Pennford Deverick is dead."

Her head suddenly and smoothly turned and Matthew was looking directly into her face. The abruptness of this made him gasp and almost topple backward, but he held his position.

"Young man," she said in a clear, strong voice, and though her expression was exactly the same as when she'd been watching the fireflies her tone carried an edge of irritation, "has the king's reply yet arrived?"

"The . . . king's reply?"

"That was my question. Would you answer, please?"

Matthew looked to the doctors for help, but neither spoke nor offered assistance. Hulzen continued to smoke his pipe. It occurred to Matthew that they had heard this question before. "No, madam," he nervously responded.

"Come fetch me when it does," she said, and then her face turned toward the window again and Matthew felt her moving away from him even though the physical distance did not alter an atom. In another few seconds she was somewhere very far away.

Ramsendell said, "That's why she's called the Queen. She asks that question several times a week. She asked Charles one day if the king's reply had arrived, and he told the others."

Matthew tried again, for the sake of attempt. "Madam, what was your question to the king?"

There was no reaction from her whatsoever.

Matthew stood up. He was still thoughtfully absorbed in watching her face, which had now become that of a statue. "Have you ever told her the reply *had* arrived?"

"I have," Hulzen said. "Just as an experiment. She seemed to be waiting for some other action on my part. When I failed to do whatever it was she expected, she went back into her dream state."

"Dream state," Greathouse muttered under his breath.

Matthew was suddenly aware that, as he stared at the Queen of Bedlam, he was also being keenly watched in turn by four other faces.

He looked up, at what caught yellow lamplight there on the opposite wall next to the window.

His mouth was very dry.

He said with what seemed an effort, "What are *those*?"

"Oh." Ramsendell motioned toward them. "Her masks."

Matthew was already walking around behind the Queen's chair, past Greathouse and the two doctors to the four masks that hung upon the wall. He hadn't seen them before, as his attention had been so firmly fixed upon the lady. Two of the masks were plain white, one red with black diamond shapes upon the cheeks, and the fourth black with the shapes of red diamonds framing the eyeholes.

"They came with her," Ramsendell said. "I think they may be Italian."

"No doubt," Matthew murmured; he was thinking of what Ashton McCaggers had told him: *In the Italian tradition, carnival masks are sometimes decorated with colored diamond or triangle shapes around the eyes. Particularly the harlequin masks of—*

"Venice," Matthew said, and looked across the room at the blue-toned painting that depicted the city of canals. "She may have visited there, at some time." He was speaking mostly to himself. Again he regarded the quartet of masks. Then back to the woman's face. Then at the copy of the *Earwig* still clutched in Ramsendell's hand.

Matthew was, in a way, measuring the distance between all these things as surely as if he were a surveyor's compass. Not the physical distance, but the space between them in terms of meaning. The Queen's face in calm tranquility, the masks upon the wall, the broadsheet, and back and forth and forth and back. From Deverick to masks, he thought. Or should that be from Deverick to *Masker*?

"What is it?" asked Greathouse, sensing turbulence where Matthew was standing.

Matthew traced with a finger the red diamond shapes around the eyes of the black mask. Yes, they were similar—*identical?*—to the wounds on the faces of the Masker's victims. He turned around again to look at the Queen, and to clarify what was beginning to form in his mind.

That she sat in her chair, a sad yet regal presence, at the center of this unknown geometry between Pennford Deverick and his killer.

Two facts made his brain burn.

Whoever had put her here cared for her—loved her?—deeply, and wished her to be watched over in some semblance of the previous wealthy life she must have enjoyed, yet this same person had gone to the length of chiselling away the maker's marks from the furniture to prevent her identity being traced.

Why?

Did she really recognize the Deverick name, from somewhere in the locked room her mind occupied? If so, again, why had that name caused her to shed silent tears?

Deverick to Masker and Masker to Deverick. But was the proper geometry really Queen of Bedlam to Masker to Dr. Godwin to Pennford Deverick to Eben Ausley?

"May I ask what you're thinking?" It was Ramsendell's voice.

"I'm thinking that I may be looking at a pentagon," Matthew replied.

"What?" asked Hulzen, as a thread of smoke leaked over his chin.

Matthew didn't answer, for he was still calculating. Not distances of meaning this time, but whether or not he thought there was any possibility of success at solving this particular problem. Where to begin? *How* to begin?

"So." Greathouse made the word sound like a note of portent. "Does she think herself to be Queen Mary? Waiting for a message from King William?" He scratched his chin, which was in need of a shave. "Doesn't anyone have the heart to tell her that William is deceased?"

Matthew had come to a conclusion. "I think we will accept this problem, sirs."

"Wait just one *moment*!" Greathouse flared up, before the doctors could respond. "*I* haven't agreed to that!"

"Well?" Matthew turned a cool gaze toward him. "Why wouldn't you?"

"Because . . . because we ought to *talk* about it first, that's why!"

"Gentlemen, if you wish to return with your answer in the morning, we'd be most grateful," said Ramsendell. "You can find rooms at the *Constant Friend*, but I have to say that the food is better at Mrs. DePaul's eating-house."

"Just so I can get a very large and very strong drink," Greathouse muttered. Then, more loudly and directed to Ramsendell: "Our fee would be three crowns and expenses. One crown to be paid upon agreement."

Ramsendell looked for advice to Hulzen, who shrugged. "Expensive," Ramsendell replied, "but I believe we can manage that if your expenses are reasonable."

"They may or may not be. It all depends." Greathouse, Matthew knew, was trying to break the deal before it was sealed. The rogue of swords was definitely unnerved by the shadow of madness; it was, after all, not something he could fight with fists, pistol, or rapier.

Ramsendell nodded. "We'll trust your judgment. After all, you're the professionals."

"Yes." Greathouse might have puffed his chest up a bit, but it was clear to Matthew that the matter of the fee had been settled. "Yes, we are."

Before they departed from the room, Matthew paused to again take in the rich appointments, the elegant furniture and paintings. Where was the woman's husband? he wondered. There was a lot of money on display here. What occupation had earned it?

He looked once more at the group of Italian masks, and then at the woman's immobile profile. She wore her own mask, he thought. Behind it might be a mindless blank, or a tortured memory.

Young man, has the king's reply yet arrived?

"Good evening to you," Matthew said to the silent Queen of Bedlam, and followed the others out the door.

twenty-seven

"MY OPINION," said Hudson Greathouse as he broke a silence that had stretched over half-an-hour, "is that it can't be done, no matter if you think the contrary. After all, I've had a little more experience in this profession than you."

Matthew let the comment sit. They were on the Philadelphia Pike, riding for New York. It was just after ten o'clock by Matthew's watch. The sun was peeking out from behind gray clouds and glinting off wet trees and puddles on the road. They had left Westerwicke this morning after a breakfast meeting with the two doctors at Mrs. DePaul's eating-house. During the night, while a thunderstorm blew and rain slammed against the shutters of the *Constant Friend*, Matthew and Greathouse had wrangled over the odds of finding a satisfactory solution to the Queen's identity. Greathouse had said Mrs. Herrald would have considered this problem a lost cause, while Matthew had maintained that no cause was lost until it was abandoned. At last, realizing that Matthew was not going to retreat from his position, Greathouse had shrugged his shoulders, said, "It's on your account then, as far as I'm concerned," and had taken a bottle of rum upstairs to his room. Matthew had listened to the storm wail for a while, drank a last cup of ginger tea, and gone to his own bed to mull the connections of that peculiar pentagon until sleep had rescued him from his own mind past midnight.

"Where are you to *begin* with this?" Greathouse asked, riding alongside Matthew. "Do you even have any idea?"

"I do."

"My ears are open."

"Philadelphia," Matthew said. He guided Dante around a puddle that looked like a swamp ready to swallow the horse to its bit. "To be specific, the office of Icabod Primm."

"Oh, *really*?" Now Greathouse gave a harsh laugh. "Well, that will please our clients, won't it? Didn't you hear them say Primm's not supposed to know anything about this?"

"My ears are also open, but I don't believe Mr. Primm is . . ." He paused, searching for the term.

"On the level?" Greathouse supplied.

"Exactly. If Primm's client cares so much about the lady's welfare, he—or she—is not going to take her out of there, no matter what Primm threatens. Where else would the lady go, to be treated so royally? Primm's client wants two things: the lady hidden out of the way, and also protected."

"I don't think those doctors will approve of it."

"They don't have to know, do they?"

Greathouse was quiet for a while. Sunlight was beginning to stream through the woods and the humid air was getting warmer. "This whole thing stinks, if you ask me," Greathouse started up again. "Those lunatics walking around without chains on their ankles. All that hogshit about *mental disorders* and *dream states* and such. You know what my father would've used on me if I'd gone into a damned dream state? A bullwhip to wake me up with, that's what! Seems to me that's what some of those people need, not coddling like they're tender violets."

"I assume, then," said Matthew dryly, "that you would give Jacob the bullwhip treatment?"

"You know what I mean! Hell, call a loon a loon and be done with it!"

"I'm sure there are many so-called doctors in the asylums of England who would agree with you. Then again, they would have no need for our services." Matthew glanced quickly at Greathouse to gauge his expression—which was dour—and then looked toward the road again. "Don't you think it's admirable that Ramsendell and Hulzen want to *help* their patients?"

"I think it's foolish and we were wrong to come here. People with mind disease can't be helped."

"Oh, I see. Mind disease, is it?"

"Yes, and don't be cocky about it, either. I had an uncle on my mother's side who got the mind disease. At fifty years of age he liked to sit around and whittle on little wooden horses. Sat me down once and went on about how he saw gnomes in his garden. And him an ex-military man, a cavalry captain! You know, you remind me of him, in a way."

"What way?"

"He was always playing chess. By *himself*. He set up his games and played both sides, talking to himself all the while."

"Imagine that," Matthew said, and gave Greathouse a sidelong glance.

"All right, then. Suppose you go to Philadelphia and see this Primm bastard. There's no law that says he has to tell you who the woman is. I expect he'll throw you out on your mental disorder. What will you do then? Eh?" When Matthew didn't respond, Greathouse pressed onward. "Are you going to walk the streets collaring people? Asking if they know a little old white-haired lady who thinks she's Queen Mary sitting in a loonhouse waiting for a message from King William? I can see the Quakers taking in a new boarder at their own asylum. And not to mention that Philadelphia is a *larger* town than New York. If you're going to make appointments with all the people there, the next time I see you you'll have a gray beard down to your shoes."

"What? You won't go to help me ask everyone in Philadelphia?"

"I'm serious! I said last night this is on *your* account. When Mrs. Herrald hears about this—about me letting you agree to this thing—I may wind up sharpening pencils with a dull knife for the next six months. So no, I will not go to Philadelphia on a fool's errand."

"It seems to me," Matthew said, "that you took their money willingly enough." He speared Greathouse with a chilly gaze. "And are you telling me, sir, that after all your blowhard speeches about being tough of body, mind, and spirit that you are *weak* in the face of a challenge?"

"A challenge is one thing. This is an impossible quest. And mind who you're calling *weak*, boy, because I could knock you off that horse with my little finger."

Before Matthew could think twice about it, he was wheeling Dante in front of Greathouse's horse. Matthew's cheeks had flamed red, his heart was pounding, and he had had enough of the dish Greathouse was so eager to spoon out. Greathouse's mount snorted and backed up as Dante stood his ground. Matthew sat in the saddle seething with anger.

"What the hell's wrong with *you*?" Greathouse shouted. "You might have caused my horse to—"

"You hold your tongue," Matthew said.

"*What?*"

"I said, you hold your tongue."

"Well, well." Greathouse wore a tight grin. "The boy has finally cracked."

"Not cracked. Just ready to tell you what I think of you."

"Really? This should be entertaining. Shall I get off my horse and prepare to twist you around that tree over there?"

Matthew felt his nerve faltering. He had to go ahead and speak before his good sense forbade it. "You're going to sit there and listen. If you want to try to twist me around a tree when I'm done, so be it. I have no doubt you could do that, or knock me off my horse with your little finger as you so eloquently spoke, but I'll be damned if I'll let you talk down to me anymore."

Greathouse narrowed his eyes. "What's gotten up your bum?"

"Mrs. Herrald has chosen me for a reason. A very good reason. I'm fairly intelligent and I have a history that intrigues her. No, more than fairly intelligent. I'm very smart, Mr. Greathouse. Probably smarter than you, and you know that. Now I can't *fight* as well as you can, or use a rapier worth a damn, and I haven't stopped any assassination attempts in the last few months, but I *have* saved a woman from being burned at the stake as a witch, and I *have* uncovered a murderer and a plot to destroy an entire town. I think that counts for something. Don't you?"

"I suppose it—"

"I'm not finished," Matthew plowed on, and Greathouse was silent. "I don't have your experience or your physical strength— and maybe I never will—but I intend to get one thing from you that you seem unwilling to offer: your respect. Not because I turn into who you want me to be, but because of who I am. Now Mrs. Herrald seems to trust my judgment, so why shouldn't you when I tell you I *can* find out who that woman in the hospital is. And not only that, but I think it's vital to find out, because I believe she has some knowledge of Mr. Deverick's death and perhaps even of the Masker."

"That's stretching things, don't you think?"

"I won't know until I explore it further."

"Explore *away*, then!" Greathouse gave a sweep of his arm that Matthew thought would have knocked him to Sunday if it had hit him. "What the hell should I care if you go off on a goose-chase and squander Mrs. Herrald's coin?"

"It's not her coin," Matthew reminded him. "The doctors are paying expenses."

Greathouse squinted and looked toward the sun, perhaps to burn from his eyes the image of a fool. Then he focused his attention on Matthew again and he said gruffly, "All right, now it's my turn to speak. Yes, Mrs. Herrald has confidence in you. More than I do, by the way, but that ought to be obvious. There's more to this business than mind-work. I've known several very smart gents who walked into a blind alley believing there was an open door at the end of it, and now they lie in graves so only the worms appreciate the size of their brains. *Experience* counts for a lot of this, yes, but also something you haven't got, which is *instinct*. I have an

instinct you're going to fail at finding out who this woman was—
is—and you'll cause more harm than good trying to do it. As far as
respect, sir Corbett, you get that from me by one way and one way
only: by earning it. So you might be riding a tall horse today, and
feel all the flush for your height, but I can tell you that the earth is
very hard and unforgiving when you take a fall."

"I'll have to fall to find out then, won't I?"

"Yes, but at least fall doing something with a *possibility* of
success."

Matthew nodded. He refused to look away from Greathouse's
baleful stare. "I think we should agree to disagree, sir, because contrary to your opinion I have the instinct that the Queen has a connection to both Pennford Deverick and the Masker and I intend to
find out what it is."

"And I think her Highness is a lunatic whose family put her
away to keep her from drooling on the breakfast bacon."

"Something more than that, I believe," said Matthew. "Much
more. The maker's marks being either rubbed or chiselled off the
furniture tells me she was put there to be invisible. Actually, it
sounds more to me that Mr. Primm's client *fears* having the lady's
identity discovered. Why should that be?"

"I don't know. You being the chief investigator on this, you
enlighten me."

"People who wish to draw a curtain over their activities usually
have a secret to hide. I should like to find out what that secret is."

"Now we've gone from finding out identities to finding out
supposed secrets."

"Well," Matthew said, "call it an instinct."

Greathouse snorted. "Boy, I'll bet you could drive someone
mad with that attitude of yours."

"You have your blades," Matthew answered, "and I have
mine."

"So you do." Greathouse regarded Matthew with perhaps a
hint of new appreciation, but if it had really been there it was gone
in an instant. "You'll notice that while we've been jawing, the road
to New York has not gotten any shorter."

They rode on, with Dante now taking the lead by a nose.

The clouds parted and drifted away like so much mist, the sun strengthened and thrust golden swords between the trees, the air shimmered with insects, and the birds sang their delight at life in the modern century. The only other disruption during the trip was the wait for about an hour for the ferry at Weehawken, as an oar had broken on a drifting treetrunk on the New York side, but then the trip was made and Matthew and Greathouse at last guided their horses off the flatboat onto Manhattan mud.

Greathouse said he would report back to Mrs. Herrald and also return to town within the next couple of days to get the list of the upper island residents Magistrate Powers was procuring for him, and then he wished Matthew well and bid him good day. At the stable Matthew relinquished Dante—a "very good horse I hope to use again," he told Mr. Winekoop—and walked up the Broad Way hill for home in the deepening shadows of afternoon. He was used to long rides, for with Powers he'd made many trips to deliver legal documents or scribe cases being heard by the magistrate in smaller towns, but his ass was hurting. A three-day jaunt to Philadelphia was not something he wished to consider at this point in his discomfort.

He was mulling over the fact of the four masks on the wall of the Queen's room—and wondering if his so-called instinct in asserting his determination to solve this problem in front of Greathouse wouldn't result in that topple from a tall horse before all was said and done—when he heard a voice to his right call, "Matthew! Ho there, Matthew!"

He looked around and saw two figures approaching him from the corner of Maiden Lane. A wagon went past, hauling barrels. Matthew stepped back to let the vehicle trundle by. Then the two figures were crossing the Broad Way toward him and he saw Marmaduke Grigsby's gap-toothed grin and stoop-shouldered shamble. The other person wore a round-brimmed straw hat and a bright violet-colored gown decorated with rather loud examples of green lace at the throat and sleeves. Matthew realized he was about to be formally introduced to Beryl Grigsby, whose taste in colors made him feel vaguely seasick.

The last he'd seen of Grigsby's granddaughter was as a mud-colored lump fainting down with relief and exhaustion into a chair at the printmaster's house. Matthew had put the girl's bags on the floor, wished everyone well, and gotten out of there before he caught a bad case of mildew.

"Matthew, I want you to meet Beryl. Now that she's present-able, I mean." Grigsby came on like a four-horse coach while the girl lagged behind. It occurred to Matthew that possibly she didn't care to be supervised any more than he wished to be her supervisor. "Come, come!" Grigsby urged the girl, who kept her face cast down in the shadow of that hat as she obeyed and walked up to stand alongside the old trumpeter. Matthew almost instinctively took a step back, but his manners did hold him steady.

He was surprised to see how tall she was, as he'd expected a female gnome in the mold of her grandfather. Yet she was only two inches shorter than himself, which was a rare height for a woman. Well, Grigsby's loins have begat a giantess, Matthew thought; and a nervous giantess too, for she held her hands clasped together and shifted her weight from foot to foot as if late for a pressing appointment with a chamberpot.

"Matthew Corbett, please meet a rested and recovered Beryl Grigsby. Oh." The old man gave a smile and a wink. "She's informed me that she's no longer called 'Beryl.' It's *Berry* now. These youngsters!"

"How do you do, Miss Grigsby," Matthew said to the shad-owed face, and he caught a quick, reluctant "How do you do, Mr. Corbett," in return and—horrors!—a glimpse of a smile from a pretty-enough mouth but within it a gap between the front teeth that shivered his timbers. "Well," Matthew said, "very nice to meet you and I hope you have a successful stay in our fair town. Good day to you both." With a polite but firm smile to Grigsby, Matthew turned and began walking—quickly, quickly—up the hill toward the pottery shop.

"Uh . . . oh, Matthew! Please wait a moment, won't you?"

Matthew certainly did not wait. He glanced back over his shoulder and saw that Grigsby had seized the girl's hand and was coming after him. The devil of this was that Matthew was well aware of the printmaster's powers of persuasion. If he let Grigsby set a hook, he'd have this blowsy girl harpooned to his hip before he could say Jack Robinson. He kept going, feeling as if he were in a foot race and wouldn't be safe until he was up behind his blessed trapdoor.

"We have a question to put to you, Matthew!" Grigsby said, unwilling to take no answer for an answer. "Rather, Berry does! Please, Matthew, just give us a moment!"

Matthew was almost knocked off his feet by a pair of dogs that, chasing each other with wild abandon, squirted out between two houses and darted across the Broad Way. He had time to see that the chaser, a dusty yellow dog with as near a grin as an animal might conjure, was wearing a rope collar and trailed a long length of rope behind itself, having broken loose from a recent confinement. Up ahead was the pottery, and also coming south along the Broad Way was a farmer sitting up on a one-horse wagon, behind which was being towed the biggest bull Matthew had ever seen. He realized in another few seconds that his entry into the pottery was going to be blocked by the bullwagon until it creaked past, and so he gave himself up to his fate and turned to meet the Grigsbys just as the old inkspotter nearly fell upon him.

"My Lord!" Grigsby's forehead sparkled with sweat and his eyes were huge behind his spectacles. "What's the hurry?"

"I've had a long, hard day. My hurry is to get home, have supper, and go to an early bed."

"Understandable, of course, but your plan may coincide with our question. Would you care to dine with us this evening?"

Matthew still had not gotten a good look at the face beneath the hat, though he caught a glimpse of curly red hair. He focused his attention on Grigsby. "I'm sorry, Marmy. Some other time, really."

"Whoa, whoa!" the farmer called to his horse, and he lowered his wagon-brake almost exactly in front of the pottery's display window. He clambered down as Matthew glared at him. Behind the wagon, the bull stomped and snorted. "Watch him!" the farmer cautioned. "Brutus has got a bad temper!"

"Thank you, sir," Matthew shot back. Then, as the farmer tended to drawing tighter the thick rope that tethered Brutus from nose ring to the wagon before they got further into town, Matthew turned again to Grigsby. "Not this evening, but some other time. Honestly."

"You do look beat. What were you up to today?"

"I was—" *out of town*, he began to say, but thought better of it lest his trip to visit the Queen of Bedlam become broadsheet fodder. "Just busy."

Grigsby started to speak again, but what he was going to say would have to wait.

For what occurred next happened very fast, starting with the black blur that Matthew realized was a cat streaking under the wagon from the other side of the Broad Way.

Following the feline almost at equal speed was one of the pair of rowdy dogs. Barking with bloodlust, it darted nearly under the horse's hooves, which made the horse jump in its traces and jerk the wagon two inches forward even against the brake. This motion was enough to trap beneath the right rear wheel the trailing rope of the second dog that came racing after its companion, and suddenly the animal was barking and snarling and tangled up in rope under the bulk of Brutus the bull.

"*Oh*," Matthew thought he heard Berry say, or perhaps this was the noise of breath from the farmer's lungs as the man was knocked through the air like a watermelon when Brutus bucked up off all four legs. The entire rear of the wagon lifted from the ground and the yellow dog shot free and scurried for its miserable life. Brutus, however, was not willing to forgive or forget such an affront so easily, for as the wagon crashed down the bull violently twisted his head and suddenly the plank of wood that secured the metal hook to which Brutus' nose-ring rope was attached splintered and tore away.

"Great God!" the printmaster hollered, as he backed into

Matthew and almost laid both of them low. The bull had done some injury to himself and was bleeding from the nostrils. He began to jump and spin like a monstrous top only mere feet away from where Matthew, Grigsby, and the girl had squeezed themselves together as if to make the thinnest possible target, yet they were all frozen with fear at the sight of a rawhide mountain in the process of earthquake. The ground trembled, the horse screamed and dragged at the wagon, and the farmer was crabbing across the street with his right leg bent oddly at the knee. Brutus leaped and spun and the rope with its attached splintered plank and metal hook shrieked over Matthew's head.

When Brutus slammed down again and the dust welled up from his hooves, he suddenly stiffened and lowered his head as if to charge. Matthew had an instant to see the reflection of the bull's face in the pottery's window glass, and then Brutus gave an enraged bellow and the glass was no more for in a tremendous shatter and crash the bull went right through it and much of the pottery's front wall.

"Get out! Get out!" Matthew shouted toward the gaping hole by which Brutus had just entered the pottery, but in all this hellation of noise it would have been impossible for anyone to hear. The sounds of destruction within were cataclysmic, as if Armageddon had come to New York with the intent of breaking every cup, platter, and candle holder shaped by the hand of Hiram Stokely. The door, which was hanging by a hinge, abruptly burst from its single restraint. Scrambling out of the doomed shop came Stokely, his face white as a pearl beneath his snowy beard, followed at his heels by Cecily, who Matthew thought might have given a greyhound a run for the money.

The disaster was summoning a crowd from the nearby shops and houses. Someone grabbed the frantic horse's reins and several other samaritans rushed to aid the hapless farmer. Matthew was in no mood to help anybody; he was wincing at every crash that issued through the hole and pile of debris where the window had been, and now he clearly heard the snapping of a timber like a bone breaking. Brutus had just hit one of the support posts that held up the garret floor. He saw the roof tremble. Shingles popped up like jack-in-the-boxes.

Patience Stokely came running from their house on the other side of the shop, wringing her hands with terror. She saw her husband and flung her arms about him, at the same time burying her face against his shoulder as if she couldn't bear to witness the onrushing future. Hiram was either stoic or in shock, it was hard to say which, and Cecily just circled 'round and 'round as if trying to bite her tail.

Dust was rolling out of the pottery from a hundred chinks where treenails had exploded from their joints. Still Matthew heard the noise of destruction as Brutus' fury continued. Somewhere in that cacophony he heard a second timber break. Another support post, he realized, and as he watched the roof tremble again like an old man in a nightmare it dawned on him that one man's ceiling was another man's floor.

With another series of explosive crashes, silence fell. Some foolhardy soul tried to look through the hole at the innards of the place but was forced back by the dust.

The silence stretched. Little tinkles of falling glass sounded like sweet music notes, but the concert had been atrocious.

Then suddenly through the ragged aperture came Brutus, a ghostly gray. He pushed himself out like a dog as men shouted and women screamed and surged back to give the beast of the Broad Way room. Brutus stood on the street looking around as if wondering what all the fuss was about, while a few supremely brave or awesomely stupid men crept up on either side and were successful in seizing the nose-ring rope. Brutus gave them what might have been a shrug of his massive shoulders and small glittering pieces of pottery slid off his flanks.

Matthew breathed a sigh of relief. The Stokelys were safe, and that was the important thing.

"Thank God that's over!" said Marmaduke Grigsby, at Matthew's side.

There was a noise like a behemoth's belch, followed by the ominous noise of a hundred boards breaking. The roof seemed to lift upward and hang there for a few seconds, and then as Matthew watched in horror the roof collapsed like a flattened cake. From within the building came the tumult of the gods and a wave of wind and dust that in a matter of seconds had sent a London fog rolling down the Broad Way and turned every man, woman, child, and animal in the throng into a gray-daubed scarecrow.

Matthew was half-blinded. People were staggering around, coughing and hacking. Matthew felt tears in his eyes and thought this would surely make the first story of the next *Earwig*. It wasn't every day that an entire building was knocked to the ground by a rampaging bull. He made his way through the murk toward the hole where the window had been, and he was able to see all the way up to the crooked beams of the roof, for no longer was there a ceiling nor garret floor. Amid the wreckage spread before him he could make out a few items that made his throat clutch: here a broken bed, there the pieces of a clothes chest . . . and, yes, over there what remained of a bookcase that used to have burned underneath the bottom shelf the name and date of Rodrigo de Pallares, Octubre 1690.

He backed away from this sickening scene, and when he turned around he saw through the drifting pall the girl watching him.

She had either removed her hat or lost it, and the long curly tresses of red hair that had been caught up underneath now spilled in waves over her shoulders. Though she was as dusty as everyone else, still she seemed oblivious to this discomfort. She said nothing, but perhaps she saw the hurt in his eyes for she too had a wounded look as if sharing the pain he felt at the destruction of his home. She had a finely chiselled nose and a firm jaw that on a smaller girl with more delicate features might have been too wide or too strong, but she was neither small nor delicate. She simply looked at him, sadly, as the dust floated around and between them. Matthew took a step forward and felt terribly light-headed. He sat down—or rather, sank down—upon the street, and that was when he realized that he was the object of a second female's attention.

Cecily was sitting on her haunches nearby, regarding him with a slightly tilted head. Her ears twitched. Was there a shine in those piggy little eyes? Could a pig smile, and in so smiling say *I told you, didn't I?*

"Yes," Matthew answered, recalling all those knee-bumps and snout-shoves. "You did."

The disaster had at last arrived, as Cecily had predicted. He listened to the last few notes of falling glass and popping treenails, and then he drew his knees up to his chin and sat there staring at nothing until Hiram Stokely came to clasp his arm and help him to his feet.

twenty-eight

Two hours after the destruction of Stokely's pottery, Matthew sat drinking his third glass of wine at a table in the Trot Then Gallop with a half-finished platter of whitefish before him. Sitting with him at the table were Marmaduke Grigsby and Berry, who had taken him to dine and joined both in his tribulations and his drinking. A pewter cup that had been set at midtable, put there by Felix Sudbury to garner donations from the Trot's regulars, held in total three shillings, six groats, and fourteen duits, which was not a bad haul. Sudbury had been kind enough to give Matthew his dinner and drink free this evening, and of course the consolation helped but did not lift Matthew's mood from the basement.

He was shamed by his distress, for though he'd lost his living quarters the Stokelys had lost their livelihood. Going through all that wreckage, with Patience sobbing quietly at Hiram's side, had been a torment of grief. Almost everything except the odd cup or plate had been shattered, and all of Matthew's furniture broken to bits. He'd been able to salvage some clothes and he'd found his small leather pouch of savings which totalled about a pound and three shillings, all of which now sat on the floor beside him in a canvas bag Patience had brought him from the house. A few of his cherished books had survived, but he would gather those up later.

It had heartened him to hear Hiram vow to take his own savings and rebuild the pottery as soon as was possible, and he had no doubt that within a month the building would start rising again from the shards.

But it had been a damnable thing. The whitefish didn't go down very well and the wine wasn't strong enough to put him to sleep. The problem being, *where* to sleep?

"It was *my* fault, you know."

Matthew looked across the table into Berry's face. She had scrubbed the dust off in a bucket of water, and by the glow of the table's lamp Matthew could see the fine scattering of freckles across her sunburned cheeks and the bridge of her nose. The red hair shone with copper highlights and a curl hung down across her forehead over one unplucked eyebrow. She had clear, expressive eyes the exact shade of deep blue as her grandfather's, and they did not melt from Matthew's gaze. He had already judged her as more an earthy milkmaid than an erudite teacher. He could see her pitching hay in a barn, or plucking corn off the stalks. She was a pretty girl, yes, if you didn't care for the dainty type. Out to make her way in the world, a little adventurous, a little wild, probably a lot foolish. And then there were those gap-spaced front teeth, which she hadn't shown since that first quick smile from under the hat, but he knew they were there and he'd been waiting for them to pop out. What else about her resembled her grandfather? He would not like to think.

"*Your* fault?" he answered, and he took another drink of wine. "How?"

"My bad luck. Hasn't he told you?" This was punctuated by a nod of her head toward Marmaduke.

"Oh, nonsense," Grigsby replied with a scowl. "Accidents happen."

"They do, but they happen to me all the time. Even to other people, if I'm anywhere nearby." She reached for her own glass of wine and took down a swig that Matthew thought Greathouse would have approved of. "Like what happened to the preacher, on the *Sarah Embry*."

"Don't start that again," Grigsby said, or rather *pleaded*. "I've told you what the other passengers have verified. It was an accident, and if anyone was to blame it was the captain himself."

"That's not true. I dropped the soap. If not for that, the preacher wouldn't have gone over."

"All right." Matthew was weary and heartsick, but never let it be said that a good argument couldn't revive the spirit. "Suppose you *do* have bad luck. Suppose you carry it around and spread it out like fairy dust. Suppose your just being on the spot caused that bull to go mad, but of course we'll have to forget about the cat and the dogs. Also about the bull seeing his reflection in the glass window. I don't know the particulars of any other incidents, but it seems to me that you would rather see happenstance as bad luck because . . ." He shrugged.

"Because *what*?" she challenged, and Matthew thought he may have gone a red hair too far.

"Because," he said, rising to the bait, "happenstance is *dull*. It is the everyday order of things that sometimes explodes in unfortunate chaos or accidents, but to say that you have bad luck that causes these things elevates you above the crowd into the realm of . . ." Again, he felt he was treading near quicksand that had a bit of volcanic activity going on underneath it, so he shut his mouth.

"Let's all have another drink," Grigsby suggested, giddily.

"The realm of *what*?" came back the question.

Matthew levelled his gaze at her and let her have it. "The realm, miss, of rare air where resides those who require a special mixture of self-pity and magic powers, both of which are sure magnets of attention."

Berry did not reply. Were her cheeks reddening, or was that the sunburn? Matthew thought he saw her eyes gleam, in the way that light had leaped off the rapier blade Greathouse had swung at him. He realized he was sitting across the table from a girl who relished a good tangle.

"Be nice, be nice," Grigsby muttered in his wine.

"I can assure you, sir," said Berry, and there came a little glimpse of the gap as she gave a fleeting smile, "that I have neither self-pity nor powers of magic. I'm simply telling you what I know to be true. All my life I have been plagued by—or caused others to be plagued by—incidents of bad luck. How many to count? Ten, twenty, thirty? One is enough, believe me. Fires, coach accidents, broken bones, near drownings, and in the case of the preacher a *sure* drowning . . . all the above and more. I take the incident today as part of my spread of 'fairy dust,' as you so eloquently put it. By the way, you still have a lot of fairy dust in your hair."

"Unfortunately I have not been able to bathe today. I regret the inconvenience to your sensibilities."

"Children," Grigsby said, "I'm glad we're all getting along so well, but it might do to consider the hard earth of reality for a moment. Where are you going to sleep tonight, Matthew?"

A good question, but Matthew shrugged to mask his uncertainty. "I'm sure I'll find a place. A boarding house, I suppose. Or maybe Mr. Sudbury would let me sleep in the back for just the one night."

"The time to clear streets is getting near. It wouldn't do to be walking from house to house after eight-thirty. Unless, of course, you *wanted* to sleep in the gaol." Grigsby drank down the rest of his wine and pushed his glass aside. "Listen, Matthew, I have an idea."

Matthew listened, though he was wary of Grigsby's ideas. Berry also seemed to be giving her grandfather her full attention as he worked himself up to speak.

"I'd offer my house, but with Beryl . . . uh . . . Berry there now, I think you'd find it somewhat restrictive. I *do* suggest a second option, though. The Dutch dairy, beside my house."

The brick outbuilding where Grigsby kept printing supplies and press parts. Matthew knew that as a former "cool house" where milk and other perishables had once been stored, it would certainly be a nice change of temperature from his garret, but there was at least one problem. "Doesn't it have a dirt floor?"

"Nothing a throw rug couldn't fix," said Grigsby.

"Last call, gentlemen! Last call!" shouted Mr. Sudbury, with a pull on the bell that hung over the bar. "Closing in ten minutes!"

"I don't know." Matthew avoided looking at Berry, though he could feel her eyes on him. "It would be awfully *small*, wouldn't it?"

"How much room do you *need*? Berry and I could clear some space for you, and I have a cot you might use. As you say, just for one night. Or however long you wish, as my guest."

Ah, Matthew thought. Here's the catch. Putting him in close proximity to Berry, so that he might be talked into beginning his duties as a supervisor. "No windows in the place," he said. "I'm used to a view."

"What are you going to look out at, in the dark? Come, Matthew! It's just serving as a storeroom now. Plenty of space for a cot, and I could probably find a small writing desk for you as well, if you'd need that. A lantern to brighten the place, and it's home for a night."

Matthew drank some more wine and considered it. He *was* terribly tired, and didn't care where he slept tonight as long as it was clean. "No mice, are there?"

"None. It's as secure as a fort. Lock on the door and the key's in my bureau."

He nodded and then cast a swift glance at Berry. "What do *you* say about it?"

"I say, do as you please. Unless you fear another stroke of my bad luck."

"What, doesn't it ever run out?"

"Not that I've noticed."

"I don't believe in bad luck."

"But surely, sir," she said with false sweetness, "you believe in *good* luck? Why should you not believe that a person might be born under a dark cloud?"

"I think your dark cloud is self-made," Matthew answered, and again he saw the warning glint in her eyes. He kept going nevertheless. "But perhaps it's not attention you're seeking after all. Perhaps it's a dark cloud to hide under."

"To hide under?" Her mouth gave a slight twist. "What might I be hiding from?"

"The *issue* at hand," interjected Grigsby, which was fine for Matthew because he didn't wish to fence with the girl any further, "is not dark clouds but where to spend a dark night. What say you, Matthew?"

"I don't say." If Berry had indeed been born under a dark cloud, she had the knack of raining all over other people as well. Matthew realized he'd finished his third glass of wine yet he thirsted for a little more numbheadedness.

"Well, Berry and I ought to be going. Come, granddaughter." Grigsby and the girl stood up from the table, and she walked on out of the tavern without a backward glance. "Forgive her, Matthew. She's on edge. You understand. That with the ship and all. Can you blame her?"

"Her luck may be questionable, but her bad manners are unfortunately not."

"I do think she feels she had something to do with the disaster. Her mere presence, I suppose. But don't concern yourself, she'll warm up to you very soon."

Matthew frowned. "Why should I care if she warms up to me or not?"

"Just a neighborly comment, that's all. Now listen, I meant what I said about the lodgings. Would that suit you?"

"I haven't decided, but thank you anyway."

"If you *do* decide in the positive, I'll leave a lantern for you next to the door and on the door a cord with the key. All right?"

Matthew was going to reply with a shrug, for Berry's petulance was catching, but instead he sighed and said, "All right. I'm going to have another drink first."

"Mind the decree," Grigsby cautioned, and then he also left the Trot.

Matthew asked Sudbury for another half-glass of wine and drank it while he set up a chess problem on one of the boards and played it out. Sudbury announced closing time, as it was eight o'clock, and finally Matthew picked up his bag of dusty belongings, thanked Sudbury for his kind hospitality, and left the man a shilling from his donation cup. He was the last customer out, and heard the door being bolted behind him.

It was a warm and pleasant night. Matthew turned right onto Crown Street and then took the corner south onto Smith Street. He was planning on walking a circle, to turn left onto Wall Street and then back up Queen Street along the waterfront to Grigsby's house. He needed some air and some time to think. A bit of wooziness softened his vision, but he was all right, mostly. The street-corner lamps were lit, stars sparkled in the sky, and far to the east, over the Atlantic, a distant thunderstorm flickered. Matthew passed a few people rushing to get indoors before the decree began at eight-thirty, but he kept his pace unhurried as he walked along Wall Street. His mind was not on Brutus the bull nor the destruction of the pottery, but instead on the mysterious lady at the asylum.

A trip to Philadelphia was indeed in his future, but if Primm would offer up no information, then how was the Queen of Bedlam to be identified? By stopping every citizen of that town on the streets and describing the woman? Greathouse was right; it was an impossible task. But then, *how*?

That girl was maddening. Bad luck and a dark cloud. Ridiculous.

Back to the problem of identifying the woman. He felt now as if he'd overplayed his hand with Greathouse. *You being the chief investigator on this*, Greathouse had said. Did the man mean for Matthew to go to Philadelphia *alone*, and this basically his first case for the agency? That was a fine initiation, wasn't it?

And the girl needed a lesson in manners, too. But there was something else in her eyes behind that flash of anger, Matthew thought. *Perhaps it's a dark cloud to hide under*. Was there more truth to that than he'd realized?

He came to the corner of Wall Street and stopped in the glow of the lamp there to check his watch. Almost quarter after eight. He still had time, for Grigsby's house was just two blocks north up the harbor street. He took a moment to rewind the watch and then started off again, his mind moving between the mad lady and the maddening girl.

Once more lightning flashed, far at sea. The dark shapes of ships stood on his right, their spars and masts towering overhead. The commingled smells of tar, pine, and dockwater drifted to him. He was about midway between Wall Street and King Street, his mind fixed now on the demands of a six-day journey to Philadelphia—three days there and three back—when he heard a *crunch* behind him.

It came to him that it was the noise of a boot on gravel or an oyster shell, and he was about to be—

At the same instant as the hair raised on the back of his neck and he started to twist around, an arm seized him by the throat, bodily lifted him off the ground, and pulled him hard against the rough brick wall of a shopfront to his left. He had dropped his bag, for he was fighting for voice and breath and could find neither. His legs kicked, his body thrashed to no avail, and then a voice muffled by a wrapping of cloth whispered, very close to his ear, *"Be quiet and still. Just listen."*

Matthew was in no mood to listen. He was trying to get the wind back in his lungs to shout for help, but the arm around his throat tightened and he felt the blood pound at his temples. His vision swam.

"I have something for you," said the voice. An object was pressed into Matthew's right hand, which convulsively gripped and then opened again to let the thing fall. *"I have marked a page. Pay heed to it."*

Matthew was near passing out. His head felt about to explode.

The muffled voice whispered, *"Eben Ausley was—"*

A moving lantern came around the corner of King Street, and suddenly the pressure of the arm was gone. As Matthew slumped to the ground, his eyes full of red sparks and blue pinwheels, he heard the noise of someone running south. Then the noise abruptly vanished and his thought through the mindfog was that whoever it was had slipped between buildings farther along the street.

The Masker's trick, he realized.

He must have made a sound of some kind—possibly an animalish grunt or a ragged whistle as he drew air into his lungs—because suddenly the lamplight was directed down at him as he sat there stupidly blinking his eyes and rubbing his throat.

"Oh, looky here!" said the man behind the lantern. It was the nasty voice of a predatory little bully. "Who do we have but the *clerk*?"

A black billyclub came down and rested on Matthew's left shoulder. Matthew made a gasping noise but still could not speak.

Dippen Nack leaned forward and sniffed the air. "Drunk, are you? And so near the clearin' of streets, too. What am I to make o' this?"

"Help me," Matthew managed to say. His eyes had watered and he tried to get his legs under him but was having no success. "Help me up."

"I'll help you up, a'right. I'll help you right to the gaol. I thought you were such an abider of the *law*, Corbett. What's old Powers gonna say about *this*, eh?"

The billyclub rapped Matthew on the shoulder, which made him determined to get up the next time he tried. As he put his hand down to the ground for support he felt the object that had been forced upon him. He retrieved it and saw it was a small rectangular shape wrapped in brown paper. Sealed with plain white wax, he noted. He angled it toward Nack's light and saw quilled on the paper in block letters his name: *Corbett*.

"Come on. Up. I'd say not only are you stinkin' drunk, but you've violated Cornhole's decree." Again the billyclub struck Matthew's shoulder, harder this time. A sting of pain coursed along Matthew's arm. "Five seconds and I'm draggin' you up by the hair."

Matthew got up. The world spun around him a few revolutions, but he lowered his head and gulped in air and the dizziness passed. He held the brown-paper object in his right hand and dug for his watch with the left.

"I'm arrestin' you, in case it's so hard to figger out. Start walkin'," Nack commanded.

Matthew opened the watch and offered it to the light. "It's eight-twenty."

"Well, maybe I can't afford a fancy watch like that—and Lord only knows how you got it—but I don't need one to know my duty. You're drunk and it's a good walk to the gaol. 'Bout a ten- or twelve-minute walk if I know my streets."

"I'm not drunk. I was *attacked*."

"Oh, were you, now? Who attacked you?" Nack gave a chortle. "The fuckin' *Masker*?"

"Maybe it *was* him, I don't know."

Nack thrust the lantern into Matthew's face. "So why aren't you *dead*?"

Matthew couldn't supply an answer.

"Let's go," said Nack, and pressed the billyclub's tip up against Matthew's throat.

Matthew stiffened his legs so he would not be moved. "I'm not going to the gaol," he said. "I'm going home, because I'm not in violation of the decree." Home being a windowless Dutch dairy or not, he planned on waking up in the morning a free man.

"You're resistin' arrest, is that it?"

"I'm telling you what I'm going to do and advising that you go about your business."

"Is that so?"

"Let's just forget this, shall we? And thank you for your help."

Nack wore a crooked grin. "I think you need to be knocked down a peg." He lifted the club and Matthew realized the man meant to brain him.

But if Nack thought that Matthew was drunk and incapable of defense, the brutish constable was presently and unpleasantly surprised, for Matthew shifted the paper-wrapped object to his left hand and used his right fist to protest violently against Nack's mouth. The sound was like a fat codfish being smacked with an oar. Nack staggered, his eyes wide, and the billyclub cleaved empty air where Matthew had stepped aside.

Nack had perhaps three seconds of stunned immobility. Then the constable's face took on the enraged snarl of an animal—a maddened muskrat, perhaps—and he came in again, once more lifting the club. Matthew stood firm. Something that Hudson Greathouse had said during their first fencing lesson came to him very clearly: *you must take dominance of the action from your opponent*. Matthew figured that applied to fist-fighting as well as rapiers. He took a step in to block the blow with his left forearm and let fly with his right fist into Nack's nose. There was a wet-sounding *pop*. The constable fell back, almost skidding on his bootheels. He coughed and snorted and blood spurted from both nostrils, and then he cupped a hand over his wounded snout as the tears of pain flooded out of his eyes.

Matthew showed Nack his fist, cocked for another greeting. "Do you wish some more, sir?"

Nack just made a mewling noise. Matthew waited for another attack, which tonight would be the third he'd endured. Then Nack lowered his head, turned around, and walked swiftly back the way he'd come, taking the left onto King Street and carrying the lantern's light with him.

Good riddance! Matthew almost shouted at the man's back, but now with the light gone he didn't feel so brave. Whether Nack would go running to find another constable, Matthew didn't know nor did he particularly care. He picked up his bag, looked behind him to make sure no one was sweeping in on him again to lock an iron arm around his throat, and began walking at his own rapid pace toward Grigsby's house.

Never had Matthew been so glad to see a light, even if it was just the punched-tin lantern sitting on the ground beside the outbuilding's door. The cord with the key hung on the doorhandle, as promised. Matthew unlocked the door, went down three steps with the lantern, and found himself in a space about half that of the garret. The hard-packed dirt on the ground was the color of cinnamon. The walls were plastered and painted, suitably, a cream color. An uncomfortable-looking deerskin cot had been set up for him. Well, it was better than the dirt. Or was it? To the credit of Grigsby's hospitality, though, Matthew saw that he'd been supplied a small round table on which sat a waterbowl, a few matches, and a tinderbox. On the floor next to the cot was a chamberpot. He would have to share the space with a stack of wooden boxes, some buckets, an assortment of press parts, a shovel, axe, and other implements and unknown items wrapped up with canvas. Because the floor was so low and there were air-vents in the bricks just below the roof, the place was comfortably cool. For one night, it would do. The only problem, he realized soon enough, was that there was no latch on this side of the door. It would stay closed, but of course would not be locked. He would have to figure out how to somehow secure it.

Matthew then turned his attention to the object that had been so roughly gifted to him. He opened the wax seal and the paper unfolded to reveal a small black notebook with gold leaf ornamentation on the cover. His heart gave a kick that Brutus might have envied. He'd never seen the gold leaf design up close before. It was a square of scrollwork, too elegant for its owner.

Eben Ausley's missing notebook. Here in his hands. Given to him by whom?

The *Masker*?

Matthew sat down on the cot, pulled the table near, and put the lantern on top of it with the lid open to afford the most light. *I have something for you*, the muffled voice had whispered.

It was incredible, Matthew thought. Yet here it was. For whatever reason, the Masker had to have taken the notebook from Ausley's body, and for whatever reason delivered it by means of an arm around the throat. But no blade *to* the throat. Why not?

I have marked a page. Pay heed to it.

Matthew saw that a page was dog-eared toward the last third of the book. He opened it to that leaf, noting the brown stain that ran along the top of the book and had stuck some of the pages together, for there was evidence a blade had been used to cut them apart. He held the dog-eared page to the light, and saw written by Ausley's crimped hand and lead pencil a strange listing.

Ben Hepburn	4	4	6	5	Rejct	5/9
Thomas Lawry	7	5	5	8	Chapel	5/9
John Tappan	8	6	4	6	Chapel	5/9
Jacob Two	5	3	7	4	Rejct	6/20
Daniel DeBois	7	7	5	7	Chapel	6/20
Silas Oakley	7	8	8	5	Chapel	6/20
Jack Bell	3	5	4	6	Rejct	6/28
Samuell Slythe	8	7	6	9		

After that page followed a few blank pages. Matthew went back to the first page and skimmed through what he soon realized was evidence of Ausley's disordered mind. Matthew had been not far wrong in assuming that the headmaster was as addicted to his note-taking as to his gambling, for scrawled down were amounts paid for food and drink for his charges, amounts due from various charities and the churches, notes on the weather, listings—of course—of winnings and losings at the tavern tables, notes on the playing styles of different gamblers, and—yes—even jottings on what the man had been eating for lunch and supper and the ease or difficulty of his bowel movements. It was a combination ledger book and personal journal. Matthew found his own name several times in such listings as *Corbett the bastard follows me again damn his eyes* and *Corbett again the shit something must be done.* Dark stains on some of the pages may have been patches of Ausley's blood or spilled wine from a boisterous night at the tables.

Matthew returned to the dog-eared page and once more read over the series of names and numbers.

The Masker had said *Eben Ausley was—*

"Was what?" Matthew asked quietly, of the lantern's flame.

Though he wished to read the notebook carefully from beginning to end, he was being overcome by weariness. It made no sense to him whatsoever, that the Masker should give him this book. Should mark a page for him. Should refrain from cutting his throat, for wasn't murder the Masker's motive?

Murder, he thought. Murder. Yes, but for a purpose.

It does not serve his purpose to murder me, Matthew realized.

It serves his purpose for me to understand this page he has marked.

My God, Matthew thought. The Masker wants me to *help* him.

Do *what*?

He couldn't think about this anymore tonight. He closed the notebook and put it atop the table. Then he got up and set the lantern on the first step, where the opening door would knock it over and give him at least a warning. It was the best he could do. He decided against extinguishing the candle; let it go out on its own.

He took off his shoes, stretched out on the deerskin, and quickly fell away into sleep. But the last image in his mind was not the skulking Masker nor the silent Queen of Bedlam nor Reverend Wade weeping in the night nor any number of things that might have been; it was Berry Grigsby's face across the table in the Trot, golden and freckled in the lamplight, her eyes penetrating his and her voice asking, as if in challenge,

What might I be hiding from?

twenty-nine

IT WAS AN EERIE MORNING to which Matthew awakened, for when he came up from sleep he wasn't certain that the events of yesterday hadn't been just a wretched dream. Therefore when he found himself on the deerskin cot in the dim light that filtered through the air-vents, with Eben Ausley's notebook on the table, his body stiff and sore from being yanked off his feet by the Masker's arm and the memory of the pottery's destruction still crashing in his mind, he squeezed his eyes shut again for a while and lay still as if to avoid life itself until he felt strong enough to receive it.

Oh, his back hurt! He got up, wondering how the Indians could bear it. His first task was to get a match aflame and light the lamp. The candle had burned down to almost nothing, yet there remained a small stub and a bit of wick that sputtered but finally accepted the fire. He felt the same as that wick. Then, in the meager illumination, Matthew picked up the notebook to make sure it was real. He turned again to the dog-eared page, held it nearer the light, and examined the names and numbers pencilled there.

Matthew assumed they were the names of orphans. The *Two* beside the *Jacob* would mean he was the second Jacob in the group but his surname was unknown; the same as John Five. The lines of numbers were a mystery. And then there were the other markings:

Rejct, Chapel, and what might have been dates. The ninth of May, twentieth and twenty-eighth of June. The last entry bearing no notation or date. He looked at the word *Rejct.*

Reject? Why had Ausley not simply added the second *e?* Or was it a shorthand for *Rejected?*

The word *Chapel* next drew his attention. He knew the orphanage did have a chapel. Just a small room with a few benches in it, really. In Matthew's time there, the churchmen occasionally came to make sure the orphans were following the righteous path. Otherwise the chapel would have been just another chilly chamber for bunks.

Matthew had a sense of unease about that word. Was he looking at a record of Ausley's more recent "punishments"? And had that bastard committed his sickening deeds in the *chapel,* of all places?

But the notation *Rejected* did not fit, in that context. If that was really the word, then *Rejected* for what? And by whom? Why also was there no notation next to the last name?

He reasoned that he would have to put together a time span for this notebook. When Ausley filled up one, he likely went right to the next. The notebook might have been his fifth or fifteenth. Just going by the dates on the list, this particular volume of Ausley's great deeds would have been started around the second week of May.

The wick began to spit again. Matthew decided it was time to rejoin the world. His stomach was also making itself heard, calling for breakfast. When he checked his watch, he was shocked to see the time was nearly eight o'clock. He'd been more weary than he'd realized, as he usually woke around six. He spent a moment splashing cool water in his face, but there was neither soap nor towel. After getting some breakfast he intended to visit the barber for a shave and bath, for he had both the grit of travel and the dust of disaster in his pores.

He took a clean—*clean* being a relative term—light blue shirt from his bag and put it on, along with a pair of fresh stockings. The two pair of breeches in the bag were about as grimy as the pair he'd slept in, so he made no change in that regard. Then he put Ausley's notebook into the bag under the breeches and the bag under the cot. He walked out into a brilliant sunshine that at first blinded him; it was darker than he'd thought in the Dutch dairy, which was of course the purpose. He locked the door behind him.

Marmaduke Grigsby answered his knock and invited him in, and soon Matthew was sitting at the table in Grigsby's kitchen as the printmaster cut slices of salted bacon for him and broke two eggs into a pan over the hearth's small fire. A cup of strong dark tea tore away the last cobwebs in Matthew's mind.

Matthew started in on his breakfast, which was absolutely delicious, and drank down a mug of apple cider before he asked, "I presume Berry's sleeping late?"

"Sleeping *late*? That girl hardly sleeps at *all*. She's been up and out almost before sunrise."

"Really? Where to so early?"

"Gone up Queen Street. Looking for a place, as she put it, to catch the morning light."

Matthew paused with a piece of bacon half-chewed in his mouth. "Catch the light? Why?"

"Her fascination," said Grigsby, as he poured a cup of tea for himself from the pot. "Didn't I tell you? That she has hopes of becoming an artist? Well, she already *is* an artist, I mean, but she hopes to make some money off it." Grigsby sat down across from Matthew. "Your breakfast all right?"

"Fine, thank you, and I do appreciate your hospitality." Matthew finished his bacon before he spoke again. "An artist? I thought she planned to be a teacher."

"Yes, that's the plan. Headmaster Brown's going to interview her for a position next week. But Berry's always been interested in drawing and such, even as a little girl. She got the tar spanked out of her once, as I recall, for fingerpainting the family dog."

"Somehow, I'm not surprised."

Grigsby smiled at Matthew's tone of voice, but then he frowned and said, "Aren't you due at work? I know that might be difficult today, but surely you ought to at least speak to Magistrate Powers."

"I've been discharged," Matthew answered, and then wished he hadn't because instantly the printmaster's gaze sharpened and he leaned closer over the table.

"What's happened? Was Powers fired?"

"No. I might as well tell you that the magistrate is leaving New York. He has an offer for a better job in the Carolina colony. Working with his brother on Lord Kent's tobacco plantation." Matthew knew the shine in Grigsby's eyes behind those spectacles meant an item of news was being born for the next *Earwig*. "Now listen, Marmy, that's not to be printed. I mean it." If an *Earwig* could get to the asylum in Westerwicke, one could also find its way to Professor Fell. "It's important that you understand, the information is confidential."

"And why is it so confidential, then?" Grigsby watched him carefully. Absentmindedly, the printmaster reached over to a bowl of walnuts and removed one. "It's a change of residence and position, yes? Or is it something more?"

"It's just confidential, that's all. I expect you to refrain from printing it."

"*Refrain.*" Grigsby grimaced. "Now that's a strong word, isn't it? Particularly to a man in my profession." The hand with the walnut in it flew up against his forehead. There was a pistol-shot *crack* and with no ill effect whatsoever Grigsby separated nut from broken shell. "You know, with the Masker not killing anyone since the decree began, I have to take the news as it comes. It's my duty to report the facts, so to have to *refrain* can be difficult." He paused in his chewing of the walnut to sip at his tea with a slurping noise and then looked at Matthew over the cup's rim. "What do you honestly think of Berry?"

"I have no thoughts."

"Surely you do." He chose a second nut from the bowl. "She made you a little angry last night, didn't she?"

Matthew shrugged.

"She did. She has that way about her. Speaks her mind. All

374 · Robert McCammon

that malarkey about the bad luck. I'm not sure if she really believes it or not. But you may be right." *Crack!* shattered the shell.

"About what?" Matthew busied himself with finishing the eggs. How did the man *do* that? And not a mark on his forehead. The skull must be made of iron, the flesh of leather.

"Her creating a dark cloud to hide under. I think it's because she likes her freedom. She doesn't want to give it up to anyone. Particularly a husband, though she came close to the altar with that young man who broke out in the blotches. Also I think she doesn't want to be hurt. That could be a reason for creating a dark cloud, couldn't it?"

"Yes, it could be," Matthew agreed.

"You know," Grigsby said, chewing, "you have the damnedest way of pretending *not* to pay attention when you're taking everything in. It's infuriating."

"Oh, is it? I'm sorry."

"Well, I don't *want* her to be hurt," Grigsby went on. "You know what I mean. Berry's not exactly a clothes-horse, nor does she give a fig about the latest fads. She couldn't care less about those French hairstyles and the new dances, which seem to consume the minds of almost every girl her age in this town."

"The ones who aren't married, at least," Matthew said.

"Yes, and that's another thing." A third nut was selected, forehead-cracked, and eaten. "The young men around here are not to be trusted. Listen, I could tell you stories that would curl your hair about what some of these young gents get up to with the girls on Saturday nights!"

"Told to you by the widow Sherwyn, I presume?"

"Yes, and others as well. These young men are like ravenous wolves, eager to snap up whatever innocent morsel they can find! I think it must be something in the water."

"Spoken like a true grandfather." Matthew tipped his teacup to the man.

Grigsby sat back. He pushed his spectacles up onto his forehead and rubbed the bridge of his nose. "Ah, me," he said. "Seeing

Berry again . . . it takes me back, Matthew. She reminds me so much of Deborah. The red hair, the fresh face, the glorious *youth*. I wasn't so squat and ugly in my own younger days that I couldn't attract a pretty girl. It also helped that my father's printshop did very well and we lived in a nice house. But I wasn't the landcrab you see before you now, Matthew. Far from it. You know they say a man's ears, nose, and feet grow larger all his life. True in my case, very true. Unfortunately many other parts grew smaller. Oh, don't look at me like that!"

"I wasn't," said Matthew.

"Here's the rub." Grigsby returned his spectacles to his eyes, blinked heavily once, and then focused on his guest. "I'd like you to move into the dairyhouse for a while, so you can watch Berry. Keep her out of trouble and away from those young serpents I've mentioned. You know who they are, those youngsters of Golden Hill who tear through the taverns and end their evenings on Polly Blossom's pillows."

"Indeed," Matthew said, though this was news to him.

"I can't keep up with her. And she certainly doesn't want me tagging along. So I thought you might introduce her to some people more her age. Pave the way for her, so to speak."

Matthew was slow in answering, as he was still taking in the *I'd like you to move into the dairyhouse*. "If you haven't already noticed," he said, "I'm not at the center of the social whirl. The last time I looked, clerks were not being invited to join the Young New Yorkers, the Bombasters, or the Cavaliers." Naming three of the social clubs that held dances and parties throughout the year. "I am not one for loud gatherings and so-called merriment."

"Yes, I know that. You're steady and dependable, and that's why I want you to be an example for Berry."

"You mean her *guardian*."

"Well, you might learn something from each other," Grigsby suggested, with a twitch of his eyebrows. "She to be more responsible, and you to be more . . . merry-making."

"Move into the *dairyhouse*?" Matthew decided to steer toward a firmer shore. "It's a dungeon in there!"

"It's a cool, cosy summerhouse. Think of it that way."

"Summerhouses usually have floors and at least one window. There's not even a latch on the other side of the door. I could be murdered in my sleep."

"A latch is no problem. I could easily have one put on the door." Grigsby then pounced on Matthew's silence. "You can live there free of charge, as long as you please. Eat your meals here, if you like. And I also could use your help with the printing, so I'd pay you a shilling or two per job."

"I already have a job. Hopefully it will turn into a *profession*." He saw that Grigsby was all ears. "Do you know that notice I had you place? For the Herrald Agency? I've joined them."

"That's well and good, but what do they *do*?"

For the next while, Matthew explained to the printmaster his meeting with Katherine Herrald and the agency's purpose. "She thinks I can be of service, and I'm eager to get started. I understand she and her associate, Mr. Greathouse, are close to renting office space."

"Problem solving?" Grigsby shrugged. "I suppose it might go over. Especially if the agency hired out to City Hall to help with criminal cases. I'm not sure what Bynes or Lillehorne would think of it, but there's the possibility." He cast a sharp eye at Matthew. "Ah *ha*! You're working on finding the Masker, aren't you? Has the city already given that over?"

"No. I *am* working on finding the Masker for Mrs. Deverick, though. As a private concern. I'm waiting for her to respond to some questions I sent her in a letter. The agency has some other things going on, as well." He dared not mention the Queen of Bedlam, for he wished that to remain his own business. Neither did he want to speak the name of Professor Fell. "So you see, I do have a future." He quickly corrected himself. "A job, I mean."

"I never doubted that you had a future." Grigsby finished his tea before he spoke again. "I still would like for you to move into the dairyhouse and keep watch . . . I mean keep *company* with Berry. Whatever you wish to do with the dairyhouse as far as making it more comfortable, I am at your service. And I do have some money saved up to work with."

"I appreciate the gesture, but I expect I can find a room somewhere. That's not to say I wouldn't be willing to help you with the print jobs, if time allows it."

"Very kind of you, very kind." Grigsby stared at a pineknot on the table. "But you know, Matthew, it would be difficult for me to *refrain* from printing a certain item concerning Magistrate Powers if you weren't . . . say . . . living on the premises."

Matthew's mouth fell open. "Tell me," he said quietly, "that you didn't just stoop to what I think you stooped to."

"What did I stoop to?"

"You know what! Marmy, I *can't* nursemaid your granddaughter! And I'll bet she'd brain you on the skull with that frying pan if she even knew you were suggesting it!" Little good the frying pan would do, he thought.

"Then she ought not to know, for the sake of my skull."

"She ought to find her own way here! She doesn't need my help! I'd say she can take care of herself well enough, bad luck or not."

"Possibly true. But I'm not asking you to nursemaid her or watch her every move. I'm simply asking you to show her around. Introduce her to people. Take her to dinner a time or two. Listen . . . before you decide anything, will you at least go *talk* to her? Try to get to know her a little better? I hate the idea that you and she got off on the wrong foot." He watched Matthew scowl. "You being one of my favorite people, and she being another. Just go and talk to her for a little while. Would you do that for an old addlepated grandpa?"

"Addlepated is right," Matthew said. Then he drew in a long breath and let it out and figured he could at least *speak* to the confounded girl before he went on his way. Grigsby wouldn't print the item about Magistrate Powers; he was bluffing. Wasn't he? Matthew pushed his chair back and stood up. "Where did you say she went?" he asked glumly.

"Up Queen Street. Looking for—"

"A place to catch the morning light, yes, I know." He started for the door and then turned back. "Marmy, if she bites my head off I'm not going to have anything more to do with her. Is that agreed?"

The printmaster regarded him over the lenses. "I'll go ahead and get the locksmith to work. Does that suit you?"

Matthew left the house before he said words no gentleman should utter. Since he was going walking, he decided he ought to take his bag of dirty clothes to the widow Sherwyn, so he went back into the dairyhouse—was the place even smaller than it had been last night?—and retrieved the bag from beneath his cot. The notebook was problematic. He didn't wish to leave it lying about if the locksmith did come today, nor did he wish to be carrying it around town. He lifted one of the shrouds of canvas and found of all things a burlap-covered archery target, well-punctured. Some of the hay stuffing was boiling out. He widened a rip, slid the notebook down into the target, and covered it over once more with the canvas. Then he noted something leaning in the corner alongside the shovel and axe: a rapier with what appeared to be an ivory grip. There was no scabbard. The blade was splotched with rust. Matthew wondered how the sword and the target had gotten in here, but he had places to go and things to do. With the bag in tow, he left the dairyhouse and locked the door behind him.

It took him almost twenty minutes and a walk of well over a mile before he found Berry Grigsby. She had gone north along Queen Street past the hubbub and clatter of shipyards and wharfs until she'd found a pier to her liking. The place was shaded with overhanging trees, and the river washed around house-sized boulders that had been set here by the hand of God. She was sitting out about fifty feet from shore at the very end of her chosen pier, her straw hat on her head and in her lap a pad of sketching paper. She was wearing what looked to be a dress sewn together from patches of a dozen different eye-startling costumes, in colors of peach, lavender, pale blue, and lemon yellow. He didn't know if he'd be talking to a girl or a fruit bowl.

He bit his lip and called, "Hello!"

Berry looked around at him, waved, and then continued her drawing. She seemed to be concentrating on her view of a green and rolling pasture across the river in Breuckelen. Gulls were swooping over the water, following the white sails of a small packet boat making its way south.

"May I come out?" Matthew called.

"As you wish," she answered, without pause in her creative labor.

Matthew thought it was a lost cause, but he started out along the pier. It took him only three steps to realize Berry had chosen a wharf that must have been used by the first fur trader to have ever skinned a beaver in New Amsterdam. The thing had been battered by the prows of many long-forgotten boats and spaces gaped between the weather-beaten planks. He stopped, thinking that one misstep or the breaking of a worm-eaten board beneath his feet could give him a bath and douse his clothes at the same time. Then he felt her eyes on him, and he knew he had to go the distance. Besides, the girl had made it, hadn't she? But why the devil had she chosen this old broken-down pier, of all places?

He kept walking. Every creak and groan sent a shudder up his spine. At one place there was a hole the size of an anvil. He saw dark water below, and he almost stopped and turned around but he was more than halfway to where the girl sat, crosslegged Indian style, and he felt somehow that this was a mission of honor. Or a dare. Whichever, he edged around the hole with its jagged boards and eased forward, step after nervous step.

When he reached Berry, he must have breathed a sigh of relief because she angled her face up at him from under the straw hat and he caught the brief glimpse of a mischievous smile. "Nice morning for a walk, isn't it, Mr. Corbett?"

"Invigorating." He felt a bit damp under his arms. She returned to her drawing and Matthew saw she was pencilling a very pleasant scene of the pasture and rolling hills. Beside her was a small box, open to display an assortment of different-hued crayons.

"I don't think I've caught it yet," Berry said.

"Caught what?"

"The *spirit* of the place," she replied. "All that energy."

"Energy?"

"Forces of nature. Here, this one I've finished." She flipped up her sketch to display the sheet of paper below it, and Matthew thought his eyes might bleed. This previous work, the same scene as the present one, had been attacked with vivid emerald green, pale grass green, streaks of yellow, and splotches of fiery orange and red. It looked to him more like the interior of a blacksmith's forge than a sunny pastoral view. It was an act of war against Mother Nature, he thought as he looked out across the river to make sure he was seeing what she did. Obviously, he did not. He wondered what the good, witch-fearing folk of Fount Royal would have thought about this picture and the artist who'd created it. Thank God bad taste in art wasn't a sign of demonic possession, or Berry would have been hanged by her blue stockings. *I wouldn't show that to anyone*, he almost said, but he bit his tongue so hard the blood almost bloomed.

"This is the rough work, of course," she said. "I'll put it to canvas when I get it right."

He had to open his mouth. "You know, I don't see any red or orange over there. Only green. Oh! Was that the sun coming up?"

She let the new drawing fall back to cover the first, as if saying he wasn't intelligent enough to view it. Her sketching continued. "I'm not trying to capture what *is*, Mr. Corbett," she said, with some frost. "I'm trying to capture the essence of the place. You don't see any red or orange, which is my interpretation of the creative fire of the earth, because you're only looking at the pasture."

"Yes," he agreed. "That's what I see. A pasture. Is there something I'm missing?"

"Only the element at work *beneath* the pasture. The surge of life and fire from the heart of the earth. Almost like . . . well, a cooking fire, I suppose. Or—"

"A blacksmith's forge?"

"Ah!" Berry smiled up at him. "Now you've got it."

Matthew thought she should never mention phrases like *the*

heart of the earth unless she wished to leave town under tar and feathers en route to Bedlam herself, but decorum prevented putting the thought to voice. "I suppose that's the modern art style from London?" he asked.

"Heavens, no! Everything's gray and gloomy on the canvases over there. You'd think the artists washed their brushes with tears. And the portraits! Why is it that everyone wishes to be viewed by history as tight-assed fops? The women even more than the men!"

Matthew had to recover his wits after this scandalous outburst. "Well," he ventured, "possibly because they *are* tight-assed fops?"

Berry looked up at him and this time allowed the sun to catch her face. Her blue eyes, clear as diamonds and potentially as cutting, appraised him with a genuine interest for a few seconds, and then she lowered her head and the sketching pencil scratched on.

Matthew cleared his throat. "May I ask why you chose this particular pier? I think it might collapse at any moment."

"It might," she agreed. "I didn't believe anyone else would be foolish enough to walk on it and disturb me while I'm working."

"Pardon the disturbance." He gave a slight bow. "I'll leave you now to the furnace."

He had just turned to retrace his path over the rickety structure when Berry said, very calmly and matter-of-factly, "I know what my grandfather is asking of you. Oh, he doesn't *know* that I know, but he disregards my . . . call it . . . intuition. He wants you to *watch* me, doesn't he? Keep me out of trouble?"

"Not exactly."

"What, then? Exactly?" Berry put down her pencil and turned around to give him her full attention.

"He's asked me to squire you around a bit. Help you get settled." He was beginning to be annoyed by her sly little smile. "New York may not be London, but there *are* pitfalls here. Your grandfather simply wishes you not to step into one."

"I see." She nodded and angled her head to the side. The sun gleamed on the red curls that fell over her shoulder. "You should know, Mr. Corbett, that you're being foxed. Before I left England, my father received a letter from Grandda telling him not to worry, for my grandfather was making a vow to find me a husband. You, sir, seem to be the candidate for groom."

Matthew smiled broadly at the nonsense of that last sentence, but when Berry's face remained steadfastly serious he felt his smile collapse. "That's ridiculous!"

"I'm glad we're of a single mind on the subject."

"I don't plan on being married to *anyone*, anytime soon."

"And before I marry I plan on making a living from my art."

An impoverished spinster for life, Matthew thought. "But your teaching is important to you also, isn't it?"

"It is. I think I have value as a teacher, and I do like children. But art is my true calling."

More like a yodel at midnight, he thought, but he kept a straight face. "Listen, I assure you I'll put your grandfather on the straight road about this. He's been hounding me about moving into the dairyhouse, and now I know why."

Berry stood up. Her height almost put her eye-to-eye with Matthew. "Don't be so rash, Mr. Corbett," she said silkily. "If Grandda puts all his eggs in your basket, he won't be trying to foist me off on a succession of boring imbeciles whose idea of a plum future is an easy chair and an easy maid. So if you were to play along, it would be to my favor."

"Really? And what favor would *I* get out of it? A dirt floor and a dungeon?"

"I'm not saying you would have to . . . as you put it . . . squire me around very long. A month, possibly. If that. Just long enough for me to impress my will upon my grandfather." She blinked and thought better of that last statement. "I mean, impress to my grandfather how important my freedom is. And the fact that I can find my own young man, in my own time."

"A *month*?" That word left a sour taste in Matthew's mouth. "I'd be just as comfortable in the gaol. At least the cells have windows."

"Think about it, at least. Will you? I'd be in your debt."

Matthew didn't wish to give it a moment's further thought,

but here was the point of the pickle: if he did consent to stay in the dairyhouse and at least pretend to serve as Berry's squire or guardian or whatever the blazing hell Grigsby intended, he could keep that item about Magistrate Powers from turning up in a future *Earwig*. One month? He could stand it. Maybe.

"I'll think about it," he agreed.

"Thank you. Well, I believe I'm done for the morning." Berry knelt down and began to put away her crayons. "May I walk back with you?" It was obvious now that she was warming to him, as this business of the New York groom had been overcome.

"I'm not going all the way back to Grigsby's, but you're welcome to accompany me." So saying, he cast an uneasy eye along the fifty feet of rotten pier and fervently hoped Berry's bad luck would not sink them both.

They made it over, though not without Matthew thinking more than once that the next step would take him into the river. Berry gave a laugh when they reached solid ground, as if what was for Matthew an ordeal was for her an adventure. He had the impression that her problem might not be bad luck, but unfortunate choices. Still, she did have a nice laugh.

On their walk back along Queen Street, Berry asked if Matthew had ever been to London and he said regrettably not, but that he hoped to go before long. She then proceeded for the next while to entertain him with descriptions of some of the sights and streets of London that were clearly remembered by the eye of the artist, so richly were they fashioned. He found it interesting that Berry described several book stores she used to visit, and one book seller in particular who sold coffee and chocolate at a counter right in the shop. After her telling of it, Matthew felt he could smell the fresh paper of the books and the wafting aroma of the hot black coffee on a rainy London afternoon.

They were nearly back to Grigsby's house when, with Berry talking about her life in the Great City and Matthew listening as if walking the cobblestones at her side, there came the sound of horse hooves and jingling traces behind them. A high-pitched bell was rung, and they stepped aside as a double-horse carriage approached. As it slowed, Matthew saw in the seats behind the driver Joplin Pollard and Mrs. Deverick, he jaunty in a beige suit, waistcoat, and tricorn and she again grim in black gown and hat, her face pallid beneath white powder. The leather top of the carriage had been put up to throw shade over the passengers.

"Ah! Corbett!" said the lawyer. "Mrs. Deverick and I were just on our way to the printmaster's house. We've been trying to find you."

"Oh?"

"We made a stop at Stokely's house. He told us you'd left with Grigsby after that ghastly mishap yesterday. Not much left of the pottery, is there? And who might this be?"

"This is Miss Beryl . . . Berry Grigsby. Marmaduke's grand-daughter. Berry, this is Mr. Joplin Pollard and . . . the widow Deverick."

"Charmed, my dear." Pollard touched the rolled rim of his tricorn, and Berry gave a nod in return. The lady in black swept her gaze across Berry's clothes and then looked at her with narrowed eyes, as one might regard a strangely colored lizard. "May we steal Mr. Corbett away from you for a little discussion?" Pollard didn't wait for Berry's response, but clicked open the carriage's door. "Climb up, Corbett."

"If you're going in that direction," Matthew said, "might you give Miss Grigsby a ride home? It's just—"

"A *private* discussion," Mrs. Deverick interrupted, staring straight ahead.

Matthew felt a bit of heat in his cheeks, but when he looked at Berry she just shrugged and gave him a glimpse of the gap between her front teeth when she smiled. "It's all right, Matthew. I think I'd rather walk. Will you join us for lunch?"

"I have some errands, but I'll see you later."

"Fine. I'm sure Grandda will appreciate that. Good day, sir," she said to Pollard, and to Mrs. Deverick, "Good day, widow." Then Berry walked on along the harbor street, carrying her valise and sketchpad, and Pollard said to Matthew, "Come, come! We have some business."

thirty

W ITH MATTHEW SEATED across from his two carriage companions, his clothes bag on the floor at his feet and the
horses clip-clopping south along the harbor, Mrs. Deverick looked
pointedly at him and asked, "Have you sworn off shaving, young
man?"

"Forgive the stubble. One of my errands today is to Mr. Reynaud."

"I hear he does a good job," said Pollard. "Though I wouldn't
let a slave with a razor anywhere near me."

"Mr. Reynaud is a free man," Matthew reminded him. "He's
been free for nearly five years, I understand."

"You're a braver man than me, then. I'd be afraid he'd choose
the moment of my shaving to forget he's living in civilization and
revert back to savagery. So. I—and Mrs. Deverick also, of
course—regret to hear of your recent inconvenience. Where are
you living?"

"In Grigsby's dairyhouse." From the corner of his eye he saw
Mrs. Deverick put a black-gloved hand to her mouth. "For the
time being. A month, maybe."

"A dairyhouse." A quick smile flickered around the edges of
Pollard's mouth. "I assume you'll have all the milk you can drink?"

"It *used* to be a dairyhouse. Now it's—" He decided to stop playing at civilities. "There was business you wished to discuss?" He turned his gaze upon the woman. "Privately?"

"Oh, yes." Pollard reached into his coat and brought out an envelope. "Your questions to Mrs. Deverick. She wishes to respond to them, in my presence."

Matthew kept his focus on the widow. "Madam, do you need a lawyer to answer some simple questions?"

"I think it's best," Pollard offered. "After all, protecting my client is what I'm paid to do."

"In this instance, protection against what? *Me?*"

"Mr. Corbett, we're all striving for clarity in this situation, are we not? I would be present if Mrs. Deverick were to answer questions like these before High Constable Lillehorne, or any magistrate. Surely I ought to be present if a *clerk*—no matter how intriguing or intelligent he appears to my client—asks them. And forgive me, Mrs. Deverick, but I have to repeat my objections that this entire arrangement is farcical. What can this fellow learn that trained professionals can't—"

"Objection noted," said Mrs. Deverick. "Now shut your wine keg and sit back. You'll earn your fee with silence as well as with prattling." She took the envelope from his hand as he settled back with a soft hissing noise, his brown eyes glinting with both defeat and disdain. "I decided not to put anything in writing," she told Matthew as she pulled the letter free. "On the advice of my lawyer. Particularly concerning my thoughts on . . ." She paused for a few seconds, as if willing herself to speak the following names. "Dr. Julius Godwin and Mr. Eben Ausley."

"Very well," Matthew said. "Nothing in writing, then."

"I'll answer your questions in the order they were asked. First, having to do with any discussion Mr. Deverick might have had with me concerning business matters: the answer to that is *none*. As I have previously stated to you, Pennford kept his business affairs strictly to himself. I was required to run the household, raise the sons, and comport myself as a wife ought to. I never asked about business. It was not my realm. Next question: having to do

with any recent trips Pennford made, either for business or pleasure."

Matthew was listening, though he had the suspicion this was
not going to get him anywhere. The horses clopped on, and
Matthew began to think of how good a hot bath was going to feel.

"As *recent*, I assume you mean within the last six months," Mrs.
Deverick continued. "The answer to that, also, is *none*. Pennford
did not care to travel, as he had digestive problems."

"No need for that detail, madam," Pollard spoke up.

She gave him a withering glare. "Again, charging per word, I
presume?"

"What about *less* recent?" Matthew asked. "Say, a year or so?"

"Adding to the questions now, are we?" was Pollard's rebuke.

"Within a year or so, the answer is the same," said the widow.
"None."

Matthew nodded and rubbed his scratchy chin.

Mrs. Deverick put the letter in her lap and smoothed it out.
"The third question, and most odious, concerns my displeasure
over your mention of those two men in connection with my late
husband. I shall state emphatically and under the eye of the Lord
that Pennford had no dealings with either Dr. Godwin or Eben
Ausley. They weren't worth the scrapings off Pennford's boots."
She turned to Pollard as he was about to protest this detail and put
a finger in his face. *"Shut."*

Matthew let Pollard settle back like a strawman in collapse
before he ventured further. "It's my understanding that Dr. Godwin had a sterling reputation, madam. Even though he was physician to Polly Blossom's ladies. After all, *some* physician had to take
that job."

"Ah, but Julius Godwin *enjoyed* it too much. He practically
lived there the last few years. Became a sobbing drunk and nearly
a lunatic, spending all his time with what you charitably and fool-
ishly call *ladies*. Those are demons in disguise, and before I draw
my last breath I pray to see Polly Blossom thrown onto a ship like
a pile of rags and deported from these colonies."

"We are keeping our emotions about us," Pollard advised.

She ignored him. "I cannot *stand* a weak man, sir," she said to Matthew, her face nearly contorted with disgust. "Weak men go through those doors. You ask me why I detested Julius Godwin, well there it is. And plenty of eligible—and fashionable—widows available to him, but he preferred to go to the whores. Pennford told me Godwin was sick, and that's why he drank so much and spent his . . . his *energies* with those filthy creatures."

"Sick?" Matthew was no longer thinking about the bath; his mind was questing. "You mean mentally ill?"

"I mean he could have been married long ago, but he threw himself away. And I recall when Dr. Godwin first came here, he was a fine upstanding physician. A clean man. Had come from London, to start anew. He was all right, until his weakness killed him."

"I think it was the Masker who killed him," Matthew said.

"The Masker finished the job Godwin's weakness began," came the reply. "I don't know, maybe the Masker is some maniac who was incensed over where Godwin put his dirty instruments."

Matthew let that one go. Pollard was just looking blankly out at the ships as the carriage progressed toward the Great Dock. Matthew wondered if Pollard might be thinking what Mrs. Deverick would say if she knew that one of her own lawyers was as much a whore-monger as Godwin had been. It seemed that the upper class had all the money, but the lower class—like the widow Sherwyn—had all the knowledge. But of course, according to Grigsby, there were plenty of Polly Blossom's customers living on Golden Hill.

Matthew leaned forward. "You said Dr. Godwin came from London to *start anew*. When was that?"

"I suppose it was . . . at least fifteen years ago. Probably nearer twenty."

"And start anew from *what?*"

"I don't know for certain. It was a phrase Pennford used. But it was well-known that Godwin's wife died of fever, when they were both very young. He told it around town. Possibly that had something to do with the drunken wreckage he became, but I had no sympathy for him."

A silence stretched, as Matthew pondered this last statement.

Pollard came out of his trance. "Where do you want us to drop you, Corbett?"

"Eben Ausley," Matthew said to the woman. "What about *him*?"

Mrs. Deverick gave an unladylike snort of derision. "You being an orphan, as Mr. Pollard informs me, I'm surprised you don't know what was whispered about him. That he was a . . . well, I hardly can mention the word. That he took *liberties* with his charges. Hadn't you *heard*? Pennford despised him, too, and said that if any orphan ever came forward to testify about such indignities he personally would have that monstrous heathen hanged in front of City Hall."

"Really," Matthew said, as the world seemed to spin around in one dizzying revolution.

"Absolutely. It could never be proven, though. Evidently the rumor went that Ausley was reeking drunk at a tavern and made some mention of . . . that practice to one of the whores. She told someone else, and . . . but, as I said, it was never proven. Still, that man made my flesh crawl. I didn't like him, just on principle."

"But who can trust a whore?" asked Pollard, with a shrug.

"You were Ausley's lawyer. How is it you could represent Pennford Deverick and also Ausley?"

"Where's the problem? My firm inherited both accounts from Charles Land. I handled Ausley's legal and financial affairs, not his morals. And if you're wishing to stir up muddy water between Mrs. Deverick and me, you'll be disappointed to know that she understands—as did her husband—that a lawyer is a tool for a purpose. It was not my place to pass judgment on anyone."

"Though now that Pennford is gone, there might have been a change of legal firms if Ausley had remained alive," Mrs. Deverick said. "Tool or not."

"Another question for you." Matthew kept his gaze on Pollard. "Since you handled Ausley's financial affairs, how is it he could afford to lose so much money at the gaming tables?"

Pollard's reddish-brown eyebrows lifted. "How is it you know how much money he lost? If indeed he lost *any?*"

"I saw him lose money on many occasions."

"Did you? What were you doing? *Following* him?"

"I just . . . saw him, that's all. In the taverns."

"I'd presume," said Pollard, "that on some nights he lost and on some nights he won. If you do the math, you might find he came out even or a little ahead."

"He was *repulsive.*" Mrs. Deverick returned the letter to the envelope. "And Godwin was sickening. So there are your answers, Mr. Corbett." She held the envelope out to him. "Helpful in some way, I hope."

Not really, he wanted to say, but then again he had to put his mind to what the woman had told him and sift through the information as if it were fine sand. He took the envelope and settled against his seatback, the horses' rhythm causing the carriage to rock back and forth.

"My opinion, if I'm allowed to give one," said Pollard, who paused to make sure his nose wasn't clipped before he went on, "is that this Masker person has left town. I think the decree has had its effect, as much as we regret having to lose income to suit Lord Cornbury's grievances against the taverns. I mean, if *I* were the Masker, why should I wish to dawdle at the scene of the crimes?"

"Possibly because your work might not be done?" Matthew asked, looking sharply at him.

"My *work?* And what work might that be, sir?"

"I don't know."

"Did you hear that, madam?" Pollard's voice was almost gleeful. "Your investigator *doesn't know.* Corbett, I'll give you some free advice, and pay heed to it. Return to your role as clerk and give up this amusing attempt to play at high constable. You'll be ever so much the better for—"

"One moment," Matthew interrupted. "Repeat that, please."

"Repeat *what?*"

"You said, 'I'll give you some free advice, and—' "

"I have no idea what you're going on about now."

" 'Pay heed to it,' is what you said," Mrs. Deverick spoke up. She looked quizzically at Matthew.

"Yes. Would you repeat that phrase, Mr. Pollard?"

Pollard grinned and frowned and grinned. "Has your brain gotten too much sun?"

Matthew watched him carefully. *I have marked a page*, the Masker's muffled voice had said last night. *Pay heed to it.* "Just speak it. Won't you?"

"I've said it once, why should I say it again? Because you demand it?"

"Because I'm asking."

"For the mercy of *Christ*!" scowled the widow. "Say it, Pollard!"

"All right then, what do I care if a lunatic demands that I speak a phrase I hardly even recall saying? Pay heed to it, pay heed to it, pay heed to it! Does that send you into a rapture?"

Matthew had been listening for something—anything—that might remind him of the voice from last night, but he heard nothing recognizable in tone or cadence. Still, the voice being so muffled, probably disguised behind a cravat pulled up over the mouth . . . it was hard to tell whether Pollard was shamming or not. Inconclusive, he thought, but he still kept a watchful eye trained on the man.

"I suppose I'll get out here," Matthew said, as the carriage reached Hanover Square. Micah Reynaud's shop was only two blocks away, across from the Jewish synagogue on Mill Street. With a command from Mrs. Deverick to her driver, the carriage was at the curb. Matthew retrieved his bag, clicked open the door, and stepped out.

"Do get a shave, Corbett," Pollard said. "A bath might go well for you, also."

"Thank you, sir." Matthew paused on the last carriage step before easing down onto the paving stones. He wanted to try one last time with the lady. "Mrs. Deverick, can you think of *any* trip your late husband might have taken? Not in recent memory, perhaps, but within the last few years?"

"This interview is over," came Pollard's cutting voice. "Mr. Deverick's trips have no bearing whatsoever on——"

"I'm trying to find a motive," Matthew persisted. "A clue. *Anything*. Please, Mrs. Deverick. Any information you might have would be helpful."

"Do not *beg*, Mr. Corbett." She glowered down at him. "It is a sign of weakness."

Matthew felt his mouth draw into a tight line. Damn it all, he thought. He'd done his best, but this seemed to be a dead-end. "Thank you for your time, madam," he said, rather grimly, and stepped down onto the stones.

Her powdered face with its thin arched eyebrows leaned toward him. "If it would be *helpful*," she said, "there were the trips to Philadelphia."

Matthew froze where he stood.

"Madam?" Pollard again, trying to regain his authority now that Matthew was out of the carriage. "I don't think you are obligated to——"

"*Hush,*" she snapped, and he hushed. Then, to Matthew, "Pennford made several trips to Philadelphia. Several years ago, though. I do know that our firm handles the brokerage duties for taverns there, as well."

"Oh, I see. How did that come about?"

Pollard leaned out to give his two pence. "Mr. Deverick bought a Philadelphia brokerage firm. That was in 1698. Ancient history, as far as business goes."

"You handled the papers?"

"No, it was a few months before I arrived. The transaction was managed by Charles Land. May we go on our way now?"

"And," said Mrs. Deverick, "Pennford did take the trip to London. I think that was . . . early autumn of 1695."

"London?" Matthew was intrigued. "Did you accompany him?"

"I did not."

"So you don't know who he visited?"

"It was *business*, I'm sure. Pennford would not have made such a journey as that for any other reason. When he came back, his stomach pained him so much Dr. Edmonds put him in bed for a week."

"The Philadelphia brokerage firm," Matthew said to Pollard. "What was its title?"

"It bears Mr. Deverick's name."

"Yes, I understand it bears his name *now*, but who owned the firm before Mr. Deverick bought it?"

Pollard laughed harshly. "Clerk, *what* are you driving at? That there is some connection between Mr. Deverick's murder and the brokerage firm in Philadelphia? You might as well accuse the man in the moon!"

"I'm not accusing, I'm asking. Who owned the firm before Mr. Deverick bought it?"

"Dear God, you're an arse-pain! Excuse my language, madam."

"Mr. Pollard?" Matthew said, willing to grind the man down. "Why won't you answer my question? Do you know, or don't you?"

"It was a man named Ives, who is still employed by the Deverick company as manager there. So what does that tell you?"

"That I'd hate to perform dental surgery on you, sir, as the extraction of your teeth would have to be done with explosives."

Pollard's face had reddened. His thoughts, Matthew reckoned, must have been equally as crimson. The lawyer sat back in his seat, and Matthew saw that Mrs. Deverick had enjoyed this little combat because she was smiling wickedly.

"I have to say," she commented, "you're an entertaining young man, Mr. Corbett."

"Thank you, madam."

"Is there anything else, then?"

"No, but I appreciate your candor and your time."

"Our arrangement still stands," she said. "I'd like to pay you the ten shillings, if only to see you move into something more suitable than a dairyhouse."

"I intend to collect the money," Matthew replied, "but the dairyhouse will suit me for a while."

"As you please. Good day, then." To the driver she said crisply, "*Drive on!*" and the carriage promptly pulled away, leaving

Matthew in bustling Hanover Square with his mind again turning toward the Queen of Bedlam.

It was interesting, he pondered, how the Queen had been placed in the asylum by a Philadelphia lawyer, and now came news that Deverick owned a brokerage firm in the Fount of Brotherly Love. He doubted that there was as much money to be made in the Quaker town as in New York. Why had Deverick bought the firm? Simply for the desire of acquisition? He recalled something Robert had said, answering questions about his dead father in McCaggers' cold room: *Here he had no competition.*

Deverick had obviously amassed quite a fortune in New York. Was it not enough for him? Did he wish the challenge of starting over again in Philadelphia?

The London trip. *Pennford did not care to travel, as he had digestive problems.*

So why had a man with digestive problems gone for a sea voyage of many weeks to London? Business? What kind of business was it that would call for Deverick to make such a sacrifice of time and suffering of health?

Interesting, he thought.

Matthew believed now more than ever that all roads led to the Queen of Bedlam. She sat there in her sublime silence at the center of all mysteries. It was his task to somehow make her reveal the answers.

Hefting his bag, he started toward Micah Reynaud's shop, looking forward to a keen razor and a cake of sandalwood soap.

thirty-one

The black freedman Micah Reynaud, who had a chest like an ale barrel and hair the color of smoke, was quick yet painstaking with his razor. Matthew also found him an excellent conversationalist, as Reynaud owned a brass telescope and studied the heavens as well as being an inventor of note. In one corner of the barbershop was a cage in which a squirrel was afforded a tread-mill, which was attached to pulleys and gears that turned a wooden spindle connected by another set of pulleys and gears to a second wooden spindle held in a tin sleeve at the ceiling. This second rod, when revolving, also caused the parchment blades of a ceiling fan to rotate, providing a breeze beneath which a customer might wish for the ebony barber to be less quick in his duties. The squirrel was named Sassafras and loved boiled peanuts.

After Matthew got a hair-trim, it was off to the bath room where Reynaud's wife, Larissa, poured hot water into one of the three wooden tubs and left a gentleman to soak and ruminate. Matthew stayed there until he wrinkled. When he left Reynaud's he was shaved, clean, and as bright as a new duit, but there was still the matter of his dirty clothes.

A stop at the widow Sherwyn's relieved him of that particular problem, and he was about to leave when the widow asked, "Am I to take it that due to the disaster the rest of your clothes are now beggars' rags?"

"Yes, madam. I might find some more in the debris, but right now I am clothing-impoverished."

She nodded. "Mayhaps I can help you, then. Would you be skittish about wearing a dead man's suits?"

"Pardon?"

"Julius Godwin was my customer," she explained. "He left six shirts, four pair of breeches, and two suits with me a few days before he was murdered. They're clean and ready to be taken. I was about to donate them to the orphanage, and then Ausley bit it." She eyed him from shoesole to collar. "Godwin wasn't so tall as you, but he was slender. Do you want to try the clothes? The suits are right high quality."

So it transpired that Matthew found himself in the widow's back room appreciating the deceased's taste in clothing. One suit was dark blue, with a silver-buttoned dark blue waistcoat; the other was light gray with black pinstripes and a black waistcoat. He noted frayed cuffs on the shirts, which might speak to the state of mind Mrs. Deverick had mentioned. Shirts and suit coats were a bit tight across the shoulders, but they would do. The breeches likewise fit him imperfectly, but not enough to be discarded. He decided the old adage of beggars not being choosers was highly appropriate; he thanked the laundress and asked her if she might keep his new wardrobe until after lunch.

"Won't walk off and leave," she said, as another customer entered the shop. "Say hello to the Duke for me, won't you?"

At twelve-thirty Matthew was sitting at a table in the Trot with a bowl of barley soup before him and a mug of cider at hand. Several regulars came up to commiserate his circumstances with him, but he was past the tragedy and just smiled and nodded at their well-wishes. He was fixed on the immediate problem of the Queen's identity, and how he was going to find out anything more about her in Philadelphia. The first task was to *get* to Philadelphia, and then to visit Icabod Primm. He thought the lawyer might rage and posture over removing the lady from the Westerwicke asylum, but he didn't think any action would be taken in that regard. He doubted a better or more humane place could be found. It was a risk, of course, and counter to what the clients expected, but if it was results they—and himself as well— wanted, then Primm's office had to be the first stop.

"Matthew?"

Yet what would happen if Primm denied all knowledge of the lady, as was likely? Philadelphia was a big town. How was one to discover the identity of a single person, amidst all that populace? He needed something more than a verbal description of the Queen, or as Greathouse had said he'd be walking the streets of Brotherly Love until he had a beard down to his—

"Matthew?"

He blinked, retreated from his thoughts, and looked up at who'd addressed him.

"I hoped I'd find you here," said John Five. "Can I sit?"

"Oh. Yes. Go ahead."

John took the chair across from him. His face was ruddy and the sweat of labor still sparkled at his hairline. "I only have a few minutes. Got to get back to work."

"How are you? Would you like something?" Matthew lifted his hand to signal Sudbury. "A glass of wine?"

"No, nothin'." John glanced back at the tavernkeeper and shook his head, and then he regarded Matthew with a gaze that could only be described as dour.

"What is it?" Matthew asked, sensing trouble.

"Constance," John said. "She followed the reverend last night."

"She . . . *followed* him?" Matthew didn't want to ask *to where*. "Tell me."

"It was long after the clearin' of streets. Ten o'clock or so, she said. He left the house, tryin' to be quiet about it. Constance said she heard the board creak near the door, and she knew. After what happened . . . you know . . . at the church, she's been torn up over him. I swear, Matthew, she's goin' to pieces just like *he* is."

"All right, calm yourself. So Constance went out after him?"

"She did. Twice she saw her father dodge a constable, and once she herself almost walked into a lantern. But she went on after him, God bless her heart, and . . . I just wanted to know, Matthew. Where did he go the night you followed him?"

Matthew shifted uneasily in his chair. He picked up his cider and set it down again.

John Five leaned closer and said in a whisper, "Constance said her father went to Petticoat Lane. I can hardly believe it but I know she's tellin' me the truth. She said he stood across the street from Polly Blossom's house. Didn't go in, thank Christ, but just stood there. Then, after maybe five or six minutes, a man came out and spoke to him."

"A man came out? Who?"

"She couldn't tell. He spoke to Reverend Wade for a minute or so, touched his shoulder, and then went back into the house. She said she could see lights inside, and while she was watchin' two other gents went in and the reverend stepped back out of sight. So the place was still doin' business, even after the decree."

"Bribes have a way of making constables blind, I'm sure," Matthew said. He had no doubt Polly Blossom was making payments even to Bynes and Lillehorne. Also, with the Masker making no further bloodlettings, the power of the decree was weakening no matter what Cornbury wished. "All right. Did the reverend go anywhere else?"

"No. Constance said she followed him back in the direction of home and had to run a different route to get ahead of him. She barely got back before he came into the house."

"And what happened then?"

"She got into bed. He cracked the door open to look in on her and she pretended to be asleep, but I can tell you that she slept no more last night. She was at the smith's shop when I got there at dawn."

"Has she mentioned any of this to the reverend?"

"She said she almost told it all, but he looked so wretched at breakfast she couldn't bear to. I said to keep silent, 'til after I'd talked to you."

Matthew reached for his cider and took a long drink.

"What does it *mean*, Matthew?" John's tone was almost pleading. "I'm tellin' you, Constance is a wreck over this, and I'm thinkin' that Reverend Wade is involved in some dark business that sooner or later has to come to light. And what'll happen to him *then*?" He closed his eyes and pressed a hand against his forehead. "What'll happen to Constance then?"

Matthew continued eating his soup where he'd left off, his gaze vacant. He had made up his mind what needed to be done as soon as John had mentioned the second man.

"You're takin' this calm, I see. Good for you, but it's a tragedy for Constance. And for the reverend. What's he gotten himself *into*?"

Matthew took one more taste and put down his spoon. "I'll take care of the situation from here."

"Take *care* of it? How?"

"Just go back to work. When you see Constance, tell her there's to be no mention of this to her father. Not yet. Do you understand?"

"No."

"Listen to me," Matthew said with enough force in his voice to crush all resistance. "It's vital that Reverend Wade does not know Constance followed him. There's no use in pushing this in his face before . . ." He trailed off.

"Before *what*, Matthew?"

"Before I have all the pieces. But I intend to get them, you can be sure of that. Now promise me there'll be no word to the reverend. I mean it."

John hesitated, his expression tormented, but then he lowered his eyes and grasped the table's edge as if fearing to be flung off the world. "I trust you," he said quietly. "Thought you were crazed in the head many a time, but I do trust you. All right. No word to the reverend."

"Go back to work. One more thing: tell Constance to stay at home tonight, no matter if he leaves again or not."

John Five nodded. He stood up, and Matthew could see how much his friend loved Constance Wade in the abject pain of his eyes and the slump of his broad shoulders. John wished to do something—anything—to help his love, but in this case the strength that drove a hammer was meaningless. "Thank you," he said, and he left the Trot at a stumble.

Matthew watched him go and then finished his soup. He called for another mug of cider and drank that down. Two of the regulars were playing a game of chess over in the far corner. He decided to watch them, and if needed to give pointers to either party.

It was time, he thought, to meet the mysterious Grace Hester.

When he returned to Grigsby's house with his bundle of dead man's clothes, he learned from Marmaduke that the locksmith could not do the job until the next morning, but he was content to wait another day. Grigsby commented on how good he looked with a fresh shave and haircut, which he took as an invitation to come in and speak to Berry, but he simply informed the old fox that the arrangement of which they'd spoken was—after much deliberation—suitable to him for the time being.

"Glad to hear so, my boy!" Grigsby said, with a face-splitting grin. "You won't regret it!"

"I don't plan on regretting it. Now do you think I might be able to get a real bed in there? Something small, of course, but more comfortable than deerskin. I'd also like a mirror and a chair. A lapdesk, if there's not enough room for a larger one. Also a shaving stand. And do you think I might get a rug for the floor, just to keep the dirt settled?"

"All those can be arranged. I'll make a mansion out of it for you."

"I also have some . . . uh . . . new clothes. Anything that would help me in keeping them stored would be appreciated."

"I believe I can put up some pegs for you. What else?"

"I'd like to have that junk cleared out," Matthew said. "May I ask why there's an archery target and rapier among the current furnishings?"

"Oh, all that stuff. You'd be amazed what people barter with to settle their debts. The sword belonged to a militia officer who wanted a book of poems printed for his lady. Married her and they moved to Huntington, as I recall. The target is more recent. It was payment from the Green Arrows archery club for an announcement in the first *Earwig*. When it was the *Bedbug*, I mean."

"You might want to insist on coin of the realm for your labor," Matthew advised. "In any case, if all those buckets and boxes were out I'd have more room in my mansion."

With that list of demands delivered, Matthew returned to the dairyhouse, lit his lantern, and retrieved Ausley's notebook from the straw inside the archery target. He sat on the cot and began to go over the notations page-by-page in the steady yellow light.

It didn't take him long to realize this particular notebook had been started near the first of May, according to jottings on the weather and the date of a particularly large loss of two crowns, four shillings at the Old Admiral on May fifth. Ausley won three shillings on the seventh of May, then lost another crown on the eighth. So much for his breaking even at the tables. In fact, judging by the angry scrawls and wine-spottings throughout the portion of the notebook that dealt with Ausley's gambling habits, the man was in continual dire straits. Yet where was his money coming from? Surely he didn't draw enough from the town to afford such losses.

Matthew saw that Ausley kept the items in his notebook separate from each other. That is, scribblings on his gambling woes were in one section, health woes in another, meals and regurgitations in yet another, and so on. And then there was the cryptic list of names and numbers, which was on a page following the section that concerned amounts due from the various charities and churches. Some of the social clubs, such as the New Yorkers and the Cavaliers, also were jotted down as being sources of charitable funds.

Was Ausley pocketing some of that money? Matthew wondered. And that's how he was paying his debts? For the gambling debt section clearly showed payments to several brothers of the bones in amounts that dwarfed the charities. If anything, it appeared from the notebook that Ausley was quick to erase his losses, as he wouldn't have been allowed back at the tables otherwise.

But the list of names and numbers. What to make of them?

The names of orphans, yes. Matthew accepted that much. What did the dates mean? The notation *Rejct* and the word *Chapel*? He studied the numbers, trying to find a pattern or some sense of them. A code of some kind? Or a form of shorthand? Whatever they were, their meaning had died within Ausley's brain.

He returned the notebook to its sanctuary within the archery target, covered the target over with canvas, and at six o'clock attended supper at Grigsby's house, where he ate chicken and rice with the printmaster and Berry. Afterward he played Grigsby a few games of checkers while Berry worked on applying outlandish colors to one of her landscapes, and as the hour grew later Matthew excused himself and retired to his humble abode.

There he kept track of the time and wondered what a gentleman wore to a whorehouse, as he himself had never crossed such a threshold. At nine o'clock he dressed in a white shirt and cravat, the dark blue suit and waistcoat with silver buttons, and put a few shillings in his pocket though again he had no idea what the going rate was. He debated carrying a lantern or not and decided against it. Then, as ready as he thought he'd ever be, he left the dairyhouse, locked the door behind him, and started off toward Petticoat Lane with an eye peeled for a constable's lamp.

Tonight he was the skulker, for he moved furtively along the streets. He didn't fail to think that the Masker might be coming up behind him at any moment, but he doubted the Masker would harm him. The notebook had been given to him for the purpose of deduction; the Masker wanted him to see that mysterious page and figure out what it meant, thus there was no point in murder. He realized that in some strange way he was now working at the Masker's behest.

Matthew heard loud and drunken singing and put his head down as three sots staggered along Wall Street, passing without seeing him. He saw the glimmer of a moving lantern at the end of the block and turned left onto Smith Street to avoid the approaching constable. There he kept his wits about him and froze in a doorway as another constable—this one carrying a hatchet to go along with his lamp—strode past on his way to apprehend the melodic trio. Matthew kept going, turning right onto Princes Street and then crossing the Broad Way. At the corner of Petticoat Lane he almost collided with another man who was walking north at a fast clip, but the incident was over and his fellow decree-breaker moving away so rapidly that Matthew's heart barely had time to jump.

A few more paces and Matthew stood before the two-story pink brick house. Candles shone through the gauzy curtains. As he watched he could see figures moving past the windows. The pink-painted iron gate between the hedges barred his way, but it was simply a matter of a firm push to pass through. He eased the gate shut at his back, took a deep breath and straightened his cravat, and then he walked purposefully up the steps. He had a moment's confusion of whether to knock at the door or enter without invitation. He chose the first option and waited as someone approached on the floorboards within.

The door opened, an aroma of Babylonian gardens wafted out, and standing before him was a huge black woman in a strawberry-red gown with pink and purple ribbons adorning the straining bodice. She wore a pink wig piled high and a pink eyepatch covering her left eye; on the eyepatch had been sewn a red heart pierced by Cupid's arrow.

Her protuberant right eye inspected him up and down. In a West Indies accent and a voice like thunder over the Caribbean she said, "New blood."

"I'm sorry?"

"Ain't seen you a'fore."

"My first time," he said.

"Cash or credit?"

He jingled the coins in his pocket.

"Welcome, guv'nah," she said with a wide wicked grin, and stepped aside for his passage into a new world.

thirty-two

MATTHEW CLOSED THE DOOR behind him. He stood in a
vestibule with lavender walls and an oval mirror, the better
to check one's appearance before meeting prostitutes. In front of
him, beyond the black strawberry, was a drawn red curtain. He
heard feminine laughter from the other side, and not too dainty,
either. Then a man laughed, with a snort. He began to doubt his
wisdom at coming to this place, but there were answers here and
so be it.

Suddenly the ebony woman, who stood so close to him
Matthew felt the heat glowing through her gown, had a dagger in
her hands and was cleaning her fingernails with its deadly point.
Hidden under all that finery, he thought. Ready to come out and
stab somebody in the heart at the drop of a disagreement.

"First time here," she said as she continued her grooming,
"needs rules spelt out, unnastand?"

"Yes," Matthew answered, carefully.

"No rough play. Disrespect earn disrespect, in spades. No
weapons. Got any?"

Matthew shook his head.

"Trus'worthy face," she decided. "First trouble, a warnin'. Second trouble, you goes out in separate pieces. I keep de rules. Unnastand?"

"I do," Matthew said, in all sincerity.

"Verra good!" The dagger was flipped around on fat but nimble fingers and vanished into the abyss. "Half a shillin' rents de room for a half-hour or any part a' it. Customary to pay de lady a groat, 'fore you goes up. All money to be collected by *me*. First glass a' wine's on de house. That smooth your sails?"

"Yes, madam," Matthew said, assuming it was the correct reply.

"Not *madam*," she scoffed. "I'm jus' ole Becca Black." She grinned widely again. "We gonna be good friends," she told him, and one treelimb of an arm whisked the curtain open.

A rather luxurious parlor lay before him, decorated with dark red wallpaper and illuminated by many candles. There were chairs and settees and sofas, everything overstuffed and covered with glossy fabric in shades of red, pink, and purple. Matthew thought the place was meant to tantalize, but he feared for his vision. Within the parlor, where the pungently sweet fumes of incense curled from a Turkish lamp, sat in various postures of relaxation two men and three women. The men were not together and paid no mind to each other nor to Matthew, as all their attention was devoted to the females, who wore shockingly casual garments more like pantaloons than gowns. Brightly colored scarves covered their breasts, with ribbons around their throats. Scandalously, their midsections were exposed and one of the ladies wore a green jewel in her navel. None of them were great beauties, but the exposure of so much feminine flesh was enough to make Matthew weak in the knees. He assumed this was the normal uniform of Polly Blossom's prostitutes, designed to be shed and reapplied as rapidly as possible.

One of the doxies, a full-bodied and white-wigged wench who might have been able to throw Brutus the bull, stood up from her sofa and grinned with snaggle-teeth at Matthew, offering him the comfort of bone-crushing arms.

"Go right in, then!" said Becca Black, who seized Matthew's shoulder and nearly flung him into the room.

The whore lumbered toward him. Matthew thought he was

about to be consumed like a meat-pie when a saving angel glided between them, having come through another doorway at the left side of the parlor.

"Master Corbett, isn't it?" Polly Blossom asked, her face right up in his own. Before he could speak, she said quietly, "Sit down, Barsheba," without moving her eyes from Matthew's. He was aware in his peripheral vision of the female beast retreating to her sofa and curling herself up with a little sigh of lost love or, at least, an unearned groat. Polly leaned in so close her eyes, startlingly blue and clear, became the world. "We don't wish to frighten you away, your very first visit," she all but whispered in his ear.

In spite of the rigid design of his mission, Matthew had begun to sweat both at temples and under his arms. His stomach felt crawly. Polly Blossom was a handsome woman, no doubt. Her thick blond ringlets had no need of a whore's wig, and she wore only a modicum of blue shadow-paint above her eyes. Her full, pouting lips—so close to his own mouth!—were daubed with pink. Her color was healthy, her body with its full swell of breasts and hips clothed in a rich indigo gown embroidered with lighter blue silk flowers. He had to look down to see if she wore the metal-toed boots, and yes, for all of her gentlewoman's finery and a per-fume that smelled like peaches she did indeed wear the fearsome black kickers.

There came the sound of someone strumming a gittern. Matthew looked to one side to see that Becca Black had situated herself in a chair and was playing the instrument, her head cocked and the remaining eye half-closed as if in reverie. The woman began to sing what might have been a West Indian song, a soft and lilting tune that seemed to be half English and half the language of her island heritage. He couldn't understand most of it, due to the lady's heavy accent, but he recognized in the lovely yet wistful song the sound of a universal longing.

A hand slid into Matthew's. "Come," said Polly, her voice still hushed. "Sit with me."

She led him to a sofa, where suddenly he found himself seated with New York's notorious and beautiful whore-mistress leaning against his shoulder and offering him a sugared almond from a silver dish. When he started to take it from her, she just laughed and pushed it into his mouth.

"Tell me," she said, as a hand lay upon his thigh, "about yourself."

This water was getting deep. He had not come here for dalliance, but for information. A meeting with Grace Hester, if possible. He had to keep his wits about him, before they flew away. He wondered what Polly Blossom might say if she knew he was unsure whether he was a virgin or not, for his memory of a heated physical encounter with Rachel Howarth might have been true yet might have been produced by the strange elixirs given him by an Indian medicine man after his fight with Jack One Eye the bear three years ago. He could hear Madam Blossom say as she stared steadily at him, *After you leave here tonight, your memory will serve you well.* But he was here for professional reasons, not for yearnings of the flesh. He was here to get in and out as quickly as possible. To get to the essence of things. To . . . damn, this woman was sitting so close!

Footsteps descended a staircase. Matthew saw a narrow set of stairs at the opposite end of the parlor. Coming down and looking quite woozy, either from drink or his amorous exertions, was Samuel Baiter, whose face was still bruised from the dust-up during a dice game at his house on Saturday night. He carried his tricorn hat in one hand and the other was still tugging his breeches up. "Good night, Madam Blossom," he croaked as he passed, and the lady answered, "Good night, Master Baiter."

Then she turned her attention again upon her object of sugared almonds. "Oh," she said, "you're a very handsome young man. But surely you've been told this by *many* ladies much younger and prettier than myself, have you not?"

The question sounded as loaded as one of those multi-barreled pistols Ashton McCaggers had told him about. "I have not," he replied.

"Then I fear for the taste of the ladies of New York, sir, as well as for their sanity in letting you walk the streets without the companionship of the fairer sex. Handsome, well-bred, well-dressed, and *intelligent*, too. Oh, how my heart pounds!" She used his hand to demonstrate if not how hard her heart was pounding then how soft was her left breast.

Matthew's flag had unfurled and was rapidly rising. He thought that if this went much further he was going to lose all professional account of himself.

One of the other customers was telling a joke and both the women laughed as if they hadn't heard about the farmer's daughter and the brush salesman a hundred times. Becca Black strummed and sang and Polly Blossom regarded Matthew as if he were Eros embodied, which he knew must be part of her own professional wiles for he certainly wasn't all that.

Madam Blossom ceased her *faux* swooning to watch like a hawk as the two men chose their paramours of the half-hour and put coins into a white ceramic bowl on a table beside Becca Black, who did not pause in her playing. One of the men either was mad or had terrible eyesight, as he'd chosen the white-wigged giantess; well, perhaps he craved what was nearly about to explode from her scarf and pantaloons. They went up the stairs chatting and laughing, leaving the spurned girl—a slim brown-haired doxy with sharp features under a heavy pancake of rouge and white powder—to lean back in her chair bored to the soul and rapidly stir the air around her face with a black fan as if dissipating the odors of manly musk and bad breath.

"Master Corbett," said Polly, again all smile and flirtation, "I regret I cannot offer myself for commerce tonight, as I might wish to, but I am under Eve's curse. Might I suggest that Nicole over there would be an excellent companion? *Nicole!* Please sit up straight and show your good breeding, my dear." Nicole obeyed, with a frozen grin. "Or I have a very pleasant and highly intelligent young blond, newly arrived from London just last week, almost a virgin so fresh is she, so supple and dewy. But if it's experience you wish, and a certain exotic charm, I also have a dark-fleshed gypsy with—I'm told—the firm grip of a sixteen-year-old and sure to delight. What is your pleasure, sir?"

"I . . ." Matthew's nerves betrayed him by making his voice
crack. He cleared his throat and tried again. "I do have a request."
She watched him intently, with perhaps a little hard flint back in
those eyes somewhere. "I'd like to be introduced to—"

"God*damn*, what a night!" said a waspish feminine voice as
someone came down the stairs. "That bastard Baiter's got a cock
enough for three men!"

"Hold your tongue, missy!" At once Madam Blossom had
risen to her feet in a show of indignation. "We have a gentleman on
the floor!"

Matthew stood up as well, for on the stairs was the young
prostitute that he'd last seen hanging on Andrew Kippering at the
Thorn Bush. Her dark hair, a shade of brown so deep it was almost
black, was brushed back from her forehead and gathered behind
with a crimson ribbon. She wore, as was the custom of ladies both
high and low, white face powder and her eyebrows were drawn as
thin black arches. As he'd noted at the Thorn Bush, she was about
twenty years old and not unattractive, for her features were well-
defined and her expression catlike with a sexual cunning. She wore
the pantaloon outfit but had a flimsy violet robe thrown about her
shoulders and drawn over her breasts. Her ebony eyes found
Matthew but remained vacant. She said in an affected voice, "My
regrets, sir. I was simply remarkin' of what happens when a giant
sausage is shoved into a silk purse."

"No apologies necessary," Matthew told Grace Hester, before
the madam of the house could speak. "I understand that not all
sausages are created equal, but all silk purses have a bottom. So
my regrets to you that a so-called gentleman has no concept of
physical volume."

There was a silence. Becca Black's music had ceased on an off-
key note.

Grace Hester frowned. "Who the hell are *you*?" she asked. "A
gibberin' loon?"

"Hush!" Polly snapped, and then her tone softened though her
eyes had become as hard as her reputation. "This is Master
Matthew Corbett, my dear. A magistrate's clerk and well-known

young man about town. He featured prominently in a recent article in the *Earwig*, so he may be considered somewhat of a celebrity
and we are *honored* to—"

Grace yawned and winced as she rubbed her crotch.

"Honored to have him visit us," Polly finished. "These young
ladies!" she said to Matthew with a sad shake of her head. "They
just don't know good manners anymore."

"I'm done for the night." Grace continued down the stairs,
walking with a noticeable hitch in her roll. She had no pretense of
being a gentlelady; she was all foul temper and crudities. "Somebody get me a fuckin' drink."

"Get yourself your own fucking drink," answered the mistress
of the house, as the masks of civility began to crack. "You already
owe me two shillings for your liquor. When are you going to pay?"

The girl shrugged and passed Matthew and Polly, heading for
a sideboard on which stood three open bottles of wine and a few
glasses. Suddenly there was a yawp of female laughter from
upstairs followed by an incomprehensible shout from a man. Becca
Black returned to her gittern, this time playing a more stately and
intricate tune that had no words. Matthew was impressed by her
musical talents and he wondered what her story might be; but he
was here for Grace Hester's tale, and it was time to work toward
his aim.

"That wine's for the customers," Polly said, advancing toward
the girl before a bottle could be tipped. "You'll pay me what you
owe, or you'll have more than a pain in the puss."

"Pardon me," Matthew spoke up, before these two cats began
to scratch. "The lady may have *my* glass." They turned as one to
glare at him, as if he were the lowest creature ever born. "I am
afforded a free glass of wine, am I not? If so, the lady may have
mine."

Polly Blossom, to her credit, was quick to swing between her
roles of whore-warden and flirtatious businesswoman. It was,
Matthew thought, the key to her success. She lowered her eyes
demurely. "How gracious of you, sir. How kind. We thank you."

Grace didn't thank anyone. She loaded up a glass and drank

most of it down before Matthew could withdraw a silver shilling from his pocket.

"I'll take this girl," he said, holding out the coin. "And to ease her discomfort, I'll pay an extra half-shilling."

"I'm *done*, I said," Grace replied, without even offering him a look.

"We do have more suitable ladies, Master Corbett." Even as she spoke, Polly Blossom had her eyes fixed on the coin. "I have a very pretty maiden of seventeen, lately arrived from Amsterdam."

"That ugly bitch saw seventeen ten years ago," said Grace as she licked the empty glass with an extraordinarily long tongue.

"*This* girl," Matthew said. "One shilling for thirty minutes. Plus two groats for the trouble."

Suddenly Polly's eyes narrowed as she smelled a rat. "Very extravagant, aren't you, sir? Why may I ask do you wish this particular companion, when I offer so many other choices?"

"She appeals to me." Matthew ignored the girl's dark chortle. The next thing he said surprised him when it came out: "I prefer the wicked ones."

"Well, there's plenty of wickedness to go around here, sir," said Polly, and with a smooth motion she took a step toward him and put her hand firmly on his crotch. Before Matthew could jump back, the woman had taken stock of his package. "He's *normal*," she told Grace. "A shilling and two groats would make a nice end to your evening."

"Hell!" Becca Black rumbled. "Pay me de money and you ain't never *seen* such wickedness!"

Matthew doubted he would live through that much. He kept his hand outstretched with the shilling in his palm. Grace was busy pouring herself another glass.

The light of avarice shone in Polly's eyes, yet she did show concern for her charges. "Go ahead and do him as your last trick," she told the girl. "I'll get you some extra ointment in the morning."

Grace drank the second glass empty and slammed it down so hard Matthew thought it might shatter. Then she turned her black-eyed, feline gaze upon him and pulled up a crooked grin. "As you please, sir." Her voice was a mockery of manners. "I won't feel you down there, anyways."

With a forefinger, Polly directed Matthew to the money bowl, where he added his coins to the collection. As Matthew followed Grace up the stairs, Polly called out sharply, "Make sure you give Master Corbett his money's worth! The customer always comes first in this house!"

No comment was given from the sullen whore. She continued up the stairs, leading Matthew into a candle-lit corridor with four doors on either side and one at the far end. In gilded frames on the walls hung scandalous drawings of such fevered intertwinings that a blush heated Matthew's cheeks. Another Turkish lamp on a small table sent out blue tendrils of incense, the spicy-sweet scent hiding perhaps the more offensive odors of sweat and musk. She opened the second door on the right and went in without a word to her customer, whose heart had begun to pound with a wild rhythm even though his intentions were honorable. He could hear Becca Black singing again downstairs, and again there was a harsh rasp of female laughter from along the hall before Grace shut the door at his back.

It was a plain bedroom with pale yellow walls and a single shuttered window. The bed was rumpled and obviously had seen hard use tonight. On a small round table sat a triple-wicked candle-holder. The flames gave the room a more romantic glow than it deserved, for Matthew did notice ugly cracks in the plaster. There was a mousy little gray chair, a chest-of-drawers with a washing-bowl atop it, and next to it an hourglass. On the wall was a small square mirror. Pegs held various items of female clothing. The place was neater than Matthew had expected, as the plank floor had been swept clean and everything was orderly but for the bed, and he wished not to look too closely at the sheets.

Grace stood staring at him, her expression blank.

Matthew had no idea what to say. So he began with "I assume you've been busy lately," and immediately winced at the ridiculous statement.

"Your name's Corbett?" she asked, and then she frowned slightly. "Have I seen you before?"

"Possibly. One night at the Thorn Bush."

She seemed to be trying to remember, but it was beyond her. She walked past him to the chest and slid a drawer open, trailing the faint odor of peppermint. At least, he thought, she kept her teeth clean.

"You can call me Matthew," he told her.

She turned around and had a light brown object about seven inches long and oily-looking dangling off her hand. She said, "Put this sheath on yourself and I'll turn the glass when you're ready, or if you want me to put it on for you I'll turn the glass now. What's it to be?"

Matthew had heard of the penis-sheaths, but he'd never before seen one. Made of sheep's gut, as he understood. He stared at the thing in Grace Hester's hand, and in spite of his excitement at being here in this den of pleasure he had a queasy sensation in the pit of his stomach.

"I won't need that," he said.

"No sheath, no fuck, and I don't care how much money you pay. I don't want to be laid up with that damned doctor diggin' a kid out of me." She held it toward him adamantly. "Go on, all the gents use it."

"Not that particular one, I hope."

"Are you *stupid*? You use it once and toss it." She nodded toward a bucket on the floor. "Thank Christ I'm not the one who has to *wash* 'em."

"I won't need it," he repeated quietly, "because I only want to *talk*."

Grace was silent. She blinked as if she'd been slapped. In the quiet Matthew could hear the gittern music and Becca Black's singing from the parlor. Then all the air seemed to rush back into Grace's lungs. "*Talk*? What the fuck *about*?"

"I would like to ask you a few questions."

She saw he was serious. She backed away from him, as one might retreat from a frothing dog. "Listen, you," she said, her voice tight. "One scream and Becca'll carve your heart out."

That threat was enough to send a shiver up his spine, but he had to keep his composure. "I hope you won't scream, as I'd like to leave here with all the parts I brought."

"You *are* a loon." Grace was nearly pushing herself into a corner. "Who the hell *talks* when they could *fuck*?"

"I came here to see you for a purpose, and it wasn't . . . uh . . . *that*. I promise you I won't touch you. All right?"

"You fool, you *paid* to touch me."

"That's incorrect. I paid for a half-hour of your time. I just have a few questions to ask, and then I'll leave. I'll tell Madam Blossom you were a wonderful . . ." He searched for the gentlemanly word. "Hostess. I won't touch you, and I certainly won't *hurt* you. Please." He kept his voice low and soothing. "Trust me."

Grace gave a bitter laugh. Her eyes were no longer vacant; now they held the steely glint of suspicion. She said, with nearly a spit on the planks, "I trust *nobody*."

Matthew decided to put himself where she might consider him the weakest. He sat down on the bed.

Her mouth twisted. "So now you've changed your mind?"

"No. I just want you to see that you can get out of the room at any time you please, and I won't stop you."

"You *couldn't* stop me."

"That's probably true," he agreed. He reasoned she might have a dagger or two hidden around here for her own protection, in case Becca was slow up the stairs. "I really do need to ask you a few things. Important things."

Grace just watched him without speaking. The penis-sheath was caught in her fist. "If you'll answer them as truthfully as possible," Matthew continued, "I'll go on my way and you can get to bed. To *sleep*, I mean."

Still she made no response, but Matthew saw she wasn't going to scream. At least for now his heart was safe.

She took a hesitant step forward and then passed him, pulling herself away so she wouldn't graze his knees. She returned the penis-sheath to the drawer and then closed it. Her right hand came up and turned the hourglass over, and the sand began to slither through. Before she faced him again, she opened the chest's top drawer and brought something out that Matthew couldn't see at first. She went directly back to the corner in which she felt safe and when she turned toward him Matthew saw she was holding close to herself a small, dingy cloth doll with a red-stitched mouth and black buttons for eyes.

"What do you want to know?" she asked warily.

"First of all, what your relationship is with Reverend Wade."

"Who?"

"William Wade. The reverend at Trinity Church."

Grace stared blankly at him, with her doll nestled in the crook of an arm.

"You don't know Reverend Wade?" Matthew asked.

"I suppose I've heard the name. I hear a lot of names. But why should I know him?" An evil little grin stole across her face. "Does he come here in *disguise?*"

"No." He noted she looked a bit disappointed that the reverend wasn't walking on the fiery edge of Hell. He himself was dismayed by the response, for he thought it to be truthful from her tone of voice and lack of reaction to the name. "What about Andrew Kippering? I presume you know—" She was already nodding vigorously, so there was no use in finishing it.

"*Andy*, you mean. Oh, he's a right fine gent. Big and handsome and the money flows out of him like water under London Bridge. He comes here two, three times a week. Sometimes stays the whole night. Gets a deal from the old dragon. He's a lawyer, you know."

"Yes."

"Wait." Grace had been warming, but now she froze again. "Andy's not in any kind of trouble, is he?" She took a step toward the door that made Matthew almost bolt to his feet, expecting the shrill scream for Becca Black. "Hey, who are you to be askin' questions about Andy? I'm not gonna be helpin' you put the finger on him, no matter what he's done."

"I didn't say he'd done anything."

"You can ask any of the girls here. The *ladies*, I mean." Grace thrust her sharp chin at him as she crushed the doll against her breasts. "Andy's made of sterlin'. Just who the hell are *you*, anyway?"

"I mean no harm to Mr. Kippering," Matthew said calmly. "I was only trying to settle the fact that you knew him. I saw you together at the Thorn Bush, but I wanted to hear it from you."

"All right, I know him. So does every other lady here. Even the old dragon takes him to bed once in a while, and I hear it's for *free*." Grace spoke that word with disgust.

Matthew couldn't fathom how to proceed from this point. If Grace Hester didn't know Reverend Wade, then what had Kippering been going on about that day at the dock? *What is it you know about Grace Hester?* Kippering had asked, there in the shadows of the masted ships. *This can't get out, do you understand?*

Matthew decided to change course. The sand made a faint hissing noise as it collected at the bottom of the glass. "How long have you been here?"

"Since the end of April, I suppose. Why?"

"Dr. Godwin," Matthew said. "Did you know him?"

"That old fart? Got himself killed good and proper, didn't he?" The subject of her dear sterling Andy behind them, Grace was beginning to warm up once more. "They say he nearly had his head cut off," she said, with a delicious glee bordering on the obscene.

"He took care of you ladies, yes? Before Dr. Vanderbrocken stepped in?"

"And Godwin poked us, too, while he was at it. Old bastard had a cock on him. And at his age! You see Nicole downstairs? The skinny one? Godwin was on her every time she turned around. Gave her some fuckin' dinner plates for her birthday, the very night he got his neck opened. Said he *loved* her. Can you believe it?" She made a face. "*Love*, in a place like this!"

"It *is* amusing," Matthew agreed, but actually he thought it was very sad. The plates, he recalled, had been crafted by Hiram Stokely.

"If Nicole wasn't such a fuckin' gin-fiend, she'd be rich from all that silver Godwin paid her. And she said some nights after he shot his cannon and lay there sleepy he called her a different name. When he started sobbin' on her shoulder, she kicked him out, silver or no. A whore's got her pride."

"A different name?" Matthew asked, intrigued. "What was it?"

"Nicole said it was . . . Susan, I think. You'll have to ask her yourself. Anyway, Godwin was a strange old bird. Drunk half the time, and his hands were always cold, too."

"I may have to speak to Nicole," Matthew said, mostly to himself. "I'd like to find out more about Dr. Godwin."

Grace grunted. "Now you're soundin' like *him*."

Matthew brought his attention back. "Sounding like who?"

"Andy. Wantin' to know when Godwin was here, and what time he left and all that. He talked to Nicole about the old bastard. Nicole said he stuck his cock in her and shot in his sheath and then all he wanted to do was ask questions about Godwin, like that was the real reason he came. I mean . . . the real reason he was *here*."

"Is that so?" Matthew asked, watching Grace rub the doll and realizing she was unconscious of needing the security of a bit of dirty cloth stitched over a stuffing of straw. A relic from her past, he thought. So too might the name *Susan* be a relic from Godwin's past. Could it also have had something to do with his murder? "Miss Hester," he said, "just one more question. Did Andrew Kippering never mention to you the name of William—"

"Stop," she directed. "What did you call me?"

"Miss Hester," Matthew said. "Your name."

"*My* name?"

Matthew had a sudden piercing insight as sharp as a dagger stab. "Your name isn't Grace Hester."

"Hell, no. I'm Missy Jones," she answered. "Grace Hester's in the room at the end of the hall. She's the sick girl."

"The . . . sick girl?"

"Consumption. Gotten worse and worse these last few days. Becca says she'll be passin' soon. Why she's got the biggest room in the house, I don't know."

"Oh . . . I've been stupid," Matthew said in almost a gasp. He stood up, and to her credit Missy Jones did not back away. "I've been very, very stupid."

"Stupid about what?"

"The meaning of things." He levelled his gaze at her. "Miss Jones, can I get in to see Grace Hester?"

"The door's kept locked. Grace is a rounder. Even sick, she wants to go out to the Thorn Bush and cull a trick. Last time she got out, Andy had to go bring her back."

Matthew knew now. He knew, and it had been there in front of him the very night Eben Ausley's stomperboys had introduced his face to a mound of horse apples. "Is there any way I can get in to see her? Just for a moment."

"Door's locked, as I say." She had begun to look nervous again. "Why do you want to see her? You don't . . . uh . . . favor *sick* girls, do you?"

"No, it's nothing like that. It's honorable, I promise you."

"I don't understand it," Missy said, but then she chewed on her lower lip and stroked her doll and said, "I . . . suppose . . . I can trust you. Can't I?"

"You can."

She nodded. "The old dragon won't like it. Neither will Becca. You'll have to be quick." Then she hugged her doll close and said with her eyes downcast, "The key's up on top. The sill over the door. If anybody catches you, you'll be in for it. And me too."

"Nobody's going to catch me," he assured her. "And even if they did, I can promise you that neither one of us will be harmed in any way. Do you believe that?"

"No," she said. Then, with a frown that brought her brows together: "Maybe. I don't know."

Matthew went to the door, and she quickly moved aside. "Thank you for your time, Miss Jones. And thank you for your help."

"It's no matter," she answered. His hand was on the doorlatch when she said, "You can call me Missy, if you like."

"Thank you," he said again, and he offered her a smile. He

might have wished for a smile from her in return, but she was already crossing the room to her waterbowl to wash the makeup off her face and the doll was pressed up against her cheek. He wondered what she looked like underneath the powder, and what story was hidden in her soul. He had no time to linger; he went out, quietly closed the door, and walked down the hall.

He found the key quick enough. As he started to push it into the lock, he thought that a scream from the real Grace Hester would bring the house down upon him, but if this were a game of chess he held a bishop against a pawn. He heard Becca still singing in the parlor, this time a happier West Indies tune. He slid the key home, turned it, and opened the door.

This bedroom was practically the same as Missy's, though perhaps a few feet wider. On the floor was a wine-red rug. Two candles burned, one upon the bedside table and another atop the chest-of-drawers.

The sheets moved and the girl who lay there, her face pallid and her dark hair sweat-damp, sat up with an obvious effort. She had high cheekbones and a narrow chin, and in some long-ago time she might have been pretty but now she was wrecked on the coast of desolation.

The heavy makeup had masked her sickness, and the strong drink had given her false strength. She was the girl Matthew had seen stagger out of the Thorn Bush in the company of Andrew Kippering, that night the stomperboys had darkened Matthew's complexion.

Grace Hester stared at him, her mouth open. Becca sung in the parlor and the gittern played its lilting, sunny notes.

"Father?" the girl asked, her voice slurred and weary yet . . . hopeful.

Matthew said quietly, "No," and he backed out of the room before his heart might break.

thirty-three

HE WAS FISHING in his favorite spot, at the end of Wind Mill Lane on the west side of town, just where John Five had said he would be.

Along the lane were a few houses, a carpentry shop, a cornfield, and a new brewery in the first stage of construction. The Thursday morning sun shone on the river and a wind stirred the green woods of New Jersey on the far side. The fisherman sat amid a jumble of gray boulders at the shore, his line trailing from an ashwood rod into the water. Just beyond him was the hulk of an old merchant vessel that had been shoved by a storm into the rocks and, its hull impaled and broken, was slowly collapsing before the infinite progress of time and currents. Up on a hill, and near enough to cast its shadow upon the fisherman, was the tall windmill for which this lane was named; its revolving head atop a stationary tower had been positioned to take advantage of the breeze, and its canvas sails billowed along the slowly turning vanes.

Though Matthew took care to be quiet as he came along the rocks, he knew his presence had been noted. The reverend had glanced at him and then quickly away again without a word. Wade didn't look much like the erudite minister of Trinity Church this morning. He wore gray breeches patched at the knees and a faded brown shirt with the sleeves rolled up. On his head was a shapeless beige cloth hat that had evidently seen many summer suns and rainshowers alike. His fishing clothes, Matthew thought. Beside the reverend was a scoopnet and a wicker basket to hold his catch.

Matthew stopped ten yards away from the man. Wade sat perfectly still, waiting for a bite.

"Good morning, sir," said Matthew.

"Good morning, Matthew," came the reply in a voice from which no hint of emotion could be read. Neither did he look in Matthew's direction.

A silence stretched. A breath of wind furrowed the river and made the windmill's vanes creak.

"I fear I'm not having much luck this morning," Wade said at last. "Two small fellows, not sufficient for a pan. They fought so hard it seemed wrong to land them. I'm after a carp I've seen here before, but he always foxes me. Do you fish?"

"I haven't for a long time." He once caught fish to *live* on, in the rough days before he went to the orphanage.

"But you do catch things, don't you?"

Matthew knew his meaning. "Yes sir, I do."

"You're a very intelligent young man. You wished to be a lawyer, Andrew tells me?"

"I did. More than anything, at one point. Now it hardly matters."

Wade nodded, watching the floating red fly where his line met the river. "He says you're very strong on the concept of justice. That's to be commended. You've impressed me as a young man of high character, Matthew, and therefore I'm puzzled why you should wish to throw yourself into the low business of blackmail." His head turned. His eyes were somber and dark-rimmed. Sleep must have been a stranger last night. "I've been expecting you, ever since Andrew told me. And to think that *John* is part of this, when he professed to love Constance and I came to regard him as dear as a son. What do you think that does to my heart, Matthew?"

"Do you really *have* a heart?"

Reverend Wade didn't reply, but looked out again upon the river.

"I told Kippering an untruth. John Five doesn't know anything about the girl. He came to me for help because Constance thought you were losing your mind. Did you think you could go out and about at night without her wondering sooner or later *where* you went? I followed you myself, to Polly Blossom's. I saw what I would term a pitiful sight. And the last time you went out—just Tuesday night—Constance followed you."

The reverend's face had paled under the shapeless hat.

"She saw where you went. She saw Andrew Kippering come out and speak to you. Oh, she didn't see his face, but I'm sure it was him. He *is* the go-between, isn't he?"

There was yet no answer.

"Yes, he is," Matthew went on, as a swirl of wind whipped around him. "I presume the money to keep Grace in that room comes from you and passes through Kippering? And his good relationship with Polly Blossom has convinced her to let the girl die in the house? Yes? I presume also that Madam Blossom was the first to discover that one of her doves was the daughter to the reverend of Trinty Church? Did Grace tell her, when she realized she was going to die?" He gave Wade a space to speak, but nothing came forth. "I'd think you might look upon Madam Blossom as a saint, because if anyone was going to blackmail anyone it would have started with her. What's her reward for this? A place in Heaven for a woman who fears Hell?"

Wade lowered his head slightly, as if in an attitude of prayer. Then he said in a care-worn voice, "Madam Blossom is a businesswoman. Andrew framed the agreement as a matter of business. It's what she understands."

"I'm sure it also doesn't hurt Madam Blossom to have a minister on her side. If, say, certain socially powerful members of the church might wish to shut her house down."

"I'm sure," Wade answered, his head still bent forward. "But I had no choice, Matthew. The upward path—the right path—was too dangerous. What I always have preached . . . I could not practice, when called upon. I'm going to have to live with that for the rest of my days, and don't think it will be easy."

"But you'll still be a reverend," Matthew said. "Your daughter will be dead, without having heard her father's forgiveness."

"Forgiveness?" Wade looked at him with a mixture of incredulity and anger that passed across the minister's face like a stormcloud. He cast aside his fishing-rod and stood up, his chest thrust out as if in readiness to fight the world. "Is *that* what you think she wants? It is *not*, sir! She has no shame and no regrets for the life she's led!"

"Then what is it she wants?"

Wade ran a hand over his face. He looked as if he might sink down to the stones again, and lie there like a rag. He pulled in a deep breath and let it slowly out. "Always the impulsive child. The girl who must have all the attention. Who must wear the bows and bells, no matter what sin buys them. Do you know why she wishes to die in that house? She told Andrew she wants to die in a place where there's *music* and *laughter*. As if the gaiety in that house isn't forced through the teeth! And her lying in there, on that deathbed, with me standing outside on the street . . ." He shook his head.

"Weeping?" Matthew supplied.

"Yes, weeping!" The answer was harsh and the anger had returned. "Oh, when Andrew first told me what he'd found out from Madam Blossom, you should have seen me! I didn't weep! I nearly cursed God and sent myself to Hell for it! What was in my mind might have cast me into eternal fire, but there it was and I had to deal with it! I thought first of *Constance*, and only her!"

"She doesn't know?"

"That her elder sister is a whore? Certainly not. What was I to tell Constance? What was I to *do*?" He stared at nothing, his eyes dazed. "What *am* I to do?"

"I think that the situation will take care of itself soon enough. Isn't that what you said to Constance?"

"Dr. Vanderbrocken tells me . . . that there is nothing he can do except try to keep her comfortable. She may have a week or two, he says, and how she's holding on he doesn't know."

"She may be holding on," Matthew said, "because she's waiting for a visit from her father."

"Me, go in that place? A man of God in a whorehouse? That would be the end of me in this town." Wade's expression was pained, and now he sank down to sit upon the boulder again. For a moment he watched the breeze moving across the hills, and then he said quietly, "I have wanted to go in. I have wanted to see her. To speak to her. To say . . . I don't know what. But something to comfort her, or bring her some peace if that is possible. Evidently . . . when she arrived here in May she was sick, of course, but she hid her condition very well from Madam Blossom and Dr. Godwin as well. She always had a silver tongue, even as a child. I'm sure she talked her way right through that odious examination. Then, according to Andrew, the exertions of her . . . occupation . . . wore her down. She collapsed in that house, Dr. Godwin was summoned . . . and to keep from being thrown out into the street, she told Madam Blossom who she was. I presume Andrew was taken into confidence because of his credentials. As a lawyer, I mean, not as a whore-monger."

Equally qualified in both areas, Matthew thought, but said nothing.

"An agreement was drawn up," the reverend continued. "Andrew kept me informed of Grace's condition, and as I understand he even went out after her a few times when she managed to talk someone into setting her loose. She particularly liked the Thorn Bush, he told me."

Matthew had realized this: Kippering thought Matthew had seen the lawyer and Grace together *inside* the Thorn Bush on one of those occasions, instead of just staggering out the door that night, and had put together in his mind the idea that somehow Matthew, the sammy rooster, had discovered her identity.

"The night of Mr. Deverick's murder," Matthew said. "You were summoned by Dr. Vanderbrocken because Grace had taken a turn for the worse? And he feared Grace might die that night?"

"Yes."

No wonder, then, that Wade had said he and the doctor were

travelling to different destinations, Matthew thought. It would have been hard to explain to High Constable Lillehorne where they were going together on such an urgent mission.

"And one of Madam Blossom's ladies went to Vanderbrocken's house to tell him?"

"Yes. She came with him to fetch me, and waited at the corner outside my house."

That accounted for the woman Constance had seen, but it raised another question. "You said Andrew Kippering was the go-between. Where was he that night?"

"I have no idea. I do know he enjoys his liquor far more than a Christian man ought to." Wade took off his hat and wiped his forehead with the back of his hand. His dark brown hair was thinning on top and gone to gray at the temples. "Yes," he said, as if thinking of something he should have reacted to but had let pass at the moment. "I *did* say to Constance that the problem would be solved, soon enough. And it will be, by the strong hand of God."

Matthew decided he wasn't going to let the reverend off so easily, and may the Lord forgive him for his audacity. "Did you think that, all those nights you stood outside Madam Blossom's house? Knowing that your daughter was on her deathbed in there, and at any time she might pass? *I* saw you shed more than one tear, Reverend. I know you were trying to gather the courage to go inside. Did you think that one night you might free yourself of the social bridle? Of what the church elders would say, if they knew a father could still love a daughter who was a prostitute?" He paused, to let those wasp-stings settle. "So I believe that even if the strong hand of God does solve this problem—soon enough, as you say—a broken man may be left behind, if you fail to see her."

"I'll be broken if I do see her," came the firm reply. "If I stepped into that house, I would be putting at risk everything I've devoted my life to. You don't know how some of those Golden Hill families would swoop down on me, if they were to find out."

"You couldn't do it in secret?"

"I'm already keeping one secret from my flock. You were present at the church, weren't you, when I had my little moment up there? I couldn't bear to keep another secret. I'd be no good for anyone or anything."

Matthew sat down on a boulder near the reverend, but didn't wish to crowd him too closely. "May I ask how your daughter came into her profession?"

"She was born with a willful spirit." Wade looked Matthew full in the eyes, his cheeks reddened, and Matthew wondered if this willfulness wasn't inherited. "Early on she delighted in disobeying, and in running with boys day and night. What more can I say? I don't—and never did—fully know her heart." He clasped his hat between his hands and stared downward, a vein ticking at his temple. "Grace was the first child. Eight years older than Constance. We had a boy, in between, who died. Hester—yes, that was my wife's name—passed a few days after Constance was born. A complication, the doctor said. Something unforeseen. And there I was, with two daughters and my Hester gone. I tried. I *did* try. My sister helped, as much as she could, but after Hester died . . . Grace became more and more undisciplined. At ten she was out in the streets, throwing rocks through storefront windows. At twelve, caught with an older boy in a hayloft. And me, trying to advance my career and the word of God. The plans for success that Hester and I had made . . . they were coming apart, because of Grace. How many times did someone come to my door with a complaint against her, or a demand for money because she'd lifted an item from a shop and taken to running!"

Wade was silent, lost in his memories, and Matthew thought for a moment that the reverend looked eighty years old.

"When she reached the age of fourteen," Wade said, "I had to do something. I lost a position at a church because Grace attacked another young girl with a knife. In a more primitive time, she might have been considered *demonic*. She was beyond control, and her spiteful attitude was affecting Constance, too. God protect Constance, she was never fully aware of all the problems. I tried to shield her, as best I could. A six-year-old child should be shielded from wickedness, shouldn't she?" Wade glanced at Matthew, who remained quiet. "I . . . arranged for Grace to be sent to a boarding school, a few miles out of Exeter. It was the most I could afford. Barely a year went by before I received a letter from the headmistress to the effect that Grace had taken her belongings and left in the middle of the night . . . unfortunately, according to another girl, in the company of a young man of dubious reputation. A few months later, I received a letter from Grace with three words: *I am alive.* No address, no intent to seek reconciliation or intent to return to either school or my house. Just those words, and then nothing else."

The reverend had been working the shapeless hat with his hands, and Matthew wondered if it had been a dignified tricorn before being molded just like this, into a fisherman's topper.

"My star did continue to rise, after I had sent Grace away," Wade continued. "I was on the verge of realizing the success that Hester and I had imagined. Then came the opportunity to take the pastorship at Trinity Church, with the understanding that I would return to England in four or five years when an opening presented itself, preferably in London. Grace must have been following my progress from afar. She must have read in the *Gazette* of my assignment here. And so she took a handful of dirty money, boarded a ship, and proceeded to New York. To spend the last days of her life doing what she has done so well for so many of her twenty-five years . . . dealing out pain to me."

The reverend aimed a bitter smile at Matthew. "Yes, I did weep. Many times, and many tears. Whatever Grace is, she is still my daughter and I am fully aware, thank you, of my responsibilities. But I have so much to consider now . . . so much at stake. Hester and I . . . our dreams of making a shining example of a church and advancing God's plan . . . all of it could be destroyed, if I walked into that house. There is Constance to think of. She knows only that her sister fled the boarding school and disappeared. And if John Five knew, what would *he* say?"

Matthew recalled John Five's reluctance to bear witness against Eben Ausley, for fear of what Reverend Wade might say. "I think," Matthew countered, "that John would say he loves Constance, no matter what her sister is, and no matter that her father will struggle with this decision for the rest of his life if he doesn't do what he knows to be correct."

"*Correct*," Wade repeated, his head lowered. "What is *correct* in this situation?"

"My opinion?"

"Let's hear it."

"Constance has to be told, first thing." Matthew saw the reverend wince when he said it, but he knew Wade had already figured out it had to be done, since Constance had followed him to the Blossom house. "If she tells John, so be it. How she'll react to the news, if you're asking my opinion, will be a mixture of sadness and relief, with relief winning the day. Now to Grace herself: it seems to me she may have journeyed here for no other reason than to say goodbye. Or perhaps she came to test you."

"Test me? How?"

"To find out if you still had any love for her. Enough to make you—a man of God—walk into a house of prostitution, for the sake of a wayward daughter. I doubt if she planned to die here, but I imagine a sea voyage did not help her condition. For all she may be, she must have tremendous strength of will."

"Willful, as I said," the reverend agreed.

"I think," Matthew said, "as you've asked my opinion, that your eldest daughter does not need a minister, a pastor, or a reverend, but a simple and honest father." Wade gave no response to this. "At least, the attention of a father for . . . say . . . ten or fifteen minutes?"

"So you're suggesting I walk into there and throw my and Hester's dream away, is that it? To give fifteen minutes to a daughter I haven't seen for eleven *years*?"

"I would point out, sir, that your wife has long departed to the gardens of Paradise and I'm sure only wishes the best for her husband and *both* her daughters who must remain on this less-than-perfect earth. And I am suggesting that you do what you feel to be correct."

Wade was silent. At last he put his crushed hat back on. "Yes." His voice was distant. "I thought that might be your suggestion."

They sat together for a further time but said nothing, for all had been said. Matthew stood up, and Wade retrieved his fishing rod. He reeled the line in and watched the river moving toward the sea. "That carp," he said. "I'll get him, someday."

"Good luck," Matthew told him, and started across the rocks, back the way he'd come.

"Matthew?" Wade called, and when Matthew turned around the reverend said, "Thank you for your opinion."

"My pleasure, sir," Matthew replied. He continued along Wind Mill Lane and then across to the east side to the little dirt-floored dairyhouse he was beginning to think of as home.

A little plume of smoke rose from the kitchen chimney of the Grigsby abode. Matthew went into the dairyhouse, soaped his face, and began to shave by lamplight, as he had neglected to do so in his haste to see John Five early this morning. He had no idea what Reverend Wade would do. The correct thing? And what really was the correct thing? To enter the whorehouse for a few minutes with a dying girl he probably wouldn't even recognize, or to continue—as Wade put it—the dream of advancing his career and the plan of God? Well, what was God's plan, anyway? Who could say, from this side of the veil? It seemed to Matthew that it took a man with a full belly of himself to say that he knew what was the plan of God. But Matthew did know that Reverend Wade had a conscience to go along with his heart, and that if Wade went to see Grace he couldn't keep it a secret even if no one from his congregation saw him in the rose-colored house. The reverend would sooner or later either tell the church elders or speak the truth from the pulpit, and then what might the outcry be? To send the father of a whore packing, or commend him for his fatherly concern? Matthew mused, as he finished shaving, that this situation might become a test of the mettle of Trinity Church as well as a test of strength for Reverend Wade. The correct thing? God only knew, but the reverend would have to decide.

Matthew washed his face and dried it on one of his shirts, remarking to himself that it would be wise to go shopping for a handtowel. He determined to see the Stokelys today, to see how they were holding up. Thinking of all of Stokely's work that had been destroyed was wrenching, but if anything Stokely was an industrious man and if he could keep his bearings away from melancholy over the wreckage he would soon get to rebuilding the place. Hopefully this time it would be strong enough to withstand a maddened bull, which seemed vital for a pottery shop.

Matthew started to pull the canvas away from the archery target to get at Ausley's notebook again, but somehow his hand was diverted. He grasped the rapier's ivory handle and lifted the sword. It was about the same length and weight of the sword he'd used in training with Hudson Greathouse. He'd wished to have a sword of his own for further exercise; here it was, if he wanted it. He stepped back, positioning himself as Greathouse had directed—*Make your body thin. Show only your right side. Feet not too close. Sink down as if you're about to sit. Left arm behind you, like a rudder. Step forward with your right foot, keeping left arm, body, and sword in line. Thrust!*

Matthew hesitated. What else? Oh, yes. *Keep that thumb locked down!*

He thrust forward with the sword and then came back to the first position. He began to repeat that movement over and over, aiming for speed and economy. From time to time he varied the motion, by thrusting to left or right and then always bringing himself back to the center, everything in control and steady. It quickly became an effort of mind over muscle. As he continued his exercise, he thought of the question that had come out of his talk with Reverend Wade. *Where was Andrew Kippering the night Wade and Vanderbrocken went to the Blossom house?* Of course he might have been anywhere. At his boarding house, for instance, or at one of the taverns. Even working in his office. But Matthew couldn't help but wonder if Kippering hadn't been available to go fetch Reverend Wade or Dr. Vanderbrocken personally, in his role of go-between, because he'd been involved with another pressing appointment. Namely, the murder of Pennford Deverick.

Thrust left, return to center. Thrust right, return to center. A little quicker now, and keep the sword tip up.

He drinks himself into stupors, throws his money away gambling, and almost has his name burned on a door at Polly Blossom's. Doesn't that sound to you like someone who pretends to enjoy life but really is in a great hurry to die? the widow Sherwyn had asked.

Take care of your footing. Not too close, or your balance suffers. Thrust center, return to first position. Again, more smoothly.

Wantin' to know when Godwin was here, and what time he left and all that, said Missy Jones.

And from Kippering himself, the night of Ausley's murder and the discovery of the blood smear on the cellar door: *I think the Masker might also be a gambler. Don't you?*

Thrust right, return to center. Steady now, don't weaken! Thrust left, return to center. Make your body thin, moonbeam. And keep that thumb locked down!

Matthew stopped. His shoulder and forearm were thrumming. How did anyone get used to the weight of these things? A swordsman had to be born, he'd decided. It had to be in the bones.

He pushed the rapier's tip down into the dirt and leaned on the sword. In spite of the dairyhouse's coolness, he felt the sparkle of sweat on his face.

He was thinking that Andrew Kippering had shown a great interest in Dr. Godwin, possibly for the purpose of timing the man's visits to Nicole. Why? To choose the right time for a throat-cutting?

Who do you think the high constable should be looking for? Katherine Herrald had asked.

And Matthew had answered, *A gentleman executioner*.

Someone who had approached Pennford Deverick on the street, and caused Mr. Deverick to offer a hand of greeting. Someone Mr. Deverick knew. Someone who wanted the doomed man to see his face.

And what, then, of Eben Ausley? Why those three men, throat-slashed and cut about the eyes?

I would look, Ashton McCaggers had said, *for someone who has experience in a slaughterhouse.*

Was Andrew Kippering that man? A gentleman executioner?

With experience in a slaughterhouse? Was the man who pretended to enjoy life but really was in a great hurry to die also a gambler with the lives of other human beings? The Masker?

But for what reason? If execution was the sentence, what had been the crime? What linked Godwin, Deverick, and Ausley together in such a fashion that they should be put to death for it?

Matthew rubbed the rapier's ivory handle. He thought once again that all roads led to the Queen of Bedlam, who sat locked at the center of a secret. The masks on the walls. The painting of Italy. The furniture defaced so as to prevent identification of the maker. Deverick. The rich trappings of a wealthy woman. The mysterious client, who hid in the shadows behind Icabod Primm. *Has the king's reply yet arrived?*

"Matthew?"

He came out of his brown study. Someone was knocking at his door. "Yes?" he called.

"It's Berry. You have a visitor."

"One moment." He put the rapier back where it had been. Then he opened the door and found himself looking not just at one pretty girl, but at one pretty girl and one beautiful lady.

Berry wore an apron over her dress. Her hair was pulled back from her face by a red scarf. She looked a bit flustered, her cheeks ruddy, and Matthew wondered if she'd been helping her father with lunch in the kitchen. In contrast to Berry's homespun clothes, the elegant lady who stood just beside and behind her had stepped from a Parisian portrait of modern fashion. She was tall and willowy, with thick curls of light blond hair and eyes the color of the bittersweet chocolate cakes in the window of Madam Kenneday's bakery. She wore a pale blue gown with fine white lace along the sleeves and billowing at the throat. On her head was a small and very fashionable curled-rim hat, of the same fabric and color as her dress, adorned with a white feather. Matthew couldn't help notice that she was indeed a striking-looking young lady, about the same age as he if he judged age correctly. She had fair unblemished skin, high cheekbones, perfect cupid's-bow lips brushed with pink, and a lovely slim-bridged nose. Her blond eyebrows lifted as she saw him take her measure. A beauty mark dotted her left cheek, and at her side she held a white parasol.

"Master Corbett," she said, speaking it like music, and stepped forward to offer him a white-gloved hand.

"Yes." He fumbled with her hand and didn't know what to do with it, so he quickly let it go. He caught Berry looking at him askance, and then she blotted the perspiration of kitchen heat from her forehead with an old rag. "What . . . uh . . ." Matthew felt himself coming to pieces. The young lady's eyes were beautiful, but they penetrated through his skull. "What may I do for you?"

"I am Miss Charity LeClaire," she announced, as if he might recognize the name. "Might we speak in private?"

There was an awkward moment in which no one moved. Then Berry explosively cleared her throat. "Matthew, Grandda's gone to get you some things. He'll be back by eleven, he said. Lunch'll be ready by then."

"All right. Thank you."

Still Berry lingered. She cast a furtive eye up and down Charity LeClaire while trying to hide behind her kitchen rag.

"In private, please," the young lady repeated, her music just a note or two strained this time.

"Oh. Of course. Privacy. A very important thing," said Berry, as she began to back away toward the house.

"Yes," Miss LeClaire answered cooly. "Useful, also."

"If you need anything, let me know," Berry said to Matthew. "You know. Some water or anything."

"I'm fine, thank you."

"Back to the kitchen, then. Did I say lunch would be ready at—"

"Eleven," Miss LeClaire interrupted, with a slight smile. "Yes, we got that."

We? Matthew thought. What was this about?

"Good day, then," Berry said, and Matthew saw her blue eyes go cold. Obviously Miss LeClaire was not to be invited to lunch today. Berry turned around and went back to the house, and never did Miss LeClaire's calmly appraising gaze leave Matthew's face.

"How may I help you?" Matthew asked. He remembered his manners, as the morning was growing warmer. Unfortunately he had no shade to offer but his humble dairyhouse. "Would you care to step inside?"

"No, thank you." The white parasol went up, opening with a quick *pop*. "I have been directed to you by a Mr. Sudbury at a tavern you are known to frequent. I have a situation in which your aid is needed."

"Oh? What situation?"

"I might tell you that I have visited Mr. Ashton McCaggers in his charming domain. He tells me that I am not the first to remark upon an item missing from the belongings of the deceased Eben Ausley."

Matthew's heart gave a little kick. He said nothing and attempted to let nothing show in his expression.

"Mr. Ausley, God rest him, was my uncle," said Miss LeClaire. "I am searching for a particular notebook that was likely on his person the night of his unfortunate demise. I presume you have seen this notebook, since you asked Mr. McCaggers about it." She paused, and Matthew knew she was trying to read his face. "Would you happen to know where the notebook might be?"

He was still reeling from the shock of hearing that someone so vile as Ausley had such beauty in his family. He swallowed hard, his mind moving options like chess pieces. If he gave up the notebook, he might never learn the meaning of that strange page of code. And for this lady to suddenly show up on his doorstep asking if he had it . . . well, it was an odd picture.

"No, I don't," he replied. "After all, I did mention to McCaggers that it was missing."

"Ah, of course." She smiled and nodded under the parasol's shadow. "But why would you be looking for it, sir?"

"May I ask the same of you?"

"Business reasons."

"I was unaware that Mr. Ausley was involved in business."

"He was," she said.

Matthew remained silent, and so did she. The silence stretched.

Then Miss LeClaire tapped a finger against her lower lip. "I have a carriage just up the street. I believe my employer would like to meet you, and I am empowered to offer you such a meeting. It would be a ride of several hours, but I think you might find it worthwhile."

"Your employer? Who might that be?"

"His name," she said, "is Mr. Chapel."

thirty-four

"MR. CHAPEL," Matthew repeated. The name was heavy in his mouth. Had his face shown a reaction? He wasn't sure. The lady was watching him intently.

"Do you know the name?"

"No, I don't."

"Little wonder. Mr. Chapel values his privacy."

"And privacy can be very useful, can't it?" Matthew asked.

"Yes." She allowed a small smile to creep across her mouth, but it had the effect of making her eyes appear hard. "My question to you was: why were you interested in my uncle's notebook?"

"I happened to see your uncle with a notebook many times. In the taverns, that is. He obviously liked to take notes."

"It would seem so." Miss LeClaire's gaze did not waver. "Pardon me, but you said '*a* notebook' instead of '*the* notebook.' Do you suggest there was more than one?"

She was trapping him, he thought. Pushing him into a corner. Trying to get him to admit that he'd been following the bastard over the course of two years. What did she know about that damned notebook, and all the other notebooks that must have preceded it? Whoever she was, her interrogative abilities might have made a good addition to the Herrald Agency. "I only saw what I saw," he told her.

"Ah, of course. But the real question is: who saw it *last*? Not you?"

It was time to start throwing doubt, before he buckled. "I imagine there must have been a crowd around the body. Someone may have picked it up."

"But left his wallet?"

He felt he had met his match in this cool player. He could only summon up a tight smile and say, "Perhaps his killer wished to read your uncle's notes."

"Perhaps," she agreed, in an unconvinced voice. Then she smiled and shifted the parasol so a bit of sunlight sparkled upon her moist pink lips. "You might care to meet Mr. Chapel, Matthew. May I call you Matthew?"

"As you please."

"One evening and a dinner at Mr. Chapel's estate, and you'll be brought back in the morning. I can attest that Mr. Chapel hosts very fine dinners. Will you come?"

Matthew hesitated. He caught a movement from the Grigsby house and saw Berry duck away from the kitchen window. Miss LeClaire followed the line of his vision, but Berry did not reappear. Matthew had to focus on a decision. He had no doubt that meeting Mr. Chapel might give him some insight into what game Ausley had been up to. "An estate, you say?"

"Yes. A vineyard and a fledgling winery, as well. Some fifteen miles north along the Hudson River."

"Really." Matthew felt a creep of dread. That distance would put it four or five miles beyond the Ormond farm, where the eyeless dead man was found. In what Greathouse feared was the realm of Professor Fell, if his instincts were correct.

The lady was waiting.

"I do have business to take care of tomorrow," Matthew said, eager to throw himself a land-anchor. "Some people might be very upset if I'm late."

"If you're an early riser, you'll be back by this time Friday. Would that be a problem?"

Matthew decided to take the risk. It was the only way. "No

problem," he said, trying to keep his voice light. "Let me tell my friend I won't be attending lunch. Pardon me." He closed the door behind him and locked it. He noted how attentively she watched the key go into his pocket, and he had the sudden clear insight of a fist gripping the doorhandle and a length of burglar's key sliding in to spring the lock as the moon shone down. Whoever this Mr. Chapel was, he had sent a professional to fetch Matthew; she might not be Ausley's niece, after all. Family papers could be forged and presented to a coroner. In fact, one of Matthew's cases with Magistrate Powers had concerned that very same thing. As Matthew walked around to the front of the Grigsby house with Miss LeClaire following at a distance, he thought he should not assume another professional wouldn't arrive tonight to search through his belongings. If the archery target was torn open . . .

He knocked at the door. By the time Berry deigned to open it, Charity LeClaire had taken up position a few paces to his left and behind him. He said, "I won't be joining you for lunch. I'm going on an overnight trip with Miss LeClaire."

"Oh." Berry blinked and looked from Matthew to the lady and then back again. "All right. I'll tell Grandda, then."

"If you would." He added a hint of irritation to his voice. "And remind him, please, to remove the junk from my house. Particularly that archery garbage. Yes?"

"I'll tell him."

"Thank you." Matthew wished he could warn her that if any sound was heard tonight from the dairyhouse they should remain in their beds, but he hoped if a burglar did arrive the man would be skilled enough to be noiseless. Then he bid Berry good day and followed Miss LeClaire up the street to where a handsome dark brown lacquered road coach with tan trim awaited, complete with a four-in-hand team of matched gray horses. He doubted that such a fine conveyance had been seen even on Golden Hill, and people were already gathering around to gawk at the vehicle. Made by a master craftsman in England and shipped over? he wondered. If so, it had been at fabulous expense. A husky young driver in a light blue suit and tricorn hat sat up high holding the reins, while his whipman climbed down off the seat to spring the door of the enclosed compartment open for Miss LeClaire and her employer's guest.

In another moment they were on their way, turning right onto King Street. They passed the almshouse at a clatter. Matthew, who sat in the vis-à-vis position facing Miss LeClaire, noted that the lady did not bother to glance at her so-called uncle's last earthly place of occupation. The coach turned right onto the Broad Way and on the outskirts of town took the Post Road. Matthew settled back against the black leather upholstery as the horses picked up speed. The coach fairly flew along the road, its well-balanced construction hardly shuddering as its wheels went over the ruts and potholes.

Under an ambitious whip, the horses were making quick progress. Matthew waited until New York was perhaps two miles behind them, and then he said to the drowsing lady, "Was Eben Ausley really your uncle?"

Her eyes remained closed and no reply was offered.

"What makes this particular notebook so important?"

Still no response.

He tried a third time. "What was your uncle doing for Mr. Chapel?"

"Please," she said in a voice that was by no means slurred by sleep. "Your questions are wasted on me, sir."

Matthew had no doubt she was correct. Through his crescent-shaped window he watched the woods blur past. He had the sensation of being observed, even though the lady's eyes were shut. As the distance between himself and town increased, he began to regret his decision. He was going willingly into what was most probably a dangerous lair, and he must be very careful lest the creature who owned it ate him alive.

He was able to sleep for a total of about an hour, a few minutes at a time. Once he opened his eyes to find Charity LeClaire staring straight at him in a way that sent a shiver up his spine. She, too, looked ravenous. Then she closed her eyes again, seemed to drift away to sleep even though the rocking of the coach over the Post

Road was no one's cradle, and Matthew was left once more with sweat gathering under his collar.

He marked the road that turned off toward Mrs. Herrald's house. They swept past it, leaving a cloud of dust. In a little while came the turnoff that led to the Ormond farm, and that too was passed in a hurry. Then there was just woodland, the occasional farmfield and a few windmills until the coach veered left where the road split into two around a dark little swamp. He didn't need a map to know they were heading toward the river.

It was about an hour later when Matthew felt the coach's speed begin to slow. At once Miss LeClaire was awake, if she had ever really been sleeping. Matthew looked out his window and saw a wall of rough stones about eight feet high. Vines and creepers dangled over it, while tree branches hung overhead. The coach was following a road close-set along the wall. Then the driver shouted, "Whoa, there! Whoa!" and hauled back on the reins. Now the coach was just barely rolling. Matthew saw a huge wooden slab of a gate set in the wall. His first thought was that they were about to enter not an estate but a fortress. The driver pulled the team to a halt and the whipman rang a bell that must have been secured under the seat. Within a few seconds the gate opened inward and the coach began moving once more.

Matthew caught sight of a young man who had emerged from a small white-washed gatehouse that had windows of multi-paned glass. The gatekeeper waved to the coach crew as the coach continued on, and then the coach travelled along a driveway that curved to the right and on either side stood thick woods. Matthew reckoned they'd gone about a hundred more yards before the coach slowed again. He saw a green sward of grass where a flock of sheep grazed and a few lambs pranced around. A large two-storey manse of mottled red and gray brickwork came into view, its handsome front adorned with many windows and a gray-painted cupola at the top with a copper roof. Chimneys jutted skyward. The driveway made a circle around a lily pond that stood a few yards from the front steps, and it was at these steps that the coach finally halted.

At once the coach door on Miss LeClaire's side, closest to the house, was opened and a man perhaps only a few years older than Matthew offered a hand to the lady. "Good afternoon, miss," he said, and then nodded at Matthew. "Good afternoon, sir. I hope your trip was pleasant."

"Very pleasant, Lawrence. We made a quick pace," said Miss LeClaire as she allowed the man to help her out. Matthew followed. As soon as Matthew set foot on the ground, the man shut the door again and motioned to the driver. The coach rolled away, following the circle and then continuing along another road that led off to the left between the trees.

"I'm Lawrence Evans, Master Corbett. Assistant to Mr. Chapel." The man shook Matthew's hand with a firm grip. He was tall and slim and wore an elegant pale gray suit with polished silver buttons. His dark brown hair was tied back in a queue with a black ribbon, and he wore spectacles that made him look, of all things, like nothing more sinister than one of the studious clerks at City Hall. His brown eyes were friendly and intelligent, his manner gracious, and as he stepped aside to allow Matthew and the lady entry to the manse he said, "Welcome to Mr. Chapel's home."

The foyer was panelled in glossy dark wood. The arched doorway of what appeared to be a large parlor was on the right, with a smaller room on the left. Overhead from the high ceiling hung an iron chandelier with eight candles, and directly ahead a set of stairs covered with red carpet ascended to the upper realm. A corridor decorated with pastoral tapestries led past the staircase toward the rear of the house. Everything was clean and polished and glowed with the golden afternoon light that streamed through the windows.

"Mr. Chapel regrets he'll be busy until the evening meal," Evans was speaking to Matthew. "I'm to show you to your room. As I know you must be tired and hungry, you might care to take a nap but first the kitchen has supplied a platter of bacon, biscuits, and jelly as a light sustainment. I'll be glad to fetch you a glass of wine, if you'd like."

"Yes," Matthew said gratefully, though his guard was still up. "Thank you."

Miss LeClaire was peeling her gloves off. "I need a cool bath. Would you arrange it?"

"Absolutely, miss. Will you come with me, sir?"

Matthew followed Evans up the stairs, while Charity LeClaire drifted away down the corridor. He was shown along another hallway to an opulent chamber that had surely never known a poorer guest than himself. The walls were golden pinewood, the floor adorned with a circular red-and-gold Persian rug. There was an ornate beige writing desk, a chest-of-drawers, a wash-stand and basin, two red-covered chairs, and a canopied bed. Heavy gold-colored drapes were open on either side of a glass-paned terrace door. Before one of the chairs was a small round table with the fresh platter of victuals Evans had mentioned, complete with silver utensils.

"Please make yourself at home," Evans said. "I'll bring your wine up and a pitcher of water also. We have a well here that provides excellent water, unlike that sulphurous liquid in town. Can you think of anything else you might wish?"

Matthew walked to the wash-stand and saw arranged around the basin of water a clean white facecloth, a cake of soap, a straight razor, a comb and hairbrush, and a small dish of baking soda for the teeth. An oval mirror was set on the wall. Whatever Mr. Chapel's game, the man required his guests to be presentable. "I think everything's here," Matthew answered.

"Very good, then."

As Evans moved toward the door, Matthew said, "One thing. What's my host's first name?"

"Simon."

Matthew nodded. When Evans left the room, Matthew listened for the sound of a key turning in the outer lock but it didn't come. Obviously he was not a prisoner, if one took a liberal view. Neither was the terrace door locked, for Matthew stepped outside and looked down upon a large garden of flowering trees, hedges, and ornamental shrubs that would have caused Mrs. Deverick to grind her teeth with envy. Dissecting the garden were pathways of white gravel. Beyond the garden there were more trees but over their leafy branches Matthew could see the blue width of the Hudson River, shimmering in the sunlight. A single flatboat with spread sails was slowly travelling southward, past the green wooded hills. Aiming his gaze a few degrees to the northeast, he saw more forest and then the disciplined rows of the vineyard about a quarter-mile distant. He could see also in that direction the roofs of other buildings that Matthew guessed to be a stable, the coachhouse, and structures having to do with the winery.

Simon Chapel. The name of course meant nothing to him, but for Ausley's notations. It was a farce that Charity LeClaire was Ausley's niece. That deception had been for the coroner's benefit. The documents must have been well-forged, for McCaggers to be taken in by them. It all seemed like an elaborate effort, but what was the purpose?

Matthew went back inside and sat down to enjoy the bacon, biscuits, and a dab of apple jelly, for the mind would be sluggish without nourishment. He also had the feeling he was going to need his full complement of wits about him. Soon Evans returned bearing a silver tray that held a glass of very dark red wine and a pitcher of water.

"Anything more you require?" the man asked.

"Nothing more, thank you." Matthew tried the wine. It was somewhat thick to be an afternoon libation but otherwise satisfying. "This is the estate's grape?"

"Unfortunately not. That particular bottle was purchased in New York. Our vines have yet to produce a grape worthy of Mr. Chapel's approval."

"Oh." That led to a question he'd been hoping to ask. "How long has the vineyard been here?"

"Many years. Mr. Chapel purchased the estate from a Dutchman who actually made his fortune in the shipping trade and let his son grow the grapes. They did produce a wine, though we consider it to be beneath our standards. The soil's a problem, you see. But Mr. Chapel has great aspirations."

"He must enjoy a challenge."

"He does."

Matthew wasn't content to let Evans retreat without another try. "So the vineyard is Mr. Chapel's chief occupation?" he asked as he spread jelly on a biscuit with a silver knife.

"Oh, no sir. Just one of many. If you'll pardon me now, I do have some tasks at hand." Evans offered up an easy smile. "I'd suggest you take a moment to browse the library downstairs, just to the right along the corridor."

"I do enjoy books. Oh . . . might I walk in the garden?"

"Of course. The entrance to the garden is through the dining-room at the rear of the house. Dinner is served at seven o'clock. You'll hear the bell being rung. Good afternoon, sir." And then Chapel's assistant was out the door before he could be troubled with any further questions.

Matthew took his leisure finishing the food. At length he drank the last of the wine followed by a glass of water and then stood up. He had brought his silver watch, in the pocket opposite where his key currently resided, and checking it he saw the hour hand neared four o'clock. Chapel's hospitality was excellent, but it was time to explore this velvet cage.

He returned the watch to his pocket and went out into the corridor, where he followed the Persian runner back to the staircase. The house was quiet; if there were other servants about, they were discreet to the point of invisibility. He walked downstairs, making no effort at stealthy treading, for after all he was an invited guest. Then he went back along the tapestry-adorned corridor, past other rooms and alcoves, and going through an archway he found himself presented with the dining-room Evans had mentioned. He stopped and took stock of the place.

To call this a dining-room was like calling City Hall a meeting house. A long table suited for a dozen guests stood at the room's center, its stocky legs carved in the shapes of fish. Six elaborate brass candelabras taller than Matthew were placed at intervals around the room, ready to throw light from ten wicks apiece. The plank-and-peg floor was the color of honey and indicated a healthy history, though it appeared many of the bootmarks had been eased by judicious sanding. A large fireplace of red and gray bricks, in keeping with the external construction of the house, held logs behind a brass firescreen. Above the table, a simple oval-ring chandelier held eight more candles. When this room was fully lit up, Matthew mused, tinted glasses would be required.

But what both interested him most and caused not a little twinge of concern was the room's display of weaponry. Above the fireplace and on either side of it were gleaming swords, displayed business-tip northward and fixed in place in fan-shaped arrangements under small crested shields. There were six swords in each display. Eighteen swords, and not all of them rapiers. A few of them had darkened blades and looked as if they'd tasted blood.

This was not a room in which to linger, he decided. Ahead of him, at the far end of the chamber, was a closed door off to the left and a set of glass-paned doors between wine-red drapes. He crossed past the fireplace and the swords, which seemed to hiss at him as he went by. The double doors were unlocked, and he stepped out into the warm sunlight onto a brick terrace that had a wrought-iron railing and a set of steps leading down to a garden path.

Just below the terrace was a small pond where goldfish swam amid waterplants. A turtle eased off a rock and vanished into the murk. Matthew followed the path deeper into the garden, walking between all manner of flowers and shrubs, through the cool of the shadows of trees and then into sunlight again. Birds chirped and called from all sides. An occasional bench was positioned to welcome the wanderer, but Matthew was not inclined to do any more sitting after that jolting coach ride.

Soon, by following one path that intersected with another, he came to a hedge wall. He walked along it a distance and discovered an iron gate about six feet high, topped with spear-points. Beyond the gate the path continued through an untamed thicket. A chain and padlock told him he was not going out this particular way. Further on he found a second gate in the hedge wall, also similarly locked. He paused and rubbed his chin. Evidently his explorations were meant to be contained, and this realization struck him like a glove smack across the face. After all, it was not only Mr. Chapel who enjoyed a challenge.

Matthew continued walking, mindful that he was now definitely seeking a way out. After a few further paces, his attention was caught by the glimpse of a red cardinal in the lower branches of a nearby tree. He saw the cardinal take flight, perhaps alarmed by his approach, and as it soared up into the sunlight Matthew took a moment to admire its grace and color.

Suddenly something darted in like a blur and hit the cardinal in midair. There was a sound of impact, like a fist on flesh. Red feathers whirled down.

The cardinal was gone.

Matthew caught sight of a large brown-and-white bird speeding away with a crimson mass clutched up underneath it. It sailed off to the right and was lost from view beyond the higher trees.

Some kind of hunting bird, he'd realized. Most likely one of the favorite predators of the medieval monarchs, a falcon or a hawk.

The speed of that flight and the quickness of the kill was stunning. The intrusion of violent death—even the demise of a cardinal—on this sunny afternoon, in this hedge-walled garden with locked gates, gave him a crawl of unease deep in his belly. He hoped it wasn't an omen of his night to come with Simon Chapel. He thought it wise to turn around and go back to the house, which seemed to loom over him like a threat, but what was it Mrs. Herrald had said about going forward? In any case, he wanted out of the garden and he didn't intend to let a lock or two stop him.

When he found the third padlocked gate, he decided he was climbing it. He looked around and saw a bench under a nearby tree. Dragging it to the gate, he stood up on it and set about trying to clamber over and avoid the spear-points, which were distressingly sharp. Careful, careful! he thought as a point snagged his breeches at the crotch. One slip and a fall on this thing and he'd be known henceforth as Mattina. But then he had pulled himself over and landed on the ground in not too untidy a splay. Before him the path went through vines and thicket. He dared not glance back at the house, because he didn't care to see Evans or some other person watching him from a balcony. He set off along the path.

There was nothing to see but woods on both sides. The path curved to the right. Matthew didn't know what he was expecting, but he had to be going somewhere Chapel didn't want him going. He'd been walking for two or three minutes when he heard the distinct *crack* of a musket shot, somewhere off to the right and farther distant, but the noise was enough to make him stand stock-still until he could make his lungs pull in air again. He went on, more cautiously now, watching the underbrush for any sign of a human predator.

The path emerged from the woods. Before him was a dirt road, and on the other side more forest. Matthew noted mounds of horse manure steaming in the sun. The coach team had gone this way, probably heading to the stable. He reasoned that if he went left along the road it would lead him to the vineyard and the buildings there. He knelt down, pondering if he should risk his luck anymore. After all, what was he thinking to find?

An answer, he thought, and he stood up.

He had taken two paces toward the road when a hard voice said, "I think you'd best stand where you are."

Matthew froze. A few yards to the left and across the road, a man stood at the edge of the woods. He was dressed in dark brown breeches and boots, a gray shirt and a brown leather waistcoat, and he wore a wide-brimmed leather hat. He was shouldering a musket. At his side, gripped in his left hand, was a hunter's pole from which dangled four dead hares.

"Out a distance from the house, aren't you?" the man asked. And then he added, as an afterthought with a sneer in it: "*Sir.*"

"I was just walking," Matthew answered. The hunter's face was shadowed by the wide brim, but there was something familiar about it. The deep-sunken eyes. The voice, too . . . familiar . . . unsettling.

"Just walking could get you shot. What if I'd put a hole through you?"

Matthew stepped toward the man, who stood his ground. The

musket came off the shoulder and even though its death-snout pointed away, Matthew stopped.

"Do I know you?" Matthew asked, sure that he did. From somewhere . . .

"Get back to the house. Go on. That way." The chin jerked to Matthew's right.

Matthew had no desire to argue with a gun. He said, "Very well, I'll go." He felt a stirring of anger and from it he said sarcastically, "Thank you for your hospitality." Then he turned and began walking in the direction of the house, wishing to get as much distance from a musket ball as quickly as possible.

"*My pleasure*," the hunter replied, with equal disdain.

And then Matthew knew him.

He had heard that same phrase, just before his face was thrust down into the pile of horse figs on Sloat Lane. He turned around. The man had not moved. Matthew said coldly, "Which one are you? Bromfield or Carver?"

"*Sir?*"

"What's your name? So I might compliment Mr. Chapel for his choice in servants."

"My name," said the hunter with perhaps the slash of a dangerous smile in the hatbrim's shadow, "is trouble. Do you want some?" Now the musket's stock came to rest against the man's knee and the barrel drifted a few inches toward Matthew before it was checked.

Bromfield or Carver, one or the other. Ausley's stomperboys. On loan to him that night from Simon Chapel to do a roughneck's work? Matthew and the man stared at each other, neither one willing to yield. But Matthew realized it was a fool who taunted a musket, and he didn't wish to be someone's tragic accident. He gave a mock bow, turned around again, and began walking away. The small of his back tensed, as if the muscles there expected a hammerblow.

"Corbett!" the hunter called. "My compliments to Mr. Chapel for his choice in guests! Make sure you wash your face before dinner!"

Matthew kept going. Well, at least the bastard had been drawn out enough to make that last comment, which secured the fact. Before the road curved, Matthew glanced back and saw that his rude acquaintance had disappeared. He had no doubt the man was not far away, though. Watching him. As perhaps other eyes were, as well.

He looked forward to dinner. One could fence without using a sword, and he expected this night would see a match that would make even Hudson Greathouse quake.

thirty-five

WHEN THE DINNER BELL RANG, Matthew was just finishing his shave before the oval mirror. He rinsed the blade off in the washbasin, wiped the remainder of soap from his face with the damp washcloth, and then combed his hair. Regarding his reflection in the polished glass, he knew he had come a long way from the orphanage to this moment. He was looking at a gentleman who had in his eyes not only the bright spark of curiosity but also the steely glint of determination. He was no longer who he once had been, and though he was not yet suited to a sword he doubted he would be fully suited to a pen ever again.

Time to go downstairs and meet the man in Ausley's notebook.

He breathed deeply a few times to clear his head, and then he walked out of the room.

Lawrence Evans had been aghast this afternoon when he'd answered Matthew's knock at the front door, which had obviously been key-latched to keep the guest from straying. *Oh sir, how did you get out there? You shouldn't have gone out the front, sir. It's not wise to go roaming, as there are wild hogs on the property.*

"Yes," Matthew had replied. "I did meet a pig on the road."

You'll keep this to yourself, won't you, sir? If Mr. Chapel found out I let you roam around, he'd be most displeased.

"I won't tell him," Matthew had said, though he'd wondered if word would get back to the estate's master through the road-pig.

Now, as Matthew came down the staircase and turned along the corridor, he heard voices from the dining-room. They were hushed, almost like whispers of wind. Matthew braced himself for the moment, squared his shoulders, and walked with as much confidence as he could muster into the candle-flamed room of eighteen swords.

"Ah, here's our young nobleman!" said the man who sat at the head of the table, as he scraped his chair back and stood up to greet their guest. He walked toward Matthew with a large hand offered in friendship, his boots clumping thunderously on the planks. "Simon Chapel, sir! Very pleased to meet you!"

Matthew took the hand, which nearly crushed his own into a lifeless cuttlefish. The man was huge, standing at least six-foot-three and as solidly built as a brickwagon. He had a sturdy jaw and grinned with a set of peglike teeth that might bite a bulldog in half. His eyes, a shade approaching topaz, were large and luminous under spectacles with square frames. In contest to his physical magnitude, his nose was a small English heirloom turned up at the tip as if smelling spoiled violets. Above it the forehead was a slab of blue-veined marble, his hair a scatter of sparkling gray sand upon a skull slightly pointed at the crest as if suited for a battering-ram. His mouth twisted and twitched with some explosive remarks still being formed. He wore a royal-blue suit with a cream-colored waistcoat, a white shirt, and a blue silk cravat with small red and cream squares upon it.

He was a picture to behold, yet Matthew didn't know quite what he was looking at.

"Sit!" Chapel said. "Right there!" He clapped Matthew on the shoulder with his right hand and with the left pointed to a place set for him on the other side of the table next to the chair he'd so energetically vacated.

Matthew took stock of the three other members of the dinner party. At the long table, which gleamed with silver trays, bowls, utensils, dishes, and cups under the fury of orange candlelight, sat

Charity LeClaire, positioned directly to the right of Matthew's waiting chair. Across from her, and also standing to greet Matthew, was Lawrence Evans, whose presence here indicated he was several leagues above being a mere servant.

It was the other man at the table, the man who had chosen not to stand, who riveted Matthew's attention. He was eating an apple that had been cut into slices on a small silver fruit tray about the size of an open hand. He was a slim dandy, perhaps thirty years old or thereabouts, with hair so pale blond it was almost white. The hair was pulled back into a queue and tied with a beige ribbon. His eyes were piercing green, yet lifeless as they examined Matthew. The face was both handsome for its regal gentility and fearsome for its utter lack of expression. He wore a light brown suit and waistcoat, and flowing waves of European lace spilled from the front of his crisp white shirt and cuffs.

Matthew had last seen this man at night, walking around the corner of King Street near the almshouse, and had first seen him firing apples into the face of Ebenezer Grooder at the pillory before City Hall.

The pitiless grenadier, Matthew thought. He nodded at the man, who watched him but did not return the gesture.

"Allow me to introduce Count Anton Mannerheim Dahlgren," said Chapel, as he steered Matthew toward the head of the table. The blond-haired man now gave the slightest nod, but his relaxed and almost somnolent posture said he was not interested in introductions. He continued eating an apple slice with small birdlike pecks and staring at Matthew as Matthew took the seat across from him.

Chapel sat down again, the grin fixed in place. "I fear Count Dahlgren doesn't speak much English. He's come over from Prussia and he's very . . . well . . . *Prussian*, if you know what I mean. Yes?" That last word was directed to Dahlgren.

"Yas," came the quiet reply in an accent as thick as the Black Forest, with a brief show of gray teeth. "Var' *Prussian*."

Chapel picked up a little silver bell next to his platter and rang it. "Let's eat, shall we? Matthew, I hope you're hungry?"

"I am, sir." If he could get anything into his stomach, which was so tense amid this crew that it felt squeezed by iron bands.

Presently through a door at the right side of the room came the first wave of this feast: a procession of bowls, platters, and trays filled with sliced melons, stewed apples, honeyed strawberries, green salads, and other enticements brought in by three boys about fourteen or fifteen years of age, dressed in white shirts and black breeches, and two older women wearing kitchen aprons. Wine red and white was poured into glasses and Chapel proposed a toast with his glass lifted high: "To new friends and new prosperity!" Everyone drank. The glasses were immediately filled again by one of the boys, a wiry youth with shoulder-length brown hair that looked to have been brushed back from his face with bee's-wax pomade. His purpose seemed to be standing nearby over a cartful of wine bottles, ready to pour when a glass showed its bottom.

The meal progressed, as candlelight flashed off the fine silver and was reflected upon the walls like streaking comets. Matthew was aware of the swords at his back while he carried on a conversation about the weather with Miss LeClaire, Chapel offered some observations about the size and shape of clouds, Evans borrowed a remark or two and reworked it so it sounded as if he'd come up with it on his own, and Count Dahlgren drank a glass of white wine and watched Matthew over the brim. The conversation then turned to the beauty of Chapel's silverware, and when he stated between sips of wine that his father had impressed upon him the idea that no gentleman was a true gentleman without fine silver on the dinner table Miss LeClaire clapped her hands as if he'd made a pronouncement of discovering a medical cure for dropsy.

Then came the second wave, this one a flotilla of bowls bearing soups and chowders: mushroom and bacon, oyster and corn, she-crab and cream. Chapel took pinches of pepper from a mound in a silver bowl and threw them with gusto into his food, so much so that the lady had a fit of sneezing that a napkin could hardly contain. Evans went the salt route, while Dahlgren ignored his spoon and drank directly but delicately from the bowl in what Matthew thought must be the Prussian way.

Matthew was waiting for the first sound of a blade sliding out of its sheath, and twenty minutes into the feast Chapel cleared his throat with a peppery rumble.

Evans and Miss LeClaire had been chattering about the value of oysters to a healthy diet. Both of them suddenly went mute.

Chapel reached into his coat, brought out an object, and laid it on the table in front of Matthew, after which he returned to his pepperpot.

It was Ausley's notebook. Matthew's heart twisted on its root. He feared the book might have been the one in his possession, and stolen from the dairyhouse even as he'd been brought here today. But no . . . compose yourself, he thought. He could see there was no dried blood on it. This was one of Ausley's less recent books, but identical in every way to the one Matthew had.

"You know what this is, I presume?" Chapel asked. There was a little *ting* as Dahlgren tapped the rim of his wineglass with a fingernail.

Matthew had had his fill of mushroom-and-bacon soup. He pushed the bowl aside. "I do." Careful! he cautioned himself. "I've seen Ausley writing in it."

"Not this particular one, maybe. He had a box full of them, under the bed in his room. A strange bastard, wasn't he? Scribbled notes on everything under God's sun. You know, I once knew of a lunatic in London who made balls of dust. Hundreds of them. Kept them in his attic. It was in the *Gazette*, wasn't it, Lawrence?"

"Yes sir."

Chapel nodded his conical head with satisfaction that his memory had been served. "I think Ausley was one notebook away from dust balls. All that about his gambling debts and his bowel habits . . . ridiculous. Of course you suspect by now that dear Charity here is not in any way related to Ausley, unless you consider nymph's itch as a kind of lunacy." He showed his peg-teeth to the lady, who looked straight ahead and continued drinking her white wine with no sign of perturbance except for a metallic glint of the eyes. "We found the box of notebooks when we searched his room," Chapel went on, speaking to Matthew again, "but as he was known to always carry one on his person, there was—and *remains*—the notebook missing from his personal belongings." He smiled faintly. "Do you have any idea where it might be, Matthew?"

"No sir," came the steady reply.

"I'm sorry to hear that, for it would have made things so much easier. Now we have to go about *searching* for it. And *where* to begin? With his murderer? Do you think his murderer might have taken the notebook, Matthew?"

"I have no idea."

"Oh, but you *must* have an idea! An opinion, at least. Why would his murderer have taken the notebook but left his wallet? Eh?"

Matthew knew Chapel was waiting for a response, so one must be given. "I suspect Ausley's killer wished to read it."

"*Exactly!*" Chapel lifted a thick forefinger. He was grinning as if all this was the most wonderful merriment, but the topaz eyes were stone-hard. "So this was someone who killed Ausley for a purpose, just as he's killed Dr. Godwin and Mr. Deverick. Their wallets were likewise left undisturbed? Lawrence, the *sheet* please." He held out a hand. Evans reached into his own coat with an eagerness that bordered on the frantic; from an inside pocket he brought out a many-times-folded sheet of paper that Matthew already knew was the *Earwig*. Evans unfolded it, smoothed it out, and slid it past Matthew and Count Dahlgren to the smiling host.

"A long way to go, to match the *Gazette*," Chapel said as he looked over the article on Deverick's murder. "But a good beginning, I'd say. I suppose there'll be another sheet out soon with an article about Ausley? Or is he old news by now?"

"I'm sure there'll be another sheet out within a few days. Mr. Grigsby has to gather enough news to fit first."

"Of course. Economy must be observed, and why would Ausley rate a sheet all to *himself*? You know, we found your name in several of those notebooks. He had a very interesting combination of respect for your intellect and hatred for your principles. I think actually he was *afraid* of you. In any event, he was glad to be rid of you to that Magistrate Woodward."

Matthew was shocked. "He was keeping notebooks *that* long ago?"

"Indeed. Only he didn't write as much in them or go through them as quickly as later, when he went off the pier's end with his gambling and personal lecheries. But as I say, he was afraid of you." Chapel returned to his soup and dabbed a little she-crab from his chin with a white napkin. "He feared you were going to get another boy as witness to tell everything to Magistrate Powers and then the church might step in. Also, you made him nervous just following him around like that, night after night. He made a convincing argument for my help, so that's why I let him use Carver and Bromfield, my hunters. I think you saw Bromfield this afternoon?"

Matthew glanced quickly at Evans but said nothing.

"Oh, don't mind what Lawrence told you. It's no matter. I would've been highly disappointed in you if you *hadn't* gotten out and exploring. You did take a risk, though. Bromfield has a nasty streak. Are we ready for the main course, friends? Let's be at it, then!" He rang the little silver bell again, as Count Dahlgren held out his wineglass to be refilled.

More platters and trays were brought to the table. This time the offerings were substantial: grilled lamb with dill pickles, sweetbreads in mustard sauce, a hunk of red meat that Matthew thought must be a calf's tongue, and thickly sliced ham with a burnt sugar glaze. Accompanying these stomach-busters was wild rice, creamed corn, and a pile of biscuits. Matthew looked in vain for the hares. Who had Bromfield been hunting for?

But it was all Matthew could do to keep his mind about him, for this scene of feast coupled to the strange conversation with Simon Chapel was more like a dream than reality. He was full already, and the serving boys were loading up another plate for him. Then, quite suddenly, one of the boys spilled wild rice over the front of Matthew's breeches and cried out, "Pardon, sir! Pardon, sir!" as he wiped the offending food away with a napkin. Matthew stood up from the table as the boy's hand rapidly darted here and there to clean off the debris and Matthew finally said,

"It's all right. Really. I'm fine." He brushed the last bits off himself and returned to his seat, while the boy—a small-boned lad with a mass of curly brown hair and the fast movements of a weasel— wadded up the napkin in his fist and started toward the door that presumably led to the kitchen.

"Silas, Silas, *Silas*!" Chapel said, with an air of exasperation. "Stop where you are, please!"

The boy obeyed and, turning around toward the master, had a crooked grin on his red-cheeked face.

"Give it up," Chapel instructed. "Whatever it is."

"Give it up, Silas!" jeered the young wine-guardian.

"*Now*." Chapel's voice had begun to lose its humor.

The boy's grin faded. "I was jus' practisin'," he said. "Gonna put 'em back later."

"Return them to Mr. Corbett. This moment, or you and I will have some difficulties."

"Awwww," Silas said, in the manner of any boy caught red-handed at a mischief. He approached Matthew, opened the napkin, and deposited from it both the silver watch and the dairyhouse key onto the table next to Matthew's plate. Instinctively and with abject amazement Matthew checked his pockets, which had been picked so quick and cleanly he'd had no sensation of looting fingers.

"Go about your business, Silas," Chapel instructed, as he began to slice the calf's tongue. "No more nonsense, now."

"No more *nonsense*," smirked the wine-boy, who flinched as Silas balled up a fist and made a threat of striking him, but then Silas thought better of it and went out through the door to the kitchen.

"Silas has a little habit." Chapel pushed the tongue platter toward Matthew. "We indulge him sometimes, as he does no harm. He *is* quick, isn't he?" His gaze locked on the watch. "Very fine, that is. How come you to have such an expensive time instrument?"

"It was a gift," Matthew answered, aware he was again edging on shaky ground. "From . . ." His wits failed him.

"Oh, it's not Mr. *Deverick's* watch, is it?" Chapel made a wide-eyed expression of mock horror that was almost comical. "*You're* not the Masker, are you?"

"No." His mind started up again, like Sassafras running on the treadmill at Micah Reynaud's barbershop. "It was a gift from the man who founded the town of Fount Royal, in the Carolina colony. Given for clearing up an important matter."

"The witchcraft thing? Yes, Ausley told me. I might mention that my Carolina source says Fount Royal dried up and blew away last summer, so sad to relate. But life goes on, and so does time. Ah, what's *this*?" Chapel plucked up the dairyhouse key even as his mouth was gobbling tongue.

Matthew, who felt as if Dr. Godwin's breeches were already about to burst at the belly, had passed the tongue on down to Miss LeClaire, who stabbed herself a piece. Evans was intent on his small portion of ham and across from Matthew, Count Dahlgren put a fork to the grilled lamb and chewed steadily while watching Chapel inspect the key.

"This is an *antique*," Chapel remarked once his mouth was clear. "Charity tells me you live in an outhouse."

"A dairyhouse," Matthew corrected.

He shrugged his massive shoulders. "Outhouse, dairyhouse . . ."

"*Whorehouse*," the lady sniggered, with a shiny look that skimmed past Matthew. One of her blond curls had come unpinned and was hanging down over a chocolate eye. Her wineglass was empty. The wine-boy poured another.

"Here, mind she doesn't get *too* much!" Chapel told the boy. "She'll have us all on the table devouring us like Sunday sausages!" He returned his attention to Matthew. "Why does a young man of your aptitude live in an *outhouse*?"

"My aptitude, sir?"

"Your *brains*. Your gumption. You're not *lazy*, I know. Also I know you have curiosity and you're not afraid to strike out on your own. Why an outhouse, then? Do you have no *ambition*?"

"I have ambition. I am where I am, for right now."

"Where you *are* right now," Chapel said as he set the key down beside Matthew's silver plate, "is *here*. It's where you're going tomorrow morning that I think shameful."

"Sir?"

"Back to that noxious town. Full of those cretins and clodfoots. Pigs in the streets and horse manure . . . well, need I mention that to you? I think you have such potential, Matthew! Such a mind as yours should not be put to waste . . ." He paused and took a sip of wine.

"To waste, sir?" Matthew asked.

"Doing menial labor," came the reply. "Isn't that right, Lawrence?"

"Yes sir." The *s* was perhaps a shade slurred.

"Listen to him, for Lawrence was once a legal clerk himself. Drowning in ink and debts. But look at him now, Matthew. Dressed in such finery and performing tasks more suited to his skills. And with a great future yet ahead of him!"

Matthew was watching Dahlgren, who watched Matthew. "Does the Count also work for you?"

"In a sense. He's a guest, but he's also my fencing instructor. I'm a bit late in taking it up, I fear, but I'm trying to learn. It's damned *hard*, though."

"Hard?" Miss LeClaire stirred and seemed to be rocking back and forth in her chair, her eyes flicking from one man to another. Her voice was thick. "Who's hard?"

"Hush," Chapel said. "I meant to say *difficult*, Matthew. One must take care around Miss LeClaire, lest her condition leap out and romp us to death."

Matthew finished his glass of wine and put a finger to the rim, allowing no more, when the boy rushed forward to pour again. Sense had to be made of this strange cornucopia, and he knew of only one way in the situation to start finding some answers. The frontal assault. "Mr. Chapel," he said, and at once the man was listening attentively, "may I ask exactly why Ausley's notebooks are so important to you?"

"Of course. They hold, amid his ravings and chamber-pot tribulations, the names of the orphan boys he's sold to me."

"*Sold* to you?"

"Well, I suppose *rented* is a better word. You know. To work here, as grounds and house staff and in the vineyard. Good help is so difficult to find. We clean them up, of course. Educate them and give them a trial period. If they fit in, they stay. If they don't, they return to the orphanage." Chapel continued eating. "A simple solution to my needs. I suppose I could have bought slaves, but I don't wish black hands on the grapes."

"Black hands," Miss LeClaire slurred, both eyes now obscured by fallen curls. "On the grapes." And then she snorted a laugh that made clear threads of snot shoot out of both nostrils.

"Dear Lord! Lawrence, do something about her, will you? Mind your stones, she's got a claw of iron. Where were we? Oh, the orphans! Well, this arrangement's been going on since I— Lawrence in my stead, I mean—approached him . . . oh, back in 1696, I suppose. And when did you leave the orphanage? 1694, wasn't it?"

"Yes." Matthew tried not to look as Evans cleaned the lady's nose and tried to make her stop rubbing herself back and forth on the chair's seat. The nymph's itch, indeed.

"We just missed you. It works well for us, and well for Ausley . . . until he was murdered, I mean. Now we've got all the books but the last one, and we really must find it."

"Why?" Matthew asked. "What's so important about the names?"

"Actually, there's only one name I care about in the books. My own." Chapel offered an apologetic smile and a tilt of the battering-ram. "You see, Ausley was not removing the names of his charges from the rolls after they were sent to *me*. Therefore he could continue to get the same amount of money from the charities and the churches because his numbers stayed the same. I suppose I paid for much of his gambling adventures, plus he took the extra charitable funds. Now that the poor wretched bastard is dead, I'd think someone in a position of responsibility will be going over the official ledgers and records of placement. The notebooks, you understand, are highly *unofficial*."

Chapel leaned toward Matthew in an attitude of sharing a secret. "I told him, through Lawrence, not to write my name down *anywhere*. I wanted there to be no trail of paper leading to me. Hate those. Well, what do we find when we get the notebooks from under his bed? Yes, there it was, all right! My name, in glorious scribble! I had a suspicion, after Bromfield and Carver told me they got a glimpse of one of those damned books the night they hired out to him, that my name was in them somewhere. Now it may have been true that just my family name is there and possibly no one would ever have connected me to the scheme, but still . . . care saves trouble, as my father used to say. I have not advanced to my present situation by lack of planning, I promise you."

Matthew nodded. This information didn't surprise him in the least. But what of the numbers? The code Ausley had written down? Of course he couldn't ask, though he nearly had to lock his teeth together.

"I'm not a *monster*," Chapel continued. He knifed butter from a silver tray and bathed a biscuit with it. "The boys here are all volunteers. No one has to stay if they don't like it. How many are here presently, Lawrence?"

"Nineteen, sir." Evans was trying to free himself from the hands that were earnestly working at the buttons of his breeches front.

"Many various ages, from twelve on up," Chapel said. "They live in a very comfortable building at the vineyard. When they reach the age of eighteen, they are free to go out into the world on their own if they choose. I had a ready source of labor, Ausley got his money, and all was right with Simon Chapel's little world." His visage darkened. "Until this Masker came along. And who the *devil* is he, anyway? Why these three men, Matthew? Does anyone have any ideas?" His gray eyebrows went up. "Do *you*?"

It wasn't right, Matthew thought as he pushed his plate aside and folded his hands on the table. Something . . . was . . . not . . . *right*. Why should the Masker be interested in Ausley's scheme with Chapel? He remembered that before Dippen Nack had scared the Masker away, there'd been a whispered *Eben Ausley was* . . .

What was the finish of that declaration to be?

Eben Ausley was selling orphans as vineyard workers? As household and grounds staff?

Why in the world should the Masker have a care for what Ausley did with the orphans?

It wasn't right, Matthew thought. No.

"Tell me about this, then," said Chapel, as he slid the *Earwig* toward Matthew. His index finger tapped a small item. Matthew saw the broadsheet had been turned to its second page, and Chapel's finger was on the lines of print that read *The Herrald Agency. Problem-Solving. Letters of Inquiry to go to the Dock House Inn.*

thirty-six

"THE PRINTMASTER'S YOUR FRIEND, isn't he?" Chapel looked at his fingertip and found it was marred by a small darkening of ink. He wiped it on his napkin. "Do you know who brought that item to him?"

Matthew was startled as Count Dahlgren suddenly got up from his chair, walked across the room with a half-glass of white wine in his left hand, and with his other pulled a sword from the display on the right side of the fireplace. It came out with a shrieking sound.

"Tell me," Chapel said, his intense topaz gaze fixed upon Matthew. The reflection of orange candleflames on his spectacle lenses made it appear that his eyeballs were burning.

Behind Matthew, Dahlgren began to thrust and parry at a phantom opponent. Matthew dared not turn around, but could hear the sword's high *whick*ing noise as air was cleaved left and right.

"Do you know these agency people *yourself*, Matthew? Have you met them?"

"I . . ." What a pit had been opened for him! Would that it not become a grave where he might lie rotting and filled up with roaches. He swallowed hard as Dahlgren swung his blade through a candle and the waxen stump flew over Matthew's head into the wild rice. "I have—"

He didn't know what he was going to say, but before he could say it a drunken load of woman jumped into his lap, driving the breath out of him and almost causing him to spew forth sliced melons, stewed apples, salad, mushroom-and-bacon soup, and every other foodstuff deposited in his belly-bank. This leap of wanton faith was accompanied an instant later by a tongue—of the feminine human variety—winnowing itself into his mouth like a river eel. He tried to push her off but she was stuck fast, her arms going around his neck and her fleshy red rag nearly down his throat. He had the feeling that he might strangle on it, while as if in some nightmare formed from bad codfish Count Dahlgren lunged around the room whacking candles, Evans grabbed the itching nymph to give Matthew some air and Chapel said sourly, "Well, damn it all," and beckoned the wine-boy over for another glass.

When Evans got Miss LeClaire unsealed and unseated and she began to try to get his breeches pulled down, Chapel leaned toward the hard-breathing and red-faced young nobleman and said, "Listen now, Matthew. Very important. Will you run a simple errand for me when you get back to town?"

"What . . ." He ducked as the upper half of a candle, its wick still smoking, sailed between them. "What is it?"

"Don't mind Count Dahlgren." Chapel waved a dismissive hand in the swordsman's direction. "This is obviously some kind of Prussian after-dinner thing. But about the errand: will you go for me to the Dock House Inn and find out if anyone named *Herrald* is staying there?"

"Herrald?" Matthew asked, as Dahlgren began to deliver an unintelligible chant in a strange, staccato rhythm while he swung the sword back and forth with lightning speed, the blade hardly a blur. Matthew saw him switch hands, whirl around, almost drop to the floor, and then smoothly switch hands again and strike out as if piercing an enemy's heart.

"The Herrald Agency. The *item*. Wake up, is the wine taking you under? I want to know specifically if a Mrs. Katherine Herrald is staying there, or has lately *been* there. I also want to know who's gone to see her and what company she keeps." Chapel grasped Matthew's shoulder with a steely claw that reminded him of Jack

One Eye the bear. "Also, get what you can from the printmaster. Bring me back this information within three or four days and I'll make it worth your while."

"Worth my while, sir?"

"That's right. How about a pound sterling, to start with?" Chapel waited for the sound of that immense sum to sink in. "We've got to get you away from that outhouse *somehow*, and this seems a good place to begin."

"All right," Matthew said, for he wished to return to New York in a single package. "I'll see what I can do."

"That's the boy! Also keep your eyes and ears open about that notebook, won't you?"

"I will."

"And please, not a word to *anyone*. You wouldn't want old Simon in the pillory, would you?"

"No."

"Excellent! Let's have a drink on it! Jeremy, open the new bottle!"

The wine-boy uncorked a hitherto untasted vintage, poured thick red liquid into two fresh glasses, and set them before Matthew and Chapel. "To victory!" Chapel said, lifting his glass. Matthew wasn't sure what battle was in the future, but he also lifted his glass and drank.

"Now, now!" Chapel chided when Matthew started to put his drink aside. "Bottoms up, young Corbett! Bottoms up!"

Matthew saw no option but to finish the glass, knowing that at least this bizarre dinner was almost over and he could get up to bed. But then came the servers again, this time bearing a huge white-iced cake, some kind of fruit pie, and a plateful of sugared cookies. The sight of the sweets diverted Miss LeClaire from her mission of removing Evans' breeches, and with a cry of girlish delight she staggered drunkenly toward the cake, her hair hanging in her face. As the lady attacked the cake with her fingers, Evans hoisted up his breeches, Count Dahlgren chanted and fenced, and Chapel watched everything with firelit eyes and a thin-lipped smile, Matthew thought he knew the real meaning of the word *bedlam*.

A piece of cake the size of a brick was placed before Matthew, who had not the stomach for a pebble. Following this was a slice of pie from which red cherries oozed. He noted that the room's furious light had faded somewhat, as Dahlgren continued to chop away at candles. The smells of burnt tallow and smoke whirled about him, scorching his nostrils. At the back of his throat, now that the acidic tang of the wine had subsided, was a sulphurous taste. Whatever vintage he'd just drunk, he thought, it was not yet suited for public consumption.

He heard Miss LeClaire laugh with her mouth full and then Evans said something he picked up only as a distant rumble. Looking through the slithering smoke, he watched Dahlgren wielding a sword like a clockwork automaton, back and forth across the room. Say what you please, he told himself, the Prussian was damned good with that blade. The man moved in a blur, the sword a sharp sparkle of light as it twisted, turned, and bit. Matthew figured Dahlgren certainly knew how to keep his thumb locked down.

Matthew watched Dahlgren's shadow thrown monstrously upon the wall, emulating its master's moves. Then, quite suddenly, Matthew realized he was watching Dahlgren fencing his shadow, and the shadow was making its own moves and countermoves. Now *this* is interesting, he thought happily, aware of a red haze beginning to creep around the edges of his vision.

Wait, he heard his own voice say, or perhaps it was spoken only in his mind. It sounded like an echo from the bottom of a well. He repeated it, and it came out *Wayyyytttt*. When Matthew blinked heavy eyelids and looked at Simon Chapel through the creeping haze he saw that his host was growing a second head to the left of the first. It was coming up like a warty mass, bulging the collar of the man's shirt. From the birthing head a single eye with a red pupil like a flare at the end of a candlewick found Matthew's face, and in the darkness below it a scarlet mouth opened in a smile to show a hundred teeth the size of needles.

Matthew's heart begin to pound and writhe. Cold sweat bloomed on his face. He wanted to look at Chapel's real face, for he knew in the recess of his mind yet untouched by whatever drug he'd ingested that the terrifying vision was false yet he could not, could not, look away. He saw a hand with seven fingers reaching for him, and a voice that stung like hot wax whispered *Let go, Matthew, just let go . . .*

He did not want to let go, but he couldn't help it, for in the next minute or second or whatever time had become he felt himself falling forward as if off a precipice and it was not the blue river beneath him but the white icing of cake. He felt his body sag off the chair, he heard a mean little peal of laughter and a sword hiss through the air, and then he was all alone and drifting in the dark.

It occurred to him in this small country of darkness that Chapel had not seemed affected by the drug. How was that so, when they'd both drunk from the same unopened bottle? It was a curious thing, he thought, as his body began to become elongated and his legs and arms splayed out until he was as thin as a kite.

He was coming down for a landing. He felt something rushing up at him, though he knew not what. He hit a soft surface, someone—a man's voice, hollow in the distance—said *he's all yours but don't kill him, dear*, and then a wild animal seemed to jump upon him because hot breath bathed his neck and claws dug into his shoulders.

Were his breeches being tugged off? Was his skin still on his bones? He opened his lips to cry out and a burning mouth caught the cry and tore it up between gnashing teeth. The mouth sucked at his lips so hard he thought they were being torn away. Then the mouth moved southward along with the fingernails and when the ultimate destination was reached at midcontinent the suction lifted his buttocks up and held him suspended.

Through eyes that would not open beyond slits he saw flickering candles and a wild-haired shadow humping with the ferocity of the damned. His backbone cracked, his teeth chattered, and the brain rattled in his skull. There was a savage twist and a searing pain and he feared his manhood had been tied in a knot by the pulsing wet orifice that squeezed so mightily around the member. Then the pounding continued with no abate and no tender mercy.

In his drugged state, his mind in a stupor, and his body roused to a sweating fever, he had no doubt what was being done to him. He had been thrown to Charity LeClaire and was serving as a scratch for the nymph's itch. All he could do was be battered and beaten, tossed and trumpled, rowdied and rompled and rigidified. Up was down, down was up, and at some point the bed broke and the whole heaving world slid sideways. A mouth sucked his mouth, a hand grasped his hair, a second hand caught his beans, and eager thighs slammed down in a spine-bending maneuver both frenzied and frantic.

He was half off the bed, but which half he didn't know. Blond curls fell in his face and damp breasts squeezed against his chest. A catlike tongue darted and flicked. The hammering of the lady's pubic mound against Matthew's groin beat from him a grunting rhythm, broken when the demoniacal damsel screamed in his ear. Then after a respite that seemed as long as eight seconds, Matthew felt himself seized by the ankles and dragged along with the bed-sheets upon the chamber's floor, where Miss LeClaire continued her demonstration of the lusty art. Matthew swore he felt his soul trying to float free from his body. After so many explosions of energy, probably helped along by the wicked drug, he was now only shooting forth blue air.

But the lady screamed and screamed again, and to stifle another scream chewed on his right ear as if it were a cornbread muffin. He was only vapor now, a ghost of his former self. In this half-viewed, orange-daubed debaucher's paradise he thought Miss LeClaire could teach Polly Blossom things the madam had only seen in opium dreams.

At last, at long last: a cessation of motion. The weight of a body lying across Matthew's chest, and the sensation of steam pouring forth as in hot sun after rain. His neck was kinked and his back crooked. His eyes, like cannonballs, rolled across devastated fields. He fell away into the void.

It was with an abrupt start that Matthew returned to the world of the living. He was being roughly jostled back and forth, which at first made him think the tireless nymph was again at work, but then he saw through swollen eyes the padded interior of a coach. Early morning had arrived, as the red sun was just rising to the east. He realized he was dressed, more or less, in the clothes he'd come with, and he was being returned to New York.

The seat opposite him was empty. He heard the crack of the whip and felt the vibration of the four horses hauling the vehicle southward. A rear wheel hit a particularly brutal pothole and lifted his bottom off the seat, and when he came down he landed on a sore nut and almost shouted God's name in vain. It would do to find a way to steady himself, for the sake of his bruised stones. The horses were making a quick clip and the coach was a rolling symphony of creaks, cracks, and groans. He knew the feeling.

The darkness rose up and took him once more, and when he awakened this time—again to the aches and pains of spent passions—he blinked in the stronger light, as the day had advanced by perhaps two hours. Still he was hazy and had to concentrate to keep his eyelids from sliding shut. The drugged wine, Matthew thought, had been a potent vintage. But no, no . . . his mind was yet working properly. He reached up and rubbed his temples, so as to move the sluggish blood.

It had not been the wine, he realized, or Chapel also would have fallen under its spell. The drug must've been smeared inside his glass. Yes. Inside the glass, so an unopened bottle might be shared by two but a victim made only of one.

Whatever that had been about, he had no idea except to guess that the other men had given him up to Charity LeClaire as a way to save their own foreskins. If she was like that every night she must nearly have put them all in a grave. Well, there could be no doubting now of his status as an ex-virgin, though this had been more assault than sex. The damnable thing was if he might start in the next few days—or after an ample time of recovery, at least— wondering about what it must be like to meet her in the bedchamber without being drugged almost immobile.

There must have been another reason to it as well, Matthew mused as he lifted up off the seat with every shudder of the suspension. He'd been drugged to keep him from roaming around at night, after his host had gone to bed. Charity LeClaire had just been the icing on the cake.

It made no sense to him. That business about the orphans being put to work as servants and vineyard workers. Of course there'd been the serving-boys in the room. But what would the Masker care about it?

Matthew remembered the boy who'd picked his pocket and he immediately felt to see if his watch and key were still there. They were. *Silas has a little habit*, Chapel had said. A habit indeed.

Matthew quieted his mind and tried to rest again, as his body demanded it. Soon the coach's wheels were rolling over more familiar dirt and they passed through the outskirts of town. The silver watch reported ten-thirteen. On the streets this Friday morning was the usual traffic of wagons and pedestrians, all hurrying about their business in the way that Matthew had begun to think of as "New Yorkian." The coach's team was slowed to a walk but steered toward the harbor to set its passenger off at his destination, and that was when Matthew caught in the air the sharp scent of smoke. This was no surprise, due to the number of industries that required fire, but when the air became tinted with murky yellow about a block from Grigsby's house Matthew realized something nearby was well and truly aflame. He peered out the crescent-shaped window and to his absolute horror saw smoke and a lick of flame rising from just ahead, on the printmaster's property.

His dairyhouse was burning.

He shouted, "I'm getting out *here*!" to the driver and whipman, popped the door open, and jumped down to the street. His knees gave way, his groin ached like a stab wound, and he staggered forward on the edge of collapse but he kept going against the pull of gravity itself. He had no doubt about it; the dairyhouse was going up, and so then were the last of his meager belongings.

But as he got onto Grigsby's property from Queen Street he saw it was not his miniature mansion aflame. The smoke and a flurry of ashes were rising from well behind the dairyhouse. Matthew walked—or rather, limped—toward the conflagration, his heart pounding, and saw the printmaster and his daughter engaged in tending a bonfire, each of them armed with rakes to herd off errant flames in the grass.

"What is *this*?" Matthew asked as he neared Grigsby, and he noted that when Berry turned around she glanced first at his sallow face and then quickly at his crotch as if she knew where it had spent the night.

"Matthew, there you are!" Grigsby grinned, his face puffed by the heat. Ashes clung to his little tuft of hair and a black streak lay across his nose. "Where've you been?"

"Just away for the night," he answered, as Berry turned her back on him and raked dead a crawling fist of fire. Ashes billowed from the flames and blew around them like gray snow.

"What are you burning?"

"Garbage," Grigsby said, with a twitch of his eyebrows. "On your command, sir."

"*My* command?"

"But of course. Anything to please the master of the house."

"Master of the—" Matthew stopped, for he'd peered into the flames and saw in that red hotpot a melded mass of shapes that might have once been a pile of old buckets, boxes, implements, and unknown items shrouded with blazing canvas. He caught sight of a well-punctured and smouldering archery target an instant before its straw-stuffed interior ignited and then exploded into a small inferno.

His first impulse was to grab Grigsby's rake and attack the fire; his second was to pick up the bucket of water he saw on the ground nearby and try to save what he knew to be hidden within the target, but the burlap was nothing but blaze now and it was too late, much too late. *"What have you done?"* he heard his own voice cry out, with such anguish that both Grigsbys looked at him as if he'd caught flame himself.

The printmaster's spectacles had slid down to the end of his sweating nose. He pushed them back up, the better to see Matthew's horror-struck face. "I've done what you asked!" he said. "I've cleaned the dairyhouse out for you!"

"And set everything on *fire*?" He'd almost screamed the last word. "Are you *mad*?"

"Well, what else was I to do with all that junk? I mean, the press parts and tins of ink I kept, of course, but everything else had to go. My lord, Matthew, you look ill!"

Matthew had staggered back from the heat and almost gone down on his rear, but if he busted another nut he'd have to be put in a wheelbarrow and carted to the public hospital on King Street.

"Matthew!" Berry was coming toward him, her red curls in wild disarray and black smears of ash on her chin and forehead. The deep blue eyes saw much. "What *is* it?"

"Gone," was all he could say.

"Gone? What's gone?"

"It was in there. The target. Inside there, where I hid it." He realized he was babbling like a brook, but he was unable to make sense. "I hid it, right in there."

"I think he's drunk!" Grigsby said, raking away a piece of blazing burlap that had escaped the furies.

"Very important," Matthew rambled on. He felt as if he were again under the effects of Chapel's drug, his vision blurring in and out of focus. "Very important I keep it, and now it's gone."

"Keep *what*?" Grigsby asked. "Aren't you pleased I did this for you?"

Berry put aside her rake and took Matthew's hand. "Settle down," she said, in a voice like a firm slap to the jaw. He blinked and stared at her, his mouth half-open and the taste of ashes on his tongue. Berry said, "Come with me," and pulled him gently toward the printmaster's house.

"Everything's cleaned up for you!" Grigsby called after them. "I got a rug for you and a new desk! Oh, and the locksmith came this morning! Your old lock was sprung!"

In the kitchen, Berry guided Matthew into a chair at the table and poured him a cup of water. He looked at it for a few seconds, uncomprehending, until she put the cup into his hand and waited for him to press his fingers around it. "Drink it," she said, and he obeyed like a pole-axed dullard.

"What's this about?" she asked, when he'd put the cup down.

He shook his head, unable to speak it. What might have been a vital part of this puzzle, now turned to ashes and smoke. Not knowing what secret the Masker meant him to discover was too much to bear. He realized Berry was no longer in the room with him. He sat stupidly looking at the watercup as he heard her foot-steps approaching across the boards.

She stopped just behind him. Suddenly, with a small sharp *smack*, was laid on the table before him an object risen from death by fire.

"I helped Grandda move the junk yesterday," she said. "I needed some more straw for my mattress. That was in the second handful."

Matthew reached out to touch the gold-ornamented note-book, to make sure it was real. He swallowed, his mind still reel-ing, and said the first thing that came to him: "Lucky for me."

"Yes," Berry agreed, in a quiet voice. "Lucky for you." Then: "I looked through it, but I didn't show it to Grandda. I found your name in it."

Matthew nodded.

"You hid it in there?"

Again a nod.

"Would you care to tell me why?"

He was still all pins and nerves. He picked up the notebook and opened it to the cryptic page. One glance at the list of names and he saw:

Silas Oakley   7   8   8   5   *Chapel*   *6/20*

This, he presumed, very well might be the Silas with the little habit—and huge talent—of picking pockets. The date might have been when the transaction was made with Ausley, but what was the meaning of the other four numbers?

"Well?" Berry prompted.

"It's an involved story." Matthew closed the notebook and put it down, but kept his hand on it. He recalled as if from a dream

Grigsby saying *Your old lock was sprung.* Had someone come in the night to search his house? "You took the items out of there yesterday?"

"Yes, a few hours after you'd left."

"And you found the notebook then?"

"That's right. Then we just left the stuff out behind the house until Grandda could get a city permit for an open fire."

"I see."

"I *don't* see." Berry came around the table and sat down facing him. Her no-nonsense stare promised him no mercy. "What's it about and why'd you hide it?" A light of realization glinted. "Oh. Does that ladybird have something to do with it?"

After a moment's deliberation he said, "Yes." It was best to continue, for he had the feeling that once Berry had seized upon a subject it was a subject under siege. "Has Marmaduke told you about the Masker?"

"He has. I've read the broadsheets, too." Her freckled cheeks suddenly flushed and she leaned forward with urgent excitement. "It has something to do with the *murders*?"

"It does." He scowled at her. "Now listen to me, and I mean it: not one word to your grandfather. Do you hear me?"

"I hear. But what does the lady have to do with it? And where did you go last night?"

"I have no idea, is the answer to the first question. To the second, it's probably best that you don't know."

"And the notebook, then? All that scribbling about gambling and food and all the rest of it?" Berry made an unpleasant face. "Why's it so important?"

"Again, I have no idea." Matthew decided against all wisdom to give her *something*, as she *had* saved this chestnut from the fire. "I'll tell you that there are other people who want this book, and it's vital they don't find it." He ran a hand through his hair, his energy almost sapped. "I think someone may have broken into the dairyhouse last night to find it, so thank God and all the lucky stars that you found it first. Now: can you do me a great favor and keep it here somewhere, but out of Marmy's sight?"

476 · Robert McCammon

"*Me* keep it?"

"That's right. I'm going to have to make a trip to Philadelphia soon, and I want that book to be here when I get back."

"To Philadelphia? What for?"

"Just never mind." He waved her questions away. "Will you keep the book for me, or not?"

It didn't take Berry long to consider. There was a note of eager excitement in her voice when she said, "I'll put it in the bottom drawer of my chest, under my crayon box. You don't think anyone will break in *here*, do you?"

"That I can't say. I think they suspect I've got it, but they don't know for sure."

She looked at him steadily for a few seconds, and Matthew saw her gaze drop to the front of his shirt. "You're missing three buttons."

In his state of weariness he was unable to formulate a response, so the best he could do was shrug his shoulders and offer a faint, lopsided smile.

"I'd better get back out to help Grandda, but I'll put this away first." She retrieved the notebook and stood up. "Oh . . . a man brought a letter for you. It's on the table in the front room."

"Thank you." He waited until she'd gone, as he feared that when he stood up some dull ache or stabbing pain might cause him to give a groan and she'd want to know what was hurting. The less said about that, the better. When Berry went back outside, Matthew eased himself up and went into the front room, where he found a white envelope sitting on the small round table next to the door. A quick inspection showed him it was sealed with red wax that bore the impressed initial *H*.

He opened the envelope and read: *Dear Matthew, if at all possible please come today before three o'clock to Number Seven Stone Street. With All Regards, Katherine Herrald.*

He refolded the letter and returned it to the envelope. Interesting, if both Mrs. Herrald and Hudson Greathouse were in town. He'd have to promptly go see what this was about, and catch some decent sleep later this afternoon. It would be a good opportunity to relate his tale of last night, as well.

An item that he'd not noticed before caught his attention. Set up near the east-facing window was an artist's easel. A chair was situated before it, turned to the side. On the easel was one of Berry's works in progress, and Matthew stood in the yellow shards of light examining her effort.

It was a rough pencil drawing of Marmaduke Grigsby, seen in profile. The tuft of hair sticking up on the bald scalp, in the moon-round face a large eye behind a spectacle lens, a heavy eyebrow ready to jump and twitch, the massive vein-shot nose, the low-hanging cleft-gouged chin, folds and wrinkles that even in still-ness gave life and character to the expression: all were there. It was really very good, for Berry had captured the strange construction of her grandfather's face with neither the artificiality of emphasis nor restraint. It was therefore not a flattering portrait, but an honest one. He wondered what colors it might be when Berry finished it. Bright red for burning curiosity, and deepest purple for *Earwig* prose? He continued to stare at it for some time, thinking that it took real talent to be truthful. Here was not a gloomy caricature of a tight-assed fop, as Berry would put it; here was the study of a singular human being, with all flaws on display.

A real talent, Matthew thought.

The seed of an idea came to him and began to grow roots.

Absent-mindedly he reached down to fasten buttons that were no longer there, and then he hurried out of the house in the direction of Stone Street.

thirty-seven

NUMBER SEVEN STONE STREET was a brown door that opened onto a narrow and rather steep stairway squeezed between, on the left, the office of Moses Leverich the peltry buyer and on the right the shop of Captain Cyrus Donaghan, who crafted quadrants, astrolabes, and other navigational tools for the shipping trade.

Matthew went up the stairs and found himself in a loft that demanded a good going-over with a scrub-brush and bristle-broom. He had no idea what business had existed here, perhaps during the reign of Peter Stuyvesant, but traces of its grandeur remained like flecks of gold in a mudpuddle. At the top of the stairs was an oak-paneled outer room that held a clerk's multi-drawered desk and a chair with a broken back. Behind the desk was a cubbyhole-chest suited for holding rolled-up maps, documents, and the like. Across the floorboards, and right at Matthew's feet, was a disturbingly large dark stain that he sincerely hoped was not ancient blood. Beyond this room was another closed door. The window shutters were open, allowing the strong sunlight full entry, and the windows themselves—their glass panes filmed with smoke and grime—had been unlatched and pushed ajar to allow for the circulation of air. Through two windows below the over-hanging gray slate roof could be seen the full expanse of the Great

Dock and the ships awaiting destinations and cargo. It was an intriguing view. The whole busy picture of the wharf was on display from this height, as wagons trundled back and forth across the cobbles and citizens went about their errands against the backdrop of buildings, smoke-belching chimneys, shipmasts, furled sails, and the spark of sun off the blue harbor water.

"Hello!" Matthew called. "Anyone here?"

Boots thumped on the boards and the other door opened with a squeal of angry hinges.

Hudson Greathouse, dapper in a dark blue suit and waistcoat with brass buttons, stood in the doorway. "Corbett!" he said, not without a faint smile of welcome that was quickly extinguished. "Come in here, will you?"

Matthew walked into the second room. It was twice as large as the outer chamber, with two desks set side-by-side and behind them against the wall three wooden file cabinets. A pleasant addition was a small fireplace of rough gray and tan stones on the left. Overhead at the center of the room was a wrought-iron chandelier that still held eight old melted stubs. A pair of unshuttered and opened windows gave a view of New York to the northwest, the wide river and the brown cliffs and emerald hills of the Jersey shore.

"What do you think?"

Matthew looked to his right. Standing there was Mrs. Herrald, elegant in a gray gown with an adornment of white lace at the throat. She wore a gray riding-cap, again tilted at a slightly rakish angle but with neither feather nor other decoration. Her blue eyes were fixed on him, and her eyebrows went up. "Well?" she prodded.

"A nice view," he said.

"Also a nice price. It's been vacant, obviously, for many years." She reached up to brush aside a dangling spider's web. "But Hudson and I think it will do as an office. What's your opinion?"

"A bit dusty. What used to be here?"

"A coffee-importing business, begun in the years of the Dutch colony. The real-estate broker tells me the business perished in

1658 and the space has only been rented a few times since then. I agree it needs cleaning, but it *does* have potential, don't you think?"

Matthew looked around, avoiding Greathouse's stare. "I do," he decided. "It's certainly large enough." He just wished he'd found this place before she had and claimed it as his living-quarters, but then again he was sure the rental—though it could hardly be regal—was surely beyond his means.

"Room to grow, yes," Mrs. Herrald said firmly. She walked past Matthew and stood beneath the chandelier, which Matthew realized hung at a crooked angle. "I think this will suit our purposes very nicely. If we're all in agreement, then?" She paused for one final check of the two gentlemen, who both nodded. "I'll sign the papers this afternoon. And don't worry, Matthew, I won't impose upon you or Hudson to get the place cleaned up and cart furniture in. I'll hire some men for the job."

He was glad to hear that. The mere idea of sweeping this dirty floor and scrubbing the soot off the windows, in his present condition, was enough to rekindle the throbbing ache in his groin.

"You look like hell," Greathouse said, getting right to the point. "What have you been into?"

"Hudson!" the woman chided.

"It's all right," Matthew said. "As a matter of fact, I was taken on a trip yesterday and I stayed the night at an estate about fifteen miles up the river."

"Really?" Greathouse looked at him quizzically. "What was *that* about?"

"I'm not quite sure, and I can't explain it. But do either of you know a man named Simon Chapel?"

Mrs. Herrald shook her head and Greathouse replied, "Doesn't ring a chime."

"How about a woman named Charity LeClaire? Or another man called Count Dahlgren?"

"Never heard of them either," Greathouse said.

Mrs. Herrald came a few steps closer to Matthew. "What's this about, please?"

Matthew took aim at Greathouse. "You haven't told her yet? About Ormond's farm?"

"No, I have not." The man's face had tightened.

"Don't you think you should? I have some suspicions about Simon Chapel. I don't fully know what he's up to, but his estate might be where the body came from."

"The body," Mrs. Herrald repeated. She turned to also aim at Greathouse. "*What* body?"

Greathouse gave Matthew a look that said *Thank you for bringing this up now, fool.* He reached into his coat and brought out a folded piece of paper. "I was going to go over this with you later," he said to Matthew, "but since you've chosen this moment to air the subject, I'll tell you what I've found out from the survey office." He unfolded the paper, which Matthew could see was a listing of names in black ink. "North of Ormond, just as he told us, are farms owned by Gustenkirk and Van Hullig. Then there's a few miles of forest deeded to an Englishman named Isaac Adams. He lives in London. Up above that, there's an estate and vineyard owned by—"

"Simon Chapel," Matthew interrupted. "That's where I was last night."

"Wrong." Greathouse's attention never left the paper. "According to the records at City Hall, the estate is owned by another Englishman named Garrett Stillwater. He bought the estate from a Dutchman in 1696. About three miles north of the vineyard is a farm deeded to William Vale, and then an apple orchard and cider mill owned by Zopher Rogers. After that you're at the ferry and the end of the island." He looked up. "None of those names fit any alias that I know to be used by any associate of . . ." He trailed off, but Matthew knew he could feel Mrs. Herrald staring at him.

"Go on." The way she spoke it said she already knew. "Any associate of whom?"

Greathouse refolded the paper, taking his time about it, and put it away.

"He's here," Mrs. Herrald said. "Is that what you mean to

say?" She went on without waiting, her chin lifted in indignation. "You suspect he's here, and you didn't tell me? Because you weren't sure—and *aren't* sure—and you wished to investigate further? Or you wished to spare me the emotion of *fear*? Is that correct?"

He was silent, thinking it over. Then at last he replied, "Yes. All that."

"You found a body, then? In a condition we've come to recognize?"

"Yes."

"Hudson." She shook her head, her eyes lit with both anger and sadness. "Why didn't you *tell* me? You know I'm not a fainting flower. I've been expecting this, but just . . . not so soon. Why didn't you *tell* me?" Her voice cracked, just a little bit.

"If I told you I was trying to protect you, would—"

"There is *no* protection," said Mrs. Herrald. Though this had been spoken quietly, the tension in her voice made Matthew flinch. "There is only foreknowledge and preparation."

"Of course." Greathouse decided it was best to avert his eyes to the floor. "My pardon."

Mrs. Herrald went to the window and peered north, as if trying to locate her enemy by a darkness on the horizon. It was at least fifteen seconds before she spoke again. "I presume we can't be sure?"

"No, but the body bore the marks. I've told Matthew about your theory."

"The gauntlet, yes." She glanced quickly at Matthew and then out the windows again. "I'm not the only one with that theory, by the way. How many stab wounds in this particular corpse?"

"Eight. A young man, the arms tied behind the back. He washed up nearly three weeks ago on John Ormond's farm. You know, where I've gone to buy produce. The coroner had already buried the body, so Matthew and I had to . . . um . . . do some shovel work."

"That must have been *lovely*."

"The method of execution appears to be the same except for

one interesting difference," Greathouse continued. "In all the cases we know about, the skulls of the victims were broken from behind. Probably when they were kneeling on a floor bleeding to death. In this particular instance, the *front* of the skull was crushed."

"Speculation?" asked the lady in gray.

"Well, it may mean nothing. Then again, it may be that one of the professor's students has put his own mark on the way the gauntlet's done. Or it may mean that some variant of the gauntlet was held out-of-doors. I think the victim cheated the blades by either jumping or falling from a high cliff, and he bashed his skull on the way down." He held up the paper. "I got this list of property owners intending to find out where the body might have drifted from. Again, there's no name on the list that I recognize."

"A new world," Mrs. Herrald said, her eyes heavy-lidded, "calls for new names."

"And speaking of names," Matthew said, "Chapel knew *yours*. He had a copy of the broadsheet announcement and wanted more information. I'm supposed to ask about you at the Dock House Inn and report back to him within a few days."

Mrs. Herrald pursed her lips and released a small, quiet puff of air. "I don't like *that*. How is it you went to see this Chapel person in the first place?"

"It has to do with the Masker. Specifically, with Eben Ausley's notebook."

"Is this some kind of riddle?" she asked, frowning. "What's this about a notebook?"

"Corbett's on a tear about this damned Masker," Greathouse spoke up. "He's told Pennford Deverick's widow he can find out who the bastard is, and for that he'll get ten shillings."

"Ah." Mrs. Herrald regarded Matthew with a knowing expression. "An independent job, is that it?"

"She wants the Clear Streets Decree overthrown, as it's costing her money. Until the Masker is found, Lord Cornbury's going to keep the decree in force. It's a simple matter of economics." Matthew shot a glance at Greathouse, then back to Mrs. Herrald. "But no, it's not *entirely* an independent job."

"Meaning?"

"Meaning," Matthew said in a calm but firm voice, "that I believe these current events are by no means independent of each other. I think they hinge together, in a way I can't yet explain. The Masker, the three murders, the notebook, Chapel . . . even the woman at the Westerwicke asylum. I think all of them are linked."

"There's a good one!" Greathouse's face wanted to grin, but Mrs. Herrald's lifted hand stopped his chortle before it began.

"Again you mention a notebook," she said. "A notebook belonging to whom and signifying what?"

Matthew took in a deep breath. The moment had arrived. "A notebook taken from the body of Eben Ausley by the Masker, and given to *me* by the Masker. Before you ask: no, I wasn't able to see his face. Chapel wants the book, and I believe he's sent someone to break into my house to find it. I think it shows that Ausley was selling orphans to Chapel for some reason the Masker wants me to discover."

If he was expecting an immediate response, he was disappointed. Mrs. Herrald stood silent, her head cocked to one side and her hands clasped before her. Hudson Greathouse was also struck mute, but his mouth was open and if his eyes had gotten any bigger they might have popped from his head.

The silence stretched on, until finally Mrs. Herrald busied herself with rearranging the folds of lace at her throat.

Greathouse found his voice, though it sounded nearly strangled. "As I said before, what have you gotten into?"

"What we're supposed to be into. A problem that needs a solution."

"Be careful you don't get your throat cut trying to solve it." Greathouse turned to appeal to Mrs. Herrald. "If Chapel—whoever he is—has some tie to Professor Fell, then Corbett's in water way over his head. You know how cunning they are. Chapel might already know Corbett went to meet you at the Dock House. He was just fishing. If he goes back there, and Chapel does happen to be one of the professor's disciples, I wouldn't give a rat's ass for his survival."

"If he was going to kill me, he would have done it last night," Matthew said, but he did think he'd nearly been killed, after all.

"Precisely," Mrs. Herrald agreed, maintaining an admirable composure. "So—if indeed he *is* a confederate of Professor Fell— why did he let you go, suspecting you were working with us?" She paused just a beat before she went on. "Because you obviously have something he values. The famous notebook, I presume. I won't ask where it's hidden, because I don't wish to know. But I'd say if it *had* been found last night, you'd be dead by now. So he sent you back, and now you're being watched."

"Oh." He hadn't thought of that possibility, but it made diabolical sense.

"Spoken like someone who forgot to brush their brain this morning," Mrs. Herrald said. "What indeed happened last night? You don't seem yourself."

Matthew shrugged. "I'm just tired, that's all." The understatement of the new century.

"Well, it's likely you're being watched in the hopes that sooner or later you'll bring that book out. Be very careful, Matthew. These people are professionals. They leap on mistakes, and in this case a mistake can be fatal. Now I also presume you can't directly prove any wrong-doing from this notebook, or you would have already taken it to the high constable?"

"That's correct."

"And you feel it would be wrong to present it to him, without this proof?"

"He wouldn't know what to do with it."

"Do *you* know what to do with it?"

"For now," Matthew answered, "just to keep it safely hidden."

"At your discretion," she said, with a slight nod that gave her approval. She came forward until she was right in his face. Her eyes were cold. "But listen to me well, Matthew. I don't think you know what Professor Fell and his compatriots are capable of. Have you told him the whole story, Hudson?"

"No," came the hollow reply.

"Then I shall do the honors. My husband Richard, who

founded the agency. Do you have any idea what happened to him when he came into conflict with Professor Fell?"

Matthew shook his head.

"Richard was successful in having one of the professor's more notorious associates cast into prison charged with a scheme of arson and extortion. The man was in Newgate only three hours before he was stabbed to death by an unknown killer. Then, several days after that, Richard received the blood card. A small calling-card, with a single bloody fingerprint upon it. Might you guess for yourself what that means?"

"A death threat," Matthew said.

"No, not a death threat. A death *vow*. When you receive the blood card, you might as well prepare your funeral. Nathaniel Powers knows all about it. The blood card he received caused him to uproot his family, leave a long-established law practice, and board a ship to New York. But he knows, deep down, that Professor Fell never forgets, and whether it takes one week, or one month, or one year, or *ten* years, that vow is going to be acted upon. Such was the case with my Richard." She blinked and looked toward the window, her face paled by the sunlight. "The months passed by. We knew, both of us, what the card meant. We were careful. We were aware of strangers around us, of how dangerous crowds could be, or how deadly might be a silent street. All we could do was wait, and all I could do was pray to God that when the knife or the strangle-cord came Richard would see it in time. Do you know what it does to you, Matthew? Living in fear like that, day after day? For more than five *years*? Do you have any possible *idea*?"

"No," Matthew said grimly. "I don't."

"I pray you never do. It erodes your humanity. It saps all joy, and extinguishes all light. And no one can help you, Matthew. No one." She returned her gaze to him, and in that space of seconds Matthew thought she had been aged just by the memory of those terrible five years and her eyes had sunken into dark-rimmed pits. "We threw ourselves into our business. Our *purpose*, as Richard called it. There were more problems to be solved, more clients to be served. But always . . . always . . . the shadow of Professor Fell was there, waiting. My nerves almost went to pieces sometime during the sixth year. I'm not sure I ever really recovered. But Richard was steadfast. No, he said, he didn't wish to leave the city. He didn't wish to run and hide, because he wanted to be able to look at himself in the shaving mirror. And I steadied myself, as well, and went on. One goes on, because one must." She pulled up a horrible, glassy-eyed smile and glanced at Hudson. "Listen to me prattle like a simpleton. It's hell, getting old."

"You don't have to say anything else," Greathouse told her, but she waved his objection away.

For a moment she stood looking down at the floor between herself and Matthew. Beyond the window a seagull cried out as it flew by and a dog barked stridently down on the street.

"On November the tenth. In the seventh year," she said, in a pained and hesitant voice, "at four o'clock in the afternoon. A rainy day. Cold to the bone. Richard left the office to meet his half-brother at the Cross Keys Tavern two blocks from our door. I remember telling him I'd be along soon, after I'd finished writing a report. The case was . . . a missing emerald ring. Stolen by a maid named Sophie. I remember that, very clearly. I told Richard . . . I told him to wear his muffler, and to get some hot tea. He was suffering from a sore throat. The London chill, you know. I told him I'd be along . . . and he walked out the door, bound for the Cross Keys Tavern . . . and he never, ever got there. Not two blocks. He was not seen leaving our building. He was not seen . . . anywhere, by anyone." She lifted her head to stare again out the window, and Matthew wondered just what she was seeing. She started to speak, but words failed her. After a moment she tried once more. "The morning . . . of November the thirteenth," she said, "I found a package at our front door. A very small package."

"Katherine." Greathouse had swiftly moved to her side and taken her elbow. "Don't do this."

"It's a *history* lesson," she answered wanly. "A cautionary tale, for those who have no choice but to go on. I was saying . . . about the small package. Matthew, do you know the agency used to have a motto? Painted on our sign, and printed on our cards. 'The Hands and Eyes of the Law.' "

Matthew recalled Ashton McCaggers telling him about it, up in the coroner's attic.

"I should not have opened that package. I never should have." Something broke in her voice and a tremor passed over her face. "They had left his wedding band on. Very kind of them, in their depravity. They wanted to make sure . . . absolutely sure . . . that I could recognize . . . what remained." She closed her eyes. "What remained," she said again, in nearly a whisper, and beyond the window gulls flew past as white as seafoam and someone on the street began to holler about buckets for sale.

Mrs. Herrald had finished her story. She stood between sunlight and shadow in the room, her head bowed, and perhaps there was a dampness at her eyes or perhaps not, for Matthew thought she in her own way was a soldier, and soldiers only wept alone.

"I was the half-brother Richard was going to meet," Greathouse said to Matthew, as he released the woman's elbow. "Eight years between us. Also the width of a world. He was always lamenting my choices in drink, women, and mercenary adventuring. Said I ought to turn my formidable talents to the support of the law. _Formidable_. Have you ever heard such shit?"

"Shit or not," said Mrs. Herrald sharply, as if emerging from her trance of agonized memory, "you're here, aren't you?"

"Yes," he answered, directly to her. "I am here."

"So . . . I presume you were going to tell me about this _before_ Monday morning?"

"I was going to get around to it."

"Monday morning?" Matthew asked. "What happens then?"

"Then," Mrs. Herrald replied, and now her face had regained its smooth composure and her voice had strengthened, "I walk aboard a ship and, God willing, set foot in England within ten weeks if the wind is providential."

"You're going back to _England_?"

"Yes, I believe that's what I just said. I have other offices of the agency to run, and other business obligations. You and Hudson will oversee this office."

"He and I? By ourselves?"

"Really, Matthew!" She frowned. "You must need a good night's sleep! You and Hudson will do fine, by yourselves. One or two more associates may be hired later, at Hudson's discretion, but for the time being I think things are in order. Except for this ghastly place, and once it's scrubbed and the furniture brought in it'll be ready for business. We'll hang a sign, and there you are. *Oh!*" She looked at Hudson. "Give him the money."

With obvious distaste, Greathouse brought a small leather pouch from within his coat and held it toward Matthew.

"Go on and take it," Mrs. Herrald urged. "It's to cover your travel expenses when you go to Philadelphia." When Matthew hesitated, Mrs. Herrald sighed heavily and said, "Well, you *do* plan to go, don't you? How else are you going to pursue this problem of the . . . what's she called?"

"The Queen," said Greathouse, with a dark smirk. "Of the Loonhouse."

"They call her the Queen of Bedlam, but only in the most respectful way," Matthew said. He took the leather pouch. "I think I've figured out a way to help identify her, but I'll have to go back to the asylum first."

"As you please. Hudson thinks it's wasted money and I would usually agree, but then again . . . sometimes a horse needs to be given its head, don't you agree, Hudson?"

"Yes, and a jackass sometimes needs a kick to the—"

"Play nicely, boys," she advised. "Matthew, I've given you enough money to take a packet boat from here to Philadelphia and back. That will cut the trip to one day, back and forth, instead of three or more by road. Do what you feel is necessary, but do not throw my money away on frivolities, is that clearly understood?"

"Yes, ma'am. Clearly."

"And Hudson, in light of this information from Matthew, I

want you to immediately start finding out everything you can about this Simon Chapel. Someone in the taverns may know the name, but—again—be very careful. All right?"

"Always," he promised.

"Professor Fell may not be here in person," she continued, "but if his influence is here, it's for a reason. I shudder to think. Both of you, watch yourselves and proceed with extreme caution. I shall return, God willing, in May or thereabouts. Any questions?" She lifted her brows, looking from one man to the other.

"I . . . suppose I have a question," Matthew said. "About this office."

"What about it? Other than it being at the moment a spider's paradise?"

"Well . . . I was wondering . . . exactly what's wrong with it."

"What's *wrong* with it? Meaning what?"

"Meaning . . . it's a large space, with a good view and a central location. I was just wondering what must be wrong with it, since it's not been rented in so long."

"Oh, that." Mrs. Herrald smiled thinly. "Nothing's wrong with it, except that it's haunted."

"Haunted," Matthew heard himself repeat, like a dull bell.

"If you believe the tales. I presume you saw the bloodstains out there on the floor? The two original owners of the coffee-importing concern killed each other in an argument. One was stabbed and as he fell he evidently pushed his former partner down the stairs, where he broke his neck. Both the downstairs tenants, Mr. Leverich and Captain Donaghan, have said that on several occasions they've heard heavy boots on the floor and ghostly voices tangled in discord. That does tend to keep a space vacant. Oh, Hudson, that reminds me. We need to find a railing for the stairs."

"My thought as well," Greathouse said. "I don't want Corbett pushing me down the steps in an argument over who has the largest beans."

"I can see you two will get along famously. But most important, to the both of you . . . I expect professionalism and results. I expect you to go forward, even when the road is uncertain. I expect . . ." Mrs. Herrald hesitated, and then she offered Matthew a half-smile that overcame the last remnant of sad memory in her eyes.

"Your best," she said.

There was nothing left to do here until the brush and broom finished their work and the furniture turned a vacant space into an office. Matthew's mind was already turning away, focusing on first Westerwicke and then Philadelphia and—specifically—a lawyer named Icabod Primm.

He felt answers—to the identity of the Queen of Bedlam, the unmasking of the Masker, and the purpose of Simon Chapel— were close at hand, but for this task he needed a good-luck charm by the name of Berry Grigsby.

Matthew followed Hudson Greathouse and Mrs. Herrald down to the street. As he was last out the door, he was the one who thought he heard at his back not ghostly wrangling but rather the small sigh of some watchful soul who was also intrigued by things to come.

thirty-eight

BERRY LEANED FORWARD, her face radiant in the early morning light that streamed through the window. She was deep in concentration, a single furrow between her brows, her eyes fixed first on her subject and then the pad of paper held on a lap desk across her knees. The tip of her charcoal pencil was ready, but her hand was not.

Matthew watched the copper gleam in her thick red hair, and found himself admiring the way it fell about her shoulders. Natural, without artifice. A single ivory comb served to restrain any errant curls from tumbling over her forehead. He saw her in profile from his position in the room, and wondered how that firm jawline and narrow, slightly upturned nose could have been born from Marmaduke Grigsby's comical flesh. Matthew enjoyed looking at her. The blue eyes had taken on a hint of steel, as they surveyed and calculated. She wore today what she'd worn yesterday, a light sand-colored dress with white lace trailing along the sleeves and decorating the cuffs. Not the most comfortable attire for a day-long horseback ride, but she'd obviously had riding experience— probably in the company of that young equestrian with the broken tailbone, Matthew surmised—and had managed the trip without complaint. Wearing the round-brimmed straw hat at a sporty angle on her head and the way she kept her steed apace with Matthew's horse Dante, she might have passed for a high-wayman's dolly. He was pleased that she'd agreed to come. It wasn't every girl who would've done it, as the road between New York and the Westerwicke asylum was no easy jaunt.

One more check between subject and paper, and then Berry's pencil moved to make a single curved line. She had begun her portrait of the Queen of Bedlam. Matthew glanced over at the two doctors, Ramsendell and Hulzen, who stood at one side of the room watching the procedure. Hulzen was smoking his clay pipe, puffing thin clouds of smoke that drifted out the window, while Ramsendell had one arm hooked under the other elbow and his bearded chin supported by a thumb.

Matthew's watch reported the time as four minutes after eight o'clock. When he and Berry had arrived yesterday, Saturday, it had been almost dark. She hadn't wanted to do the task by candleglow. Matthew had told the doctors that he wished to take a likeness of the lady to Philadelphia as a means of identification, and when they'd assented he'd asked if Berry could do her drawing in the morning light, as Berry had said that would be the optimum as far as getting the details down. Then he and Berry had found two rooms at the *Constant Friend*, eaten supper at Mrs. DePaul's, and gone to bed equally saddle-sore but equally excited about the work to be done. In fact, a half-bottle of port had been required to unwind Matthew enough for sleep to take him.

The morning light illuminated also the face of the lady who sat mute and motionless in the high-backed dark purple chair. She stared out as before, her soft brown eyes directed toward the garden. Everyone else in the room—indeed, in the entire world—might have been a phantasm, unworthy of note. As before, her cloud of white hair was neatly brushed. Her unadorned hands gripped the armrests. She wore the pink slippers decorated with small bows. The only difference at this meeting was that her frail body was wrapped up in a silken homegown not pink as a rose but instead the color of the yellow butterflies that fluttered back and forth amid the garden's flowers. To say she was absolutely motionless was not exactly true, for again her lips moved every so often, as if posing to herself unanswerable questions.

Berry sat where she could catch the lady's profile, just as she'd drawn her grandfather's.

Draw who? she'd asked at the kitchen table on Friday evening.

The face of a woman in an asylum for the mentally infirm, Matthew had told her. *At Westerwicke. That would be New Jersey, a trip of about thirty miles.*

An asylum? Marmaduke Grigsby had quivered, scenting a story over the smell of the chicken livers on his plate. *What woman? Matthew, what secrets are you keeping from me?*

No secrets. I told you I've joined the Herrald Agency and their purpose is the solving of problems. Well, one problem is that the doctors at this asylum wish to put an identity to an unknown woman. How to do that, without first a description? And what better description to offer than a portrait? He'd then turned his attention to the girl. *I'll pay you something, if you think you can do it.*

Of course I can do it, Berry had replied. *I used to go out every weekend to the park and find people to draw. If I happened to sell a portrait, more the better. What, did you think I just did the landscapes?*

I don't know about this, Grigsby had said with a scowl. *It sounds dangerous. Mad people and all. And a day's ride to New Jersey? Absolutely not! No, I refuse to give my approval.*

Which actually had been for the best, since for Berry her grandfather's disapproval was like throwing gunpowder on flames. And then, just past dawn on Saturday as they'd waited with their horses for the ferry to cross from Weehawken, came the question from Berry that Matthew had been expecting: *If I'm going all this way with you to draw a madwoman in an asylum, don't you think I should know the whole story? And not just bits and pieces of it that you gave Grandda, either. I mean everything.*

Matthew hadn't spent much time thinking it over. He realized he needed her support, more than anyone's. *Yes,* he'd agreed. *I do think you need to know.*

During the course of their trip he'd given her the story, beginning with his obsession to bring Eben Ausley to justice. He'd told her about the ambush on Sloat Lane, about the night of Pennford Deverick's death, about his arrival on the scene of Ausley's murder and his subsequent chase of the Masker. He'd related the events of his being hired as an associate by the Herrald Agency and his arrangement with Mrs. Deverick to find her husband's killer. He'd shaped for her his visit with Ashton McCaggers and his realization that the notebook was not among Ausley's last possessions, and then described what it was like to be seized from behind by the Masker and given the book to be deciphered. The names of orphans were in the book, he'd told her, and some kind of code to distinguish them. He'd presented to her his recollections of the Queen of Bedlam, and how the lady had reacted to Deverick's name. The Italian masks on the lady's walls; were they some clue that tied her unknown past and her present condition to the Masker? He'd told Berry he thought the answer to many mysteries was in Philadelphia, but to have any chance of success he needed the portrait.

When Matthew had finished his recounting of events, he'd left out only two things he thought she should not know: his investigation into the agony of Reverend Wade, and his night of physical assault at the hands of Charity LeClaire. The first was private and the second was damned embarrassing.

My, Berry had said when he'd done, and Matthew couldn't tell from her tone of voice whether she was impressed or overwhelmed. *You've been busy.*

Yes, he decided. Best to keep that business of the nymph's itch to himself.

As Berry sketched the lady's profile Dr. Hulzen had to take his leave to look in on the patients, but Dr. Ramsendell came nearer to watch the work progress. Matthew saw that Berry was doing an excellent rendition. The Queen was coming to life on the paper. Suddenly the lady jerked and her head swivelled to look directly at Berry, who caught her breath with a sharp surprised gasp and lifted her pencil from the sheet. There passed a few seconds of tension as the lady stared at Berry, as if to ask what the girl was doing in her parlor. Ramsendell held up a hand to tell Berry just to remain still, and then the Queen's eyes dimmed and she turned her head to gaze again at the sunlit garden. Berry glanced quickly at Matthew for a nod of reassurance and then continued her work.

Matthew wandered quietly about the room, looking more closely at the masks and then at the painting of Venice. In the richly appointed chamber there was only the noise of birdsong and the determined scratching of Berry's pencil. Thus he and Berry were unprepared when the lady turned her attention to her pro-filer once more and asked in her regal voice, "Young woman? Has the king's reply yet arrived?"

Flustered, Berry looked for help from the doctor, who shook his head. "No, madam," she answered cautiously.

The Queen continued to stare fixedly at Berry, but Matthew saw the lady's eyes going glassy again, her focus returning to the mysterious inner world that claimed her hours. She said, "Come fetch me when it does," and then, almost in a weary whisper, "He promised, and he has never broken a promise."

Ramsendell and Matthew exchanged glances. Berry returned to her drawing. The Queen had left them, just that quickly, and was already somewhere far away.

When Berry had finished the work just as Matthew had requested, Matthew approached the lady and knelt down beside her. Ramsendell watched intently but made no motion to inter-fere.

"Madam?" Matthew asked. There was no response, not even the flicker of an eyelid. He tried again, in a stronger voice, "Madam?" Still nothing. He leaned in a little closer. "Pennford Deverick," he said.

This time the Queen of Bedlam blinked. It was almost as if she'd been struck by a lash. Still, though, her expression was impassive.

"How do you know Pennford Deverick?" Matthew asked.

Nothing, this time. Not even the lash-stung blink.

Matthew wanted to press on, but he looked to Ramsendell first with raised eyebrows. The doctor nodded and said softly, "Go ahead."

"Pennford Deverick. How do you know that name, madam?"

Did her fingers grip the armrests just a squeeze harder? Did her chin lift a fraction, and her mouth move but make no sound?

Matthew waited. If she had indeed made a response, it had now ceased. He said, "I'm trying to help you, madam. We all are. Please try to hear me, if you can. Pennford Deverick. You know the name. You know who he was. A goods broker. Please try to think . . . what did Pennford Deverick have to do with Philadelphia?"

The word floated out like one of the ghosts at Number Seven Stone Street: "*Philadelphia.*"

"Yes, madam." Matthew was aware that Ramsendell had taken up a position on the other side of the Queen's chair. "More specifically, and please try to listen . . . what did Pennford Deverick have to do with *you?*"

There was no answer, but Matthew saw on the Queen's face a ripple that might have been emotion welling up from some deep and desperate place that she had locked and then lost the key to. It was just there for a fleeting second, but its presence was so terrible in the pain that surfaced in the twisted crimp of her mouth and the shock-glint of her eyes that he feared he had done more damage than good. Ramsendell saw it too, for he immediately said, "Mr. Corbett? I don't think you should—"

"Pennford Deverick is dead," said the Queen of Bedlam, in a strained gasp. "Never prove it now. Never."

Matthew couldn't let that go. His heart was pounding. "Prove *what*, madam?"

"The king's reply," she said, and now there came the glitter of tears. "He promised, he promised." A tear broke and ran in a slow rivulet down her right cheek.

"Mr. Corbett." Ramsendell's voice was stern. "I think that is all."

"One more thing, doctor. Please. One more, then we'll be done. All right?"

"My duty is to my patient, sir." Ramsendell leaned over to peer into the lady's face, which except for the trail of the tear was completely blank. "I think she's gone now, anyway."

"May I speak one name to her? Just a name. If she responds to it, I'll have a vital clue." He saw that Ramsendell was hesitating. "One name, and I won't repeat it."

Ramsendell paused. He rubbed his beard with the edge of his hand, and then he nodded.

Matthew leaned so close to the Queen of Bedlam that he could smell her lilac soap.

He said, clearly and distinctly, "Andrew Kippering."

He didn't know what he'd been expecting. A thunderclap? A stream of sanity flooding back into a parched mind? A gasp and cry and a sudden return to the world of reality, be it ever so torturous and full of grief?

Whatever he expected, he got nothing.

The Queen stared straight ahead. Her mouth did not move nor her eyelids flicker nor her fingers grip. She was, as Ramsendell had so aptly put it, *gone*.

As far as Matthew could tell, to her that was the name of a stranger. Nothing more.

He stood up. Berry was also on her feet, the paper rolled up in her hand. He let go a sigh, because he'd been so sure. There was something he was not seeing yet, but it was so very close. Something he ought to see, but was still blinded to. The king's reply. *He promised, he promised*.

And the intriguing, haunting gasp: *Never prove it now. Never.*

"I'd best show you out," Ramsendell said. "I wish you good luck in Philadelphia."

"Thank you," Matthew answered, still dazed. So close, so close. "I'll need it," he said, with a smile so tight he thought he might choke.

thirty-nine

UNDER A LEADEN SKY, Matthew stood on the deck of the packet boat *Mercury* and watched the town built on the hope of brotherly love slide out of the gray mist.

It was Tuesday morning, nearing seven o'clock. He was one of eight passengers, and had enjoyed a decent communal supper with his fellow travellers and the captain and then a good night's sleep in a hammock that swayed with the boat. He was dressed as a proper gentleman for today's excursion, wearing his dark blue suit with the silver-buttoned waistcoat and a new dark blue tricorn bought an hour before the *Mercury* had sailed on Monday morning. A white-and-blue-striped cravat tucked into the collar of his clean white shirt added a dash of professional flair. At his side he held a brown canvas valise with a leather shoulder strap, courtesy of Marmaduke Grigsby. He no longer resembled a clerk, but perhaps a young lawyer with places to go and people to see. The better to get into Icabod Primm's office, since he had no appointment.

The *Mercury* was sailing slowly but surely along the green Delaware River. Ahead on the port side, forest and pastures had given way to first a scattering of wooden houses, and now brick buildings were coming into view. Boatyards and piers emerged, with men already at work transferring cargo to and from other vessels. Ropes lay in thick coils; barrels, crates, sacks, and hogshead casks were stacked awaiting destinations. The smell of the river was thick and swampy, yet it was apparent the river gave Philadelphia life and certainly profits. Matthew saw larger ships "mud-docked" in the shallows, where they were undergoing refitting, having their hulls scraped of barnacles and the like. Scaffoldings had been built alongside the ships and men with mallets and other tools were clambering around like so many ants, each focused on one small part of a larger picture.

He noted especially the labor that was going on regarding a few older ships. Their nameplates were in the process of being chiselled off. Queen Anne must be given due respect, if one wished to make a living on the sea, and there were always officials standing ready with pad and pencil to mark down the offenders. Therefore any ship's name with the word *King* in it was being retitled to honor the Queen. A whole row of ancient mariners sat keel-deep in the mud, awaiting the mallet and a more politically suitable christening.

Matthew watched the work intently as the *Mercury* continued on, and then his mind turned toward the news that Marmaduke had been bursting to relate on Sunday night when the two weary travellers had returned from Westerwicke.

"An amazing moment," Grigsby had said. "When Reverend Wade stood at the pulpit and announced that he was torn between his church family and the family he and his departed wife had created. He said he'd wrestled with this decision, and I have to say at one point he was quiet so long I thought he was still trying to decide it. But then he said his allegiance had to be to the memory of his wife, and what she would want him to do. He said he would accept the consequences. Then he told the story. His eldest daughter, Grace, is ill near to death. And do you know where she's lying?"

"Tell us," Matthew had urged, as he'd spooned sugar into his cup of hot tea.

"At Polly Blossom's house! Can you fathom it?" The white eyebrows had jumped and capered. "The reverend announced to one and all that Grace was—how did he put it, exactly?—a child of the streets who had found her way home. He stood up there, looked everyone in the eyes, and said he'd been to that house to see his daughter and he was planning on going again until she passed away. Not only that, but he was going to pray over her in the cemetery and bury her in a plot he'd chosen. Well, you can be sure some of those elders flared up, and it was a near riot."

"I don't doubt it," Matthew had said.

"Constance was sitting right there in front, with that young man of hers. You know, the fellow with one ear."

"I know."

"I suppose they already knew the story, because they didn't react, but the rest of the church was in one hell of an uproar. A few of the elders were shouting about blasphemy, others turned around and walked out, and you should have seen some of the Golden Hillers sticking their noses up in the air. It would have been comical," Grigsby had said, and then more gravely, "if it hadn't been so tragic. I fear that's the last of William Wade in this town."

"Maybe not," Matthew had ventured. "He obviously has a strong character and he's meant a lot to the growth of Trinity. If enough church members come to his defense—which they ought to do, and which I intend to do—he might yet weather the storm."

Grigsby had looked at him askance. "Why is it," he'd said, "that I have the distinct impression you're not surprised by this news?"

"Surprised by the fact that the reverend is first and foremost a human being? Surprised by the fact that every human being, reverend or ribald, can be undone by capricious circumstances? Or should I be surprised by the fact that a man who teaches love and forgiveness *can* love and forgive? Tell me, Marmy, exactly what it is I should be surprised at."

The printmaster had shrugged his misproportioned shoulders and retreated, but not without a potful of muttering, a grotesque grimace or two, and the faintest echo of a bass Chinese gong.

Watching the town glide nearer, Matthew thought he should

be kinder to Grigsby but he was still rankling at this marriage business, just as Berry rankled at it. Two people should not be potted together like plants and expected to entwine their roots. No, it should be a slow process of excitement and discovery. Then let whatever was to happen run its course. Still, he should be kinder to Grigsby just for the sheer effort the printmaster had put into making the dairyhouse a home. A nice writing desk, a decent bed, a set of bookshelves that hopefully would not remain barren too much longer, and even a rug to cover the dirt floor. Of course the new and very secure lock on the door. He did wish for a view, though. But all in all, it was his own miniature mansion and the rent could not be better, either.

"Mr. Corbett?"

Matthew turned around and there stood the portly and white-bearded Mr. Haverstraw and his equally portly but fortunately nonbearded wife, Jeanine. He had learned last night that the Haverstraws, who were natives of New Jersey and owned a flour mill near Stony Point, were on their way for a few days' visit with their eldest son and his family. Haverstraw, a regular visitor to Philadelphia, had been helpful in suggesting places where Matthew might find lodging for a night.

"Very pleasant to spend time with you, sir," said Haverstraw, offering a calloused workman's hand to shake. "I hope your business is successful. A legal matter, did you say?"

"Yes sir, it is a matter of the law."

"Well, then, good fortune to you. Do remember the Squire's Inn on Chestnut Street. The beef there is excellent. Also the Blue Anchor serves a fine supper, if you prefer fish. And Mrs. Fontaine's boarding house is not so richly appointed as the Market Street Lodge, but if you're like me you'll appreciate the shillings saved."

"Thank you, sir."

The lady Haverstraw gave her husband a quick prod in the belly with her elbow, which Matthew pretended not to notice. "Oh, yes!" Haverstraw said, a bit of color blooming in his cheeks. "I meant to ask you. Are you a married man?"

"No, sir."

"Ah. Well, then. Any . . . um . . . ladyfriend of note?"

Matthew knew where this was heading. The lovely daughter of a friend's friend who had just turned sixteen and was interested in matrimony and seven children if the right young man presented himself. Matthew smiled and said, "At the moment, I am perfectly free and intend to remain so."

Some of the shine went out of the lady's eyes. Haverstraw nodded. "If you're ever up our way, come say hello." Then when his wife turned away, he gave Matthew a quick thumbs-up.

The *Mercury*'s lines were thrown and secured and along with the other passengers Matthew walked across the gangway onto the wharf planks. He saw that a fiddler was playing for coins in a tin cup and farther on two little girls were dancing for money as their presumed mother and father beat out a rhythm on drums. The same as in New York, so as in Philly.

Matthew set out for the intersection of Walnut and Fourth streets, which was where Haverstraw had said he might find Mrs. Fontaine's house. The river's mist yet shrouded the entire picture, but before him the town was not unlike New York, being houses and shops of red brick and gray stone, churches with wooden steeples, pedestrians going about their business, and wagons trundling on their routes. A nice touch was that trees had been planted regularly along the sidewalks. He quickly realized also that the streets were laid out quite differently here than in New York. It seemed to be an orderly grid pattern, as opposed to New York's often chaotic arrangement.

He discovered within another block, however, that there was a downside to this otherwise pleasing pattern. Out of the mist a hay-wagon with two horses went flying past him at a speed that would have taken him under the hooves if he'd not been paying attention, and he drew himself back up to the curb thankful for no broken bones. The grid meant long, flat, and unobstructed streets, and woe to pedestrians for Matthew noted that the drivers of some vehicles took advantage of that fact to let their horses run.

Having secured a room at Mrs. Fontaine's, shaved, and then eaten a light breakfast, Matthew headed back at midmorning with his valise toward Market Street in search of Icabod Primm's office. The sun was beginning to shine through the murk. Thanks to the help of a tailor on the corner of Market and Fourth, it was no difficult matter to find the building, which was just a block to the east and near the very beautiful and elm-shaded Christ Church.

I. Primm, Attorney-At-Law, read a brass plate on the front gate. Matthew ascended six stone steps to the slab of a door, opened it, and faced a young clerk at a reception desk. The place was as quiet and serious as a crypt, the walls the color of dark tea. The clerk waited until Matthew had closed the door behind him and approached the desk.

"May I help you, sir?"

"Yes. I'd like to see Mr. Primm, please."

The young man's eyes behind his spectacles were two bits of uncaring coal and were certainly not impressed by either Matthew's suit or new hat. "And this is concerning . . . ?"

"I just need to see him for a few minutes."

"Well," said the clerk, and folded his thin hands together. Matthew knew the signs when a person who had no power suddenly got a gift of it. "Mr. Primm has a very busy schedule, sir. In fact, he's with a client now and I doubt he'll be free within the hour. Let me see." He opened a ledger book and made a show of tapping his finger down a list of appointments. "No, no . . . unfortunately, *no.* Mr. Primm will not have time to see any *new* clients today." He looked up and gave a cheerless smile. "Might you come back tomorrow afternoon, say?"

"I'm afraid I'm taking the packet boat back to New York tomorrow morning."

"Oh, New York, is it? I thought something about you seemed different."

"Be that as it may," Matthew said, keeping his voice pleasant, "I would appreciate five minutes with Mr. Primm. Today. Would that be impossible?"

"Yes sir, I'm afraid it is. Impossible." The clerk picked up his quill and started to pretend to do whatever it was he'd been pretending to do when Matthew had opened the door.

Matthew had hoped it would not come to this, but here it was. And so quickly, too. He opened the valise, took out a rolled sheet of paper, and put it on the desk in front of the clerk's face. "If you value your position," he said calmly, "you'll take that to Mr. Primm. I'll wait."

The young man unrolled the paper and looked at the drawing there. In an eyeblink Matthew knew the clerk had no inkling who the woman was. "This has some meaning, I assume?"

"You may. Assume," Matthew answered, with a little more grit in his voice. He decided to approach this irritating road-block as Hudson Greathouse might. "Now get your 'assume' up out of your chair and take that drawing to Mr. Primm. I don't care who he's with, and he won't care either in about two minutes." For effect, he produced his silver watch and snapped it open.

It was either the tone or the watch, for the clerk took Berry's drawing and was off like a rabbit up a set of stairs behind him and to the left.

Matthew waited, and wound his watch while he was at it. One minute later, there came the sound of a door opening and closing and boots on the risers. A voice boomed along the stairway: "I should say I couldn't sit there like a muffin and let that man *strike* me, could I? And right in broad daylight at my favorite tavern! I ought to challenge the old fart to a duel, is what I should do, and to blazes with the courts!"

"I'm sure that would not be the best course of action, Admiral," came the clerk's voice, now more nettled than powerful. He appeared guiding a man of about seventy wearing a huge cock-aded bicorn and dressed in some kind of military uniform with a row of medals pinned to his chest. The old man's right eye was blackened.

"Mr. Primm promised me an hour! Either I'm more senseless than I thought or my hour has shrunken into ten minutes!" the affronted admiral protested as he was escorted to the door.

"Yes sir. But I'm sure Mr. Primm has the situation under control and, besides, as Mr. Primm says, your time and money are best spent more wisely than sitting in his office talking about a minor scuffle."

"A minor scuffle? That old seabeast strikes me, near blinds my eye, and it's called a minor *scuffle*? See here, I have a reputation to uphold!"

"Of course, sir, and Mr. Primm has your reputation foremost in his mind." The clerk opened the door for the crusty old man's exit and said quickly and rather acidly to Matthew, "Go up."

Matthew picked up his valise, climbed the stairs, and at the top faced another door. He started to knock but decided it was a waste of time. He was expected. He took a fast deep breath for courage, gripped the doorhandle, and turned it.

The man beyond the door, sitting at a central desk before a wide multi-paned window that overlooked the river, did not lift his head nor otherwise acknowledge the visitor. Before him, spread out on a dark green blotter, was the likeness of the Queen of Bedlam. The office was either a tribute to the triumph of order or, as Berry might have said, a monument to a tight-ass. In fact, two of those dreaded gray-fleshed portraits of constipated noblemen hung upon the walls. There were shelves of dozens of thick leatherbound books that looked as if they'd been recently waxed. Three granite busts of unknown but obviously revered gentlemen stood on pedestals along the right-hand wall, their faces turned toward the door as if measuring the value of whoever crossed that august threshold. On the floor was a dun-colored carpet and in the silvery light that spilled through the window not one mote of dust dared float. A spare and uncomfortable-looking chair had been positioned in front of the desk. Standing in the corner just behind Mr. Primm, and casting a shadow across his desk, was a granite life-sized statue of the blindfolded goddess Justitia, holding a sword in one hand and balancing scales in the other. It was fitting for this mausoleum, Matthew thought, for the man at the desk might also be mistaken for a statue.

Primm wore a black suit with thin gray pinstripes and a white shirt buttoned to the throat. A black ribbon-tie was wound around the collar and tied with a small ugly knot that looked like a strangler's joy. Atop Primm's high forehead sat a white wig of tight curls, which went very well with the white powder that adorned his gaunt and solemn face. Matthew thought Primm had the longest nose and smallest mouth of any man he'd ever seen; it was not so much a nose as a boulevard, and not so much a mouth as a trinket.

Therefore Matthew was not surprised when Primm spoke in a high-pitched, hushed voice that did not seem to require his mouth, for the tiny compressed lips barely moved.

"I will give you five minutes."

"Thank you. I regret to have interrupted the admiral's complaint."

"An honorary title. We humor him."

"Ah," Matthew said, and waited for an invitation to sit that was clearly not going to be offered.

Still Primm had not lifted his gaze from the paper. Long thin fingers touched the surface, meandering over the charcoalled features.

"I'd like to know who she is," Matthew said.

"And who are *you*?"

"My name is Matthew Corbett. I've come from New York."

"In what capacity?"

"I'm an associate with the Herrald Agency."

Primm's fingers stopped moving. "Their nearest office is in London."

"No sir, that's incorrect. Our new office is Number Seven Stone Street, New York."

"You have a card?"

Matthew felt a little twinge in the stomach. A card! Why hadn't Mrs. Herrald given him an official card before she'd left? Maybe it was up to Greathouse to have them printed. "The cards have been delayed," he countered.

Now Primm did tear his attention away from the portrait, and his pallid face with small marbles of piercing black deepset within it lifted to look at Matthew as one would consider the vilest dockside roach. "No card? Therefore no proof of identity?" He spoke that last word as if he were biting his teeth against a bone.

Getting me off-balance, Matthew thought. Attacking, when he should be defending. "No card," Matthew answered flatly. "As far as identity, I'm sure the doctors Ramsendell and Hulzen might vouch for me."

"They are not *present*."

"Present or not, they've hired the agency—and me—to find out who their patient is. They believe they can help her, if they know—"

"How dare you come here," Primm interrupted, and though there was coiled anger in his voice his face was devoid of emotion. "Are you a lunatic who has escaped the asylum? Are those so-called doctors deserving of a cell in their own Bedlam? Their instructions were concise and complete."

"I'm telling you, the doctors feel they can help this lady if they—"

"Get out of this office," hissed Primm. "Get out and be sure their careers will be wrecked, the lady in question moved within the week, and your own cardless and witless career dashed on the rocks of contract law."

. Matthew didn't know what to say. He felt heat rising in his face, but then he realized Primm wanted him to lose control. Indeed, Primm was banking on it. Matthew swallowed his anger, waited a few seconds, and then said, "That's a load, sir. You're not going to move the lady. She's in the best possible place. Your client wouldn't want her moved, would he?"

Primm gave no response. He had again become a statue, in emulation of Lady Justice.

"If I have three remaining minutes," Matthew went on, "allow me to use them constructively. Please look at this." He reached down into his valise and brought out the most recent issue of the *Earwig*, with its article about the death of Pennford Deverick. This he placed atop the Queen's portrait on Primm's desk. "Your client, for all his good works concerning the lady, may be involved in this murder."

"The *Masker*?" Primm's mouth squeezed in disgust and almost disappeared up his nostrils. "What nonsense is this?"

"No nonsense. In fact, your client may well *be* the Masker. Wanted now for three murders, by the way. Is your client named Andrew Kippering?"

"*Who?*"

"Yes, I've used that trick, too. To stall while you think. If Mr. Kippering is your client, sir, he may have murdered three people. I'd like to know why, and I think finding out who this mystery patient at the Westerwicke asylum is could go a long way in providing a motive. Do you agree with that?"

"I agree," said the lawyer, "that you need a rest in Westerwicke yourself."

"I'm informing you that your client may be a murderer. Doesn't that mean anything to you?"

"The only thing that has any meaning for me, sir, is *proof*." Primm's jaw thrust forward. "Do you know what proof is? It's not conjecture, nor is it fantasy. As long as I serve the law and this embodiment of justice you see standing behind me, I consider *proof* to be the alpha and omega of my profession. And proof you do not have, sir, so I will tell you to go back to New York, leave the lady in question *alone*, and I shall deal very promptly with perhaps the good-intentioned but legally uneducated doctors."

When Matthew was sure Primm's tirade was done, he said quietly, "She can be helped. It's wrong for her to sit there locked up in herself, day after day."

"Are you a doctor now, as well?"

"I just want to know her name and her story."

"Ask for the moon to come down and play the fiddle while you're at it."

"I really hoped you'd help me," Matthew said. "But if you refuse, I intend to take that portrait to every tavern in Philadelphia until I find one person who recognizes her. Or to every boarding house. Or to every church. I intend to find out her name *and* her story before I leave here in the morning, if I have to walk the streets all night."

"Ah, then. I suppose I really should help you, since you wish it so ardently." With a smile that looked like a razor cut, Primm picked up the paper, ripped it in half, and then rapidly began to tear the halves to pieces. Matthew almost lunged forward to save what he could, but he realized it was too late. The fragments of a face fell from Primm's hands. "There! Now you can get to bed early!"

forty

MATTHEW STOOD ON THE STREET outside Primm's office, wondering where to go next. He counted himself lucky that on the way out he hadn't been kicked in the bottom by that self-superior clerk.

One interesting thing, Matthew thought, is that when he'd reached down to retrieve the *Earwig* Primm had snapped it off the desk amid the pieces of Berry's drawing and with beady rattlesnake eyes had dared Matthew to try for it. That told him something, at least. Primm obviously didn't want it shown to anyone else.

The question remained: where to go next?

The sun was warm now. The mist had burned away. Two young damsels with parasols paraded past and they gave Matthew a glance but he was in no mood for flirtations. A slight breeze ruffled the shade trees along Market Street. He paused, looking to left and right. Across Third Street and north about a halfblock was a sign reading *The Good Pye* with a depiction of a piece of pie and an ale tankard. He decided that might be the place to begin, and started walking in that direction. At least he might get himself a drink to settle his nerves. As he waited for a carriage to go past before he crossed the street, he caught a movement of white from the corner of his eye.

Icabod Primm had just emerged from his office and was walking quickly and bow-leggedly south along Third Street. Matthew watched the small-framed man hurry away. Primm's right hand clutched the broadsheet in a death-grip.

Ah ha, Matthew thought. *I have smoked the powdered rattler from his hole.*

He gave Primm a few more strides, and then he began to follow at a careful distance.

In another moment Primm had turned left at the corner of Chestnut Street, heading away from the river. Matthew stood on the corner, watching the white wig bob along among the other citizens who travelled the sidewalk. He again followed, realizing that Primm was too fixed on where he was going to bother casting a backward glance. Then, half another block ahead, the lawyer abruptly turned into a doorway under a sign that announced *The Lamplighter*.

It was just an ordinary tavern, Matthew thought as he stood at the door. Several hitching-posts at the curb. A window made of the round bottoms of glass bottles, some clear and some green. He opened the door without undue haste and entered, his eyes having to adjust from the bright sunlight to the dim greenish interior where lanterns burned from hooks on the ceiling beams.

Nothing special, really. A long bar where several well-dressed gentlemen congregated over ale tankards and eight tables each set with the stub of a candle. Only three of the tables were occupied, as it was a bit early for lunch. It was no problem to spy Icabod Primm, sitting at the back of the room bent over the *Earwig* by candlelight.

Matthew approached, but at an oblique angle. Primm didn't know he was coming until he was there. Then the lawyer's black eyes spat fire, his toy mouth chewed the air, and what came out was "*You* again!"

"Guilty," Matthew said.

"Of following me. Yes, I got that part."

"You were going in my direction."

"Please continue then, all the way to New York."

A burly, black-bearded man with a lion's mane of ebony hair came up beside Matthew carrying a brown bottle and a small glass. As the man filled the glass to the brim, Matthew caught the nostril-prickling aroma of stout apple brandy.

"Leave the bottle, Samson," Primm said, and the man set it down and started back to the bar.

It occurred to Matthew that if Primm drank an entire bottle of what was usually a highly combustible mixture, not only would the lawyer's lamp be lit but his wig would burst into flame.

"Having a liquid lunch?" Matthew prodded. "It *is* unsettling to realize your client's a murderer, isn't it?"

Primm took a deep and needful drink. His eyes watered and gleamed.

"I think she's his mother," Matthew went on. It was a shaky guess, for why would the lady not have reacted to her son's name? "He hid her away in Westerwicke, and then he plotted the deaths of three men. But my real question is: what happened to his father?"

"Samson!" Primm rasped after another swallow of fire had scorched his throat. The black-bearded behemoth returned to the table, his strides making the planks squeal. "This young man is annoying me. If he speaks one more word, I'd like you to throw him out on his New York bum."

"Yes, Mr. Primm," Samson replied in a biblical basso while staring into Matthew's face from the distance of four inches. He also cracked the knuckles of one huge hand like the walls of Jericho.

Matthew decided that one more word was not worth the loss of many good teeth. He gave Primm a brief smile and bow, turned around, and got out before his own lamp was extinguished. Farther down the street he saw the sign of another tavern, this one titled *The Harp and Hat*. He approached its door, but before he went in he stopped to open his valise. He removed from it another rolled-up piece of paper, which was the second portrait of the Queen of Bedlam that Matthew had asked Berry to draw, just in case Primm's fingers didn't like the first one.

Matthew entered the tavern, carrying the lady's picture and in hopes that someone here might recognize it.

Soon he emerged with hopes dashed, for no one in the place had any idea who she might be. Just across Chestnut Street was the Squire's Inn, which Haverstraw had mentioned. Matthew went in there with the picture ready, and was accosted by a drunken wag who said the lady in question was his mother and he'd not seen her since he was knee-high to a grasshopper. Since the man was over sixty, that was quite impossible. The tavern's owner, a friendly enough gent in his late twenties, said he thought the woman looked familiar but he couldn't put a name to her. Matthew thanked one and all for their trouble and continued on his way.

By the time he reached a third tavern, this one called *The Old Bucket* on Walnut Street, it was nearing lunch and a dozen persons were celebrating the noon hour. A young man with a brown mustache and goatee and wearing a russet-colored suit took the drawing and examined it pensively while he stood at the bar drinking a glass of port and eating a plate of sausages and fried potatoes. He called to a friend rather more rustic than himself to come look, and together they regarded the picture as other customers ringed around to see. "I think I saw this woman on Front Street this morning," the young man finally decided. "Was she collecting coins while a girl was playing the tambourine?"

"No!" his friend scoffed, and pulled the paper away so fast Matthew feared it was going to be ripped asunder just as the first had been. "You know who this is! It's the widow Blake! She was sittin' up in her window watchin' me when I went past her house today!"

"I *know* that's not the widow Blake!" said the heavy-set tavern-keeper as he put an empty pitcher under the spigot of the wine cask behind the bar and filled it. "The widow Blake's got a fat face. That one's thin."

"It *is* her, I say! Looks just like her!" The rustic with the rough manner had angled a suspicious gaze at Matthew. "Hey, now. What is it you're doin', carryin' around a picture of the widow Blake?"

"Not her," said the tavern-keeper.

"She's not in any trouble, is she?" came the question from the young man with the goatee. "Does she owe money?"

"I'm sayin', it's *not* the widow Blake. Lemme see that." The tavern-keeper nearly tore a corner off it when one of his big hands yanked it away. "No, she's too thin to be her. Anybody else thinks this looks like the widow Blake?" He held the picture up for the assembly to judge. "And if you do, you're already way too drunk!"

Matthew counted himself fortunate to get out of the place with the drawing intact and no one chasing him with a cudgel for being a bill collector. He'd told the group he was trying to locate a missing person, and was informed by the grinning rustic that everyone knew where the widow Blake lived, so why should she be missing?

Matthew took to stopping a few passersby on the street to show them the picture, but none recognized the face. Farther on along Walnut Street, past an area where farmers had pulled their wagons up to offer fruit and vegetables for sale, he came to two taverns almost across the street from each other. The one on the right was the Crooked Horse Shoe and the one on the left the Seven Stars Inn. He didn't care for the luck of a crooked horse shoe, so he chose to cast his fate to the stars.

Again the lunchtime crowd—mostly a dozen or so men in business suits, but also a few well-dressed women—had come in for drinks and what Matthew saw to be a menu of baked chicken, some kind of meat pie, and vegetables probably fresh from the farm wagons. The place was clean, the light through the windows bright, and the conversations lively. On the wall behind the bar was a painted depiction of seven white stars. It was the same kind of welcoming tavern as the Trot, with its immediate feeling of belonging. Matthew made his way toward the bar, pausing to let a serving-girl with a tray of platters pass, and almost at once the tall gray-haired man who was pouring wine for a customer came down the bar to him. "Help you, sir?"

"Yes, please. I know you're very busy, but would you look at this for me?" Matthew put the Queen's portrait down before the man.

"Why, may I ask, am I looking at this?"

"I've come from New York. I represent a legal agency there." A white lie? It was all in the interpretation. "Our client is trying to identify this woman. We think she at least has roots in Philadelphia. Would you tell me if you recognize the face?"

The man picked the portrait up. "Just a moment," he said, while he fished spectacles from a pocket. Then he angled the drawing into sunlight that reflected off the bar's polished oak.

Matthew saw the man frown, and his gray eyebrows draw together.

"From New York, you say?" the man asked.

"Yes, that's right. I arrived this morning."

"You're a lawyer?"

"Not exactly a lawyer, no."

"What, then? Exactly."

"I'm . . ." What would be the right word? he wondered. Deducer? No, that wasn't it. Deductive? No, also wrong and hideous to boot. His role was to solve problems. Solvant? *No.* He might be considered, he thought, as a sifter of clues. A weigher of evidence. A detector of truth and lies.

That would do. "I'm a detector," he said.

The man's frown deepened. "A *what*?"

Not good, Matthew thought. One should at least sound professional, if one was to be taken professionally.

He made up a word on the spot and spoke it with forceful assurance: "I mean to say, sir, that I am a *detective*."

"As I said before . . . a *what*?" The man's attention was mercifully diverted by a handsome gray-haired woman about the same age as himself who had just come behind the bar through another doorway. "Lizbeth!" he said. "Look at this and tell me who you think it is."

She put aside the wine-pitcher she'd come to refill and examined the portrait. Matthew saw her also respond with a frown, and his heart jumped because he thought she *must* know something. She looked at him with searching brown eyes, and then at the man. "It's Emily Swanscott."

"That's who I thought. This young man says he's come from New York. Says he's a . . . a . . . well, a legal person. Says his client is trying to identify the woman in the picture."

"Emily Swanscott," Lizbeth repeated, speaking to Matthew. "May I ask who your client is, and from where you got this drawing?"

"I fear I have to plead confidentiality," Matthew replied, trying to keep his voice as light as possible. "You know. It's a legal condition."

"Be that as it may, where *is* Mrs. Swanscott?"

"One moment. Are you absolutely *certain* you can identify this woman as being Emily Swanscott?"

"As certain as I'm seeing you. Mrs. Swanscott didn't get out very much, but I met her in the Christ Church cemetery one afternoon. I was there to see to my sister's grave, and Mrs. Swanscott was putting flowers on the graves of her sons."

"Flowers?" He'd really meant to say *graves* but the word had stuck in his throat.

"That's right. She was very kind. She was telling me what sort of flowers attract butterflies. It seems her eldest boy, the one who drowned, liked to catch them."

"Ah," Matthew said, half-dazed. "Her eldest boy."

"A terrible accident," the man spoke up. "Eleven years old when he died, as I understand."

"How many sons did she have?"

"Just the two," Lizbeth said. "The younger one died of fever when he was . . . oh . . ."

"Not even six," the man supplied. Matthew thought he was probably Lizbeth's husband, and that they together owned the Seven Stars.

"Tom and I had heard that Mrs. Swanscott was ill." Again the brown eyes searched Matthew's face. "Up in her house. Then she just disappeared overnight. Do you know where she is?"

"I do," Matthew said, with both relief and caution.

"Then why should you need the portrait identified?" Tom asked. "If you know where she is, I mean."

"Wine, please!" said another customer, bellying up to the bar. Which suited Matthew just fine, for the tavern-keeper had to go tend to his trade and that question could be avoided.

But then again, maybe not. "Where is Mrs. Swanscott?" Lizbeth asked.

"She is indeed ill," said Matthew. "Unfortunately, her ability to communicate has been impaired."

"I wouldn't doubt it. What she went through."

"You mean the deaths of her sons?"

"Oh no," the woman said. Her mouth tightened. "That was bad enough, I'm sure. But I'm talking about the tragedy."

"The *tragedy*," Matthew repeated. "And this had to do with . . . ?"

Tom had returned and had overheard this last part. "Bad luck or criminal negligence, whichever you prefer. Nothing was ever settled, one way or the other. I mean, Mr. Swanscott *was* held liable, and the courts took almost everything. He had business insurance, of course, but his reputation was destroyed. It was a shame, because they were both good and decent people. He was always very pleasant to *me*, though I never met his wife. But with five people dead and a score sick nearly to death, someone had to be held accountable."

"Five people *dead*? How?"

"The bad wine," Tom said. "It was contaminated. No one knows how, or with what. It happened at the White Stag, over on Arch Street. Just past Fourth. Of course it isn't there now. No tavern would ever rent that space again. When did it happen?" He had directed this question to Lizbeth.

"1697," his wife answered. "High summer."

That date gave him pause. Matthew remembered: Joplin Pollard had said Deverick had bought a brokerage firm here in Philadelphia in 1698, except he'd made the purchase from a man named Ives who still remained the manager. *Ancient history, as far as business goes.*

Matthew had to ask a question, though he already knew the answer. "What was your relationship to Mr. Swanscott?"

"He was the goods broker," came the reply, which Matthew had expected but nonetheless gave him a shudder for his realization of the depth and darkness of the pool into which he peered. "For all the taverns here. The wine, the meat, the ale . . . everything."

Something Robert Deverick had said in McCaggers' cold room now came back very sharply to Matthew: *My father used to have a credo. He said business is war. And he fervently believed it.*

Plus the statement Robert had made concerning his father's credo at the Deverick house: *A businessman should be a warrior, he said, and if someone dares to challenge you then . . .*

"Destruction has to be the only response," Matthew said, thinking aloud.

"Pardon?" Tom asked.

"Nothing. Sorry." Matthew blinked and returned his attention to the moment. "I know this is a busy time. Might I come back later and ask you some more questions? Concerning the Swanscotts and the tragedy?"

"I'm certainly not the expert on it." Tom busied himself filling a pitcher from one of several small wine casks behind the bar. "I'll tell you who *would* be, though. Gordon Shulton still has a farm up north on the pike."

"That's right," Lizbeth added. "We bought some beans and corn from him last week."

"Two miles up the pike," Tom continued, putting the pitcher on the bar for the serving-girl to take to a table. "Gordon can tell you the whole story. He was the Swanscotts' longtime coachman and stable keeper. Came with them from London."

Lizbeth picked up the portrait and examined it again. "He'll be glad to know she's at least *alive*. He was so broken-hearted when Mr. Swanscott died."

"And how exactly did that happen?"

"No one knows for sure. Whether it was an accident, or . . ." She trailed off.

"Or suicide," Tom finished for her. "It was twilight. Mr. Swanscott was obviously burdened with his troubles and the fact that he was being sued out of existence and might go to prison for criminal negligence. No one knows whether he stepped in front of the carriage horses by accident, or on purpose. There was speculation that he had insurance on his life with a London company. Mrs. Swanscott had already been ill, I heard, when it happened. She was reclusive to begin with, but after that . . . no one saw her anymore."

"A tragedy." Lizbeth shook her head. "A tragedy and a shame." She gave the portrait of the Queen of Bedlam back to Matthew.

"Thank you," Matthew said. "For your time and your answers." This should be a joyful moment for him, he thought. He had the name he'd so ardently sought. Why then did he feel so sullied? "Two miles to the north, did you say?"

"I did." Tom caught the expression of anguish that had surfaced in Matthew's eyes. "What's the matter?"

"I have to admit that I'm almost afraid to go to Mr. Shulton's. You won't understand this, but I fear that after Mr. Shulton has given me the whole story I may no longer be able to tell the difference between a murderer and an executioner." Matthew put the drawing back into his valise and offered the puzzled couple a sad smile. "Good day."

Four

The Methods
of Murder

forty-one

"MATTHEW!" said John Five, with as wide and free a smile as Matthew had ever seen on his friend's face. "Good mornin'! Aren't you the dressed-up peacock today!" Then John's smile fell a hitch, for Matthew knew his lack of sleep on the packet boat last night showed in dark hollows beneath his eyes and a gray countenance to his flesh.

"Good morning." Matthew had only just left the packet boat, and was still wearing his dark blue suit, waistcoat, and tricorn and toting his valise. He'd come directly here to Master Ross' blacksmithery. In the seething heat of the forge, sparks spat and the coals glowed bright orange. John had been bending lengths of iron into pothooks on his anvil with the hammer, while the second apprentice and Master Ross were speaking to another customer across the smoke-hazed shop. "A few minutes?" Matthew asked.

"Master Ross?" John called, and the elder blacksmith saw Matthew standing there and said in a crusty growl, "Don't you ever *work*?"

"Yes sir, I do my share."

"I doubt that very much, sir. Go on then, the both of you! Three minutes, John!"

Three minutes might not be enough, Matthew thought, but he would have to take what he could. Outside, in the bright warm sunshine of Thursday morning, John squinted and clapped Matthew hard on the shoulder. "My thanks to you. I don't know what you did, but I think you must have had a part in the reverend's speech on Sunday. Where were you?"

"Working," Matthew answered.

"On *Sunday*? I wouldn't let the reverend hear that, if I were you. But listen, he told us the whole story on Friday night. As much as Constance and I were knocked down to find it out, we were just as relieved. I mean . . . havin' a sick daughter who's led such a life as that is one thing, but at least Reverend Wade's not out of his mind. Not anymore, that is."

"I'm glad to hear it."

"It took courage for him to get up there and lay it all out. It's still takin' courage, for him to go in and see her like he's done. You know, yesterday mornin' he took Constance. She wanted to see her sister, and she wasn't gonna be denied."

"I hope that went well." ·

"It did. I reckon. She hasn't talked much about it." John rubbed the back of his neck, as if working a muscle the hammer and anvil had perplexed. "I mean, nobody's *happy* about where Grace is, and why she wants to stay there. She won't leave it, you know. But I guess everything'll take care of itself in time, just like the reverend said. I know he's got a fight on his hands with some of those elders, though."

"But not all of them, I'm sure," Matthew said.

"No, not all, that's true." John cocked his head to one side. "I'd like to ask you what you knew about Grace, and *when* you knew it, but would you tell me?"

"I would not."

"Didn't think so. Doesn't matter, does it?"

"I'd like to talk about something that *does* matter," Matthew said, and his somber tone of voice made John Five draw up a frown. "About the orphanage, to be exact."

"The *orphanage*? Oh, Matthew! He's dead now. Can't you ever let it go?"

"It's not that. I left the orphanage in 1694, when I was fifteen.

You were brought there by a parson, I recall, when you were about nine years old, and you stayed until you turned seventeen and Master Ross chose you as an apprentice. Is that correct?"

"Yes. What of it?"

"In the years from, say, 1696 to when you left, can you think of anything unusual happening there?"

"Unusual," John repeated, with no emotion. Then he said heatedly, "Listen, Matthew, you've got to give this up! Forget the damned place! It's not doin' you a bit a' good to—"

"Anything unusual," Matthew plowed on, his eyes intense and perhaps a little haunted. "I'm not talking about Ausley's personal habits now. I'm talking about something that would have required boys to leave the orphanage *before* they were placed with families or offered apprenticeships. Maybe some left and came back, I don't know." He could tell John wasn't even *trying* to remember, probably because John's own experience at the hands of Ausley wouldn't let him go back to that terrible place even in his memory. "Please, John. *Think*. Something that drew the boys away from the orphanage. Maybe *you* even went."

"Oh. That," said John, who breathed a sigh of fresh relief. "That was *nothin'*. I wanted to go, but I didn't have any skills they were needin'."

"Skills? What kind of skills?"

John shrugged his heavy-set shoulders. "Readin' and writin'. Figurin' numbers. Copyin' drawin's and such. You remember Seth Barnwell? He went and came back. Said they got up in his face too much. Ran the place like an army camp. Seth wasn't there but a few days. He went to learn how to make keys, but the hell of it was that for some reason they took a lot of fellas who liked to fight and cause mischief and after Seth got his nose busted a couple of times he'd had enough."

"What *was* this place?"

"It was a trade school," John said.

A *trade school*, Matthew thought grimly. *Indeed*. "Was it up the river about fifteen miles?"

"I think so, yes. But like I said, I never went. One of my best friends went and stayed, though. You remember Billy Hodges? That long tall drink of water? He was two or three years younger than you, I guess."

"I remember him." Hodges had been a smart young man, but had always been plotting intricate ways to escape the orphanage and had great dreams of being a sea captain and sailing to the West Indies.

"He applied, and they took *him*. You know what they took him in for? Because he had such good handwritin'. Can you believe it? They wanted him so he could learn to be a *scrivener*. Keep records and such, they told him. And him with that missin' thumb."

Matthew felt a cold shock slowly course through him. He thought his face had gone from gray to pasty-white in an instant. "Missing thumb?" he heard himself ask.

"That's right. A year after you left, Billy was puttin' on his shoes one day when a spider bit his left thumb. Thing was in his shoe. I saw it, wasn't so big but it was awful black. Next thing, his thumb's turned blue and swelled up and his whole hand's killin' him. It went on for a while like that, brought him to tears and he was a tough nut, too. Anyway, by the time Ausley brought a doctor, Billy's thumb was as black as the spider. Took it off, so he wouldn't lose the whole hand. He was all right about it, though. I think he was prouder of showin' off the stump than he'd been of havin' a thumb."

"Good thing it wasn't his scrivening hand," Matthew said.

John grinned. "See, that's the thing. It *was* his writin' hand. He had to learn to write all over again with his right hand. Maybe that helped when he had to copy the script."

"Copy the script? What script?"

"Oh, some men would come now and again and give us tests. You know. Doin' numbers, copyin' script, figurin' out puzzles and such. They talked to us, too. Wantin' to know all about us and our lives and so on. What we wanted for the future. Were we sad, were we angry, did we carry grudges or get in fights. A man even came a couple of times to see if any of the older boys knew how to use a sword or a dagger. He was a Prussian fella, could hardly speak English. But he could handle a sword in both hands."

The enigmatic Count Dahlgren, Matthew thought. Not teaching Chapel how to use a sword, but instead teaching younger and more pliable students. "Whatever use would you have for a sword or dagger at a trade school?" he asked.

"One of the trades was learnin' how to sharpen swords and knives. I reckon they wanted somebody who showed an interest in blades."

Master Ross suddenly peered out through the entryway, and he looked none too happy. "Mr. Five, are you comin' back to your labors anytime today?"

"Oh, yes sir. Sorry." When the smith had gone back in, John said, "I've got to go. But why all this interest in the trade school? I'd nearly forgotten about it."

"I think it was more than a trade school," Matthew replied.

"*More* than a trade school? Meanin' what?"

"Mr. *Five*!" came the bellow from within.

John winced. "Ouch. Well, his bark's worse than his bite. Usually. You ought to have dinner with Constance and me one evenin', Matthew. We'll talk then. All right?"

Before Matthew could respond, John Five had returned to his work. He stood in the strong white sunlight. People moved about him as if he were a rock in the midst of a stream. He was thinking that Billy Hodges was now lying in a grave on John Ormond's farm, and the young man's last journey had not been as a sea captain but as a passenger of the river.

Matthew couldn't help but wonder if Hodges, the plotter of daring escapes, hadn't tried to escape the trade school, and thus brought down upon himself the judgment of the gauntlet.

He had his own work to do, and best get to it. He hurried back to Grigsby's house by the shortest route, which was along the dockside, and found the printmaster setting out type for the next *Earwig*. Berry was absent. Grigsby told Matthew she'd gone out at first light to continue her landscape pictures, and then he wanted to know all about Matthew's trip to Philadelphia and if he'd met with success.

"Not just now, Marmy," Matthew said. "Do you think Berry would mind if I get something from her drawers?"

Grigsby's eyes nearly popped. "Excuse me?"

"I mean her *chest*-of-drawers!" Matthew's face was red. "Something I asked her to keep for me."

"I have no opinion, it's just *my* house. It's apparent you and Berry are keeping secrets from me, so go right ahead and——" But he was mouthing to the air, for Matthew had already gone to open the bottom drawer and retrieve the notebook.

Matthew put the notebook in the inside pocket of his coat. He didn't have a far distance to go, and then it was a short walk to City Hall and Lillehorne's office. Chapel's cohorts might indeed be watching him, but on this day the law would also lay eyes upon Simon Chapel.

"Back later," Matthew told Grigsby as he went out the door.

"Go on, and don't bother telling me anything!" Grigsby called after him, a smear of old ink already leaped across his forehead. "I'm just the broadsheet publisher!"

Matthew considered stopping at Number Seven Stone Street to see if Hudson Greathouse was available for . . . what would be the word? . . . back-up, but as he reached the Broad Way and turned south he decided against it. No, this was a more delicate issue. There was a time for flashing swords but also a time for the quiet movement of chess pieces.

He turned left onto Wall Street, passing City Hall, and then right on Broad Street. Between Barrack and Beaver, he went up three front steps to a door with a brass knocker, proclaimed himself like the hand of justice, and waited beneath the sign that read *Pollard, Fitzgerald, and Kippering, Attorneys*.

The door opened within a few seconds and a pallid-faced man with thinning brown hair and thick-lensed spectacles peered out, as if uncomfortable with the light of day. Matthew had always thought Bryan Fitzgerald looked like a mole.

"Good morning," the lawyer said. Across his chest he held a sheaf of papers that had obviously just been pulled from a file cabinet. His shirt was marred by a small inkstain and his fingernails were chewed to the quick. He might be the one who did all the work and was well paid for it, Matthew recalled the widow Sherwyn saying, but Fitzgerald was probably more mule than mole. Fitzgerald adjusted his glasses. "Mr. Corbett, isn't it?"

"Yes sir. May I come in?"

"Of course." He stepped back as Matthew entered and then closed the door, again as if sunlight and fresh air were the enemies to solid Puritan productivity. "How may I help you?"

"I was actually hoping to see Mr. Kippering today. Is he in yet?"

"Well . . . he's . . ." Fitzgerald cast a glance up the narrow stairs. Then he whispered, "*I don't think he went home last night.*"

"Oh?"

"Yes. He's . . . well, I'm not sure he's able to see a client this morning. Mr. Pollard should be back any minute. Would you care to wait for him?"

"I won't take very long." Matthew withdrew the notebook from his coat. "May I give this to Mr. Kippering?"

Fitzgerald reached out for it. "I'll be glad to make sure he—"

"No, thank you," Matthew said firmly, and gripped his fingers tight. "This is something I think he'd wish to see for—"

"Myself," said the man who had come out of his office at the height of the stairs.

"Yes sir," Matthew answered him, with a steady and fearless gaze. "As I'd hoped."

Kippering did not move. He had one hand pressed against the wall beside him and the other clutching the decorative carved pineapple that topped the staircase railing. His face was masked by shadow. He wore black breeches that were shiny at the knees and the white of his stockings had faded to yellow as had his shirt. His sleeves were rolled up, but Matthew was certain it was not to welcome the energy of the day but to keep his cuffs from mopping up spilled liquor by night. Matthew figured there was a bottle or two up there, and plenty of dead ones tucked away. Kippering had killed a few of them last night, it appeared, for now he began to come slowly and unsteadily down the stairs, holding on to that railing like a lifeline.

"Bryan," he said in a creaky, tired voice, "will you do me a great favor?"

"Yes, Andrew?"

"I haven't had breakfast. Would you be so kind as to fetch me something from Sally Almond's?"

And then the light from a small oval window above the door caught Kippering's face, and Matthew had to draw a breath because he felt as if he'd been punched in the ribs. The young man who was in such a hurry to kill himself appeared at least three-quarters arrived at the graveyard. It had been over a week since Matthew had last seen him, but how could a human being have become so aged and infirm in such little time? Kippering was slope-shouldered and unkempt, his black hair oily and uncombed and the icy blue eyes now only so much cold and murky water. His face, once wolfishly handsome, now seemed only starved. The lines had deepened and the hollows darkened and his jaw was burdened with a beard that might have broken a razor. He looked twenty-eight years old and a century. Matthew was shocked to see that there was even the slight shaking of palsy to Kippering's head.

"What is today?" Kippering frowned, seeking the answer in a brain that may have begun to mold. "Thursday? Ah, then." He attempted a smile that was no less than horrid. "The raisin cakes will be fresh this morning. Would you go get me two of them, Bryan?"

"I'm gathering the papers for Captain Topping's case," Fitzgerald protested, but with a weak spirit. "Joplin will be back soon, and I'm supposed to have everything—"

"Shhhhhh," Kippering whispered. "It's all right, Bryan. Really it is. Go to Sally Almond's while I speak to Mr. Corbett, won't you? And here." He reached into his pocket and brought forth some coins, which he pressed into his partner's palm. "Get yourself a raisin cake, and Joplin one as well. Then do me one more favor."

"Another favor?"

"Yes, please. While you're out, go over to see Mr. Garrow at his shop on Duke Street. You know the one?"

"I do. The horn merchant."

"Yes, and tell him I'm still waiting for the papers he's supposed to have sent me on Monday. Would you do that? It's very important."

"I'm very busy myself," said Fitzgerald, though the subdued way he spoke it and the fact that he avoided eye contact told Matthew the issue was settled. "All right, then," he sighed, "if it's so important." He trundled into what must have been his own office, a little broomcloset of a space that was nevertheless as neat as a hangman's noose, and unloaded his papers upon a scarred and battered desk that might have been a refugee from Grigsby's dairyhouse. Without another word except an exhalation of breath that spoke volumes for the endurance of downtrodden mules, Fitzgerald went to the door, opened it, and paused on the threshold against the morning glare. "Did you say you wanted two cakes, Andrew?"

"Yes, Bryan. Two."

Fitzgerald closed the door, and Matthew was alone with a walking corpse.

Neither spoke. Then Kippering said, "Don't you want to keep the door open, Matthew?"

"No, sir. I don't think that's necessary."

"As long as you're sure."

"I *do* want," Matthew said, finding it difficult to look into the man's haggard face, "to see something in the cellar."

"All right, then. Shall I lead the way, or you?"

"If you'll lead, please?"

"Of course." Another quick death's-head smile, and Kippering walked past Matthew to the table on which sat a candle in a pewter holder next to an ivory tinderbox. He got the wick lit, opened the door to the cellar, and descended into the dark on the set of rickety stairs.

forty-two

"MY CONGRATULATIONS," said the lawyer, when Matthew had come down the stairs after him. Kippering stood in a meager circle of light, his eyes hooded. "I understand you had a visit with Reverend Wade. He wouldn't tell me what was said, but obviously you had an influence."

"Glad to be of help."

"You're absolutely sure you wanted to shut that door?"

"Yes." Before Matthew had followed Kippering down, he'd closed the door at the top of the steps. He didn't wish to be interrupted if either Pollard came in or Fitzgerald returned from what appeared to Matthew to be a pin-chasing errand, something that had been made up on the spot.

"The last time you were in here," Kippering reminded him with a tight smile, "you wanted all the doors left open. I thought you might be afraid of me. Would you care for some more light?"

"Always," Matthew said. He removed his tricorn and put it down atop a stack of boxes.

Kippering walked away a few paces, bent down, and rummaged in the wreckage of old discarded office furniture. He came up with a tin two-candle lantern and lit the wicks from his present flame. Then he reached up and placed the lantern's handle on a beam hook so that it hung between himself and Matthew.

"There," he said as the illumination spread. "At your command. Now what is it you wish to see?"

"Actually," Matthew answered, "the stairs themselves."

"Oh? Anything special about them that I'm missing?"

"They *are* infirm, aren't they? I recall you telling me to watch my footing on them, as they were older than your grandmother. Mr. Kippering, what is your grandmother's *name*?"

"My . . . grandmother's . . ."

"Name, yes," said Matthew crisply. "What is it?"

Kippering started to speak, but both he and Matthew knew that any name he produced would be a lie. Perhaps if he'd been less weary, or less sick, or less bitten by the brown fox of liquor, he might have carried off a lie and done it with charm. Now, though, he saw no point to it. His mouth, half-opened, slowly closed.

"You don't remember your grandmother, do you? As neither do I remember *my* grandmother. A common bond between us orphans, I think."

Kippering stared into the flame of his candle.

"May I tell you a story?" Matthew asked. "It's a tragedy, really. But yet there's hope in it, as I believe you'll see."

"Yes," Kippering said thickly, transfixed by the eye of light. "Do go on."

"Once there was a couple, very much in love. Devoted to each other. His name was Nicholas, and her name was—*is*—Emily. The Swanscotts of London. Neither one started out with great ambitions. He loved music and hoped to conduct an orchestra, and she only wished to be a good wife and a mother. But as things progressed, Nicholas Swanscott was persuaded to buy with his father's help a small brokerage business that catered to the tavern trade and so went the youthful dreams. However, in came the money. As Mr. Swanscott's personality made him not so fixated on profits, he was able to undercut other brokers—with no malice, but rather simply the way he did business—and in essence suddenly found that he was a rich young man. His rivals took note of this, but what could they do?"

"What, indeed?" asked Kippering. "Are you making this up?"

"No sir. I've been in consultation with the Swanscotts' long-time coachman, whose name is Gordon Shulton and who lives two miles north of Philadelphia on the pike road." Matthew raised his eyebrows. "May I go on?"

"If it pleases you." There was a tremor to the voice.

"It seemed," Matthew said, "that Mr. Swanscott was a great success. He turned out to be naturally adept at planning and management. Well, consider it: anyone who could interweave the chaos of violins, horns, and kettle drums into a symphony would have no trouble managing the shipments of smoked sausage, salted beef, casks of wine, and ale to clients all over London. A goods broker keeps a warehouse, you see, and stores the food and drink until the taverns need it."

"A fine lesson in tavern economics, thank you," said Kippering, his eyes quickly glancing up toward Matthew.

"Sadly," Matthew went on, "as Mr. Swanscott was a success, his wife was finding her role difficult at best. According to Gordy—that's what he asked me to call him, by the way—Emily Swanscott was a gentle, quiet woman who would rather spend time in her butterfly garden than go to the social events of the season. She was perhaps a little overcome by all the money. Perhaps, deep down, she didn't feel she deserved it."

Kippering set his candle down on a time-worn desk. "The illness of the upper class. I pity her."

"You might, well and truly. You see, her greatest desire was to have children. Her first child, a boy, unfortunately died within minutes of being born. Her second child, also a boy, died at age eleven in a swimming accident. Her third, again a boy, perished of fever when he was five. You might pity her, for thinking as she did—according to my friend Gordy—that any boy born to her was doomed to die early. One might presume that under the weight of those three deaths she might have begun to break, even then."

Matthew held up a finger. "But . . . one day . . . Mr. Swanscott came home, very excitedly, and told his wife that he'd made an interesting discovery. He'd been touring, by necessity, a slaughterhouse where he bought his beef. And who should be there on the killing line, but a handsome young orphan boy working silently and diligently in all that blood and muck. A boy who looked out of place there, but who was uncomplaining of his lot in life. A strong young boy, stout of heart and quick of mind. And merciful, too, for this young boy had developed a system by which he struck the animals in the temple with a mallet before he delivered the cut. Might Emily wish to meet this boy, for his own mother and father had perished by the same fever that took little Michael? Might Emily wish to meet this boy, when he was all clean and presentable on a Sunday afternoon? Might she wish to just have one look at him, for he was not violent in his soul. No, far from it. He only did what he needed to do, to survive in a cruel and heartless world. Just one visit, and who knows what might happen?"

Kippering turned his head away, so the light would not touch his face.

Matthew thought he heard a footfall on the floor above. He waited, but it didn't repeat. This place might be haunted like the Herrald Agency's office, Matthew mused. A one-legged ghost, perhaps. But he knew he was already looking at a ghost.

He continued, in a softer voice. "This orphan boy did have a family name. It was Trevor Kirby. Over a period of time and many visits, he endeared himself to the Swanscotts. And why not? You should hear Gordy talk about him. Smart, a quick wit, a noble personality. Under all that blood, of course. Well, he got cleaned up and the Swanscotts took him out of the slaughterhouse and put him in a proper school. Then he really showed what he was made of. A piece of gold found in dirty water. His grades soared and he was making progress by leaps and bounds. Turning into a gentleman. And he was appreciative, too. On Sunday afternoons he used to read to his . . . well, I can't call Mrs. Swanscott his *mother*, exactly, because there was the fear of sudden death that she couldn't ever really banish. That was why the Swanscotts never officially adopted him. She feared giving him the family name. But he was her sparkle of hope, Trevor was, and he brought her back from the abyss. And they *did* become his foster parents, and loved him like a real son by any measure you give it. And do you know what? Mr. Swanscott even used his considerable influence to get Trevor admitted to law school!"

Matthew grunted, as if some people had all the luck in the world. "Then, to top that off, when Trevor graduated with honors the Swanscotts took him on a trip to Italy. What a trip that must have been! What a joyous occasion! After that, Mr. Swanscott gave him a gift of money, by which to open a small law firm in the town of St. Andrew-On-The-Hill, which was Mr. Swanscott's own hometown in the north of England and where I imagine he lay on the sward and dreamed of leading his symphonies under the clouds. But do you know what, Andrew? Gordy told me that Trevor Kirby paid every cent of that money back to his foster father. Every cent and more. You see, Trevor became very successful. Oh, not a big-city lawyer by any means, but maybe that was for the best. I think sometimes lawyers in the cities lose sight of the real meaning of justice. Don't you, Andrew? I think sometimes they can become bitter, and believe that the system of justice has failed. That can have unfortunate results to a man's mind, don't you agree?"

The lawyer put a hand to his face but did not speak.

"I'm sorry, sir." Matthew felt a lump rising in his throat. "But I have to finish it. It's my nature."

"Yes," came the barely recognizable voice. "I understand."

"Unfortunately," Matthew said, his own voice husky, "when Trevor began his own life, Mrs. Swanscott began to drift away again. Oh, he visited her of course, but . . . things do get in the way. According to Gordy, she couldn't sleep for days on end. She was having visions of death and disaster. Mr. Swanscott did what he could to soothe her, but she was slowly going to pieces. And then came the day when he asked his wife to consider leaving England, and starting over again in the colonies. A hard task? Of course. Fraught with difficulties? Certainly. But the business had gotten so large and utterly consuming. He planned to leave it to another manager he'd been training. Where might they go, in the colonies, that he might take what he knew of the brokerage business and yet not be overwhelmed, that they could spend more time together? Boston? The Puritans frowned on taverns. New York? Possibly, but word was that an old business rival named Pennford Deverick had set up shop there, and Deverick was not a man who appreciated competition. Ah, Philadelphia! The Quaker town! Full of brotherly love and friendly companionship! Not so many taverns there as in New York, but that was all to the good, wasn't it?"

"All to the good," the lawyer blurted out, and kept his face averted.

"That's right," Matthew said, watching the man carefully. "But still, for all the excitement and challenge of sailing to a new land, making connections and starting over, Mrs. Swanscott must have felt a hole within herself. Do you know what she did, Andrew? She had buried her deceased infant in the butterfly garden behind their house, so she let him lie there sleeping, but she took her two other sons with her, to be laid in Christ Church cemetery. The people I talked to in Philadelphia never knew about the infant, Andrew. They never knew that Mrs. Swanscott was carrying the burden of three deaths, instead of two."

"Imagine," came the garbled voice.

"Oh, I can't imagine. Who would want to?" Matthew paused, considering how to approach the next subject. There was nothing to do but forge ahead. "Everything went well until the summer of 1697. That was the year five people died and many others were sickened near to death in a Philadelphia tavern called the White Stag. Do you know the procedure that Mr. Swanscott went through to buy and deliver wine to his clients, sir? Gordy told me. It seems that wine is shipped over from England in hogshead barrels. These barrels would have been taken from the ships and stored in Mr. Swanscott's warehouse on the Philadelphia waterfront until orders were sent from the taverns. Depending on the needs of the taverns, the wine is transferred from the hogshead barrels to smaller casks, and these are delivered to the clients. Now, during the transferral from hogshead to cask, an inspector paid for by Mr. Swanscott is on hand to taste the wine to make sure it hasn't spoiled. The casks are likewise inspected for mold or other problems. When the wine is transferred, the casks are given a seal of approval by the inspector, and the destination tavern's name is chalked upon them. The casks may sit in the warehouse under lock for another few days awaiting delivery, but no longer than that. Everything should have gone as usual, but on this day it did not."

The lawyer lifted his head and was listening intently.

Matthew said, "On this day, in the summer of 1697, five people died at the White Stag from drinking wine poured into a pitcher from one of Mr. Swanscott's casks. Many others—a *score*, I understand—were brought to death's door. Some have not fully recovered yet, but have been made so feeble they can't even walk. In October of 1697 Mr. Swanscott was brought to trial, where both he and the inspector swore the wine was suitable and that the approval was not negligent. The Swanscotts' attorney, Icabod Primm, handled the defense. A few of the family members of those who died were adamant that the wine had spoiled in the summer heat and had been passed on anyway, or that the cask had been fouled by vermin and not properly cleaned. Up until then, Mr. Swanscott's reputation had been spotless, but after that day . . . he was ruined. He couldn't prove the inspector hadn't been paid to apply a falsified seal, as some were saying. It didn't help that the inspector disappeared while the trial was going on."

"Yes," said the lawyer. He nodded. "Find the inspector."

"I don't have to tell you what was happening to Mrs. Swanscott, as she watched her husband being torn to pieces at court. Just after the incident, she had sent a letter to Trevor, explaining the situation and begging him to come help Primm with the defense. I can envision Trevor's horror at receiving such a letter, can't you?"

The lawyer did not respond, but Matthew knew the man had looked upon horror many times.

"He sent back a letter," Matthew said. "Promising to come, and to prove Mr. Swanscott's innocence. The only problem was that before Trevor could reach Philadelphia from Portsmouth, whether by accident or design his foster father stepped in front of a fast carriage at twilight on one of those long, straight streets. He lingered for . . ." There was no need to go into that. "At which point, Emily Swanscott retreated from the world and collapsed. She now sits every day at a window, staring out at a garden. But *you* know where she is, don't you, sir? You know, because you put her there."

The lawyer bent over the desk and gripped it as if he might fall.

"Mrs. Swanscott *does* speak, if only briefly and nonsensically. She keeps asking about the king's reply having arrived," Matthew told him. "On the way into Philadelphia I saw some ships whose names were being reworked to honor the Queen. It struck me that the *King's Reply* might indeed be the name of a ship. Now, of course, it would be named the *Queen's Reply*. When Gordy very kindly gave me a ride back to Philadelphia on his wagon, I went directly to the shipping office to see if there might be any record of a ship called the *King's Reply* arriving at Philadelphia probably in the first half of 1698. Actually, it arrived in early March. The clerk there found a list of passengers."

Matthew saw the man's shoulders hunch as if readying for a whipstrike.

"Your name was among them, Trevor. In your letter you'd told her the name of the ship on which you'd booked passage. You came one month before your foster mother was put into the Westerwicke asylum. I assume you arranged everything with Icabod Primm. The removal of all personal items and the makers' marks from the furniture. You wished to hide her, didn't you? You wished no one to know who she was. I'm unclear on that part of it. Why go to all that trouble?"

Trevor Kirby shook his head. It was not denial, but a vain attempt at avoiding the wasps that stung his brain.

"Did you believe that the legal system had failed Mr. Swanscott?" Matthew asked. "Did you set yourself up as an avenger? A righter of wrongs? Because his innocence could not be proven in court, did you decide to murder the men you felt respon-

sible?" Matthew dared to move a few steps nearer the man. "I realized, when I was sitting in Primm's office looking at his statue of
Justitia, that the cuts you made around the victims' eyes were not
supposed to represent a *mask*, Trevor. They represented a *blindfold*.
Your statement, I presume, that Lady Justice was never so blind as
to allow those three men to escape the law?"

"Those three *men*," came the nearly strangled reply, "destroyed
the only father and mother I ever knew." He turned now toward
Matthew, the light was cast upon his enraged face, and Matthew
decided it best to stand very still and not speak.

Kirby was sweating. His face was damp, his eyes swollen with
either hatred or torment. Probably both, Matthew thought. "Yes,
I did arrive too late. I went to the house and saw her sitting at a
window, her head lolling. One of the servants had warned me how
bad it was, but I wasn't ready. I could never have been. I stood
there and I heard her cry out, calling for Father and Toby and
Michael, but they were all dead. Then she started praying to God
and speaking gibberish and sobbing, and I could not—could
not—go to her side." He blinked, his mouth slack for a moment
until it could once more form words. "I was afraid that when she
looked at me I would see nothing in there but madness. And that
is what tears me apart every day and every night. That is why I
cannot stand to be with myself, and hear myself think. Because I
was not there . . ." He seemed to waver on his feet, and had to start
again. "I was not there, when she needed me. When they *both*
needed me. And I promised I would come and help Mr. Primm
prove he was innocent, and I failed. More than that." His face,
once so handsome, was a thing of tortured angles wracked by a
shudder. "I was ashamed to speak to her, there in that room. She
was so *broken*. It was an obscenity."

He looked hopefully at Matthew, his expression begging for
understanding. "If you'd seen her, when she was in Italy! When we
were all happy! If you'd seen her . . . what she was *then* . . . you'd
know why I couldn't bear it. Selfish, I know." He nodded vigorously. "Yes, selfish! But as I watched . . . she gave a moan. One
long . . . terrible moan, and she suddenly stopped crying and

praying. It was as if everything . . . everything had departed from her. I was looking at an empty husk. Dear God." Tears glistened. "Oh dear Christ, dear Jesus. I turned away from there and I walked out, and I went . . . I went directly to Mr. Primm. And I said . . . take care of her. Find a place where she can be . . . the nearest place to home. If at all possible. Not one of those . . . those filthy, ugly asylums. Those horrendous bedlams. Find a place, I said. Money is no object. Find a place where she can have some of her pretty things, and no one will steal them. I said find a place that is *safe*."

"And why *safe* to the degree of not even telling the doctors who she was?" Matthew asked. "Why did you remove any possibility of identifying her?"

"Because of the three men," Kirby replied. "Because I already knew what they'd done, and I already knew who pulled the puppet strings."

"Who?"

"A man. A shadow of a man. Known as Professor Fell."

forty-three

Mathew didn't say anything for a few seconds. Then: "Go on."

Kirby reached into a pocket and withdrew a white handkerchief, with which he began to blot the beads of sweat from his forehead. "I didn't receive Mother's letter until November. I'd been in Scotland, working on a case. I had other commitments as well. I'd been planning on being married . . . to a wonderful young woman, the following summer. I was going to write Father and Mother, to let them know. Then I got the post. I dropped everything, of course. I shut my office, I told Margaret I'd be gone for a while, that my family needed me. A few months, I said. Then we'd pick our wedding plans up where we'd left them." He began to carefully fold the handkerchief into a tight square.

"When I got the letter from Mother . . . I knew there had to be some other explanation," Kirby said. "I knew Father would never have made an error like that. No. He was a professional. He was *clean*. But if he hadn't made an error . . . then how was it done, and why?" He was silent, turning something over and over in his mind like a puzzle to be viewed from all sides.

"I had remembered . . . once when I visited them, a few years after they'd moved to Philadelphia . . . Father asked me my opinion of whether he should take the business into New

York or not. There were two brothers who owned the White Stag tavern. They had plans for one to move to New York and open a second White Stag. In their research, they discovered that the brokerage prices commanded by Mr. Pennford Deverick were very much higher for the very same items that Father sold. They wanted him to consider expansion into the New York market, and they would wish to invest some money in the enterprise if he did. They were sure that Father could undercut Deverick's prices and still make a profit. So . . . he asked me that day what I thought."

When Kirby hesitated, Matthew asked, "What was your advice?"

"Not to go. I just didn't think the extra work would be worth it. They had a grand life, why should they disturb what they had? Besides, Father was never driven by greed. Far from it. He simply enjoyed the management process. I left him still considering the opportunity, but I don't think he was going to do it. I don't think Mother wanted it, either."

Matthew nodded. "So when you read in your mother's letter about the incident taking place at the White Stag, what did you think?"

"That it was very suspicious. Why that tavern, of all the others? Why *only* that tavern? It would be called, I suppose, killing two birds with one stone."

Matthew thought Deverick's zeal for destruction might indeed have been set flaming by the news that an old rival was moving into his territory, whether it was only rumor heard round the New York taverns or not.

"When I got to Portsmouth, it was the height of the winter storm season," Kirby said, blinking up at the lantern that hung from the ceiling beam. "My departure was to be delayed for at least three weeks. I think I . . . had my own breakdown then. My first one. Knowing I *had* to do something, but could do nothing. I went to London. And I went with a vengeance, for as London is the center of the world, so it is the center of the underworld. Deverick had his motive, yet he needed the advice and aid of professionals. A contract might have been drawn up. Would anyone in London have any information? I decided to find out.

"I visited my attorney friends first, for names of contacts. That led me nowhere. Then . . . I suppose I might say I threw myself with a fervor into my research. My second breakdown, perhaps." Kirby's eyes glistened, but they were dead. "I went through every back alley ginpot I could find. I gambled, threw away money, drank with the reptiles, pegged the whores, and winnowed into every little shitpot that opened up for me. Suddenly two weeks had passed, and I was bearded and filthy and the lice were jumping out of my hair." He brought up a wicked smile. "And do you know who was born, during that time? Andrew Kippering himself. *Andrew* for Father's hometown, *Kippering* for the tailor at the end of my street. I looked into the grimy glass of a half-pence whore-house and lo and behold—there he stood, grinning back. Ready to get to work. To rub shoulders with the thugs and thieves, and announce that money was to be had for information. A *lot* of money."

"I almost got my head bashed in outside the Black Tail Tavern," Kirby said. "Almost was caught by a band of men and would've been beaten to death in an alley if I hadn't been carrying a knife. Suddenly everything came back. The movement of the arm, the quickness of the strike. Even the smell of blood. I cut one right across the face, pretty as you please. The second one I got in the ribs. Then they ran, and the next night the Blind Boy found me."

"The Blind Boy?"

"About thirteen or fourteen years old. Thin as a pole, but well-dressed. Dark glasses. Very articulate. Had a cane. Was he blind or not? I don't know, but his face was terribly scarred. A whore named Tender Judy brought him to my table. Said he could find out things, but it would cost me. Said he would tell me once, and I could ask no questions. Said I would never try to find him again, afterward, or it would be my death. I believed him."

"A reasonable assumption," Matthew agreed.

"I paid him half up front. Then he asked me what I wanted to know. I'd been thinking what to ask. It was very important, with these people, that you phrased things correctly. I said, 'I want to know about the contract on Nicholas Swanscott. How was it done, and who did it?' He said he had no idea what I was talking about, but he would make some inquiries."

"And he delivered the information?" Matthew prodded.

"I was walking back to my room two nights later," Kirby said. "Long after midnight. I was nearly drunk on some filth or another. Suddenly there was a man beside me. Not a big man, but a tough gent who could handle himself. He seized my elbow before I could turn around and he said right up in my ear, 'Come with me. No noise.' I thought I was going to be killed, but we didn't have far to go. A few streets, a few alleys. I was pushed into a little room with yellow wallpaper, the Blind Boy was sitting on a throne of rags, and he beckoned me nearer. 'Now listen,' he said. 'No questions. After this, we are strangers. After this, you will die if you go asking anymore. Do you understand?'

"I said I did," Kirby related. "Then he said, 'The contract was paid for by a man named Deverick, who came from New York to have a problem solved. The problem being: how to destroy someone and their business at the same time, yet leave no trace?' Done with poison, he said. The poison had been made by a New York doctor. Goodwin or Godwin, he thought was the name. There was something on the doctor in London, having to do with a prostitute and a dead baby. The name he got was 'Susan.' An abortion gone bad, he said. Local talent for the job was provided by someone named Ausley. Two crows, a screever, and a lugger."

"Pardon?" Matthew asked.

Kirby translated: "Two lookouts, a forger, and someone to carry the materials."

"Oh. Yes." Matthew nodded, as if he'd known these street terms all along. "Go ahead."

"While the crows watched for constables, the others opened the lock with a key provided by an inside-man. A cask was chosen, opened, and the poison poured in. The cask was closed with a soft mallet. The screever had a blank paper inspection seal, which was forged on the spot and fixed to the cask with red wax. The inside-man had told them the correct color to use. Then the cask was returned to its place, the team got out, relocked the door, and it was all over in a few minutes."

"And they didn't care how many people would be killed?"

Kirby didn't bother to answer. "The Blind Boy said there was one loose end to the contract, which the hornpipe—a criminal attorney, if you will—suggested correcting. He said it involved Swanscott's wife. Her name, he said, was Emily."

Matthew waited.

"The Blind Boy told me," Kirby said, "that this hornpipe considered that Mr. Swanscott would likely go to prison for many years. Would probably die there. But if the wife decided to rebuild the business, as a gesture of faith, she should promptly meet with an accident. If the contract called for destruction of the business, then destruction it should be. Signed, sealed, and delivered."

"Very civilized of them." Matthew was beginning to understand why Kirby had so desperately wanted to keep his mother hidden away.

"They have their own code." Kirby stared intently at Matthew for a few seconds before he went on. "The Blind Boy said he didn't know me—except that he knew my name was Andrew Kippering and I was a high ball playing low. He said, 'I'd like to give you some advice, sir. Go home where you belong. This contract was underwritten by the professor, and your interest in it disturbs me. Now, if you'll pay me my money, you'll be shown back to your door.' "

"Underwritten by the professor?" Matthew frowned. *"Why?"*

"I didn't know who the Blind Boy meant. I asked Tender Judy about it, later. She told me as much as she knew, which was not very much. A shadow here, a shadow there. A black carriage passing in the fog. Rumors and whispers, and a great amount of fear. Professor Fell, first name unknown. Age and description, unknown. But whoever he is, he had a hand in the ruin of my father. And I feared beyond anything that if Mother got well . . . if she came back to herself . . . someone might talk her into hiring managers and rebuilding the business again under the family name. So I did my best to prevent anyone from finding her, or to prevent anyone at that hospital from pursuing her identity. I didn't want her attracting unwanted attention." Kirby looked down at the ground, and Matthew could tell he was fighting a battle with the shame that must be festering in his soul. "I didn't want her to get better," he said softly. "To come out of her sleep. There's just pain waiting for her, when she wakes up."

"Not least of all, the fact that her son has murdered three men in the name of justice. Let me ask this: did you tell Mr. Primm what you'd found out?"

"No. Well . . . I did mention Pennford Deverick's name. I think I said . . . something about him being one of Father's fiercest competitors in London, and the fact that they'd had more than one public argument. I said it was peculiar, that Pennford Deverick now ruled New York's taverns only a hundred miles away, and this very suspect tragedy had destroyed my father. Primm didn't make any connection, and why should he? I had no proof whatsoever."

Matthew remembered Primm's declaration: *I consider proof to be the alpha and omega of my profession.* Difficult to argue with that. Matthew was also thinking about something Pollard had said. "Did you advise Primm to sell the business?"

"I did, and the sooner the better. The money could go into the fund I'd set up for Mother. Actually a buyer was already interested. I signed the papers before I left Philadelphia."

"Who was the buyer?"

"Culley Ives. He was one of the two managers. Had worked with Father for many years. We only got shillings on the pound, but I was satisfied with it."

"Ives," Matthew repeated.

Matthew recalled Pollard saying that Deverick had bought a Philadelphia brokerage firm in 1698. To Matthew's question of *Who owned the firm before Mr. Deverick bought it?* Pollard had answered *It was a man named Ives, who is still employed by the Deverick company as manager there. So what does that tell you?*

Matthew said, "You might wish—or perhaps not—to know

that Mr. Ives probably paid those shillings on the pound in money given to him from Pennford Deverick's pocket. I wouldn't doubt that Mr. Ives might have been the inside-man."

A hideous smile slowly, terribly, spread across Kirby's mouth and stretched it until Matthew thought the man might scream. But instead Kirby only said, quietly, "To the victor go the spoils. Isn't that right? You see how tough I've become? How . . . shall I say . . . resigned to fate?"

"Obsessed might be more accurate." This kettle and pot were both black, Matthew thought grimly. To understand the depths of obsession all he had to do was think back two weeks, when he was nearly insane that Eben Ausley had escaped justice for his crimes against the orphans. He shook it off. "I presume you found it difficult to return to being Trevor Kirby when you'd had a taste of Andrew Kippering's life? And you decided to find a position here, to better stalk your prey? What did you do, go back to London and buy screeved . . . um . . . *forged* documents to present yourself as a lower ball than you are?"

"Exactly that," came the reply. "I came here to kill those three men, and to speak Father's name in their ears before I did it. I was very fortunate indeed to get a position with Pollard. Even if it was a fraction of the money and work I was used to. Pollard wanted someone who was a brash gadfly, and perhaps a little dull. I could tell that at once. He wanted a tavern partner. More for show than work, and I'd made up a story about my past sins that I could tell intrigued him. You see, Joplin needs the help, but he wants to run all the horses. But attorney to Deverick and Ausley! I'd be able to mark their comings and goings with ease."

"Dr. Godwin, too?" Matthew asked. "You began spending time at Polly Blossom's to mark his . . . if I may say . . . comings and goings?"

"That's right. I waited for the moment, until it came."

"And the night you killed Deverick? The same night that Grace Hester became so ill? I presume, since you were the go-between, that the prostitute sent out to find you searched your usual haunts with no success, since you were probably down here removing your black clothing, and she wound up having to go fetch Dr. Vanderbrocken himself? And she went with him and stood at the corner outside the reverend's house while Dr. Vanderbrocken went to the door?"

Kirby shrugged. "You know, *you* had a part in the deaths of Deverick and Ausley."

"*Me?* How?"

The lawyer made a noise between a grunt and a laugh. "When you stood up before Lord Cornbury and suggested more and better-trained constables. I was afraid he would agree, and so I thought I'd best hurry and finish the job."

Matthew almost said *Glad to be of service.*

Kirby spoke. "Would you like to see the Masker?"

"Sir?"

"The Masker," Kirby repeated, and just that quickly he slipped out of the light and into the gloomy fringes.

Matthew glanced nervously back to see how far the stairs were. He heard a sliding movement off to the side amid the cellar's boxes and wreckage. Then he jumped and his nerves jangled as something metal crunched into brick. There was the noise of what might have been bricks being moved aside. Then, seconds later, a brown canvas bag came flying through the air and landed with a dusty *thump* in front of Matthew's shoes.

"He's in there," came Kirby's voice, and then Kirby himself reentered the light's realm.

Matthew leaned carefully down and looked into the bag. It contained black clothing—one cloak, if not more, and a hooded coat. A woolen cap. A pair of black gloves. No, two pair. He could smell the heavy odor of dried gore. A smaller object caught his attention. When he picked it up by its wire-wrapped grip, he found the thing surprisingly heavy. Its business end was a tongue-shaped piece of black leather that felt as if it had a fist of lead sewn up within. The gentleman executioner had not forgotten his slaughterhouse system: first the blow to the temple, then the knife to the throat.

He was aware, very suddenly and joltingly, of Kirby's boots in the dirt beside him. When Matthew looked up, Kirby was holding the evil little knife with its hooked blade.

To his credit Matthew did not cry out, though he did feel the blood drain from his face. He got to his feet, watching for the strike and wondering which way to dodge it when it came.

Kirby turned the knife around and offered him the ebony leather handle. "It's very sharp," he said. "Easy to cut yourself." When Matthew wouldn't touch the thing, Kirby dropped it back amid the other items in the bag. It was then that Matthew realized Kirby was also holding the strange pair of hammered-brass fireplace tongs. "Oh." Kirby held the tongs up for Matthew's inspection of the chiselled ends. "You drive these into the cracks between two loose bricks that I found one day. Pull out the first brick and a few more and you've got yourself a nice hidey-hole. I couldn't go *home* wearing bloody clothes, could I? Not with Mary Belovaire watching me. I found the two cloaks and pairs of gloves at the bottom of that old trunk. They fit me fairly well. The blackjack came off a sailor willing to part with it. The knife I bought from a higgler in New Jersey. You know, you nearly caught me that night. If you hadn't been chasing me and I hadn't been trying to hold on to the notebook, I wouldn't have left that blood smear on the door."

Matthew held up the notebook. "Tell me about this."

"*You* tell me about it."

The front door suddenly opened upstairs. Both men were silent. The door closed, and footsteps could be heard ascending the stairs. Then a voice, calling, "Andrew? Andrew, are you here?"

"Joplin," Kirby said to Matthew, keeping his own volume low.

Pollard came back down the stairs. The front door opened and closed again.

"Poor fellow. An insecure boy, actually. He's wanting a pal at the bar," said Kirby. "You know, the only one who really works around here is Bryan. We both dump our papers on him. Joplin told me that Bryan's very unhappy if he's not burdened down. *Now:* the notebook. You saw the page I marked?"

"I did. I appreciate your rough treatment that night, by the way."

"Nothing personal. I was planning on leaving the package at Grigsby's door. I saw you by the corner lamp on Wall Street, so I had to move quickly. On that particular page, those are the names of orphans. Am I correct?"

"I believe so, yes."

"And the numbers beside them? Any guess?"

"A code."

"Of course a *code*, idiot! Meaning *what*?" Anger poured into the dead eyes. Even as the shade of what he'd been, Kirby was still a formidable and frightening presence. "*Think*, damn it! I've tried and failed, but if anyone can figure it out, it's you!"

Matthew opened the book to the page and held it under the lamplight. He scanned the numbers, back and forth.

"This is the problem I hoped you'd solve for me, Matthew," the lawyer said. "I saw Ausley scribbling in that notebook time and again, and I thought I had to get hold of it in search of a clue. I know what parts Godwin, Deverick, and Ausley acted in this, but who put the play *together*? Professor Fell? One of his compatriots? It wasn't Ausley, he wasn't smart enough. But it had to be someone here, on this side of the pond. A headmaster, if you will."

"*Headmaster*," Matthew repeated, looking up from the page. Something had clicked into place.

"I was going to say, that night, that *Eben Ausley is selling his orphans to the underworld.* Not all of them, but some. Maybe some who are talented in ways this headmaster can use. Can forge and shape, as he pleases. Look at that word *Chapel* there. Could that be a name?"

"Yes," Matthew said, but he was thinking furiously. *Headmaster. Trade school.* "It *is* a name." *Some men would come now and again and give us tests,* John Five had said. *Doin' numbers, copyin' script, figurin' out puzzles and such.* "Simon Chapel." *Wantin' to know all about us and our lives and so on.* "I think . . . these might be . . ." *What we wanted for the future.*

"What?" Kirby asked, closer now.

A man even came a couple of times to see if any of the older boys knew how to use a sword or a dagger.

"I think," Matthew said, and then he stopped himself. "I *believe*," he corrected, "that these are grades. I believe Eben Ausley was assigning grades to some of the boys. Maybe . . . for special talents, or something as mundane as how well they could understand and carry out orders. Many of the orphans would have come from violent circumstances, like John Five. Maybe they were graded on cruelty, or the ability to fight. Maybe how well-suited they might be for a life of crime. And here . . . this means *Rejected*. Either by Ausley, who had the first choice of whom to present to Chapel, or by Chapel himself later on." He thought of Silas. Silas with the quick hands and light touch. Silas Oakley, who was presented with high grades to the headmaster Simon Chapel on the twentieth of June, hardly more than a month ago.

I was jus' practisin', Silas had said.

For what future purpose? Surely not just shilling crimes; those were beneath Professor Fell. No, these would be more monumental, more grandiose in their evil. The theft of a key to a box where a diplomatic pouch lay, with the fate of kings and nations in the balance? The theft of business letters, or of guarded seals of state, or of perfume-touched messages between lovers that might lead to scandals, executions, and the overnight collapse of an empire . . . if the right price was not paid for the return?

This contract was underwritten by the professor, the Blind Boy had told Kirby.

Because, Matthew thought, the professor was interested in seeing the orphans in action.

A new world, Mrs. Herrald had said, *calls for new names*.

Not just new names, Matthew realized.

New blood.

Kirby was waiting. Matthew closed the notebook. He said with grim certainty, "Professor Fell is financing a school for criminals. North along the Hudson, about fifteen miles from here. It's run by a man named Simon Chapel. I don't think he's the professor. I may be wrong. But what better place to find potential 'students' than an orphanage full of boys who've already known hardship and violence? Diamonds in the rough, wouldn't you say?"

Kirby nodded. The light of understanding had also dawned on him, though his actions had doomed him to a prison's darkness.

Matthew drew himself up tall. Again, he marked the distance between where he stood and the stairs. "I'm going to take this notebook to City Hall," he said, in a voice that fortunately did not betray his gut-clenched fear. "I'm going to give it to Lillehorne, and I'm going to tell him everything." He hesitated, while that sank into the lawyer's blood-fevered brain. The only thing that moved about Kirby was a quick twitch of the mouth. "I'd like you to come with me."

forty-four

SOMEWHERE THE FERRY WAS CROSSING the river under the bright blue sky. Somewhere birds sang in the green Jersey hills. Somewhere children played, in all innocence and happiness, a game of Jack Straws.

But in the gloomy cellar of the attorneys' office on Broad Street, the Masker wore a smile full of pain. "You know I can't do that, Matthew."

"I know you *have* to. What good is the notebook without your testimony?"

Kirby stared at the floor. "You said . . . this tragic story had hope in it. May I ask where it might be?"

"The hope," Matthew said, "is that if you give yourself up today—right now—I can promise you that I and influential people will make certain you see your mother before you go to prison."

"Oh. You and influential people."

"That's right. It's my promise."

"Well." Kirby grinned tightly. "I should feel so much better now, shouldn't I?"

"What did you think you were going to do, Trevor? Did you think that I was going to uncover the headmaster of this scheme and you would get a chance to *murder* him, too, before he went to the docket?" Matthew scowled. "You must be truly mad, to think it would end there. Don't you want to kill all the orphans who were involved? What about Ives? Don't you thirst to slash his throat, too?" He let that hang because Kirby had given him a hollow-eyed, dangerous glare that made him think he'd gone a slash too far. Still, he pressed on. "I think if you took up shaving again and viewed yourself in the mirror, you'd see what effect murder has had on you. You're not a killer at heart! Far from it! Even Andrew Kippering, for all his vices, isn't a killer. It's time to let this go, and for the law to finish what you've begun."

"Oh, now you're going to tell me about the power of the law! The majesty of the courts! How *justice*, that blindfolded whore, always wins the day!"

"No, I'm not," said Matthew. "As a lawyer, you know better than that. Mistakes can be made and wrong decisions delivered by even the most auspicious court. That's *life*. But what I'm telling you is that your testimony could bring more villains to justice than your knife. You can't kill them *all*. I don't think, in your heart, you would want to. But your testimony could put them all behind bars. Yours is a compelling story, Trevor. Don't sell the truth so short."

"The *truth*. I can prove nothing."

"This is a beginning," Matthew told him, and held up the notebook.

Kirby wavered on his feet. He blinked heavily, stared up at the lantern, and then focused on empty air. "I . . . have to think." A hand drifted to his forehead. "I'm tired. I'm so tired."

"I know you are," Matthew said, and then gave the man his last cannon shot. "Your mother sleeps, even with her eyes open. I think she dreams of hearing that the *King's Reply* has arrived, and of seeing you walk through the door. That's what she's waiting for, Trevor. Her son, to come wake her up. If you walk to Lillehorne's office with me, right now, you'll get that chance."

A tremor passed over Kirby's face. Just that quickly, tears leaped to his eyes. It was like watching a shored-up house be torn apart under a bitter storm, so fast did Kirby's face contort and the wretched sob burst from his mouth. Matthew thought it was not a sound any human should ever have to utter; it was the cry of the damned, cast out from Heaven. As the tears streamed down Kirby's cheeks and his face truly became a mask—though this one of agony far beyond any punishment known to Man—his knees buckled, he crumpled to the dirt, and amid the boxes and papers of the profession's underbelly he crawled like a dying animal to crush himself against the unyielding bricks.

Matthew had to steel himself, lest he too be overcome. Kirby had given up everything. His position, his bride-to-be, his life. He had fought to avenge a terrible injustice, and had lost his soul in that unwinnable fight. For it seemed now to Matthew that vengeance, in the end, always consumed the innocent as well as the guilty, and burned them both into only so much cold ash.

But, Matthew thought, there was one thing no one could ever doubt about Trevor Kirby.

He was a good son.

"I'm going to go now," Matthew heard himself say, and the man's sobbing quietened. "Will you follow me, when you're able?"

There was no answer. Kirby remained pressed against the wall, his face hidden.

"Please," Matthew added. "For the both of us." Then he retrieved his tricorn and put it on, held the notebook close and firm at his side, and turned away to climb the stairs. He flinched as he heard Kirby move, but no attack ensued. Matthew went through the door at the top of the steps, then out the front door into the same bright light where the ferry sailed, the birds sang, and children played their joyful games.

He started walking north along Broad Street toward City Hall, his pace neither brisk nor particularly slow. He was simply giving a good but misguided son the chance to make up his mind. The air smelled of salt sea and the occasional puff of tobacco as pipe-smoking gentlemen walked past him. He kept his focus on the building ahead, putting together in his mind what his first words would be to Gardner Lillehorne. How was he to explain this, if Kirby failed to appear? It would be so much chaff to the wind. *Constable Lillehorne, will you listen while I tell you about an insidious plot to mold orphans into professional criminals in service to—*

The hard grip of a hand against his right shoulder jarred him out of his thoughts. Startled, he looked to that side and into the sunken-eyed, vulpine face of Bromfield, who wore the same wide-brimmed leather hat and similar rustic clothes as he'd been wearing that day on Chapel's estate.

"Look here!" A second hand snatched the notebook from Matthew's grip. "An added reward, I'd say!"

Bromfield put his arm around Matthew's neck like an old friend bending in to tell a secret and pushed him off the sidewalk into the shaded alcove of a doorway.

"Careful, careful," said the second man, who held the notebook. "All geniality and lightness, please. Mr. Corbett?"

Matthew blinked, stunned, and looked into the smiling face of Joplin Pollard.

The boyish lawyer leaned close; his mouth retained the smile, but his large brown eyes were sparkling not with grand good humor but with the razor-sharp glints of cruelty. "I want you to be very quiet now, all right? No trouble. Show it to him, Mr. Bromfield."

The hunter brought up his other hand and displayed a terribly familiar straw hat. He couldn't help himself; he took Matthew's tricorn off and pushed Berry's straw topper down around the younger man's ears.

"Your lovely friend has been taken on ahead." Pollard kept a hand pressed against the center of Matthew's chest. "Sadly, she gave Mr. Carver a kick to the shin that rattled even *my* teeth. So when you see her again she may be a bit bruised, but you should know that her life depends on what you do and say—or rather, *not* say—in the next few minutes."

"What's this . . . what's . . ." But Matthew knew, in spite of his mental fumbling. It hit him in the face like freezing water. Charles Land, the attorney whose practice Pollard had taken over, had supposedly inherited a large sum of money and returned to England to become an art patron and a dabbler in politics. That had been Professor Fell's method of clearing the way for a new investment.

Pollard is the one with ambition, the widow Sherwyn had said.

"*You.*" The word came bitterly from Matthew's mouth. "You're in charge of everything, aren't you?"

"Everything? A large blanket, I think. No, not everything. Just making sure people do what they're paid to do, and all goes smoothly. That's my job, really." He showed his teeth. "To smooth the rough roads and make sure they all connect. Thank you for the notebook, Mr. Corbett. I didn't expect to get hold of *this* today."

"Can I tweak his nose, sir?" Bromfield asked hopefully.

"Certainly not. Let's keep our decorum on the public street. Mr. Corbett, you're going to come with us and do it without protest or drawing attention. If you're not delivered to Mr. Chapel's estate within a reasonable number of hours, the very lovely Miss Grigsby will die a death I can't begin to explain to you without losing my breakfast. Therefore, I'd suggest you follow my instructions: keep your head down, move quickly, do *not* speak to anyone else even if you're spoken to. Ready? Let's go, then."

Whether he was ready or not was beside the point. Matthew, with Berry's hat obscuring most of his face, was pushed along between the two men, who steered him left onto Barrack Street and past the place where he'd found Ausley's body.

"We've been searching all over for you this morning," said Pollard as they kept a steady clip. "I met Bryan on the street a little while ago. He told me you were in to see Andrew. Would you mind telling me what that was about?"

Matthew did, so he didn't.

"No matter," the lawyer answered to Matthew's silence. "I'll have a little talk with Andrew and we'll get to the bottom of it. Am I right to feel a little *uneasy* around Andrew these days? What say you?"

"I say, you can put your head up your—" That gallant but foolish statement was censored by a pair of rustic knuckles that drove into his ribs through coat, waistcoat, and sweat-damp shirt.

"Easy, Mr. Bromfield. No need for that yet. Ah, here we are."

Ahead at the corner of Barrack and the Broad Way sat a coach with four horses. It was very different from the vehicle that had carried Charity LeClaire and him to the estate. This one was dusty and ugly, meant to look more like the regular, road-weary landboats that travelled the hard track between New York and Boston, and so would not gather as much notice amid the movement of pedestrians, cargo wagons, farmers' carts, and higglers' wheelbarrows.

A driver and whipman, both boys about fifteen or sixteen years old, sat up top. "Get in," said Pollard, guiding him forward. Quickly Bromfield tossed the tricorn through the window into the coach and unlatched the door. As Matthew was about to enter, he glanced to the right and saw his friend and chessmate Effrem Owles approaching along the sidewalk not twenty feet away. Effrem's head was lowered, his eyes lost in thought behind the spectacles. It came to Matthew to cry out for help, but just that fast the thought perished for not only might these men take Effrem as well, but Berry's life hung by a slender thread. Effrem passed by, so close Matthew could have touched him.

Then Matthew felt Bromfield's hand balled up in the small of his back, and he let himself be pushed into the coach. Already within sat the wiry, long-haired youth whose job had been to pour the wine at Chapel's feast. Jeremy, Chapel had called him. Pomade glistened in his hair. He had drawn a knife as soon as the door had opened, and greeted Matthew with its blade.

Matthew sat on the bench seat facing him. Bromfield sat beside Matthew, reached over, and pulled the canvas sunshade down over the opposite window.

Pollard leaned in through the door and gave the notebook to Bromfield, who instantly tucked it down in his leather waistcoat. "Good man," Pollard said to Matthew. "No need for unpleasantries. Mr. Chapel just wants to speak to you."

"To *speak* to me? You mean, to *kill* me, don't you?"

"Relax, Mr. Corbett. We don't waste talent, even if it is misguided. Our benefactor keeps a nice village in Wales where people can be educated as to the proper meaning of life. I *would* like to know, though: how did you come upon the notebook?"

Matthew had to think fast. "McCaggers was wrong about it not being with Ausley's belongings. His slave, Zed, had moved some of the stuff to another drawer. I went back to McCaggers and he'd found it."

"Is that so?"

"Yes."

"Hm." Pollard's eyes, much more alert than Matthew had ever seen them, examined Matthew's face. "I'll have to ask Mr. McCaggers about that. You trouble me, sir, just as you trouble Mr. Chapel. It's time something is done."

"The girl's not part of this."

"Part of *what*, sir?" Pollard kept the thin smile. "Oh, you mean your *intrigues* with Mr. Greathouse, is that correct? We know all about your going to dig up a certain grave on a certain farm. Mr. Ormond was glad to talk to a young representative from the coroner's office who wished to tie up some loose ends."

"I have no idea what—"

"Spare me. Good, dependable, and stupid Bryan has a little game he plays with his laundress. He tells her a secret, she tells him a secret. I think that's his only vice, God pity him. On Tuesday Bryan tells me his laundress has heard that there have been *four* murders instead of only three. A corpse was found washed up out of the river onto a farm about ten miles out of town. A young man, still unidentified. The body pierced by multiple stab wounds. And this mysterious informant has actually *seen* it. Well, Mr. Ormond saw our young representative yesterday and provided the names of the two men who came to dig up the grave. Hudson Greathouse and—lo and behold—his *associate* Matthew Corbett. How about *those* apples?"

Sour, Matthew thought.

"Be sure we'll deal with Mr. Greathouse in due time. First you. Goodbye, sir." Pollard withdrew from the coach and shut the door. "Drive on!" he called up, as Bromfield reached across Matthew to draw the second canvas sunshade down with a definitive *snap*.

A whip was applied and the coach began to roll. In the yellow-tinged cabin, Matthew was sweating. He heard the workaday sounds of New York passing as the coach trundled north on the Broad Way. His eyes kept going to the knife in Jeremy's hand. It looked very eager.

He had to figure a way out of this. Unfortunately, there was no way out. He reached up to take off Berry's hat and at the same time the knife flicked toward him like a rattlesnake's tongue and Bromfield clasped an iron hand to his shoulder. Then the two rapscallions realized what he was doing and allowed him to de-hat. He put it on his lap, thinking that if he were a real hero pressed from the mold of Hudson Greathouse he would wait for a particularly vicious pothole, flick the straw topper into the boy's eyes, seize the knife, and plunge it into the largest target, which would be Bromfield's chest. Of course, getting through that leather waistcoat and the notebook tucked behind it might prove an ill adventure. He decided there was only one Hudson Greathouse, and no place for a hero in this coach.

They were moving faster now, turning onto the Post Road and leaving the town behind. The whip was striking left and right and the four horses were hauling ass.

A nice village in Wales, Pollard had said. Just the place for Berry and I to spend our old age, Matthew thought. If we live long enough to have one.

We, he realized. He had not thought of anyone that way, in conjunction with him, since the incident with Rachel Howarth at Fount Royal. He imagined he'd loved Rachel, when instead he'd wished to be her champion. Love was something he wasn't sure he yet understood. He knew desire, and the need for companionship . . . but *love*? No. He was far too busy for even the idea of it.

Now, however, he looked to be facing a long period of—at the best—retirement. He wished suddenly that he'd been a little less serious and a lot more . . . how did Marmaduke put it . . . merrymaking. Less chess, perhaps, and more dancing. Or, at the very least, more appreciation of the pretty girls in New York, and yes there were quite a few. It was interesting how a knife pointed at you could direct one's mind to things that a few weeks ago seemed frivolous and now seemed only sadly lost.

But wait, he told himself firmly. Just wait. He was still alive, and Berry was still alive. Hopefully. There might come a time, and unfortunately very soon, for wailing and lamentations. Now was not that time. He had to remain calm, focused, and ready to act if the situation presented itself.

The coach hit a pothole the depth of his misery and bounced. Matthew's moment to swat Jeremy's face with his topper passed. No heroes in this coach. But wasn't it heroic enough just to hold the nerves together, as they strained and screamed under his skin?

What are you going to do, moonbeam?

The boy had lowered his blade to the seat beside him. Bromfield's head leaned back, his eyes half-closed as the coach rocked.

"Hey," Matthew said to Jeremy. Instantly Bromfield's eyes opened fully and he sat up.

The boy stared blankly at Matthew.

"How old are you?" Matthew asked.

Jeremy glanced at Bromfield, who shrugged, and then back to his questioner. "Fifteen."

"I left the orphanage when I was fifteen. I was an orphan too, you know."

"Is that so?"

"What's your specialty?"

"My *what?*"

"Your talent," Matthew said. "What got you out of the orphanage and into Chapel's school?"

"Ain't a school. It's . . ." Jeremy frowned, calling up a word. Obviously, quick wit was not his ticket. "It's a *university.*"

"I'm sure you'll go far upon graduation. What's your talent?"

The boy picked up his knife and looked almost lovingly at the blade. "I can throw this," he said with a full measure of pride, "and hit a fella square in the back from twenty paces. Killed me an Injun kid one time, stealin' from my papa's chickencoop. Got him in the back and then I cut his red damn throat and took me his scalp, too."

"Laudable. You were how old when this happened?"

"Eleven, I reckon. Then them Injuns came and dragged my

papa off. They tied me to a fuckin' tree and torched the house down. That's how I got left on my own."

Matthew nodded. A fledgling assassin, perhaps? A killer able to strike at long distance from the shadows? It occurred to him that Ausley had possessed the talent of recognizing the inherent ability—call it the seed of evil, either inborn or created from any of life's more brutal circumstances—in some of his charges, and Chapel refined that raw substance into a valuable commodity. "What does Mr. Chapel offer you, in return for your loyalty to this . . . *university*?"

"Good food," the boy replied. "A bed. Nobody fuckin' with me. And I get all the pussy I can handle."

Ah, Matthew thought. So Charity LeClaire was also a valuable commodity. "Have you killed anyone else since you were eleven?"

"That's enough," Bromfield warned. "Shut up and keep shut."

The voice was harsh enough to tell Matthew he should pursue this no further if he cared to keep his teeth. Matthew settled against the backrest. He watched as Jeremy continued to admire the knife as if it were his declaration of power in a world that ground young men into pulp beneath ten-league boots.

At last—and much too soon—Matthew felt the coach slowing. He heard the whipman ring his signal bell and there was a pause as the gate was opened. Then the coach rolled forward, gained speed once more, and a hundred yards later came the cry, "Whoa! Whoa!"

The coach creaked to a halt, the door on Matthew's right was opened and Lawrence Evans, well-dressed and immaculately groomed, stood there in the bright spill of afternoon light. But he was certainly not alone, for around him and peering into the coach was a crowd of young faces of every description and, as Chapel had said, a variety of ages between twelve and eighteen, with possibly two or three a few years elder. Nineteen of them, according to Evans. Maybe so, but to Matthew it seemed there were enough to fight an English brigade.

Bromfield got out first and then Matthew, followed by Jeremy and his knife. The boys instantly began to hoot, cat-call, and snicker, until Evans said crisply, "That is *enough*. Show respect, even to the enemy. Make way, now."

As the whip cracked and the coach was driven away toward the vineyard, Matthew was escorted into the manse. Quickly, though, he noted that the university's "students" were all dressed more or less the same, in white shirts and black or brown breeches with cream-colored stockings. Notable also were paper badges that they worn pinned to their shirts in crayoned colors of crimson and royal blue and in different shapes of square, triangle, circle and—glimpsed only briefly and belonging to the oldest boys—a combination of blue circle within a red triangle within a blue square. Medals of some kind? he wondered. A way to distinguish between "years" for the students, as a real university would classify first year, second year, and so on? He was through the door and the door was closed behind him as one of the boys shouted, "You'll get what's comin'!"

He dreaded to think.

He was escorted—rather roughly by Bromfield with a hand to the nape of his neck—past the staircase and into the tapestry-draped corridor. Further back, the huge dining room with its fan-shaped arrays of swords had been recently the site of a late and obviously recently interrupted luncheon feast, for platters full of chicken bones sat amid the gleaming silver trays, salt and pepper bowls, and the other implements that Chapel felt created a gentle-man's table. Matthew felt a bit of satisfaction, thinking that his arrival might have propelled Chapel up from his repast.

The door to the left of the room was open. Within it a staircase curved upward. Light glowed through a long, narrow window. "Up, please," Evans said as he ascended first. A shove almost knocked Matthew up the stairs before he could take the initial riser. The stairs rose to an office with circular windows overlooking the garden like the portholes of a ship. Everything was dark oak and black leather. It was the same as might be the office of any man of means: a wide desk, chairs, a file cabinet, and on shelves bookcases with many leatherbound volumes that in happier times Matthew might have wished to prowl through.

The two things in this particular office that stood unpleasantly out were Simon Chapel seated behind the desk, the light slanting across his face, the bulk of shoulders and battering-ram head, and Berry Grigsby in a peach-colored dress with yellow lace trim. She was sitting in a chair off to the side. Her hands were bound behind her with white cords, and likewise was she bound around her waist to the back of the chair. Her hair was wild and tangled, her eyes were wild and very frightened, and a vivid blue bruise lay across her left cheekbone.

"Hello, Matthew," Chapel said, his elbows on the desk's green blotter and his fingers steepled. The light lay fiery in his spectacles. "Pardon me if I don't stand up."

Matthew had no witty remark to throw at him. His mouth was a dry well. He saw Charity LeClaire, as elegant and beautiful as she was wretched and soul-ugly, standing directly behind Berry. In a chair on the opposite side of the room, the lizardy Count Dahlgren in his elegant beige suit sprawled as if basking on a warm rock.

"*Matthew*," Berry said hoarsely, her lower lip cut and swollen. He saw fingermarks on her neck where Carver had throttled the beginnings of a scream. Her eyes begged for rescue, as if this were the most terrible mistake and surely it would be all right, now that he'd come in like Sir Lancelot.

The knight of the moment noted something very disturbing indeed. On the floor beneath Berry's chair was a spread of sail-cloth. To protect the expensive brick-red rug, he thought. From what? Again, he dreaded to think.

"He was carryin' this, sir," said Bromfield, as he fished the notebook free and put it down on the desktop blotter. Chapel immediately picked it up and opened it to the page that had been dog-eared by the Masker's thumb.

"Ah, yes. Very good." Chapel's smile was a wet gash. "The last book! Now I can rest easy, can't I." It was a statement, not a question.

Matthew saw there was one other person in the room. Over on the right, in the shadows that clung to the bookshelves like black cobwebs, was a boy of indeterminate age. Small-boned, pale of skin, and weirdly fragile. His silky hair was the color of dust. He wore the same uniform as his fellow students. His shirt-badge was the circle. He had a long thin scar running up through his right eyebrow into his hairline, and his eye on that side was a cold orb of milky-white.

"Restrain him," said Chapel, as he paged through the notebook.

Bromfield had moved behind Matthew, and now he locked an arm around Matthew's throat while Lawrence Evans displayed that an ex-clerk could have a suspiciously good relationship with a rope. Matthew's arms were pulled back, the cord was tied around his wrists, knotted so hard he thought he would pee in his breeches, and then he was shoved down into a chair so graciously slid beneath his buttocks.

Chapel took snuff from a silver case. One pinch up each nostril, *snort* and *snort*, but only in the most gentlemanly way. He used a white lace handkerchief to brush the refuse from the coat of his suit, which was the color of rich brown tobacco anyway.

"I want to know," he said as he folded his handkerchief and put it away, "from where you got this notebook. Will you tell me that, please?"

Matthew got his dry well watered enough to rasp, "Certainly. Very simply, the coroner had misplaced it. In a different drawer. I returned to his office and—"

"Why would he give it to *you*, sir?" The topaz eyes flared, just a fraction.

Careful, Matthew thought. "He trusts me. I told him I knew Miss LeClaire, and that I would give it to her. Of course I was going to bring it here." He took advantage of the pause. "I told Mr. Pollard the same thing. He's going to go speak to Mr. McCaggers."

"He knows everything," Bromfield said, which made Matthew want to kick him in the nuts.

"I *know* he knows everything," Chapel replied irritably. "Perhaps not everything, but enough. All right, Matthew, let's put aside the notebook for a moment. I want to talk to you about the Masker. Do you know who he is?"

"No, I don't."

"Are you positively *sure* about that?"

"I'm . . . I'm sure," Matthew said, and damned his nervous stutter.

"Well, the reason I ask is that the Masker has killed three men who featured large in our project. You know what project I'm talking about, don't you?"

"No sir, I don't." And he quickly added, "You don't really have to tell me, either."

"Sir?" It was back-stabbing Jeremy. "He asked me in the coach what my talent is. He called our university a fuckin' *school*."

"Watch your language, please. That's demerits off." Chapel returned his languid, scorching attention to Matthew's sweat-sparkling face. "Who dog-eared that particular page?" Matthew went deaf and dumb. "The page with the orphans' names," Chapel prodded. "Who dog-eared that? Mr. McCaggers?"

"I suppose so, sir. Possibly I did it, I don't exactly—"

"You are slobbering bullshit," said Chapel, very quietly. It was odd, how sometimes a quiet voice could make your backbone shiver. "I think you *do* know who the Masker is. I think the Masker killed those three men particularly *because* of one of our endeavors. I think he has some grandiose scheme of vengeance, which means he has a connection to the Swanscott family."

"The *who*, sir?" Matthew asked, though strangled.

"Mr. Bromfield, if he speaks without being spoken to again, I want you to make a violent response. Do mind the carpet, though. It's new and I don't want blood on it."

"Yes sir."

"I was *saying*," Chapel continued, "that the Masker has a connection to the Swanscott family. Obviously. I think, you being an associate now of Mr. Hudson Greathouse and that highly lauded woman's agency, that for whatever reason and whatever bizarre circumstances the Masker approached you because of that notice in the broadsheet. So it must be someone you know, and who knows your current association. He presented you with the note-book he'd taken off the body of Eben Ausley, that dead asshole. Now the Masker had a problem: he wished to know who might have engineered the adventure in Philadelphia, in . . . what was the date, Lawrence?"

"1697, sir."

"Yes, quite correct. He wishes you to find out who put the plan together, so he might strike that man down. If you haven't figured it out yet, we're talking about *myself*. I don't take very kindly to having to watch my throat, sir, even if this Masker would be step-ping into a slaughterhouse were he to set one foot over that wall. So . . . I should like to know his name, that I might bring him here and empty his head of its brains. You're going to tell me his name, sir. You're going to tell me his name within one minute. Mr. Ripley?"

The boy moved sinuously from the shadows. Instantly Charity LeClaire grasped two handfuls of Berry's hair and jerked her head back. Lawrence Evans, a jack of all evils, stepped forward and fixed some kind of metal clamp to Berry's right eye which held the lids apart as much as she cried out and tried to struggle. For good mea-sure, the elegant lady shoved a dirty leather glove into Berry's mouth.

Ripley slid from his pocket a long and terribly sharp blue knit-ting needle.

forty-five

THE BOY FLOATED like an angel of death. There was a grace about him, an ethereal blue glow. Or perhaps that was just light glinting off the needle.

He came steadfastly forward, neither in haste nor with time to waste. Berry tried to kick at him but he neatly and effortlessly sidestepped. He might have been a shadow, though he was fearfully real. When Berry attempted to overthrow the chair, the beautiful lady behind her simply applied more pressure to the red locks.

Ripley reached his victim. Without hesitation, he pushed forth the needle toward the center of Berry's trapped eyeball.

"I'll tell," Matthew said.

"Stop, Mr. Ripley," Chapel commanded. The boy immediately obeyed. His living eye on the side sinister, which was a black marble, twitched toward his headmaster. "Step back, but remain ready." Chapel got to his feet, said to Dahlgren, "Get up," and when the grenadier sluggishly obeyed Chapel took his chair and dragged it over to face Matthew. "Hold her just as she is," Chapel told the lady and Evans. He sat down with his knees nearly touching Matthew's, and he leaned in so close Matthew might have watched the oil leaking from his pores and could positively smell the baked chicken on his heated breath.

"Now then." Chapel smiled, all sunny and light. "You were going to give me a name."

"Can I have a drink of water? My throat's—"

"I won't stop him next time, Matthew. What do I care if she loses an eye? The *name*."

"All right." Matthew licked his lips. A bead of sweat ran down to the tip of his nose and hung there, quivering. It wasn't easy to talk while Berry alternately murmured in pain and tried to blow a shout through the glove jammed in her mouth. "I have to tell you *about* him first." He saw Chapel turn his head, about to order the young torturer to continue. "Sir! *Please!* Let me explain to you that he is the Swanscotts' *son*!"

Chapel paused. His huge blue-veined brow furrowed. "I think I recall . . ." He tapped his head with a forefinger, as if to jog a memory. "The Swanscotts had two sons who died early in life, according to our findings."

"Oh, the two sons—Toby and Michael—died, it's true enough, but this boy was found working in a slaughterhouse. He was unofficially adopted by the Swanscotts. They raised him as their own, sent him to school. Everything that parents could do."

"Really?" Chapel drew closer, almost nose-to-nose. His eyes bored relentlessly into Matthew's.

"Yes sir. He's made quite a bit of money. He's disguised himself. I think he put it as . . . a high ball playing low."

Chapel scratched his chin. "Go on."

"He made some inquiries in London. Put money on the street for information. He knows all about it. The poisoned wine, and all the rest."

"Is that so?"

"Yes sir. He did give me the notebook. Wanted me to figure out the meaning of that page. What the grades meant. I mean, the numbers."

"Very good." A slight smile surfaced. "They *were* grades. At least, from Ausley's limited point-of-view. He used them to dicker over prices. I gave my own marks later."

"He did hope that I might lead him to you. I told him he ought to give himself up, that he has a compelling story to tell."

"And *did* he give himself up?" Chapel correctly read Matthew's expression. "Of course he didn't. He's come all this way, he's probably near insane by now. Why should he give himself up? And you've told this story to who else? Hudson Greathouse and Mrs. Herrald, I presume?"

"Neither of them. This is my investigation."

"But you and Greathouse dug up the body of Billy Hodges, didn't you? Why?"

"McCaggers told me about it. High Constable Lillehorne didn't want anyone else to know. I thought . . . it might have some bearing on the Masker."

"In a roundabout way," Chapel said. "Poor Billy. An *excellent* forger, but unfortunately a weak mind. You know, he was the screever who forged the inspection label in Swanscott's warehouse. It's intriguing that very often a person who has to learn to write with an unnatural hand can more easily master the art of forgery. He was a wonder, that Billy. Did some work for us in Boston, as well, but just minor items on the order of deeds and such. He was an instructor for the younger lads for several years . . . then, sadly, he wished to leave us. Ah, that Billy."

"I'd rather you not tell me, sir," Matthew said.

"Oh, it's all right! I'm not *angry* with you!" Chapel slapped Matthew's left knee. "Lord, no! I understand this is just business! You wished to make a name for yourself with the Herrald Agency, am I right? But tell me . . . how did you feel about helping a murderer plan a *murder*?"

"I suppose . . ." Matthew swallowed. "It was just business."

"There's the spirit!" Chapel smacked his hands together and looked at the others in the room, as Berry thrashed and writhed to no avail. He was beaming. "True industry at work, friends! The ultimate commingling of what some would call the angelic and the demonic! He wants to get ahead in life, so he plots with an insane murderer! Can you beat it?"

"Very humorous," said Lawrence Evans, with no trace of humor.

Chapel turned his face back toward Matthew, again almost nose-to-nose. His smile was gone. Matthew could see his own face, scared witless, in the lenses. "The *name*."

"His name is . . ." Matthew hesitated, his heart pounding. No one was going to save either Berry or him. He had to do what he could, to buy them some time and figure a way out of this.

"Mr. Ripley is waiting," Chapel whispered.

Matthew said, "His name is Dippen Nack. He's a constable."

The room seemed frozen.

Chapel looked at Evans. "*Dippen Nack?* What kind of name is that? Do you know him?"

"No sir."

"Bromfield?"

"No sir," said the hunter.

Chapel returned his attention to his prisoner and began to fidget with the silver buttons of Matthew's waistcoat. "Mr. Evans, get the census book and find out if indeed there's a Mr. Dippen Nack included on the list. Beautiful buttons, by the way."

Evans removed the eye clamp from Berry's orb, which must have been nearly dried out. She blinked rapidly, as if trying to push it back into its socket without benefit of her fingers. Evans went to the desk and opened a drawer. He came out with a thin brown leather book. Matthew recognized it. A copy of the New York census, undertaken last year by order of the late lamented Mayor Hood. Matthew felt the sweat dripping under his arms. If Nack had a wife and a houseful of kids or lived with his mother, it was all up.

"Dippen Nack is an alias," he said, to relieve his steam. "I don't know his real name."

Evans' index finger was searching. "Here he is, sir. Dippen Nack. Lives on Nassau Street." He brought the book over to display the name and address.

"Very good. Well, there *is* such a man. No wife or children, I see. Tell me, Lawrence, do you recall the names of the Swanscott boys? Were they Toby and Michael?"

"I think they were, but it'll just take a moment to look up the file. I'm sure we have that jotted down somewhere."

"Go ahead, then."

Evans went to the file cabinet, opened a drawer, and began going through papers.

Matthew squirmed in his chair, as much as he was able. He heard Berry make a muffled sound between a cry of pain and an oath. Her hair was still being gripped by Miss LeClaire's pitiless hands. "Please, sir," he said to Chapel, "won't you let her go?"

"No," came the reply. "But I suppose we needn't be so harsh. Charity? One hand only."

"Found it, sir!" Evans announced. He leaned forward, reading something. "Yes, that was their names. But hold on!" He paused. "Now *that's* interesting," he said, in a voice that sent a coursing of fresh terror through Matthew. "It seems the Swanscotts had——"

Matthew decided to take a chance, and if he was wrong it might be the last thing he ever spoke. "A third son, yes I know. An infant who died right after birth."

Evans was silent, still reading.

"Well?" Chapel asked.

"He's correct, sir. There's a small notation here. An infant who died soon after birth, according to the medical copy from London." He held up the yellowed parchment. "Care to see it?"

"No." Chapel grinned. "Dippen Nack, eh? The only way Matthew could have known about that dead infant was from a family member. A *fourth* son! Unofficial, of course. It makes sense, doesn't it? The Masker being a *constable*? He could creep around all night, stalk his victims, and then . . ." A finger across the throat completed his point.

Someone was climbing the stairs. It sounded like a pegleg. Matthew looked to the side as Carver, the sandy-haired, thick-set, and heavy-lidded second hunter and sometime stomperboy, limped into the room.

"Mr. Chapel!" he said. "Pardon, but the fellas want to know if we're havin' a game today."

"Yes, we certainly are." Chapel stood up. "Tell them, and tell

Edgar and Hastings to get everything ready. Oh . . . wait. After you've done that, I want you and Mr. Bromfield to take your horses and ride back to town. Go to the stable there and secure a third horse. Then proceed to . . ." He checked the census book. "Number Thirty-Nine Nassau Street. Wait until dark if you have to, but bring back a man named Dippen Nack. Be careful, as he may be very dangerous and quite mad, but do not—I repeat—do not injure him in such a way that any further injury would be redundant and ineffective. All right?" He glanced at Evans. "Who's on the gate today?"

"Enoch Speck, sir."

"On the way out, tell Mr. Speck he may join in the game after he locks up tight. Go, the both of you!"

When the two hunters had gone, one in obvious distress from a bruised shin, Chapel made a motion to Jeremy, who cut the cords binding Berry to the chair. Miss LeClaire released Berry's hair, but Matthew noted she had many red strands stuck between her fingers.

"Up, the both of you." Chapel extended his hands and motioned them to their feet with a waggling of his fingers. "Get that out of her mouth, please."

Berry turned toward the elegant bitch to have the glove extracted. Matthew saw it before Miss LeClaire did: a crimson glare in Berry's eyes, like the distant watchfire on a rocky coast proclaiming *Danger, many ships have perished here*.

Before the glove was halfway out, Berry suddenly leaned her head back and then swiftly crashed her forehead into the slim bridge of Miss LeClaire's nose. There was a noise Matthew equated to what a melon might sound like if it fell from a one-hundred-storey building, if indeed such an edifice was possible. Even as Chapel reached to restrain Berry and the pale torturer-in-training Mr. Ripley gave not a cry but an emotionless hiss of alarm, Miss LeClaire fell back with eyes already turned inward toward a world of long sleep and painful recovery. The bridge of her nose was flattened, as if smacked by a skillet. Her head crunched into the wall behind her, her hair seemed to explode into a mass of writhing blond Medusa snakes, and as she sank down to the floor the blood shot in two fine arcs from the small holes of her nostrils onto her lacy dress and a black bruise spread across her twitching face as quickly and hideously as the plague.

Berry spat out the rest of the glove. It landed square atop Miss LeClaire's head, like a new style of Parisian hat.

It occurred to Matthew that Grandda Grigsby was not the only one in his family who could crack walnuts on an iron forehead.

Chapel spun her around, but kept an arm up in case Berry tried for a double score. A red blotch of anger had surfaced on each cheek, but because he was a man of firm self-control and perhaps also fatalism they cleared just as rapidly. He even managed a guarded smile of approval as he regarded the collapsed dolly. "Nicely done," he said.

"You bastards!" Berry seethed to the room at large. "What do you think you're *doing?*"

"Language, please," Chapel cautioned. "We can always find another glove." His arm was still up, protecting his brainpan.

Matthew didn't like this talk about a *game*. In fact, it made his knees weak and his bladder throb even more than having his hands nearly dead from the pressure of the cords. "They're going to send us to a nice little village in Wales," he said, by several shades too brightly. "Aren't you, Mr. Chapel? The village the professor keeps?"

The emotion drained from Chapel's face. It was now a wax replica. "Hold this vixen, Lawrence." When Evans had cautiously taken the position, Chapel entertained himself with two more sniffs of snuff. At length he said, "For all his worth in keeping the affairs in order, Mr. Pollard has demonstrated a very large and disorderly mouth. Our benefactor's business is not any of yours, sir. In fact, it is up to my discretion whether you should be passed on further into the system or if you should not. *Be,*" he added, for clarification. "I have decided on the latter course." A bell began ringing in the distance. Ringing and ringing. He gazed at Matthew and behind the square-rimmed spectacles his hard eyes softened. He seemed to wear a little gray cast of regret. "You have the *mind,*

Matthew. You have the *resources*. You might have been very useful to our benefactor, in time. But I fear—and the professor would agree—that you're too far gone."

Chapel shook his head. His decision had been painfully made. "You should at least have let us take *one* eye before you ratted out Mr. Nack," he said. In Matthew's stunned and apprehensive silence, Chapel returned to his desk, picked up the notebook, and put it into the top drawer. The bell was still ringing. A merry sound for a funeral, Matthew thought. Berry was looking at him for some kind of reassurance, but he had none to give her.

"Let her sleep," Chapel instructed when Jeremy bent down to tend to his source of that which starts with *p* and ends in *y*. "God knows we all could use the rest. You first down the stairs, Jeremy. Don't step in blood and get it on my carpet, for the sake of *Christ*! All right, move along. You next, Mr. Ripley." Matthew noted that even Chapel drew back from the young creeper. "After you, miss," he told Berry, who started to plant her feet obstinately but was pushed forward by Lawrence Evans with a hand gripped to her neck. "Mr. Corbett and Count Dahlgren, please proceed."

In the dining-room, the group waited for Chapel to descend the stairs. He came down as a whistling, convivial spirit. All was right with Simon Chapel's little world. Matthew watched as he closed the office door behind him, took a key from a coat pocket, locked the door, and returned the key to its home. Miss LeClaire probably wouldn't wake up until September.

Matthew threw a glance at Berry, who caught it and returned one of her own that said, in quite explicit language: *What the hell are we going to do?*

He didn't know. What he *did* know, he didn't intend sharing with Berry. The cords around their wrists, at once lighter and more strongly woven than regular barn or household rope, were the same as had bound the wrists of Billy Hodges.

"We're off," beamed Chapel, as the bell kept ringing.

"Sir," Matthew said before Count Dahlgren could shove him along again, "don't you think we ought to *wait*? I mean, just to be sure I've told you the truth about Dippen Nack?"

"Why?" Chapel's face loomed, moonlike, into Matthew's. "Was it *not* the truth?" To Matthew's contemplation of how to respond to this knitting-needle of a question, Chapel laughed explosively and clapped his prisoner's shoulder. "Your problem," he said with damnable good humor, "is that you're much too honest. Come along, now."

forty-six

IT WAS A LONG WALK to a bad end, with the bell pealing a spritely dirge.

Matthew and Berry were side-by-side as they progressed along the road toward the vineyard. Ahead of them strode Chapel, deep in conversation with Evans. Arrayed around the hapless prisoners in a dangerous triangle were Jeremy, Ripley, and Count Dahlgren. And keeping pace were the boys, hooting and laughing with joyful glee, jostling one another for closer looks at Berry, darting in and plucking at Matthew's coat or Berry's dress and then being chased back by an almost playful feint from Jeremy's knife or a backhanded threat and Prussian yell from the count. No one bothered Ripley and Ripley reacted to no one; he'd put on dark-tinted spectacles to shield his eyes from the sun and walked with a solemn but inexorable forward motion.

"What are they going to *do* to us?" Berry pressed up close beside Matthew, flinching as a yellow-haired boy of about fourteen ran in and pulled at her dress. She started to turn and shout at him, as she'd done to several others, but as that had just brought about a storm of laughter she decided it was wasted breath.

Matthew wanted to say *I don't know* but the time for that lie was well and truly done. After all, he was so damned *honest*. "They're going to kill us," he said.

Berry stopped. She stood gaping at him, her blue eyes scorching holes through his head, until Dahlgren gave her a shove that almost propelled her into Matthew. Oh, how the boys did convulse themselves! One—a little brown-haired imp not over twelve—started massaging the front of his breeches and grinningly pranced a jig, his boots kicking up dustpuffs.

"Kill us?" she gasped when she could speak. "*Kill us?* What have you got me into?"

"An adventure," he replied. "I thought you liked those."

"I like adventures I can *live* through!" Her mouth was so close to his right ear Matthew thought she was going to bite it off. Her hair was wild and tangled and whitened by dust. She looked desperately around and saw only woods beyond the laughing faces and capering figures. "We can run, can't we?"

"Not faster than they can catch us."

"They're not going to kill us!" Her mouth twisted. Her eyes were wet. "They're just going to *frighten* us, aren't they?"

"I don't know. I don't think I could be any more frightened."

"You're supposed to *do* something!" she insisted, again right up at his ear.

Matthew just grunted. *What are you going to do, moonbeam?*

He could cry, he thought. Break down in tears and let them see his real courage. Let them see what happens when a chess-loving moonbeam plays . . . what was that word he'd conjured up in Philadelphia? *Detective.* Ho, ho, what a joke! One has to survive his first investigation, Matthew thought grimly. He gave another pull at his bonds, as he'd done at least half-a-dozen times, but the cords were only going to come off when his wrists had thinned a little more.

"Someone's coming, aren't they?" Berry pleaded. Her voice cracked and she caught herself. "Tell me. Someone's coming."

"No one's coming. And the gate's locked." Was he being too cruel? He thought to put an arm around her, but found how quickly he had forgotten about the cords. His mind was swimming in the blood of the future. The very near future. Well, his heart might explode and he might fall down and die without further injury.

But not further insult, for he realized he had just stepped into a pile of manure left by the coach horses on their way to the stable. The laughter and hollering swelled up and someone called him a "shitfoot." Could someone actually die of embarrassment? he wondered. Regrettably, no.

"Mister!" Berry shouted. Then, louder to be heard over death-bell and merriment, "Mister *Chapel*!"

Chapel interrupted his discussion with Evans and drifted back. "Yes, miss?"

"We won't say anything!" she told him.

"That's right," he agreed.

"I mean it! We'll be quiet! Won't we, Matthew?"

"Yes, you'll be very quiet," Chapel said.

Berry suddenly sat down on the ground. At once Chapel motioned for help and a swarm of boys rushed in to oblige. Matthew thought Berry's clothes were going to be torn off, and her breasts and private area squeezed and felt by every hand on an arm. She got up red-faced, swollen-eyed, and fighting, until Count Dahlgren came forward, grabbed a handful of her hair, shook her head back and forth, and hollered, "You vill *valk*!" into her ear. His fist was ready to strike before her forehead could. Matthew saw her eyes go blank and her mouth slack, and a pain beyond agony pierced his heart as she staggered forward and the little parade marched on.

"She's not doing well," Chapel remarked as he walked at Matthew's side.

"This is her first time to be murdered," he answered, in a stronger voice than he'd ever imagined he could summon up, if he'd ever imagined such a situation at all.

"Just don't run very far," Chapel advised, in the manner of a friendly confidant. "Far enough to give them some exercise. Then just lie down and let them have at it. It won't take long."

"Am I being murdered or having a tooth pulled?"

Chapel laughed softly. The bell stopped, which made Matthew's guts churn like a barrel of fresh-caught cod. "Being *disposed* of," the man replied. "As any commodity might be used up and thrown away. That's what all human beings are, really, when you get down to things. Correct?"

"If I said yes, would I and the girl live?"

Again that soft laugh.

"So that's what all this is about?" Matthew saw at the end of the road the vineyard and the arrangement of buildings all constructed from chalkwhite stone. One of the buildings had a small belltower. "Creating commodities for use by Professor Fell?"

"Yes, and for use by anyone willing to pay. Come on, Matthew! Surely you understand how important it is for the . . . how shall I phrase it . . . ?"

"Criminal underworld?" Matthew supplied.

"Brotherhood," said Chapel, "and *sister*hood, also, to replenish itself. We are commodities, too. All our talents make us valuable to different degrees and different worths. Take Billy Hodges, for instance. As I said, he did some wonderful work for us and became an instructor in the screever's art. See that building off to the left, there? Beside the one with the belltower? That would be our primary classroom. Billy taught his pupils in there. Some of them advanced to take other positions in the colonies, where they are waiting for certain signals. Some have been sent to England to work. The same as with all our classes: the art of self-defense, the study of finance, the techniques of human management, the art of communication . . . and on and on until you get to the more defined studies of assassination, arson, blackmail, theft, extortion, cardsharping, dipping, forgery, and—"

"Poisoning?" Matthew interrupted. "How to concoct drugs to kill five innocent people in a Philadelphia tavern?"

"Oh, those five people were unfortunate byproducts of the contract. *Someone* had to drink that wine. We couldn't exactly ruin Swanscott and his business if *no one* was poisoned, could we?"

"Lovely."

"*Necessary*. Don't you see that this is a business? Really, Matthew! This is a business with a great future. It's been sailing along in England and Europe for many, many generations. Now, with the new world opening up and all its potential ahead, we'd be pretty foolish not to want to get in the door too, wouldn't we?" He sighed, because he knew he wasn't making much of an impression. "As for the poisoning, you might be interested to know that when Mr. Nack committed his acts of revenge, only Mr. Deverick had any idea *why* he might be getting his throat cut." He slid a sidelong glance at Matthew to gauge his interest, then went ahead anyway when Matthew showed none. "Ausley only supplied the human commodities, without knowing their exact use. As for Godwin, the doctor was involved with a young whore in London after his wife died. We found out her name was Susan. He fawned over her, and she used him as her *ponce*. Made a real fool out of him, as the tale goes. I suppose he'd do anything to stay around her, for that is the illusion we call love. Me, I would have ripped her gutless and thrown her out a window. But Godwin must have thought himself a noble soul who would someday wean his sweetheart off the throbbing cocks of other men and lead her to a better life. Until she got herself knocked up and he killed both his sweet Susan and the little bastard on the abortion table. An accident, I'm sure. But you know, he was always drawn to the doves. A sad episode in an otherwise exemplary life. However, we thrive on such episodes. They make our business so much simpler. Therefore when we approached the good doctor about making a small batch of poison for us—out of belladonna he purchased at the Smith Street Apothecary, by the way—he was at first very reluctant until we brought all that up about Susan. Could we prove it? Witnesses could be found and letters written, we said." Chapel gave a broad wink. "We have ladies with great imagination and not a little experience. But Godwin was a weak nut. Guilt-ridden and pliable, so not much pressure had to be applied. We were going to kill him ourselves, if he tried to approach the high constable. We would have found someone else. A commodity. You see?"

"A tragedy," Matthew replied.

"A business. Like any other, except . . ." Chapel thought about it. "It made me, a poor but ambitious tinker's son, very wealthy."

The boys suddenly rushed ahead. Ominously so, Matthew

thought. They disappeared around the corner of the belltower building.

"Ah, the ragged schools give us such dedicated pupils," Chapel said, with a hint of wicked delight. "Now listen, do as I say. Run a little bit to get them excited, then lie down. Tell the girl, if she's in any state to hear you. But you won't be able to run very far, anyway."

"What'll you do to us afterward? Throw our bodies in the river?"

"Certainly not. Billy jumped off that cliff over there," and here Chapel motioned in the direction of the Hudson, "before he could be stopped. He was half-blind, as it was. Couldn't see where he was running to or from. Ordinarily, we would have buried him back in the woods where we bury all our mistakes and failures. Which are unfortunately many, as we have very exacting standards, the same as any university. Out of all the candidates sold to us by Ausley, we only pass through about six a year. Now this Ausley situation is a problem. We're going to have to find a replacement for him and get our own representative heading up the girls' orphanage, so we have a lot of work to do the next few months."

Matthew's mind had latched on to something Chapel had just said. "Half-blind? What do you mean, Billy was half-blind?"

"Oh, his eyes were all torn up. The birds, you know."

"The *birds*?"

"That's right. My hawks." And then they turned the corner and there around a large canopy-shaded aviary the pack of boys were waiting. Three of the biggest ones had hooded brown-and-white birds of prey perched on their leather gloves and forearm-guards.

Berry made a sound as if she'd taken a blow to the stomach. Her knees buckled, but the gentlemanly Count shoved her forward with sadistic relish.

"You are one bastard," Matthew said to Chapel, his teeth gritted so hard they were about to break. Chapel shrugged, as if this were a compliment.

"Young men!" Lawrence Evans had picked up a basket and

was passing it around. "Arm yourselves, please. Watch the blades, we don't want any accidents."

The boys, who Matthew noted had removed their colored badges so all were equal in this endeavor, were reaching in and coming up with knives. There was a disturbing variety of blades: short, long, hooked up or down, wide, thin, stubby, elegantly evil. The boys walked around sticking and stabbing the air, some delivering a brutal twist, some slashing as if trying to destroy the last vestiges of childhood before they stepped across the threshold of no return.

They all appeared to have done this before, though several—including the light-fingered Silas—looked just a bit green around the gills. But they too hacked and sliced the air with abandon.

"Your version of the professor's gauntlet," Matthew said to Chapel; or more correctly, heard himself say, as his face and mouth seemed numbed by frost.

"Correct. My version, utilizing a long-cherished hobby. Mr. Greathouse has been schooling you well. He'll be out here soon enough himself, you can mark that." He waited for Dahlgren to shove Berry into earshot, though she still looked too dazed to comprehend their fate. "Mr. Edgar? Where's Mr. Edgar?"

"Here, sir," said a large, stocky young man with close-cropped dark brown hair. He came forward out of the building's shadow cradling a small lamb in the crook of a meaty arm, and in the other hand a wooden bucket that held of all things a paintbrush. Edgar had a slight limp and a pock-marked face, his eyes also dark brown and obviously nervous for he was blinking rapidly. When he reached Chapel, he glanced up and said almost shyly, "Hello, Matthew."

Matthew was struck dumb for a few seconds. Then his mouth moved and he said, "Hello, Jerrod."

"I heard you might be coming out. How've you been?"

"Fine, thank you. And you?"

"I'm all right." Jerrod Edgar nodded. His dull eyes did not show the most intelligence in the world, but Matthew had known him as a decent fellow in 1694, when Matthew was fifteen and Jerrod twelve. Jerrod had unfortunately been the target of some of Ausley's most frequent and intense attentions, and Matthew had watched him withdraw into himself and pull all his shame and anger into the shell with him. Then Jerrod had stolen a burning-glass that Ausley lit his pipe with during one of the punishment sessions, and afterward he was always setting fire to either leaves or donated prayer book pages or grasshoppers or his own plucked-out hair. When another boy had tried to steal it, the boy had left the orphanage for the King Street hospital folded up in a cart and obviously died there, as he'd never returned. "I guess I'm doin' all right," Jerrod repeated, as he gave the lamb to Simon Chapel.

"May I ask what you're doing here?"

"I don't know. Just playin' with fire, mostly. It's what I like."

"Knife, please," Chapel said, to no one in particular.

Matthew saw that the other boys were settling down. They had stopped swinging their blades. Their muscles were warmed up, and they were saving their energy. Matthew looked back into Jerrod's disturbed but fathomless eyes. "Jerrod?" he said quietly.

"Yes, Matthew?"

"Are you going to kill me?"

Evans had brought a hooked knife to his master. Matthew realized it was the exact kind of slaughterhouse implement Kirby had used so well. Chapel stroked the lamb a few times and said, "There, there," to its pitiful call for its mother. Then he drew the head up and back with one hand while the blade in the other sliced the white throat from ear to ear. The bright red blood burst out and flooded into the bucket that Evans had taken from Jerrod and now held steady beneath the torrent.

"Yes, Matthew," said Jerrod. "I suppose I am."

"You don't have to," Matthew told him.

Jerrod cocked his head, listening to the blood spilling into the bucket. The three hawks began to shiver with excitement and clench their claws on the leather gloves, scoring deep grooves even deeper. "I do," Jerrod answered. "If I want to stay, I mean. They're good to me here, Matthew. I'm somebody."

"You always were somebody."

"Naw." Jerrod's mouth smiled, but his eyes did not. "I was never nobody, out there."

Then he looked at Matthew a moment longer, as the convulsing lamb emptied and the bucket filled up and the hawks stirred and made little eerie skreeling noises, and finally Jerrod went over to the basket on the ground to get himself a knife.

Matthew started to go over to stand beside Berry, to say— *exactly what, pray tell?*—something to her to get her mind focused, but suddenly Evans grasped his upper arm and a bloody paintbrush that smelled of old Dutch copper duits was being liberally applied to his face: forehead, cheeks, around the eyes, circling the mouth, down the chin, and done.

One of the hawks, the largest of the birds and perhaps the one that had torn the cardinal to shreds over Matthew's head in the garden that day, twitched its hooded head back and forth and made a soft, high keening noise.

"They're trained to go for the color," Chapel explained, in all earnest seriousness. "Many hundreds of blood-soaked field mice and hares have gallantly given their lives. They smell the odor too, of course, which helps them home onto you, but their eyesight is simply magnificent." He had deposited the lamb's carcass into a black box with a lid on it that he now closed, so as not to give the birds a confusing signal. Lawrence Evans walked over, carrying the gore-bucket to paint Berry's face with the brush. She looked at him as if he were mad, tried to kick him and then strike his head with her own, but had to relent when again Count Dahlgren seized her hair, shoved a fist against her spine, and threatened to break her back before the game even began.

"You'll be given a running start." Chapel walked a few paces away to a horse trough to wash his hands. The boys were striding back and forth, also eager to hunt. No one was laughing and whenever someone spoke the voice was tight and clipped. "To the first row of vines," Chapel continued, motioning toward the sunny field some seventy yards away. "Then I'll signal the handlers to release their birds. It'll take them a few seconds to reach you. They'll see your face as just another bloody little animal, though perhaps a more difficult challenge. They seem to particularly like the eyes. At my discretion, I'll then send the boys. Everyone gets some exercise, everyone gets some experience. Everyone forges a *bond* to his brother. Do you see?"

Matthew was watching Berry shudder as the brush left her face bloodied in the same pattern as his own. The rings around the eyes were the worst. Billy Hodges had leaped to his death not only to escape the blades, but to escape the beaks and claws. "If we're going to die anyway, why should we run?"

"Well, there's no way you can get off the estate because of the wall all around, that's true, but in several instances we've had young men who've fled from the vineyard into the woods and hidden there for a day or so. Sometimes the birds do get tired and distracted and they turn away. We *have* had to go into the woods on hunting expeditions. Very bothersome, but again it's experience. Now: are you sure you want to stand there and die without resistance? Of course I would recommend that you *not* try to get into the woods, as it would simply prolong your inevitable deaths, but if you're interested in perhaps spending a last night communing with your Maker before you go, or hanging on to life as we know it to be, then you *will* give us a good display, won't you?"

Matthew looked at the group of young killers. Nineteen had never seemed so many. Had a few ghosts of previous failures slipped in among them, to rectify their failings? Movement at an upper window of one of the buildings caught his attention. Someone had just pulled a curtain aside and was peering out. An indistinct face. One of the instructors, perhaps? Was that their living quarters?

"Oh . . . one last thing. Mr. Hastings!" To Chapel's summons came a burly, thick-shouldered boy of about seventeen, who carried a knife with a long slim blade. "Clear his pockets, please," Chapel directed. Hastings came up with some coins and the silver watch, which Chapel immediately took charge of. "I'll give you a little time to ready yourselves," he told Matthew, as he wound his new possession.

Matthew walked to Berry's side. She was trembling and tears

had rolled down through her bloodmask, yet her eyes were no longer scorched blue blanks. She was hanging on.

"Listen to me," he said, looking her square in the face. "We have two choices." One of the hawks loudly skreeled. He felt his own nerve quickly ebbing. "We can fall on the ground and wait for them to kill us, or we can run. The hawks are going to be after us first, then the boys. We can cut across the vineyard and try to reach the woods. That way." His gaze ticked to the right. "We might get there. If we can find a place to hide—"

"Where?" Berry asked, with welcome fury in her voice. "Hide *where?"*

"If we can find a place to hide," he continued, "long enough to get these ropes off." How that was to be done without a knife he didn't offer. "We might be able to climb the wall."

"Ready, Matthew? Miss? Ready, young men?" Chapel called. A few of the boys crouched down, Indian-style, with one knee to the ground.

"Keep *going*," Matthew said. "Don't fall." He feared he was losing her, as she blinked heavily and wavered on her feet. *"Berry, listen!"* He heard a raw edge of panic. His arms gave a final convulsive wrench against the cords, which would not be loosened. "Just keep going, do you—"

"Time!" Chapel shouted, and instantly the boys began to shout with voices as sharp as their blades.

Berry set out like a deer, even as Matthew said, "—hear me?" Then he followed right on her heels and immediately tripped over his own feet and fell to his knees to a chorus of frenzied laughter. He hauled himself up, cursing under his breath, and caught up with her. She was running faster and more nimbly than he would have expected, her hair flowing back and her face grim as the grave beneath the blood. He kept pace with her, and though she staggered once and crashed against his side neither of them fell this time but kept going onto the vineyard itself.

As they neared the first vine row, Matthew realized the true vintage on these few acres of Hell was the wine of corruption. The field was overgrown with weeds and the gray clumps of grapes were rotten and shrivelled. A sickly-sweet odor akin to graveyard decay wafted in the sun. He felt the urge to look back but dared not. He cried out, "This way!" and ran along the row toward the green line of forest perhaps another hundred yards distant. A gnarled root caught at his right foot and he pitched forward, out of control for a few seconds before he righted himself. Berry was close beside him, her hair whipping into his face.

A shadow passed over them, followed by a second and a third. The boys were silent, waiting.

Eighty more yards to the woods, Matthew judged it to be. They were still running at full speed. A giddy spark of hope flared in his heart that they would make the forest. He glanced back to see if the boys were coming yet, and the hawk that was swooping down right on top of him spread its wings wide and struck.

forty-seven

MATTHEW THREW HIMSELF ASIDE as the hawk sailed past his right shoulder, its talons grasping at empty air. A second bird of prey came in from the opposite direction, this one moving in a blur, and almost before he could register that it was right there in his face he felt a searing pain across his left cheek and knew he'd been hit.

The third hawk came down almost lazily and grazed Berry's forehead. She gave a wounded cry but her stride never slowed. She kept her head down as another hawk sped by with a high shrill shriek and began to turn a slow circle for its next pass.

Sixty yards to the forest. Suddenly Matthew had feathers in his face and talons jabbing for his eyes. He hunched his shoulders up and head down and felt the sharp claws rip furrows across his left shoulder. There was no time to waste; he had to keep moving, just as Berry was not letting the next attack—even so close as it came to taking out her own left eye—make her lose her speed and determination to live.

Two birds passed close over Matthew's head, one from the right and one from behind. A third darted in, again shrieking, and this time slammed into the left side of Berry's face. As it flew on she stumbled and fell to one knee. Matthew stood over her shouting, *"Get away! Get away!"* as another hawk skimmed her head. She got up, breathing raggedly, and then Matthew looked back and saw the boys coming.

Sunlight glinted off their knives. Three of the smaller and faster boys were already halfway to the first vine row. He saw Simon Chapel watching, standing between Lawrence Evans and Count Dahlgren. Four other adults Matthew did not recognize—three men in suits and tricorn hats and a woman under a dark blue parasol—stood with them. The instructors had emerged to watch their pupils in action. The desire to live caught flame within him. If they could get their wrists free . . .

Berry was up and moving again, still heading toward the forest. Just above her left eye what was lamb's blood and what her own was difficult to tell. Matthew ran after her. A hawk flashed by his face with a noise like bacon sizzling in a pan. An instant later, a pair of talons were scrabbling at his forehead and the fresh pain told him he was going to be cut to pieces out here in the open. A red haze shimmered before his eyes. If he fell or was overcome, he was most certainly dead. The hawk's shriek pierced his ears, but he ducked his head down before further damage could be done.

Forty yards to go, and with every stride the forest neared.

Matthew could imagine what the hawks must have done to Billy Hodges. Three on him at once; it had been a cutting party before the boys had even—

The largest hawk was suddenly upon him. From which direction it had come, he had no clue. It was just there, its wings outstretched as if to enfold him. His instinctive turning of his head and squeezing his eyes shut probably saved him from being blinded, as the claws caught at the front of his coat and the hooked beak, intending to pierce his left lamp, tore flesh a half-inch beside it. The bird's talons ripped shreds of cloth from his suit and through slitted eyes Matthew saw a flurry of beating wings and a blur of red-spark eyes and flashing beak. He was hit again on the cheek just under the right eye, a pain like a burn, and then what felt like a broomstick clobbered him across the back of the head and talons were caught in his hair. He heard himself cry out with pain and abject terror and he did the only thing he could do: he crashed himself headlong into the grapevines with the strength of the damned. As he rolled on the earth, he realized the large hawk was still clutched to his coat and the beak was trying to hook an eye. Matthew desperately twisted his head back and forth, his shoulders hunched and his eyes tightly sealed against the onslaught. Then the bird gave a sudden human-like grunt and near-squeal, and Matthew opened his eyes to see the hawk whirling away on the toe of Berry's shoe.

"Get up!" she shouted. She thrust her foot under his armpit and he got his legs beneath him and stood up. The world spun and the sun burned down but the air had one less predator, for a hawk lay at the base of the grapevines twitching on a broken wing.

Berry ran and Matthew followed. Twenty yards to go. He glanced back and saw sweat glistening on the three faces of the fastest boys, who were about fifty yards behind. Beyond them came the other sixteen.

The pursued were nearly to the woods, which offered no safety but a modicum of cover from overhead attack, when one of the birds swooped down on Berry again with a fierce show of nature's will at work. The creature struck at her forehead, which caused Berry to scream and double over to protect her face but she kept staggering forward. Matthew saw the hawk get tangled in Berry's hair and almost lift her off the ground as it fought itself free. Then it was loose and sailing up into the blue once more, and as Matthew dodged the attentions of the second hawk and it shrieked its indignation the forest took them in.

Yet in the sun-dappled glade there could be no pause, for the shouting of the boys was coming ever nearer. Here the going was rougher, over ancient tree roots and sharp-edged rocks. Matthew thought one of those edges might serve to sever a rope, but there was no time to find out with nineteen killers breathing down their necks.

"This way!" Matthew shouted, and he tore off at an angle to the right between two massive oaks. Berry followed right behind. He had no clear sense of where he was heading, other than to get as much distance between them and the knives as possible. He looked up and saw the two hawks trailing them above the green treetops. All the boys had to do was look to the hawks to mark the progress of their soon-to-be-victims.

There was a gully ahead. Matthew ran along its edge, his eyes searching for any sign of the estate's wall. But how to climb the damned thing, even if it was anywhere near? He ducked under low branches, Berry at his heels, and suddenly one of the hawks flashed past his face. He kept going, into a dense thicket where vines and thorns clutched at his suit. Another hawk came zooming down through the branches and skreeled so loud it was a sure call to the young killers. Matthew realized that even if he and Berry found a place to hide, the hawks would either attack or give them away. There was no stopping.

He heard crashing through the woods over on their left, but he couldn't yet see anyone. Then a damned hawk went screaming over his head and he felt its talons go through his hair like razors.

Suddenly the forest thinned and parted and Matthew and Berry emerged onto the road that led from the vineyard to the main house. As he stood for a second thinking what direction they ought to go, the two hawks flew in almost side-by-side and left Berry staggering from another gash across the cheek. The hawks went up and started circling for a renewed attack. Matthew looked toward the vineyard, then in the direction of the house. He was aware of shouting in the woods behind them and the shadows of the hawks on the road. It came to him that Chapel had asked Lawrence Evans a question: *Who's on the gate today?*

Enoch Speck, sir, was the answer.

On the way out, tell Mr. Speck he may join in the game after he locks up tight.

The gate, Matthew thought. It was unguarded.

The gatehouse had windows.

Glass.

"Come on!" he told Berry, whose face—like his own—was well-marked under the lamb's blood. He began running at full speed toward the house, his knees starting to go wobbly. He could hear her breathing harshly behind him, or was that his own breath? The road curved to the right. A glance back. The pack hadn't yet come out of the woods. Then around the curve, the hawks flew at them again and once more the largest chose Matthew as a target. It came down like the devil's own fury, the beak stabbing for his eyes. He thought he'd been struck again, or at least grazed, but everything was hurting now from chin to hairline and as he ducked his face down he knew it was just a matter of time—and seconds, at that—before a beak or claw rendered him if not completely blind then one-eyed. The hawks climbed, trailing their eerie cries.

Matthew took three more strides and then saw on the road before him the mounds of fresh horse manure he'd stepped into. When he abruptly stopped, Berry slammed into his back.

He had very clearly remembered the taunting voice of Eben Ausley.

You might even scare the carrion birds away with that face, Corbett!

The hawks were circling. Their shadows, growing larger.

"What are you *doing?*" Berry asked through gashed and swollen lips, her eyes bright blue against the glistening red.

They're trained to go for the color, Chapel had said.

"Trust me," Matthew said, and heard his own mangled voice. He dropped to his knees, pressed his lips together, and squeezed his eyes shut. He pushed his face into the pile. When he struggled up again, his face was freighted with a mask of manure.

"You have gone *mad,*" said Berry, who was backing away from him.

"We'll find out," came Matthew's answer, as he looked up and saw the hawks coming down.

Berry realized what he was doing. The hawks were almost upon them, shrieking as they came.

"Oh, *sh*—!" she started to say, but then she dropped down as he had done, leaned forward, and with a muffled groan applied her own grassy brown mask.

The large hawk darted in first, its talons extended. Matthew stood his ground, his eyes half-slitted. He was ready to dodge if his stratagem turned out to be a stinking failure.

The bird's wings spread. It was about to strike. Matthew caught the red gleam of the predator's eyes. He tensed, his heart hammering.

A few feet from Matthew's face, the hawk suddenly pulled its claws in and accelerated. He felt the wind of its passage as it streaked by with a blur of wings. The second hawk skimmed over Matthew's head but its talons had also retracted. Berry got up off the ground, the blood on her face covered by muddy dung. They saw the two hawks make a ragged searching circle above them and then, in the manner of any practical killer, call off the hunt. The birds flew back toward the vineyard, in the direction of their aerie.

If the boys were watching the hawks to lead them, this might offer some time. But very little. "The gatehouse," Matthew said, and together the two dirty crows flew along the road toward the only way out.

There was no one around the house. Dragonflies flitted over the lily pond, which enticed Matthew and Berry to wash their faces yet they both knew there was no time to pause. They kept running past the pond, both of them sweating and their lungs afire. A hundred yards farther on, and there stood the white gatehouse with its multi-paned windows. The gate itself was secured by an iron rod. Matthew tried the gatehouse's door and it swung open. Inside there was a small desk, a chair, and on the wall some clothes pegs. A brown coat hung from one of the pegs, and from another dangled a canteen with a leather strap. Matthew judged how best to break the nearest window. His mind felt sludgy. The upper lid of his left eye was swollen and his lips felt shredded. He said to Berry, "Put your back against mine and stand firm."

In that position he put his foot through the window, careful not to break out all the glass at the bottom. Then, after the explosion of breakage that he thought surely must bring the deathpack running, he said, "Guide me!" and Berry directed him as he twisted his body and leaned backward to rub the cords against the edges of glass.

He worked with haste but not without pain, for glass cut skin as well as rope. If he sliced an artery, all was for nought. He did cut himself but it wasn't bad enough to stop. He just gritted his teeth, shifted his position, and kept sawing.

"That's it!" Berry said. "You've got it!"

Not yet. Damn these cords, they were as strong as Hudson Greathouse's breath.

What are you going to do, moonbeam?

"I'll show you what I'm going to damned do," he said, and Berry asked, "What?" but he shook his head and concentrated on the cutting. Something foul crept into Berry's mouth and she spat violently.

"Keep watch!" he told her, but he thought—hoped—the boys were still searching the woods for them. His shoulders were about to burst from their sockets. Was anything happening? This was like trying to get through the Gordian Knot with a butterknife. *Ow*, that was skin! Come on, come on! Damn the pain, keep cutting!

He wrenched at his bonds. Nothing yet. Then he felt the pressure lessen just a fraction and he sawed with a maniacal fury. He imagined he heard the cords part with a quick *pop*, but whether he'd actually heard that or not, suddenly his wrists were coming unbound and he fought them free. The blood roared back into his hands as the cords fell away. He immediately went to work on Berry's ropes, though his fingers were still mostly long lengths of dead meat.

When Berry's hands were free, she gave a deep sob and began to cry but Matthew caught her filthy, beautiful face by the chin. "Stop that. No time." She stopped. He reached for the canteen, uncorked it, and poured some liquid into his palm but it was not water. Rum, he thought as he took a taste. There had to be some reward for the gate-watcher. He drank a swallow that burned his mind crystal clear and passed it to Berry, who in spite of a glob of horse shit on the canteen's mouth also took a drink. Matthew restrained himself from going through the coat and the desk drawers. He said urgently, "Come on," and led Berry to the gate. The iron rod was not so heavy that one older boy couldn't pull it free from the wooden guides on which it rested. He pulled the gate open.

"Stay off the road," he told her, as he stared into her eyes. "Just keep going, no matter what. I'll be along as soon as I can."

"You're coming too," she said; a statement.

"Not yet. I'm going back for the notebook."

"Matthew! You're mad! They'll—"

"Shut," he ordered. "Don't waste time." He pushed her out with his new-found and much-appreciated hands.

"You can't go back! If they—"

"I'm leaving the gate open. If they see it they'll think we're both out. That's why I say you've got to stay off the road, because they'll send riders. *Go!*"

She hesitated, but only for a few seconds. Then she went, fast as a hare before a hawk.

But sometimes the hares did escape, Matthew thought as he returned to the gatehouse. Especially a hare who did the unexpected. He took a longer drink of rum and saw stars. Going through the coat and the desk drawers, he found nothing useful. Like one of those multiple-barreled death-dealing pistols Ashton McCaggers had told him were being developed in Prussia. He had the feeling he'd been born fifty years too early for this particular occupation. Still, here he was.

If Chapel destroyed that notebook—and he would, as soon as he thought Matthew and Berry had escaped—then all Matthew had to show Gardner Lillehorne was a madman in a cellar.

Get in quickly, break that office door open, and get out quickly. Would someone be guarding the house? Or were they all at the game? What about the women who'd cooked their feast? He could stand here and second-and-third-guess himself to death. He started to take a last drink of courage, but instead he spat some shit out of his mouth and ran toward his fate.

forty-eight

BEFORE MATTHEW VENTURED into the manse he was compelled to kneel beside the lily pond and drink. Then he thrust his face into the water, for his makeup was drawing flies. He got as much of the mess off as he could. His fingers found the wounds of beak-jab and talon-scrape, his left eye was on its way to swelling shut, and there was a gash on his right cheek that felt so deep the bone must have a clawmark on it. A pretty little scar to go with his collection, he thought. At this rate he'd have to wear his own mask to be presentable in public.

But he had his vision and he wasn't dead, nor was he severely wounded enough to *wish* to die. He had his hands back, and that was a blessing. Quick in and quick out, and pray to God they didn't put a boy on the gate before he was done.

It was deadly dangerous to be out here in the open. He heard shouting off in the distance, to the right. They were combing the woods, but it wouldn't be long before they did discover the gate. At any second he expected someone to come running along the road, knife in hand, to take up position on the front steps. He got himself up, his heart pounding so hard it shook his body, climbed the steps, and tried the door. It had not been locked by Chapel or Evans on the way to the game, and Matthew walked into the house. He shut the door behind him. The place was silent. He hurried through the corridor to the dining-room, his senses questing for movement or sound, and there stood before the door that separated him from Chapel's office and the last remaining notebook.

Of course he'd seen it locked, but out of the habit of humans to not trust their eyes Matthew tried the handle. Locked then, locked now.

Now what?

Nothing to be done but the way of the brute. Matthew set himself and kicked the door as hard as he could manage. Then once again, when it wouldn't budge. It seemed colonial oak was equally as strong as the English variety. The thing wasn't opening so easily, and in the bargain the noise would awaken the eyeless failures in Chapel's cemetery.

Matthew desperately looked around. The tall brass candelabras that shed so much light upon the glittering silverware. Their bases looked sturdy enough. He picked one up and found his muscles straining under the weight. This is what a moonbeam can do, he thought. Sir Lancelot he was not, but he backed up nearly the length of the room and held the candelabra's base as a medieval knight might have hefted a jousting lance. If the door didn't give this time, his ribs were going to be caved in.

He set off running. Hit the door under the handle with his makeshift lance and had an instant of feeling impaled upon it. Was that his ribs, making such a cracking sound?

No. It was the door, which burst open and crashed against the wall behind it. The battered thing hung limply on a single hinge. He had felt similarly unhinged after his drugged escapade with Lady LeClaire, who he remembered was a sleeping not-so-beauty at the top of the stairs.

Someone began to clap their hands together.

Matthew caught his breath and spun around, the candelabra still in his arms.

"A wonderful example of how to wreck a perfectly good door, sir," said Simon Chapel. Beside him and behind a few paces stood Count Dahlgren, his face devoid of emotion but the green eyes glittering. "What do you think you're doing, otherwise?"

Matthew couldn't get his tongue working.

"Oh," Chapel said, with a quick mirthless smile. "I see. Returning for the notebook, is that it? Surely. You have nothing without it, correct? Even Mr. Nack knew that." His topaz eyes behind the square lenses ticked right and left. "Your ladyfriend? Where is she?"

"Gone," Matthew said. "Out the gate."

Chapel's mouth may have twisted just a fraction. "Out the *gate*?" He composed himself, like any ambitious son of a poor tinker would. "Well, it's a long way to town, isn't it? A long way also to the nearest farm. We'll find her." He looked Matthew over from dirty shoetips to top of his touselled and claw-ripped hair. "Maybe you *ought* to go to that village in Wales, Matthew. I'm sure the professor would find some use for an escape artist of your caliber. And you got out of the cords, too! Fascinating. But some of the boys are just out front and their knives are very hungry, so you can tell me how you gave my birds the shake while we—"

He was interrupted, quite firmly, by a shouting and hollering outside the house that even Matthew could tell was not rough-housing boys eager for a killing. There was some panic in the voices that went up and up like the hawks fleeing bitter earth. "What is *that*?" Chapel said to Count Dahlgren, and he was answered not by the Prussian but by the *crack* of a pistol shot.

"Sir! Sir!" It was Lawrence Evans, shouting from the doorway. "Someone's gotten in!" The voice was high and thin, squeezed by fear. "Riders!"

Chapel shivered. In an instant his face went pallid, as if he were freezing to death.

"Mr. *Chapel*!" Evans squawled, and now could be heard through the open door and along the corridor a small thunder of horse hooves, more panicked shouting, and a second pistol shot that made the master of the house shake in his shoes as if his little world had suddenly been knocked out of the sky by one of Increase Mather's comets.

Chapel turned like a force of nature, however wounded, and grasped the front of Dahlgren's beige coat to shove the man aside.

But then he glanced back at Matthew, his face contorted and saliva glistening at the corners of his mouth. Beneath the mask of a gentleman was a mad dog. He said to Dahlgren, "Cut him to pieces."

Chapel rushed from the room along the corridor, and Dahlgren suddenly moved with the speed of quicksilver to draw a sword from one of the displays beside the fireplace.

Matthew glanced toward the doors that led out to the terrace and the garden. They were shrouded by the wine-red drapes. He thought that if he had to spend more than two seconds trying to get through the drapes and the doors, he'd be skewered in the back. Even if he made it, he would die amid the flowers.

Dahlgren was advancing. The sounds of conflict outside the house made no impression upon him; his orders had been given.

Matthew had to move. He thrust forward with the candelabra, aiming at Dahlgren's chest. The Count nimbly stepped aside, grabbed the knight's lance with one hand, and tore it out of Matthew's grip, at the same time bringing the rapier's deadly point up in a strike at Matthew's belly.

Matthew backpedalled out of range. Dahlgren followed, throwing aside the candelabra with Prussian disdain. Abruptly Matthew found himself pushed back against the other display of swords on his side of the fireplace. His hand chose a rapier before his brain could tell him it was a stupid thing to do, yet he pulled the weapon free. Instantly Dahlgren went into a combat posture, turning his body to make a thinner target and putting his free hand behind him like a rudder, knees bent but not too much, feet spaced for balance, hand closed firmly around the sword's grip and the thumb locked down. All the damned things Greathouse had tried to teach, Matthew thought grimly.

He knew he had not the chance of a spit in a skillet to survive the next minute, let alone a concentrated attack. When Dahlgren realized he was facing a moonbeam, the headstone carver ought to get his chisel.

Someone was out there. Riders, Evans had said. How many? Two pistol shots and pandemonium. If rescuers had somehow arrived, he had to live long enough to be rescued.

To bluff was his only option. He emulated Dahlgren's posture. What was the bastard looking at? His sword? No, his eyes. Reading the fear in them? Matthew stared also into Dahlgren's eyes, which now held a spark of interest. With sweat oozing from his pores he waited for the next thrust even as he shifted carefully to the left.

Dahlgren's sword struck. A feint. Too late, Matthew reached out to check it and was off-balance. The blade hissed in, twisted, and struck at Matthew's face like a viper's tongue. Matthew jerked his head aside and stumbled backward, but now Dahlgren was coming in on him with a death's-head grin.

In panic, Matthew threw his sword like a spear even as he realized the action would stamp him as a rank pretender. Dahlgren reached out with his own blade and casually flicked the flying sword aside. It clattered across the silverware on the table. At once Matthew had bounded back to the array of weapons and pulled another one out. Dahlgren was almost upon him, the sword's point rising toward Matthew's throat. Matthew braced his legs—to hell with the form—and knocked the point aside. Dahlgren's arm seemed to rotate with supernatural speed and again the rapier's tip was a flash of steel, this time aimed at Matthew's chest. Matthew dodged in an ungainly sprawl but was not quick enough, for the sword tore through the cloth of his right upper arm. When the point came out, there was blood on it but Matthew was beyond feeling pain. He stepped forward, his teeth clenched and his face a rictus of terror. He lunged at Dahlgren's face but in the next instant his rapier was broken in half and his wrist almost with it.

Matthew pulled a third sword free. As he was turning to face the Count, the enemy's rapier tip almost pierced his nose. He ducked down and scrambled away to give himself room.

Dahlgren followed.

Matthew tensed, his nerves screaming. Dahlgren made a quick feint to the right, but Matthew was too slow to respond and didn't go for it. Then Dahlgren's knees bent a little more, and Matthew knew the next attack was coming. He backed up and hit the table.

Dahlgren's rapier tip moved slowly from right to left, with mesmerizing effect.

Matthew took an instant to dare a glance at the table. Dahlgren sprang forward, but Matthew had already seen and picked up Chapel's silver pepper bowl with his left hand. He threw the contents into the swordsman's eyes.

Dahlgren cried out and threw an arm across his face, the sword thrust went wild over Matthew's right shoulder, and for a second Matthew had the clear image of a chessboard where his next move had to be offensive. He took a rapid measure of distance followed by a single quick lunge toward his opponent. The point of his sword pierced cloth and entered Dahlgren's chest on the right side. It was not the same as striking a bale of hay; this was more like sticking a side of beef. Dahlgren wrenched himself backward off Matthew's sword and kept going back, his own rapier thrusting left, right, and center in a blur and his free hand working to clear his eyes.

Matthew rushed upon the man. He swung with all his strength, intending to hit Dahlgren on the side of the head. There was a brittle *clang* as the two swords met and half of his broken rapier again flew across the room. Dahlgren blinked rapidly but his eyes though shot with red were cleared. He swung a back-handed blow at Matthew, who once more fell against the table with a grip and eight inches of rapier in his hand.

Dahlgren sneezed pepper from his nostrils. His chest convulsed. He spat bright blood upon the floor, and then settled himself into his formal combat posture.

Matthew dropped the broken blade, picked up a silver plate full of chicken bones, and threw it at him. The plate passed over the man's head and crashed against the fireplace bricks. A second thrown plate glanced off his shoulder. Matthew reached to the table a third time and brought up a knife, still glistening with chicken grease.

Dahlgren retreated to the nearest array of swords and slid free a second rapier.

Matthew looked dumbly at his own little chicken-skinner. His fingers opened, it fell to the table, and he retrieved his original sword that lay amid the carnage of lunch.

The Prussian advanced, the two swordpoints making small circles in the air. Outside the house there was a third pistol shot, and now from beyond the corridor came the noise of fighting: the smack of a blow against flesh followed by a shrill cry of pain.

Dahlgren came in like a juggernaut, his face perfectly composed and a red thread of blood spooling from his lower lip.

One rapier thrust high while the second thrust low. Matthew parried the first without losing his own sword, but the other blade was aimed at his groin. There was no way to escape it without growing wings. He twisted his body for protection and was almost gratified when the rapier slid into the flesh of his left thigh. He'd thought he was beyond pain, but this nearly paralyzed him. A grunt escaped his lips, fresh sweat bloomed on his forehead, and he struck with his own blade into the Prussian's face. Dahlgren jerked his head aside but his lung wound was telling; the tip of Matthew's sword went through the man's right ear and just that quickly Dahlgren gasped for air and stumbled backward. Matthew's sword left the wounded ear and Dahlgren's blade retreated from the wounded thigh.

Then Dahlgren began to circle, keen for another opportunity. His back was to the open door of Chapel's office. He made feinting motions with both rapiers, watching for Matthew to react. Blood was welling up on Matthew's breeches leg, and as he backed away he feared his strength was a short-lived proposition.

Dahlgren took a quick stutter-step toward Matthew with the tips of both rapiers crossed, and that was when a figure with a black and swollen face came screaming and staggering out of the doorway behind him and grabbed him around the shoulders in agonized supplication.

Matthew saw his chance while the Prussian tried to fight off the nearly deranged Miss LeClaire. He thinned his body in the way Greathouse had told him and lunged as best he could with one thigh feeling like a melon. Dahlgren battled his blade away even as the man struggled to get loose from his encumbrance. The swords clashed and rang and Miss LeClaire shrieked like a cat on fire. Matthew struck high and low and high again and always the two blades were there to defend, yet Dahlgren could neither shift his position nor attack with the baggage hanging off him. Then the Count threw one sword away, turned, and seized the woman. With a shout that might have been a Prussian oath, he ran her through stomach to back. He pushed her off his blade with a disinterested boot and still parried Matthew's next strike. Miss LeClaire stumbled against Matthew, who swung at Dahlgren's head and was rewarded by having his sword knocked from his hand. It spun away as the lady crumpled to her knees and pitched forward onto the remains of her beauty.

Dahlgren's face was contorted, the blood coming up through his coat. Perhaps eager to finish his opponent, he now charged Matthew not with the cool logic of a swordsman but with the fury of a wild animal. The sword flashed at Matthew's ribs. He sidestepped the wicked point, grabbed at Dahlgren's rapier arm to pin it, and drove his fist into the man's face. Bloody spittle flew from the mouth. They locked together and fought at close quarters. Matthew saw the green eyes, flamed with red, right in his face. He slammed his fist again into Dahlgren's mouth, splitting the upper lip, and then he too received a stunning blow to the side of his head from the hilt of Dahlgren's sword.

In this blurred and frantic struggle, as Matthew's knees threatened to give way and he hung on to the sword arm for dear life, he saw Dahlgren's free hand start to go up under the man's waistcoat. And with that betraying motion he knew.

Before the hand could reach its destination, he gave Dahlgren an uppercut on the chin that rocked the man's head back. He took another blow from the rapier's hilt that made a red haze briefly blind him, and suddenly he was falling across the table and dragging the gentleman's silverware with him in an ungodly crash of platters, trays, and soup bowls. He lay on the floor on his stomach amid the debris, his arms pinned up underneath. When Matthew sat up with bells ringing and beasts roaring in his head, Dahlgren was staggering around the table after him, his rapier ready for the kill and blood drooling from his mouth.

Matthew stood up.

He shoved a chair at Dahlgren but it was kicked aside. Then Matthew flung himself at the man even as the rapier thrust, its tip penetrating Matthew's coat but luckily no flesh. Again he caught the sword arm and again they fought face-to-face, Matthew battering at Dahlgren's head, Dahlgren trying to get in a blow with the rapier's hilt and clawing at Matthew's face with his other hand. They caromed off the table and went 'round and 'round like battling tops.

As Matthew fought for his life, he had one thing in mind.

Something Hudson Greathouse had said.

You'll someday cross swords with a villain who'll long to get a short blade in your belly. You'll know him, when the time comes.

Matthew knew him.

He saw Dahlgren's left hand go under the waistcoat. He grabbed at the wrist to trap it, but another blow from the hilt rattled his brains. Where was Dahlgren's hand? Panic flared in him. Where was—

Suddenly Dahlgren's hand emerged. It had six fingers, one formed of steel and deadly sharp.

With a whuff of air and a burst of demonic strength, the Count drove his hidden dagger squarely into Matthew's stomach.

There was a sudden loud *crack*. No more, no less.

Dahlgren screamed like a woman. He fell back, the dagger dangling and then dropping from the hand that hung off a broken wrist. His rapier also clattered to the floor. His eyes were wide with shock, and perhaps they widened even farther when Matthew reached under his own waistcoat and pulled out the silver fruit tray—about the size of an open hand—that he'd slid down to protect his belly from the dagger attack that Greathouse had warned him in the wisdom of experience to anticipate.

One thing could be said about Dahlgren, Matthew thought. The man certainly kept his thumb locked down.

Dahlgren shook his head back and forth, his damp blond hair standing up like horns. Matthew took the opportunity to smash the fruit tray into his face. When Dahlgren retreated a few paces and made a dazed circle with the broken wrist clutched to his chest, Matthew hit him again. Then a third time, and the Prussian fell into the wine-red curtains that hung over the garden doors but due evidently to his status as a grenadier did not allow himself to fall. Matthew dropped the fruit tray back into the silver debris from whence it had come. He tore the curtains off their hooks and wrapped them around the man's head. Then, moving slowly and painfully but with definite purpose, he managed to pick up a chair and with it clouted Count Anton Mannerheim Dahlgren a final soul-satisfying blow that sent the swordsman crashing out the doors and over the terrace railing into the goldfish pond, where he sputtered and feebly kicked beneath his wrappings.

Matthew fell to his knees.

It couldn't have been very long before he could move again, because though the commotion out front had subsided there were still shouts and an occasional curse to be heard. He crawled to Charity LeClaire and ascertained from her moaning that she was still alive, and if she lived long enough to think about it she would surely reconsider her purpose in this world.

He got to his feet and unsteadily went through the corridor.

Lying in the doorway was Lawrence Evans with a huge blue bruise at the center of his forehead. His nose was also pretty much a pulp. A knife was on the floor near his right hand. Sitting not far away with his own hand pressed to a circle of blood on the shirt at his left shoulder was Dippen Nack, whose nose was covered with a white plaster and both eyes dark-shadowed courtesy of Matthew's fist. The black billyclub rested beside him, a good afternoon's work done.

Matthew thought he'd taken too much of a beating, for surely he was seeing what was not there. He blinked and looked again.

Nack growled, "What the damned hell are *you* lookin' at?"

Matthew walked on, stepping over Evans' body into the sunlight.

The battle that had raged in front of the house was over, though the dust raised by hooves and boots still lingered. It was clear to see who had won and who had lost. Standing with hands upraised were the boys—at least, the ones who were not on the ground nursing injuries—and standing victorious around them with hatchets, cudgels, and swords were some of the very constables Matthew had thought to be so moronic at their tasks. He counted eight men. No, two more were just coming along the road, herding five boys at the point of axe and musket. A dozen or so horses either nervously pranced around or calmly grazed in the grass along with the sheep, oblivious to the conflicts of men.

Matthew peered through the drifting dust and saw a diminutive man who wore a canary-yellow suit and tricorn hat and held a pistol limply at his side. He was standing over a body.

As Matthew approached, Gardner Lillehorne glanced up at him with wounded eyes. In the harsh light, his skin was pale white and his dyed hair pulled into a queue with a yellow ribbon was more blue than black. He looked down again upon the body, and when he spoke his voice was crushed. "I had to shoot him. He wouldn't stop coming at me. He's . . . not dead, is he?"

Matthew knelt down. The ball had entered very near Jerrod Edgar's heart. The boy's eyes were open, but his flame was out. A large knife was still gripped in the right hand.

Matthew stood up, wincing as a pain rippled through his wounded thigh. "He's dead."

"I thought so. I just . . . didn't . . ." Lillehorne stopped speaking for a few seconds, and then tried again. "I didn't want to kill anyone," he said.

"Chapel," Matthew said, dazed by the loss of blood and the strange illusion that he was actually feeling sympathy for the high constable. "What happened to Chapel?" He ran a hand over his forehead. "What are you *doing* here?"

"Kirby," Lillehorne replied. "He told me everything. I got as many constables as I could find. Brought us here. My God, Matthew!" He blinked heavily, looking around at the boys who were being told to sit down with their legs crossed underneath them and their hands cupped behind their necks. "They're so *young*!"

They were young once, Matthew thought but he didn't say it. Perhaps a long time ago. The hardship, cruelty, and violence of the world had begun their education. Ausley and Chapel had refined it. Professor Fell had put it to use. And as Jerrod Edgar had said, *I was never nobody, out there.*

"Where's Kirby?" Matthew asked, and was answered by a half-hearted motion from the high constable, directing Matthew toward the road to the vineyard.

Matthew set off.

Not long after, he came upon the body of Simon Chapel, stretched out on his belly in the dust of the road. Possibly interrupted on his journey to get a horse from the stable, Matthew thought. Just as Lawrence Evans might have been interrupted by Dippen Nack on his way to get the last notebook or some of the more sensitive papers in that file cabinet. On Chapel's left temple was a black bruise about three inches long. The face had been severely deformed by either fists or, more likely, a pair of boots. It was far from lovely, and in fact Matthew's gorge rose at the sight of such a mess that a human face might become. But there was no pool of blood around the throat, and as Chapel's raw lips moved and made incoherent sounds it was clear he had not yet departed the earthly scene.

"I wanted to kill him," said Kirby, who sat on the other side of the road in the shade of a tree. A black horse with a white face stood nearby, grazing. Kirby had drawn his knees up to his chin and was holding the blackjack. "I gave Lillehorne my knife before we left. But I could have picked up a knife here, from one of the boys. I could have cut his throat, very easily."

Matthew walked over to him, if just to get away from the sight of the large green flies crawling over the bloodmask that Chapel's face had become.

Kirby said, "Pollard described him for me. So I'd know him. You see . . . I followed you from the office. I was going to go with you. To see Lillehorne. Then I watched Pollard and that other man stop you. When I saw Pollard take the notebook . . . I knew. I followed him back to the office, and I had a talk with him." Kirby's eyes closed and he leaned his head back against the treetrunk. Sweat sparkled on his forehead and cheeks.

"Where is he now?"

"Dear Joplin? My dear tavern pal? Well, first . . . before he talked he fell down a flight of grandmotherly stairs. Then . . . *after* he talked, my good pal shattered both his knees on a pair of fireplace tongs." He opened his eyes and stared at Chapel's body. "I made sure I got to him, before anyone else, because I *was* going to kill him. Beat him to death, if I had to. But I stopped beating him." He frowned, thinking. "Why did I stop, Matthew? *Why?*"

Matthew also took some time to consider. "Because," came his answer, "you know that from this point on Justitia will see Simon Chapel and his crimes very clearly, and by murdering him you only kill yourself a little more."

"Yes," Mrs. Swanscott's son said. He nodded. "That must be it."

Matthew eased himself to the ground in the treeshade. He was drowsy, the sleep of exhaustion pulling at him. Yet where was Berry? Was she all right? He didn't know. He had to trust that she was. But what about all the boys? Had everyone been captured? What about the instructors? Was there anyplace all these people could be confined until a trial? It would be Lillehorne's worst nightmare . . . if he could get over the bad dreams of shooting down a young man who in his soul had probably welcomed the release of death.

It was a strange place, this world that men had made. The new world perhaps even more strange than the old.

The sun of a summer afternoon shone down, the birds sang, the yellow butterflies flitted, and the green flies buzzed.

Matthew lay back in the shadowed grass, closed his eyes, and let himself rest for just a little while.

forty-nine

THE DOCTORS WERE WAITING.

One stood composed and steady, the other nervously puffing his pipe. Who could tell what this would accomplish? Still, it had to be tried and both doctors were in accord.

The afternoon's golden light spilled through the open window. In her high-backed purple chair, the Queen of Bedlam—a small woman, fragile in her pink homegown—sat as she always did, viewing the garden without comment or change of expression from moment to moment.

Matthew Corbett walked into the room.

He was dressed suitably for the long ride from New York. The tan-colored breeches, white shirt, and stockings were brand-new. So too were his dark brown riding boots, fashioned for him by the shoemaker Bulliver Martin. It helped to have a good-paying job in New York. Alas, he'd been unable to collect the ten shillings from Esther Deverick, for even though he'd put an end to the Masker's career and the Clear Streets Decree, her condition of being the first informed had not been met. In this case, he would rather be alive than have ten shillings thrown on his grave.

'Twas a pity, then, that his discovery of the Masker's identity and the subsequent story as it appeared in the *Earwig* meant that Deverick's widow could not pack her belongings soon enough for the voyage back to England. The residents of Golden Hill of course appreciated money, but they did not appreciate a murder plot. At least, one that had been found out and so shamefully printed for all eyes both noble and common to read. *So, farewell Mrs. Deverick!* read a letter in the following week's *Earwig*.

> *Take your black gowns bought with even blacker money and depart from us so that we might breathe afresh once more, and that the honest business persons of this town might know what it means when greed and corruption are placed on a higher pedestal of value than the law of God, Queen, and Country.*
>
> *I Beg Our Lord Grant You A Safe And Rapid Journey To Your Final Destination.*
>
> > *Yours Sincerely,*
> > POLLY BLOSSOM

It was perhaps a bit harsh, and glided over the concept that Mrs. Deverick had been completely unaware of her husband's dark adventure. Yet also Mrs. Deverick had been the most ferocious wind at work trying to blow Reverend Wade from Trinity Church, so without her Machiavellian turbulence that particular ship failed to sail.

Of the long-suffering Robert Deverick, however, there was a different story.

Matthew walked to Mrs. Swanscott's side. He favored his left leg a bit, but the infection from the swordbite in his thigh had been caught and drained, the swelling subsided, and Dr. Vanderbrocken—who had decided a retirement of playing the violin and otherwise fiddling around did not suit his fiery nature—had declared him out of danger and whacked him on the back of his head for even causing him to consider the amputation saw. Of Matthew's other wounds, there was not much to speak of if one did not mention the large medical plaster that covered the nasty gash just beside his left eye, the second and third smaller plasters on both cheeks, sundry scuffs, scrapes, and bruises and the strong odor of comfrey-and-garlic ointment that lubricated the healing gashes beneath the plaster on his forehead. Would he bear any further battle scars? The question asked of Vanderbrocken had caused the ill-tempered but highly efficient doctor to glare at Matthew over his spectacles and say, *Do you wish to bear any further scars, young man? If you don't shut up about scars, keep the wounds clean, and use that ointment as I tell you, I'll give you the damnedest battle you ever fought.*

The worst pain, if one wished to speak of pain, was not the sword cut on his right arm—for that was fortunately a shallow nick and not worth troubling—but underneath the comfrey-and-garlic damp bandage at his left shoulder where one of the hawks had torn through his coat cloth and shown in an instant how a cardinal could become nothing but a whirl of red feathers. It was also healing, but Vanderbrocken wanted to check that wound most often, as it was bone-deep and did cause Matthew to clench his teeth sometimes when it hurt like a screaming bastard usually in the middle of the night. The same arm, he knew so well, that Jack One Eye had thoroughly busted three years ago. He was going to be living on the starboard yet.

Otherwise, he was in tip-top health.

He had the fear, as he stood beside Mrs. Swanscott and she stared dreamily at the garden beyond, that this mass of plasters, scrapes, and bruises normally called "a face" would so frighten the woman that she might forever lose the power of speech. He glanced at the two doctors. Ramsendell nodded, while Hulzen looked anxiously on and pipesmoke billowed from his mouth.

Matthew said quietly, "Mrs. Swanscott?"

The Queen of Bedlam blinked, but she did not shift her gaze from the flowers and the butterflies. Matthew knew: it was all she had.

"Madam Emily Swanscott?" he repeated. "Can you hear me?"

She could. He knew it. Had her color changed, just slightly? Had her skin tone begun to turn more pink, starting with the ears?

"Emily?" Matthew asked, and gently put a hand on her shoulder.

Her head abruptly turned. Her eyes were wet, though still

without true focus. Her mouth opened, but no words emerged. She closed her mouth, drew a long breath, and Matthew realized that somewhere inside her a voice of reason might be saying *I will ask this question for the last time, the very last time, before I go away forever.*

One tear rolled down her right cheek.

Her face was impassive. Regal. Her mouth opened, as if by superhuman effort of will.

"Young man," she said, in a strained whisper, "has the *King's Reply* yet arrived?"

Matthew answered. "Yes, madam. Yes, it has."

And on that signal, Trevor Kirby entered his mother's room.

He had been made handsome again, in a gray suit with black pinstripes and a gray waistcoat. The suit of a successful lawyer, donated by the Herrald Agency. The black, highly glossed shoes, likewise. Hudson Greathouse had thrown a fit, but Matthew was adamant and when Matthew got adamant time ceased to move on the silver watch he'd retrieved from Simon Chapel's battered body. The watch had also taken a licking, but . . .

It still worked.

With a bath, a shave, a hair trim, some decent food, and a few nights—and days—of relatively peaceful sleep, Trevor had lost some if not all of the gaunt fever in his eyes and the hollowed-out sharpness of his cheekbones. He looked to all the world, with his thick black hair combed, his fingernails clean, and his stride purposeful, as far from being a thrice-time murderer as Simon Chapel from being a university's headmaster.

Matthew saw Trevor's purposeful stride falter, in spite of what Trevor had planned to do when he came into the room. He stopped, a cloud of indecision passing across his face. His gaze caught Matthew's, and only Matthew would know the depth of shame and anguish that he saw displayed there in Trevor's eyes.

Mrs. Swanscott gave a gasp. She was looking past Matthew at the apparition. Her spine seemed to go rigid for a few seconds, as she clenched and released and clenched and released the armrests of her chair.

Then, slowly, she relinquished her throne and began to stand up.

As she stood, her eyes streamed the waters that had been dammed up by the mind's necessity, and she said, very clearly, "*My boy.*"

Ramsendell and Hulzen stepped forward to catch her if she fell, for she trembled so violently all in the room feared it. Yet she stood steady and firm, like a willow that bends and bends but does not, never, ever, never does it break.

Without a word Trevor came the rest of the way, and Matthew always would remember that it was not far, but oh it was such a distance.

Son clasped mother, and mother laid her head against her son's shoulder and sobbed. Trevor wept also, unashamed and unafraid, and if any man had said there was not true blood between them, Matthew would have struck him down even if it had been ten times a Hudson Greathouse.

He had to turn away, go to the window, and stare out at the same garden that had been the lady's salvation. The Queen of Bedlam was no more; God rest her.

"I think," Ramsendell said as he came up beside Matthew, "that I'll go fetch everyone some tea."

In time, Trevor helped his mother into a chair beside the bed and pulled a second chair over for himself. He held both her hands between his, and listened while she dreamed awake.

"Your father," she said. "He's gone for a walk. Out just a little while." Fresh tears welled up. "He's been so worried lately, Trevor. It's because of . . . because of . . . the . . ." A hand floated like a butterfly to her forehead. "I can't . . . think very well today, Trevor. I'm so sorry."

"It's all right," Trevor answered, his voice infinitely kind and even more patient. "It's I who am sorry. For not coming when I said I would. Can you forgive me?"

"*Forgive . . . you?*" she asked, as if puzzled by the very thought. "What is there to forgive? You're here now. Oh . . . my throat is so dry. I can hardly speak, it's so dry."

"Tea," said Ramsendell, as he offered both of them a cup.

Mrs. Swanscott looked at the doctor and frowned, trying to make out who he was. Then she cast her gaze around the room and even Matthew could tell that some image in her mind was coming loose from its scroll. Unravelling, like a long spool of thread along a dark and unknown corridor. To find her way back to what she knew, she simply stared at Trevor and took a sip of tea. "Your father," she tried again, when the tea had gone down, "will be back soon. Out walking. A lot on his mind right now."

"Yes, I know!" Trevor said.

"Look at you!" A smile came out, though the sadness in her face would not be banished. "How *handsome* you are! Tell me . . . how is Margaret?"

"Margaret is fine," he decided to say.

"A beautiful day." She had turned her head so as to view the garden once more. "The baby is buried right out there. My little one. *Oh.*" Something had struck her deeply, for she lowered her head and her shoulders sagged as if under a tremendous, crushing weight. She remained in that posture, as everyone in the room waited.

"Just stay as you are," Ramsendell suggested, keeping his voice casual.

Fifteen or twenty seconds crawled by. Then suddenly Mrs. Swanscott took a breath as if she had forgotten how to breathe, lifted her head, and smiled at her son, her eyes scorched and empty. "Your father is out walking. Soon, very soon. You can tell him all about Margaret. *Oh.*" Matthew had thought it was another strike of anguish, but Mrs. Swanscott had just touched Trevor's knee. "Your sea voyage. The *King's Reply*. Was it a comfortable ship?"

"Yes, very comfortable."

"I'm glad. Now . . . you were coming to visit for . . . I can't think clearly, Trevor. Really. I'm getting so old they're going to have to put me in a box."

"Mother?" He took her teacup, put it aside, and again held both her hands in his. "Listen to me."

"All right," she said. Then, when he hesitated: "Well, what is it?"

"It's about me, Mother."

"All right."

He leaned closer. "I'm not going to be able to stay very long. I have some business to attend to. Do you understand?"

"Business? No, I don't understand business. Your father does. He . . ." She had obviously run onto the rocks again, for she went silent and staring for a few seconds before she recovered. "You *are* a lawyer," she told him. "Your father is very, very proud of you."

"And I am proud of our family," Trevor replied. "Of what we have accomplished together. We've come a long way, haven't we?"

"A long walk? Yes, but he'll be back soon," she said.

Trevor looked at the two doctors for help, but they had become simply mute witnesses as had Matthew. It was up to Mrs. Swanscott's son to find the way home.

"Father may be late," he said.

She did not respond.

"Father . . . may not come back." He quickly added, "For a while, that is."

"He'll come back. Of *course* he'll come back."

"Mother . . . something may have happened. Something that was . . . very bad. An accident, perhaps. I don't know, I'm just saying. Something may have happened."

A finger went to Trevor's lips. "Shhhhh," she said. "You don't know. Ask anyone. Ask Gordon, he can tell you. When Nicholas goes for a walk, it's because . . . it's because he has to *think*. About a problem. Some problem that's troubling him. A trouble, that's it. He's gone for a walk because there's been . . ." She swallowed thickly. "There's been some trouble."

"Yes," Trevor said. "Do you know what the trouble *is*?"

"I don't . . . know. There's something . . . the wine was . . ." She shook her head, trying to cast a recollection away. "Nicholas has been very worried lately. The lawyer was here. That Mr. Primm. I think . . . he *did* stay for dinner, yes. He said . . ." Here she winced, as if she'd been physically struck, and it took her a little while and an effort to continue. "He said we have to prove it. Prove it. Very important, he said. To prove it." She suddenly looked at her hands and spread her fingers. "Oh my," she said. "My rings need to be cleaned."

"Mother? Look at me. Please."

She lowered her ringless hands and obeyed.

"Do you see that young man over there?" Trevor motioned toward Matthew.

"Yes." Mrs. Swanscott leaned closer to her son and whispered, "Speaking of accidents."

"His name is Matthew Corbett. He's a friend of mine, Mother. Now, as I said I'm going to be very busy here for a while. Very much . . . tied up. I won't be able to see you as often as I'd like. I may not be here again." He caught the ripple of dismay on her face. "I mean, for . . . who knows how long?"

"You're a very busy and successful lawyer," she said. "Every penny worth it."

"Matthew is going to come and see you, from time to time. He'll sit with you and listen if you want to talk, or talk if you'd like to listen, or read to you if you'd like that." He gave her hands a squeeze. "I want you to know," he went on, "that when Matthew is sitting beside you, I also am there. When he is reading to you, so I am, and when you speak to him I hear. Can you understand that?"

"I think you're a little brain-addled after that long trip." She pulled a hand free and gently touched his cheek. "But if it makes you happy, and you're so busy, then yes. Your father and I certainly won't mind if a friend of yours comes to the house from time to time. Will he want to stay for dinner?"

Matthew heard, and replied, "Yes, madam. I would."

"He's not a freeloader, is he?" This question was directed to Trevor in a whisper.

"No, he's quite respectable."

"Good. Well, he *would* be, wouldn't he? If he's a friend of yours?" She stroked his cheek, as Matthew thought perhaps she had when he was a small, smart, and industrious boy and she saw all the possibilities ahead. "It *is* late, isn't it?" she asked.

"Late, Mother?"

"Late for *me*. I'm such an old dotty. But you . . . you have everything wonderful ahead of you. Your life, and Margaret. And *children* of your own, don't forget that. What you might become, Trevor. The man you shall grow to be. You know, your father's still a boy in so many ways. I think he shall never fully grow up. How can it be, that you and he are so alike?"

"I don't know," came the answer. "I only know I loved . . . I love Father, and I love you. And I shall always love the both of you, and hold you the highest in my heart."

"Oh!" She playfully cuffed his chin. "That's what all sons say, until they have sons of their own."

Trevor lowered his head for a moment. Matthew knew then why he could get away with hiding behind the mask of Andrew Kippering who hid behind the Masker, because when Trevor looked up at his mother again he was smiling as if he had no care under God's heaven. He kissed her cheek, and she said, "I think I'd better go to bed. I'm so tired from all this."

All this was not explained, but Trevor helped her into bed as the two doctors watched. When Trevor got her situated and the covers pulled up, she smiled at him and held his hand. "Promise me," she said.

"Promise you what?"

"Promise me . . . you'll go to the kitchen and ask Priscilla to make you some chicken soup before you leave."

"Oh, I can't leave without a bowl of Priscilla's chicken soup, can I?"

"Perish the thought," said Mrs. Swanscott, in a voice that was beginning to drift. "When I wake up," she said, "everything . . . will be so much brighter. Don't you think?"

"Yes, Mother. Much brighter."

"One can only hope," Matthew heard her say, in nearly a whisper. Then she sighed, let go of Trevor's hand, and just that quickly she was gone.

Ramsendell and Hulzen came to the bedside, but only to check her breathing and make sure her chamberpot was within easy reach. Ramsendell rubbed the back of his neck. "A long way to go, but at least now we know in which direction."

Trevor was on his feet. "Will she ever recover? I mean . . . back to how she was?"

"Debatable. I really don't know. We shall have to begin slowly, of course. First of all, to let her understand where she is and who *we* are. Then we'll approach the loss of Mr. Swanscott, but only when we're sure she can accept it. That may be a long and difficult task for all of us. But I think it's a very good idea for Mr. Corbett to return and spend time with her. That's something I'm sure she'll look forward to and see as a . . . well . . . as a visit from *you*, since you put it so eloquently."

Trevor nodded. He had turned his face away from the bed, and regarded the doorway with grim resignation. At last he said, "All right. I'm ready." Before he left he kissed his sleeping mother on the forehead, and then he preceded Matthew from the room.

Outside, the wagon was waiting. Wearing a riding suit the color of cream with a bright red vest and a cream-hued tricorn accented by a red feather, Gardner Lillehorne was standing next to his horse at the hitching-post. Matthew's horse Dante was also tied at the post. Up on the wagon, the driver and a constable named Uriah Blount were ready to receive the prisoner. Lillehorne had the manacles and chains in hand. They jangled with heavy finality as Lillehorne walked to meet Trevor Kirby.

"May I ask that Mr. Kirby not be manacled?" Matthew asked when Trevor thrust his wrists out.

The small black eyes flashed. "And why not, sir? Because your heart is bleeding?"

"No, because I think it's unnecessary. Mr. Kirby has vowed to cause no trouble. We should take him at his word."

"Oh, is that why he was manacled on the trip *here*, sir? Because we took him at his word?"

"Do me the favor," Matthew said flatly.

Lillehorne grunted and started to close the ponderous cuffs around Trevor's wrists, but then he scowled and stepped back with them still undone. "I have already done you *the favor*, as you put it,

622 · Robert McCammon

by allowing this highly unofficial visit to be *made*. The prisoner will get in the wagon. Mr. Blount, give him aid, please. And keep your pistol ready at all times."

"Yes sir."

"Thank you, Matthew," Trevor said before he climbed up to be guarded all the way back to New York. "Thank you also for agreeing to come see her. Let me ask this: do you think she'll be safe?"

"I think so. There would be no profit in harming her, and no lesson to be made out of her for the underlings. So yes, I do think she'll be safe."

"Let's *go*, gentlemen." Lillehorne mounted his horse. "Or shall we all shuffle to the nearest tavern and weep in our beers?"

On the ride, as they followed the Philadelphia Pike, Matthew urged Dante up next to Lillehorne's horse. They were proceeding at a walk. "I do appreciate the favors," he said. "Both of them."

"Spare me."

"I just wanted you to know that it meant a great deal to Trevor to see his—"

"What is this *Trevor* business? Are you his best *friend*? Don't you recollect that he killed three men, mangled the legs of a third, and might have killed a fourth?"

"I recollect that he turned himself in to you and saved my life. Best friend, perhaps not, but friend yes."

"You were knocked about up at that damned estate one too many times," Lillehorne said sourly.

Matthew held his tongue. Gardner Lillehorne had returned to his usual form. Of course it was understandable, since Lillehorne was in one muddy mire of a mess. The gaol was full, the cold room had been turned into a makeshift gaol, and the judicial fabric of New York was straining under the pull of so many criminals they could hardly be housed, much less fed. The entire scene was a merry disaster, with boys throwing slop buckets and pissing at whoever came near the bars. Two prisoners who seemed determined to piss and holler their way out of the cells were Bromfield and Carver, who'd been caught on their way to pick up Dippen Nack. The two hunters had run smack into Lillehorne, Kirby, and the constables, and Kirby had recognized Bromfield as the man who'd been with Pollard. A chase had ensued, with Bromfield's horse throwing him into a briar patch and Carver being stopped by a pistol ball past his ear.

Add to the festivities the complications—and mysteries—of the files and papers that had been found in Chapel's office, and little wonder Lillehorne's temper had become a tinderbox. The prosecutors of Charles Town, Philadelphia, and Boston as well as a dozen other smaller localities had to be notified due to the staggering number of forged deeds and bills of sale, plans for arson, extortion, kidnapping, document theft, and even the counterfeiting of money that had either been already hatched or in their initial stages, using the services of those boys—and young men—who had previously passed through the criminal university and been placed in those towns waiting for a signal to act. It was a law officer's delirium, to have to deal with thirty or more acts of crime in the planning stages all up and down the Atlantic coast while holding on to twenty-five sharkers some in need of medical attention. And some, like Chapel and Pollard, bound up in beds at the King Street hospital. So Matthew could pardon Lillehorne's foul disposition, as the situation truly was dire.

But, as Matthew considered, it was just his job to catch the criminals. It was Lillehorne's job to hold on to them.

"Gardner," Matthew said as their horses walked side-by-side, "I have an idea about that central constable's station I was talking about. You remember, at the meeting with Lord Cornbury? If this constable's station was built, it could be combined with a new gaol. A modern facility, with . . . say . . . twenty cells. With a kitchen also, so meals could be made on the premises. You know, there might be a small medical facility there as well, so wounded prisoners would not be taken away to—"

"Silence!" the man snapped. "*What* did you call me?"

"Pardon?"

"I said . . . *what* did you call me?"

Matthew thought back. "Gardner. Your name."

"No, *sir*. You are *not* allowed to call me by anything but High

Constable Lillehorne or *Mister* Lillehorne. Certainly not . . . what you called me. How *dare* you! And you think because of . . . you know . . . what happened at that estate and my brief stumble that you can rise to my level?" Lillehorne's immaculate black goatee actually twitched. "I am a public official, Corbett! You are a private citizen, not much more elevated than a clerk, if you really want to know my opinion, no matter how highly you think of yourself and this agency that will in the future be shown as a foolish and ridiculous endeavor! This is *my* town, Corbett! Do you hear me? It certainly doesn't belong to you or that lout Greathouse, and if you think you can weaken my authority and throw mud in my face in front of Lord Cornbury, then I'll vow before my honor that you'll have a fight on your hands! Do you hear? A fight! And if you think Gardner Lillehorne has ever backed away from a fight, ever in his life, well then I'm here to look you right in the eye and tell you . . ."

Matthew let the high constable continue this loquacious rant, as if there were anything he might do to plug it up. He was sure Lillehorne would still be talking when he decided to listen again about five minutes from now. He was instead transfixed by the way the red feather jiggled and shook on Lillehorne's tricorn as the man raged on, and he wondered where were the hawks when you needed them.

fifty

THE SUN ROSE AND THE SUN SET. The moon moved across the nights, changing shape as it progressed. Tides swelled high, then fell low. The summer ended, and September had arrived.

Matthew checked his watch. It was just after nine o'clock. He would have to be getting home soon, as tomorrow morning he had a case to scribe in the record book and then in the afternoon he had two hours of sword practice with Hudson Greathouse. Not something he looked forward to, but he had learned the valuable lesson of heeding the voice of experience.

"Your move."

"Yes, I'm aware of that." Matthew reached out and took a drink from his cup of cider, making Effrem Owles wait that much longer. The chessboard on the table between them was an example of the decimation that could be wrought when two equal opponents decided to cast aggression to the wind. Matthew, playing white, had two knights, two rooks, and six pawns left on this pinewood battleground to defend his king and win the war, while Effrem's black arsenal held a bishop, a knight, two rooks, and six pawns. Effrem's king sat at d7 and Matthew's hugged the corner at h1. Matthew drank slowly, for he didn't like the way this game was turning out.

"The move is apparent," Effrem said.

"All right, then." Matthew wasn't so sure. Effrem's rook at h8 was going to take his pawn at h3, no matter what he did. The exposure was just too much. Well, something had to be done. He slid a rook from a1 to e1 and was rewarded by Effrem's rook crashing down upon his hapless pawn. Now he had five.

They sat in the lamplight of the Trot Then Gallop. Matthew had joined his friend for dinner at Effrem's invitation, had enjoyed a meal of baked fish, fried potatoes, and green beans, plus a couple of cups of the very tart and delicious cider. Nowadays he drank sparingly of the tavern liquors, particularly wine from newly tapped casks, but he had come to the conclusion that one could not truly live with the idea in mind that the next sip of anything might bring death by belladonna. Still, it was a hard idea to shake.

He moved another rook and Effrem without hesitation took a white knight with one of his own rooks at h2.

Gak! Matthew thought. Perhaps he'd overstayed his visit here tonight. He and Effrem had played two previous games. Matthew had won the first with a feint up the middle and an attack on the right, the second game had been a stalemate, and now this one was looking grim. Effrem was definitely getting better. Then again, Matthew was getting better at handling the rapier. It would be a kick in the breeches, he thought, if as he became more accomplished at swordplay he became a dunce at chessplay.

But not tonight, friend Effrem! Matthew captured the offending rook with his king and sought a way out of the trap that was being developed involving the black knight and the remaining rook. Not tonight!

There did happen to be some things on his mind that chewed at his concentration.

His health was good, that was on the plus side. All the plasters had come off except the one beside his left eye and the one under his shirt at his left shoulder. He still smelled of comfrey-and-garlic liniment, but by now everyone understood.

What gnawed at him, among other things, were the murders of Simon Chapel and Joplin Pollard.

It had happened in the King Street hospital two weeks ago.

Chapel had been put in a bed there to recover from the condition of having his face very nastily rearranged. Infection had set in, and fever, and beneath his bandages Chapel had remained silent to any and all questions posed to him by High Constable Lillehorne. Likewise silent was Joplin Pollard, whose shattered knees had caused him to bite on a stick whenever Dr. Vanderbrocken or Dr. Edmonds merely touched them. If he'd lived he would have likely been wheeled in a pushcart to the hangman's rope.

As Pollard and Chapel were the only other patients on that particular ward—the so-called "prisoners' ward," which was locked up tight behind two doors—and both of them depended on rather stupefying drugs to even allow them a twilight sleep, their departure must have been a relatively quiet affair. But no less sinister for its degree of quiet. They were found dead by the first of the hospital's attendants to arrive, a young man born in New York and known for his scrupulous care of the patients. It appeared in the reports made by Ashton McCaggers that death had been administered sometime between two and three in the morning, and had come about due to a long thin blade driven through the right eye of each man, and hence into the brain. Whoever had picked the locks had left only faint scratches as a signature.

Matthew was particularly bothered about this. Not simply because Chapel and Pollard had escaped the noose and taken their knowledge of Professor Fell with them to the demonic world, but that Mr. Ripley had not been among the boys captured on the day of reckoning.

A black knight moved, getting into position for attack.

"That's far too easy," Matthew said, as he moved his king.

"Yes," Effrem answered. He tapped his chin, his brown eyes magnified large behind his round-lensed spectacles. "I suppose it is."

Other things also whispered to Matthew from the dark. The power of Professor Fell to demand loyalty might as well have caused Lawrence Evans to swallow his tongue, for all the questions he would answer. Evans sat in a cell at the gaol, ever silent. A look of sublime peace had settled upon his face. Did he think he would also be leaving the scene far before a judge read his sentence? If so, he was prepared for the voyage.

Bromfield and Carver were mules. They took orders and knew nothing. Likewise the terrified Dutch-speaking women who cooked the meals and turned out to believe they had been part of a great experiment in the process of education. Charity LeClaire, who occupied a bed in the women's ward on King Street and waxed and waned like the moon, might have wanted to talk to avenge a sticking, but when she began feverishly babbling it was all about being plucked from a London bordello by Lawrence Evans in 1696, cleaned up and dressed up, and under the duress of drugs having to satisfy the wanton and cruel—yes, cruel, I say!—desires of what sounded to be enough young criminals-in-training to fill New York twice over. Details were copious. Matthew had noted that Lillehorne and Bynes had paid close attention to her testimony and the clerk had broken two quills. Unfortunately, though Miss LeClaire obviously had a strong constitution for someone so thoroughly skewered, she was also useless beyond her ability to titillate.

Effrem's hand moved the second rook. He gave a shrug and sigh as he set it down, as if it didn't matter to the game a whit. Matthew saw where it would be going in two moves, and again shifted his king.

He realized he was caught strictly on the defensive. A bad place to be, according to Greathouse.

Other things. The raid on Chapel's estate had netted two men, one in his forties and the other nearly sixty, who had evidently been employed as instructors. The younger man had confessed an aptitude in both the art of blackmail—"priming the pigeon," he called it—and the usage of various methods of extortion. The older man was a financial expert, whose only crime seemed to be that he could discourse on international monies, exchange rates, and patterns of market behavior in such things as hog bellies and rare jewels until his questioners wished to seal his mouth with a hot poker. Both men confessed to witnessing many killings at the estate and would show Lillehorne the cemetery where the bodies lay, but the story of their employment was a tangled web that could not be followed without travelling to London's underworld . . . and even then, no sure thing.

The problem, Matthew thought as he stared at the chessboard, was that he'd seen *four* people whom he'd taken to be instructors. Of the third man and the woman with the blue parasol, there was no trace.

Effrem made a mistake. A simple one, but telling. Matthew leaped a knight upon the black bishop and saw a glimmer of light at the end of the tunnel.

Effrem shook his head. "Oh, I should've moved that rook!"

Misdirection, Matthew thought. He's trying to get me to go after the rook. Well, I won't unless I have to.

And then there was Count Anton Mannerheim Dahlgren.

This was another set of teeth that bit him. When Matthew had left Trevor Kirby in the shade of the tree that afternoon, he'd gone back into the house, through the wrecked dining-room and out onto the terrace where, armed with a rapier, he'd intended to go down the steps, and pull Dahlgren from the garden's goldfish pond.

The curtains had still been in the pond, but Dahlgren was gone.

Four men and Matthew searching the manse, the buildings, and the stable came up with nothing. The evil grenadier might have spread his own leathery wings and flown back to Prussia, so cleanly had he vanished. It was amazing to Matthew—almost incredible—how someone so badly battered could have gotten away so quickly. Again, the word *demonic* came to mind.

Effrem started to move his rook and hesitated. "You know, I asked you to meet me here for a particular reason, Matthew."

"Right. Dinner and chess."

"Well . . . not exactly." He moved the rook, which threatened Matthew's knight. "I wanted to know if . . ." He shifted in his chair. "If . . ."

"Go ahead and spit it out."

Effrem cleared his throat. "If I were to ask Berry Grigsby to go with me to the Young Lions Ball a week from Friday, do you think she'd go?"

"*What?*"

"Berry Grigsby," Effrem repeated. "The Young Lions Ball. A week from Friday. Do you think?"

Matthew sat back. "The Young Lions? Since when are you a member?"

"I joined last month. The day after I turned twenty-one. Well, don't look at me like *that*, Matthew! The Young Lions are a really fine group of fellows! All of them the sons of various crafts-men . . ."

"I know who they are."

"And they have these really fine dances. They're holding this one at the Dock House Inn."

"Wonderful." Matthew moved his king.

"I can't believe you did *that*! What's wrong with you?" The black rook captured Matthew's last knight.

"I'm trying to get it through my mind that you've joined a *social* club. I thought you were so dead-set against those! I thought you said they were a foolish waste of time!"

"No, Matthew," Effrem replied. "That's what *you* said. Your move."

"Now wait a minute, just wait. You want to ask *Berry*? Why?"

Effrem laughed. "Are you insane, Matthew?"

"I wasn't before I sat down at this table."

"Listen." Effrem slid a pawn forward. "Haven't you looked at Berry? Haven't you talked to her? She's a beautiful girl, and she's got a lot of . . . a lot of . . . well, I don't know exactly what it is that she's got, but whatever it is I like it. She's *different*, Matthew. She's . . . exciting, I suppose is what I'm trying to say."

"Exciting," Matthew said. He countered the pawn with one of his own.

"Yes, absolutely. I saw her sitting there on the wharf one morning, doing her drawing. That was the morning I stepped on that damned black cat and fell in the drink, thank you very much for laughing, but it was what brought us together. She helped me climb out. I sat . . . we sat . . . for a long time, just talking. I like the way she laughs, I like the way she smells, I like—"

"Well when the hell did you *smell* her?"

"You know what I mean. You just get a whiff sometimes of a girl's hair, or her skin. It's a nice smell."

"The last time I smelled her, it wasn't so nice."

"Pardon?"

"Nothing." Matthew tried to force his concentration back to the game and failed miserably. Suddenly he seemed not to be able to tell any difference at all between pawn, rook, or king.

"My original question," Effrem plowed on, "is whether or not you think she'd go with me if I asked her."

"I don't know. How should I know?"

"You *live* in the house right behind her! You take almost every meal in the kitchen with her sitting across the table! What's wrong with you?" He smacked the rook down. "Checkmate."

"That is *not*!" Matthew objected, but then his vision cleared and he saw the deadly triangle trap of black pawn, rook, and knight that had converged upon his king. "Damn!"

"I'm thinking of giving her flowers when I ask her," said Effrem. "Do you think she might like that?"

"I don't know! Give her weeds, for all I care!" And then Matthew took a good long look at Effrem. He realized why his friend was suddenly so well-dressed in his nice dark blue suit, white shirt, and waistcoat and his brown hair with the gray streaks at the sides was no longer such a bird's-nest but so well-combed and he had the scrubbed appearance of a young lion with places to go and a bright future as a New York tailor.

If Effrem was not yet in love with Berry Grigsby, he was on the way.

"Pah!" Matthew said. He grabbed his cider and swigged it.

"What? Really, Matthew, you're not making any sense. The flowers, now. What kind of flowers should they be?"

"Flowers are flowers."

"Granted, but I thought she might have . . . possibly . . . told you what kind she liked. Roses, or carnations, or lilies, or—" He shrugged, lost. "I have no idea." A quick adjustment of his glasses, and he leaned forward. "What kind would *you* get her, Matthew?"

"I don't know anything about flowers."

"Just *think*. Surely there's something she might like."

Matthew thought. It was ridiculous, asking this of him. Absurd. He rubbed a hand across his forehead and winced because some of the scratches there were still tender. "I suppose . . . I might get her . . ." What? he asked himself. "Wildflowers."

"Wildflowers?"

"Yes. Just pick them from a field somewhere. I think she'd prefer wildflowers to roses, or carnations, or . . . any of those."

"That's a grand idea!" Effrem slapped his palm down on the table for emphasis. "Wildflowers it is, and they won't cost any money, either. Now: what color would you suggest?"

"Color?"

"Color," Effrem said. "Blue, yellow, red . . . what color might she like?"

Matthew considered that in his years of knowing Effrem this was the strangest conversation they had ever shared. Still, one could tell from Effrem's expression—his shining excitement, as it were—that for some reason Berry Grigsby had impressed him and come to have a meaning for him. As outlandish as that was. Those two together! A couple! Dancing at a Young Lions Ball! And maybe more than dancing, given time and the curve of Cupid's bow.

"Any ideas?" Effrem urged.

"Yes," Matthew said after a moment's reflection. He stared at the chessboard, at the pieces that had trapped his king, but he was seeing fifty feet of rotten pier and the sun shining down upon a green pasture across the river in Breuckelen. "Have you ever looked into a blacksmith's forge?"

"I have. Once I had a sty on my right eye, and you know the heat is good for bursting them. If you stare into the forge long around, you feel the sty . . ." He stopped. "What's a blacksmith's forge have to do with wildflowers?"

"Those are the colors," Matthew said. "The heart of the earth."

"The *what*?" Effrem's brows came together. "I think you may have had one cider too many."

A slim brown box about ten inches long and wrapped with white ribbon was suddenly placed on the table in front of Matthew.

fifty-one

S TARTLED, MATTHEW LOOKED UP into a craggy face with a formidable nose, deep-set eyes dark as tarpits, and the left charcoal-gray eyebrow sliced by a jagged scar.

"Good evening, Mr. Greathouse," said Effrem. "Would you care to join us?"

"No, thank you, Mr. Owles. I'm just passing through. As I know your haunts by now, Matthew, I figured I'd find you."—he gave the chessboard a disdainful glance—"doing whatever it is you do in here. I wanted to bring that to you." He nodded toward the box.

Matthew picked it up and shook it, making something shift within. "What is it?"

"A gift from Mrs. Herrald. She bought it for you before she left. Asked me to hold on to it until that situation with the lady was over. Mrs. Swanscott, I mean. I suppose I wanted to wait until I saw how you did on your second problem."

Matthew nodded. He had no idea what was in the box, but as for Matthew's second problem, he'd just solved the mystery of the Eternal Maidens Club and their coconut pies. It seemed that the Eternal Maidens had put their money together to buy a very expensive "pharaoh's nut," a coconut, and the best cook of the club—Granny Farkason—had baked two pies from it. The pies had been put on a windowsill to cool and lo and behold they vanished. A neighbor known to eat her weight in biscuits was accused. Matthew had traced crumbs and clues to a travelling troubadour who had made camp in the shadow of the windmill on Wind Mill Lane and whose trained monkey, unbeknownst to him, had learned to slip his chain and go galavanting about town while his owner slept. The monkey had already disposed of one of the purloined items and had hidden an uneaten portion of the second in a hollow log. A *gratis* performance for the Maidens was arranged, including a great deal of flirting from the handsome troubadour that made several of the elderly maidens rethink their obligations to the club, and things ended as happily as possible when money, a monkey, and two coconut pies are involved.

Not much of a problem, but it beat what Greathouse was working on: a more mundane thing in which he was tasked to follow the wife of a wealthy shipyard owner who suspected a young lover in the shadows. But it was work and money, and Greathouse told Matthew that as the word got out about the agency the solving of problems would become more numerous and hopefully more interesting.

"May I open this?" Matthew asked.

"You might, but I think Mrs. Herrald intended you to open it in private."

"I see." He didn't, but it was the polite thing to say.

"There you go," Greathouse said with a scowl. "Saying the polite thing."

"I'll open this when I get home, then."

"And I'd suggest a good night's sleep." He glanced around the Trot, which was definitely too tame for his wild streak. "Regardless of whatever enjoyment you get out of this tomb." He started out, stopped, and came back to their table. "Oh . . . Matthew. I don't give compliments lightly, but I might wish to say you did the agency very proud in that business with Mrs. Swanscott. I still think it was a headstrong risk, but—hey—you showed me up."

"It was not my intention to show you up."

"As you please. I might wish also to say that the business with the Masker and Simon Chapel was recounted to its full extent in the letter I've just sent off to Katherine, and I can tell you she will discuss the matter with her associates and the legal officials both in England and in Europe forthwith. Your name shall gain a boatload of fame." He grinned. "How do you like my formal language? You have to know that junk when you're writing a letter."

"It doesn't suit you."

"I don't think so, either. That's why from now on I'll leave all the letter-writing up to you. Unless we feel the need to hire a clerk, which presently we don't." Greathouse paused but did not remove himself, and Matthew knew more was coming. "There's a good and a bad to your name being known," he said, more seriously. "If you haven't already come to the attention of a certain person, you *will*."

"I've thought of that possibility."

"Just so you're aware."

"I plan to be," Matthew answered. "Aware."

"Good. Oh . . . we're going to start training in hand-to-hand combat soon. End of the week, probably."

"All right." The brightness of his interest was not exactly solar. He'd certainly needed to know hand-to-hand combat, battling that monkey there in the high grass. Then again, he thought of a pair of wine-red curtains in a goldfish pond. "The sooner the better."

"You might want to stop by the apothecary and get some liniment," Greathouse suggested. "For sore muscles and such. And while you're at it . . . get enough for me, too. Goodnight, gentlemen," he said, and then to Matthew from across the Trot, "Don't let that candle burn too late, moon—" He stopped himself short. "Mr. Corbett."

Then he was out the door and gone.

Matthew picked up the mysterious box and got to his feet. He promised Effrem that when the time was right he would put in a good word for him with Berry, and then with a last hard look at that triangular king-trap he set off for home.

It was a beautiful night. A million stars were showing and a cool breeze that promised autumn blew from the sea. Fiddle music and laughter could be heard from another nearby tavern, and many other citizens were out on their way to somewhere. As Matthew walked east along Crown Street and crossed the intersection of Smith, he saw to his right the green glow of a constable's lantern moving south, and a second green lamp coming north. All along Smith Street, on each corner, stood a wooden post with a lantern attached. The project of putting up lamp-posts on all street corners in town was not yet completed, but every small candle helped to illuminate the larger dark.

In another moment he looked up at a sign on the left-hand side of the street and saw there the newly painted announcement *Crown Street Coffee Shoppe*. The shop was dark, but Robert Deverick hoped to have it open within the month and serving customers until the late hours. He had defied his mother, which must have taken the courage of Perseus, in making his decision to remain in New York. As Matthew understood, Robert had decided his education must be good for something, so he'd elected to go into the coffee-importing business as a silent partner with a young man, newly arrived from London, who had some fanciful ideas about . . . of all things . . . the use of flavored cream in coffee. Matthew wished Robert well and hoped to sometime partake of what would certainly be a novel beverage.

Matthew continued toward the harbor. As he turned right en route to his home, he saw by the light from the lamp on Crown Street's corner that approaching him with a brisk stride was none other than the tall figure of Polly Blossom. She wore a full-skirted gown, puffed by petticoats, a feathered hat and white gloves with rings on the fingers. Her face was lowered, her broad shoulders slightly stooped as if in contemplation of her role in the salvation of a reverend.

Matthew neared her and said, "Good evening, madam," with a quick nod as he passed, and too late he saw the curls of the long white wig and the horsey face beneath it.

"Good evening, sir," replied Lord Cornbury, as the sharp *clack-clack* of high French heels on solid English stones took New York's governor away on his nightly constitutional.

It was all Matthew could do not to say *Nice shoes* but he did manage to resist.

With a few more steps he paused along the harbor street, drew in a long draught of night air, and looked at the houses, the shops, the taverns, and the sparkling lamplights before him.

He had realized that the real Queen of Bedlam was a town on an island between two rivers.

In this town of soon to be more than five thousand persons there was a governor who wore a dress, a reverend who loved a prostitute, a printmaster who could crack walnuts on his forehead, a high constable who had killed a boy, a magistrate who was once a tennis champion, a laundress who collected secrets, and a coroner who collected bones. There was a barber who owned a squirrel named Sassafras, a tailor who could identify a dead man from a suit's watch pocket, and a black giantess who would put aside her gittern just long enough to kill you.

If a town, like a ship, could be given feminine attributes, then this Queen of Bedlam sat regal on her throne and kept her secrets in a golden cup. This Queen of Bedlam might smile at tears, or weep at laughter. This Queen of Bedlam saw all the swirl of humanity, all its joys and tragedies, its wisdom and madness. This Queen of Bedlam threw dice, and drank hearty, and sometimes played rough.

But here she was, in her gown of night with the lamps ashine like yellow diamonds. Here she was, silent in her thoughts and loud in her desires.

Here she was, on the new world's edge.

Matthew walked on.

His house was now a home. The dairyhouse did still have a dirt floor, true, but a very nice dark red rug covered most of it. There was a small writing desk, a shelf of a few books with room for more, his comfortable bed, and a fine though much-battered brown leather chair Grigsby had procured for him. On the walls were pegs to hang his clothes, and below an oval mirror a wash-stand to hold his water basin and grooming items. Other than that, there wasn't much room for a mouse to chase its tail, but thankfully there were no rodents nor . . . dread the thought . . . roaches.

But of course there was the new window.

When the shutters were open as now, Matthew could look out through the glass panes and see the harbor and a slice of moonlit river, as well as a piece of Breuckelen green by day. Grigsby was giving the brickmason, carpenter, and glazier free mentions in the *Earwig*, and Matthew had insisted on shouldering some of the cost with a portion of his first salary earned from solving the Swanscott problem.

It wasn't exactly a mansion, but it was his home. For now, at least. He was too busy to go house-hunting, and really he couldn't afford anything else. The window to the world made all the difference. The next step was the addition of a fireplace, if just one suited for a gnome, as a comfortable summerhouse did not necessarily make an inviting winterhouse.

Matthew had upon entering already touched a match to the two candles on the wash-stand, next to the door. Now he lit a second match and touched the candle on his writing desk and the one that sat on the windowsill, for he'd noted the candle burning in the kitchen window beyond.

He took off his coat, hung it on a peg, loosened his cravat, and sat down in his leather chair next to the window. He had removed the white ribbon and was about to open the gift from Mrs. Herrald when there came a knock to the door.

"One moment!" It took him three seconds to get there. Matthew put aside the box, opened the door, and stood face-to-face with Berry.

She carried a lantern and wore a loose-fitting green gown that said she'd been getting ready for bed. Copper highlights in her brushed red tresses caught the light, her face was scrubbed and fresh, her bright blue eyes sparkling. The scrapes, bruises, and cuts—save for two deeper than the others under a plaster on her forehead—had faded, just as his had, under the benevolent care of time. The children at the Garden Street school, where she'd begun teaching as an aide to Headmaster Brown at the first of September, had eagerly wanted to know what kind of tree she'd fallen out of.

She hadn't spoken to Matthew for a week after the incident. Then, only a few words the second week. But Matthew understood that a girl stumbling around the woods for five hours with horse muck on her face might hold something of a grudge for the person who got her so mucked up, though in truth she'd washed the manure off in a pond a mile or so from Chapel's gate. The Dutch-speaking farmer Van Hullig had certainly learned the meaning of the word *Help*.

"Hello," Matthew said brightly.

" 'lo," she answered. "I saw your candle." She lifted her other hand to give him a pitcher.

"Thank you." He accepted it. Matthew had taken to getting a pitcher of water from the nearest well at night, and sometimes Berry had already drawn it and had it ready as she did tonight.

"We missed you at dinner."

"Ah. Well, a friend of mine. Effrem Owles. You know Effrem, don't you?"

"He was the one who stepped—"

"—on the cat, yes. Unfortunate incident. He asked me to dinner. I went directly from the office."

"The *office*. That sounds so official."

"It should. You know. Office. *Official*. Anyway, we wound up playing chess and . . . you know how time gets away when you're drawing. That's how it is."

"I see."

"Yes." Matthew nodded, not knowing quite where to let his eyes rest.

Berry nodded also. Then she said, "A very lovely night." A slight frown passed over her face. "Are you all right?"

"Yes, I'm—"

"I just thought you looked—"

"—all right, perfectly—"

"—a little troubled about—"

"—all right."

"—something," she said. "Are you?"

"Me? Troubled about something? No. Absolutely not. As you say, it's a very lovely night."

"Well," she said.

"That's where this came from," he said, holding up the pitcher and giving a grin that he knew must be the stupidest expression to ever slide across the face of a human being.

"Matthew!" She cuffed him on the shoulder. Not the wounded one, because she remembered.

"Listen," they both said together.

"Go ahead," Matthew offered.

"No, you."

"The lady should go first."

"All right, then." Berry set her chin; something was coming. "As you have agreed to be my . . . shall I say . . . *guardian* and have so far done a . . . fair job of it, I'd like to ask you a question." She paused and Matthew waited. She chewed on her lower lip and then she looked him square in the eyes and said, "There's going to be a social a week from Friday. I was wondering, just thinking really, if you might like to go. As my guardian, I mean."

"A social? Uh . . . a week from Friday, did you say?"

"Grandda's printing the posters. It's going to be at Sally Almond's."

"Ah. Sally Almond's. A week from Friday." He also chewed on his lower lip, aware that Berry was watching him carefully. "I . . . I really don't *dance*, you know."

"I didn't say it was a dance. I said it was a social. Just meeting some people. I think there's going to be music. But dancing? I don't know." She cocked her head slightly. "Why *don't* you dance?"

"I've never learned."

"It's not all that difficult. You just do what everyone else is doing."

"Yes, but tell that to my feet." He sighed. "I really can't go, Berry. Not a week from Friday. In fact, I think I . . . may have to take a trip on Friday morning and I won't be back until Saturday."

"A trip? To where?"

"I think it's probably time I went to see Mrs. Swanscott again."

"I understand, but on *that* particular Friday?"

"It might be the only time I can get there for a while." He cast his eyes down, realized she might see the untruth in that gesture, and quickly looked up at her again. "Really."

"Really?"

"A lot of work coming in," Matthew said.

"I'm disappointed," Berry admitted, "but I know you have your work. Listen, then. Do you think it proper that I go alone? I really would like to meet some people my own age."

"Oh . . . yes. Then again . . . there's . . . Effrem."

"Effrem?"

"Yes, Effrem. As a matter of fact, if you like to dance"—here something caught at his throat and he had no idea what it was but he had to keep speaking lest he choke—"I happen to know that Effrem is a member of the Young Lions club and *they* are having a dance that particular night at the Dock House Inn. So. If you and Effrem were to"—again that choking sensation—"go to the social first, you might attend the dance afterward. Does that make sense?"

Berry stared at him. Then her eyes lit up and she smiled, in all innocence. "It *does* make sense! But how in the world am I going to get Effrem to escort me?"

"You forget," said Matthew, "that my business is solving problems."

"All right, then. You may guard me at the *next* social, and please please *please* say that someday you'll let me teach you how to dance."

"I'll say I'll let you try. Someday."

"A fair enough bargain." She searched his face; he let her at least do this, though he did not know what she was searching for. Whatever it was, he could tell she didn't find it. "Oh . . . what did you mean to ask me?"

"You know," he said, "I'm so tired I fear it's slipped my mind. Must not have been very important."

"Perhaps you'll think of it later."

"I probably will," he agreed.

She nodded, and a breath of wind stirred her hair and brought to him its faint aroma of—what was that? The grassy scent of wildflowers? She motioned with a tilt of her head toward the house. "I'd best get to bed."

"Yes. Me too."

"Goodnight, then. Breakfast tomorrow?"

"Bright and early," Matthew said.

Berry retreated from the door and started to walk away. He watched her go, and wondered if a rapier through the heart felt like this. But *why*? They were friends, and that was all. Just friends. Only.

She turned toward him again. "Matthew?" she asked, her voice concerned. "Are you sure you're all right?"

"I am," he replied, and kept his own voice steady with supreme effort. "Sure."

"I just wanted to make certain. Goodnight and sleep well."

"You too," he said, and watched her return to the house before he closed the door. And locked it.

Matthew retrieved the box, went back to his leather chair before the window and the candle, and opened it.

Within was an object about eight inches long, wrapped in blue velvet. A letter was included.

Matthew,

There is in the Herrald Agency a time-honored tradition. Richard created it, and so shall I keep it. If you are reading this, then you have passed your initial trial. You have successfully solved one problem of the first three assigned to you. I welcome you fully and completely no longer as a junior associate but as a full investigator with all the respect and strength of my husband's name at your command. With this name and the value you have displayed, doors will open for you that you have never dreamed existed. Now take this gift as a measure of my confidence in you, and know that through this the world may be seen more clearly than before.

With All Respect and Admiration,
KATHERINE HERRALD

He opened the blue velvet and found a magnifying glass. Its crystal clarity reminded Matthew of Mrs. Herrald's purpose, while its handle of rough-hewn wood reminded him that tomorrow he was going to be sword-fighting with Hudson Greathouse again. He was reminded also of a small bit of windowglass given to him by the aged Headmaster Staunton, who had originally brought him into the orphanage and taught him the wonders of reading and education, and the disciplines of self-control and self-knowledge. Then as now, the gift was a clear view unto the world.

It was time for rest, but first there was the other thing.

Matthew got up, went to his writing desk, and opened the first drawer. From it he withdrew the blood card that had been slipped under his door three nights ago in a plain white envelope sealed with a dab of red wax. Then he took it with him to the chair, sat down once more, and turned the card between his hands.

The envelope was not from Mr. Ellery's stock. He'd gone there first. Did not care to show him the card, but he was sure it had likewise not been purchased from Mr. Ellery.

A plain, elegant white card with a single bloody fingerprint at its center.

A death vow.

Whether it takes one week, or one month, or one year or ten years . . .

Professor Fell never forgets.

He continued turning the card between his hands. A small thing. A trifle, really.

The question was: who had slipped it beneath his door? If not the professor, then someone acting on the professor's authority. A surrogate son? Or daughter? *Who?*

Matthew had known, really, what Berry had been searching his face for. It had been there, hidden all the time. But he couldn't let her see it. No. Never. For if he let himself care about anyone, if he *dared* to care . . . then two might die as cheaply as one, for a soul could be murdered as well as a body. Ask Katherine Herrald to talk about Richard.

She had come close to being killed at Chapel's estate. He wouldn't let that happen, ever again. She would be kept at arm's length. A friend. That only.

That. Only.

Matthew picked up the magnifying glass, and through it by candlelight examined the fingerprint.

He wondered if he compared it to the print on the blood card possessed by Magistrate Powers, would it be the same? No, this was his chain to drag. The magistrate was in the Carolina colony now, with his wife Judith and younger son Roger, getting settled in the town near Lord Kent's tobacco plantation to work with his elder brother Durham. God guide him in his progress, and God protect a good man.

But Professor Fell, the deadly hand, never forgets.

Matthew held the glass close to the fingerprint and narrowed his eyes.

How like a maze a fingerprint was, he thought. How like the unknown streets and alleys of a strange city. Curving and circling, ending here and going there, snaking and twisting and cut by a slash.

Matthew followed the maze with his glass, deeper and deeper, deeper still.

Deeper yet, toward the center of it all.

About the Author

Robert McCammon is the *New York Times* bestselling author of fifteen novels, including *Swan Song, Stinger, The Wolf's Hour, Gone South, Mystery Walk, Usher's Passing,* and *Boy's Life.* There are more than four million copies of his books in print. He lives in Birmingham, Alabama, with his wife and daughter.